Fractured Symphony

Volume 2 of the Two-Part Series

'Til The End Of Time

By

JENNIFER LARMAR

"An epic love story that readers want to dive into ... get this into readers' hands as it's something lovers of romance will want to read..."

Hannah Brown Gordon, Literary Agent, New York City

Jennifer Larmar was born in Brisbane, Australia. She and her husband have recently moved from an apartment in the Brisbane CBD to run a luxury B&B in a small former gold rush town located in the foothills of the Victorian High Country to be closer to her only daughter and young grandson.

Fractured Symphony is Volume 2 in a two-part series entitled *'Til the End of Time*, commencing with her first published novel *Silken Images*.

To connect with Jennifer, you can visit her *Facebook* page:
https://www.facebook.com/JenniferLarmar/
or email her at *sbandta@optusnet.com.au*

For more titles and samples of her novels, or to keep up with news of Jennifer's other ventures and blogs, pop on over to her webpage:

http://sbandta.wixsite.com/jenniferlarmar

Both have links where readers can purchase her novels. Or if you contact the author personally via her Facebook page or email, she offers them at a discount rate plus postage – along with a tasty little treat!

Let's have some fun ... to see how far Jennifer's books travel around the world, please take a picture with some way of identifying where you were at the time, e.g. with a signpost of some kind, a hotel napkin (or anything else you can think of) and then either post it to her Facebook page Jennifer Larmar – Australian Author or send an email to sbandta@optusnet.com.au and she will reply in person.

Jennifer is currently working on a standalone novel entitled *Broken Pieces*. This contemporary work tells the story of Sally and Ben, Australian medical professionals who volunteer at a remote district hospital in Rwanda. Following their arrival several years after the devastating and horrific months of the genocide, they use their expertise to bring new life and hope to many of their new friends. Until, one day, an unexpected and tragic event brings far-reaching consequences.

DEDICATION

...To Lucy Maunder...

From the moment you stepped onto The Lyric Theatre stage at QPAC on 23 July 2011, you held me enthralled by your superb portrayal of my favourite fictional character, Lara Guishar-Antipova.

Your exquisite voice hitting every note and bringing those haunting lyrics and script to life was the major influence for this series to come into existence.

Offstage, you're just as delightful!

Maybe one day we'll get to wander in a forest similar to the one mentioned during our amusing ride in a certain little red chariot after your brilliant performance in 'Noël and Gertie' at Glen Street Theatre – only this time simply to enjoy the serenity. Steve and I always share a chuckle when we think of that spontaneous trip and quip!

Such a generous spirit proves the woman you are.

I have said it many times before and I will say it again ...
your voice is like liquid chocolate – smooth warm and sweet
as it oozes into every pore of a listener's soul.

May God bless and keep you and those you love always in His care...

WORDS OF ENCOURAGEMENT

"I am so pleased for you that your writing career is taking off, and I am delighted that our work on Dr Zhivago was a catalyst for you ... my thanks for your enthusiasm and support for our creative work ... I think you are the original Zhivago fan. We are grateful for your undying support and for your faithful spreading the word."

Lucy Simon, Composer, Doctor Zhivago – A New Musical

"Best best best of luck with the book! ... Bless you for your boundless heart and talent ... I am excited for the book to take wing!"

Amy Powers, Co-Lyricist, Doctor Zhivago – A New Musical

"I'm so glad you enjoyed the show. I am very sad to let Zhivago go, it was an incredible nine months and that final performance was super emotional as you saw! ... Congratulations too for your book – you must be over the moon ... A great achievement! ... Thank you always for your love and support..."

Lucy Maunder, Australian Entertainer
... and the inspiration for this series

Dear Reader, The greatest gift you can give an author is to write a review to encourage others to purchase novels that have touched your heart in some way. Amazon, Goodreads and Bookbub sites, any Book Clubs or Book Pages you may belong to, as well as adding a review to the author's personal Facebook Page in the section entitled 'Recommendations and Reviews' are excellent ways to do this. Oh, and don't forget, word of mouth is an excellent recommendation.

With sincere thanks, Jennifer

WITH HEARTFELT THANKS

to all of those involved in the stirring production of

Doctor Zhivago – A New Musical

performed at The Lyric Theatre, Brisbane, Australia, throughout July and August of 2011.

The part you all played in this magnificent piece of musical theatre was the catalyst for me giving birth to this story out of a special place in my heart.

It was always there – it just needed your inspiration so I could form the words and bring these beloved characters to life.

... the *amazing cast*, whose blending of voices was exceptional, delivered with the clearest diction I have ever heard in such a large company, and with each of you singing every piece with purity and passion.
You will always deserve to have your own Cast Album made!

... the brilliant *Kellie Dickerson*, Musical Director, along with a *very talented orchestra*. Thank you for affording me the privilege of sitting in a darkened theatre and being transported to 'a taste of heaven' by your wonderful interpretation of a superb score. And for those few precious moments following the final Australian show when you opened up your heart and spoke about your beloved Rob – such a beautiful tribute.
I will never forget what you shared.

... the talented Associate Musical Director, *Ben Van Tienen* and the *gifted young lady who played bass* (I'm only sorry I didn't ask for your name to include it here) – both of whom performed at the final Australian performance of this stirring production – for your readiness to chat during the interval through your musicians' 'cage', as well as showing such willingness to help ensure I had the correct version of that one elusive lyric! Thank you so much, and I wish you all the best in the future as music fills your lives to stir the souls of so many.

... *Johanna Allen, Anton Berezin, Caitlin Berry, Luke Joslin, Toddy Keys, Lucy Maunder, Elise McCann, Stephanie Silcock, Ben Van Tienen, Anthony Warlow* and *Jamie Way* for your willingness to allow me to include you in these pages. Sending each and every one of you a huge Aussie 'chookas' for continued success as you tread the boards of theatres both in Australia and around the world.

To *Anne-Maree McDonald* and *Stuart Maunder* – Lucy's parents – delightful folk who certainly know how to put on a show that sets an audience's toes tapping. It is an honour to include you on these pages. Thank you for providing treasured memories of a very special occasion in the Riverside Theatre back in March 2013, along with so many other times when your beautiful girl has been performing on a stage. What a surprise and thorough delight it was to be able to lift my voice with Stuart's for a few lines of *Honey Bun* during that marvellous production of *The Sound of Rodgers* while Anne-Maree tickled the ivories. The two of you have always been so generous with your time – along with a few glasses of wine! – and in offering the warmest of welcomes. Whenever I think of you, it is always with sincere gratitude and a warm smile.

With sincerest thanks...

... to *Lucy Simon* for a stirring score and *Amy Powers* and *Michael Korie* for poignant lyrics which still cause my heart to sigh each time I hear them. No words could ever express how privileged and honoured I felt to receive your kind permission to include the exquisite lyrics of *On The Edge of Time* from *Doctor Zhivago - A New Musical* in the pages of my novel and for your heartfelt words of encouragement. One of the highlights of my life was being invited to the Broadway opening of this magnificent musical and then being welcomed to your private pre- and post-show functions where I could thank each of you personally. A night I will always treasure...

With special thanks...

... to *Anthony Warlow* and *Lucy Maunder* for an exception rendition of the magnificent *On the Edge of Time* – the flawless blending of your voices made my spirit soar. This poignant piece perfectly portrays the words that were always residing in Adam and Lara's hearts for their absent soulmate.

Anthony, my sincere thanks for the generous amount of time and the encouragement you gave me outside QPAC on a Friday afternoon in April 2012, and again in Melbourne in August of that same year just before it was time for you to head to the bright lights of Broadway.

And finally...

To the delightful *Lucy Maunder* ... I have to save this last tribute for you

Luce, you have been a true inspiration from the moment I first saw you on that QPAC stage on the afternoon of 23 July 2011. Since then, I have been touched over-and-over by your exquisite talent with both music and prose in so many different productions – including your own, *Songs in the Key of Black,* on two separate occasions in two different cities. Your voice leaves a lasting impression on everyone who has the chance to hear it, and your gracious spirit has touched my heart every single time. A true professional, the dedication you devote to your craft is second-to-none. I hope to see you on many more stages, both in Australia and overseas as the years unfold.

Your portrayal of my favourite fictional character – the same name chosen for one of the central characters on these pages – helped to make this story what it is. By pure coincidence and a significant twist of fate, two of my favourite names have always been Lara and Lucy!

Thank you from the bottom of my heart.

INTRODUCTION

The idea for this story has been a part of my life for many years in one form or another. For the last few, snippets of ideas or lines have come to me, often in the middle of the night, and I quickly jotted them down, never truly believing they would ever come together.

In July 2011, I sat in a darkened theatre and set out on a wonderful journey as the pages of Boris Pasternak's evocative novel *Doctor Zhivago* came to life on a musical theatre stage. Lucy Simon's haunting score blended beautifully with stirring lyrics from the pens of both Amy Powers and Michael Korie. I was mesmerised to see this tragic love story, which had always been one of my favourites, fall from the mouths of a brilliant cast, with music giving it a new and touching dimension. The entire production moved me so much that I returned again ... and again ... and again – another three times over the same amount of weeks – and every time I came away wanting more.

This was the beginning of Lara and Adam's story. As soon as I arrived home from the first show, I knew a seed had germinated – I could feel the tiny sprout stirring inside my heart as it pushed and prodded to break free. Nine months later more than eight hundred completed pages sat in a file on my computer, telling the story of two people who were always meant to be together despite formidable obstacles, hardships and tragedy trying to keep them apart.

Now their tale is contained in two volumes – this one, *Fractured Symphony*, along with its companion, *Silken Images*.

I hope you gain as much pleasure in reading about them as I did in bringing them to life.

Jennifer Larmar
Brisbane, Australia
14 August 2014

PROLOGUE

Cortona, Italy

He came to her as he always did – and in the only way he could now – in breathtaking dreams emerging from the depths of her heart ... that secret place where he alone dwelt.

Their time together had been their own private place ... a fragment of space in the vastness of the universe ... and yet those glorious hours had touched her world every moment she took breath ... and nothing could erase him from her memory.

She didn't have the strength to regret the decision made so long ago – she knew if she did, she couldn't live with the pain...

...but she would always long for him in that secret place...

...the one she had made in her heart especially for him...

...every day, until she was no more.

PART ONE

Brisbane, Australia

January 1989 to mid-November 1989

Chapter 1

Each day inched by slowly – like a tiny snail crawling through thick sludge on the lookout for its next form of nourishment.

While each new sunrise put on a glorious display, and despite long daylight hours bathed in summer sunlight, the crushing heaviness contained in two lonely hearts was like the depths of a winter snowstorm as Lara and Adam battled the raging internal blizzards ever threatening to consume them. The icy reality of aloneness meant they missed each other dreadfully and nothing either one could do was able to ease that terrible ache.

Lara had already organised with David, her boss, to take a few weeks off over the Christmas season, hoping Adam might find a chance to pop in during his lunch breaks. She could never have anticipated their separate tidings heralding in the New Year would be whispered vows about never seeing each other again.

For Nikki's sake – the delightful little girl who was now the only sunshine in her lonely life – Lara went through each day trying to pretend everything was fine. In reality, her heart felt as though it had been shattered into millions of tiny shards. Whenever she tried to recall the loving sentiments Adam had whispered into her ear during their last phone call, the venomous threat his vengeful wife had spewed down the line just before it went dead soon washed them away.

She was back editing another feature film at her flatbed two weeks later, albeit only going through the motions. Nothing managed to penetrate the thick shroud of heaviness squashing her spirit. Each day, she sat in her office like a robot programmed to perform its tasks.

When David tried to draw her out, she was able to muster up the makings of a smile. "Don't worry; it's nothing really. Nikki's just about to start school and I'm not sure I want to let her go just yet. There's a big bad world out there and I don't think she's ready for it – I know I'm not..."

"Oh I'm sure she'll be alright – nothing ever seems to faze her – it's you I'm worried about. What's going on? Since the holidays you just haven't seemed your normal self."

For the space of a moment, Lara gazed out the window as though searching for something. Then with a heartfelt sigh, she turned back and shrugged, "Oh,

I'm alright, Davey. Probably just tired from all the excitement of Nikki's fifth birthday followed closely by Christmas with all its preparations. Did I tell you Suzie put on a fancy-dress party to celebrate the incoming new year? That big sister of mine sure goes all out when it comes to celebrating! It's been a hectic time, so I'm glad to be back."

Despite her reassurances, David was certain there was a lot more she wasn't saying. He had grown used to hearing Lara singing at her desk. Now the silence pervading the little editing suite meant going to work was no longer one of the brightest spots of his week – he missed his talented sidekick's cheery ways.

"Well, why don't you take another week off. That way you'll have a bit more time with Nikki before the big event."

At first, Lara didn't answer as she contemplated the tempting suggestion, but then she shook her head. "I couldn't do that – we have the deadline for that big ABC doco coming up. Not having me here means you'll have to work around the clock to get both of them finished."

"Don't worry; I can do them – besides, there's not much more to be done on this one. It'd do you good to get out of here for a few more days, and I'm sure that little moppet would like to have some fun with her mum before the big event."

He peered over the rim of his glasses with a determined stare. She knew he was right. Having a few more days off would probably be a good thing after her recent mindless responses, although it also meant long days without her soulmate – and no work to take her mind off the longing.

§

On the morning following that memorable phone call when Trina spat out mouthfuls of hatred and shattered all of Adam's dreams, the husband and wife sat stony-faced around a small breakfast table in a sunny corner of the kitchen he had designed nearly six years earlier. The frosty looks and cutting remarks emanating from her side of the table were enough to fill him with dread.

"I'm warning you, Adam, I'm the woman you married and that's how it's going to stay. How dare you turn to one of your little theatre floosies when I've always been here waiting for you! If you so much as even pick up the phone to call her, I'll do everything in my power to make both of you very, very sorry. Since coming home from that rotten clinic – the one you and those stupid doctors forced me into – I've done everything I could to please you and haven't touched a drop since..."

"Okay, Trina. I'm not going to argue. You made your point last night," he answered despondently, looking through the window to the peaceful scene outside and comparing it to the battle zone raging within the stately home. Although their house was located in the affluent suburb of Brookfield on the outskirts of Brisbane, the atmosphere inside was more suited to the killing fields of France over four decades earlier.

He was astounded at how easily the lies tripped off her tongue. It was obvious she had been drinking just over a week ago after turning up for the final performance of *Beauty and the Beast*. Miraculously, she seemed to have forgotten one pertinent fact. Before ending up in a drunken coma on their kitchen floor a few months earlier – the catalyst for her stint in rehab – she was never home, preferring the party scene rather than spending time with him. Nevertheless, Adam refused to get into another fight when she was in this frame of mind. The worried man held serious doubts as to how far he could trust her not to wreak revenge on Lara and would to do everything within his power to ensure his beloved soulmate's safety, including putting up with this living hell.

Every weekday morning as the first signs of daylight crept over the curtains, Adam rose from his bed in the guest room anxious to leave the house before his wife wandered downstairs. At the other end of the day, he stayed on late at the office, seeking out any excuse to put off returning to the cold, friendless house.

When the weekend rolled around, he needed to fill those long waking hours with things to take his mind off all he had lost. After spending Saturday morning weeding the garden, in the afternoon he grabbed up his keys, hoping to find Elizabeth and Charles at home. Their place was set high on the banks of the Brisbane River and offered a welcome respite from his turbulent home life. He wanted to be with people who cared rather than trying to appease an angry wife. After losing his parents in a tragic accident as a teenager, the Ashworths were the only family he had left now. His foster parents would help to fill the hours previously reserved for Lara and Nikki each week.

The next day was a blur of deliberate avoidance – with Adam once again pottering around in the sprawling gardens while Trina watched TV or chatted on the phone with Judith, her long-time party friend.

Midnight hours were the longest of all. Nothing could make time go any faster. Night after night Lara and Adam lay tossing and turning in their lonely beds, miles apart and wondering how their other half was coping. She understood the reason for his continuing silence, but it didn't make life any easier. Their only solace was having confidence in the strength of their love, even though they needed to keep it lying dormant in their hearts. They were learning to keep their feelings at bay or else it would be pure torture having to cope with the constant ache. Even so, even the slightest reminder was enough for that ever-present yearning to take on a life of its own again.

Lara only needed to catch sight of Mt Coot-tha with its four television towers piercing the sky. The well-known landmark was visible from most areas around Brisbane, and its grassy knoll and lookout at the top had been host to many happy times for the pair of them. One small glimpse and her heart rose from its lonely grave and started beating a lively tattoo in her chest ... until a relentless sense of loss overwhelmed her once more, and the tears flowed unchecked.

The hilltop was even visible from her bedroom window. Sometimes in her darkest hours she stood transfixed, simply to feel alive again for a few moments as memories from times past stirred her soul. At other times, searching fingers brushing across the corner of the kitchen bench where Adam had often perched himself while sharing late-night suppers and tender kisses. It was as though an invisible string always drew her hand back to that one cherished spot.

For Adam, a small glimmer of comfort came from his regular trips to the Gold Coast when he went to check on last-minute details for his latest architectural project. He recalled the laughter and love shared during a few special days when he and an adorable little girl had built sandcastles, along with memories of the touch of a woman's hand in his at the top of a lookout. They were from when his life had been full of hope. So often he longed to sweep by a serene cottage in Paddington and carry them back to that place ... and stay there forever.

His greatest consolation came from a set of beautiful albums Lara had fashioned especially for him, depicting two of the best periods of his life. One was alive with keepsakes and memories from their time together onstage during *Show Boat's* run; the other contained photos and entries of all the places they had seen and fun times they had shared during a few precious weeks spent travelling through Italy and Austria.

Most nights just before turning out the light, when his spirit craved most to be with her, he would bring them out from the safe hidden behind a painting in his room. If they couldn't physically be together, her presence was in every little nuance or word, and each one helped to nourish that all-consuming hunger to be with her again.

§

The new school year was fast approaching. With Nikki enrolled in an independent private school, the excited little girl begged Lara to invite Adam over so she could show off her brand-new uniform.

"I know you want to see him, Missy Tuppence," she answered, straightening the stiff collar as Nikki twirled a strand of Lara's long, chestnut hair through her fidgety fingers. "But he just can't come over to visit us at the moment."

"But *why* Mummy? He *always* used to come and see us, but he hasn't been for sooo long! I've got heaps to tell him, and I want us to go back and build another sandcastle – he's the bestest sandcastle builderer, and we haven't been to the beach for ages! You just *have* to ring him and say he has to come over – pleeeaaase..."

She jumped up and down with her little fists clenched in excitement, imagining sharing this latest bit of news.

"I really want to, little one, but I can't. Uncle Adam's very busy and he has to look after a friend who's been sick so he can't get away just now."

It broke Lara's heart to see her daughter's crestfallen look, but there was nothing else she could say. Instead, she took Nikki in her arms and tried to kiss away the effects of having to relay this disappointing news. Despite her best efforts, over the next few days the inconsolable child moped around the house, eyes darting to the door whenever she heard a car slow down and then sighing loudly as it continued down the street.

One Sunday afternoon towards the end of January, Lara called Elizabeth in desperation to ask if they could drop by for a quick visit. Adam's foster mother was thrilled to hear her voice and quickly invited them to stay for dinner.

She and Charles came out as soon as they heard the crunch of tyres on the driveway. This was the first time either of them had seen Lara and Nikki since the fateful night of the pantomime and they were anxious to ensure both the young woman and her small offspring were okay. The older couple well knew how much their son was missing the mother and daughter duo – whenever he dropped by for a visit, his haunted dark eyes told their story. Elizabeth was also concerned as to how Lara was coping with the separation. The women had spoken on the phone a couple of times, but she was reluctant to intrude too much.

The Ashworths' warm greeting was just what Lara needed to lift her spirits. It was a fine Brisbane day with the hint of a cooling breeze coming off the river, so the two families gravitated to the shady terrace. Since their very first meeting, Elizabeth had assumed a motherly role – seemingly taking the place of Lara's own mother after two separate tragedies within the space of a few months had left her parentless. It was just one of many parallels the young couple shared and made for a common bond drawing them even closer.

For Nikki's sake, the adults initially skirted around any talk of Adam and the enforced estrangement, though the caring looks Elizabeth sent her way convinced Lara she still had an ally. Ever since that horrible night, the young woman had been anxious his parents would be reluctant to see them again. Any of those fears were soon laid to rest when she saw the love and concern oozing from their eyes.

"Do you want to have a look at my new school uniform?" Nikki hopped excitedly from one foot to the other waiting for their response.

"Of course we do, don't we, darling," Elizabeth enthused as Charles vigorously nodded his head.

Off she ran to grab the brand-new tartan backpack from its temporary home beside the kitchen bench. After a mad scramble inside its dark confines, she came back with the miniscule garment pressed proudly against her tiny body.

"See, isn't it pretty? It's even got a special crest on the pocket – look!" She pointed to the badge and turned to her mother. "Can I put it on to show them, Mummy?"

"Alright, but be careful. We don't want it getting dirty."

"Yay!" Nikki squealed loudly, running off to the downstairs bathroom with Lara following closely behind.

"Oh, you look so cute!" Elizabeth exclaimed when she pranced out a few minutes later, dressed in the red, black and green checked tunic that matched the same tartan pattern on the new backpack.

"*Och aye*, a bonnie wee lass!" Charles concurred, jumping to his feet and dancing a lively Highland Jig. He had Nikki – along with the others – in fits of laughter as she joined in.

They were in their usual spot on the shady terrace attached to the back of the elegant plantation-style mansion. It was perfectly positioned to overlook the Brisbane River at Fig Tree Pocket and had played host to many special times, especially in the last few months. It wasn't long before the little girl started skipping around the table, impatient to change into her riding gear for a quick ride on Clancy before dinner was served.

While Charles took Nikki off to visit the Welsh Mountain pony restlessly pacing backwards and forwards along the fence-line since Lara's car pulled in, the two women settled back to discuss what was uppermost in their hearts.

"How are you really doing, my dear girl?" Elizabeth couldn't hide her concern. "I've been so worried about you."

Lara nodded slowly and gazed across the river, her eyes fixed on nothing in particular. "Mmm, I'm okay … at least I'm getting there. I try to keep my mind on other things as much as I can – but, you know … that old ache never takes a holiday. At least Nikki keeps me busy, so that's a blessing. Don't worry, I'll be alright," she finished with the makings of a smile.

There was no way she wanted to reveal the true depths of her despair … no one could do anything to help, and she certainly didn't want to add to Elizabeth's worries. Somehow, she just had to learn to live without him.

Adam's mother wasn't at all convinced and decided it was high time the truth about her son was brought to light. Hopefully, it might also help Lara to open up and possibly even lend a hand in bringing about their reconciliation. No matter how hard she and Charles tried over the years, Trina was never interested in spending time with them and hadn't been to their house in years. It was inevitable their only concern was for Adam and his needs – along with this delightful young woman and the little child he loved with all his heart.

She squeezed Lara's hand as a way to soften the aftermath of what was coming. "My dear, there's something you really need to know, and I'm not going to beat around the bush. My poor Adam is devastated. I've never seen him looking this despondent. He misses you more than I could ever say; so much so, I'm becoming quite concerned."

The news had the desired effect and a sob caught in Lara's throat, although she couldn't get any words out over the huge lump lodged there.

"He tries hard to pretend everything's okay, but those eyes tell a different story. And he's so worried about how you're coping, it's eating him up inside, but he won't let us do anything to help. I'm afraid he's just about reached breaking point."

Lara swallowed hard. "I miss him so much, Elizabeth ... sometimes I can hardly breathe..."

"Oh, my darling girl, I'm so sorry. Come here."

She gathered the broken woman in her arms as the dam wall finally burst. Learning the true extent of Adam's heartache had been the final straw. Because there had been no word from him for almost a month, Lara had assumed he was getting on with life. Hearing this news compounded her own heartache, and anguished sobs rose from deep in her spirit.

"I just wish there was something I could do to help. It breaks my heart to see you both like this," his mother crooned.

Her arms provided a level of shelter and comfort the other one so desperately needed. Even so, when Lara eventually managed to dry her tears, the depth of her misery was still plain to see.

"I thought he might be coping better by now. I just want him to be happy – I *need* him to be happy ... that's all that matters." She clutched at the other woman's arm. "You have to make him forget about me, even if it means telling him we're getting on with our lives. I don't want him worrying about us with everything else that's going on over there. I'll be okay as long as I know he's alright."

Elizabeth had listened to her son utter these exact same sentiments for more an hour the day before. He well knew how much Lara would be fretting and didn't want her wasting her life on a dream that may never come to fruition ... she had been through enough in her short life.

His mother was astounded at how the pair of them always put the other one's needs above their own. It was what made them so special ... and so right for each other. But she wasn't going to lie. What they were asking went against everything she believed in. They belonged together, even if things seemed impossible right now.

§

Dinner itself turned into a light-hearted affair as Charles regaled them with tales of his time as a young man in comedy theatre. Lara was sure it was his way of trying to cheer her up, especially as she watched him mesmerise Nikki with a few of the memorable characters from those days. Despite the sombre talk on the terrace, these few hours had brought some much-needed sunshine into an otherwise hopeless situation.

When they were saying goodbye, she hugged him close. "Thank you. We both needed that."

His answering nod and a soft kiss on her cheek conveyed a measure of his care and concern. "Good, that's what I was hoping. Now keep in touch, young lady. We don't want to have to worry about you, too."

"Mmm, I will, I promise. And thanks for being so free with your love and support. It means everything to both of us."

"You're very welcome and don't leave it so long between visits next time."

"I won't," she finished with the glimmer of a smile before driving away.

Charles placed a comforting arm around his wife's shoulder as they walked back into the house. He pulled her even closer as a film of sadness clouded her eyes. "Don't worry, my darling. All we can do is pray for them and be there when they need us. The rest is up to God."

A downcast nod and deep sigh were all Elizabeth could manage as she pressed closer into his side.

§

Later that night while Charles was sound asleep, his wife made one of her monthly calls to a charming villa in Tuscany, Italy – one arm of their many business concerns. When a familiar voice answered, she settled down for a long chat.

Claudia was thrilled to hear from her Australian friend. Though she and Antonio were technically only the managers of the vineyard, Charles and Elizabeth had never treated either of them as anything other than family. After their usual chatter, Claudia enquired after Adam, Lara and Nikki. The trio had taken up residence in the Italian *Nona's* heart during their short stay only a few months earlier, so she was always eager to catch up on any news.

"Actually, that's one of the reasons for my call. I need to ask you a favour, my dear."

"*Si,* of course, *Elizabetta,* 'ow can I 'elp you?"

"Oh, it's so terribly sad, Claudia ... Adam and Lara are no longer together. Trina—"

The other woman broke in. As usual, her words were a jumbled mix of both languages, especially whenever she was upset. "*Oh, no ... è terribile!* My poor Larissa... And Adam – they are sooo in love. Trina *è una mucca orribile* – 'ow you say ... ummm ... a 'orrible cow! He should 'ave left 'er years ago. Oh, *mama mia*, this news is no good..." Her voice trailed off, laden with disappointment and sadness.

"I know ... that's how we feel, too. Since Trina left rehab, she's started getting up to her old tricks – even drinking again on at least one occasion – and just before Christmas, she found out about their relationship. Normally I could never condone an affair, but after all the grief she's given him over the yea—"

"Adam needs to leave – you must tell 'im, *mia caro amico* – make 'im go! Larissa, she is *molto buono* – aaahhh ... ummm ... *si* – she is very good for 'im ... and Nikki, that *preziosa bambina* – oh 'e loves 'er like 'is own..."

She was heartbroken and in typical Mediterranean fashion, her voice was loud with emotion.

"Yes, it's awful. Nikki's missing him terribly. Oh, Claudia, it's so sad to see. We love them both like our own, and they're so good for him, too – I've never seen him so happy as when they were together. It's just tragic."

"Oh no, 'ow will I tell 'Tonio! He will be 'eartbroken..."

Her mind went back to images of them all laughing around the table during the trio's two-week visit to the villa when her husband tried to show Adam how to 'romance his woman' in the true Italian way.

"I know. We all are..."

The two women commiserated with each other for several minutes until Elizabeth finished with, "So I need you to include them in your prayers, my dear friend. When you go to early morning mass in the old church down the road, please send up a prayer for them as well."

Claudia's stilted English dripped with sadness. "Of course, my sweet *Elizabetta*, I will pray every day, and I know *Our Signora Maria* will answer – she 'as done *molti, molti miracoli* in that special place, so this will just be one more. I will truly be asking for a miracle. *Dio* will answer, you will see."

"Thank you, dear one. I knew I could rely on you."

With promises to ring if she had any further news, Elizabeth put the phone back in its cradle. The call had brought a glimmer of hope into her sad heart.

§

Suzie was just as worried and had been ringing Lara regularly to make sure she was okay. With Nikki's first day of school looming, the sisters made plans to meet at the school gate. The older one had no trouble imagining how hard Lara would find it having to say goodbye to such a special phase in their lives. Watching her little girl take those first real steps towards independence would be a huge wrench on her heart.

"Hi, Lara-Lu ... hello, my little pumpkin!" she called out, waving madly through the swarm of mothers and children.

Nikki's face lit up and she took off at a run, the large backpack swinging from side to side on her tiny frame as her long plait bounced freely against her derrière, both keeping time to the slap of brand new shoes on the bitumen footpath. The new tartan tunic reached down past her knees, almost making the excited youngster trip up. Being so petite, everything seemed to swim on her.

Suzie caught the mini tornado in full flight, wrapping her in a smothering bearhug while a pair of thin arms wrapped themselves tightly around this much-loved auntie's neck.

"You came ... you came! I'm going to *big* school today and I can't wait!" came the excited reply as the brand-new pupil let go and twirled around proudly for Suzie to see. "I'm going to make lots of friends, and I've even got a new uniform."

"You look sooo grown up, little miss, and I bet you'll have a boyfriend by the end of the week! None of the boys will be able to resist you, especially with that gorgeous smile."

She tweaked her niece's cute button nose and made her laugh.

"I've already got a boyfriend. His name's Joshua, and I really like him. He used to be horrible and mean, but now he's really nice."

Lara caught the last few remarks after fighting her way through the ever-increasing throng. For the space of an instant, another conversation caused a sharp pang in her heart as she recalled Nikki assuring Adam he was her 'fabourite boyfriend'. She pushed the thought back to where it belonged. This was Nikki's day, and nothing was going to spoil it.

The grade one classroom was nearest to the front gate, and the family mingled with other mothers and excited students just outside the door. It wasn't long before Nikki's teacher arrived, meaning it was time for Lara to leave her only offspring in the care of a total stranger. Thankfully, the little girl was far too eager to find out what 'big school' was all about to get upset about saying goodbye.

After lots of tight hugs and assurances as to how much she would miss her, Lara watched with a heavy heart as her only child took those first poignant steps away from toddlerhood. Not surprisingly, it ached just that little bit more when the door closed with a defining click. It didn't matter how much she enjoyed watching Nikki develop and mature, a stubborn, selfish streak still wanted to keep her young and innocent ... and all to herself.

Suzie couldn't help noticing the sadness creeping into her sister's eyes, so she linked arms with her as they dawdled back to their cars.

Unbeknown to either of them, the same dark eyes that had once followed Lara when she was lost in the music on a shadowy stage during *Show Boat's* first rehearsal, now became silent witnesses to the tears glistening in those sapphire blue ones watching as her precious daughter spread a new set of wings.

Even though a fierce yearning assaulted him and he wanted to rush over to be the one offering her comfort, Adam didn't dare. He was too afraid of the temptation to throw caution to the wind just to get lost inside those mesmerising eyes again. With Trina's sinister threats still ringing in his ears, Lara's safety was paramount over any selfish desires on his part.

All night he had wrestled with wanting to be there and needing to stay away. In the end, the cry of his heart won out. Even if it meant only being able to witness a little girl's first solo adventure from afar, anything was better than this endless wondering.

"Go with them, Lord," he whispered.

Then with the heaviest of hearts, Adam slumped down in his seat – dreading the thought of having to drive away from the only woman he would ever love.

§

The day couldn't go fast enough. Lara's mind was constantly on her young daughter in the company of complete strangers. No matter how many times she scolded herself for being ridiculous, the truth was it had only been the two of them for many years. It was only natural she was feeling the weight of separation so much. The bond they shared was stronger than most, and more than likely Nikki would be the only child Lara would ever have. Trusting the little girl's future to folk she didn't know made the separation even more difficult.

Her first project after lunch was syncing the vision and audio of a woman in the throes of labour. Sitting in front of the array of rollers, buttons and large flat spools littering the flatbed's vast surface, an overwhelming sense of loss bubbled up from deep inside. Even if she and Adam did eventually end up together, Lara would never have an opportunity to carry his baby. And it was all Trina's fault. Even though he had always wanted children of his own, his wife had badgered him into having a vasectomy many years ago.

From the depths of Lara's anguished spirit came a ceaseless yearning. *Oh God, if I couldn't have all of him, why couldn't I at least have known the joy of having his baby – something of his to love and cherish forever? Even having just a part of him might have helped to fill this gaping hole in my heart.*

A heart-wrenching sob bubbled up from her throat, and she couldn't control the tears as they poured down her cheeks. Thankfully, her boss was out of the office, so there were no witnesses to this new form of torment.

Will nothing help to take this misery away?

§

Lara was standing at the school gate just as three o'clock ticked over. David was aware of how hard she worked and knew how important it was for her to be there for Nikki. It was his idea to adjust her work hours to ensure she could pick the little girl up from school each day. He also offered a comparable pay rise to ensure she didn't lose any of her much-needed income. His generosity had taken a heavy load off the young mother's mind, and she was grateful to have such an understanding boss.

As soon as the little girl spied the familiar figure waiting by the school gate, she rushed down the path with her arms outstretched and the school hat bouncing around her neck.

"Mummy, you came! I missed you sooo much."

Lara clasped the precious little bundle close. "Of course I came, Poppet. I missed you too, as big as the sky, and I couldn't leave my bestest girl to walk home all by herself now, could I?"

Hand-in-hand they made their way to the car with Nikki babbling on and on about all she had done and how many new friends she had made.

"Did you find yourself a new boyfriend?"

Rolling her eyes, the youngster scoffed, "Of *course* not. I love Joshua and he loves me!"

The declaration was so matter-of-fact Lara let out a loud chortle. This was the first time she had laughed since before Christmas, and all because of a bubbly little girl.

§

"Mummy, you *have* to eat up all your dinner. That's what you always tell me."

The food on Lara's plate was congealing into a gluggy mess as she absentmindedly dug at it with a fork. This was the third time Nikki had scolded her in a matter of minutes, so she made another attempt to look interested to appease the little girl.

Suddenly there was a loud knock on the door. The little pocket-rocket raced to the window, only to let out a loud squeal of delight when she caught sight of Suzie and her new boyfriend smiling back at her. Spying a large box of popcorn under his arm was added incentive, so she flung open the door and rushed out to greet them.

"Hello, gorgeous girl," Suzie said with a chuckle, bending down to kiss the giggling mass covered in long hair so like her sister's now clinging to her thighs. "I've come to hijack your mum for a while, and Uncle Ben's going to watch *The Sound of Music* with you. It's about time he learned the words to all your favourite songs!"

"*Yippee!* Uncle Ben, you're going to *love* it! Come with me and I'll show you where the video player is." Suzie soon found herself abandoned as Nikki dragged him inside by the hand.

She went straight out to the kitchen and discovered her sister hurriedly scraping what looked to be food still covering half the plate into the bin.

Knowing how frugal Lara normally was, she sent a worried frown her way, speaking with just as much concern as determination. "Okay, young lady, you and me are going out for a coffee. It's about time we got into some quality chitchat and tonight's the night. I'll finish off here while you get changed out of that disgusting old tracksuit. The only place it deserves to be is in the bin!"

Lara knew exactly what she was up to and quickly protested; clinging to the plate her sister was trying to wrestle from her hands. "You don't have to do that, Suze. I'm fine. How about we just stay here with the others and watch the movie, too."

"And have to endure listening to 'My Fabourite Things' again for the hundredth time this year – you've got to be kidding! Besides, just once would you do as you're told! Now scoot ... I want you back out here in five minutes, okay?" Sending a playful scowl over her shoulder, Lara went off to the bedroom but not without receiving one last command. "Oh, and next time eat *all* your dinner just like you tell a certain little person every night!"

A short time later, the two women wandered into a little cafe not too far from Lara's home. They gave their order to the cashier before choosing a spot in a quiet corner.

Recognising the pain still plainly visible in Lara's eyes, the comfortable sofa for two would be the perfect setting to soften any necessary harsh words. It was obvious she couldn't continue going down this miserable path, so it was time Suzie took a few desperate measures.

"I know you don't want to hear what I have to say, but I don't care anymore – you need to hear it. Just look at how much weight you've lost – those clothes are starting to hang off you. You're beginning to look like a shell of your former self. I know it's hard, but you can't go on like this or you'll make yourself sick. Then who's going to take care of Nikki? She needs you now more than ever."

The force of her words caused Lara to crumble, and the anguish in her whole demeanour broke the other one's heart. "But I miss him so much I don't know how to go on. I try, but the pain's unbearable and ... oooh, what's the point..."

Once again, concern for her niece took priority. Suzie grabbed Lara by the arm and forced her to look at her. "Did you hear what you just said? *Nikki's* the point. Even when things get so rough you're sure the ship's about to sink, you *have* to think about her."

Her message was harsh but also a necessary wake-up call. Lara let out a deep-seated sigh, but it wasn't enough to put an end to the diatribe.

"I mean it! I know you miss him, and you're fretting for all Nikki's lost too, and I understand how hard it is living without the physical side, but you can't let what's happened to eat you up like this. Your whole life is still ahe—"

"But, Suze, you don't understand! It wasn't just the physical side ... he filled my mind and my heart and every cell of my being ... the only time I feel whole is when I'm with him. It's like I'm only half a person now." Big glistening tears formed tracks down her cheeks as she stifled a sob.

Waves of compassion softened the older one's heart. Suzie was familiar with that dead feeling inside after losing her fiancé in a motorbike accident. All of the former frustration melted away, and she was filled with a rush of motherly concern remembering how much the two of them needed each other when their parents died. Drawing the broken woman into her arms, she rocked her gently as the grief overflowed.

"Oh, sweetie, I'm so sorry. I knew you were finding it tough ... I'd forgotten how bad the pain is. You're doing a great job raising Nikki – she's a real credit to you – but promise me you'll take better care of yourself. I've only got one sister, and I couldn't bear to lose any more of my family ... you and Nikki are all I have left..."

Lara nodded slowly, wiping her cheeks and under her chin with a tissue that had somehow found its way into her hand.

"Okay, I will, I promise. I know things'll get easier eventually; I just wish they'd hurry up. I'm so tired of missing him all the time..."

"I know, hon, but I'll always be here when you need me."

All Suzie could do was hold on tight, trying to impart a new lease of life into a soul that was seemingly withering before her very eyes.

Chapter 2

Those few minutes Adam spent watching Lara and Nikki at the school gate had been a bittersweet encounter. Even that tiny glimpse was enough to feed the constant hunger; until he saw the sadness in her eyes coupled with the knowledge he could do nothing to help, then the missing became so much harder.

Still fearing for their lives, he was determined not to do anything that might tempt his wife back to seeking solace in a liquor bottle in case it set her off on a tirade of hate and destruction with Lara as her main target.

Every day he made a deliberate effort to include Trina in his everyday life, even though he was living with a broken heart and longing for someone else. The onus was on him if she was to gain any semblance of trust again.

In recent weeks, his pattern of leaving for work at the crack of dawn had changed to a more decent hour. Each morning, Adam put together something healthy for breakfast, and most times waited for her to join him before starting his own. Initially, Trina was suspicious of his motives, but as the days turned to weeks, she relaxed into this new routine and even looked forward to hearing his plans for the day over the shared meal.

Three weeks after the school gate incident she entered the kitchen to find her husband just popping a last crust of toast in his mouth.

"Oh, there you are. Sorry, I have an early appointment this morning so I couldn't wait. What are you up to today?" he asked, settling back in his chair to take a long swig of coffee. Seeing her dressed in exercise gear was certainly something out of the ordinary. He looked her up and down with a puzzled frown.

"Oh, Judith and I thought we might join a fitness club that's just opened around the corner. I don't know how we'll go, but it'll be good to give it a try." She was looking far healthier now her diet had improved. As far as Adam could tell, she hadn't indulged in any of her previous liquid sustenance since the notable slip-up nearly five weeks earlier.

He was pleased to learn she was looking into doing something constructive to fill the day – a lot of her problem had been not having anything to focus on. Maybe this would help.

"That sounds great ... enjoy yourselves," he said, wiping his mouth with a napkin before pushing back his chair. He grabbed an oven mitt hanging on a hook by the stove, then took a freshly made omelette from the oven before placing it on the table in front of her. "Better have this before you go then to keep your strength up. Oh, and say hello to Judith for me."

"Yeah, if I remember," she replied, tucking into the tasty fare. There was still no warmth in any of her responses, although he was used to that after so many years.

Regardless of the recent improvements to his home life, as he finished dressing, Adam's thoughts turned to the woman who had taken up residence in his soul.

His gaze fell on a distant mountaintop with its four tall television towers clearly visible. "I miss you, sweet lady," came a heartfelt whisper.

Letting out a deep sigh, he deliberately set his shoulders, knotted his tie and with a heavy tread made his way downstairs again.

Trina was flicking through a magazine when he passed through the kitchen on his way to the car.

"See you tonight. Have fun."

Without so much as even a glance his way, she mumbled, "Mmm, whatever."

Adam paused by the door for a moment, wondering if she would look up and actually acknowledge him, but her nose remained firmly buried in the gossip columns as she drained the final dregs from her coffee cup. Not much had changed after all.

He pulled out of the driveway just as the soulful strains of Willie Nelson's classic rendition of *Always on My Mind* travelled across the airwaves. His eyes blurred and a sudden rush of longing caused him to pull over to the side of the road. As the evocative words filled the cabin of the silver Mercedes, he remained motionless for several minutes. Every line and inflection could have come from his heart, and once again he was assailed with an excruciating sense of loss, along with the realisation he would hanker for her until the last breath left his body.

§

After the recent heart to heart with her sister, Lara still wasn't coping as well as she made out. On the surface, she came across as her old self, while deep down it was as though her soul was slowly dying and nothing was able to lift her spirits. If she didn't have the responsibility of a certain little person in her life, Lara would have preferred to curl up all day in a darkened corner of her bedroom listening to soulful music. Nikki had become her sanity and the only reason she got out of bed in the morning ... everything else seemed pointless and held no meaning anymore. Even work had become a hard slog, although she always managed to put on a happy face so David wouldn't worry.

Late one night, Lara started pacing the floor looking for anything to take away the loneliness. Nikki had already been asleep for hours when she opened the fridge door and spied a full bottle of Moscato lying half-buried behind a pile of other things on the bottom shelf. It was the one Suzie had brought over so many months ago – on the day Adam made up his mind to leave Trina.

She remembered thinking they would use it to celebrate later that same afternoon. It didn't take long before memories of the excitement of sharing a future with him dropped by to keep her company ... along with recalling how those few hours of hope had suddenly disintegrated into fear and despair – and all because of the inebriated actions of a woman with revenge on her mind.

"Not much point in keeping *you* for any sort of celebration now, is there? How about you 'n me have a party instead," she scoffed into the thick cloak of night as the cork popped and flew into the air.

Lara had never really liked the taste nor the after-effects of any form of alcohol. On the rare occasions she did indulge, it was only to partake in a single glass. But tonight was different – tonight she couldn't care less. There was no one else to see and maybe it would help make the dark hours scurry away.

Sitting on the veranda with only a few streetlights to keep her company, she looked westwards to where Adam had mentioned he and Trina's country estate was located. She raised the glass of pale liquid high into the air.

"Here's to you, Trina ... cheers!"

She sculled the bubbly potion in several deep gulps.

Over the next couple of hours, the wine bottle's contents slowly diminished as the silvery shape of a half-moon crept across the starry sky. When the grandmother clock chimed one, Lara dribbled the last remaining drops into her glass.

With an elaborate flourish she raised it above her head and slurred across the miles, "But you'd better take care o' him or *I'll* be the one makin' threats next time."

Several hours later, a pair of glassy eyes opened gingerly when the sun's persistent rays danced across her eyelids. Blinking rapidly, she quickly shielded them with her hands. A throbbing head and heaving stomach were unwelcome reminders of the previous night's foolishness.

"You stupid idiot, wouldn't Adam just *love* to see you now!"

She stumbled out to the bathroom to splash cold water over her face and down her parched throat. Looking in the mirror and loathing what she saw, it suddenly dawned on her she was behaving just like his wife.

"He's better off without you if you're going to act so dumb," she muttered disgustedly to her reflection before gripping the basin hard to stop from swaying.

Screwing up her nose at the remnants of dark shadows under her eyes, she swiped at her cracked lips with the back of a shaky hand. The motion caused a foul odour to waft into her nostrils.

"*Pfaw*, you're *repulsive!*"

Shuffling back into the bedroom, she noticed the curtains billow in a gentle breeze and realised she must have forgotten to close them during her stupor of the night before. Still blinded by the summer light, she went over to draw them closed. Instinctively, her gaze fell on the lofty hills of Mt Coot-tha with its television towers clearly visible in the distance. As though pierced by an arrow, Lara felt a sharp sting in her heart. Memories of Adam's declaration about standing guard over her from that same spot caused her head to drop in shame.

In the light of day, her recent alcoholic love affair hadn't helped one bit – in fact, it had only brought more heartbreak when she realised how badly she had let him down ... as well as putting her precious daughter's life at risk. A heartfelt whisper carried on the wind with a vow never to permit anything like that to happen again.

Inadvertently, her actions of the night before had become a blessing in disguise. The pathetic encounter had brought her back from the brink and become the turning point on a long road leading away from the dark abyss that had been threatening to engulf her.

Between wracking sobs and feelings of deep regret, she came to the hardest decision of her life. "I...I don't deserve him any...more – he's all yours now, Tr...ina ... but I'll never e…ver stop lov...ing him. And you'd be...tter look after him and give him lots of rea...sons to smile..."

With one last gut-wrenching sob, her voice gave up and she flung herself across the bed – broken and bereft.

§

It was the middle of February, only a few days after Lara's brush with despair, when Paul rang Adam to announce they were about to cast the roles for a new production of *Oklahoma* due to open in May and he wanted him for the lead.

"And I've just offered Lara the role of *Laurey*. So hopefully, between the two of you, every show should be a sell-out just like *Show Boat*."

Adam's breath caught in his throat. So many times he had wanted to shout her name into the air, purely to bring a semblance of her spirit into his lonely world. Hearing it roll so easily off Paul's tongue was exquisite agony. More than anything he wanted to see her again. Now he had the perfect excuse, even if it meant sharing her with the rest of the cast.

For a split second he pondered whether he could risk not saying anything to

Trina, but the idea soon fell by the wayside. She had been taking an interest in everything he was doing lately, even if only to ensure he wasn't meeting with Lara behind her back. It wouldn't be plausible trying to attend weekly rehearsals without saying anything. There was really only one real choice left to him – come clean and face the music.

"Sounds great! When do rehearsals start?" he asked, hoping for a couple of days to talk Trina around.

"Next Thursday at the usual time. Nearly everyone has committed to this one, although I'm still waiting to hear back from Lara."

Once again, he felt that familiar tug. "What did she say when you told her?"

Paul's was surprised to hear Adam's response, expecting they would have discussed it already after inadvertently witnessing one of their furtive encounters during rehearsals the year before.

His tone was quizzical. "She couldn't give me an answer just yet – said she wanted to check with Charles first. I have to admit I was surprised, but she was adamant so I told her I was prepared to wait a few days before making a final decision. What's going on, mate? I could've bet my bottom dollar she'd be eager to jump on board, especially after the audiences' response to her solo last time."

Adam realised the director needed to hear what was going on – it was only fair to tell him the truth if they were to work together.

After learning what happened, Paul's concern was genuine. "Oh, I'm really sorry, mate. I can't begin to imagine how hard this must be on you. Both of you did a great job hiding your true feelings from everyone, but it was obvious to me almost from the beginning something was going on."

"It wasn't easy ... but it was sure better than this..."

Paul heard the pain in Adam's voice, and his tone softened even more. "I'll bet. I always had an idea living with Trina must be pretty tough – Charles filled me in on some of it when you missed opening night a few years ago – he mentioned about her 'problem'." Pausing for a moment, he then added quietly, "I also remember that black eye you tried to hide under all those layers of makeup. I didn't need to be a detective to understand what was going on."

"Mmm, we've certainly had our ups and downs, but these last seven weeks've been a living hell trying to stay away from Lara. I really want to say yes, only I'm worried how Trina'll react."

"That's okay. I can give you the night to think about it – just get back to me tomorrow sometime. If you want my two bob's worth, I reckon you'd be a fool not to take it. Trina just has to understand the theatre's a major part of your life. It's unrealistic expecting you to give it up just like that." As an added incentive, Paul threw out the one enticement he hoped would tip his star over the edge. "Besides, if Lara agrees, you'll be able to spend time with her without the need to worry."

Adam gave a half-hearted laugh that barely disguised his good-humoured sarcasm. "Thanks, pal ... why don't you go all out in making it *really* hard on a mate!" He thought for a moment before adding, "Look, I'll suss it out with Trina and get back to you, okay?"

"Sure, but you're going to regret it if you don't," came the sombre reply.

§

As soon as Trina wandered into the kitchen the following morning, Adam got up from his seat at the table to pull out the one opposite. She sat down with an uninterested grunt as he placed a plate of scrambled eggs in front of her, along with a fresh cup of steamy coffee.

With mounting trepidation, he took his place again, leaned back and looked her straight in the eye. There was nothing Adam had done to be ashamed of, and he refused to act as if there was. Even so, he suffered a few niggles of angst about raising a subject that had been eating away at him all night.

After the usual stilted greetings, he plunged straight in. "Paul rang last night – he wants me for his new musical. It means I'll be out every Thursday night 'til the middle of May and he expects it to run for about four weeks after that."

Trina had been watching her husband intently during this pre-rehearsed speech and her reply was cool. "So what's the show?"

"*Oklahoma.*"

"And I suppose *you're* playing the romantic lead. So who's your leading lady?"

Aware she was baiting him, he was ready. "Well, yeah, he's offered me the role of *Curly,* but it's still up in the air who'll be playing *Laurey* ... but just so you know, he did mention about asking Lara." It was pointless pretending he didn't know what she was getting at.

"What? Doesn't she want it?" Trina's eyes narrowed, and her response was matter-of-fact. It was obvious she wanted to find out just how much he knew.

"I wouldn't have a clue. All Paul said was that he'd asked her, but she hadn't given him an answer yet. If she does end up taking it, we'll only be seeing each other at the theatre with everyone else around. You've made your point, and I'm pretty sure I've proved over the last couple of months that you come first."

Trina couldn't argue, although she still wasn't convinced just how much he could be trusted. She had caught the looks passing between them on stage and remembered how stunning the other woman was. Glancing in the mirror behind Adam's head, she flicked at her fiery tresses; almost as if to convince herself she was just as attractive as her much younger adversary ... and would do whatever it took to ensure Adam felt the same.

"Anyway, she's probably just like every other wannabe actress, flitting from one leading man to the next depending on who takes her fancy. I wouldn't be at all surprised if you were just her holiday season fling and now she's moved on to greener pastures."

She was enjoying besmirching her rival's name, along with any feelings he might still be harbouring ... but Adam knew Lara far better than his wife realised. Trina still had no idea their relationship had been going on long before she ever learned about it ... and if he had anything to do with it, she never would.

He was quick to grasp onto the unintentional opportunity suddenly placed in his lap, so his response was immediate. For the first time in a long time, it was quite cutting too.

"You might be right, but I'm not getting into this anymore. I refuse to live my life waiting for you to pounce at every little thing that comes along, especially when you know how much I love the theatre. Either you accept I'll be staying with the company – *and* we'll be working together if Lara decides to take the role – or you and I might as well just call it quits now. I'm not playing your stupid, petty games anymore. If you can't see how often I've put you before everyone else, then our marriage isn't worth the paper it's printed on."

Taken back by his tone as well as his intent, Trina suddenly realised the precarious line she was treading. She didn't dare risk losing him, nor all the benefits staying married to him brought. She also recognised there was no substance any more for this constant jealousy. Adam was home most nights, and on the odd occasion he was away, he always called to let her know what was going on. Even so, she still felt a pressing need to hold the upper hand.

With a quick flick of her wrist as a way to dismiss his threat, she answered nonchalantly, "Alright, if that's what you want then, go ahead. They're putting on an extra class at the fitness centre on Thursday nights. While you're off with her, I'll be eyeing up the cute instructor."

She couldn't resist throwing out that final barb.

Adam rose from the table and threw his napkin on the plate. The only response worth uttering was to roll his eyes and throw out the shortest reply.

"Suit yourself. I'm off to work; see you tonight sometime."

§

As far as Charles was concerned, Lara and Adam belonged together. Sometimes he wanted to shake his son, purely to make him see what he was doing to all their lives, including Trina's. But then he also knew how stubborn Adam could be once his mind was made up.

You sure can be such a stubborn mule at times, my boy. Look at everything that's happened and all because of your pigheadedness. If you'd only listened to my advice about marrying her, we wouldn't be in this blasted mess.

When Lara eventually got around to ringing Charles, his response was exactly what Paul had hoped for.

"My dear girl, you have to take the part. Playing *Julie* in *Showboat* proved your amazing gift and this new role would suit your voice perfectly. You can't possibly say no!"

"But I can't take it, Charles. Seeing him will break my heart all over again – especially knowing we can never be together."

"But then again it might be a blessing, after all. Sometimes the best way to move forward is to face your fea—"

"I *can't*. You know how much I still care."

She had no idea Charles was actually looking far deeper. He understood how important this was, not only for her musical career but also as a way to bring their shared agony to a head. By facing each other, he hoped Adam would come to his senses and leave his wife for good. It was impossible to ignore the pain in their eyes whenever either one dropped by the Ashworth home, albeit days apart.

"Lara, all I'm saying is, take this one chance ... please. Then if things get too hard or messy, you can always join another company when this production's done. Any one of them would snap you up in an instant after *Show Boat's* rave reviews. But at least give Paul – and yourself – another opportunity to showcase that God-given talent, especially after all the hard work he's put in to elevate the company to the next level. He deserves that much after trusting you with the role of *Julie*."

His response was harsh, but he needed her to see how important this was for both of them.

Oh great, and just after I've made a vow never to see him again.

There was silence for a few moments ... and then he heard a heavy sigh of resignation. "All right ... I'll do it, but only for Paul's sake. You're right; he has been generous to me. But what about Trina? How's she going to react when she finds out?"

Charles was thankful Lara couldn't see the relieved response he sent to the heavens. "Don't you worry about Trina. Too many people have been putting her needs first. For once think about yourself and what you want."

He had to strain to hear her response.

"I only hope you're right. I couldn't bear the thought that he was suffering even more because of me."

"He's suffering far more without you. You've made a wise decision; I'm sure it'll all work out fine. See you on Thursday. And Lara" —he paused for a moment and his final two words dripped with emotion— "thank you."

Placing the receiver back on its cradle, Lara could only hope her decision would bring no dire repercussions ... but for the first time since Christmas Eve, she felt alive again.

§

The following day Lara rang Lucy. She was still in two minds and needed her best friend's wisdom to help put everything into perspective. The women had been in touch regularly and Lucy had been heartbroken when she heard about the breakup.

"Oh Lars, that's *fabulous* ... I'm over the moon you said yes! You'd be a fool to go anywhere else after making such a name for yourself already with this company. Besides, there's no one else I ever want to share a dressing room with – who else'd put up with my constant chatter ... and all that clutter!" She grinned as she caught Lara's faint chuckle. "We're a twosome you 'n me – I can just see the headline – *Paul's Frolicking Fillies* – and we're going to have a ball! And if that old cow comes around again, well these old pins of mine are much longer than hers so I'll soon kick her off the set, just you wait and see."

A sudden image of that vivid word picture flashed into Lara's mind and she burst out laughing. "Oh, Luce, what would I do without you in my life! Thanks, hon ... now, just make sure you keep those amazingly long pins on your side of the dressing room. I can't afford a broken leg after what happened to my..."

The unspoken word hung between them, but Lucy was quick with a kind word of reassurance. "Hey, I'm going to be right there beside you all the way. And if things get tough and you need a shoulder to cry on – or even just someone to make you laugh – make sure you come to me, okay?"

"Okay, I'll remember. And thanks heaps."

For the first time in ages, Lara spent the whole day with a smile on her face.

Chapter 3

Waves of nervousness kept lapping at Lara's stomach when she was getting ready on Thursday night. The only thing to bring her any form of ease was by taking slow deep breaths.

Just like so many months ago, her bed resembled a jumble sale with its dishevelled array of discarded clothing piled from one end to the other. She was scared of dressing too stylishly and making a fool of herself, but then again looking too casual was out of the question as well. Though they were no longer together, she still craved Adam's approval ... even it if was from afar. If she had been able to see inside his mind, Lara would have realised he couldn't care less what clothes she wore. Simply a glimpse of the love in her eyes was all he was hankering for ... those fathomless sapphire pools never failed to make him catch his breath whenever their eyes met.

"*Mummy!* Look ... at ... your ... *bed!*" Nikki exclaimed with her hands raised in astonishment as she walked into her mother's room. "You're *never* going to be able to find it to sleep in tonight! You might have to come and sleep with me, 'cept my bed's not very big."

Lara smiled to hear the phrase she so often used now coming from the one it was usually directed at.

Suzie and Ben were just knocking on the front door when they overheard the taut rebuke and exchanged bemused grins. Nikki heard the loud rap and ran across to let them in. Pressing a quick kiss on her niece's forehead, Suzie then marched straight to her sister's bedroom to find out why the little girl was making such a fuss.

"One guess where your mind is ... and don't worry, I'd be the same," she chuckled, watching as her sister pulled yet another dress over her head only to have it join the others at the top of the pile. "And this all looks familiar – I seem to remember another time when your bed looked like a tornado had hit!"

Suzie was pleased Lara had decided to go back to the theatre, even though her nerves were obviously getting a good workout at the thought of seeing him again. Secretly, she was hoping Adam would take one look, grab her sister by the hand and ride off into the sunset without looking back.

From their very first meeting, Suzie had felt drawn to him. Watching their relationship grow over the following months, it was easy to see how good they were for each other. No one had ever made Lara's eyes shine the way they did whenever Adam was around. Her greatest wish was to see them end up together, especially when she learnt how ghastly his marriage was.

"Stop it!" Lara warned sternly. "You have to be my anchor in this ... it's hard enough without you adding your two bits worth..."

"Okay, I'll give it a go, but you can't blame a big sister for trying," Suzie quipped, trying unsuccessfully to wipe the smirk from her face as Lara pulled another dress from the cupboard and yanked it over her head.

"Well, be a *good* big sister and help me do this zip up, please."

Lara turned around so Suzie could fasten the cobalt blue and white strapless dress – the same one chosen for their first outing to the beach on the day he and Nikki met. Like an obedient child, Suzie did as she was bid and a small grin flitted across her face at the eye-catching choice of outfit.

Crikey, if this doesn't get his attention, nothing will!

While checking her reflection in the long mirror, Lara's fingers smoothed the French cotton material where it hugged her full breasts and then inched down over her flat stomach, almost as though she was imagining another pair of hands taking that same path.

Catching the expression on her sister's face, she quickly retorted, "Stop it!" before grabbing a bag hanging from a hook behind the door. Slinging it over her shoulder, she rushed into the living room trilling, "Hi Ben, 'bye Ben," to the handsome man reading a story to the excited five-year-old perched on his knee. "And you too, Missy Tuppence," she added tenderly, brushing Nikki's rosy cheek with her lips.

Before the little girl could respond, Lara nodded and tweaked her chin. "Yes, I haven't forgotten. I promise to give Uncle Adam your love and tell him you miss him."

The mother and daughter had already suffered through another long discussion as to why he couldn't drop by. Eventually, the little tot realised no amount of persuasion was going to make any difference to the status quo. Oh well, a second-hand message was better than nothing at all.

Lara pressed the tip of a brand-new lipstick to her lips as she passed the mirror, before rushing out the door with a last-minute wave.

"I think she might be a little bit excited." Suzie's eyes twinkled as she grinned at her boyfriend. "Oh, I just wish Adam'd realise what a gem he has in her and dump that rotten old cow once and for all."

"Has Uncle Adam got a cow as well as Clancy? Can I go and pat it ... *please? I really love cows," a little voice piped up.

§

Lara's heart was racing as she turned into the street and caught a glimpse of the old theatre's well-remembered facade. Part of her yearned to see a dearly loved figure waiting in the shadows like before, while common-sense quickly brought her back to earth. She knew Adam's heart too well – his deep sense of integrity wouldn't let him hurt her again by offering any false sense of hope.

Her eyes instantly fell on the Mercedes parked in the farthest corner. Searching the dimly lit surroundings, she found nothing but empty space.

Stop it, you idiot! You knew he wouldn't be there. Get a hold of yourself.

She had to pause and take a deep breath before entering the hall, preparing mentally for her first glimpse of him in nearly two months. A stream of tears threatened to fall, so she deliberately pictured the large school fees bill waiting on the bench at home – anything to quell the hunger rising in her spirit – and with a few short, sharp blinks, she managed to bring them under control.

Things had been much the same for Adam. Turning into the car park, his eyes immediately sought out the little maroon Corolla. Finding no sign of it meant he could enter the hall without automatically seeking her out, but there was nothing he could do about the sharp pang of disappointment wondering whether she may have chickened out after all. Just in case, he made sure his back was to the door when he went over to join the others. A fear of having wounded her so deeply she wouldn't want anything more to do with him was enough incentive to keep his eyes averted – and deep down he wouldn't have blamed her. His biggest worry was wondering how he would prevent his hands from reaching out for even the slightest of touches if she did happen to turn up.

Clusters of people stood around in groups, catching up on the latest gossip and news since they were last together. The friendly chatter helped to avert his thoughts a little from what had been uppermost in his mind all day. A sudden beam of light streaming in from the door when it opened announced another new arrival. If he had been looking towards Lucy and Charles and caught the looks they exchanged, Adam would have known exactly who it was ... but there was no need. He could sense Lara's presence and quickly had to pull in the reins to stop himself from rushing down the aisle and sweeping her away forever.

For a split second, Lara faltered as she glimpsed the man with dark wavy hair standing with his back to her. As though sensing her reaction, Adam swallowed hard and had to close his eyes for several seconds, hoping to calm his racing heart. From the sidelines, Lucy witnessed both reactions and her heart ached.

Charles was standing next to his son, chatting to a few of the cast when he noticed Lara slip into the body of the hall. Her entrance was so vastly different from that first time only the year before when she was running late. Then everyone had turned to see a beautiful young woman with long flowing hair burst through the door. Now a subdued young lady nervously made her way towards the stage, her gaze intentionally focused on the side staircase.

Don't look at him ... don't look at him, was the mantra accompanying her footsteps.

Lucy instinctively knew what Lara was going through after hearing about the night when alcohol had become her temporary refuge, along with a pledge made the following morning. She hurried to meet her just as she reached the foot of the stairs.

"Hi, sweetie, it's great to see you," she whispered, wrapping caring arms around her bestie. "And don't worry. No matter what happens, I'm here for you."

Lara held on tight, grateful for the comfort and distraction of a warm welcome and too afraid to look around in case her gaze fell into those familiar dark eyes.

"Oh, Luce, you're a godsend. Thanks." Breathing heavily into her ally's shoulder, she whispered, "I can do this."

"Yep, you can, and don't forget, I'm here if things get too difficult."

Lara nodded slowly, too choked up to say anything more.

Paul broke away from a small group off to one side. Taking over from Lucy, he wrapped Lara in a friendly hug. "It's good to see you, my friend. Thanks for having the courage to come back."

"Thanks, Paul ... I think I'm glad to be here." She tried hard to smile but without much success.

Stroking the back of her hand, he held her eyes with his. "You can do this." The two-sided meaning was obvious.

She nodded and swallowed hard. "I hope so. Thanks for believing in me."

He grinned and touched his lips to her cheek. "What else could I do? You were always my first pick for *Laurey*."

A few new arrivals brushed past, chatting excitedly among themselves. Sending out a quick, "Hi," they rushed up the stairs.

Just then, a young man looking to be in his mid- to late-twenties wandered in. Lucy grinned when the good-looking actor sent a friendly wink her way. She and Jeff had become quite close throughout *Show Boat's* run, and word had it that things had started turning much cosier than the lingering looks passing between them during the Christmas pantomime a few months earlier.

Before she had time to greet the newcomer, Paul announced, "Okay, it looks like we're all here. I'd better get this show underway." He raised his eyebrows playfully. "Come on, my new star, it's time to take your place in the limelight."

Lara grimaced nervously, both in trepidation for the new role and seeing Adam face-to-face.

With a gentle smile, he leaned in to whisper, "Don't worry, Luce and I will be right here if you need us."

Taking her by the hand, he led her up to the stage area and gave it one last reassuring squeeze before facing the others. His hands came together with a loud clap as he called out, "Okay, you lot. Places please!"

As though drawn like a moth to a flame, Adam's eyes had witnessed every intimate interaction between the director and his new leading lady and he was filled with an overwhelming spasm of jealousy. He ached to reach out and caress that same cheek and hand in a similar manner. Instead, he dragged his eyes away to join in on a nearby conversation rather than torturing himself with an unquenchable need to speak to the attractive woman now standing only a short distance away.

A little while later, as Paul was discussing a scene with a few of the minor players, the young couple stood awkwardly nearby. Two sets of eyes never dared cross paths, even though their hearts beat a matching tattoo. Both knew it would be impossible trying to avoid one another all night long – not only because it would seem strange to everyone else, but it was also imperative they discuss and practise their lines after taking on the lead roles. Despite this, natural instinct kicked in, imploring them to safeguard their hearts against any more pain.

Adam felt terrible. He knew how much hurt Lara had already endured because of him, so he was determined to leave it up to her to make the first move. Not surprisingly, a relentless need to feed his quenched spirit started to get the better of him. It wasn't long before the temptation became all too much and his eyes kept darting across for just a small glimpse.

Charles and Lucy exchanged knowing looks. They recognised the longing in his eyes but thought it best to leave it up to the two of them to sort it all out.

Lara understood his dilemma. With her heart beating furiously, she took a step closer ... those anxious blue eyes at last resting on the man who continually inhabited her dreams. There was no hiding anymore, although they were like two wary butterflies flitting over the other one's features – anxious to alight, but still unsure whether to trust either themselves or that much sought-out resting place only found in their soulmate's presence.

"Hello, Adam."

Her voice was like liquid chocolate ... warm, smooth and sweet as it flowed into every pore of his soul. It took all of his willpower not to reach out and pull her into his arms. She looked stunning in a dress that evoked memories of a glorious day on a faraway beach ... and suddenly it seemed like only yesterday when they were all there together. He wanted to meld Lara's body into his and carry her away with him ... back to that place, never to be separated again.

His fingers grasped the back of a chair to keep from reaching out to her. All he could murmur was a timid, "Hello, Lara," while every part of him wanted to cry out, *Thank God you're here, my darling. I couldn't bear going another day without seeing you...*

The parallel conversation continued – one on his lips and the other in his heart. "It's good to see you." *It's so wonderful to see you ... you look beautiful ... I've missed you more than you can possibly imagine ... I'm so sorry ... please come back to me.* "How's Nikki? I bet she's growing." *How's our delightful daughter? She'll always be our daughter in my heart ... I miss her ... and you ... so much...*

He didn't dare ask how she was doing – he couldn't have handled hearing her answer either way.

Lara wanted to reach out and brush her mouth against those lips she knew so well. Instead, she responded in a manner similar to his.

"It's good to see you, too." *You look so sad, my darling ... but that's not the way it's supposed to be ... you made your choice, and it was supposed to be the right one ... only it doesn't look like you're alright ... you look miserable. I wish you could come back to me so we can be made whole again.* "She's doing okay ... she's at school now – and getting taller by the minute." *She misses you so much ... we both do ... we wanted you to be there for her first day of school ... she looks so grown up in her uniform, you'd be proud of her.*

"Mum mentioned that you'd called in to see them ... she said how grown up Nikki looked in her uniform." *She looked adorable in that pretty tartan tunic. I was so proud of her ... and you too, when you turned to go ... I could see how hard it was having to leave your little girl – our little girl – behind. Yes, I was there, watching everything ... I couldn't stay away.* "Is her teacher nice?" *I wish I could come with you to the parent/teacher interview nights ...I don't want you having to go alone.*

"Yes, she's lovely, and Nikki thinks she's great – you'd like her, I'm sure." *Oh, why did I say that! ... I'm sorry, my love ... but I so wanted you to be there too.*

The silent double-sided conversation played out in their hearts, while the reality of their circumstances was like a lead weight in their souls. Neither of them dared admit the underlying dialogue was underpinned with absolute truthfulness ... along with the oneness of spirit they still shared.

§

Not long afterwards, Paul asked everyone to break into groups to rehearse any lines pertinent to their specific scenes. Naturally, Lara and Adam found themselves paired together for the rest of the night.

After some initial wariness, it was as though their communication turned into a ballet, only this time not by touch. This was a new form of body language played out in a storyline very similar to their own. They went into the first scene with both *Curly* and *Laurey* too proud and stubborn to admit their true feelings, despite the deep attraction flowing between them. Charles stood nearby observing these cautious overtures and couldn't help noting the parallels to their situation.

Throughout the first part of the rehearsal, two sets of eyes continually sought out their mate, but the instant they met, one or the other quickly looked away. Adam's father was becoming so frustrated by their antics, he wanted to shake them both and tell them to grow up ... they were far too old to be putting each other through this new form of torment. Nevertheless, he remained a silent onlooker, helpless to do anything.

When the director called for a short break, he couldn't stand it any longer. Striding over to stand between them, he whispered harshly for their ears alone, "Listen, you two ... it's about time you got your act together. If you want to play these roles to their full potential, you at least need to be able to look at one another. I understand what you're going through – truly I do – but you have to try harder for Paul's sake if nothing else."

He was right, and they knew it. The errant pair sheepishly nodded in unison, though still too reticent to look at each other properly. Lara's bottom lip ended up between her teeth, while all Adam could manage was a half-hearted prod with the toe of his shoe at a crack in the floor. They reminded him of a pair of gangly teenagers experiencing their first crush.

Desperate to break the tension, he sent them a friendly smile before extending both hands towards each of them. "Lara, I'd like you to meet Adam. He won't bite, I promise, even though he can be as stubborn as a mule at times ... Adam, this is Lara, a delightful young woman who could really do with a caring friend."

Offering a coy smile, Adam stretched out his hand to the woman who had once known its intimate caress. Somewhat reverently she placed her hand in his, responding to that all-familiar touch as though her heart had come home. At last, they were free to drown in eyes that once upon a time had been their refuge.

Hidden within Adam's nonchalant stance, she could sense a trail of delicate tendrils filled with concern flowing from those warm dark pools ... the ones now feasting on every feature of her face. They seemed to reach out and then metamorphose into the soulful caress she remembered so well.

"It's a pleasure to meet you, Lara. Unfortunately, Dad's right ... I can be a stubborn mule at times ... but I can also be an absolute fool, especially when it comes to letting the best things in life pass me by." He sent her another timid smile, and the emotion in his voice tore at her heartstrings. "I'd really like to be your friend."

He recognised the same form of loving concern in her gaze – one that never failed to touch his spirit – though she did manage to replicate his casual manner.

"It's a pleasure to meet you too, Adam. And don't worry ... sometimes being a fool happens to the best of us and there's nothing we can do about it, no matter how much we want to." Her gracious words matched the poignant smile he knew so well, assuring him of her understanding ... and forgiveness. "I hope we can be friends ... I'd really like that."

She felt his relief through their shared touch and couldn't resist stroking the back of his hand with the pad of her thumb ... but only for the tiniest fragment of time. And yet, those few seconds were long enough for kindred spirits to understand nothing could ever destroy their unique oneness of body, mind and soul.

Lucy had been keeping an eye on Lara all night long and overheard the touching exchanges. Sidling up to Charles a little bit later, she sent him a grateful smile. She missed the shared camaraderie from *Show Boat's* run when she and Lara, along with Adam and Jeff, often turned the drudgery of rehearsing lines into a form of comical theatre whenever Paul wasn't watching. Maybe now they might be able to regain a semblance of those once happy times.

His reply took the form of a satisfied wink. They were relieved to see the young couple finally talking to one another again, though it was obvious neither one would allow themselves the pleasure of getting close enough to touch again unless their parts called for it.

As soon as rehearsals were over, Lara raced up to Lucy so they could walk out together. She didn't want to put Adam in the awkward position of finding her alone ... but most of all she needed to protect her heart. It would be so easy to slip back into the habit of spending time with him in the car park afterwards.

Charles had the same thought. He lengthened his stride to catch up to his son, and the pair walked side-by-side down the side aisle. Unable to resist, Adam turned back for one more glimpse just as they reached the door. He needed these final few seconds as a form of sustenance to last through the upcoming seven long days and even longer nights.

Lara was just walking down the stairs with Lucy by her side when she sensed someone watching her. Her heart skipped a beat as she looked up and noticed his expression. Tentatively, she raised a hand in farewell. He responded in kind, accompanied by a small nod as though wishing her well. Their gaze remained fixed for an eternity of milliseconds as his mouth formed one last heartfelt smile...

Charles' placed a loving arm across his shoulders. It was time to go. Lara watched on sadly as the father and son walked slowly out into the night.

"Are you okay?" Lucy's voice dripped with concern, glimpsing the emotion reflected in her friend's eyes.

Lara nodded unconvincingly. "Yeah, I will be. It's just been so long since we were together, seeing him tonight brought all of that old longing back to the surface. How do I tell my heart we can only ever be friends..."

The pain in her voice caused Lucy to swallow her own tears.

A long, heartfelt sigh slipped through her lips as Lara added, "It's so hard, Luce ... but I have to learn to be strong if I want to do this."

There was nothing the other woman could say to help the situation. Instead, they walked in silence with their arms linked.

Pulling up beside her car, Lucy turned to Lara for one final hug. "Don't be too hard on yourself ... and don't forget I'm just a phone call away."

"Thanks, Luce ... you're the kind of friend everyone needs. I could've have done all this without you. But don't worry, I'll be okay. See you next week."

Lara's step was laboured and slow as she made her way to her own vehicle. There was none of that usual jauntiness Adam was so familiar with.

Unbeknown to anyone he had moved further into the shadows, hoping for one more glimpse before it was time to face that other nightmare again. And then his heart broke all over again as he watched the woman he adored slump into her seat and take forever to turn the key.

When she eventually drove off into the lonely night, his head dropped dejectedly as a shroud of darkness smothered his soul.

Chapter 4

Thursday nights became Lara and Adam's only focus. There was nothing they could do to make the hours hurry by and every second seemed to limp along in slow motion. When dawn broke on another rehearsal day, two hearts raced in anticipation. All day long the excitement kept building, but once their eyes met on stage, having to act as though this was just any other day gave birth to another form of agony. The bittersweet contrast of caring and disinterest contained a new type of imprisonment, and for two people lost without the other, there was no hope of escape. The only good to come out of all this shadowboxing was the practice it provided for their roles.

Rehearsals were coming along well. Paul was pleased with the effort everyone was putting in and Charles' stern words had brought about the desired effect. Whenever Lara and Adam were in character, it seemed they actually took on the spirit of their individual roles by playing off each other perfectly. But it was a different story once the sessions were over. There was nothing left to hide behind, and that old awkwardness returned. The pair of them went to great lengths to avoid the other's searching gaze behind everyday topics. Mostly, their conversation centred around work or aspects of the musical ... and being extra careful not to ask anything about their private lives unless it had something to do with a certain little person close to both their hearts.

Every week Adam asked after Nikki, but he had no control over the aching sense of loss when Lara talked about their exploits.

The only time she showed any form of animation in any of their conversations was the ready smile that appeared whenever her daughter's name was mentioned. Watching the spontaneous displays of affection light up her face reminded him of being on the receiving end of similar tokens from when they were together.

Deep down, her responses were much the same as his as soon as their eyes met ... it just took all of her willpower to suppress them.

"So how's that cute little Munchkin now? Feeling any better?" he asked a few weeks into rehearsals following Lara's announcement the week prior she thought Nikki was coming down with a cold.

"Oh, she's heaps better and as lively as ever! I don't know where she gets her energy from. It's hard to keep up with her most days."

He couldn't resist. "Have you been down to Miami Beach lately?"

She had to close her eyes for a moment as images of a driftwood doll with seaweed hair from a day filled with laughter and nervous expectation filled her mind.

When she opened them again, the subliminal message in the look she sent him was clear as she shook her head. "No, not anymore."

For a split second, there was a glimmer of relief in his eyes. The next instant, he hated himself for being so selfish and expecting her to stay away from their favourite haunt. Then the shutters came down again and when he looked at her the pain behind his expression was plain to see. "I'm sorry..."

"Don't be – it's easier this way. Now we either go for a drive in the country looking for a creek to have a cool dip, or drop by your parents' place so she can ride Clancy before going for a swim in the pool."

A small smile touched the corners of his mouth. "Mmm, I spotted the box of titbits she has stashed away in his stable. Don't let her spoil my old pony or he'll end up getting too fat!"

The expression on her face matched his as images of him teaching Nikki to ride flooded back. "I won't ... but she's sure besotted..."

Adam's fingers twitched. She had the feeling he was about to reach out and take her hand ... until Charles' voice drifted over from the other side of the stage.

"I'd better go and see what Dad's up to."

She could only nod and follow him with her eyes as he faded into the shadows.

§

One night, they were standing only a few metres apart waiting for their cue. As was so often the case, Lara couldn't resist watching him from out of the corner of her eye. Usually, she looked away before he could catch her – this time their eyes met and held. His spontaneous response was the slightest hint of a loving wink. It just flowed naturally and was so unexpected her eyes grew misty. Memories came flooding back of the countless times that same gesture assured her of his love. Now it was a much longed-for balm to soothe her aching heart.

Please God, let him still care ... at least a little bit.

Adam caught her reaction, and it tore at his soul. It was obvious how much even this miniscule token still meant to her, and the last thing he wanted was to be the instigator of any more pain.

Just then the music rose. It was time to get into character. For the rest of the night, unintentional silent messages passed between them through unguarded loving glances or little instinctive gestures known only to them. Forever they would be two halves of one spirit ... even though necessity kept them apart.

36

Waiting further back in the wings, Lucy caught both the wink and her friend's reaction. Once the run-throughs were over, and Adam and his father had left for the night, she invited Lara out for a coffee.

"It'll have to be a quick one then, Luce. Suzie's babysitting and she has to be up early for work."

"Oh, that's okay. I don't mean to keep you long anyway. I just thought it was about time we had a little chat. How about we go to that new coffee house just around the corner?" As usual, she linked arms as they left the theatre.

With the soft moonlight highlighting Lucy's blonde wavy bob and Lara's thick mane of chestnut hair reaching almost to her waist, they were easy to recognise.

Adam was just driving off when he noticed them. A sharp jab of jealousy grabbed at his heart. He missed those night when he and Lara would invite Lucy and Jeff to join them for a late-night snack at one of the local cafés. Under his breath, he wished the duo well while his eyes still followed their every move.

As the girls faced each other across a secluded table, Lucy didn't even wait for the coffee to arrive. "Okay, so tell me how you're really doing? And don't act as though you don't know what I'm talking about."

There was no use pretending any more – Lara knew she needed to get everything out in the open. Apart from Suzie, Lucy was her closest ally.

"Honestly?"

"Yes, honestly."

"I feel like I've been cut in half ... I'm still walking around, but the most important part of me is missing. I do my job okay ... eat when I have to ... and get out every now and then, but to be honest, nothing really seems to matter anymore ... except for Nikki. If I didn't have her – well..." She shrugged her shoulders. "Yeah, I know that sounds morbid and depressing ... but you wanted the truth..."

Lucy reached out and squeezed her friend's hand. "Oh, Lars, I'm so sorry. This is *ridiculous*. You two belong together more than anyone I know. It was obvious right from the start how much you both cared – and still is to those of us who know the truth, even though you try to hide it. I just wish there was something I could do."

Lara returned the gesture with a strained smile. "Thanks, Luce; I don't know how I'd deal with all this if I didn't have your friendship. Knowing that you care sure helps" —she shrugged her shoulders again and sighed deeply— "but there's really nothing anyone can do. Adam and I just have to get through it somehow, and hopefully come out the other side good friends ... I just have to trust he'll be okay. He'd better be – I send enough prayers his way!"

"Well, I may not go to church as often as you do, but I'll be praying up a storm for both of you. It's easy to see Adam isn't the only one needing some divine intervention."

§

The following Saturday, Adam woke with a feeling of dread. The day stretched ahead of him like a prison walking track – boring and predictable ... and going nowhere. He struggled out of bed and trudged over to the French doors to pull the heavy curtains aside. A blaze of sunlight greeted him as his gaze fell on a forest of blue-tinted eucalypt trees crowning a mountain range in the distance. It reminded him of Saturdays once spent with Lara and Nikki. Wanting to be alone with his thoughts, he decided to take a leisurely drive up to Mt Glorious, a picturesque hilltop village less than an hour from the centre of the city.

Set on a panoramic ridge, a line of lookouts offered views down to deep green valleys riddled with large areas of grazing land dotted with cattle and horses. Looking east, the landscape extended across Brisbane's suburban sprawl to the blue waters of Moreton Bay. It would do him good to take in some country air and blow away the cobwebs. Mostly, he wanted to just have some time to himself without Trina continually checking up on him.

Over a late breakfast, his plans came up in conversation. Before he had a chance to finish, she accused him of making up excuses to be with Lara.

"Look, you don't have to worry. I'm not going anywhere near her."

Though it defeated his purpose, he invited her to join him. At least then she would know he was telling the truth.

"You've got to be kidding! Why on *earth* would I want to go for a drive in the back of beyond when I can spend the afternoon with Judith. At least *we* have things in common. You know how much I hate the country. It's bad enough living way out here without going all the way up to Hicksville!"

Exasperated, he raised his hands in defeat. "Suit yourself then. I'll be gone for most of the afternoon. See you when I get back." Pushing back from the table, he grabbed his keys and headed out the door.

Adam was so fed up with her constant accusations while making no effort to keep their marriage alive herself, he couldn't even be bothered cleaning up. All he could think about was getting lost in memories of better times. His wife had been slowly slipping back into her old habits. Thankfully, so far he hadn't come across any alcohol stashes hidden around the house. As long as she remained sober and Lara was safe, he could put up with any of her sudden mood swings.

Driving along a tree-lined road spanning the ridge that ran between the outer suburbs and Mt Glorious township, he imagined Lara's response if she had been on the receiving end of his invitation. No matter where they went or how mundane a chore was, somehow she always managed to turn everything into fun. Every shared hour overflowed with laughter and love – along with the delightful giggles of a little girl.

One of the restaurants had a large balcony that overlooked all of those magnificent views. For several minutes, he sat sipping on a strong cup of coffee while his eyes flitted across the scenery below. Somewhere down there were the two people who constantly filled his thoughts. He couldn't help wondering where they were and what they were doing.

The friendly owner could tell something was on his mind and tried to tempt him with a large piece of homemade lasagne and a fresh side salad. Although he wasn't really hungry, Adam eventually gave in, but only managed a few mouthfuls before pushing the plate away. Feeling wretched and depressed, he paid the bill with a heartfelt apology before climbing back behind the wheel.

A little further down the road, he spotted a sign for a bushwalking track leading through dense rainforest. After pulling into the carpark, he wandered along a leaf-littered path dappled with warm splashes of sunlight that penetrated the thick canopy overhead. The pretty warble of a magpie and the clear ring of a few bellbirds accompanied his footsteps ... but the only sound he was aware of was an echo of that much-loved voice from two nights earlier...

The walk took longer than expected and he arrived home just as dusk was falling. There was no sign of Trina's car in its usual space, and he let out a long sigh of relief. He wasn't ready to face another inquisition. A pile of dirty plates left over from breakfast was congealing in the sink. At least the clink of dishes being washed would help to fill the silence.

In a replay of lunch, Adam sat on the living room sofa half-heartedly watching the television while picking at a light dinner from the tray resting on his lap. All the while, his thoughts kept returning to a beautiful woman with splashes of glistening chestnut in her hair. His mind produced images of Lara and Nikki sitting at the dining room table in her cottage, happily sharing stories as they tucked into one of her delicious meals. A kaleidoscope of snapshots followed, showing their laughing faces as they wandered the fascinating streets of both Italy and Austria. He couldn't help comparing those happy times to the life he was now leading.

If only. It was always *if only...*

When Trina's car pulled into the driveway, he was already lying in bed with only the darkness to keep him company. It wasn't long before he heard a brusque expletive when she stumbled up the stairs leading to the front door. A clay pot suddenly bumped against the railing with a loud rumble, and then he recognised the clink of keys as she rattled around in her handbag. Finally, after making several unsuccessful attempts to insert one into the lock, he pulled on his robe and went downstairs to open the door.

"Oh, *there* you are, finally found your way home, hey?" she said sarcastically, pushing past him and ducking her head behind a thick curtain of red hair.

Shaking his head in dismay, he sighed, "*I'm* finally home? Where have *you* been? I thought you said you were going out with Judith. She rang looking for you hours ago."

Although there was no discernible smell of alcohol on her breath, he could tell something strange was going on. When she straightened up after picking up a shoe that had fallen off, he couldn't help noticing traces of bright red lipstick smeared above her mouth and along her chin line.

"So do you want to tell me who you've been with? And don't try to pretend differently – the evidence is all over your face."

"As if *you* can talk, Mr *Never-Do-Wrong* ... don't you *dare* start preaching at me," she hissed, punctuating each word with a shaky finger. "I've been out with friends, people *you've* never met before, but I don't have anything to hide. How do I know you weren't with *that* woman ... or someone else just as trashy this afternoon? You *never* want to spend any time with me."

Turning on her heel she continued up the stairs, stumbling awkwardly while trying to walk in one shoe.

Adam thought about reminding her of his invitation to join him, but he didn't have either the energy or the desire to set the record straight. Arguing with her was just a waste of time. Instead, he waited until her door slammed shut before trudging back to his room.

Lying in the darkness afterwards, he felt a measure of guilt recalling her words. She was right ... he had been with another woman – thoughts of Lara had been with him all day.

Drifting off to sleep, memories of a night in Cortona – the first time he had known the feel of Lara's soft, warm body lying beneath his – followed him into his dreams.

§

In the harsher light of day, the conversation from the night before became paramount in his mind.

How dare you accuse me of anything when it's obvious you've been with someone else! You can't deny it because of those telltale lipstick marks – and who knows what else happened. I've given up the only woman who'll ever mean anything to me ... and for what? So you can play the field with any poor fool you meet! Why can't you fall in love with someone else? At least then we'd both have an excuse to let go of this sham of a marriage...

He knew it sounded hypocritical, but last night's episode was the final straw, especially after all her threats. For the last few months, he had been trying hard to maintain some form of commitment to their marriage vows when deep down his only desire was to walk away and never look back.

By the time Trina came downstairs, it was nearly eleven o'clock. Adam was ropeable and had to restrain himself from giving her a piece of his mind. Taking a deep breath, he waited until she poured herself a cup of coffee. Then he let fly...

"I know you were with someone last night – and don't deny it because there was lipstick smeared all over your face." She started to protest, but he'd had enough. With each word, his voice grew louder and less controlled. "I don't want to hear any more of your lies, Trina. I'm sorry for hurting you last year, but how dare you accuse me of being with anyone else when you're the one who's obviously playing around now!"

His hand came down hard on the kitchen bench and she jumped like a startled cat. She had never seen him this angry before and had no idea what else was coming. Realising her taunts must have pushed him to the end of his limits, she burst into tears.

"And so you should be – what you did hurt me deeply, Adam, but I didn't mean to upset you either. I was just so hurt after finding out about you and that little tart, all I could think about was finding some way to retaliate. It was nothing ... really. When I was leaving, one of the guys started fooling around – we only shared one kiss."

She moved to his side of the island bench and pulled on his arm, forcing him to look her ... but he couldn't. He felt nothing but repulsion at her attempts to get back at him.

"Look at me ... *Adam,* I'm warning you, if you hadn't done anything in the first place, I wouldn't've been tempted to hurt you back." When he still wouldn't look at her, she spat out, "Anyway, it's all your fault!" Without warning, a large glob of saliva landed smack on his cheek.

Pushing her away in disgust, he swiped at it with the back of his hand and strode to the door. Pausing for a few seconds to calm his raging anger, he then turned to look her straight in the eye. "In that case, we might as well get a divorce. It's obvious you don't care, and now you're doing everything in your power to turn me against you. I've had enou—"

Her rage echoed through the cold expanse of the sprawling house. "*Noooo,* you *can't* leave. It's *you* I really love, not him!" Glaring at his retreating back, she stood her ground with clenched teeth and both fists rigid by her side. "Come ... back ... *here!* If you don't, I'm going to do something that'll make you regret speaking to me like that. I *mean* it, Adam. Don't you *dare* leave me!"

He turned around slowly, a piercing stare reflecting the icy emotion that was all he had left, and his tone was low and steady.

"You can't do anything more to me, Trina. And don't you *dare* say you love me. You've never loved me, but you've sure killed off any love I once felt for you – and stolen away any hope I had of being a father." He turned to go and then faltered ... looking her straight in the eyes again. "*And* taken away the only two things that ever mattered in my life."

As soon as that last sentence left his lips, Adam knew he had gone too far. He had forgotten how venomous she could be.

She didn't care about his reference to the secret abortion – nor the vasectomy she'd forced him into. The only thing that registered was Lara. "*See! I knew* you still carried a torch for that whore, no matter how much you deny it." She spat at him again. "I can easily find out where she lives – it won't be hard – and *then* we'll see whether you leave me or not."

"Trina, I'm *warning* you—"

"*No*, Adam, *I'm* warning *you*. Either you prove I'm the most important person in your life or..." Her voice trailed off, and the look in her eyes sent shivers down his spine.

"You wouldn't dare." His tone was just as menacing.

The fingers on her right hand brushed against a knife resting near the sink. "*Oh, wouldn't I?* Why don't you just try me then?" She just stood there, glaring back at him.

Raising his hands in defeat, he walked backwards through the door. "Alright, I give up, you win. But I need to get out of here for a while ... and before you think the worst, I'll be over at Mum and Dad's. If I don't get out of here right now, I'm likely to do something I'll regret, so just *leave* me alone."

He slammed the front door, but her voice still penetrated the heavy timber.

"That's right, run home to Mummy and Daddy and don't forget to tell them all about *bad, bad Trina!*"

All four wheels spun in the crushed bluestone as Adam took off down the driveway. His sole focus was to be with people whose moods were always predictable. More than anything, he needed to be around people who truly cared.

They were pottering in the garden as he swept through the gates, tyres squealing when he took the corner hard. Sending his wife a worried frown, Charles rushed over and she hurried after him.

"What's the matter, son? What's happened?" he asked anxiously as the car door slammed with a resounding bang.

Adam's only response was to shake his head as he tried to suppress the rage still threatening to erupt. Elizabeth went straight over and wrapped her arms around his tense shoulders.

Holding him close she murmured, "It's okay, love, Dad and I are here. Come inside. I'll make us all a cuppa while you tell us what's going on."

He slumped against her and sighed. "Thanks, Mum."

Together they walked to the house, with the husband and wife glancing at each other with concern.

While Adam gathered his thoughts, both men sat opposite each other at the kitchen table. Charles' forehead creased into a worried frown and Elizabeth sent him a nervous look as she bustled around putting the kettle on.

Sucking in a deep breath, the troubled young man didn't hold back, even including a graphic description of his threat to leave and the extent of his anger.

Everything was fine until he got to the part about Trina's warning. Suddenly all of that former control slipped away. Letting out an anguished cry, he slumped against the table with his head in his hands.

"I just can't take any more of her threats. One minute she's accusing me of still seeing Lara and vowing to do something drastic. The next thing, she blurts out about locking lips with someone else while stressing how much she loves me." He looked up wearily and a mantle of fear caused heavy shadows to dull the light in his eyes. "And do you know how stupid *I* am? Too damned scared to leave 'cause I've got no idea what she's likely to do."

Elizabeth could only listen with a look of horror on her face, while Charles' concern was evident in both his tone and expression.

"Well, you just can't stay there, son, not with all of that rubbish going on. It's time to be sensible and think about your future. There's obviously no love lost between the two of you, and she's likely to do anything."

"I know, Dad, and that's why I *have* to stay. Lara and Nikki's safety is far more important than anything else at the moment. At least while I'm there, I can control what happens. But I dare not risk Trina finding out where they live. There's no telling what she might do. I just have to try and keep her happy ... that way I'll know they're safe."

Elizabeth turned to her husband in desperation, worried their beloved son was on the verge of a breakdown. Charles' face was a picture of concern as he tried to talk reason to the distraught young man.

"But my dear boy, you can't live under this much strain for the rest of your life. Trina knows how to push your buttons, and you're playing right into her hands."

"I know, but I can't risk it, Dad. I'd *never* forgive myself if anything happened to them. Lara's given me more happiness in these last few months than in all the time Trina and I have been together – at least I have memories to hold onto. Maybe her stint in rehab was the perfect opportunity. I should've left then when I had the chance. Now it's too late..."

His despair was heartbreaking, but as much as they tried to make him see reason, he was determined to stay. It was the only way he could ensure Lara and Nikki were safe from Trina's wrath.

§

The following Saturday morning, Lara's phone rang. It was Elizabeth, and her tone was serious. "Lara, I need to talk to you urgently, but I need it to be on neutral territory so Nikki doesn't hear."

The young woman had never heard Adam's mother so upset. "Okay, I can come over now if you like."

There was a load of wet washing ready to go out on the line, but it could wait a few hours.

"No, I think it'd be better if Charles and I came over there. That way he can look after her while you and I go out for a coffee. What I have to say is extremely important."

Their faces were grim when the sleek silver Jag pulled into Lara's driveway. Elizabeth didn't even bother getting out. Instead, she waited for Lara to join her. Charles snatched Nikki up in a warm hug when she rushed down the stairs, while Lara only had time to land a quick kiss on his cheek as she hurried past. From the look he sent her way, it was clear Elizabeth was anxious to get going.

The two women greeted each other sombrely when Lara dropped into the passenger seat. Ever mindful of Elizabeth's heart condition, she didn't want to delve into what was going on while she was driving. Thankfully, the coffee shop was only a few streets away, so she didn't have long to wait before finding out what was going on.

Elizabeth spotted a secluded table in a far corner and made a beeline for it. They sat opposite one another, but she didn't even wait for Lara to get comfortable before the words spilled out.

"My dear, I'm sorry you've been hurt so dreadfully by everything that's happened, and I know you're trying to get on with life as best you can, but I need to talk to you about something important to all of us. I might be stretching the boundaries with what I'm about to ask, but you're the only one who can make a difference. I would never bother you if I thought there was any other way."

"It's okay, Elizabeth, just tell me what's going on. Is Adam alright?" She didn't have to be a mind reader to work out this meeting had something to do with him.

"Oh, my darling girl, it's horrible. He's distraught, and I'm scared for his safety – both mentally and physically."

Lara gasped as Elizabeth related how devastated her son was, making sure she didn't leave anything out and providing a full picture of his state of mind. She went on to reveal how Trina had been with another man, her threats and the accusations made, as well as his despair after losing the two of them.

She was horrified. "What? No! Oh, Elizabeth, he has to get out of there!"

"Charles and I have already told him that, but unfortunately he just won't listen. Maybe you can make him see reason. He'll always listen to you."

Lara knew she was right, but there was more at risk than just the two of them. Her mother-heart couldn't go beyond the safety of her child. "I want to help, believe me, but I can't ignore her threats. If you'd heard Trina on the phone that night, you'd understand why he's taking her so seriously. I can still hear the hatred in her voice – I have to think of Nikki first."

Elizabeth fully understood where she was coming from; nevertheless, concern for her son outweighed everything else. Like a mother hen protecting her chick, she pleaded with the younger woman.

"Of course you do, but I'm sure she's all noise and no action – Trina wouldn't dare do anything after the way she behaved in hospital and the rehab centre. The doctors would soon make a case against her if she tried anything. As much as this goes against what Adam said, he needs you desperately. Please, Lara, I'm begging you ... please go to him. He's not coping, and it breaks my heart to see him like this. If you could just tell him how you feel, I'm sure he'll come to his senses. I'm so worried; I wouldn't ask if there was any other way."

The young woman could feel her heart breaking as she contemplated everything Elizabeth said. She ached to go to him, but there was also a real fear of putting them all at risk, especially her innocent daughter ... besides, how could she go against Adam's direct wishes. Making things harder on him was the last thing any of them needed – and there was no telling what he would do if Trina really did let loose.

Seeing her quandary, Elizabeth leaned across to pat Lara's arm. "At least think about what I've said ... please? You're my only hope ... and his." She prayed those last two words would help sway the young woman.

The other one nodded sombrely. "I will, I promise."

§

Later that night Lara sought out the solitude of her veranda, pondering everything Elizabeth had said. The quiet little corner often drew her in the midnight hours when she missed him the most. Her heart ached for all he was going through, but how could she demand he throw away everything he believed in when it came to a commitment made in good faith. And how could she risk Nikki's safety?

At the forefront of her mind was a vow made in all good conscience – a promise never to see him alone again ... and she was too afraid to break it.

Her life was in turmoil ... and she knew his was too.

Chapter 5

Opening night played to a packed house. Seats had been selling steadily since it was confirmed Adam and Lara had the leading roles. By Friday afternoon, patrons wanting to pre-book were going away empty-handed. Even the Lord Mayor ordered her tickets early when she learned how popular those 'in the know' expected the show to be.

Saturday afternoon was a mixture of both anticipation and reflection in two separate households. As they were getting ready, Lara and Adam remembered all of excitement and nervousness happening at her place just prior to *Show Boat's* opening the year before.

This time they practised in front of bathroom mirrors where the acoustics were best, alone with their thoughts and praying for a clean delivery with no fluffing of lines. Ahead of them, were two love scenes with intimate overtures. The wedding scene towards the end was especially poignant and uppermost in their minds as they made their separate ways to the theatre.

During each rehearsal, both had managed to sidestep around any physical closeness when it came to what should have been quite passionate scenes, using the excuse of one then the other coming down with a sore throat. Other members of the cast found this quite plausible knowing how important it was to protect their voices for the big night.

Paul had already pulled them aside separately at the final dress rehearsal to offer a warning. "Listen, guys, don't forget, this is the real thing. I need you to be convincing, even if it does mean feeling uncomfortable for a few minutes."

He understood their reticence and was lenient in the most part, but when people paid good money to be entertained, he expected only the best from his performers. Lara and Adam were too professional to give anything less, so their firm reassurances set his mind at ease.

Adam decided it was best to invite Trina along to the opening as a way to allay any fears she may have of anything going on between him and his leading lady. In the past, she had never shown any interest in anything her husband was involved with, so he never bothered.

She was surprised by the invitation and quickly rang Judith to ask if she wanted to keep her company on the likely chance she grew bored. The two women made plans to go out for dinner beforehand, leaving Adam to his own devices until it was time to leave for the theatre.

He arrived early to prepare for the onslaught of emotions certain to accompany his performance. Lara was just getting out of her car as he drove into the car park. Aware of how ridiculous it would be trying to avoid one another, she waited for him to catch up.

Their eyes locked as he made his way towards her and she had to stifle a cry when she saw the look on his face. All of the loneliness from the past three months seemed embodied in his gaze, and a host of suppressed feelings came bubbling to the surface.

He longed to reach out and touch her, and for a fraction of a second, she sensed his hand almost seemed to have a will of its own ... until she caught sight of a set of white knuckles obviously keeping it in check as he drew closer.

His gaze fell on a sparkling pendant in the shape of treble clef lying in the crook of her neck. Inevitably, his eyes drifted down to its significant counterpart: a sapphire and diamond ring gracing her right hand where he had placed it only a few days before Christmas. Instinctively, her thumb brushed across the brilliant stones – something that had become a regular habit to ensure it was always safe.

She planned on turning the setting around so it was lying against her palm when she was performing. A thin strip of flesh-toned tape would ensure it stayed hidden from the audience. Her earlier vow never to take the ring off was a promise she always meant to keep, so this seemed the perfect solution to make sure no one caught sight of it.

"Hello, Lara. Another opening," he whispered softly, remembering another held in this same hall less than a year ago.

Even the sound of her name on his lips increased the longing and her tone matched his. "Hello, Adam. Yes, here we are again."

She understood his hesitation and wanted to reach out a few inches to caress his hand. Not too long ago their entwined fingers helped to create a host of moving symphonies and ballet routines across one another's skin by a simple touch. She missed the silent music they made together – although it was now a place neither of them had the courage to revisit.

Together they walked side-by-side with only a few millimetres separating them. Both could sense the very hairs on their arms reaching out to draw their missing half closer. It took all of their concentration to put one foot in front of the other.

Lara was struggling to keep up the pretence after seeing the response in both his eyes and hands as he approached ... and most especially when she remembered Elizabeth's recent plea.

"How've you been?" he asked cautiously, trying to subdue the urge to pull her around the corner and claim her mouth with his. A thought flashed through his brain, *At least it'd be good practice for the passionate kiss we have to deliver in the final scene – the one we've been avoiding all these weeks.*

Their footsteps kept perfect time as they approached the hall. All of a sudden and out of nowhere, all of that former reasoning fell away. With eyes downcast, her voice floated across the space between them like a gentle summer breeze. "I miss you ... I try not to ... but I can't help it."

The strangled cry she had been wrestling with ever since rehearsals first began came out as a whimper. He recognised the sound from the many times desire had enlivened her words, only none of those had been tinged with distress. Lara's fingers pressed hard against her lips as she tried to swallow, anxious to stifle the gut-wrenching sob rising in her throat.

A river of emotions suddenly found their release when he pulled up abruptly and went to grab her hand. "Oh, Baby, I'm sooo sorry."

His whole focus was a desperate need to go back to the way things used to be – even if only for a moment.

Lara could only shake her head and keep up the steady pace. "Don't, Adam… We can't do anything. But I won't pretend any more – I can't ... not to you."

He ignored her plea, walking backwards in front of her and reaching out once again to force her to stop.

Again, she shook her head. "*Pleeaase* don't look at me like that."

Her heart was begging ... and he knew she was right.

In an uncanny coincidence, the sorrowful call of a curlew came from beneath a nearby bush. Its sad tune matched the cry of her heart. This time both of them stopped dead in their tracks as though recognising their mate's call. Lara could sense Adam's eyes fastened on her face, but she had to look away. All he could do was nod slowly. In unison, they set off again, with the night bird still giving voice to all that remained unsaid.

They passed other early arrivals in the back corridors and exchanged that distinctive Aussie cry of 'chookas' instead of the usual showbiz phrase, 'break a leg'. The air of anticipation was a welcome distraction from the turmoil playing out in their hearts.

Just before reaching Lara's dressing room, he remembered to warn her of Trina's impending appearance.

"Okay, thanks for letting me know. And don't worry. I'll be careful to stay in character the whole time," came the sober response.

Neither of them could afford to risk letting their guard down – not after the horrible aftermath of last time – and he nodded gravely.

Outside her door, he turned again, willing her to look at him. "I hate having to leave you but..."

A host of unspoken words floated in the air. All she could do was hold his gaze and send him an understanding nod.

"You'll be a knock-out – I just know it," he added with a distinct catch in his voice. "The audience is going to love you, and I'll always be in your corner urging you on. And don't ever forget – I'm your biggest fan ... even if I can't let the rest of the world see."

This time the temptation was too strong. The expression on her face conveyed everything she wanted to say but wasn't game enough to put into words. "Thank you ... I hope you know I feel the same about you. Please be careful out there and don't take any risks." He nodded solemnly, his gaze never wavering when she looked deep into those eyes she knew so well. "It's an honour to be your leading lady, even if it is only on a stage. I hope I make you proud."

The pain she saw in their smoky depths broke her heart ... though his response cradled it securely. "You always do, sweet lady." Sending her one final heartfelt look, he added, "And while we're out there, that's our world ... no-one else's."

She nodded sadly as he turned abruptly and hurried off, both trying hard to push aside thoughts of how different life had been the last time they appeared in a show together.

§

Backstage was the normal hive of activity as the cast performed last-minute warm-ups of both their voices and muscles. The dance numbers were full on, and no one could risk an injury with a packed house expected each night. Paul could feel the nervous tension as he wove his way from one group to the next, offering encouragement and checking all was in readiness to wow the audience waiting expectantly on the other side of the velvet curtain.

A few minutes before the call came, he approached his two stars. They were waiting motionless in the wings with only a bare hand's breadth separating them. It was easy to feel the electricity flowing between them, but it was obvious they weren't brave enough to respond.

"This is it, folks, the night you prove to the critics we've found the new Fred and Ginger and *Show Boat* wasn't just a one-off! I've heard there's an agent from Morgan and Chalmers here tonight. Apparently, he's determined to get your names on their books if you can live up to those last performances." Leaning close, he grinned sheepishly, "And when it comes to the wedding scene, just pretend you're back in Europe and give it all you've got ... for the sake of the audience and me, if for no other reason."

Sending them an affectionate wink he wandered off, leaving behind images of those magical nights. It was exactly the boost they needed as two sets of eyes glowed with the memories.

When the music swelled, they each took a deep breath and exchanged pensive smiles, then two tiny familiar gestures lifted both of their spirits in a way nothing else could. His loving wink and the responsive wriggle of her nose brought a sudden rush of reminiscing from those precious few seconds leading up to all their former performances. It didn't matter what manner of subterfuge they were about to re-enact to the world, deep down their love was still as strong as ever.

From the moment that thick black veil opened, ushering eager onlookers across the miles to a bustling farmyard in Oklahoma, Lara and Adam turned into consummate professionals determined to ensure the show was a success for the director's sake. To those watching in the audience, all they observed were a pair of brilliant performers giving their all with no hint of the emotion playing out below the surface. And from what she could see from her VIP seat, even Trina had no cause to worry.

Standing on stage as the first act drew to a close, the applause was thunderous. From his seat in the centre of the eighth row, Max, the head of Brisbane's foremost talent agency, was confident his earlier expectations were spot on.

Heading backstage, those from the cast chatted back and forth about the reaction of the crowd. Lucy took her friend's arm as they walked the stark white corridors back to their dressing room. Lara had already mentioned Trina would be somewhere in the audience watching like a hawk. Like any true friend, Lucy was determined to stay close in case Adam's wife decided to try anything.

With Jeff cast in the role of *Jud Fry, Curly's* main rival for *Laurey's* hand, his and Adam's friendship picked up where it had left off the year before. Jeff was happy to shadow his co-star during the break after Lucy asked him to keep Adam occupied whenever they were off stage. She wanted to cover all bases on the off-chance Trina tried to confront her husband.

"Places everyone!" the call came.

In no time at all, the curtain rose again for Act II. It was the scene of the picnic box social and everyone played their roles to perfection. Paul was thrilled at how well his new 'baby' was being received when he glanced across the seated crowd. It was easy to see the storyline had everyone enthralled, even though a good majority were already familiar with it. Their reactions, along with the hush settling across the hall, confirmed he had another hit on his hands.

The action was only a few minutes in when there was a sudden movement in the centre of the auditorium. Paul noticed two women get out of their seats, squeeze past other patrons and exit the theatre, whispering as they went. Unless it was an emergency, he wondered why anyone would need to leave partway through the second act. Just as quickly, his focus returned to the stage – two disappointed onlookers from a packed house weren't too much cause for alarm.

The tiny disturbance occurred during the bidding for one of the picnic hampers. As neither Lara nor Adam was involved in the immediate dialogue, they noticed the interruption at the same time.

Recognising his wife in the ray of light streaming through the large entrance doors, Adam guessed she was probably bored. He well knew she only had a short attention span for anything not revolving around herself. Obviously, his and Lara's interaction had drawn no cause for concern. He suspected she had gone off to look for better things to do with her time.

With that pressure gone, it meant the crucial wedding scene could be delivered with the full scope of passion required. Adam dared to glance across at Lara, who was already watching for his reaction. The look of relief he sent her way resulted in a smidgen of a smile to touch the corners of her mouth. With Trina no longer around, they could relax for the rest of the show.

During the showdown for *Laurey's* hamper, Adam and Jeff's characters were totally convincing with their fiery exchanges growing even more heated. Lara's encouraging glances caused Adam to put all of his ardour into the scene until *Curly* eventually won her basket over his rival. Loud cheers from the crowd had both of them grinning – although the reason had nothing to do with their reactions but everything to do with pure anticipation for what lay ahead.

Her heart was pounding a rapid beat when it came time for the main characters to reveal their true feelings. This would be the first time either of them had the chance to play their roles to the full. Both were nervous, wondering whether they would remember their lines and spots or become too caught up in the moment and forget everything to do with the storyline.

With exquisite tenderness, their lips met. Instantly they were back in a bed in Tuscany, submitting to that all-consuming passion denied for so long.

Unfortunately, the kiss ended far too soon for their liking.

The script called for *Curly* to push *Laurey* away and it took all of Adam's willpower to keep on track when his sole focus was to drag Lara into his arms and keep her there forever. Staying true to their task, her heavy eyelids and the veiled look sent his way were enough confirmation she was feeling exactly the same. And all the while, their lips tingled from the encounter. Thankfully, it wasn't too long before the script had them in each other's arms again while crooning the lullaby *People Will Say We're In Love*.

It was the perfect case of reality following fantasy as *Laurey* took *Curly's* hand in hers and sang lines that fitted their true persona's mood exactly ... *"Just keep your hand in mine ... your hand feels so grand in mine."*

When the song reached its emotional conclusion, Adam couldn't look away as the audience erupted into thunderous applause. His expression conveyed everything he had been longing to say ever since setting eyes on Lara during the first rehearsal. Her reply was to run gentle fingers sensuously over his palm in that old familiar way. It was easy for observers to imagine this was all part of the scene, while to them it became a private declaration of their ongoing love.

No matter what was to come in the future, this poignant encounter would always be a never-to-be-forgotten homecoming.

The young couple was disappointed when the scene changed and other storylines played out. Even so, it provided a necessary reprieve and gave the butterflies in their stomachs a chance to dissipate ... while the memory of those few precious moments lingered on.

It wasn't long before they had to focus again when their characters were suddenly thrust into the centre of attention once more. A party was in full swing, and it was soon apparent to the audience this was *Curly* and *Laurey's* marriage feast. The walls echoed with happy sounds when the wedding guests joined the happy couple in singing the title number. But just as they were preparing to leave for their honeymoon, the tempo changed into drama and rivalry as a very drunk *Jud* arrived on the scene. Angry and jealous he exploded full force, wielding a knife at the surprised groom. During the scuffle, *Jud* was the one felled by the weapon instead of *Curly*. The silence was deafening as he lay dead on the floor.

The reality of the situation hit a little too close to home for Adam. Trina's threats against Lara if he didn't stay away from her still echoed in his ear. It was a relief knowing she hadn't stayed to witness the fight and its dreadful outcome.

The next scene depicted a makeshift trial. Much to everyone's relief, *Curly* was declared not guilty. Amongst all the revelry, Lara and Adam's eyes met for a moment. Their expressions conveyed a touch of wistfulness as they dared to imagine celebrating their own special day. Though neither one was brave enough to go down that track, it wasn't too hard to imagine something of a similar vein being the catalyst for them becoming husband and wife.

Thankfully, no one else noticed the exchange.

As the happy couple drove off into the sunset in the famous 'surrey with the fringe on top', the audience rose to their feet with shrill whistles, shouts of acclamation and deafening applause mingling together. The show was clearly another rousing success, and not surprisingly, Paul's applause was loudest of all.

Throughout the curtain call, individual groups moved to the edge of the stage, both humbled and grateful to receive the recognition they so richly deserved. Starting with the ensemble players and then moving through the minor characters to the second leads, as each set moved forward the level of applause increased significantly until eventually Adam and Lara stood hand-in-hand with the spotlight focussed solely on them.

The crowd erupted into cheers, and loud shouts of "Bravo!" and "Brava!"

echoed from all four corners. It was a huge relief to have made it through those crucial scenes without the worry of Trina's watchful eye, and Adam raised their joined hands in the air. Exchanging broad grins, the pair then bowed low.

After almost a minute of deafening applause, he beckoned for all the cast to come forward. Adam wanted the full company to be on the receiving end of all this rousing acclaim, and also provide a chance for each of them to acknowledge those in the orchestra pit. More shouts of approval erupted around the room. As a final gesture, the entire ensemble joined hands across the stage for one last bow. It was the perfect conclusion to a successful opening night.

Once the curtain fell, several of the show's backers went over to congratulate Paul for all his hard work. They were ecstatic, confident the reviewers would refer to it as a 'big hit', which in turn would ensure a long run.

Backstage the atmosphere was electric. It had been an exhausting time for all, both physically and emotionally, from the energetic dance numbers and an intense storyline. Any signs of fatigue soon fell away as the corridors echoed with the sound of actors slapping each other on the back for a job well done.

Charles had also been involved in the wedding scene. He knew only too well the emotion portrayed by Lara and Adam had nothing to do with their roles. Secretly he was thrilled to witness so much joy on their faces after being downcast and discouraged for so long. When Elizabeth came backstage to join him, her expression mirrored his with eagerness and hope.

All of a sudden, a little whirlwind burst through the door and straight into the arms of the man she hadn't seen for many months.

"Uncle Adam, Uncle Adam, I've missed you *sooo* much!"

Nikki's touching cries pierced his heart as she clung to his neck.

"Hello, my precious little Munchkin. I think I've missed you even more…"

Lara's eyes filled with tears as she watched him hold her daughter close and burrow into her hair. Nikki's love for this caring man who had changed both their lives and turned their worlds into a full-blown family made her heart ache. For months, she had deliberately pushed away any thought of the bond these two shared. Now she was overwhelmed by a tidal wave of guilt for having kept them apart ... even though she didn't have any other choice.

Adam's heart broke when their eyes met and he witnessed her tears. Sadly, there was nothing he could do to comfort her with so many people milling about. The only positive was the relief that came from knowing Trina wasn't there to witness his and Nikki's reactions – their touching reunion would have been instant proof of every single one of his wife's accusations.

Lucy and Jeff rushed over to join them. She threw her arms around Lara in much the same manner as Adam longed to do and his eyes followed their every move. When she sent him a sympathetic grimace, he responded by mouthing a heartfelt, "Thank you," followed by a miniscule dip of his head.

As the surge of congratulations flowed, Charles and Elizabeth hurried over with the director and a well-dressed man following close behind. The two men were chatting animatedly between themselves, and Paul's face was beaming as he introduced the visitor to his two leads. It was apparent their performances had impressed the newcomer from the mountain of warm praise he handed out.

Paul tried to contain his excitement as he broke in. "Max is *the* Morgan of Morgan & Chalmers. I'm sure you've heard of them – especially you, Adam. They're one of the most respected agencies in the business."

Adam tried just as hard to temper his reply. Everyone in the industry had heard of Max's reputation, so he was surprised to find the head of the company at the opening rather than sending along one from his middle-management team. It didn't take long for the famous agent to get down to business.

"That was a magnificent body of work – especially what I just saw from you two. Our company is keen to add your names to our client list. Now I just need to know when you're free to come to my office to flesh out a deal..."

Both Lara and Adam were speechless. The excitement of opening night had been thrilling enough; hearing his offer magnified the entire experience with a massive rush of adrenalin. This could be the start of something much bigger than either of them could ever have imagined, even though Paul had always said it wouldn't be long before agents came calling.

Lara was flabbergasted at the thought of being approached by such a prominent agency. Adam was more familiar with their reputation and knew Morgan & Chambers carried only the biggest names on their books. He was both surprised and flattered to even be considered. Several of his peers now sported high profiles after being offered roles in some of the biggest shows due to the efforts put in by Max and his partners, so it was a high honour.

"Goodness, I haven't had any time to think about it," Adam answered eventually, trying hard to keep his tone on an even keel. "Ummm ... I'm not too sure – maybe I could come in one day this week if that would suit."

Lara was still in shock. She was finding it almost impossible to take in what this could mean for her future. All she could manage was a hasty, "Umm ... well ... heavens, I'm not even sure when I'm free. Can I get back to you in a few days? I have a young daughter and my day job to consider."

Max was fully understanding, realising she very likely had no experience with the contracting process. With a keen nose for business, he fished out a small leather pouch from his coat pocket. "Of course, that's fine. Here's my card ... how about I get back to you within the week?"

"Oh, um, that – that would be great, th-thank you," she stammered, still feeling overwhelmed from the unexpected offer.

As he was going, the agent smiled and extended his hand to each of them. "I look forward to working with both of you. Now go and enjoy the party."

On his way out, Max made a mental note to follow them up later in the week. He was convinced Lara and Adam were destined for great things and wanted to have them locked in with his company before another came along with a better offer. There was no way he could afford to have them slip away after those stellar performances.

As the troupe and their entourage of family and friends made their way down to a nearby restaurant, the streets echoed with happy chatter. No agency had ever approached anyone from their ranks before, so this was even more reason to celebrate.

The maître d' greeted them with a huge smile, gushing about the stories already coming out of the theatre from other guests. He led them to a room already booked for the entire cast and crew and pointed to a table large enough to cater for nine.

"Please enjoy yourselves and congratulations on a successful show."

Elizabeth had already organised for the young couple to have seats next to each other and Nikki was quick to claim the vacant one on Adam's other side. All night long she kept leaning over to touch his arm or hand. His heart melted to see those big brown eyes shining up at him. He missed the little girl almost as much as he had Lara and having her there was the perfect culmination to a wonderful evening.

Lucy and Jeff, as well as Suzie and Ben, made up the table of nine and with so much laughter and chatter going on, it was easy to disguise the furtive looks and quiet whispers passing between the reunited pair. They tried hard not to be obvious, though any astute observer would have no problem recognising the signs of two people attempting to play down their attraction. Fortunately, those seated around other tables had too many other things to talk about rather than concern themselves with what was happening between their co-stars.

Halfway through the evening, Paul wandered over to their table and pulled up a chair for a chat with the talented duo.

"What'd I tell you!" His elbow nudged Adam's as he sent Lara a big grin. "I knew it wouldn't be long until agents came beating down your door!"

"Hang on! They're not exactly coming in droves – that was one tentative offer, and we haven't even agreed yet."

"You will, my friend, you will!" Paul assured him as Charles joined in.

"Absolutely, my boy! I always said you were both destined for much bigger stages and now Max's company is proving me right. Here's to our new stars." He raised his glass. "To Adam and Lara!"

Lara's cheeks turned pink, while Adam only shook his head and chuckled when those around the table raised their glasses to toast the success of the still astonished pair.

Not too much later, Nikki drifted off to sleep with her head resting on Adam's lap. As much as Lara hated the thought of leaving, it wasn't fair to keep the worn-out youngster from her bed any longer. While she gathered up their things, he nestled the little girl over his shoulder. As the duo said their farewells, the rest of the cast were quick to reiterate their congratulations and it took nearly ten minutes to get through them all. Eventually, they managed to make their way through the mass of bodies and out to the entrance.

"I can take her from here if you like." The expression in Lara's eyes belied her suggestion, but she had no wish to presume anything or put him under any more pressure.

"No, it's okay. Please let me carry her out to your car. I'm not ready to say goodbye just yet."

They walked in silence ... not quite touching, yet close enough to feel the heat emanating from every pore. Slow footfalls ensured whatever time he could spare stretched out that little bit longer. The evening had stirred up a heap of emotions, but they were reticent to bring them out into the open because of an uncertainty for the future, especially with Trina's threats always looming on the horizon.

The little Corolla's distinctive shape loomed much too soon for Adam's liking. He took his time strapping Nikki safely into the booster seat. Lara felt that familiar, loving tug as he positioned a pillow to cushion her head. Once again, his actions became a tender reflection of that kind heart she knew so well.

He could feel her eyes following his every move, though neither one could do anything about the raw emotion clawing at their souls. They had too much to think about and needed the light of day to gain a true perspective as to how, when and where they could seek out an answer to their dilemma.

Despite his best efforts, Adam couldn't prevent his hand from reaching out to stroke her cheek as he wished her goodnight. Closing her eyes, she took advantage of those few precious seconds to lean into that familiar touch. It felt as if a kaleidoscope of desires scurried across her soul, rousing it to life. She raised her head, and all either of them could do was gaze at each other as mirrored expressions reflected the desperate yearning that had become their constant companion.

Lara had far too many thoughts swirling around in her head and each one needed to be processed when she was alone if she wanted to gain a proper perspective without his presence influencing her in any way. With a final lingering glance, she whispered a tender goodnight before climbing into her car.

Adam watched her drive away, his heart aching knowing they were both going home to the stark reality of lonely lives.

It had been an emotion-charged day, not only because of the open acknowledgement of their love, but also the surprising offer from Max. Both events could be the turning point to the rest of their lives.

§

Adam arrived home to a house shrouded in darkness, and he was quick to notice the empty space where Trina's car usually stood. Thankfully, this meant there would be no pointed questions – at least until morning – and he let out a long sigh. There was too much to ponder regarding his future to try and deal with her inevitable third-degree inquisition.

Soft moonlight spilled through the half-open curtains in two homes separated by several miles. Sitting in its silvery glow, a pair of heartbroken soulmates begged God for another chance while basking in the imprint of their other half on her cheek and his palm.

§

And in another realm, two skilful hands that had once fashioned an intricate tapestry outlining the story of a young couple's intimate journey, reached out to gather up several strands of luxurious silk. The colourful threads had been left blowing aimlessly in the wind of life for what seemed like an eternity of earthly time.

This canvas – a masterpiece of perfection depicting two entwined lives – emphasised a oneness of spirit that had lain dormant and lifeless for the same period of time.

Ever so carefully, expert fingers threaded the trailing pieces into the eye of a needle made from the purest gold. Then with miniscule stitches, a delicate pattern emerged across a surface where more recently and for far too long there had been only a yawning void. This newly formed image represented a stave of musical notes; a brand-new melody able to breathe new life into whoever heard it – while at its heart was the single word, *Hope*.

Below in Earth's dark cocoon, the two young people symbolised by this silken chorus fell asleep with the touch of a smile taking them into dreams laden with possibilities and laughter, rather than the recent despair that had been their sole companion on many a long and lonely night.

Chapter 6

A dam was just finishing off a mug of coffee at the kitchen bench when Trina made her way to the fridge the next morning.

Even though she was looking a little worse for wear, there was no hint of a tell-tale odour of stale liquor.

"'Morning. Where did you disappear to last night? I was expecting to find you at the after-party."

"Oh, Judith decided she'd seen enough, so we went to a nightclub for a bit more excitement. Mediocre re-runs of a backwoods shindig aren't really her thing – nor mine for that matter. And no, I didn't drink anything I shouldn't have, just in case you're wondering. I stuck with lemon, lime and bitters all night."

Even though the bitters component contained a small amount of alcohol, Adam felt it was easier to let it slide rather than start an argument when he was still feeling on top of the world. He certainly wasn't going to allow any of her caustic sarcasm to burst his bubble.

Deep down, he was delighted she felt that way and hoped this would mean she wasn't interested in attending any other performances. That way he and Lara could relax, especially in those last vital scenes. The corners of his mouth formed the makings of a smile at his choice of word. They weren't exactly relaxed when it came to kissing each other. Thankfully, his wife still had her nose in the fridge and missed the spontaneous gesture.

"Anyway, what about you? Did you enjoy partying with all your *friends?*"

Her emphasis on the last word was clear, but he decided to ignore it.

"Yeah, it was great, and you might be interested to hear I've been approached by a well-respected agent, so it looks like good things might come of this. He's asked me to drop by his office sometime this week."

Her head snapped up, and he couldn't miss the excited gleam in her eye. "What *sort* of good? Fame and mixing with theatrical royalty instead of that old flea-bitten company I witnessed last night ... now wouldn't *that* be a nice change from your *usual* crowd."

The blatant dig at his father and Lara was obvious, but he couldn't be bothered responding. Taking one last swig from his cup, he grabbed a set of keys from the dish on the bench. "I'm off to get the papers and read the reviews. Is there anything you want while I'm out?"

She responded with a disinterested shake of her head and poured herself a cup of coffee. "No, I'm off to Judith's shortly – I'll probably be gone when you get back."

Her answer was the ideal response for a quick change of plans. Sending her a hurried, "Bye," over his shoulder, Adam made a bee-line for the garage. If she couldn't be bothered with what the papers had to say, his parents certainly would.

§

Suzie burst into the cottage with several newspapers clutched under her arm just as her sister was making breakfast. Lara was stifling a long yawn when the uninvited visitor plonked herself down at the dining table.

Between the sweet sensation of Adam's lips against hers and the adoring looks he had sent her way during the wedding scene, not to mention the later meeting with Max and everything he was proposing, Lara's sleep had only been fitful ... but she didn't care. For the first time in months, there was a big smile on her face.

"Oh, that smells good, but how about you take it off the stove for a while and come and check out what the papers are saying. Wait 'til you see!" Suzie called.

The excited exclamation brought Nikki running in from the backyard where she had been riding an imaginary pony; whenever she hadn't seen Clancy for a few days, Trilby was the next best thing. She rushed up to her aunt with a loud 'neigh' of welcome.

Suzie pulled the little girl onto her lap and then spread the papers across the table with an exaggerated flourish. "Hello, Miss Filly, come and look at what I've got here ... but first of all" —she kissed the cute little button nose that now had a few specks of grass on it— "would you like some juicy orange carrots for breakfast to fill up that hungry tummy?"

"No," Nikki giggled, tickling her aunt's chin. "I'd rather have some orange *juice* and lotsa toast with Begemite! But what are all these papers for?"

The sisters exchanged bemused grins at her unique take on the popular Aussie breakfast spread.

"They've got lots and lots of great reviews all about your mummy and how good she is! Now you'd better go and call her over so we can read them together."

"*Mummy*, come *quickly!* Aunty Suzie said you're really good and you need to come and read all about it!" She shuffled her few square inches of butt over to make more room. "Come *ooon* – you can sit on her other knee next to me and then we can look at all the pretty pictures together."

"We're not having toast today," Lara said, ignoring the endearing request while the cheery sizzle of bacon and eggs kept her company. "I thought I'd do one of your favourites, and if I come over there, everything might get burnt. Why don't you ask Aunty Suzie to read them out instead?"

Her thoughts went back to the last time when Adam had joined her so they could browse the papers together. Today she needed to keep busy to help cope with the painful reminders. Not surprisingly, she wondered what he was doing and whether he had seen them yet.

Suzie rifled through the pages. "Hang on, let me just find them ... mmm ... oh yeah, here's one. *'Another Magnificent Performance by Two Up-and-Coming Young Stars'* and that's just the headline!" she prattled off with an excited grin. *"'Last night, in similar performances to their excellent work in last year's* Show Boat, *Adam Peters and Lara Jennings kept the audience spellbound with their brilliant portrayal of* Curly *and* Laurey *from Rodgers and Hammerstein's much-loved* Oklahoma.

"'With voices blending perfectly and an energy that bounced off every corner of the theatre, they brought to life this wonderful tale of jealousy and love. Paul Storey certainly picked two winners when it came to casting the lead roles, and as usual, his direction was superb.

"'I predict this show will run for a long season as the people of Brisbane flock to be entertained by two of its finest new stars.'"

Lara couldn't contain the rush of adrenalin as her sister opened another. "And then there's this one, *'A Duo Made in Heaven'.*"

The headline made Lara's heart skip a beat. *Please, God.*

"'The inhabitants of the little town of Claremore in a south-central state of the USA came to Brisbane last night as the familiar old classic Oklahoma *played to a packed house in Spring Hill. It sounded like everyone in the audience had their feet tapping along as Lara Jennings and Adam Peters sang up a storm in their roles of* Laurey *and* Curly. *These two young performers are proving Brisbane can produce just as many talented stars as Sydney and Melbourne.*

"'Ms Jennings' breathtaking soprano perfectly matched Mr Peters' powerful baritone and their harmonies created a new flavour for the brilliant musical score. I predict these two gifted actors will soon be treading the boards of all the major theatres around the country and their names will be on everyone's lips.

"'Paul Storey seems to be putting his unique stamp on revised musical productions as the entire ensemble brought this old favourite to life in an energetic and toe-tapping way. The raw energy on display throughout the dance routines was evidence of the long hours of practice put in to make this show a success – Lucy Palmer and Jeff Castle were two other standouts in a finely-tuned group, along with a great line-up of ensemble players.

"'Bravo and Brava to everyone involved in bringing this fabulous musical to our rapidly emerging entertainment scene.'

"What'd I tell you ... oh, and look at *this* one! There's even a *photo* of the two of you!" Suzie gushed.

This time she couldn't resist. Quickly taking the pan off the stove and setting it aside on the marble countertop, Lara went and glanced over her sister's shoulder. Her stomach started doing somersaults at the sight of those gorgeous dark eyes staring back at her. And as always, every part of her ached for him.

Suzie's voice rose with each new sentence as she read the next piece. *"Two Talented Stars Light Up Brizzie's Theatre Circle. Last night Brisbane shone with the talent of two new stars of the stage in Paul Storey's excellent adaptation of* Oklahoma, *the beloved musical that has entertained the masses since the early forties.*

"'Already wowing audiences last year in Show Boat, *it took last night's new offering to cement these two fine young actors as performers with the entire world at their feet. This reviewer sat enthralled at the magnificence of two voices perfectly highlighting the other.*

"'There was even a glimpse of Max Morgan, the famous agent, heading purposefully backstage when it was all over. I predict musical lovers won't be at all surprised to learn of these two talented artists being offered lucrative contracts – they most definitely have long and successful careers to look forward to from the rousing reception of the Opening Night crowd. Personally, I hope to see them gracing our Queensland theatres for many more years to come.'

"So ... my little sister's now a fully-fledged star, and I'm super proud of her! It's obvious you have another hit on your hands," Suzie chuckled, looking over her shoulder to check for Lara's reaction. "No wonder Max wants to sign you up so quickly. He knows there'll be plenty like him banging down your door."

Lara was blown away with the write-ups and wondered again whether Adam had seen the reviews ... and added an anxious prayer that his wife hadn't.

§

Several kilometres away, Adam joined Charles and Elizabeth on the wide terrace of their home overlooking the Brisbane River. Reams of newspapers littered the alfresco table as they enjoyed fresh mugs of coffee and poured through the same reviews. His parents' happy exclamations and proud smiles matched Suzie's over at the Paddington cottage.

"Well done, my boy. Mum and I have always been proud of your achievements. Having you join our family has brought more happiness into our lives than we ever dreamed possible. It's high time you received some well-deserved praise."

Like a doting father, Charles patted him on the back. There was a slight catch in his voice as he pictured how delighted Adam's first parents would be if they were still alive.

His son caught the underlying message and nodded in thanks. The subliminal message added another level of poignancy to an already emotion-charged weekend.

§

The first matinee was held that same afternoon. When the two stars ran into each other backstage, it was easy to use the glowing reviews as a means to grab a few stolen minutes. Two sets of eyes sparkled as they shared their joy while being careful to keep things on the same keel of the last few months. It would be too risky opening up their hearts fully with Trina's threat forever lurking in the back of their minds. Even so, all the tender nuances underpinning their conversation were constant reminders they were always meant to be together.

Everyone else in the cast was abuzz after reading them too. Several contained references to their individual performances and there wasn't a bad one among them. Paul was ecstatic and went from dressing room to dressing room offering his congratulations for a job very well done.

The show started right on time with those same silent messages being exchanged by the main leads just as the curtain went up. To anyone else, they came across as insignificant little gestures, while to the recipients they offered a feast of soul food able to set the tone for more stellar performances. As the first act progressed, those in the audience enjoyed the rollicking tale, along with the stirring score and lively lyrics bringing it to life.

Without the fear of Trina's scrutiny, their performances provided a true homecoming for Lara and Adam's hearts. Having the freedom to display the emotion required by their characters right from the start meant *Laurey* and *Curly* weren't the only recipients of this shared lovemaking. The former lovers, who lived and breathed to be together, relished every morsel.

Sadly, once the curtain came down again, that awful reality returned. The only sign the emotional storyline hadn't been left abandoned on the now-empty stage was the ongoing spate of stolen glances – and each one made their hearts race.

§

Early the following week Adam called Max, agreeing to come to his office to mull over the details of the proposed contract. The family solicitor accompanied him to the meeting to ensure everything agreed upon was in his client's best interests. After a couple of hours, the details were finalised to everyone's satisfaction.

It was all very exhilarating, although it also meant major changes would be necessary to his everyday life. If the agency's plans came to fruition, he needed to make himself available for much larger productions. This could entail touring the country and appearing in eight shows a week instead of the four *Oklahoma* currently had scheduled. As soon as he got back to the office, Adam made an appointment with his bosses at the architectural firm.

Several executives from the company had been at the opening after reading about his success in *Show Boat*. None were surprised to hear he was suddenly in demand and Max's agency was eager to add him to their books. Adam explained he didn't want to give up his work commitments entirely and hoped they would be willing to allow him to cut back only when necessary. It was a huge request and he waited nervously for their response.

It didn't take long for them to agree to work around his commitments, at least on a trial basis, to see how things panned out over the next twelve months. His contributions to the company were invaluable, so they were prepared to grant him some leniency, especially after all the successful feedback following the lectures he delivered in Salzburg the year before. With his unique talent in designing, it wasn't surprising he was a hot-ticket item in this cut-throat world.

§

After waiting several days, Max eventually rang Lara himself. The agent was so keen to sign her, he suggested coming to her home after work to iron out a deal. Talk around the traps was the upcoming star would be in demand right around the country, so he was worried one of his rivals would convince her to go with them if he didn't act fast. Being shut away in her editing room for most of the day, Lara had no idea what was going on. When the call came, she was bewildered as to why such an illustrious firm would be so keen to have her on their books.

When Charles heard about the appointment and Lara's concerns as to how these changes would affect Nikki, he was quick to pick up the phone, offering both himself and his lawyer to sit in on the negotiations. He wanted to ensure the contract contained a clause providing for a nanny and tutor so the little girl could accompany her mother whenever a new production was playing in another part of the country.

Things were moving along rapidly until the conversation turned to what Max's expectations would be once the signed contract was in place, especially what consequences this would have on her current editing commitments. Lara hadn't really considered this aspect in all the excitement – and doubt – of the last few days. She quickly excused herself to make a call to her boss. David had been at *Oklahoma's* opening and already knew of Max's initial offer.

"Of course you have to take it, you silly nong. This is every singer's dream."

"Are you sure, Davey? I don't want to just up and leave you in the lurch."

"Don't worry about me; this is far more important. I'm sure we can work something out so you can do both."

Secretly he was prepared to agree to anything to keep her on staff. Her skill in putting together award-winning pieces meant Lara was often a director's first choice when it came to working on their latest project.

Due to the rave reviews in Sunday's papers, when it came to finalising the deal, Max was more than willing to fit in with each clause put forward by the lawyer. By the end of the visit, every stipulation had been laid out in meticulous detail. Lara's stomach felt like a host of butterflies had taken up residence, while Charles' gentle encouragement assured her she was doing the right thing.

"Congratulations, young lady," Max said, extending his hand and reassuring her with a warm smile. "I know you won't regret this. Welcome to Morgan & Chalmers, we're thrilled to include you in our excellent talent fold."

Giving a nervous grimace and taking a very deep breath, she placed her hand in his, acutely embarrassed by the slight film of moisture that had formed there during the negotiations. Thankfully, his kindly manner set her mind at ease.

"Thanks so much, Max. This really is quite daunting, but it's very exciting at the same time. I only hope I don't let you down."

"You won't, I know it. We're going to share a great partnership. I look forward to seeing your name up in lights all around Australia – and, if my instincts are correct, in many of the famous theatres of the world!"

Only a week ago, Lara could never have believed those words would ever be directed at her, but Charles' warm hug confirmed it really was happening. She returned his embrace with an excited shiver when she saw the look of pride in his eyes. Inside, his heart ached, wishing more than anything Adam could be there to share in her joy.

Nikki's school principal was most obliging when Lara phoned the next day. She was more than willing to provide worksheets so the little girl could keep up with the rest of her classmates. Lara was confident as long as she was the constant in her life, Nikki would be able to adapt to wherever this new career path took them.

The only thing she didn't want to think about was how far it would take them from her soulmate as they travelled from city to city.

§

Oklahoma was a huge success with a run that lasted eight weeks. The schedule included performances every Wednesday, Friday and Saturday nights, along with a matinee on Sunday afternoons. Paul was thrilled with ticket sales as most shows sold out long before the doors even opened.

Lara and Adam savoured having this chance to see each other on a regular basis, though they were still vigilant when it came to any form of interaction … and not only in front of anyone else; both were just as wary around each other. Their hearts were too fragile to risk having to cope with all that pain again.

Charles was always conscious of their plight and noticed the efforts they put in to keep the relationship on a purely amicable basis. Secretly he applauded their control, although he still worried about how Adam was faring at home, especially with Trina's extreme mood swings.

Much to both his and Adam's relief, Judith kept Trina so busy she hardly ever gave a thought to the show anymore. She felt certain Lara would have moved on from her 'ever so boring' husband and Adam was well used to treading on eggshells whenever his wife was around. He was still wary if ever the musical came up in conversation, but even that was getting easier. Trina's sole focus was on his new contract and anticipating how many famous doors this could open up for her social life.

Late one Wednesday night a few weeks after the opening, Jeff banged loudly on the girls' dressing room door. "Hey, you two, hurry up and get out here! My stomach's growling and Adam's champing at the bit."

"Hang on, we're coming, give us a break!" Lucy called back, winking at Lara who was running a quick brush through her hair. It was a relief feeling it swing free after being shoved under one of the itchy theatrical wigs for so many hours.

Lucy and Jeff had taken to inviting the others to join them for a quick bite to eat after a show, similar to the shared camaraderie of the year before. To make things easier, Suzie suggested Nikki stay over at her place rather than Lara having to organise somewhere quiet backstage away from all the hustle and bustle happening between scenes. With the school being located only a street away from her usual route to work, it was easy to drop her niece off each Thursday. When weekends rolled around, they got up to all sorts of adventures – usually with Ben adding to the fun – before Lara swung by to pick her up. It was a good arrangement and meant the single mum had no reason to worry about being late home.

Over hot drinks and a pizza, or sitting around a shadowy booth at the local coffee shop, Lara and Adam's attempts at friendship blossomed while keeping their true feelings locked away. They missed the freedom of being able to touch, though their souls still seem fused together. Often they went to finish the other one's sentences and then quickly had to stop themselves ... and all the while those sparkling 'windows to their souls' conveyed the truth sealed inside their hearts.

§

Home-life in the Peters' household continued much as it had for the last few months. Trina regularly went out on the town with Judith, while Adam endeavoured to keep the peace by getting home at a reasonable hour. Even on show nights, he was usually home long before she was. This helped to keep any of those earlier threats safely buried in the past.

Whenever he was alone, Adam invariably locked himself away in the study, listening to soulful music with the lights turned low and envisioning Lara nestled beside him with their hands performing a stirring duet. This ritual soon became his only real form of relaxation. Rousing himself from memory-laden dreams a couple of hours later, he trudged upstairs to a cold, empty bed.

Sometimes in the sanctity of his room, he took the photos journals from the hole in the wall and spent an hour or so reliving every moment of that other life. Every now and then, when the yearning became too much, a tentative hand picked up the phone beside the bed ... but just before dialling the last digit, the handpiece landed back on the cradle and he turned over, desperate to find oblivion in sleep.

Following another hour or so of tossing and turning, eventually the sound of heavy breathing wafted from beneath a mound of pillows, while memories of long silky hair spread across his chest kept him company in nightly dreams.

§

Adam and his father met for their regular lunch one Saturday towards the end of May. Charles was still concerned about his son's state of mind and hoped he would be able to draw him out if they were away from Elizabeth's listening ear. Because of the scare with her heart, both men tried to shield her as much as possible from anything that may cause distress.

They were seated at one of the tables located beneath a leopard tree at their favourite haunt in Paddington. With Lara's cottage only a few streets away, it didn't take long for Adam to experience that all-familiar ache. Not long after the breakup, Charles had suggested it might be better to meet somewhere else, but Adam was adamant there was nowhere else he wanted to be.

"So how have you been, my boy? Trina hasn't started drinking again, I hope. From what you mentioned the other day, it sounds like she's out socialising most nights – maybe it's time to consider where your future lies."

Fear for his son's safety was his biggest worry. Over the years, Adam had been on the receiving end of countless injuries, and there was always the chance she could lash out again. Most men would have either hit back or left years ago, but he had remained resolute – continuing to put up with her vicious moods while filling his life with music, theatre and work ... at least until the middle of last year. Lara had changed him ... but not enough to make him see sense. His commitment was something that still baffled Charles. While admiring the young man's integrity, his greatest wish was to see him make a new life for himself – and with Lara by his side.

Adam understood his father's thinking, and deep down he felt the same, but that vow made all those years ago was always like a noose around his neck. No matter how much he wanted to leave, it kept tightening its grip. Exhaling loudly, he pondered how to get his point across when it didn't even make sense to him. Then...

"Yeah, I'm getting there, thanks, Dad. As far as I can tell, she's staying right away from it, thank goodness. With her being out so much, it means we get to live separate lives most of the time, although every now and then she almost seems to care and I start thinking maybe things'll get better after all. But then I realise it's probably only because of the new contract – almost like she's too scared I'll up and leave if she ignores me completely."

"Well, there you go – that should be a good enough reason..."

Adam grimaced and shrugged his shoulders, absentmindedly played with the cutlery. He appeared to be staring into another world unseen by others ... until a deep sigh slipped through his lips. "I miss the little things more than anything."

It wasn't hard for Charles to recognise his son's focus had changed to Lara.

"You know ... walking along the beach or chasing each other through the waves, having her tickle me while doing the dishes and not being able to get away without ending up in a bubble fight..." The corners of his mouth lifted into a crooked smile as he thought back to those times. "Hearing her laughter when Nikki comes out with one of her priceless sayings..." He sighed loudly from deep in his soul. "Nothing or no one will ever be able to fill that void ... I miss them both. That little Munchkin was able to wriggle her way into my life as much as her mother did."

"I know. The love you all shared was definitely something unique. Mum and I could feel it every time we saw you together."

Adam glanced across at his father with a pensive smile. Suddenly his face clouded over. Once again, he seemed to retreat into another world, only this time to a much darker place.

His next response was similar to a robot and without a single inflection. "I just can't bring myself to leave yet. I want to – more than anything – but I can't find the courage to leave Trina to her own devices. She's been walking a thin line for so long, I'm not sure what's going to happen – what she's likely to do."

He hung his head in shame, and his voice came out as a whisper. "I adore Lara with everything within me, but I know she's strong enough to cope." The expression on his face was one of self-loathing. "And I hate myself every day for putting her through this living hell." Deep worry lines furrowed his brow.

Charles didn't respond. He could see Adam was battling some tormented memory. All of a sudden, the younger man leaned forward, staring at his father with fire in his eyes as a wave of emotion streamed from his mouth.

"That poor woman's had to deal with the *worst* life can throw her ... *and* managed to come through it all – though God only knows how." His eyes grew misty, and he had to blink the tears away. "The last thing she needs is having to worry about being on the end of Trina's wrath. As long as Nikki's in her life, Lara will do everything possible to make their lives happy. We may never have the chance to be together properly, but at least we can be friends, even if I do have to hide how I feel from the rest of the world."

The older man had to bite his lip listening to this sad revelation. Deep down he knew his son was trying just as hard to convince himself what he said was true.

When Adam looked up and saw the concern in his father's eyes, all he could manage was a disheartened shrug. "I know that makes me sound like a fool – I'm certainly no martyr – but I can't help it. No matter how hard I try to justify leaving, deep down, those vows made between us keep echoing in my head – even though I've broken nearly every single one of them. I try to ignore them ... with every part of me – but I just can't – not while Trina has no one else to turn to. Judith's just a party girl – not someone she can rely on – even though Trina's convinced she's a true friend."

It was almost as though he was trying to prove to himself why he had to stay. Charles went to respond, but Adam still hadn't finished.

"I know it's hard to understand, Dad – to be honest, I don't even really get it myself – but I have to stay if only to make sure she's okay. At least then I can live with the guilt of loving someone else. God only knows she doesn't want me as a husband. I'm just the provider – but if I were to leave, there's no one else who cares what happens to her—" He broke off, shaking his head, "Oh, it's too hard to explain, but you don't have to worry, I'll be okay. As long as you and Mum are in my life, I can get through anything."

Charles knew exactly what he meant. He had seen his son go through far more struggles than most since joining the family. Having his parents pass away at such a young age, and then his unborn child, as well as all the other hardships resulting from his marriage. Losing Lara was the hardest of all, but he never lost sight of the things that had turned him into the man he was today. In a roundabout way, the death of his parents was the catalyst keeping Adam bound to his wife, especially now with Trina's own parents showing no interest. No matter how bad things became, he could never abandon her the way they had deserted their only child.

"I understand, son, truly I do, but I still can't help worrying. I hate the thought of you being hurt over and over again. Mum and I witnessed the difference Lara made to your life. And that's all we've ever wanted – to hear you laugh and enjoy life the way you used to before Trina came along. I know I'm being blunt, but it's how I feel."

That same wistful look returned. "They were the happiest days of my life, and I'll always keep them in my heart – nothing will ever take them away. But I have to look at reality, and at the moment Trina *is* my reality. If she had somewhere else to turn, it would be a different story ... but she doesn't, so..."

Charles shrugged his shoulders. He well knew how determined Adam could be. "Fair enough. I won't try to get you to change your mind again. You know what's best, but don't forget Mum and I are always here for you."

"I know, Dad, and I really appreciate your support."

"But I need to be honest, too. Lara and Nikki have become as much a part of our family as you are, and we want to be there for them as well. Your mother thinks of her as the daughter she never had ... and Nikki ... well, you know how much we love that little girl."

Adam's face lit up in a way his father hadn't seen all year. "It means everything knowing you feel that way ... they need the support of parental figures – now more than ever. I *want* you to keep them in your lives ... if I can't be there for them, at least they'll have you." The smile vanished as his eyes grew damp again and he rubbed at them with the heels of his hands.

"Don't worry, we will – you're all family in our eyes," Charles finished kindly.

Adam let out a heavy sigh. "So long as you and mum keep them in your lives, I'll feel like a part of me is looking out for them, too. Thanks, Dad."

Charles reached across and squeezed his son's arm. It was the only display of affection Adam could deal with in such a public arena without breaking down fully.

And through it all, their exchanged looks conveyed just how much they meant to each other.

§

The next day Lara had just finished scrubbing off the heavy layers of make-up from another matinee when she recognised a book spine wedged between a couple of others in Lucy's area of their dressing room. The temptation was too hard to resist. Perching on the arm of the sofa, she turned the familiar pages with a melancholy smile. Memories of the countless hours she had spent compiling all the photos and diary entries from *Show Boat* intermingled with those of the man featuring on so many of its pages. A heavy sigh rose out of her chest.

Lucy was just wiping away a few last smudges of lipstick when she caught her friend's reaction in the mirror. The suffering clearly evident in Lara's eyes as her fingers brushed across each page made Lucy's heart ache. There was no need for a psychology degree to guess what she was thinking.

"They were special times," Lucy said softly. "Don't worry, I often go through it too, reminiscing about all the fun we had." Hers and Jeff's relationship had begun during the same show, so it held fond memories for them as well.

Without taking her eyes or fingers from the pages, Lara nodded slowly. "Mmm, the best. So often I wish we could go back there..." The sentence trailed away and Lucy could almost feel her pain.

She went across and softly stroked Lara's back, pointing to one of the photos and hoping to bring back a smile. "Remember that day? I can still see the look on Adam's face when you dropped a handful of ice down his back just before rehearsing your big solo. Remember how he was jumping up and down trying to get it all out? None of us could stop laughing!"

Her ploy worked, and they both sniggered at the image of Adam with his shirt half hanging out and a look of agony on his face.

"I can still hear him yelping even now *and* see him jumping around like a jack-in-the-box," Lucy went on. "Remember how Paul had no idea what was going on. He thought he was having some kind of seizure or something and was just about to dial emergency when Jeff grabbed the phone and told him everything was okay."

"That's right, he looked ridiculous and *sooo* cute!" Lara gave a bittersweet grin and turned the page. "Oh, and look at this one! That's when Jeff forgot his lines. I remember you secretly passing across that page from the script so he wouldn't get in trouble with Paul. I think it was the last rehearsal before opening night and you were scared he'd replace him with the understudy."

"Oh, that's right! I'd forgotten all about that. Thank goodness he pulled it off, and Paul was none the wiser."

"Yes, but only because you taped that scrap of paper with those particular lines to Charles' back so he could see them. Then Jeff followed him around for the whole scene and Paul kept telling him to get back into position. He never did figure out what was going on! Gosh, that was a fun day!"

For the first time in ages, Lara broke into a burst of loud chuckles, and Lucy soon joined in. Only a minute or so later, there was a sharp rap on the door and the subject of their humour popped his head around the corner.

"What's all the carry-on in here? We can hear you all the way down the hall!"

"Come and look at this," Lucy beckoned Jeff inside with a welcoming grin.

She pointed to the photo of him surreptitiously peering at the paper pinned to Charles' shirt and a rueful smile accompanied his reply. "They were great times ... I still miss them ... it's not quite the same now."

As soon as the words left his mouth, he felt like sinking through the floor. Both he and Lucy glanced at Lara as the smile left her face. She could tell what they were thinking and quickly crossed her eyes and poked out her tongue. It was just what they all needed to lighten the mood again.

"Well, after that bad case of verbal dysentery, I'd better stop looking like a cowboy and climb back into the twentieth century," he laughed, offering both of them a cheeky kiss on their cheeks, before leaving them to reminisce over more shared stories and other crazy antics from those days.

Lara put the album back where she found it with a resigned sigh. "I miss those days, too. This show's been great; but Jeff's right, it's just not the same."

She remembered when Adam used to come to their dressing room, both before and after every show. These days he wasn't brave enough to open the floodgates of seeing Lara dressed in a robe, nor be there to witness the intimacy of her changing behind a flimsy screen the way he used to. Now he stayed away and it was Jeff who popped in to see how the women were getting on.

The flood of reminders suddenly hit too close to home. Without warning, Lara slithered onto the sofa, burying her face in her hands as wracking sobs filled the small room.

Lucy hurried over and pulled the distraught woman into her arms. "Oh, Lars, I'm so sorry. I hate how hard this has been on you. Please don't cry."

The tears soaked into her blouse but she didn't care. All she could do was rock her friend and croon softly.

When Lara eventually lifted her head to blow her nose, Suzie pleaded, "Listen, you *have* to tell him how you feel. You can't keep pretending you're strong all the time. It's not fair on either of you."

"He already knows how I feel, and I don't want to make things harder for him. Don't worry, I'm okay until I start thinking about everything we've lost."

A wry smile crossed Lucy's face. Even though her answer dripped with scepticism, there was a touch of affection there as well.

"And how often is that, pray tell? From what I can see, missing him is the biggest constant in your life. You can't fool me."

Lara quickly scrambled to her feet and dashed away any remaining tears. "And that's *exactly* why I have to stop thinking about him."

"Pfft ... and pigs might fly! Come on, let's grab the guys and get something to eat. I'm starving!"

Chapter 7

It was easy for Lara and Adam to slip back into the habit of sharing after-show suppers with their best friends. To everyone's relief, that earlier cautious rapport had been replaced with a much easier light-heartedness. Several weeks in and it was almost like old times.

Gales of laughter once again filled the old corridors as they donned their street clothes, though Adam still avoided entering the girls' backstage dressing room. He was too afraid of what might happen if he found Lara alone. These little trysts were the only chance the pair had to relax and enjoy quality time together, so they basked in the freedom ... and yet always between them lay a chasm of their own making.

But they didn't dare build a bridge ... if they crossed it, they might never come back.

§

Lara's bedroom was shrouded in thick darkness. It was the night before the finale and she was lying wide-awake trying to subdue the swirl of bleakness rising in her spirit. Tomorrow would be the last time she and Adam could legitimately see each other on a regular basis.

Throwing back the covers and then the thick curtains, she stood by the window and took in the view over to four twinkling towers standing tall on a distant hill. An indigo sky was the perfect backdrop for the full moon to reflect those imposing silhouettes. She could picture Adam's sleepy form touched by the glow of the silvery orb.

It had been a lonely six months. The only happy memories in all that time were of nights spent in the old theatre and the much-anticipated suppers afterwards. For the rest of the time, she had felt like a long-abandoned shell lying in the crevice of a rock after its previous tenant had found somewhere else to set up home.

Across town in an elegant bedroom now constantly infused with regret and longing, Adam stood at his window gazing up at the same glowing disk. From his perspective, that recognisable grin appeared to be mocking him.

You're probably right, old fella. I doubt I'll ever feel like wearing a true smile again once this show finishes its run.

He was anxious for the day to begin, but he was also battling a feeling of dread because of everything it would mean.

With a resigned sigh, he crept back to bed, pummelling the pillow like a punching bag – something that had become a regular habit over many nights as he tried to chase away the wretched creatures that had taken to taunting him continually in his dreams.

§

The following morning Adam was making breakfast when Trina stumbled into the kitchen. Her satin nightgown was hanging off one shoulder as she wiped the sleep from her eyes.

"What time is it?" she mumbled, picking up the piece of toast he had just buttered and taking a big bite.

"Just after nine. I'm off to see Mum and Dad once I've had this. I want to run through the songs one last time. I know how much it annoys you when I have to practise here, so I thought I'd get out of your hair for a few hours."

His parents wouldn't mind if he turned up unexpectedly. They were always glad to see him, and he would much rather spend the last few hours with them before heading to the theatre instead of moping around here by himself all day. Hopefully, it would also help to take his mind off the coming night and everything it would signify.

"Suit yourself," she shrugged. "Judith and I are off to the races – she and John have just bought a share in a horse that's running at Eagle Farm this afternoon. What time do you think you'll be home?"

"Can't say for sure. I'll be staying for the after-party, and it'll probably go late. I'll make sure to be quiet when I come in so as not to disturb you."

"Oh, I'll probably be out anyway. If the horse does well, we'll be off celebrating too. I might even stay over at their place overnight if that's the case. I'll just play it by ear." Waving the last bit of toast in a brief farewell, she went off to get ready.

It was a relief hearing about her plans. Hopefully, the horse would win and everything would pan out just as she said. The last thing he needed was for Trina to turn up for the final performance. Tonight would be difficult enough as it was without having to put on a happy face for her sake.

For the first time in a long time, Adam's cheery whistle filled the kitchen. If she stayed out all night, there would be no need for him to leave the party early. It also meant he could spend those last few treasured hours taking advantage of being with Lara instead of worrying about seeing his wife's face in the crowd. As long as she and Judith were together, Trina was sure to forget all about him.

§

Cruising down the long driveway, Adam's gaze fell on the maroon Toyota Corolla parked in front of the four-car garage at his parent's home. His heart started beating a merry dance, to the point where he felt sure it would burst through his skin.

Talk about perfect timing! He raised his eyes to the sky and grinned. *Thanks, Lord."*

A little girl's happy chatter filled his ears as he approached the side of the house. That earlier excitement bubbled over at the thought of seeing her again. He didn't dare contemplate what it would be like being there with her mother after so long. His footsteps faltered as he approached the edge of the leafy terrace and he had to stop to take a deep breath before letting it out slowly.

Instinctively, Lara looked up from the table. Her eyes seemed drawn to that same corner just as he came into view, almost as though an unseen cord connected their hearts.

Her quick intake of breath and the expression on her face caused Charles and Elizabeth to glance over too. Their faces lit up as Adam walked towards them. No amount of planning could have orchestrated a more perfect encounter.

Nikki also heard her mother's gasp. When she looked across and caught sight of Adam, her riding boots hardly touched the ground as she rushed into his arms. Lara longed to do the same. The look the former lovers exchanged confirmed they knew exactly what the other was thinking ... and it was enough for now. He walked towards her with Nikki still in his arms, unable to look away from those familiar blue eyes. He remembered that all-familiar tug on his heartstrings whenever they were together in this relaxing sanctuary far from the cares of the world ... and nothing had changed.

His parents exchanged joyful grins, albeit that was all as they observed their son and his one true love's emotion-laden interaction. The atmosphere was too intense to spoil it with any unnecessary chatter. They felt like unseen albeit welcome onlookers to a touching moment in time.

As usual, Nikki brought them all back to earth as she prattled on and on in his ear. Nothing had changed in six long months, and neither Lara nor Adam could hide their faint smirks, remembering this same scenario being played out so many times when they had eyes only for each other.

"Shhh, Nikki," Elizabeth said kindly, recognising their need to simply savour the moment. She put a finger to her lips, and the little girl fell silent, her face beaming with excitement as those tiny fists clenched and shook in anticipation.

"Hello, Adam..." Lara's words floated across to him – like a whisper with wings. The easy smile accompanying them lit up his soul with what seemed like hundreds of candles, similar to the ones permeating the darkest corners of all the churches they had visited during their trip the year before.

"Hello, Lara..." His response matched hers – with the same degree of emotion and through a smile that made her heart skip a beat.

They held each other's gaze. Love poured from her eyes with no restrictions or fear of being seen, feeding Adam's spirit from a banquet it hadn't partaken of for far too long.

As though waking from a beautiful dream, he dragged his gaze away to smile at his parents— "Hi, Mum, Dad" —then finally back to Nikki who was still clinging to his neck— "and *you*, my littlest Munchkin! *You're* certainly a sight for sore eyes." He hugged her close and tickled under her chin with his nose.

A loud chuckle bubbled up from her throat. "Stop it, that tickles!"

He did as he was bid and gently pinched the tip of her nose between his fingers instead.

She copied him exactly as the giggles disappeared. "No one told me *you* were coming, Uncle Adam! Wait 'til you see how I can ride Clancy now. I've been practising just like you taught me!"

"Have you? That's excellent!" He put her down carefully and ruffled her fringe. "Then I'll have to come and watch you later, but I'd better say hello to everyone else first, or they might get cranky at me."

Breaking into another happy giggle, she went across to lean against her mother. Lara's eyes were sparkling beneath those long dark lashes he had kissed so often. She pulled her daughter close and wrapped a loving arm automatically around her waist as a tender kiss landed on the youngster's forehead. The whole time her gaze still hadn't shifted from the unexpected visitor. Charles and Elizabeth had no trouble guessing each gesture was subconsciously meant for their son.

Everything about the visit was a reminder of old times.

Elizabeth was in her element spoiling them with big mugs filled to the brim with the best brand of coffee and a much smaller hot chocolate for Nikki. Platefuls of sweet treats were pulled from the kitchen pantry, and the sound of cheerful humming wafted through the window across to where the others waited for her to join them again.

A little bit later Charles brought out his new vintage for the adults to sample. The conversation hardly stopped as they caught up on everything that had been happening with their respective jobs as well as the recent excitement over the contracts with Max. Lara and Adam hadn't physically touched, though the energy flowing between them was like an electric current. His parents kept exchanging furtive smiles. It was easy to see that special rapport was still very much a part of the young couple's lives.

The morning flew past, much faster than they wanted. Just before noon, Lara joined Elizabeth in the kitchen to prepare lunch while the men took Nikki down for a quick ride on Clancy to show off her new skills.

"Did you know he was coming?" Lara's sceptical smile made it obvious she wondered if this had all been a set-up.

"Of course not!" Elizabeth was quick to assure her, throwing out a carefree grin accompanied by an enthusiastic arm around her waist. "But I can't say I'm disappointed. And I think I can say the same for someone else from the look on your face when he came around the corner."

Raising a perfectly tapered eyebrow, the sparkle in Lara's eyes confirmed she was right.

With arms laden, they carried the food out to the table as Lara called across the paddock, "Come and get it."

Nikki heard the summons and let out a disappointed sigh.

"Come on, Munchkin. Here, I'll help you," Adam said, unbuckling the girth and pulling the saddle from Clancy's back while she left one last lingering pat along his soft nose.

Just as they turned to go, the little girl suddenly remembered and slipped the pony a piece of carrot she had squirrelled away in her pocket. Rubbing his neck one more time, she whispered, "See ya, old boy."

The trio came through the paddock gate just as Lara looked up from pouring Elizabeth's homemade fruit punch into four tall crystal tumblers and a much smaller plastic one. When they drew closer, two sets of eyes remained fixed on their mate – still drawn like moths to a flame and too much in tune to try to pretend anything else.

"Thanks for the invite to stay for lunch, Mum, and for putting on this great spread. Mmm-mmm, this looks delicious," Adam said, smacking his lips and helping himself to a generous serving of Thai chicken salad. "Sorry I didn't warn you I was coming."

"Don't worry; we're always pleased to see you ... but don't thank me, thank this one." With an affectionate smile, she put her arm around the young woman's shoulder. "It's Lara's, and as usual she's outdone me with her culinary skills."

His mouth split into a proud smile. "I should've guessed! She's the best cook around – oh sorry" —he leaned over with a cheeky grimace and planted a firm peck on Elizabeth's cheek— "after you, of course, mother dear!"

Lara broke into a sudden giggle – she missed their playful exchanges.

Elizabeth flicked a hand at him and gave an amused chuckle. "Oh, get off with you! Don't flatter me, young man. Besides, you're right, she *is* a fantastic cook – far better than I'll ever be." Her clear blue eyes twinkled as she turned to their guest. "Somehow I think you must've sensed we'd have another mouth to feed!"

Lara couldn't say anything. Instead, her eyes said it all as they flitted almost shyly between the mother and son.

After a leisurely lunch and with their appetites sated, Charles looked at his watch. Time was marching away, so Lara and the two men went off to the music room for a short rehearsal. Elizabeth took Nikki's hand and they settled on a comfortable sofa in the library, happy to read a few stories to each other. The little girl enjoyed showing off her new reading skills and Elizabeth delighted in playing the role of grandma.

An hour later, they all gathered in the living room for a quick cup of tea before it was time to leave for the theatre.

Charles was staring through the window deep in thought as he took a long sip of the strong brew, then he looked across at his son and settled the cup back in its saucer.

"I think it'd be a good idea if you and I went with Lara in her car. Then Mum and Nikki can bring ours later. That way you can get a ride back with us after the party, and they can go straight home instead of having to come back here again. Our place is on your way, so I think that's the most sensible option."

His unspoken reasoning was a wish to guard both their hearts, especially if Trina ending up staying at Judith's place. It would be far too easy a temptation for Adam to spend the night with Lara after the euphoria and ultimate sadness of the final show.

The young couple looked at each other and shared a resigned nod. They understood the wisdom behind his suggestion ... but it didn't lessen the longing.

§

Lara handed Adam her keys and he took them with a smile. He was remembering other times behind the wheel of the reliable little car – and a cheeky reference to the sunroof just after their first meeting – so this was an unexpected and welcome thrill. The conversation was easy and carefree after the relaxing afternoon. Charles' presence ensured the journey remained light-hearted instead of turning into a maudlin affair with the unwanted parting looming later in the evening.

Backstage corridors echoed with the excited chatter of the cast, and the three newcomers quickly joined in. Lara and Adam were determined to make the most of their last performance, especially when everything was about to change so drastically. Their new contracts meant it would be rare for both of them to obtain roles in the same production and this was playing heavily on their minds.

Following a final run-through for a couple of significant numbers, Paul put his hands together. "Well done, everyone. You've made me very proud. The show's been a resounding success because of all your hard work. Now let's make this last performance the one everyone will be talking about for years."

He looked across at his two leading stars and continued the applause. "And let's make it especially memorable for these two! They're sure to be in big demand across the country after all the recent reviews. It's hard saying goodbye, though no doubt we'll be hearing about their exploits for many years to come."

With a more serious tone, he added, "Just make sure you come back to join us when either one of you gets a few months' break, okay? After all, we're family, and things just won't be the same without you."

Everyone applauded loudly, reiterating his sentiments, while the recipients of all this attention gave promises to return if ever they had the chance. Both felt they owed it to Paul after everything he had done for them.

"Okay, that's enough of all this emotional guff. Off to your dressing rooms, the lot of you!" the director declared, shooing them away with his hands. "Just beyond that curtain is an eager audience waiting to see you do your thing ... so go on, get outta here!"

The corridor erupted into laughter as they all scurried away. His final upbeat order was the perfect counterpart to any of those earlier sombre layers.

Lara and Lucy were just putting the final touches to their costumes and makeup when there was a soft knock on the door. Adam's tentative smile greeted Lucy when she poked her head out. Fully expecting to find Jeff standing there, she did a double-take.

His expression was almost pleading as he whispered, "Is it okay if I come in for a minute?"

Her eyes glistened with a film of tears when she saw what he was carrying. Without saying a word, she gave a heartfelt nod and gestured for him to come inside.

Lara was still sitting in front of the mirror with her back to the door, so she had no idea what was going on.

"Hi, Jef—" The word caught in her throat when she turned to see Adam standing there with a large bouquet of deep red roses accompanied by the loving smile that always captured her heart. "Oooh, Adam ... they're beautiful!"

It was the first time he had been to their room since rehearsals began. Without saying a word, he handed her the stunning arrangement. Holding them close, she quickly buried her nose in the fragrant blooms as though inhaling the heady fragrance. Only the roses themselves were party to the secret she was blinking back a multitude of tears.

Lucy slipped out the door as quietly as possible, though the other two didn't even notice. They were focussed solely on one another, with no thought for anything else.

Adam's face was a picture of compassion and longing. "I'm sorry. I didn't mean to upset you. It's just" —his voice faltered for a moment, and he had to swallow hard before continuing— "this could be the last time we perform together, at least for a very long time. I wanted to let you know how much I'm going to miss sharing a stage with you." There was so much more he wanted to add, but he didn't dare.

Lara had to close her eyes ... the reality of their future was too painful to contemplate. Taking a deep breath, she managed to look up at him, and it broke his heart to see her face awash with tears.

Her voice was so soft, he had to strain hard to hear what she was trying to say. "Of course you haven't upset me" —she pushed the lump in her throat down as hard as she could— "but it's just like the last night of *Show Boat*. I never wanted that night to end – I thought it would be too hard to leave this place ... but at least we were together then. Now..." Anything more fell away as she fought through the sadness.

"I know, Baby." Unwittingly, the endearment fell from his lips, and he had to fight the urge to pull her into his arms.

His use of the pet name broke her heart all over again as it brought back images from the past. She knew anything more was a fantasy just out of reach and no amount of wishing could change the reality of their situation.

Fighting an urge to run into his arms, she turned and started arranging the flowers in a tall vase on her dressing table. Adam couldn't help himself and moved in closer, as though driven there by an invisible force. She could feel his presence and longed to lean into his chest ... to melt inside him and stay there forever. But she didn't ... she wasn't brave enough.

Just like a puppeteer was choreographing their responses, Adam reached out and gently traced a solitary finger down her spine, all the way to her waist. His touch was delicate – almost a form of gratifying torture. The emotion even this miniscule contact evoked became too much to bear. With a stifled cry, she spun around and wrapped her arms tightly around his neck. She pressed her face hard into his shoulder, oblivious of its effect on either her makeup or his costume.

Once again, that unseen choreographer pulled on those invisible strings. A long veil of hair caught the delicate touch of her lips, so the fabric on his shirt remained pristine.

Sadly, it was an entirely different story for Adam's heart as it silently broke apart.

He held her close and ran gentle hands down and across her back, while an underlying yearning filled them both with exquisite pain. The minute hand on the wall clock ticked over and over, though neither one even noticed as his finger ballet continued. They were oblivious to time and everything else apart from each other.

Eventually, Lara raised her head and they stood looking into their soulmate's eyes – two spirits wordlessly crying out to one another. He cradled her face between tender hands as loving fingers brushed away the long wisps of hair caught in the trail of tears.

"Please don't cry, my darling."

He wanted to promise her everything would be okay. Instead, he bit his tongue ... empty vows would only break her heart along with his.

Just then and without warning, a loud rap sounded on the door and a voice called, "Ten minutes, Ms Jennings."

As quickly as it had disappeared, reason returned. They fell apart, and Lara quickly dabbed at the remaining moisture around her eyes before rushing to the mirror to repair any makeup smears. Adam stood watching with his heart on his sleeve.

"*Please* don't look at me like that," she pleaded to his reflection. "I can't bear to see the pain in your eyes."

He gave an understanding nod and summoned up the glimmer of a smile. Then with one last gentle caress along her forearm, he turned and walked to the door, his tread slow and resolute. She couldn't miss the gentle lift of his shoulders as he steeled himself to leave, nor the soft murmur of a sigh accompanying the gesture.

Still, he couldn't bring himself to go – not yet – not like this. Turning back, he stole one final glance. "I'm so sorry, Baby. I didn't mean to make it any harder on you. I shouldn't have come ... I just needed to see you one last time befo—"

"Please don't ... I'm glad you came – truly I am." Sending him one last heartfelt look, she murmured, "The flowers are beautiful ... and so are you. Thank you, Teddy."

The much-loved endearment was the perfect parting gift.

Nodding slowly, Adam sent her an almost indiscernible wink. Then he slipped out the door, leaving behind the sweet fragrance wafting from the roses … and a heart that was slowing falling apart.

§

A few minutes later, the whole company stood in readiness as the overture began. The curtain quivered just before opening. Offstage, Lara and Adam dared to share one last glance. After his recent parting gesture, she screwed up her nose in the old familiar way – two intimate signs to prove their love had never waned.

Through the remnants of one last tender smile, Lara and Adam faded away and *Curly* and *Laurey* made ready for their final appearances.

§

The audience was abuzz during interval, and the atmosphere backstage was just as exciting. Everything was going off without a hitch – no forgotten lines and the entire cast had their moves down pat with impeccable timing to ensure everything flowed smoothly. Costumes flew in all directions and were hastily replaced with others, while make-up and wigs received last-minute adjustments before it was time to get ready for the second half. Lucy and Jeff shared a joke as they stood in the corridor and their ready laughter brought smiles from those passing by.

Lara was just hurrying to her spot when out of nowhere she felt someone grab her hand and pull her into one of the darker recesses at the back of the stage. There was no need to guess who was behind this unexpected abduction.

Adam clutched the top of her arms as he turned her around to face him. The look in his eyes and his earnest whisper made her heart beat even faster.

"I just wanted to tell you how wonderful these last few weeks have been. And during the wedding scene tonight, they might be *Curly's* sentiments, but it will be my lips claiming yours – not someone plucked from a make-believe world." His hand reached up to stroke her cheek. "And just so you know, no matter where I go, you'll always be with me."

A pair of eyes swimming with unshed tears held Adam's fast as her hands rested against his chest – that welcoming refuge she knew so intimately – and she whispered, "Oh sweetheart, I feel the same. Nothing's changed and it never will. You'll always be a part of my life, wherever I am – tucked away safely in here." She patted her heart.

For months, his emotions had been held in check and he had to close his eyes as her words flowed over him. Pressing loving lips against her forehead, the delicate touch of her breath played over his neck as she spoke from her soul.

"You're the most special man I've ever met and having the chance to play your leading lady has been everything I ever dreamed it could be. I hate having to pretend you're nothing more than a friend away from the spotlight, but at least up there you're mine again – even if it is only for a little while."

Before he could respond a voice echoed down the corridor, "Places everyone."

Needing one more tender moment, she touched her forehead to his, nuzzling in close as though imprinting him under her skin. He couldn't answer through the lump in his throat. Instead, he breathed in her scent with their mouths only centimetres apart.

And then it was time…

§

The chemistry flowing between *Curly* and *Laurey* was stronger than ever before. Whenever the make-believe lovers' lips met, it was Adam and Lara's own desire that was the driving force. They held the audience captive by their raw displays, and the blanket of darkness couldn't muffle a few sounds of discreetly blown noses nor the movement of hands as tears were wiped away.

In the second act when *Curly* got down on one knee to ask *Laurey* to marry him, the longing in his eyes almost made her throw away the pretence and speak from her heart rather than the scripted prose. Thankfully, she managed to restrain herself in time and the scene continued without missing a beat.

As he took her in his arms to seal the promise while singing the final line from *"People Will Say We're in Love"*, their embrace lasted longer than ever before. Adam couldn't bear the thought of having to let her go again. He cradled Lara's face for one last lingering kiss before having to force himself to turn to the gathering crowd waiting to congratulate the happy couple.

Lucy watched them with tears coursing down her cheeks as reality played out before her eyes ... and she hurriedly had to brush them away to prepare for her next line as *Aunt Eller*. Anyone who noticed her reaction believed the emotional display was all part of the storyline ... while the heartbroken pair stood with hands still clasped, unwilling to break this one last link.

A little while later in the finale, when the music swelled and the newlyweds rode off into the sunset, the whole place exploded into deafening applause. A few jumped to their feet cheering and calling for more. Paul's wish had most certainly been granted. Tonight's performance had been the most emotional one of all and those witnessing it would remember this night for a long time to come.

Curtain calls lasted for several minutes and hands burned as the applause grew louder and louder. The cast and crew had worked tirelessly to take the audience to a faraway place where love was victorious, and patrons were quick to show their thanks. Along with the thunderous ovation, vocal tributes soon followed. When it came time for Adam and Lara to receive their well-deserved acclaim, many of those already on their feet called out in one voice, *"Bravo, brava!"*

She found it was impossible to hold back the tears. Standing before her adoring fans, she threw out a grateful kiss with trembling fingers. The gesture brought even more enthusiastic responses, and both she and Adam bowed low before raising their hands above their heads to reciprocate the crowd's appreciation.

At his signal and as a fitting tribute, the rest of the cast then joined in for a rousing rendition of the chorus from the title number. Tears ran down many faces as they trilled those well-loved lyrics for the final time. They were all aware this was possibly the last time any from their ranks would work with the talented leads. It was a strange feeling not to be sharing another stage with them.

After offering a lingering wave, the whole troupe turned as one and hand-in-hand left the footlights behind. Once again, Lara had to wipe a few stray tears away. Withdrawing behind the velvet curtain, Adam reached across and brushed a shiny droplet from the edge of her nose.

"Thank you," she whispered so only he could hear. Simple words that held more meaning than anyone else could ever realise. Looking down at her, his expression was laden with both elation and sorrow, proof he was trying to deal with that same sense of loss.

Paul was waiting backstage with a beaming smile and clapped loudly as everyone filed past. Lashings of praise filled their ears when he patted each actor on the back and offered hugs to every actress – just like any proud father. The champagne flowed freely as the entire troupe congratulated each other on a job well done.

And then it was time to climb out of the old-time southern costumes and put those much-loved characters to bed once and for all.

A little while later, Adam was just leaving his dressing room when he caught sight of Lara pulling her door closed. She was cradling a magnificent bouquet of roses in her arms, and he watched as she paused to draw her name plaque from the door bracket. For a moment, her eyes closed as she pressed it against her chest and then tucked it securely inside her bag. He could feel her pain, and it broke his heart.

The slight click of his door closing carried down the corridor. Lara glanced across, and their eyes met and held as she waited for him to catch up. He pulled up right in front of her, dreading the thought of saying goodbye in a few short hours.

Catching hold of her free hand, he pressed his lips into her open palm as his gaze stayed fixed on her face. Lara's breath caught in her throat as his mouth continued its delicate trail across the sensitive skin, and her fingertips tingled when he folded them over the place his mouth had just been. She swallowed hard as her eyes stayed focused on every intricate move.

They shared one final heartfelt look before going out to join the others, hands not quite touching but spirits entwined by invisible cords that could never be broken ... and all the time her fingers held his kiss captive.

§

Paul had arranged the after-party at The Summit Restaurant, a place often chosen to celebrate special occasions by Brisbane's many residents. As Adam was driving Lara's car up the steep mountain road, the pair exchanged reflective smiles. Paul couldn't have picked a more fitting venue to celebrate this memorable occasion. The restaurant was situated at the same lookout where they had shared so many treasured moments during their months together.

As usual, invitations included family members so Suzie and Ben, along with Elizabeth and Nikki, were part of the gathering. It was a triumphant celebration until midnight rolled around when Lara looked across at her daughter and felt that dreaded check in her spirit. The little girl was exhausted and needed her bed. It was time to bid farewell to the man of her dreams all over again.

Suzie followed Lara's gaze and noticed Nikki struggling to keep her eyes open. "Hey Lara-Lu, how about I take this little one home with me for the night? She's worn out, and Ben and I are just about ready to go anyway. That way you can hang around a bit longer to say proper goodbyes to everyone."

She had also caught Adam's downcast look and wanted to give the two of them a bit more time together before it was time to end another chapter in their lives.

"Are you sure?" Lara responded with a look to match his, though she tried hard to summon up a smile.

"Course, we'll have a great time, won't we, Missy?"

"Mmm, but only if we can have pancakes for breakfast," came the sleepy reply.

"You little humbug, that wasn't part of the deal," Suzie laughed, relieved to have something to lighten the mood a little.

Nikki hugged Lara and landed a sloppy kiss on her cheek before turning to Adam to do the same. "See ya, Uncle Adam. Don't forget how much I love you and maybe you can come and see me again sometime at our house." A loud 'mwah' accompanied her kiss.

"I could *never* forget that, little one." There was a catch in his voice noticeable to the adults, though the little girl was too tired to understand. "I love you too, even more than the furtherest horizon and I'll always be out there watching over you, even when I can't come and see you. That way, whenever you think of me, maybe you can look way out there and send me a wave – and if you look really closely, maybe you'll see me send one back."

"Okay, I'll try to benember, but if I forget, maybe you can wave to me first."

Nodding soberly, he dared to look in Lara's direction only to find her eyes glistening with unshed tears. They both had to swallow hard before he added, "Of course I will, but now you need to promise me you'll go straight to sleep for Aunty Suzie, and don't let any naughty bed bugs bite those cute little toes of yours, okay? I'm the only one allowed to do tha—" His voice caught on the massive lump in his throat.

She was too tired to notice, and a faint giggle accompanied her response. "I won't, and don't let them bite yours either!" Sidling up between Suzie and Ben, she placed both hands in theirs. Sending him one more smile, she turned to leave but then turned back again. The little girl held his gaze, with an earnest look on her face. "Make sure you take care of my mummy tonight 'cause I won't be there to look after her."

All he could manage was a hoarse, "Okay, Munchkin, I'll try, but then you'll have to do it for me when you get home tomorrow, okay?"

"Okay, I will. See ya later."

"See ya, precious girl." He watched her leave with Suzie and Ben and had to blink several times as he struggled to keep it together. When the trio reached the door, she turned and blew him one last kiss. It was almost his undoing, though he made sure to keep a smile on his face until she was out of sight.

Lara had seen and heard everything. Sadly, there was nothing she could say or do to ease his suffering, though the expression in her eyes assured him she understood and was facing the same battle herself.

For the rest of the evening, they mingled mostly with either Jeff and Lucy or Adam's parents. A mask of sadness cloaked both actresses' faces when they realised this could be the last time they worked together for a very long time. Their friendship had been solid right from the start, so it was inevitable they would still catch up every now and then, but treading the same stage and sharing the intimacy of a dressing room was something both would miss.

Most of the other guests had already left when that moment Lara and Adam had been dreading crept in like a stealthy thief. His parents were waiting patiently near the door, so it was pointless trying to avoid the inevitable.

"'Bye, my dear," Elizabeth crooned with a reassuring hug and an undisguised sheen of sadness filling her eyes. "Don't be a stranger now; Charles and I still want to see you regularly."

"I won't, dear friend, and thanks for everything," came the sad reply as she held on tight. "I don't think I could've done this without your support."

Charles was next to approach, reiterating the invitation, and Lara went into his arms with a silent nod. He rocked her gently for a moment and then raised his eyes to his son. Adam looked as though the world he knew was coming to an end ... and in a way, it was – at least for the two young lovers.

Sending a sad look his father's way, Adam reached out and took Lara by the hand. Slowly the pair of them sauntered down to where the Corolla was parked, leaning heavily into one another without a word being spoken. Charles and Elizabeth followed along behind, ensuring they left a fair distance between. Thankfully Lara was parked three spaces further down from Charles' Jaguar, so there was no need for them to intrude on these final few minutes.

Lara leaned with her back against the door and Adam stood only a few centimetres away as his eyes feasted on every curve and feature. He wanted to imprint this moment on his memory forever.

Cautious fingers stroked her hair until the urge became too strong. Inching across, they caressed her lips like the brush of a butterfly's wing and then inched further to trace along her cheek. She nuzzled against that beloved touch, eyes closed as if she was trying to draw him under her skin. Knowing it was nearly time to let him go, at least these few moments were hers to squirrel away. Her chest heaved at the thought of going back to a life completely separated from both his presence and his touch.

With raw emotion, the words poured from his heart. "I don't think I can leave you again ... being with you is the only part of my life that makes any sense." Her stifled cry was almost his undoing, and he had to stop himself from pulling her into his arms. "Please don't make this any harder, Baby," he implored, those brown eyes filling with the tears he had held in check since waving goodbye to Nikki.

"I'm so sorry," she begged. "I just don't know how I'll be able to live with all that emptiness again." Her voice broke as the tears fell. "I'm going to miss you so much." Instinctively she pressed a hand against his chest, and he clutched it over his heart – so hard she could feel every beat.

As though of its own accord, his free hand reached out and brushed away all her tears. His touch was delicate and reiterated how much he cared. "Don't cry, my darling, or I'll fall apart, too. I have to believe one day soon we'll get another chance to share a stage ... at least up there I can pretend you're mine."

"Oh, Teddy, it's too hard. I don't know how to say goodb—"

Before she could finish, he placed a gentle finger over her lips. "Don't ... we're *never* going to say that, remember. But you have to promise to take care of yourself ... *and* stay true to your dreams."

"You're my only dream, don't you realise that?" she entreated, tears still streaming from her eyes.

"Oh Baby, of course I do ... and you're mine ... for always and *in* all ways."

Gently he caressed each of her fingers, playing them like the strings of a harp ... and hers soon joined his in composing a brand-new masterpiece. The intimate exchange caused their spirits to both swell and ache. And while their hearts beat faster at the familiar touch, all too soon they realised the full unfinished symphony dwelling in their souls would only ever bring forth this one farewell opus on a stage made by loving hands. Sadly, the solitary composition would be their heart's only sustenance for an expanse of time neither of them could predict.

Lara was overcome by the feeling of desolation welling up inside as she remembered what it was like living in a world without him. The thought of watching him walk out of her life again was suddenly all too much. She pulled away and fumbled for her keys in a vain attempt to open the door – her focus solely on driving away without looking back. It was as though her spirit had been punctured with a sharp dagger and all the life was slowly draining away. With a stifled whimper she slumped against the door, defeated and broken.

Adam's wave of agony matched hers. Intuitively he pressed against her, aching to feel her body against his one last time.

Then he placed a tender kiss on the back of her head and whispered so softly it made her heart ache even more, "You'll always be a part of me, my darling ... no matter where I am or what I'm doing. I'll love you forever, my Lara."

He left her with a strangled cry, too afraid to look back. His steely gaze never fluctuated as he approached his parents' car. Both of them recognised his need for silence rather than comfort when he slumped down in the back seat.

Charles and Elizabeth watched on helplessly as Lara struggled with the door before collapsing into the driver's seat. Behind them, Adam sat with his head in his hands, too afraid to look up. The young woman's silhouette was illuminated by an overhead lamp as she embraced the steering wheel almost as though trying to find some form of solace to sustain her through this terrible grief.

Elizabeth's mother-heart broke into tiny fragments as she witnessed Lara's distress. She grasped the door handle until Charles covered her hand and whispered, "We must let her be, my dear. There's nothing more we can do for her now. She'll get through this, but she has to find her way."

He tilted his head slightly, drawing her attention to their son sitting just as dejectedly in the back seat ... and she understood. Both Lara and Adam needed time to come to terms with their awful loss – and without any form of interference, no matter how well meant.

The sound of a car engine shattered the silence. Three sets of eyes stayed fixed on the car ahead as Lara edged away from the curb. Charles pulled out behind, wanting to shadow her as she negotiated the steep incline.

All the while Adam's gaze remained fixed on the red tail lights ahead – his last lifeline to the woman he adored. When she reached the corner and turned left, a loud sigh emanated from the back seat ... but the man who had made it was oblivious. Adam had no idea he had even been holding his breath. The only thing he was able to focus on was the yawning emptiness waiting to swallow him up again. Sad, dark eyes followed the path she was taking as Charles turned in the opposite direction ... until those little red beacons disappeared from sight.

Father, please go with her and keep her safe always.

§

The unspoken prayer carried across the natural into the spiritual where a half-finished tapestry hung on a gilt-edged easel.

All of a sudden, a command went forth. Lara's constant guardian – the same comforter who had been with her from the moment she first took breath – forced his way through an almost impenetrable thicket of sorrow. And while his precious charge took the lonely path home, majestic wings beat time with her grieving heart.

Chapter 8

Trina didn't come home that night. When Adam entered the empty house, the full reality of just how alone he was hit him like a sharp punch in the belly. He trudged upstairs, despondent and beaten, then fell across the bed fully clothed. For the first time in his life, he longed to enjoy the taste of alcohol. How else could he drown out this relentless loneliness? Anything just to help him forget – even that liquid demon he had always considered his worst enemy. Though deep down, he knew nothing could deaden the relentless ache.

A few suburbs away, Lara was feeling just as alone. Her only recourse was to wander up and down through unlit rooms filled with memories of the man who had taken up residence in her heart. If she sat down, it was too tempting to pick up the phone, and that would only make things harder. She had already tried going to bed, but memories of being with him were everywhere.

In the end, she hoped a long hot soak in the claw foot tub might help put her to sleep. She lay with her eyes closed, listening to soothing music and tried to push aside those other longings. With the gentle strains of Beethoven's *Moonlight Sonata* floating around the bathroom, she realised her only option was to take things one day at a time and just pray the pain and loneliness would eventually ease as each day gave way to another.

§

Work was all Adam had to make the time pass. He quickly got into the habit of staying late at the office, furiously sketching new ideas as the lights of the city flickered on outside. As the moon inched its way across the dark expanse, his fingers flew across the pages. This welcome burst of inspiration meant he usually arrived home late enough to fall into bed and dream away the pain.

Trina was too busy with her fitness classes and socialising with Judith to take any notice. Any fears she may have originally harboured about Adam's nightly whereabouts soon eased when she bumped into his boss at the local supermarket. Reece raved about the inspired ideas her husband was producing when his colleagues left for the day. He was also quick to assure her the business would have more than enough designs to keep them going for several months once Adam joined a production for his new and exciting career path.

"He's a multi-talented man, that husband of yours. We'd hate to lose him altogether, so hopefully juggling both will work out for everyone. Now, I'd better run or I'll be late for my next appointment. See you, Trina – and hey, you're looking good!"

Rumours had worked their way through the office. Most of Adam's close workmates knew about her long hospital stint the year before, though none were privy to the full details.

"Oh, thanks, Reece. I'm feeling much better now. 'Bye."

So that's what you've been up to ... mmm, just as well for your sake.

With each new day, Adam turned the overnight sketches into drawn to scale projects and the partners' enthusiasm for each finished product became his only highlight in otherwise uneventful days. His innovative ideas were proof as to why he had been invited to deliver the lectures at the Salzburg conference the year before. Socialising with colleagues was the furthest thing from his mind, and this was why his door stayed shut for most of the day. The only constant in his life was work ... along with images of a woman he could never forget.

With Trina usually out galivanting, he went back to eating takeaway dinners from the Chinese restaurant across the road or a new Thai place that had just opened around the corner. The friendly office cleaner often found him hunched over his worktable with empty food containers scattered around, while his pencil flashed across a raft of drafting paper.

David's workload had tapered off, which meant Lara had to revert to her former part-time hours. After picking Nikki up in the afternoon, the pair often headed to the Botanical Gardens only two suburbs away. The inquisitive little miss was in her element exploring all the nooks and crannies making up the serene grounds. Most of the time they had fun playing tag through the flowerbeds and rainforest area or watching nobbly old water dragons and a few ducks chase each other around a vast array of lakes and creek beds. The extensive parklands became Lara's salvation; a place to blow away the jumbled nest of cobwebs clogging up her mind throughout the long empty hours when she wasn't at work.

Whenever she was alone, only one face remained at the forefront of her thoughts ... everything else faded into the background. That gossamer hideout became a much sought-out refuge where she could nurse the constant ache. Thankfully, a few hours later, a certain little girl's laughter on her quest to discover new wildlife friends helped to pull Lara away from that other world – the one she had made into a private sanctuary of bittersweet memories.

Unfortunately, she wasn't able to hide in her work the way Adam could when night-time rolled around. Instead, she kept her hands busy fashioning thick journals similar to the ones crafted for the cast of *Show Boat* ... only this time they were restricted to the few cast mates who were privy to their story. Lara had no desire to share memories of those special days and nights with anyone who wouldn't understand the true meaning behind each photo or written recollection. The look on her face fluctuated between one of deepest sorrow to loving reflection depending on whichever portion she was currently working on.

§

Nearly three weeks had passed since *Oklahoma's* closure when Lara received a phone call from her best friend suggesting they get together for lunch and a chat. The thought of Lucy's company offered a welcome relief after so many long-drawn-out days. She was pleased the journals were complete and quickly grabbed a couple before racing out the door.

One already stood on a small bookcase in her bedroom – the third instalment of a matching set from two other special occasions. They were a much sought-out distraction for those times when sleep became an elusive commodity. Another waited in readiness for her next visit with Charles and Elizabeth, while secreted away at the back of her dresser drawer was one more...

The Three Monkeys was a unique little eating-place located across the river at West End, one of Brisbane's inner-city suburbs. Its unique theatre-world ambience and tasty fare took patrons to exotic corners of the earth. Every corner was riddled with low-lit, intimate-style rooms or partitioned areas where people could relax and enjoy the unusual flavours while admiring a host of quirky items and signed posters adorning the walls and ceiling. Outside in the leafy courtyard, an array of mosaic tables had been positioned perfectly so any sunlight dapples were quick to dissolve winter's icy chill from customers' shoulders. The little café was a much-loved hangout for those with a creative flair, so it was only natural the two women felt right at home.

The besties greeted each other with big smiles and warm hugs before making a beeline for one of the tables positioned in a secluded corner. The minute they sat down, Lara dipped into her bag and brought out two parcels wrapped in cellophane and tied with colourful ribbons.

"Here you go ... a couple of keepsakes for you and Jeff."

Lucy recognised what they were immediately and was thrilled to have a reminder of that special time. She threw her arms around her generous friend.

"Oh my goodness, another one! I can't believe how much work you always put into them ... I love it, thanks heaps! Jeff's going to love his, too," she enthused, rifling through the pages and soaking up the memories. "Wow, I can't believe how you're able to remember everything – this one's just as fabulous as that first lot!"

"It helped to keep me busy, so they've been a great distraction."

They poured over the pages, reminiscing over familiar snapshots or special keepsakes from those times. Astute as always, Lucy couldn't miss the shadows behind her friend's smile whenever a pertinent piece conjured up images of happier days.

When their coffee arrived, she tucked the journal away in her bag. Her sole reason for this meetup had been to keep Lara's mind from travelling down those sad paths again. Mementos like these did nothing to help her cause. Now it was time to get down to the real reason for her invitation.

"Okay, so what's the go with Max? You're destined for far more exciting stages than our dusty old theatre, my friend – it's about time he found you something. Have you heard anything yet?"

Lara sent her a scowl, though there was a hint of playfulness in her eyes. "That 'dusty old theatre' as you put it, holds heaps of great memories I'll have you know! And, if it weren't for Paul and *that* place, I wouldn't be where I am today."

The flippant comment hit home with a thud. Not only did it apply to the contract and any new opportunities about to open up, but it was also the main culprit for the current state of her heart.

Lucy could easily guess where Lara's thoughts had taken her and quickly moved on. "Well, have you had any offers yet?"

"Funny you should ask. Max actually called yesterday to say there's something in the wind. He's scheduled a meeting for next week."

"Yay, that's brilliant!"

"Hang on, hang on. He wasn't giving anything away on the phone – it was probably simply to touch base and maybe put out a few feelers. I'm not exactly sure how everything works, so I just have to trust him."

With a beaming smile and an exaggerated flourish, Lucy spread her hands in the air, "*Starring Ms Lara Jennings – The New Sarah Brightman!*"

"Get outta here! You're crazy – but the nicest kind." Lara reached over and squeezed her friend's hand. "Thanks for making me smile … oh, and scratch that 'get outta here' line ... I really *do* need you in my life."

"You'd better believe it," came the reply, accompanied by a mischievous grin.

For the next hour, they caught up on each other's news, with Lucy making sure the conversation stayed away from any mention of a certain someone. Just after two, she looked at her watch.

"Oh heck! Lars, I'm sorry, but I'm going to have to run. I'm meeting Jeff's mum and dad tonight, so I'd better go and make myself presentable. They flew down from Cairns yesterday and he's cooking dinner for all of us."

"What! Whoa, that sounds serious..."

"Scary more like it!" She gave a sudden shiver, though an excited grin gave away her true feelings. "Anyway, don't forget to let me know what happens next week. This *has* to be your lucky break."

"I will, for sure. And ring me tomorrow, I want to hear all about tonight – oooh, I'm so excited for you!"

Lucy giggled like a nervous sixteen-year-old when she brushed lips with Lara before racing off down the street. Her friend was nowhere near as eager. As usual, Lara faced that unceasing dilemma of working out how to fill the final hour before it was time to pick Nikki up from school.

§

During one of her lunch breaks the following week, Lara walked up to Max's office. The building was situated on a very steep hill only a few hundred metres from the editing suite. She had to stop to catch her breath several times before going inside.

The reception area had been designed using frosted glass, recessed lighting and chic furniture. On one side, three curved sofas were positioned in a semi-circle, while high-end glossy magazines adorned a large coffee table in the centre.

"Ms Jennings, it's nice to finally meet you," the receptionist greeted her with a friendly smile. "I'm Lauren. If you'd like to take a seat, Mr Morgan is just finishing up a phone call with another client, so he'll be with you shortly. I've already ordered a lunch platter ... it shouldn't take long to arrive. In the meantime, can I get you something to drink?"

Lara was puzzled, wondering how the young woman could possibly know who she was when she hadn't even had the chance to introduce herself yet. Then her gaze fell on a large photograph now part of a vast wall montage of headshots advertising the firm's clientele. Looking back at her was the publicity shot she had featured in from *Show Boat* days.

She wasn't quite sure whether to feel embarrassed or excited, but her cheeks turned a telling shade of pink. Then her eyes moved across to the portrait hanging directly beside it. Inside a matching black frame was the face of a handsome man with dark hair and eyes highlighting a smile she had been on the receiving end of hundreds of times ... and her never to be trusted heart skipped several beats.

Seeing their faces lined up next to each other, all she could stammer was, "Oh ... h-hello. It's nice to meet you too, Lauren. Uuummm ... maybe ... coffee? Yeah, coffee would be perfect – white with one ... th-thanks."

Just then the intercom buzzed, and Lara dragged her gaze from the wall. The young woman stood up and beckoned her. "That's good timing. Mr Morgan's free already, would you like to come with me."

Lara followed her down a long hallway with a luxurious soft grey shag-pile carpet muffling their footsteps. Glancing at the rows of photographs displaying stars she had only ever seen on a stage or television, and often in the usual array of magazines found in doctors' waiting rooms, did nothing to steady her nerves.

Max was waiting at the door with a warm smile. He greeted her with a kiss on both cheeks in the European way.

"Lara, it's lovely to see you again. Welcome to your new career home. Come in, come in."

He led her to a plush lounge area in an alcove attached to his glass-walled office. She sank into the soft leather sofa and glanced around nervously. It was a sumptuous space compared to her cramped little editing suite, and then she remembered this was where the cream of stage and screen were entertained while striking new deals. She was used to working with directors on tight schedules who only had time to get down to business so their latest project could be in the can as soon as possible. Her world contained none of the pampering those in front of the cameras so often demanded.

They shared the usual pleasantries as Lauren delivered an impressive array of finger food choices. Lara was too nervous to eat and only picked at a club sandwich, though the tall mug of steamy coffee was a welcome distraction for her quivering fingers. Max had often seen new clients react in this way and quickly turned the conversation around to the reason for their meeting, hoping to put her at ease.

"Okay, young lady, we've had a couple of offers from producers who specifically went to see you and Adam in *Oklahoma* after reading all those glowing reviews. Just this week I've been negotiating the best deal possible."

Lara's throat went dry as her fingers gripped the mug's handle and all she could do was take a nervous sip.

"I didn't want to waste your time until I'd stipulated our conditions and negotiated what I think is a good deal for what they were prepared to give. Now I'm pretty sure you'll be excited to hear what we've managed to come up with."

Didn't want to waste your time ... stipulated our conditions ... prepared to give. These were all foreign terms. Lara was used to directors laying down their demands and having to work to their tight deadlines rather than the other way around. She found it hard to believe she was the one now in negotiations.

"The Sydney Performing Arts Group is putting on *My Fair Lady* for an eight week season at the Theatre Royal, and ... wait for it ... they want you for the lead..." He paused for a moment, looking over his glasses in anticipation of her response to his next statement. "They've already drawn up a contract, and now it's just waiting for your signature on the dotted line."

Max wasn't disappointed when she looked at him in astonishment. "But I haven't even auditioned! How can they already have a contract drawn up without knowing how I'll go in the role?"

"I told you producers would be beating down your door!" he responded with a satisfied smile. "Seriously though, there was another production already booked for The Royal, but it ran into major problems which meant they had to pull the plug. That left a major gap in their program schedule, so SPAG quickly negotiated to take its place. Because there was no time for auditions, you were their first choice."

Lara was stunned. "But how do they know what I sound like?"

"Oh, that was the easy part. I got onto Paul and he had a reel of you performing *Bill* from *Show Boat*. Lauren then organised to have the footage rushed down by overnight courier, and it was enough to convince them they didn't need to look any further. Rehearsals begin at the end of the month – only three weeks away – with opening night on the twenty-third of September. Oh, and they've agreed to all your conditions regarding a nanny and tutor for Nikki – pretty good all round if you ask me." He brushed his hands and gave another satisfied smile.

Lara's eyes opened wide. *Sydney ... for nearly four months! And playing* Eliza Doolittle, *one of musical theatre's most coveted roles!*

Swept up in the fairy-tale as it came to life ... with her next breath, the reality of all the complications that came with such a diverse character made her hands tremble again.

"But what about the different accents I'll have to master? I haven't done anything like that before – at least not to this calibre."

"Yes, you have. That Deep Southern accent of yours was perfect in *Oklahoma*. But there's no need to worry – they've hired the most experienced dialogue coach, and she's due to commence working with you next Monday, well before rehearsals begin. It'll mean coaching lessons every day for a couple of hours to make sure you're fluent with the accents when it's time to fly to Sydney."

Lara could only shake her head and gasp, "Goodness, I don't believe this is all happening! What about *Professor Higgins?* Have they cast anyone yet?"

His answer was accompanied by a broad smile. "As a matter of fact they have, and I'm sure you'll be pleased with their choice ... it's someone you're already quite familiar with."

Lara found herself holding her breath, but she didn't dare hope too hard.

"The producers were thrilled with how well you two worked together, so they want both of you for the leads."

Her heart started pounding a mile a minute, and she couldn't disguise the look of anticipation in her eyes.

"I met with Adam yesterday, and he's agreed to take the role. In fact, when I told him they were offering you *Eliza*, he almost jumped out of his seat and couldn't wait to sign. Now I just need you to do the same to get the ball rolling.

Oh, and I need your signature on the agency contract we drew up the other day to make it all legal. Congratulations, my dear – looks like your star is definitely on the rise!"

§

Lara left Max's office grinning like a Cheshire cat. Even with her limited experience, she was aware it was almost unheard of for a newcomer in such a competitive industry to land on their feet so quickly – and without even an audition. She couldn't believe her good fortune but wasn't game enough to try and process the other news yet for fear of being run over crossing the street.

With the legal business out of the way, now it was just a matter of time before she could begin perfecting those vastly different accents ... and see his beloved face again. Her step was decidedly lighter as she made her way back to the office, even though it meant breaking the news to David about needing to be away for at least four months. Despite already having his go-ahead, the reality was more than mere words thrown into the air. She began composing in her head the best way to phrase everything. There was no going back now with the contract already signed, and she had to restrain herself from running all the way down the hill.

Her boss was just as excited and had no hesitation in granting her the time off. One of his young nephews was eager to learn the trade and would be more than willing to take Lara's place during the show's run. David knew he would be hard pressed finding anyone as thorough at their work, but he would never dream of asking her to pass up such a golden opportunity.

A phone call from Max just before dinnertime confirmed the dialogue coach would come to her home every afternoon once Nikki was home from school. Lara smiled to herself, imagining the little girl picking up the accents as the lessons progressed. Even as a toddler, she was always an avid pupil and this would be just another learning adventure for the eager young miss.

Later that night, Lara finally had the chance to just sit and reflect on everything that had happened. Of course, the fact that Adam was about to become a major player in her life again took precedence over everything. She could feel the excitement bubbling away in her spirit ... along with a huge smile lighting up her face as she pictured seeing him again.

Oh, darling, I don't know if this is God, but I want to believe he's the one bringing us together again.

§

Adam's office was located on the 28th floor of one of the city's tallest skyscrapers. For the last several hours he had been willing himself to concentrate on the half-finished sketch in front of him. Mostly, his gaze kept straying through the window across to a line of foothills only a few kilometres away. One of those lights dotting the highest one was Lara's, and he felt certain she would have

95

heard the news by now.

Max had mentioned she was dropping by his office so it was only natural for him to wonder how she was feeling, though he wouldn't have blamed her for turning down the role after all the grief he had caused. Even so, underneath all his misgivings there was a faint spark of hope.

"Hi, Mr Peters, staying late again?" The cleaner's nightly greeting woke him out of his musings.

"Oh, Ellie, you startled me! Sorry, I was miles away."

As usual, they chatted for a few minutes, with him asking about her family while she went about her work. A new grandbaby had arrived recently, and he was always happy to peruse her latest photos before turning his attention back to the latest task in his busy schedule.

Just before bustling away, she gestured to the remains of a takeaway dinner spread across his workbench. It was barely touched, but he just waved a dismissive hand in the air.

"Thanks – you can take it all away. I'm not really hungry tonight."

He heard the distinct click of her tongue as she cleared away the remnants and then sent him a motherly goodnight. Ellie saw how hard he worked night after night and wished he had somewhere more exciting to be instead of sitting in a lonely office building 'til all hours.

As soon as the door clicked shut, Adam made up his mind. Unsteady fingers dialled the number tattooed on his brain, while his heart played a constant drumbeat in his chest.

Please be there, darling ... and please don't be upset ... I just need to hear your voice and find out how you feel about the news.

"Hello?"

The drumbeat quickened even more, and he was almost certain she could hear it down the line. He had to swallow hard before answering. "It's me."

Her sharp intake of breath caught at his heart, while the emotion in her voice brought butterflies to his empty stomach. "Adam! I *knew* it was you!"

"I'm sorry ... I just had to ring. I know you saw Max today. Are you upset ... or was it a welcome surprise?"

She could hear his concern and her anxious response spilled down the line in a rush. "Upset? Of *course* not. A welcome surprise? *Absolutely!* I can't *wait* to share another stage with you – though I still can't believe it's all happening!"

He could feel the relief course through his veins. "I was so worried you'd turn him down, even if you didn't want to."

She was dumbfounded. "Why would you think that?"

"I wasn't sure you'd want to be part of it once you knew I'd been offered the *Professor's* role. I thought – I was certain you wouldn't want to see me again."

"Oh ... Adam..." Just two words floating out on a sad whimper – and then her voice broke. "How could you *ever* think that? After all this time and everything we've shared ... don't you realise how much you mean to me?"

He had been too afraid to hope ... hearing her response was an elixir to his broken spirit. "Oh Baby, I'm sorry – I was just scared. Listen – um ... what do you thin – would it be oka—" After stumbling and stammering for what felt like forever, eventually he managed to get the words out. "Lara, how would you feel if I dropped by on my way home? Please? I'll only stay for a few minutes." The desperation in his voice broke her heart.

"Of course you can, and stay as long as you want. Where are you?"

"At the office still. I can be there in ten minutes, as long as you're sure you don't mind."

"Oh, darling, just come ... come as soon as you can!"

With a hasty farewell, he made a mad dash for the car, anxious to see the woman whose voice had just brought his spirit back to life. And tonight's half-finished drawings lay forgotten on the worktable.

§

She was standing in the doorway ... a familiar silhouette offering his first glimpse of the woman he adored in over four weeks. The dark, smouldering gaze she had seen so often sent her heart racing all over again as he pulled into the driveway.

Two sets of eyes locked as he walked up the stairs, although their greetings were almost tongue-tied, similar to another introduction so long ago. And just like that other reunion during *Oklahoma's* first rehearsal, they were awkward with one another, but only because of the amount of emotion being held tightly in check ... and a determination on both sides not to put the other one under any pressure.

He went first. "Hi..."

"Hello..."

"Do you mind ... are you okay with this?"

"No."

"Huh?" Adam's foot faltered, and the hint of a smile quickly faded away. "I'm sorry, I shouldn't have come..."

"Oh no – I meant, no, of course I don't mind."

"Oh ... phew."

Tiny echoes of nervous laughter confirmed they were feeling exactly the same way.

Lara led the way inside, fighting a deep-seated longing to reach out and touch him. If Adam had looked down, he would have noticed her hands trembling, but all he could focus on was that long sweep of hair and her slender waist as he followed closely at her heels. For an instant, his starved fingers reached out to caress the full length of that shiny cascade ... but then they drew back, curling in on themselves, so his fingernails dug into the soft flesh as a much-needed deterrent.

She went straight out to the kitchen. His soul seemed to sigh with contentment as he mirrored her footsteps – he was home. This was the place they could just be themselves – and always with some form of laughter or tender moments thrown in. The French provincial style with its antique white cabinetry and blue and white striped tier curtains with just a hint of lemon always brought a sense of calmness to whatever other dramas were playing out in his life.

It was only natural for him to spring onto the marble bench-top in the spot he had come to think of as his own ... the same corner Lara's fingertips sought out whenever she was alone with her memories. Both realised at the same time and exchanged knowing smiles, although she didn't dare do what her instincts were urging – to go and stand between his legs while they composed a new symphony with their fingertips. Instead, she kept busy putting the kettle on and organising a light supper. Hardly a word was uttered except a vague mention of how cool it was outside. Their eyes became the only form of communication needed, returning time and time again to their mate.

He carried the steamy mugs out to the living room and deliberately chose a single lounge chair for himself. Sharing their usual sofa meant the temptation would be too great and he wasn't sure he could handle being so close without touching her in some form. Lara placed a plate of fresh macaroons on the coffee table before claiming the chair opposite.

Both were keenly aware of the undercurrents flowing between them, yet neither one was quite sure how to respond ... instead, their eyes drank in those beloved features. Purely out of habit, Lara's shoes came off, and she tucked her legs up and off to the side while sipping on the hot tea. The hem of her dress rode up a little way, revealing long stretches of smooth flesh along her shins to the lower part of her knees. The picture she made was breathtakingly beautiful. Adam had to make a concerted effort to take shallow breaths.

Another fit of nerves made them dive in together…

"What have you—"

"How have you—"

Both instantly broke off and chuckled again, only this time without the strain of fear keeping them company.

"Let's start again. You go first," he offered.

"Sure, okay. I was just wondering how you've been." The look sent his way was a dead giveaway as to how much she still cared.

"Let's *not* go there..." His answer confirmed everything she had suspected. All she could do was nod sadly and wait as he took up his interrupted query. "I was going to ask what you've been up to."

She shrugged. "Mmm, you know, keeping busy with work ... that's about it really ... oh, apart from taking Nikki to the park most afternoons to run off some of that boundless energy."

He smiled wistfully, imagining them together, those ever candid 'windows to his soul' still held captive by hers.

Suddenly her face lit up. "Oh ... hang on a minute. I *have* been doing something else." She hurried into the bedroom with his eyes following her every move. Seconds later, she was back with a parcel wrapped in gold embossed paper and held together by a bold red ribbon. Smiling shyly, she held it out. "This is for you. I hope you like it."

Adam's brow furrowed as he took the gift, though it didn't take long to guess its contents. His instant smile lit up the dark, lonely corners of her heart. "I was wondering whether you'd make another one. You have no idea how many hours I've spent poring through the other two over the past umpteen months."

Curling up in the same chair again, her teeth caught and held the fleshy part of her bottom lip as she watched him. It was one of her unique quirks whenever she felt uncertain or emotional. Adam could almost feel his heart sigh when he caught sight of it, remembering all those intimate habits he missed so much.

Lara waited anxiously as he turned the pages. Watching his face light up or the sight of a pensive smile touch his mouth was all the reward she needed. When he reached the end, his fingers kept stroking the cover and along the edge – both up and down and in small circles. This seemingly insignificant little gesture reminded her of the harmonies their hands used to create ... and that all-familiar longing returned.

"Thank you, it's beautiful ... one more keepsake to treasure, along with so many others." His grateful smile blazed a trail into her soul.

"I was hoping you'd like it," she whispered, loath to break the spell.

Still his fingers kept up their steady rhythm, and she couldn't look away. The silence took them to a place of reflection ... meandering down well-remembered paths with cherished titbits waiting around every corner.

A wistful sigh brought him back to the here and now. Leaning back in the chair, he set his mind on the present. "So, what did Max tell you about the new show? Anything about when you need to be in Sydney?"

The questions brought Lara back with him. She had to close her eyes for a moment as though fighting through a maze of old memories. "Oh, umm ... just something about rehearsals starting next month. A dialogue teacher is flying up on Monday to start coaching me in the different accents. I'm really excited, although feeling a bit daunted, too."

His eyes lit up as he leaned forward, fingers interlocked and with both forearms resting just above his knees. "Don't worry, you'll be fine! Can you believe *both* of us are getting to play the leads? I'm still in shock – our first big break and already we're together again!"

Like a magnet was drawing her, she leaned forward too, and her eyes shone. "I know ... me too! I couldn't believe it when Max said we'd both been chosen." Her excitement turned into a well-remembered grin. "I can't believe he didn't guess there was more to it after seeing the look on my face. It must've been a dead giveaway!"

"Don't worry, I would've looked exactly the same when he told me ... though deep down I was petrified you might turn it down."

"No way! How could I ever say no to playing *your* leading lady again?"

There were so many intimations wrapped up in her words, but neither one dared open that door.

All of a sudden, Lara thought of something she hadn't even considered in all the excitement. She looked across at him in fear. "Oh no, what about Trina? How's she going to deal with having me there? We'd better tell Max not to put us up at the same hotel."

A gentle smile touched the corners of his mouth. "Don't worry, she has no idea you'll be playing *Eliza* and isn't one bit interested in coming with me. When I mentioned all the time needed for rehearsals and how the show itself will keep me far too busy for socialising with Sydney's theatrical elite, her exact response was, 'Well don't expect me to come, I'd be bored out of my wits. I'd rather stay here and mix with Judith and her new racing friends than sit in a dreary old hotel room all day.'"

His news took a huge weight off her mind. Another comfortable silence settled over them as they sipped on their drinks and shared matching smiles. Lara could feel her heartbeat as those loving eyes held hers. Words had never been necessary to convey their true feelings – the expression contained in every sustained look was conversation enough.

This silent contemplation continued ... until the sound of heavy breathing drifted under Nikki's door. Tell-tale smirks lit up their faces as memories from their European trip floated in from the past. These innocent messengers had been a failsafe way of ensuring the little girl was fast asleep before making love.

"How is she?" His question was tender and filled with emotion.

"She's okay – keeping me busy ... and tired ... and always asking questions!"

This brought a ready grin from both, as more memories dropped by to keep them company.

She talked about their daily adventures, along with Nikki's happenings at school. Her vivid descriptions brought a momentary rush of sadness as Adam realised just how much of their lives he was missing ... though he was quick to shrug it off before she noticed.

For over an hour, they chatted about his work and Lara's latest projects – laughing easily when she told him about the blooper reel she had just put together. It was so natural simply being in each other's company, for the first time in months, time raced away.

Another hour passed as they talked about the lonely, unshared things ... pathways travelled the other would never see ... but never a word of that other life he knew – the one keeping them apart. And then...

She had to push down a groan when he glanced at his watch. No other words were necessary when he mouthed a despondent, "I'm sorry..."

They walked to the door, making sure to leave a few inches between them as their footsteps kept perfect time. Then without warning, Adam turned and placed his back against the doorframe, stretching out a hand to take hers. He was cautious but couldn't bear the thought of leaving without making at least some form of physical connection.

She was hesitant to begin with – unsure whether to trust her racing heart. As their eyes followed the line of their arms, tentative fingers touched – barely at first. Their skin came to life with goosebumps and a delicious trembling in every pore – and then they picked up the rhythm of a well-remembered hand ballet as though it were only yesterday.

He wasn't strong enough to look directly at her, but she heard his heartfelt sigh. "I don't think I can do this, Baby."

She misunderstood and tried to pull away, but he held on tight and stared into her worried eyes.

"Not this" —he gripped her hand to emphasise the words— "I don't think I can stay away from you..."

Two large tears rolled down her cheeks when she understood.

Reaching out, he caught one with his finger. "See, this is why. You're as much a part of me as breathing ... my life means nothing if you're not in it."

She choked on a sob and instinctively leaned in close so their arms were just touching. "When I heard your voice on the phone tonight, it was as though my world all fell back into place. Everything that's been missing suddenly came home again."

He could feel her pain reaching out to him through the heat from her skin, and it made his heart ache even more.

All of that earlier resolve melted away and he pulled her close, wrapping both arms fully around her neck as though trying to fuse their bodies together. She clung to him like a drowning child and neither one was able to move – scared of losing a moment both had longed for in a host of daydreams. Adam's face stayed buried in her hair as though he was breathing in a form of life only she could give, while Lara's eyes shut tight as she fought to control the tears.

They heard the clock strike eleven. It was long past when he should be home, and she forced herself to pull away.

Just as firmly, he grasped the top of her arms, pulling her close again to emphasise his words. "Do you trust me, Lara?" Looking solemnly into his eyes, she could only nod ... anything else was hindered by the lump in her throat. "I don't know when, but we *are* going to have our time, Baby – I promise with everything within me. I can't go on if you're not in my life."

She brushed his cheek with the back of her hand. "I don't need your promise, Teddy. You're committed to Trina, I know that, and I understand – truly I do. I just need to know you're okay, even if it is just a quick call every now and then. It's the not knowing that's the hardest of all."

Adoring hands wrapped around her face and his gaze never faltered. "It's no wonder I love you so much. I don't deserve any of this – not after all I've put you through. Why can't you rant and rave like anyone else would? How come you *always* forgi—"

She pressed her index finger against his mouth. "Shhh. Because there's nothing *to* forgive. I'm the one in love with another woman's husband. If anyone's to blame, it's me." Her gaze matched his in intensity. "But I can't help how I feel. I know you by heart ... forget mirror images, you're my soul image, and I just can't let you go – not deep down ... it's impossible."

Her honesty was his undoing. This time it was Adam's turn to fall apart, those strong shoulders heaving at the weight of her words. All she could offer were arms to hold him close and a silent vow to love him unconditionally.

Wordlessly, she cocooned his body with hers until the weeping subsided and he was able to take a deep breath.

"I-I don't de-serve you," he stammered, "but I can h-handle the rest as long as I know you love me" —his head shook in disgust— "which is h-horrible and selfish and s-so unfair…"

Gentle fingers brushed across that furrowed forehead as a winsome smile touched her lips. "No, it's not. It's what I want ... it's what I *need*."

With infinite care, his lips pressed firstly against one eyebrow and then the other ... then inched down the length of her nose until, with a heartfelt whimper, her mouth joined his in a glorious homecoming.

§

After the earlier sadness, Adam's mood had lifted considerably by the time he pulled into his driveway. Tonight he had a reason to want to come home ... if only to lie in bed and savour the feel of Lara's lips on his again, along with the memory of being with her for those few short hours.

They hadn't dared go any further than that one drawn-out kiss. After such a long drought and spirits riddled with deep dry fissures, they were content just being in one another's arms again. The need to harness their passion was a small sacrifice.

Lying in bed, Adam ached to pick up the phone, but he knew it would be foolish to risk losing all they had gained for the sake of a few more stolen minutes. Folding his hands beneath his head, he smiled at the moon where it peeked through the curtains, imagining its silvery beams caressing the roof of Lara's cottage – similar to the way his fingers had caressed her face less than an hour ago. He hadn't felt this happy or contented for a very long time.

§

Across town, Lara cuddled her pillow and sent up a silent prayer of thanks. Nothing could wipe the smile from her face as she snuggled under the covers ... and then slept undisturbed for the first time in months.

§

Out in another dimension unseen by any life form except a Master Craftsman and a host of angels, two delicate silken strands formed a row of musical notes across one section of a magnificent canvas. Woven between them were the lyrics of a brand-new verse – all part of an ongoing symphony dedicated to a far off place and time.

In unison, those same heavenly beings raised their voices with harmonies perfect and clear. At the core of this magnificent choral chorus lay an underlying message, bringing new life to soul mates whose hearts had just been offered the slightest glimmer of hope.

Chapter 9

Instead of their usual late night calls, Adam started phoning Lara before leaving the office each day. He didn't want to risk using the phone at the house unless Trina and Judith were out together, an occurrence that was on the increase but not regular enough to know beforehand. And even then, sometimes she came home earlier than usual. It was a real game of cat and mouse.

Things were just how they used to be in the beginning – all of the excitement sharing each other's news, as well as the instant thrill of recognising those beloved voices. Those long lonely months became just a sad memory.

Every now and then he plucked up the courage to call her from his bedroom. Then, for however long he could chance it, they lay whispering in the dark, imagining the life both of them longed for. And always at the back of their minds was the excitement of soon being together in Sydney where they would be able to enjoy each other's company without any of these frustrating limitations. Days and nights now held expectation rather than loneliness and heartache.

Every weekday afternoon for the next three weeks, Lara's dialogue teacher arrived at the house. With her patience and clever techniques, Mel managed to turn what could have become a frustrating two hours into what felt like a comedy routine as she demonstrated the different accent ranges from Street Cockney through to the high-end Oxford English Lara had to adopt for *Eliza's* transformation. It made the task of mastering the different dialects entertaining rather than the daunting undertaking her nervous pupil had been expecting.

To make sure the lessons weren't interrupted, Nikki had been relegated to her bedroom. Never one to be left out, she usually sat by the door playing with Annabelle, the ragdoll Adam had given her, listening in on everything. Lara and Mel often had to stifle their giggles eavesdropping on the little mimic's attempts to try out all the different intonations on her favourite doll.

When Adam's call came through a little while later, they kept him entertained practising all their newly learned lines. By the end of the three weeks, the little girl had both the thick drawl of a common flower-seller and the refinement of a cultured Englishwoman down pat.

Any visits he did manage to squeeze in usually lasted for only a short while so as not to arouse any suspicions at home. With Nikki usually perched on his lap demanding most of his attention, there wasn't much opportunity for any form of intimacy between them, but it was a small price to pay. Just being together as a family again was enough.

When Charles and Elizabeth heard they were back together, they were tickled pink and quickly offered to look after Nikki so the young couple could share a few private moments whenever he could get away. The pagoda on their property became a favourite hangout, and the others were careful not to intrude. Each visit concluded with a casual meal on the terrace, and the grounds echoed with laughter just like old times. They were under no delusions Trina had ever really loved their son, so felt no guilt for providing an avenue of escape for the happy couple.

The little girl blossomed with all this attention – revelling in the affection of her newly adopted 'grandparents' ... along with the man she knew and loved far better than her own father.

Max had already rung them both about the accommodation details in Sydney. His secretary was able to organise two self-contained suites at a first-class hotel in the historic Rocks area. The harbourside district was in the oldest and quaintest part of town and had recently become a mecca for tourists after authorities added it to the Natural Heritage listings. Their hotel was only a few blocks from the Theatre Royal, so it suited their needs perfectly.

Because they already appeared to share a close friendship, the agent thought it only logical his two new stars would hang out together rather than just wander the vast city by themselves. With this in mind, he requested the two suites be on the same floor. Such an arrangement also had the added advantage of them being able to rehearse together as often as possible. Lara and Adam were ecstatic when they learned the rooms actually adjoined each other.

First-class plane tickets arrived via courier, and they were due to fly out Friday night, with rehearsals to commence first thing the following Monday. This meant they could settle into their new 'homes' beforehand, and it also gave them an opportunity to get to know Mrs Gillies, an experienced nanny recommended by others from Max's clientele, before lessons started. Helen was also a retired primary school teacher who would be providing private lessons each day to ensure Nikki kept up with her classmates.

On their last Sunday in Brisbane, Lara urged Nikki to put on her best dress. She wanted them to visit the local church one last time before the temporary move. Several members from the congregation had taken a special interest in the single mum and her little girl, and this would be their last opportunity to say goodbye. Nikki was worried about being away from Clancy for such a long time, so Charles and Elizabeth had organised a farewell lunch afterwards.

While the mother and daughter wandered through the beautifully manicured grounds of the old stone church, Nikki prattled on and on about the bag of apples and carrots she had stashed away on the floor of the car for her furry friend.

"So *that's* where they got to, you cheeky little ferret! I was wondering where all those apples disappeared to. That's it, just bread and dripping for your dinner then!" she laughed, tickling the little girl's ribs.

Nikki squirmed to get away. "Ewww, *yuuuck!* The doesn't sound very nice … what's *dripping?*"

"It's what all humbug little girls get to eat when they steal treats for their best friends!" Lara answered as she tickled her again.

Nikki's giggles drew the attention of a few parishioners mingling outside. Sending them smiles and waves, they hurried inside.

Many months had passed since Adam had been able to join them on a Sunday morning and he still missed the sense of serenity found behind the heavy church doors. Waking early, he lay in bed for a while, imagining the new life they were about to share and thinking back to their visits to all the spectacular basilicas in Italy. When he heard Trina's car engine turn over for her usual Sunday morning gadabout with Judith, he flung back the bedclothes and sprang out of bed.

Yanking on a pair of good trousers, he balanced precariously first on one foot and then the other before rushing around the room to grab a shirt, a matching tie, socks and a clean pair of shoes. When he was done, the bedroom looked like a bomb had gone off instead of his usual routine of leaving a neatly made bed and everything put away. But he didn't care and quickly slammed the door on the mess before rushing down the stairs. On the way, he nearly tripped over his flapping shoelaces. With a frustrated groan, he tied them quickly then grabbed his suit coat from the closet under the stairs.

There was no time for breakfast. Thankfully, being Sunday, the quiet backstreets of the western suburbs made for an easy run into the city. The streets surrounding the church were crammed with parishioner's cars, so he had to park a few blocks away. Scrambling out, he started locking the door and suddenly caught a glimpse of his reflection in the window. Blast, his hair was a mess and cleaning his teeth had been the last thing on his mind! Rummaging through the glove box, the impatient man stumbled across a half-finished packet of mint gum and popped two in his mouth before running a comb through the unruly mop. Within the space of only a few seconds, he was looking his usual impeccable self.

Lara had no idea when Adam slipped quietly into a back pew just as the service started. Rather than draw any unwanted attention their way, he sat on the opposite side a few rows behind. It was easy to spot his two favourite girls in his line of vision. When the congregation stood to sing the popular old hymns, his voice was unmistakable above the others. Lara had no trouble recognising it and glanced around carefully until their eyes met. His beaming smile and a loving wink were the perfect kindling to ignite her spirit. For the rest of the service, she could feel Adam's gaze on the back of her head, and her heart beat a mile a minute.

As soon as the service was over, she scanned the crowd for that well-known shock of dark wavy hair as several people wished them well for her new venture. Thanking each one with a ready smile, she stopped to chat with a few so as not to appear rude. Knowing time was getting away and with Adam waiting somewhere out there, it wasn't long before she grabbed Nikki by the hand and hurried off with a wave and a quick, "Sorry, we have to go. See you in a few months."

There was only one person on her mind, and she spied him waiting beside her car quite a distance up the street. Longing to run into his arms, instead she maintained a firm grip on her daughter's hand, even playing hopscotch over the pavement cracks as they went as a way to keep her distracted. The last thing she needed was for Nikki to draw attention to them by breaking into a loud squeal once she realised who was there.

Adam almost burst out laughing several times watching all her gallant efforts but managed to stop himself in time. Lara was fighting her own battle trying to contain her excitement, especially when she caught sight of his grin. The looks they exchanged were a dead giveaway to their true feelings.

As they drew closer, he hunkered down in front of them. "Hello, Munchkin, don't you look gorgeous in that pretty dress!"

Nikki's eyes lit up, and a telltale squeal accompanied her exuberant, "*Uncle Adam!*" just as Lara predicted. They were now far enough away from any prying eyes, so she let go and the little whirlwind threw herself into his waiting arms.

"You're *here!* You came to *see* us! Are you coming to your mummy and daddy's house for lunch, too?"

"I sure am, as long as that's okay with you." He winked at Lara and wrapped the wriggly little body in a bearhug.

"Yippee!" She grabbed Lara's hand to pull her closer. "Mummy, Uncle Adam's coming to lunch, too. I'll have Clancy *and* him to play with. Isn't that *exciting!*"

Lara's answering smile was the same one Adam had dreamt about all through the last six long months. He still couldn't quite believe that less than three weeks ago he was thinking all of this had been lost to him forever.

"It's *super* exciting, Munchkin, and we're going to have *so* much fun!"

As he was squatting beside her daughter, Lara couldn't resist running a careful hand across his neck. She was soon rewarded with a look that took her breath away.

Nikki tugged on his arm. "Can you come in our car ... pleeeaaase?"

Lara's ready nod and eager smile matched his.

"Alright, little miss, but only if you promise to give me a piggy-back ride when we get there!"

"You're so *funny*, Uncle Adam," Nikki giggled. "You're *much* too big to fit on my back" —an inquisitive finger travelled along the tip of his nose and across to his earlobe— "but I've got a better idea. If you patend to be Clancy, then you could give *me* one instead."

Those compelling dark eyes that looked so like his would have melted the hardest of hearts ... Adam's had already been captivated a long time ago.

"Done!" he laughed, springing up and throwing her into the air.

She shrieked with delight and squeezed him hard around the neck when she landed back in his arms. Burrowing into her hair, he pretended to choke and made her break into another fit of giggles.

Lara had missed watching them play together, and he caught her tender look. Using as much caution as her earlier caress, he brushed along her arm with the tips of his fingers. She couldn't resist and pressed into them, craving any form of contact, despite being in the middle of a busy street.

Moments later when he started the engine, their hands joined over the console, away from prying eyes.

As he drove along, the trio joined voices for Nikki's favourite songs from *The Sound of Music,* taking them back to a place where magic had been a part of their lives for five glorious weeks.

§

"Look who've just arrived, Mum!"

It was so natural to consider Lara and Nikki family, the name slipped easily off Charles' tongue when he saw them drive in. Both he and Elizabeth did a double-take to see Adam climbing out of Lara's car, but they were thrilled to bits to have him there.

As usual, his wife had a hearty lunch waiting on the terrace. Sparkles that looked like diamonds dotted the surface of the river, while warm streams of sunshine kept the winter chill at bay. Most of their chatter centred on the upcoming trip to Sydney and the adults tried to outdo each other by filling Nikki's imagination with a whole list of the amazing things to be found there. It turned into a friendly competition, and the little girl was delighted to be the centre of attention.

"There's even a great big zoo overlooking the harbour, and it's filled with all sorts of animals and birds. If you're good, I'm sure Mummy'll take you to see it one day," Elizabeth joined in.

"I remember that. We went there when I was really little, didn't I Mummy?"

Lara nodded and stroked her daughter's hair, thinking back to a hurried trip to the iconic city for an old school friend's wedding when Nikki was three.

"Can Uncle Adam come too? He might be sad if we went without him."

"I'd *better* get an invite!" he said with a loud growl, lunging for her tummy as he winked at her mother.

Once again, Lara was captivated by how much joy these two brought to each other, and her nose replied with its secret response.

With lunch over, Charles and Adam, along with their persistent little shadow, set off across the paddock to visit Clancy. He was pacing up and down the fence line, tossing his head and snorting as they approached. The women settled into a pair of comfy sofas on the terrace, laughing as the little girl gambolled along in front with the big bag of pony treats swinging from her hand. The happiness reflected in Lara's eyes reminded Elizabeth of dancing dust motes as they twinkled in the sunlight.

"You look so contented, my dear," she remarked, rubbing Lara's arm with a caring hand.

"I am, more than I ever thought possible."

"I've never seen Adam look happier either, except maybe when you were leaving for Europe. It's as though he's come to life again, despite all these huge hurdles, and I couldn't be more thrilled. This new show is the perfect gift – I only hope he comes to his senses and decides to leave Trina for good when you get back."

Lara gave a wistful smile, but she made no response. The last thing he needed was more pressure. The excitement of the upcoming adventure and all it entailed was enough for now. They would cross that other bridge when the time came.

"At least he won't have to worry about her while you're away," Elizabeth went on. "Apparently she's staying with Judith and John. Between their new racing interests and the fitness classes, that should keep her busy *and* hopefully far away from that demon drink. Although, as far as I'm concerned, she deserves whatever happens to her after the way she's treated my boy all these years."

Lara was surprised to hear the bitterness in her tone, even though she would have felt the same if Nikki's spouse ever treated her the way Trina did Adam.

Elizabeth noticed her look of astonishment. "I'm afraid I lost any respect I may have felt for her a long time ago." She waved a dismissive hand in the air. "Anyway ... enough about her. How about you and I go and sit in the pagoda while we wait for the others – it's starting to get quite warm out here in the sun."

There were sad farewells all round when it came time to leave. Charles promised they would fly down for opening night, still several weeks away. Elizabeth's eyes grew damp as she wrapped Adam in a tight hug, whispering he was to make the most of this time and forget about everything else. Reaching over, she pulled Lara into their huddle and prayed a quick blessing over both of them. Her only concern was for their happiness after everything else they had been through.

Thinking she was missing out, Nikki quickly squeezed in between their legs. Charles felt the same and decided he needed to get in on the act too. He spread his arms wide to encompass the whole family and nearly caused them all to fall in a heap on the ground. The resulting explosion of laughter was the perfect way to turn this emotional farewell into one of joy.

Waving enthusiastically as they watched the car disappear down the driveway, Charles commented to his wife, "Let's hope he finally comes to his senses while they're away."

"Mmm, well I'll certainly be praying for that to happen. I hope they can make the most of this time together ... those two deserve some real happiness after all they've been through. And Trina had better behave herself while he's away – if she gives him even one reason to worry, I'll be round there quick smart to give her a piece of my mind! I'm sick and tired of sitting on the sidelines letting her ruin his life. He's had enough grief from her to last a lifetime."

Charles kissed his wife on the forehead, just below those familiar strawberry blonde locks now flecked with silvery streaks. With a loving smile, he stroked her lips with an affectionate finger.

"Them's fightin' words, my beautiful Bessie, and it's no wonder I adore you. How about we go upstairs so I can prove to you just how much."

§

Adam pulled into the shadow of an old gum tree just down the road from where his car was parked. With Nikki sound asleep in the backseat, he decided to take advantage of some rare alone time before bidding farewell to his soulmate. Their conversation came out as loving whispers when Lara snuggled into his shoulder.

"Well, my darling, this time next week we'll be living in a different city and be able to spend time together every day. It'll almost be like Europe again," he muttered against her forehead as her hand traced delicate patterns along his forearm. The delicate touch sent exquisite sensations up and down his spine.

"Mmm, I can't wait, but I still can't believe it's all happening so fast. You'd better pinch me so I know I'm not dreaming." She nuzzled closer and softly nibbled his neck.

"I'll do more than pinch you if you keep that up!" Adam writhed sensuously under her lips when her tongue joined in this erotic dance. "Stop it, you little minx!" he groaned, imagining her lips on places that hadn't been touched for what seemed like a lifetime. "What're you trying to do to me?"

"What do you think?"

A sultry laugh accompanied her nimble fingers as they flicked open the top button of his shirt. With unbearable slowness, her mouth moved down his neck and across the exposed portion of flesh and started playing with a tuft of dark hair showing through the gap.

"Mmm ... yuuummm!" she purred between gentle kisses. "What a nice chest you have, Mr Peters."

Groaning even louder, he tried unsuccessfully to pull away from this excruciating, albeit thoroughly welcome form of agony. "Baby, don't. I'm only human, and we can't do anything with Nikki here. Please stop. Otherwise, I'll have to follow you home, and then *you'll* be the one on the receiving end of *my* kind of torture."

With Trina due home any time, Lara knew he couldn't risk staying out too long, but she was in a playful mood and not quite ready for their little tryst to end.

Those big blue eyes sparkled as her groans matched his. "Yes, please."

"You'll get me in trouble if you keep that up!" came his laughing reply as he squirmed even more beneath the agonising touch.

His words had a sobering effect, and she struggled to lift her head. "Alright, I'll stop if you really want me to, but I can't promise the same when we get to Sydney."

"Sydney's going to be a whole different matter, my love..."

He claimed her mouth with another drawn-out kiss, but had to fight to keep her hands at bay. Eventually, he managed to sidle out of the car and quickly shut the door. Lara slipped over to take his place in the driver's seat and poked her head through the window with a flirty grin. She was far too irresistible to ignore, so he bent down and stole one more kiss from those tempting lips.

After so many weeks of drought, it was as though the floodgates had opened and they couldn't get enough of each other.

She grabbed his collar to pull him even closer, and once again a stifled groan filled her ears. "Stop tormenting me, woman! Come on, I have to go!"

"Spoilsport," she retaliated with a wicked grin.

Her pleading look was enough to melt his heart, so their lips met briefly for one last time.

"Sleep well, my darling, I can't wait 'til next week. I'll ring you tomorrow – early!"

"You sleep well too, Teddy. Sweet dreams."

"And you, Baby."

Her eyes followed him all the way to his car. Then with a final wave and satisfied smiles, they drove away in opposite directions.

"This time next week!" Lara declared to the night sky with an ecstatic grin.

§

The final week of lessons went off without a hitch. Lara's ability to learn the different inflections had her sounding like a regular Cockney lass as well as a high-brow lady. Mel was thrilled at how well a certain 'little shadow' was able to imitate each one – and with almost as much panache as her mother.

At the end of their last session, she bent down and with perfect English aplomb presented a small posy of flowers, similar to *Eliza's* offerings, to the little girl. "Here you go, Miss Eliza-*ette*. I think you could join your mummy up there on stage – maybe you could be her little helper."

"Oh, wow, thanks. Aren't they pretty? I *love* pink! Do you really think I could?"

"Well, maybe not on the big stage but I'm sure everyone backstage will think you're pretty clever. I bet all of them will be begging to hear you talk in all those clever accents. You sound just like you belong in London."

"Maybe I could go there when I'm a big girl and sell flowers to all the people, too."

"That's a great idea. I'm sure you could."

She and Lara exchanged affectionate smiles as the little girl clasped the posy and did a little pirouette.

"And this is for a tremendous champion for putting in so many arduous hours to get this tricky part down pat," Mel added, presenting Lara with an original recording of the famous musical. "You're bound to wow our southern audiences, and I've already booked my ticket for opening night."

Lara was almost speechless for once, and both women laughed as she spluttered her thanks.

Mel's generosity was all the encouragement Lara needed, and she couldn't wait to show the gift to Adam. The recording was something she would always cherish as well as being an excellent tool to help keep her accent on track throughout the upcoming weeks of rehearsals.

§

It was the morning of their departure and Lara was up bright and early. Packing all their luggage had been a major undertaking, especially trying to remember everything a young child would possibly need to help keep her entertained for several months.

Her final day at the editing suite had all gone smoothly. After spending the last week meticulously teaching David's nephew her intricate logging system, she now felt confident about leaving her latest projects in his capable hands.

Wanting to celebrate this new chapter in Lara's life, David took her out for lunch to an exclusive restaurant in one of the top hotels. He was going to miss having his cheeky sidekick around, along with her bubbly personality. He was grateful it wouldn't be too long before she was back at the controls of her beloved flatbed once again. Lara was sad saying goodbye, but with so much to look forward to, there was no time for regret.

On the day of their departure, Nikki's teacher had organised a farewell lunch and so the whole class brought in something to share. Like her mother, she was sad saying goodbye to all her friends and promised to send postcards with all the exciting things she got up to so no one would forget her.

When Lara came to pick her up, Joshua ran over with a serious expression on his face.

"You ain't 'llowed to fall in love with any o' them boys in Sydney," he implored. "I'll be waitin' for you, and when we get big I'm gunna take you to the movies, 'kay?"

"Okay, I won't," she declared matter-of-factly. "I really *really* love going to the movies, but maybe we'd better wait 'til we're seven 'cause we're way too little to kiss 'cause we're only five, and the movie man might get cranky at us."

Lara overheard everything and quickly had to turn away to smother a chuckle.

Strolling down the street a little while later, the mother and daughter held hands as Lara continued the conversation. "I think that was a very good decision. You're much too young to kiss Joshua just yet. I reckon it's wise to wait 'til you're seven ... or maybe even ten might be better."

"Yeah, I've seen Aunty Suzie kiss Uncle Ben for a really *really* long time and I don't want to get any *boy* germs. They're *yucky!*" She screwed up her cute button nose.

"I think you might be right," Lara replied, imitating the little girl as she bent down to her level. "I didn't kiss my first boyfriend 'til I was *twelve* 'cause I didn't want to catch any of his germs either."

"'Sept for Uncle Adam – I like his 'cause he knows how to do it *just* right!"

Lara nodded as the hint of a grin creased the corners of her mouth. "Yeah, he's pretty special!" She couldn't resist and leaned in close. "But I've heard most of them eat worms too, now wouldn't *that* be yucky – *blergh!*"

"*Ewww – yuuuck!*"

The pair grimaced and burst out laughing as they held hands and ran to the car.

Adam's firm had organised a catered affair for his departure. Reece gave an enthusiastic speech on behalf of all the partners, wishing him well and adding a heap of praise for the excellent portfolio of designs he was leaving behind. Adam had worked on more than twenty sets of drawings for their upcoming projects, all completed during those long nights locked away in his office. It meant his absence wouldn't be as hard-felt as the management team first thought.

The only thing left for Lara to do was to drop off the house key so Suzie could collect the mail and water the plants. Everything was packed and Adam had organised a taxi for their journey to the airport.

Her sister was in the garden when they arrived, pruning branches on an overgrown bougainvillea that was heavily in flower. Nikki took off like a shot the moment she caught sight of her aunt, running as fast as those little legs could carry her. Suzie recognised the loud squeal and brushed a thick layer of dirt from her hands on a pair of already filthy jeans before being bowled over by the exuberant youngster. Using her forearm, she quickly wiped away several stray hairs from her smudged face before being smothered in kisses.

Lara laughed when she caught sight of her sister and Nikki helped pick several loose leaves from her aunt's messy mop of pale auburn hair.

"Aunty *Suzie*, you look like you've been playing in a *pig pen!*" she giggled.

"And it's nice to see you too, Miss Cheeky Little Monkey! But you'd better watch out when you go to Taronga Park Zoo, or they might put *you* in a cage if they hear all that loud carry-on!" She pretending to tickle Nikki's face with her still somewhat grubby hands and the little girl jumped away with a loud squeal.

Licking a pint-sized forefinger, and with her tongue firmly planted in her cheek, the little mischief-maker set about wiping away several dirty smudges from Suzie's chin and nose.

"Glad it's you on the receiving end of that wet offering and not me!" Lara chuckled, watching on lovingly as Nikki concentrated hard to make sure her aunt looked presentable.

"And it's just as well we share the same germs!" The grimace on Suzie's face was priceless when the sisters exchanged wry grins.

Lara felt a tug on her heart. She would miss all the fun they shared and stressed she wanted her and Ben to visit as often as possible.

A rundown of what to expect during the show's Sydney run had already arrived in the mail. Rehearsals were on a strict weekday schedule and weekends were theirs to do with as they wished. Typical of this new life, while the production was in full swing, Mondays would be their only day off. Thankfully, no one was needed at the theatre until late afternoon on a performance day, meaning they could still take in the sights of the city, catch up with any visitors or simply relax and take a few hours for themselves. She knew Nikki would miss Suzie, but at least it would be easy to keep in regular contact by phone.

After handing over the key and telling Suzie to help herself to the contents of the fridge and pantry, Lara looked at her watch. It was time to get going if they were to be ready for the taxi in just over an hour. She wanted to have Nikki bathed and in her pyjamas so she could go straight to bed when they arrived. Travelling First-Class was a blessing, as it meant dinner would be served on the plane and therefore one less load on her mind.

"Have fun, Lucy-Lu. I'm so proud of you – you're sure to have them all swooning in the aisles every night. Ben and I will be down as often as we can – I'm so excited knowing you'll soon be on a big stage! Oh, and as far as I'm concerned, you deserve all the happiness and love Adam can mete out, so just lap it up and don't worry about anything else!"

"I fully intend to, Suze! And hey, thanks for everything. I don't know what I would've done without you over the years. You're the best big sis anyone could ever ask for. And thanks for looking after my house, too. I can't wait to see you so don't leave it too long before coming down ... give Ben my love, along with a big kiss from Missy Tuppence and me."

"Don't worry I'll happily do that!" Suzie replied with a big smirk as they hugged one another tightly.

Not wanting to be left out, a little body squeezed in. "Hey, what about me? Don't I get a smooshy hug too?

The older one hoisted Nikki up and burrowed into her neck.

"Course you do, pumpkin. I'd never knowingly leave *you* out. See you later, alligator. Be good for Mummy and Uncle Adam, and remember I love you right up to the moon."

"I will, Aunty Suzie, I promise ... and I love you even bigger. I'm going to miss you, but I'll be very brave and try not to cry."

"That's my bestest girl. I'll miss you too so we can be very brave together." She ruffled the little girl's thick dark fringe and kissed her adorable upturned nose. "Bye."

§

Trina had already left to meet Judith when Adam arrived home. Their goodbyes had been said earlier in the morning, and her response had been both cold and clinical. After showing no interest when he was originally awarded the prestigious role, it came as no surprise to find she was so indifferent. As usual, if things didn't revolve around her, she wasn't the least bit interested.

"Well, break a leg or whatever it is you say to each other ... I'll probably see you when you get back," had been her parting words as he was leaving for work.

Adam couldn't have cared less about her apathy, although he did wonder how she would handle staying away from any form of alcohol without him there to keep an eye on her. Nevertheless, she was a grown woman, and he refused to turn down a fabulous opportunity like this one when it was obvious she wasn't at all interested in him.

For the space of a second, he wondered how he would have felt if she had made an effort to involve herself in his world – then just as quickly the thought was gone. For the first time in his life, Adam understood what it meant to be loved by someone who actually cared – someone with no hidden agenda lurking behind the sentiment. This Sydney adventure would be a new beginning for the three of them.

Knowing what lay ahead, he wasn't going to let anything dampen his spirits.

§

Nikki was just bundling Annabelle into her backpack when they heard a car horn sound in the driveway, followed by the thump of Adam's shoes as he bounded up the stairs. Their smiles could easily have lit up a billboard when the door was flung open.

With an excited, "*Woo-hoo!*" he picked them both up and swung them around the room as a loud flurry of laughter reverberated off the walls.

"Well, this is it, my two best girls! Are you ready for The Big Smoke and all the fun we're going to have?"

Nikki's huge grin quickly turned to a frown. "What? Smoke? Mummy said I'm not 'llowed to smoke 'cause it'll make me bomit." She turned to her mother. "Mummy, maybe we'd better stay here so I don't get sick."

Lara and Adam looked at each other and burst out laughing again as he answered, "It's okay, Munchkin, that's just another name for Sydney ... besides, I'd better *not* catch you smoking or else there'll be big trouble in *this* house!" His playful scowl soon swept away any of her concerns.

He grabbed Lara in another hug and planted a firm kiss on her mouth. "I can't wait to get down there. This is *our* time, my love."

"I know, and I can't believe it!" she grinned, returning his greeting with just as much relish. "I didn't think today would ever end, but at last you're here, and I'm so excited! Four months of bliss with my favourite man; bring on Sydney!"

She couldn't have said anything more fitting to get his heart racing. With eyes shining just like hers, he placed a grateful kiss in the palm of her hand.

After making one final check around the house and testing all the windows were secure, they grabbed the pile of suitcases and lugged them down to where the taxi was still waiting with its engine running.

As it pulled away, three sets of eyes glanced back at the little cottage Lara and Nikki had called home for the last four years.

Adam was so excited he started to sing, "*All I want is a room somewhere, far away from the cold night air...*" and the other two quickly joined in.

The driver glanced at them in the mirror and gave a chuckle. He wasn't used to having what sounded like a trio of Cockneys heading to the east end of London for the night in the back of his car. It was a nice change from the usual load of drunks sharing his cab.

Chapter 10

The hotel was perfect – luxurious and elegant with everything they needed to make it a real home-away-from-home. Views from both suites looked out across the wide expanse of Sydney Harbour, with the magnificent bridge many said resembled a giant coat hanger lit up like a Christmas tree. From several of the windows, the white sails of the iconic Opera House appeared to billow like a majestic old sailing ship above the reflections in the dark water.

Nikki had already nodded off in the taxi from the airport, so they put her straight to bed. Though her bedroom was quite small, it was more than adequate to accommodate a young child and a bag filled to the brim with her favourite toys and dolls.

She snuggled under the blankets with a mumbled, "'Night," and fell fast asleep even before Lara and Adam had made it back to the living room.

Like her, they were both exhausted after the long day. He pulled Lara onto the sofa, and they lay with their legs entwined and her body nestled against the full length of his. She had to battle hard to push the tiredness away, but lost the fight as soon as her head burrowed into his shoulder. The soft caress of his fingers travelling across her back was the final instigator to put her to sleep.

When Adam heard the soft murmur of deep breathing, he just smiled and pulled her closer. On any one of those long lonely nights making up the previous six months, images of them making love was all he had been able to focus on. But now, simply to see her asleep in his arms was more than enough and it didn't take long before his breathing took on that same even rhythm.

Several hours later, Lara stirred when her hand began tingling with the sharp sensation of pins and needles. The movement of her arm when she went to stretch it was enough to wake both of them. Sleepy smiles drew sighs of contentment when reality dawned as to where they were.

"Hello, my lovely," Adam whispered contentedly as his lips caressed her forehead.

"Mmm, hello, my darling." Lara nuzzled into his mouth with her eyes pressed shut against the bright streetlights shining through the floor length windows.

"How about I take you to bed before we catch cold out here?"

She stretched slowly, still in that dreamy half-asleep state, so he took her by the hand and made for the bedroom. Even though he was ready to make love, Adam didn't have the heart to disturb her any further. After spending days getting everything organised for the move, as well as all the hours spent practising her lines, he could see she was utterly exhausted and needed sleep far more than his body.

Lara's eyes were still heavy with sleep when he pulled back the covers and she crawled into the king-size bed. When he climbed in beside her, she automatically snuggled into his side, draping one arm over his chest while a bent leg rested across his thigh. Soft moonlight kissed her face as he tucked an arm under her head and sighed with contentment – he hadn't felt this happy since the last night they were in Dürnstein, a small hamlet in Austria.

Within a few minutes, they were both fast asleep ... heads together and hands entwined. It was as if all those lonely months had never happened. The familiarity of being in one another's arms took them back to those magical times in Europe where they had slept like this every night.

The sun had been up for several hours when a little voice drifted under the bedroom door. Lara and Adam stirred at the same time only to find themselves looking into each other's eyes. The fact their first night together only contained dreams and nothing more took them both by surprise. Even more surprising was the realisation they were both still fully dressed, which was really just as well with a certain eager visitor ready to put in an appearance.

"Come in," they yelled simultaneously.

The door flew open, and suddenly a blur of laughter and energy raced across the room and landed in the middle of the bed. The little ball of fun soon managed to make a space between them, amid a gush of giggles and a few painful groans when an errant knee landed hard against Adam's ribs. Snuggling in with a contented sigh, it didn't take long before Nikki started pestering them about all the different things they had planned for the day.

The sleepy pair exchanged amused grins. "She's back! I seem to remember a similar question when someone I know couldn't wait to visit the Mirabell Gardens," Adam mused, pretending to scowl as he tweaked her cute button nose.

She sprang up on the bed and jumped up and down, eyes wide with excitement. "Are we in *Saltburg?* Can we go back and see them today ... pleeeaaase?"

"No, Poppet, this isn't Salzburg. Don't you remember we're in Sydney?" Seeing the sad look on her face, Adam went on. "Don't worry there are lots of pretty gardens to visit here, too."

"But the *kids* won't be here, and I won't be able to sing *Do Re Mi* around the horsey fountain again."

"Hey, stop hassling Uncle Adam," her mother scolded kindly, dragging the wriggling body back down between them. "He's still half asleep and doesn't want a little person driving him crazy with questions at this hour of the morning ... *or* jumping all over him – no matter *how* cute they are!" She tickled the spot of skin showing below Nikki's pyjama top and the little girl chuckled loudly.

Adam's broad smile was sent their way, adding another layer of sparkle to those already dancing eyes. "It's okay, I don't mind." Anything was better than the empty bed he usually woke up in each day. "Well, Missy Tuppence, what do *you* want to do today – apart from singing that jolly song?"

"Have some breakfast 'cause I'm *starving!*" came the quick reply, sending both adults into fits of laughter and acknowledging their stomachs were growling too.

It was hours since any of them had eaten and a quick glance at the clock showed it was almost eight-thirty. Both Lara and Adam knew if Nikki hadn't been snuggled up between them, they could easily have stayed there all day. But neither of them really minded – they had all the time in the world to savour being back together.

§

The hotel's dining room looked out across the broad harbour. Views from their table perfectly captured the white sail-like formations of the Opera House roof where they glistened in the sunlight. It was a glorious day and the visitors were eager to explore the areas closest to the hotel. At the far end of the street, Lara noticed a line of market stalls spread out with all manner of wares.

Once breakfast was over, the trio set off to forage for treasures or unique gifts for loved ones back home. The cobblestone streets of the historic precinct brought back lovely memories of wandering similar thoroughfares in Europe. And just like back then, Nikki had a wonderful time skipping over the small blocks of stone, trying hard not to tread on any of the deep cracks. It was easy to compare this place with that once-in-a-lifetime holiday – those few short weeks were the only other time they had lived together as a family.

The Old-World charm of the village-style suburb soon found them exploring narrow laneways lined with cosy dwellings and colourful shopfronts, some over a hundred and fifty years old. These were the first European-type structures ever built in Australia and their eyes feasted on the quaintness of each stone cottage or building.

The Nurses' Walk, in particular, caught their eye with its network of passages running in and around a virtual maze of buildings. The narrow pathway was dotted with cafés and gift shops, where once upon a time it had been a haven for crime and a place where 'ladies of the night' plied their trade to any cashed-up customer. It had received its name because of the convict nurses who used to traverse these same streets on their way to toil in Sydney's first hospitals. A few trees provided a leafy canopy overhead and brought a welcome respite from the noonday sun.

After spending a couple of hours wandering in and out of the alleyways, they spied an authentic Italian café with aromas that beckoned them inside. The bower-like front courtyard was a relaxing place to sample a few of the appetising pasta dishes as throngs of tourists stroll by. Nikki's face resembled an artist's palette when long spaghetti strands left bright red tomato paste brushstrokes across her chin. Lara wiped them away with a happy chuckle, remembering a fun-filled day making pasta in a Tuscan kitchen across the seas.

In the afternoon, they went back to the hotel to unpack and rest after a hectic few days in the lead-up to this exciting new adventure. Helen, the nanny contracted by Max who would also double as Nikki's tutor, was coming over to introduce herself just before dinner and Lara wanted to have everything organised before she arrived.

While they were busy, Adam disappeared into his suite to have a proper look around and also make a quick call to his parents. Elizabeth answered and was pleased to hear his voice. Questions flew as she asked how they were and what they had been doing. The call was only short, but she didn't mind. It did her heart good to hear how relaxed he sounded away from the pressures of life with Trina, and she was quick to relay everything to Charles afterwards.

The meeting with Helen was a huge success, and Lara soon warmed to the middle-aged woman. She was a widow with a granddaughter the same age as Nikki and they quickly organised a playdate so the girls could spend some time together. Both women agreed it was important for a young child to have someone her own age to play with instead of always being around adults.

Lara was more than happy with Max's choice, and it was obvious the teacher would fit perfectly into their new lives. When Adam came back, she was quick to introduce them, though not actually expanding on how he actually fitted into their lives. It was evident from the looks the pair exchanged, and the way Nikki was so relaxed around him, he held a special place in their hearts.

They spent another delightful hour swapping stories over a fresh pot of tea. What thrilled Lara the most was seeing how Nikki automatically perched herself on the arm of Helen's chair and the warm response she received in return. Her daughter's relaxed attitude and innocent spontaneity with the caring grandmotherly figure meant she would have no need to worry when it came time to leave them alone for several hours every day – an important consideration for a mother in a new city when a virtual stranger was responsible for her only child.

Rehearsals were due to commence at nine on Monday morning. When Helen was leaving, Nikki provided the perfect farewell.

"Thanks for coming to visit us. I can't wait to go 'sploring with you when

Mummy and Uncle Adam have to go and sing!"

As they waved goodbye, the relieved young mum let out a satisfied sigh. "Mmm, I like her – she'll be perfect!"

"Me too, now can we get something to eat!"

Adam rolled his eyes as Nikki rubbed her tummy and groaned.

"Goodness, you're like a broken record – that's what you told us this morning!"

"That's 'cause I'm getting to be a big girl."

"Oh, is that right? Well, come on then; race you to the fridge!"

Lara's suite was similar to a small apartment with a compact kitchen and everything necessary to make a tasty meal. Max had obviously thought ahead when organising their accommodation, recognising her need for somewhere to cook once rehearsals were done for the day.

Routines would change when the musical officially opened as they wouldn't need to leave for the theatre until around four. Nikki's lessons would then move from mornings to afternoons, and Helen had already assured them she enjoyed pottering around the kitchen. She was quite happy to make dinner for everyone. This meant Lara and Adam would arrive home to a hearty home-cooked meal rather than having to scratch around for themselves in the dead of night.

During their morning walk through the markets, Lara had discovered a fresh produce stall, as well as a small deli selling all manner of exotic meats and cheeses. It wasn't long before the trio was cutting up a pile of vegetables and some mild salami to make a hearty soup for dinner. Despite Nikki's recent whinges, they were all still quite full from the mouth-watering lunch, so this would more than satisfy those pesky hunger pains ... and a crusty loaf purchased at a local French bakery was the perfect accompaniment to the meal.

By the time Nikki had scraped the last morsels from her bowl, she was yawning loudly.

"Okay, bath time," her mother announced, piling their plates in the dishwasher and then going off to fill the large bathtub down the hall.

As usual, it didn't take much to wake her up. What should have been a quiet clean-up, soon turned into a full-blown ruckus when the cheeky little imp squirted both of them with water from a rubber toy. By the time they were done, the adults were soaked to the skin and Nikki had foamy blobs covering her from head to toe. Even the simple process of drying her off turned into a tickle session. Eventually, she was snug in her favourite Disney pyjamas, ready to join the many quirky characters filling her dreams.

"Will you carry me to bed pleeeaaase, Uncle Adam?" she implored with a fake yawn. "My legs are much too wobbly and I might fall over."

"I think you might be telling a porker, but come on, get on!"

He squatted down, and she was soon clambering onto his back, giggling with delight. Adding to the fun even more, he danced down the hall to her bedroom warbling *Waltzing Matilda* in his best baritone before tossing her onto the bed. Another loud burst of giggles filled the suite; she hadn't enjoyed going to bed this much since the night following their Byron Bay sojourn eight months earlier.

"Can *you* say my prayers, pleeease?" she implored. "Mummy *always* says them with me, but I want you to tonight."

"Okey-dokey, Miss Cuteness, but *only* if you promise to sleep all night long."

"I promise," came the solemn vow as she hunkered under the covers with her eyes shut tight, oblivious to the meaningful look of anticipation he and Lara exchanged.

His prayer was simple, and filled with love and blessings for the little girl. Opening his eyes again, Adam was surprised to find a photo of the two of them positioned on the bedside table.

When she noticed the path his eyes had taken, Nikki sent him a big grin. "I couldn't leave *that* at home. It's my faborite photo 'cause it's got you 'n me and the huge sandcastle we made by our very own selves – and see, you're giving me a cuddle 'cause you love me, even if you couldn't come and visit us later 'cause of your sick friend."

His eyes met Lara's and a mountain of regret hung in the air between them. Thankfully, her follow-up question helped to blow it away.

"Mummy, did you benember to bring my snow globe? I want to go to sleep listening to the pretty music."

"Course I did, I wouldn't *dare* forget that!" Sure enough, just behind the photo was the much-loved Christmas gift Adam had given her.

The adults' gaze held as she wound the key. "She wasn't about to leave either of them at home ... and Annabelle had to come too. In fact, she insisted on bringing all three of them more than anything else." The room echoed with the familiar strains of *Do Re Mi*. "'Night, Poppet," Lara murmured, kissing her beloved daughter soundly on those rosy red lips.

"'Night, Mummy ... 'night, Uncle Adam." The little girl wrapped her arms around both of them as he kissed her cheek.

"Goodnight, my little angel," came his reply, smudged with the smallest hint of emotion which Lara's keen ears caught.

Adam had forgotten just how much he missed this nightly ritual.

§

As soon as the door closed, Adam pulled Lara into his arms. Between soft kisses, he said, "Now, young lady ... how about you go and put on your prettiest gown ... I'm taking you out for a night on the town."

"*What?* What could be more important than staying right here?" Her eyes danced as she looked up at him and it wasn't hard to get her meaning. "I thought we were going to bed early. And what about Nikki? I can't leave her all alone."

"Don't worry, we'll get there" —his eyes smouldered as another kiss landed on her nose— "and besides, I've already organised a babysitter through the hotel."

Lara grimaced, "Oh, I'm not too sure about leaving her with someone I don't know. And what if she wakes up?"

"Hey, don't worry. I already thought of that; the concierge assures me they use her all the time. Besides, I'm positive a certain young miss is far too tuckered out after all the walking we did today to do anything except sleep."

"Mmm ... alright ... but only as long as you're sure."

"I am, it'll be fine. Now you'd better hurry up and get ready. I can't wait to see your face, but I'm not saying where we're off to – it's a surprise. Oh, and you'd better bring that woollen jacket-style thing we bought in Bolzano, just in case it's cold."

"My best shawl? What made you think of that?"

"Never you mind, my darling, but you'd better hurry up, or we'll be late." He couldn't hide a smirk and it made his eyes gleam with mischief.

She scampered off to the bedroom, and it wasn't too long before she was back, her makeup all done and trying awkwardly to fasten the back of an eye-catching midnight blue gown. He was looking out to the harbour through the large picture window when she first spotted him. Seeing him all decked out in a formal dinner suit and bow tie, caused her to come to an abrupt halt.

"*Wow*, don't *you* look handsome!"

Her drawn-out wolf whistle grabbed his attention, and he turned around slowly with a smile that melted her heart all over again.

Adorned in the same gorgeous dress she had worn on their second night in Cortona, her style matched his perfectly. He looked her up and down with admiration in his eyes and smiled at the memory. The long velvet gown enhanced her twinkling blue eyes, and even though it fell in elegant folds all the way to the floor, nothing could hide those shapely curves. The pearl choker encircling her neck added a regal touch, and he was smitten just like a young teenager in love for the very first time.

Lara's face glowed, however, there was no time to luxuriate in his expression. Still struggling with the errant zip, she turned her back and implored, "Can you please help me with my dress, Teddy? I'm a little bit stuck!"

"On or off?" came his smooth retort as he took over trying to fix the pesky thing. She sent him a sassy smirk and landed a playful swat on his butt.

Adam had to struggle to control his fingers from slipping the plush material from her shoulders rather than doing it up, but eventually, he managed.

Nevertheless, once everything was in place, he couldn't resist, and his lips traced a delicate trail across those bare shoulders. Her whole body shivered from the sensuality of his touch, and he could feel the ripple effect where his skin touched hers.

"Mmm, maybe it *would* be better to stay home after all," he teased.

"Oh no you don't ... not after all that intrigue! If I've had to get dressed up to the nines, then the least you can do is be true to your word. Besides, we've plenty of time for those sorts of shenanigans when we get home!" The teasing grin she cast over her shoulder caused his heart to beat that much faster.

"Just you wait ... I'll hold you to that!"

She was just about to throw a cushion at him when there was a sharp rap on the door.

"Phew, saved by the bell." He ducked away to open the door, pretending to wipe his brow with an exaggerated look of relief before doing so.

A grandmotherly-type woman sporting a warm smile poked her head inside. "Hello, I'm Alice, and I'm here to look after the wee bairn."

The broad Scottish accent and kind twinkle in her eyes soon set Lara's fears at rest, especially when she spotted a half-finished bundle of knitting under her arm. With the television keeping Alice company and a list of instructions including contact details on the table – something Lara wasn't permitted to see – the young couple waved goodbye. They swept down the grand staircase with the garment Adam had suggested she bring draped over her arm.

"Where are we going, Teddy?" she pestered.

"Just you wait and see."

The concierge opened the door to a taxi while sending an admiring glance her way. Then with a simple nod to the driver, they were off. Lara looked over at Adam in surprise, but all he would offer was a mysterious grin. It was obvious even the driver was in on the secret, and she wondered at his ingenuity to be able to coordinate whatever was going on without dropping even a hint of his plans.

It wasn't long before they were pulling up in front of the modern round facade of the Theatre Royal.

Even more bewildered, she turned to her grinning companion. "Okay, now you've really got me intrigued. Why are we here? Rehearsals don't start till Monday."

Folk were milling around at the entrance, and a great throng was already streaming into the building – many of the women were dressed in elegant gowns, while the majority of men looked dapper in dinner suits.

"Well at least I'm dressed appropriately!" she added with a grimace.

A huge billboard above the entrance announced, *'The Spellbinding Musical, Les Misérables – Closing Tonight'*.

Clutching at both his arm and the expensive garment now draped across her shoulders, she let out a cry of delight. "Oh, darling, I can't believe it! We're finally getting to see a show together after your intriguing invitation on the night we met. Now I understand why you wanted me to bring this. I never thought we'd actually get around to seeing a show together and now here we are! We may not be at the Lyric, and this certainly isn't for research purposes, but I can't wait!"

He stroked her back through the delicate material. "Well, I might have the name of the theatre wrong, but we *are* on a research expedition – just pretend we're here to experience the acoustics before it's our turn to tread these boards."

Lara felt on top of the world as they joined the crowd making their way inside. Her eyes danced with anticipation. *Les Misérables* boasted a splendid cast – many of whom were the cream of Australian theatre stages. She had been disappointed to learn the current production wasn't coming to their hometown. Now she could enjoy it in this first-class place while basking in the composer's stirring score. Being seated beside the man of her dreams made everything just perfect, and her heart beat that much faster.

She turned to him with a radiant smile and his expression matched hers as his hand rested against the small of her back to guide her forward. Once again, she marvelled over his ability to surprise her. Within a few minutes, an usher appeared to show them to their seats as Adam pulled two premium tickets from his coat pocket. The theatre was buzzing with expectation, and it was exciting to be on this side of the curtain wondering what was in store.

When the thick black drape rose into the shadows above their heads, everything about the show was all Lara could have imagined and more. The heartbreaking storyline swept them back in time to the French Revolution and all the poverty and political unrest surrounding those terrible dark days. *Jean Valjean's* tragic chronicle, along with *Fantine* and *Cosette's* heartbreaking plight, had Lara struggling to contain her tears. *Le Mis,* as it was affectionately known in both literary and theatrical circles, was a tale of redemption and forgiveness that drew the audience in from the very first number. As the drama unfolded in front of them, Adam squeezed her hand and continued doing so right through to the final gripping scene.

They were on their feet as soon as the last strains faded away and continued clapping loudly until the curtain fell to the floor for the final time. Lara couldn't have imagined a more fitting performance to spur them on for their own upcoming production in this same theatre.

"Oh, Adam, that was wonderful! Now I understand why Charles is convinced Elizabeth could be a little bit in love with Anthony Warlow! He was the perfect leader of the rebels ... although Mark Sinclair was brilliant in his role as well –

and both actors are sure easy on the eye. You'd better watch out, or you may have a bit of competition if I ever get to meet either of them," she teased, peering up at him with a feisty look in her eye.

"Just so long as you're never *their* leading lady," he retorted with the hint of a light-hearted scowl. "If that's ever on the cards, watch out, young lady. I'll be waiting in the wings to drag you back to my side!"

"As if that's ever going to happen!" she laughed merrily.

They made their way to the taxi rank, both nervous and excited to think in a few weeks it would be their show about to open in that impressive theatre.

§

Following another short taxi ride and with a sincere, "Thank you," meted out to Alice, along with a couple of twenty-dollar notes slipped into her hand, Adam dashed off to his suite to change into something more comfortable. Lara did the same in hers, donning a long sheath of burgundy satin over a matching nightgown.

On his return, he found her resting against one corner of the sofa with her legs drawn up to one side. The picture she made was almost identical to the vision keeping him company for the last several months. Sending her a look that spoke volumes, he sidled in so her body nestled against his. With the rest of the night now theirs to make their own, this quiet corner was a welcome haven to unwind and reflect on the evening. He purposefully left the lights off, so the spectacle of the busy harbour became an inexpensive form of entertainment.

With the soothing sounds of a classical concert drifting from the corner stereo and their hands keeping time, they watched the lights of the ferries and cruisers crisscross its dark expanse. Similar to a pair of bookends, the magnificent light display on both the coat-hanger bridge and the opera house created silvery reflections across the water.

Lara leaned back into his chest, and he cradled her close with his mouth resting against her hair. The evening had been a delightful feast for their senses, filled with the harmonies of those haunting songs. Lying there reflecting, it was easy to relish the quietude as another form of stirring music fed their souls.

A little while later, she could sense something change in him. Twisting around to look into his eyes, she caught a glimpse of that old sadness.

With a worried frown, she sat up and cradled his jaw with her hands. "What's wrong, Teddy? What's happened?"

He couldn't answer. Instead, anxious fingertips explored her features like a blind man feverishly trying to recognise a forgotten face. It wasn't only pain but also fear she recognised in his expressive brown eyes. Once again, Lara begged him to tell her what was going on.

Adam had managed to hide it well, but at various times throughout the day, he had been wrestling with what had now become a war between his mind and soul. It was time to put his future on the line and give her one last chance to guard her heart. Letting out an anxious sigh, he tried to croak out the question he had been trying so hard to ignore for fear of losing her all over again.

"Baby ... you know how much I love you – at least I hope you do…"

Her best form of reassurance was to touch his lips with hers ... but still that frown remained as he grappled with what was obviously genuine fear and dread.

"Lara ... oh, God, how do I do this?" He swallowed hard and looked up as though pleading with that unseen deity before looking into her eyes again. "Oh, Baby ... how can you still love me or dare to put your trust in me after everything? I've hurt you over and over, but here you are – back in my arms and offering me your heart. Why would you let yourself become so vulnerable again when I still can't promise anything? I don't deserve you…"

His head dropped in brokenness, and that unashamed honesty tore at her heartstrings. Ever so gently, she lifted his face and peered into those sad, dark eyes. The answer came from the very core of her spirit.

"Oh, sweetheart, when we were offered the parts of *Henry* and *Eliza* and I heard your voice over the phone, it was as though my heart had found its true north again. From the first moment we met, you became my entire focus ... then everything became blurred and distant when we were apart – and not just our relationship, but every part of my life ... even Nikki for a little while…" She had to pause for a moment, remembering those dark days, and her voice was muffled when she went on. "I never let on to anyone, especially not her, but without you, I didn't want to go o—"

"*Nooo!*" He seized her by the arms. "You should've called me, I would've come."

Loving fingers stroked his furrowed brows, trying to erase the anguish. "No, you couldn't, Teddy ... and that's okay. I always knew you never meant to hurt me. It's not in your nature to hurt *anyone* – not even Trina. Right from the start, I knew your heart. You showed me your true self in that little café on the night you opened up about your life. And I understand why you can't leave her – truly, I do. I could never blame you, and I never lost faith either. You're my Adam ... my other half. There's no one I trust more."

He held her face and rained kisses all over her eyelids, whispering frantically, "Oh, Baby, I had no idea. No wonder I love you so much. I don't deserve you ... but I can't bear the thought of losing you either. Please forgive me."

Again, she looked him straight in the eyes, realising he needed to see the truth lying there, as well as hear it in her words. "There's nothing to forgive. We belong together ... even if it is only in secret."

Adam's frantic concern slowly melted into relief, and almost reverently, his mouth touched hers.

A spontaneous whimper coming from the deepest part of her was his undoing. With a loud groan, hungry lips sought to devour hers in their wake. Their ardour mirrored one another's as she ran strong fingers through his hair. Both were swept up in a passion that had been lying in wait for months.

Like starving children, their mouths sought out this craved-for nourishment, while eager tongues searched and claimed every crevice discovered along the way. This was a dance similar to those once choreographed by two loving hands, only this one displayed all the passion of a tango as they moved to the sultry beat coursing through their bodies ... and reached the point of no return.

Powerless to endure any more of this exquisite torture, Adam swept her up in his arms. With their lips fused as one, he carried her into the bedroom as more of those soft whimpers spurred him on.

"Oh, Baby, I want you so much," he breathed heavily into her mouth, laying her on the bed and following closely so his body lay on top of hers. "Every part of me is on fire."

Loud groans blended in perfect harmony as they rolled from one end of the bed to the other, desperate to be as close as possible, though unwilling for their unfettered need to end too soon. Clothes were peeled away as hands tried frantically to free starved flesh of any barriers ... until they lay vulnerable before one another ... naked and glistening with a thin sheen.

He gazed down at her in adoration, tracing every curve with a tentative hand ... until once again that fire consumed him and he ravished whatever skin was close enough with hungry lips. She rose up to meet him as her teeth and lips nibbled and gnawed at his neck and shoulders, ever hungry for the taste of salty flesh ... while his tongue carved its unique imprint into her flushed skin.

And throughout this welcome assault, two sets of eyes remained fixed on the image of their soulmate lying before them, needy and unashamed.

Lara shuddered from the passion engulfing her. "Teddy," she pleaded as her mouth sought out his again, "I can't wait ... it's been too long ... please!"

His body covered hers, and she moved in time with him – flowing and ebbing like the tide lapping on a deserted beach. In one smooth movement, they became one flesh, riding waves of longing far stronger than anything either of them had ever experienced before. This was passion in its purest form – the way Solomon described in his treasured *Song of Songs* – the Bible story they had both discovered on those long endless nights filled with unrequited yearning.

Until ... their desire reached that pinnacle of gratification when, with one unanimous cry, they fell back on the bed exhausted, struggling to grasp an elusive breath ... and thoroughly complete.

Time seemed to stand still as they lay in a tangle of arms and legs, simply watching one another as their chests heaved. Ever so slowly, small smiles played across bruised mouths, while hands traced a steady pattern along flushed skin.

And then … jubilant chuckles rose from deep in their bellies, confirming this outpouring of unashamed lovemaking was proof of an unbreakable bond. No words had been necessary to communicate their need. Every nuance … every look … every movement … proof of the entirety of what they were feeling. All three had taken on an almost tangible form to give truth to their love. As beloved soulmates, they belonged together, and nothing could ever change that fact.

Minutes slipped away until the only sound was the whisper of even breathing, evidence they had nothing left to give except an unshakable trust in one another. Fingers, that until only moments ago had offered intimate pleasure, now played a soft lullaby across still-damp palms, swaying to the gentle rhythm of the waves slapping against the rock wall just outside their window … and carrying them along to a place of peaceful slumber.

They were home … safe at last.

§

And in another dimension, a slender needle lying dormant at the back of an intricate tapestry for many solo scenes carefully gathered in those lustrous silken threads made of gold and once again pierced the thick woven backing. With the greatest of care, the Master Craftsman fashioned perfectly formed stitches, and soon two colourful butterflies emerged from their cocoons.

With delicate wing beats, this newly formed duo danced around each other and across the canvas with almost childlike abandon … two souls, forever entwined, once again gracing the glorious work of art.

Chapter 11

When a taxi pulled up in front of a modern skyscraper the following morning, the full realisation of what their new careers would actually mean for their lives hit Lara and Adam for the first time. The Theatre Royal was no dusty, out-of-the-way suburban playhouse. This was one of the most famous venues in the country. It had hosted some of the finest shows performed by many of the world's best-loved artistes – *Les Mis* the night before had proved that – and now it was almost their turn to tread the boards of this hallowed place.

Adam stepped from the taxi, took a deep breath and looked up. "Well, this is it, my love. No going back now." With an exaggerated flourish, he turned and held out his hand. "*Miss Eliza Dolittle*, I give you Sydney's version of early twentieth-century London!"

Following his cue, Lara breathed deeply, hoping to settle her stomach. She clutched his hand, not entirely sure whether her legs would actually support her, but nevertheless determined to muscle up the courage to take on this brash new role in the place where a poor flower seller was about to come to life.

"Why, fank ya, *Professa!* Bu' I cain' 'tirely believe we're actu'lly 'ere!"

He grinned at her perfect take on a Cockney accent and sent her an affectionate wink.

The butterflies started again when they turned around only to be confronted by a new billboard with two huge images of themselves looking back at them. Plastered across the bottom was a banner with their names in big bold letters and the words *COMING SOON*.

The director's assistant was already waiting for them at stage door. After introducing herself, she quickly led the way down a maze of backstage corridors and up two tall staircases before ushered them into an imposing office on the second floor.

A tall, lean man came out from behind a large antique desk, with a welcoming smile and outstretched hand. "Adam, Lara, it's great to meet you at last. I'm Brad, welcome to the machinations of life in a large theatre!"

Adam took his hand first. "Thank you, it's great to meet you too, Brad, and it's an honour to be here." His gaze swept around the room, admiring the impressive wood panelling lining the walls while trying to imagine others who had stood on this same spot over the years.

The director caught the look of awe in Lara's eyes as she too looked around. "Hello, Lara," he said with a smile, leaning in to kiss her on both cheeks. "I've heard many wonderful things about you, young lady. Especially how amazing that vocal range of yours is. I'm so pleased you were able to join us at such short notice – both of you." He looked from one to the other.

"Thanks, Brad, it's a fabulous opportunity. I'm really excited, although I still have to pinch myself to believe this is all happening!"

"Well, not too hard! We can't have any ugly bruises marring that gorgeous complexion when you're on stage." His friendly laugh helped to ease her fears a little. "Besides, you deserve to be here after hearing that fabulous rendition of *Bill*. The whole production team is thrilled to have you on board."

"Thank you. I'm just as thrilled to be here." The look on her face confirmed her words.

"Sorry we haven't had a chance to catch up before this. It's been quite a rush pulling everything together."

Adam joined in. "Oh, that's fine, especially given the small amount of time you had to organise it all."

"You're not wrong, it's sure been hectic. Now you're probably already aware we won't actually be rehearsing in the theatre itself – the crew for *A Chorus Line* are just about to bump in for its six-week run once the *Les Mis* crew finish up and then it'll be our turn. So, we'll just have a quick chat and then I'll take you up to the rehearsal rooms five floors above us in the office tower next door.

"Sounds great," Adam replied. "We went along to see *Les Mis* on Saturday night – such a stirring show and the sets were outstanding!"

Brad's brow furrowed with a mock scowl. "But nowhere near as good as ours is going to be!" The other two grinned and nodded in agreement. It was the perfect comeback to put them at ease. "So ... let's get started."

Hugging one corner were two fifties-style leather button lounges in a deep shade of mahogany. The director gestured for them to take a seat before giving a quick rundown of his plans for the production.

"So, as you can see our time for rehearsals is far less than usual, but with a bit of hard work and a few miracles, I'm sure we'll be able to put big smiles on the faces of all those buying tickets. So, welcome aboard – you're bound to have a great time."

They heard a soft knock on the door and his assistant popped her head around the corner.

Brad gave an answering nod and glanced at his watch. "Okay, we'd better get going so you can meet the rest of the team."

He led them down even more passageways and then ushered them into a lift that whisked them up to a vast rehearsal room. It was already beginning to fill with others still arriving. The air of expectancy sent both their hearts racing. Once introductions were over, it was obvious this was so much bigger than anything either of them had ever experienced before.

Many of the supporting cast were names they had only ever read about in theatre mags or adorning the pages of all the glossy programmes on sale at merchandising stalls when a show came to town. Adam recognised a few from musicals he had patronised on his travels, though he never expected to meet them in person. To their relief, the entire cast and crew were warm and friendly, and it helped to put them at ease straight away.

The room was buzzing and it was obvious everyone was eager to get down to business. Without further ado, Brad had them do a full read-through, including all the musical pieces, which made the morning pass in a whirl. They broke for lunch, and afterwards, the choreographer had the whole ensemble quite literally on their toes, bringing them up to speed with the tricky footwork needed for many of the numbers.

By the end of the day, Brad was more than happy with the progress. Many stood around in groups, chatting excitedly amongst themselves; others towelled themselves off or stretched tired muscles when he came out to address them for the final time.

"If you can all be back here by nine tomorrow, we'll run through those first four numbers again. And, Lara, well done with your Cockney accent. You've obviously been working hard for the last few weeks, and it's certainly paid off. Ladies and gentlemen, I give you *Miss Eliza Doolittle* in the flesh!"

He swept her an exaggerated bow and everyone broke into spontaneous applause, with a few whistles thrown in from some of the guys. Those standing close by happily patted her on the back and even a few congratulatory hugs came her way. Feeling quite overwhelmed, Lara felt her face turn pink.

Adam clapped loudest of all and his sense of pride was plain for all to see ... but he didn't care. This was her moment and he was thrilled to be a part of her coming-of-age as a performer.

§

The next few weeks consisted of long days spent at the theatre as they grew into their roles, while nights and weekends were devoted to each other and Nikki. Whenever Lara and Adam went off to work, she had a wonderful time exploring the streets of the inner city with Helen. A lot of her schooling turned into interesting geography and history lessons with so many fascinating places to explore. The substitute teacher much preferred bringing lessons to life rather than staying closeted in the confines of the hotel pouring through dull textbooks. If rehearsals ran late, they often went back to her home so Nikki could spend the night with Matilda, her young granddaughter. Their bubbly laughter over a shared secret was the perfect confirmation of a blossoming friendship.

§

After dinner one evening, Lara noticed *Doctor Zhivago* was about to air on television. The novel had been part of her Grade Twelve English curriculum and that particular period of Russian history had fascinated her ever since. The love story woven through its pages had left a lasting impression. She had always intended watching the movie, though for some reason or other was never in the right place at the right time.

Adam hadn't even heard of it, so he was happy to join in, cradling Lara against him in spoon fashion as they lounged along the couch. Both of them were soon swept up in the tale, completely mesmerised as the story came to life on the small screen, with her fingers absentmindedly rubbing along the smooth flesh of his forearms.

Learning the young woman at the centre of the story shared the same name as the one lying in his arms, Adam cuddled her even closer. They were both beautiful to look at, but there was also something extra special about each one deep down – something that touched another's heart and held them spellbound – and he could easily understand why the doctor loved his *Lara* so deeply.

Forced apart several times due to circumstances beyond their control, *Yuri Zhivago* and *Lara Guishar's* love for one another never diminished, despite enduring many long lonely years toiling in war-ravaged Russia. Lara had forgotten the main female character shared the same name and it seemed to make the story even more heartbreaking. To see her namesake having to face the same uphill battles of loving a man who belonged to another hit close to home and she feared their lives might follow the same path. For over three melancholy hours, they watched in pin-drop silence as large portions of their own story seemingly unfolded right in front of them.

When the final credits rolled across the screen, Lara lay motionless with the tears soaking into her hair. Memories of all those months spent aching for Adam broke her heart all over again – it was too hard to imagine how she would cope never being able to see him again. He felt the faint tremor as her back pressed into his chest. With a soothing cry, he pulled her even closer.

"Oh, Baby, it's okay. Don't be upset. It was only a movie." The crushing storyline had affected him in much the same way, though he didn't want her to know.

"But what if we're like that?" she cried, turning to face him. "Neither of us knowing where the other one is ... never seeing each other again. Oh, Teddy, I couldn't bear being apart from you forever. Not now ... not after all we've been through."

All he could offer were soothing words of reassurance. "Sweetheart, please don't cry. I'm here – I'm not going anywhere..." Despite his best efforts, nothing could stem the tears, and he brushed her forehead with his lips. "Come on, it's okay. That wasn't our life ... we're not going to end up like that."

"I ... can't ... he...lp it," she hiccupped. "Why did it have to end like that? They should've had their chance." She dragged herself up to look into his face and the tears continued as she recalled those final scenes. Her shimmering eyes searched his. "Why didn't she turn around? She must've sensed he was there – I can always feel you..."

"I know and I can always feel you too. I wanted them to end up happily ever after, just like you, but hey, it'll be okay. Nothing like that will happen to us."

Down deep he could feel a prayer forming. *Please God, don't ever let me hurt her again. I beg you. She doesn't deserve the amount of sorrow Yuri's Lara had to endure.*

For the first time, Adam fully understood just how deeply she loved him – and what it must have been like for her during those long lonely months of separation. It had been just as painful for him – but he was to blame and deserved it ... she didn't.

Lara was heartbroken and nothing he could do made any difference.

Long after they went to bed and several times over the course of the night, a stray tear found its way down Lara's cheek. His gentle reassurances helped, but every now and then her whole body trembled as another wave of anguish rolled in. All he could do was hold her close with heartfelt promises his love would never die.

Though never admitting it, the movie had affected him in much the same way. He couldn't imagine going back to a life where she was no longer a part of it – Lara had become the very air he breathed.

§

Over the next few days, memories of those last few agonising scenes kept resurfacing, and Lara had to turn away before Adam noticed the tears. She couldn't remember being affected this deeply by any movie and her heart ached for both characters.

Out of an old school memory, she recalled reading how the author's own life was a template for the love story in the novel. Realising the brilliant Boris Pasternak had known the agony of a secret love affair while married to another woman made the whole experience even more poignant.

As time passed, Lara managed to control her emotions, although she never forgot the anguish of watching the tragic tale unfold ... and every single time her heart broke all over again.

§

As promised, halfway through rehearsals Suzie and Ben flew down for the weekend. On the second day, they offered to take Nikki to the zoo so Lara and Adam could have the whole day to themselves – something they hadn't been able to indulge in since arriving due to long days spent practising their craft and then entertaining Nikki on weekends. The little girl was beside herself with excitement and happily went off with the visitors, holding hands and skipping along between them as they went to catch the ferry.

Adam was grateful for this time alone and hoped being away from the city might help cheer Lara up a bit. He couldn't help noticing how melancholy she had become since that night in front of the television, despite her concerted efforts to hide it. Suzie and Ben's suggestion came at the perfect time and he was soon on the phone planning a special treat for the two of them.

The weather was perfect – crisp and clear with a big blue sky beckoning them to come out and play. The concierge was happy to organise a sporty little MG so they could get away from the bustling city and spend the day in a more peaceful part of the countryside.

"Come on, gorgeous lady. Let's get outta here and enjoy some fresh air for a change."

"Where are we off to?"

"Just you wait and see, but you'd better wear something casual ... and bring a cardigan – it could get quite chilly."

Lara flew around the room, changing clothes and slapping on a thin film of make-up, while Adam waited by the door with a big grin on his face. It felt good not having to worry about deadlines or learning reams of lines. She couldn't wait to enjoy the simple pleasure of being with her man while getting back to nature, rather than navigating bustling city streets at rush hour.

The Blue Mountains were a famous Aussie landmark and driving up the steep and winding highway, passing through thick bushland for a lot of the way, they found a world of beauty and peacefulness far removed from their busy everyday lives. Breaking up the green expanse were small townships with interesting craft shops and tearooms, though Adam had his mind set on one special place for their first stop.

"Oh, Adam, look over there," Lara exclaimed from the popular Echo Point vantage point perched high above the Jamison Valley.

The Three Sisters were directly in her line of sight – unique limestone fingers rising from a deep valley floor that spread as far as the eye could see. The formations stood proudly in a row and the sheer beauty of the entire area astounded her.

"I've seen so many pictures in magazines or footage on the telly, but I had no idea how breathtaking this view really was. And it's easy to see how they came by their name – they *are* just like a family standing in a line ... and look, there's even a tiny one perched on the end," she marvelled, pointing to a much smaller craggy outcrop nestled beside the others.

She leaned back against Adam's chest with his arms encircling her waist. Pressing his mouth against a tempting ear, he whispered, "I had a feeling you'd be impressed – they call that one *The Little Brother,* and it's not hard to guess why. I've always loved coming up here ... now it's even better with you!"

They strolled along the parapet, admiring views that stretched into the valley hundreds of metres below. Their eyes moved upwards to the majestic mountain ranges lining every inch of the distant horizon. Sheer orange-burnished cliff sides and tree-lined ridges tinged with blue created a perfect frame to the panorama.

Out of the corner of her eye, Lara spotted something resembling a tram carriage and not at all where it should be. Suspended high above the chasm, this out-of-place mode of transport ran along a long parallel set of cables stretching from one ridge to another.

She grabbed his arm. "Darling, look at that! Imagine the views from way up there!"

"Well, come on; let's find out ... just so long as you're not too chicken! I don't want you freaking out on me and plunging us both to our deaths!"

Before Lara could respond with an almost certain backhand to some part of his anatomy, Adam grabbed both of her hands with one of his and tickled her ribs with the other. Giggling loudly, she struggled hard to break free.

"You blighter!" she gasped, managing to wriggle out of his grasp and swat at his butt. "Who are you calling chicken? *I'm* not afraid of heights!"

Grabbing her by the shoulders, he pretended to push her into a narrow channel only a few inches deep running beside the path. Letting out a loud squeal, she clutched at his arm.

"Not scared of heights, hey?"

He burst out laughing and pulled her close, kissing her cheek as she tried to break away.

"You're a horrible man and I'm going to get you for that – just you wait!" she threatened, tickling the vulnerable spot in the small of his back. Their playful flirting spilled onto several other sightseers enjoying the views and managed to bring amused smiles to this unexpected audience.

"Come on! Race you to the car!"

Adam took off with Lara close on his heels and minutes later both of them fell against the door gasping loudly. Being away from the pressures of work was like a breath of fresh air, and the freedom of just being themselves without having to worry about who saw them was the perfect pick-me-up. More than anything, he was relieved to see her dazzling smile back where it belonged.

The views from the *Skyway* tram were simply spectacular. Lara proved she could conquer heights similar to her recent boast when they peered through the glass floor to the lush valley below. Off to the right, thunderous waterfalls plunged beneath their feet, while a veil of fine mist floated into the air. Looking out the other side offered a magnificent view of *The Three Sisters* and beyond.

Afterwards, they went for a leisurely walk around the pretty township of Katoomba. The air was much brisker at the higher altitude, so they were grateful to drop into one of the many cafés scattered along the main street.

Soon they were tucking into platefuls of homemade Coq Au Vin with fresh vegetables, all swimming in a rich red wine sauce. A roaring fire in the brick hearth was a welcome companion to keep the chill at bay and they enjoyed soaking up the peace and quiet rather than the usual multitude of questions accompanying any meal whenever a certain little miss was around. Whispered endearments and wistful planning for the future were the only form of conversation over the mouth-watering repast.

On their way out of town, Lara spied a sign for Leura Cascades. "Oh, Teddy, can we please stop and have a look?"

It was the perfect way to end a wonderful day. Hand-in-hand they wandered through the dense forest and followed the creek where it tripped over small rocky drops on its way to the valley floor. The thick canopy overhead made the bushland quite chilly and Lara couldn't help shivering as the sun crept towards the western horizon.

Sneaking up from behind, Adam grabbed Lara and smothered her body with not only his arms but also enough tender kisses to make every part of her warm. It was rare to have the freedom to indulge in any affectionate outdoor displays, so he was quick to take full advantage while they had the chance.

Sharing satisfied smiles and with hearts fully content, they climbed back into the little sports car to join the real world again, and learn all about a little girl's exciting day.

Lara fell asleep as they motored down the steep mountain range and Adam was happy just watching her whenever the traffic thinned enough to sneak a glance. He couldn't count how many times he had imagined being with her like this; experiencing the real thing was so much better. Humming softly to himself, the rhythm of her steady breathing kept him company all the way.

"Wake up, sleepy head."

She felt his lips against her ear and came awake slowly. It took her a few seconds to work out they were in the hotel's basement carpark. "Oh, my goodness, did I fall asleep? Are we back already?"

"Yep, but don't worry, I had a great view all the way."

She grinned sheepishly. "I'm so sorry – clearly too big a dose of that fresh mountain air! You should've woken me."

"Why would I? You looked adorable and I enjoyed every minute," he said through a smile, leaning across to graze her lips with his. "Have I told you lately how much I love you, Ms Jennings?"

More grins matched her playful reply, "Not nearly enough, Mr Peters!"

It was easy to tell the trip to the mountains had been an ideal choice by the sparkle in her eyes. This time he claimed her mouth firmly with his and several minutes passed before either of them had any wish to come up for air.

§

Nikki let out an excited cry when the door opened and they greeted her with huge smiles. She barrelled towards them, eager to share her adventures and soon found herself swept up into Adam's arms before being thrown high in the air. Her giggles were a lovely welcome home, especially when she grabbed Lara around the neck and plastered a week's worth of kisses all over her face.

"Whoa, that's the best greeting a mummy could ever want. You look like you've had a great time, little Munchkin." In the middle of big squeezy hugs that left her gasping, she heard Suzie yell she was putting the kettle on. "Hang on, I'd better go and help in the kitchen; then you can tell me all about your day."

They shared another sloppy kiss before Lara went off to help her sister in the adjacent room. "Sorry, Suze, I didn't mean to leave Nikki with you all day. I thought we'd be back long before this. The weather was so beautiful it was like spending a day in paradise and time just got away."

"Don't worry, we only just got home ourselves after a fabulous time. You're looking much more relaxed, thank goodness. I was a bit worried when I saw you last night, wondering whether this was all getting a bit too much for you."

"No, I'm fine. I just needed to get away from the crowds for a while. Today was perfect, thanks again."

"Happy to help … oh, and by the way, I had no idea what a clever little mimic your daughter is. Wait 'til you hear what she got up to."

"I'm not surprised! You should've heard her when I was learning all those new accents – she was better than me most of the time."

Over a refreshing cuppa, Nikki provided a running commentary on all the animals they had encountered, and then did a great job keeping them entertained imitating many of the different calls. When she tried to replicate the gorilla, a loud grunt reverberated from deep inside her tiny body.

"What'd I tell you!" Suzie said with a laugh as her sister and Adam pretended to cower behind each other and several cushions. "Now look what you've done, pumpkin. That big scary monster you've got tucked away inside you is frightening all of us!"

The little girl chuckled and took a flying leap, landing on top of her mother and Adam, and they fought hard to push the wriggling mass of legs and arms away. Clearly, this unexpected break from routine had been good for everyone.

As dusk fell and shadows started inching across the carpet, Lara took Nikki by the hand. "Okay, Missy, it's time you and the bath became reacquainted. Look at all those bits of straw in your hair ... and that sticky mess on your chin! What else did you get up to today?"

"Nothing! That's just 'cause one of those funny old g'rillas threw a great big handful of straw at me when I patended to copy him. Then Uncle Ben bought me an ice-cream and some of it dribbled, but it was really yummy."

"Well, it's no wonder if you snorted at that big old gorilla the way you did at us just then. And that was nice of Uncle Ben – I hope you said thank you."

"I did. I benembered."

"That's my girl. Now come on, let's get you cleaned up and wash that filthy hair."

Once she was clean again, they spent a playful few minutes splashing water at each other. Nikki pretended to be an elephant, spurting out long streams from between her teeth.

Their laughter brought Adam in to see what all the commotion was about and he perched on the edge of the basin with a pensive smile. Watching them together took him down another path – one that included imaging Lara tending their own baby. He remembered her saying she had always wanted four children and her regrets about Nikki being an only child. As much as she adored the little girl, he knew she always dreamed of having another.

There was nothing he could do to change the situation but the thought stayed with him as they dressed for dinner – along with a deep regret at having been forced into having a vasectomy after Trina fell pregnant and then her choosing to have an abortion without discussing what he wanted.

It wasn't long before everyone's stomachs started to rumble, so Adam suggested a popular Chinese restaurant a few blocks away as the ideal place for dinner. They were a jovial bunch wandering down the old alleyways and cobbled streets. Echoes of laughter bounced off the brick walls when Ben put on an impromptu performance of a drunken sailor from Australia's early settlement days.

The eating house lived up to its reputation as dish after dish came out to tempt their taste buds. It wasn't long before the large lazy susan in the centre of the table groaned under the weight of the colourful fare. A lively discussion ensued around the table, expounding on their exploits between mouthfuls of the rich exotic flavours. At one stage, the men even got into some friendly rivalry by trying to outdo one another with their prowess using chopsticks.

After all their carry-on, Lara painstakingly tried to teach Nikki how to use a pair of child-sized ones, but her little fingers were too clumsy to master the unfamiliar objects. Time and time again she explained how to hold them correctly, with the little girl trying hard to get it right. Whenever the food landed with either a messy splat back in the bowl or on the table – and a couple of times even in her lap – everyone around the table burst into loud chuckles. After many unsuccessful attempts, eventually a few grains of rice made it up to Nikki's mouth, and they all let out a triumphant cheer.

Throughout the whole process, Adam had been watching their endeavours with a proud smile – and with just the smallest hint of sadness in his eyes.

I wish I could give you one of ours, my darling. Damn, Trina ... she's even stolen that away.

Lying in bed later that night, the seed of an idea was planted in his brain. He turned on his side and touched Lara's bare shoulder with his lips.

Once we're back in Brisbane, I know a doctor friend who may be able to give us a solution, Baby.

She was fast asleep and simply snuggled in closer to the warm body lying next to her, oblivious to where his thoughts had taken him.

§

The weekend flew by and soon they were back at the airport waving goodbye.

"Don't leave it too long before you come back again," Lara pleaded, hugging her sister close as the flight was announced.

"We won't, I promise. And thanks for the opening night tickets. How exciting ... my little sister with her name top billing in one of the foremost theatres in the country! Mum and Dad would've been thrilled to bits and so very proud of you."

Her words brought a cloak of sadness with them knowing two of the most important people in their lives wouldn't be there to share in the celebrations. Similar to Adam, the sisters' parents had passed away when they were still quite young.

Diagnosed with breast cancer, their mother was gone when Lara was only twenty. Their father followed only a few months later from what doctors could only describe as a broken heart. The two had been inseparable, so it wasn't surprising he found it too hard trying to cope on his own. Suzie had been the one to find him slouched over in his favourite armchair with a photo of his dead wife clutched in his hands. The doctors could find no other explanation for his sudden demise and since then the girls had been each other's only real support.

"I don't think they would've believed it, not their super shy one treading the boards – you maybe, but definitely not me," Lara responded.

"Yes, they would! Mum always said your voice was so sweet even the angels would stop to listen."

"Oh, she did not!"

"Yes, she did, and I can still see Dad leaning back at the breakfast table with a look of bliss on his face while you trilled away under the shower ... and for hours at a time, I might add! But whenever I sang along to the radio, he'd just laugh and cover his ears – or turn it up to drown me out! You always were his favourite." Suzie chuckled fondly, remembering those times.

"I was not, you little fibber!" Lara chortled. "He was *always* proud of you, especially on Awards Nights – who was the one bringing home all the trophies? Not me. You're the one with the brains. Besides, the only reason my voice didn't sound too bad was because it was drowned out by all that gushing water!"

"Oh, rubbish, Lara-Lu. Who's about to recite pages of script every night with no second chances – and who'll soon have fans coming in droves just to hear that amazing voice! The whole world's at your feet and I know Mum and Dad'd be super proud of you."

They shared one last hug just as the final boarding call sounded. Lara leaned close and whispered into her sister's ear, "Thanks, Suze, see you soon and take good care of Ben. I really like him and it's lovely to see you so happy!"

"I will, and I am!" Suzie replied, with an excited grin as she reached for her boyfriend's hand.

"'Bye, Aunty Suzie, see ya, Uncle Ben," Nikki said, throwing her arms around them both at the same time. "I miss you big much when I don't see you, so please come back soon."

"We will 'cause we miss you too, pumpkin, and be good for Mummy." She squeezed Nikki in a bearhug as Ben ruffled her thick fringe.

When they walked to the plane, Suzie turned to blow a quick kiss and send a final wave to the two people who were all the family she had left, calling over her shoulder, "See you in a few weeks. Love you..."

§

Opening night was only two weeks away and rehearsals cranked into final stages. The company had just moved into tech rehearsals ... that time when all the elements – set, lighting, costumes, sound and all the other nitty-gritty that went into a full production – came together on the actual theatre stage itself. It also meant they usually had to be there from early morning until long after dark.

Lara was finding it difficult being away from Nikki during the long days. A blanket of guilt would often be an unwanted companion in the taxi ride back to the hotel. Adam was quick to pick up on her mood and did everything he could to reassure her. Sure enough, when they walked in, the little girl was usually enjoying some game or another with Helen and showing no sign of feeling abandoned. Fortunately, weekends came around fast enough to make up for any of those lost hours.

Since arriving, their two free days turned into special times – often exploring the many picturesque little coves lining the harbour. Sometimes they hired a car for day trips to the country or visiting one of the countless white sandy beaches along the coastline. These were Nikki's favourite outings as she and Adam turned their sculpting skills into even more eye-catching sandcastles – good enough to rival their efforts on the day they first met. Lara was happy just watching them and basked in the gentle fingers of winter sunlight warming her shoulders.

Not surprisingly, Adam's suite had turned into a small rehearsal studio where they could practice scenes rather than fulfilling its original use. Drifting off to sleep in each other's arms – often after a tender night of lovemaking – brought back sweet memories of their time in Europe. On the nights they were too tired to do anything else, the pair of them lay entwined along the sofa, happy to watch television or simply chat about the day's happenings.

Weekly phone calls between Adam and his parents kept them amused with recollections of Nikki's recent exploits, along with interesting gossip snippets from rehearsals. If Charles dared to admit it, he was a tiny bit jealous, though the thrill of knowing the young lovers were sharing this incredible opportunity more than made up for it. Elizabeth couldn't wait for opening night and her excitement was always contagious whenever she was on the line.

§

Charles and Elizabeth joined Suzie and Ben to fly down on the Friday before the big night. Rooms were booked for both couples in the same hotel as the stars. When Lara and Adam arrived back following the final full run-through, the others had already checked in.

Nikki was beside herself having the family all together again, even prancing around pretending Clancy had come too. Lara's suite became a mishmash of excited chatter as the talk turned to the thrill of opening night. Not much later, everyone sauntered down to dinner at the hotel's finest restaurant.

"How are the butterflies, Lara?" Charles asked across the table.

She gave a nervous grimace and waved her fingers. "Getting more frenetic the closer the time comes! I'll be relieved when that curtain finally goes up, then we'll be on, and I won't have time to worry about anything."

"You're sure to be wonderful, my love," Adam declared, reaching under the table to stroke her knee. "You should see her, Dad. You'd think she really was a Cockney flower seller sitting on those stairs in the opening scene. I'm so proud of her and I reckon you will be, too."

"I know I will – all of us," Charles replied as Lara blushed profusely and dipped her head.

"And none more so than me," Suzie joined in, sending a big smile her sister's way.

Elizabeth was sitting next to her son and she leaned over to whisper in his ear. "Has Trina mentioned if she's coming down?"

Hearing the name he had deliberately blotted from his mind, Adam's face clouded over, and his tone changed to one of disinterest. "No, I wouldn't have a clue. I've tried ringing a few times just to see how she's doing, but she's never home. I spoke to John last week and he assured me she's not drinking, but as far as anything else goes, I have no idea. Hopefully, she won't be bothered, but knowing her, I couldn't say for sure."

"I've rung a few times myself with the same response. She and Judith seem to be out most of the time, so I'm hoping she stays up there for everybody's sake." She looked at him tellingly. "You've put up with enough over the years. Anyway, she's never shown any interest in your work before, so why would she start now. But if she does happen to make it down and tries anything at all, she'll have me to contend with … and it won't be pretty!"

The determination in her tone didn't surprise him. In the past, his mother had always tolerated Trina purely for his sake, but over the last few months, she had stopped making excuses. Elizabeth well knew the sacrifices he had made for his marriage – and with no real change to his wife's attitude. Now she was like a lioness, ready to take on anything with the gall to try to harm her cub.

Shrugging his shoulders as though shaking off any remnants of those troubled times, he smiled and took his mother's hand. "Well, let's not worry about her tonight. This is Lara's time ... she's the only one who matters. So, what have you been up to, Mum? Seen any good movies lately?"

§

Adam and Lara fell into bed just before eleven and he pulled her into his arms. "Well my darling, this time tomorrow night..."

"Mmm, this time tomorrow night I'll be as nervous as a trapeze artist without a net..."

"Rubbish, you'll be fabulous and wowing them in the aisles. Once that final bow's been taken, nothing's ever going to be the same. Mark my words ... I can already see the headlines: '*Lara Jennings, bound for Broadway!*'"

"Oh, Teddy, now you're being ridiculous ... and a little bit biased!" she laughed, nibbling all around his lips.

She could never get enough of him, even when she was exhausted, and always looked for any opportunity to plunder his mouth with hers. When they eventually came up for air, her fingers took over, trailing a slow path along his jawline and up around his nose, leaving every pore tingling in their wake.

"Anyway, what about you?" she went on. "Tomorrow night is your time too. I'm not the only one who's going to be up there in the spotlight, my love."

Adam pulled her back into his arms and this time it was his kisses inching across her mouth, reiterating every word. "Maybe ... but you're ... the one ... they'll all ... be looking at ... I know ... I'll ... only ... have eyes ... for you."

Again, she broke away, only this time to sit upright and glare down at him. The resolute stance reminded him of Elizabeth whenever she had something important to say. He tried once more to pull her back into his arms, but she was determined to have her say.

"Don't you *dare* make doe eyes at me on stage, or else Brad'll have your head. You need to be completely indifferent as far as anything romantic goes ... just the way the professor's supposed to be – no winks or furtive glances, okay! Promise me you'll behave yourself..."

His cheeky grin had her even more worried. Twisting quickly, she straddled his thighs, eyes blazing as she pressed his hands firmly against the headboard.

"Teddy, answer me! If you dare look at me like that, I'm going to kick you in the shins to bring you back to earth. Just like Eliza should after the way *Higgins* treats her. At least it won't look out of place."

"Oh yeah? *Then* who's likely to give Brad a conniption? It won't be me!"

He managed to twist free and grabbed her around the waist to tickle her ribs. Lara's chuckles echoed around the room as she tried hard to get away.

"Come back here, you," he threatened, lunging after her when she managed to break free.

His legs grabbed hers as she scrambled across the bed, pinning her down so she couldn't get away again. She put up a good fight as their arms flayed madly until he managed to turn the tables and this time it was her hands imprisoned against the headboard with her body lying beneath his.

For the longest of moments, all Adam could do was look down at her, eyes wild with desire. Then ever so slowly, his mouth descended upon her neck, and those former wriggles turned into slow writhes of desire. With aching tenderness, Lara's mouth set out on a treasure hunt of his ear and scalp, while Adam's lips and tongue continued exploring the contours of her neck and shoulders.

As her passion rose, she chose to take the masterful role. Twisting in his arms, he soon found himself imprisoned beneath those soft womanly curves as her tongue lightly encircled his chest with a ribbon of teasing. All he could do was lie there, completely vulnerable to her torturous will.

"Oh, Baby, you get me every time," he breathed into her hair as a soft moan escaped. Feverish hands raked the contours of her head, pulling her closer.

Unable to resist any longer, he swept her up and claimed her mouth as she melted into his arms. A loud groan escaped as her need intensified, returning his kisses with the same degree of ferocity. They were like two tigers coming together after months roaming the jungle alone ... on the brink of hurting one another, though never quite falling over the abyss ... and all the while burning and breathing heavily with desire.

They rolled all over the bed with mouths still joined, as though seeking to spiral into the very depths of the other one's being. Desperate hands strove to bring both pleasure and an aching yearning before that longed-for fulfilment. A duet of moans formed a frantic chorus, sending both of them soaring to the brink. Their responses grew louder and more tortured as those waves of desire continued to build. Writhing bodies struggled to scale that seemingly unattainable peak as flesh oozed with a film of perspiration from the efforts of this punishing exertion.

Dust motes danced in the glow from the streetlight below and with each laboured breath, spun like whirling dervishes caught up in a fevered dance – only to hang suspended for a few seconds until their gasping mouths once again stirred them to life.

Eventually, a woman's cry filled the room – like that of a mother bringing forth her child – and the sound was like a trigger to the man bringing her release. Hands clasped to the point of agony as his cry joined hers, filling her ears and her body with those glorious reverberations echoing throughout every pore.

Chests heaved, struggling for air when they lay bathed in that soft sheen of moisture; hair damp and lips swollen from the passion spent.

Long minutes passed and almost absentmindedly, Adam's hands played with her hair ... until he looked down at her and smirked. "Well, if that's what a bundle of nerves does, I vote we have an opening night every week!"

"I don't think so," she groaned. "I'm exhausted and it's all your fault!"

A duo of satisfied smiles kept them company as soulmates drifted off to sleep.

§

They woke to dazzling sunlight spilling over and under the curtain edges and Adam greeted Lara with just as much enthusiasm as the golden hue.

"'Mornin', *Miss Eliza,* an' top o' da mornin' t' yer. Yer lookin' moighty noice lyin' thar like tha'. 'Ow 'bou' a noice big smooch on dis ol' professa's lips to make 'im feel on top o' da world?"

A cheeky chortle accompanied her quick retort. "'Mornin' t' yer back, guvnor, bu' I ain' righ' sure I knows whos ya be. *My* professa don' sound loik tha' a' awl an' I don' jus' kiss any ol' fella, I'll 'av ya know!"

Laughing from the pure joy of simply being together and everything this day meant, they sprang out of bed, and he quickly wrestled the requested morsel from her open mouth before she could get away.

Due to all his years of experience, Charles insisted they take it easy and just hang around the hotel for the day. It was important to preserve their voices and Suzie and Ben were more than happy to entertain Nikki while they rested in the afternoon.

With sizzling memories of the welcome assault from the night before, all morning the lovers kept exchanging secret looks. Whenever an opportunity came to hide from prying eyes, they stole a few wayward kisses between muffled giggles. Suzie caught them behind the refrigerator door on more than one occasion and teased them mercilessly with raised eyebrows and saucy asides.

Exasperated, Lara pulled her sister into the bedroom to deliver a stern warning, but Suzie got in first with her eyebrows raised and the makings of a feisty grin. "It's not *my* fault! All morning you've looked like the cat that got the canary ... don't blame me if you can't keep your hands off each other and I walk in to find you acting like a pair of ravenous teenagers! What did you two get up to after we left you alone last night?"

"Never you mind," Lara tried to dismiss her, while the smirk lurking at the corners of her mouth was a dead giveaway.

"Well ... all I can say is" —Suzie's expression matched her sister's— "you look happier than I've ever seen you ... and I'm thrilled to bits! He sure must be special."

"I am ... and he is," Lara answered contentedly, planting a quick peck on the other one's cheek.

§

The plans were all in place. Once Alice turned up to babysit Nikki, all four interstate visitors would travel together in a taxi, arriving in plenty of time for the opening celebrations. A little while later the limousine Brad had organised for their red-carpet appearance would transport Lara and Adam to the theatre. This would be a completely different scenario to any of their previous opening nights. Celebrities from near and far would be walking that same ribbon of red, while jostling cameramen and reporters from all the media outlets waited in readiness to record the highlights of the evening.

At five o'clock, Lara and Adam set out for the theatre. With every minute that passed, the quivers of nervous anticipation intensified. Lara's hands were shaking during the short drive and Adam started to get concerned when he saw the mountain of fear in her eyes.

"Teddy, I don't think I can do this. What if I forget my lines? Arggghhh ... I can't even remember the first one! And what was it that Mel said to be careful of with those vowels? Umm ... *grrr* ... I can't remember *anything!* I *won't* be able to go on!" she cried, clutching at his arm as fear gave way to panic.

She was really starting to look petrified, so he freed himself from her grip and soothed her frantic hands with a gentle grip. Looking her straight in the eyes, he spoke slowly to bring a bit of calm into the situation.

"You'll be fine, darling. I *know* you will. This is just stage fright, and if you remember, it was just as bad that first time for *Show Boat* too. Look at me. Come on, you can do this."

Frantically her head began to shake and eyes filled with terror. "No, I can't! This is Sydney Central, not a quiet suburb of Brisbane and I'm getting paid big time to appear now! Ooh, I just *know* I'm going to let everyone down..."

"No, you're not, sweetheart. Come on, take a deep breath and look at me ... what's your first line? ... Come on, you *can* remember," he prompted her gently, confident that once she recalled those first few words, the panic attack would subside. Adam had seen several performers experience similar reactions when he was with the *Brisbane Harlequin Theatre Troupe* and he knew the best way to conquer fear was by getting into character straight away.

For a few seconds, she stared blankly at him ... then, "*Aaa-www-hhh!* Look where ya goin', dear! Look where ya goin'! Two bunches o' violets trod in da mud! A full day's wages!" she recited in her Cockney twang as the lines came back.

"Good girl! See I knew you'd be okay. You just have to believe in yourself. Come on, we're almost there." He pressed her hand against his lips with a confident and caring smile.

A long line of luxurious cars stretched ahead, giving them time to observe the commotion building outside the theatre. With the horde of onlookers focussing on the line-up of special guests already pulling in, they were able to steal a few private moments before joining the throng.

Cloaked by the tinted windows and shadowy back seat, Adam leaned over and touched her mouth with his. "I'll be right here with you ... nothing's going to happen, I promise. You've worked so hard for this ... don't let nerves get the better of you now."

The entrance was already swarming with people when their limo pulled up and he pressed his knee against hers as a final form of reassurance. Taking one last very deep breath, she nodded. Then grasping his hand, they stepped from the car as a male figure dressed in fancy red livery held open the door. Flashbulbs burst from every direction, making them blink several times as they made their way down the carpeted walkway.

News and magazine crews lined both sides trying to gain their attention, "Ms Jennings, over here." ... "Turn this way, Mr Peters." ... "Just one more, Lara." ... "Now, the two of you together, that's right."

Voices seemed to come from everywhere and the eager bank of photographers blinded Lara as they pressed forward, causing her to nearly trip over a wayward video cable until Adam managed to rescue her. Overwhelmed by all the attention, she clung to his arm during several minutes of turning this way and that to appease the media's constant demands.

Catching sight of Suzie and Ben in the crowd near the main door, their proud smiles gave her something familiar to focus on.

"Oh, Adam, I didn't expect anything like this," she whispered through clenched teeth, endeavouring to keep a smile on her face as they slowly made their way towards her sister.

Surreptitiously he stroked the hand draped through his arm and whispered for her ears alone, "It's okay, Baby, you're doing fine and we're almost there. Just keep smiling and try to look like you're enjoying yourself."

"That's easier said than done," she fretted, though still remembering to smile for the cameras.

A few minutes later they were inside the spacious lobby, now decorated to replicate the streets of early twentieth-century London. Suzie and Ben stood nearby, her face lit up like a Christmas tree as she proudly watched her little sister receiving all this attention. Brad was there to greet them and Max stood next to him, both men grinning from ear to ear as they welcomed the new stars.

"You look absolutely dazzling, Lara." Max held her hands at arm's length as he admired her stunning attire.

She was wearing a Grecian-style gown in an antique white tone. The seamstress had fashioned the long flowing skirt falling from just under the bustline into tiny vertical pleats and it seemed to float around her ankles as she walked.

The material was a lightweight satin that hugged her figure in all the right places, and with a crossover cut-out back giving it a distinctive flair. A layer of chiffon covered the satin fabric making up the bodice, while a thin line of gold brocade ran beneath the bustline giving her breasts the perfect silhouette. The bodice itself was fashioned into a V-shape and then tapered up to the top of her shoulders where a pair of brocade clasps adorned both straps. Soft tendrils of chestnut hair drifted around her face, and a long trail of curls fell down her back, all held in place by a matching clasp sitting high on the back of her head.

Acting with true olden-style chivalry, Max presented Lara's hand to Adam before breaking into a loud burst of applause.

The gesture was one her partner couldn't resist. He twirled his stunning co-star around so the full skirt billowed out like those worn by movie stars in a forties-style Hollywood musical. She could easily have been mistaken for *Cinderella* on her way to the ball, while Adam made a splendid *Prince Charming* decked out in an immaculate dinner suit. He was totally bewitched by her beauty and his admiring gaze made her feel like a princess.

News cameras captured this impromptu performance and the following evening it was to become the lead story in the entertainment segment on several channels. The entire theatrical world was soon buzzing with the story of these two up-and-coming Brisbane performers. In hindsight, Lara and Adam thanked their lucky stars – and God above – the clip hadn't made it to their hometown's newsfeed.

With a small glass of champagne to help steady the nerves and their agent by their side to ensure they were quoted correctly, the duo fielded questions from two of Sydney's leading newspapers, as well as a couple of minor rags whose journalists were eager to find out how the newcomers were faring in "The Big Smoke". Max knew firsthand how easily words could be twisted on the printed page, which is why he wanted to be close by. Full cast photos were called for and they found it quite overwhelming to be part of such a heady occasion.

As soon as the media call was over, they managed a hurried greeting to their families who were watching everything with huge smiles on their faces. Then the pair disappeared through a doorway, making their way down the long corridor to their personal dressing rooms. When Lara realised they would be on in less than two hours, those dreadful nerves started to resurface. Tonight, she had no Lucy to greet her or run through her lines as they helped one another get ready. Their dressing rooms were just around the corner from each other, and before Adam went off to get ready, she clutched at his hand.

"Do you *really* think I can do this, Teddy? Tell the truth," she pleaded.

"I *know* you can, sweetheart. Every run-through has been line-perfect, and once you get on stage, it'll all come back to you – I promise. Now go and get ready, then as soon as I'm done, I'll come straight back to fetch you. We can wait in the wings together before it's time to go on, just like always."

He wrapped the anxious woman in his arms and held her close until the trembling eased. She had to swallow hard to settle her nerves, but once she was able to offer him a cautious smile, Adam felt confident those horrible fears had at last been conquered.

"I think I'm alright now. I don't know what came over me." Lara was embarrassed and felt terrible to have him witness her minor meltdown.

"Hey, don't worry. It can happen to the best of us. Even the great Sir Laurence Olivier was renowned for suffering from a case of the jitters just prior to a curtain going up, along with heaps of other famous performers. You're in good company. Just you wait and see – we're going to have a brilliant time out there. Now I'd better go and get ready, then I'll be back before you know it."

With a reassuring grin and a quick kiss on the tip of her nose, he was gone.

Brad was a bundle of nerves as he flitted from one group to the next. Using two virtual unknowns in the lead roles meant he had a lot riding on this new venture. Several of his director colleagues had questioned the producers' decision to include them virtually sight unseen. After witnessing their preparations and hard work during rehearsals, he was more than confident they were perfect to carry the show.

Just over an hour before her call, Lara was just finishing changing from the beautiful white gown into a light robe when she heard a light tap on the door. Pulling it open, she found Brad standing there with a huge colourful arrangement in his arms.

"A few flowers for a special flower seller! I just wanted to show my new leading lady how delighted I am with the effort she's put in to get us to this point." He leaned over and kissed her cheek. "I know you're going to be wonderful tonight, my dear. Those accents are faultless and your delivery just perfect. I can't wait to hear the audience reaction."

Her face lit up as she invited him in. After Adam's vote of confidence and then to hear Brad's similar message, it was exactly the boost she needed to believe in herself again.

"Thanks, Brad, they're beautiful," Lara said, accepting the floral tribute. She couldn't resist and put her nose into the centre bloom, breathing in the heady fragrance.

"Hey, don't go getting hay-fever on me!" he warned nervously. "We can't have you going out on stage with a red nose and watery eyes."

"I don't know," she teased with a friendly chuckle. "Maybe it would help my Cockney accent to have a bit of nasal inflection!"

Adam was just coming around the corner and caught their remarks. He breathed a huge sigh of relief to hear her sounding like her old self again.

"Oh Adam, there you are. I was just about to come to your dressing room to see how you're doing. Are you all ready for the big night?"

"Absolutely, Brad, and I'm really looking forward to it. Thanks for giving us this opportunity and for showing so much faith in our abilities."

"I knew I was on a winner the moment I heard your voices. Now, you'd both better scoot off to hair and makeup before they send out a search party – time's getting away."

Wishing them the obligatory Aussie, "Chookas," Brad hurried away to drop by the rest of the cast to ensure they were all okay. Quick as a wink, Adam slipped into Lara's room for one last reassuring hug before it was time to metamorphose into their alter egos.

"See, I told you you'd be fine ... Brad wouldn't dare risk his baby on anyone he didn't believe could carry off the role. And Audrey Hepburn and Julie Andrews had better watch out 'cause I'm pretty sure you'll soon be their main competition!"

Lara burst out laughing at his over-the-top analogy and kissed him soundly on the lips. "I love you, Mr Peters. Thanks for putting everything back into perspective ... but *somehow* I doubt either Ms Hepburn *or* Ms Andrews have anything to worry about!"

Adam's eyes twinkled as his lips touched the tip of her nose, and thankfully they made it just in time to keep their backstage appointments.

Less than an hour later, Lara went from looking like a dazzling Grecian goddess into a dirty waif-like creature, with speckles of soot dusting those long dark tresses and thick black smudges adorning that normally flawless complexion. Ugly ragged clothing covered her from head to toe to complete the picture George Bernard Shaw first envisaged when he wrote the famous play.

When he caught sight of her, Adam burst out laughing, lifting up one of those dirty locks with a look of disdain similar to what *Professor Higgins* himself would have done. The voice that emerged was not at all what Lara was expecting.

"Wo' 'av we 'ere. Ya looks loik a righ' dir'y flah-gil," he mimicked, drawing smiles from those standing near.

"Jus' you wai', *'enry 'iggins*. I'll 'av ya guts for ga'ers, I will, if yer gunna be cheeky wiv me, guvnor, an' dem 'oity-toity friends 'o yours'll be up in arms if ya soun' like tha'. I reckin," Lara responded already in character and looking forward to the curtain rising as she received his smile and short nod of approval.

"Places everyone," echoed around the hallways and people streamed from everywhere to stand quietly in the darkness of the vast stage or wait in the wings for their cue. Adam stood in the shadows off to one side.

Lara had her face to him as she sat on a replica model of the stairs fronting the theatre in Covent Garden on a cold March night. At her feet was a large basket of flowers and the air was shrouded in mist. When the orchestra played the opening strains, he couldn't resist and sent a clandestine wink her way. In response, her dirt-smeared nose formed an almost imperceptible wrinkle. Only small gestures, but they meant the world to each of them.

And from the moment the thick curtain rose, it was as though a switch flicked on in Lara's soul ... nervousness became a thing of the past and the essence of the famous character carried her into yesteryear.

§

Every minute on stage was a triumph with Lara fully embodying the famous character during her conversion from ugly duckling to beautiful swan. Adam's portrayal of the prim professor taunting and teasing poor *Eliza* was the perfect counterbalance to her coarse character, and the audience empathised with every emotion. There was no romantic drama to portray, just continual bickering back and forth. The crowd's laughing response pervaded the stage from one scene to the next, something all actors in live theatre feed from to spur them on even further. This was definitely the case with the night's performance.

Everyone involved had honed their craft perfectly, from the lighting crew and set dresser, right up to the leads, and all under Brad's inspired direction, meaning no one left the theatre disappointed. The curtain call was a continual flow of adulation. Three encores had them returning to the front of the stage as the applause continued to build. And then with one final wave, the troupe climbed down from the heady euphoria always accompanying a packed house to put their characters to bed for the night.

Those working backstage were just as elated at the audience's response and congratulated each one as they hurried past, sporting beaming smiles and chatting non-stop. With elegant modern gowns and dress suits replacing the prim old-fashioned costumes, the whole company hurried out to join family and friends at Stage Door. Boisterous praise and more hearty calls of congratulations greeted them. As a group, they poured onto the streets and wandered around the corner to where the producers had arranged for the after-party, and the air resounded with their jubilant chatter.

Lara and Adam felt as though they were floating on a cloud as they took in everything around them. Amidst all the excitement was a certainty that life was about to become a whole lot different to anything they had ever known before.

It was late when their small party left the celebrations and they were too exhausted to think about nightcaps afterwards. Offering final wishes of congratulations and with goodnights exchanged in the hotel corridor, all three couples went off to their individual rooms. Alice was fast asleep when Adam opened the door to their suite, so Lara tiptoed across and gently nudged her awake. She quickly gathered her things after wishing them a cheery goodnight.

Not much later and thoroughly exhausted, the pair fell into bed ... too tired to do anything more than simply sleep in each other's arms. It had been an emotion-charged day and all they needed was the comfort of their lover's embrace and the luxury of a warm, comfortable bed.

"I'm so proud of you, my darling. Sleep well."

"And you, my Teddy..."

And the rhythmic soft lapping of waves against a distant rock lulled them into Dreamtime.

Chapter 12

All of the papers the following morning contained glowing reviews praising the calibre of everyone involved.

The Sydney Morning Herald had a half page spread which included, "*Hats off to the delightful newcomer, Ms Lara Jennings, for her excellent portrayal of a young Cockney flower seller. The talented young actress gave a thoroughly convincing performance with an accent to make any true East Londoner proud. Those in the audience left feeling as though they had been walking Covent Garden's cobbled streets, dodging puddles tossed from chamber pots and breathing in the pungent aromas of the markets on Drury Lane as Ms Jennings' fine efforts in the role of* Eliza Doolittle *opened the show.*

"*Adam Peters, her former Brisbane stage partner, was a most believable* Henry Higgins, *delivering that all-familiar panache while giving young* Eliza *several large pieces of his scathing tongue. The gifted Queenslander had most patrons cringing at his authentic display of one of theatre's most insensitive characters.*

"*Better keep your eye on these two – they're sure to be gracing our stages for a very long time to come. And big congratulations to the producers, along with Brad Masterton, for having the foresight to cast these two, sight unseen – a truly masterful stroke!*"

Brad's call came through before the chimes from a nearby clocktower had even struck eight o'clock. He was brimming with excitement and conveyed his thanks for all the effort they had put in to make the show such a resounding success. With so many positive comments, he felt confident packed houses would be on the cards for the entire season.

A little while later, the phone rang again. Max didn't even wait for the usual greeting ritual. Instead, he burst into an outpouring of congratulations as soon as Adam answered. His phone had been ringing hot for the last hour with other producers eager to sign them for future projects, and the variety of shows they put forward was mindboggling. Most had already been a hit on Broadway or in London's West End and he was confident his newly proclaimed stars would now be hot ticket items for the cream of future productions.

The recipients of all this acclaim were astonished by all the attention. Both had expected *My Fair Lady* would improve their profiles to some extent, but never dreamed it would happen so quickly or with such far-reaching effects, especially when the ink was barely dry on their contracts or in the press reviews.

It came as no surprise to Adam's parents and they were thrilled to bits everything was falling into place so quickly. Charles had knocked on Lara's door just after seven-thirty with a heavy bundle of newspapers under his arm. All four had been scouring through them when the calls started coming in. His face was beaming as he slapped his son on the back, while Elizabeth gave Lara an enthusiastic hug after Max's call left them both dumbfounded.

"I'm not at all surprised, my boy," Charles boasted, noting the look on the other man's face. "I always said you were destined for the finest theatres in the country rather than just our little suburban one back home."

"Thanks, Dad, but if it weren't for yours and Mum's encouragement, I wouldn't be here. It was your love of theatre that made me want to give it a go in the first place." He looked across at his co-star with a broad smile. "And without you, this gorgeously talented young woman and I would never have met, let alone had the chance to share this amazing experience together."

Lara nodded and moved closer, grasping both of their hands in hers. "He's right, Charles. If you hadn't been so welcoming, or introduced me to this beautiful man, who knows what would've happened."

"Oh, get off with you. I had nothing to do with it. It's your talent – both of you – that brought you to this place. This was always part of your destiny."

Elizabeth went over to kiss Adam's cheek. "Dad's right, dear. You were always destined to share that marvellous voice with the world. This was meant to be whether we were in your life or not." Her face glowed as she turned to Lara and cradled the young woman's face in her hands. "And you too, my dear girl. Someone was sure to pluck you from obscurity the moment you opened that incredible mouth of yours. We're just blessed to have been on the sidelines cheering you on, but it was all your hard work and dedication that got you here."

"This requires a celebratory brunch," her husband joined in. "My shout!"

"I'll be in that," Adam laughed as his stomach let out a loud rumble – whether from excitement or just plain hunger he couldn't tell.

A loud knocking came from the door and Suzie and Ben poked their heads in, waving several newspapers above their heads.

"Look what we've got!" she announced with an excited grin, grabbing her sister's hand. "You'll never guess what the papers are saying about you two!"

The others chuckled as Charles responded, "We already know – I ducked out early this morning and grabbed several copies, and now the calls are coming in thick and fast!"

Over a volley of voices and proud looks, Adam's parents relayed the gist of what had been going on.

"And now we're taking these two out for brunch to celebrate and you're coming with us!" Charles finished, rubbing his hands together with glee.

§

The meal was a relaxed affair as they enjoyed the views from one of the harbour-front cafés across to Luna Park and the famous bridge.

Their plates were almost empty when a young woman sidled over. Her eyes were fixed on Lara, although it was easy to tell she was reluctant to approach.

"Excuse me ... I'm sorry to bother you ... but did you happen to be playing *Eliza Doolittle* at the Theatre Royal last night?"

Adam couldn't resist and quickly ducked his head behind Lara so she couldn't see what he was up to. Grinning at the newcomer, he lifted his eyebrows Groucho Marx' style and nodded enthusiastically.

His antics made all of her shyness disappear. "I *thought* it was you! You look so much like her, even without the shabby clothes or smudges on your face."

Lara turned pink with embarrassment and nodding timidly until she felt Adam's breath on the back of her neck and quickly pushed his face away.

"Get away, you!" she laughed, before turning back to the young woman. "I'm sorry, yes, it was me. I hope you enjoyed the show."

"Oh, I did! The whole thing was fabulous, especially your part!"

"Thank you so much, I'm glad you enjoyed it." She gestured with her thumb to the man dobbing her in and shook her head with a look of feigned disdain. "And this is my friend, Adam Peters, who played *Professor Higgins* – well, at least I *thought* he was my friend. Not *quite* the refined gentleman of last night, as you can see!"

The young woman looked shocked and dipped her head in acknowledgement. "Oh, of course! I'm sorry I didn't recognise you. It's nice to meet you too, Mr Peters. Would you both mind signing this for me, please? I wish I had my programme here, but a napkin will have to do. I loved how you played both those characters – heck, I can't believe I'm actually getting to meet you! Wait 'til I tell all my friends! They'll be sooo jealous. We all thought you did a magnificent job," she gushed, pushing the flimsy scrap in front of Lara.

Those seated around the table exchanged excited grins as her words tumbled out. When Lara asked for her name, both she and Adam added a note of thanks to their signatures. This was their first real taste of stardom, and they were happy to repay her kindness and praise with the small gesture.

"Thank you so much! I really hope I can get back to see you again ... oh, and all the best with the rest of the season," their new fan prattled on. Finally, with a quick wave and an excited, "Bye," she continued on her way.

Lara looked around the table in astonishment. "I can't believe that just happened. How would she have recognised me? I don't look anything like *Eliza* in either persona dressed like this."

"You'd better believe it, Lara-Lu," Suzie answered, grinning at her sister. "And you'd better get used to people spouting your praises. With those striking features, a figure to die for and that long mane of hair, it won't take much for people to recognise you with your photo fronting all the posters plastered around town."

Lara wasn't convinced and quickly poo-poohed her sister's ravings, although the others had no trouble agreeing. For the next several minutes, talk centred on the chance meeting and how this was probably just a small taste of the upcoming rollercoaster ride to fame and fortune, with fans, and maybe even the paparazzi, accosting the new stars wherever they went.

Lara and Adam weren't so sure they wanted to be recognised so easily. Such a furore could cause all sorts of problems and mean they would have to be extra careful with any open displays of affection. Tabloids would have a field day if reporters sniffed out even the slightest hint of truth behind their relationship.

Despite their concerns, nothing was able to dampen Nikki's exuberance. "My mummy's famous! My mummy's famous!" came her excited chant as she skipped on ahead all the way to the hotel.

§

The weeks flew by.

When the lights of the theatre dimmed each night, every seat was full. Afterwards, flashbulbs exploded in their faces when Lara and Adam tried to slip out Stage Door. Keen fans were quick to work out the best place to wait afterwards to catch a glimpse of the two stars. They soon grew accustomed to signing the strange assortment of items thrust at them and were happy to pose for a photo or two. Both felt it was the least they could do after so many spent their hard-earned cash supporting them.

It was heady stuff. Even so, they soon fell back to earth each morning when a little girl landed on their bed, usually complaining about how starving she was.

"If I didn't know better, I'd swear you hadn't eaten for weeks, you little humbug!" Lara growled one morning when the pestering wouldn't let up. She burrowed into the little girl's neck. "I'm sure you must have hollow legs, but who cares ... I'm going to eat you up anyway – you taste sooo scrumptious."

Nikki squirmed to get away. "Don't eat me, Mummy! Helen's taking me on a ferry to Man-al-y today so we can collect shells for our social studies 'scursion and she won't be able to find me if I'm in your tummy!"

"Oh, won't she just! Well, let's see." Both mother and daughter rolled around the bed, giggling loudly as the little tot tried to get away from Lara's sharp teeth.

"I *think* she means Manly, and don't forget me – I want some of that delicious tucker, too," Adam joined in, nibbling on one of the mischief-maker's toes.

Trying hard to get away, it wasn't long before she ended up on the floor in a laughing heap, while the others fell back on the bed, exhausted.

Mornings like this became Adam's favourite part of the day.

§

Their regular Monday off turned into exciting adventures to keep Nikki amused as they explored some of the out-of-the-way places within a day's drive – either up in the mountains to the west of the city, or along the pristine beaches lining the coast, both north and south.

Sometimes they found themselves meandering around the many tiny bays and golden beaches near Gosford, a popular town located on a large inlet about an hour's drive north. Other outings had them fossicking for seashells to decorate more sandcastle masterpieces around the rock pools and beaches of Kiama, a quaint seaside village on the south coast.

On one of these visits, Nikki got the fright of her life when the town's famous blowhole suddenly erupted through a large gap in the rocky outcrop. The wind was blowing from the east and caught the sudden gush of water, drenching her from head to toe. With perfect timing, Adam was able to capture her reaction in a photo – another one to add to her mother's treasured box of memories.

Whenever they had a few hours to spare on a workday morning, the family often headed to the isolated and affluent area of Palm Beach, right at the tip of the northern coastal peninsular. It was a long ribbon of land boasting spectacular beaches quite close to Sydney. Sometimes they even managed to catch film crews shooting the new television series *Home and Away* up near the main surf club or along Palm Beach itself.

After making sandcastles on the squeaky-clean sand away from all the action, usually, they would wander across to the picturesque Pittwater Inlet with its meandering waterways and peaceful bays filled with all manner of small craft rocking on the ingoing or outgoing tide. On their first visit, the trio discovered a great little fish and chip shop along one isolated stretch. It became one of their favourite hangouts where they could bask in the sun along with the anonymity that came from wearing casual clothes and sunhats to disguise themselves, especially, Lara's long hair and Adam's small silver patch at the front of his head. She still claimed the prominent feature as her personal fingerprint.

Spring had arrived just as *My Fair Lady* opened and one of their favourite drives was to the picturesque area around Bowral and Moss Vale in the southern highlands. The rural community was a horse lover's paradise with its green rolling hills dotted with stately homes. Tiny foals on spindly legs frolicked around their protective mothers as they raced along white wooden fences. The only downside was the number of times they had to quell Nikki's pestering to take one of the little beauties home. Even so, they still had to stop many times so she could pat the mares' velvet-smooth noses.

Invariably, the explorers ended up in quiet out-of-the-way cafés, feasting on a delicious assortment of foods from the various regions. During their coastal trips, dishes containing juicy crabmeat, reef fish and plump tiger prawns were often on the menu, accompanied by all manner of sauces and salads, while Nikki nearly always chose something with an Italian flavour. When it came to country blackboard menus, succulent grain-fed lamb and beef or hearty chicken dishes found their way onto their plates, all presented in a tempting variety of ways.

Away from prying eyes, loving fingers often met underneath a tablecloth or a pair of ankles gently brushed against each other in the shadowy depths. As much as they hated having to hide how they felt, it also added a sense of excitement to their relationship. These clandestine exchanges always made their hearts flutter in anticipation of the night ahead.

§

The week before *My Fair Lady* finished its run, Adam decided it was high time they celebrated Lara's triumph at nailing the challenging role. On Sunday night following the matinee, he suggested she put on her best dress for an elegant dinner in one of Sydney's top restaurants. The rave reviews had kept up a steady stream and he knew this would probably be their last opportunity to be out in public before heading back to Brisbane and those covert lives again.

Helen had organised for Nikki to stay with her and Matilda for the weekend after putting up with the girls' constant whinging to spend more time with each other. Often after the heavy make-up had been scraped away and costumes left behind, Lara and Adam joined a few cast mates for a quick bite to eat in one of the smaller eateries or local bars close to the theatre before rushing back to the hotel and falling into bed.

This was their first chance to be on their own in public since visiting the Blue Mountains back when rehearsals were in full swing.

While they were getting ready, Lara's stomach felt like it was playing host to a rabble of butterflies and she kept sending telling grins Adam's way. Seeing her excitement melted his heart and emphasised how much he wanted to shower her with both time and experiences to make her smile.

The friendly maître d' ushered them to a quiet corner with a table set for two. Large panoramic windows offered spectacular views across the city and harbour, and out to the distant headlands. It didn't take long for Carl to recognise the young couple from all the posters plastered around the city. In a whispered aside, he was quick to offer his congratulations on their recent success.

"Thank you," they replied in similar undertones as well as grateful smiles.

His response was simply a polite nod and the trace of a smile, but it was easy to see how thrilled he was to be serving them.

"You look absolutely breathtaking, darling," Adam murmured. His eyes glowed as he looked her up and down when Carl held out her chair.

Her outfit was a deep red satin sheath that clung to her figure in all the right places. The clever design emphasised her small waist and shapely curves with just a hint of cleavage showing above the crossover neckline.

Lara blushed under his scrutiny, unaware it only enhanced the picture she made and made his pulse race even faster.

"Stop it, Teddy! Everyone can see what you're thinking. It's written all over your face!" she implored, though a faint smile gave away her true feelings. Deep down, she relished seeing the look of love and admiration in his eyes – it made her feel both desired and needed, so unlike her former husband.

"I can't help it and that's why I asked for this table. Your dress looks fabulous, and the way the candlelight reflects in your eyes would make any healthy male react the same … and I don't want any competition – not tonight. These few hours are just for us."

Adam's tone and his gaze made her catch her breath.

Their entrees arrived, and still he couldn't look away. As they sampled the tasty seafood morsels, his foot sensuously rubbed the inside of her ankle while those intense dark eyes seemingly drank her in. As she was drawn into their smoky depths, Lara felt as though she was the most desirable woman in the world. Ever so carefully her foot drew the same pattern across his, conveying its own silent message.

"It's Adam, isn't it … and Lara if I remember correctly."

The unexpected greeting made them freeze with fear. Adam carefully pulled his foot away as they tried to mask their reactions when a man and woman stopped by their table. Sporting warm smiles, both seemed familiar to the startled couple, though not enough to immediately identify who they were.

With a quizzical frown, Adam got to his feet as the other man extended his hand. "Ray Carter. We sat opposite each other at the farewell dinner in Salzburg after the seminar last year – the night we were introduced properly. You may remember Anne, my wife."

"Oh, yes, of course. It's good to see you again. I'm so sorry, I didn't mean to be rude," Adam replied, shaking the other man's hand. "Lara, do you remember Ray and Ann?"

"Mmm, yes, I do, and it's nice to see you again after so long. How are you?" Her manner was warm – masking the sense of panic churning inside – and the two women exchanged smiles … one open and friendly, the other more cautious.

"Fine thanks and what a nice surprise to find you here! Ray and I are just having a night on the town. We hardly ever get out much because of the kids, but he decided it was time to give this place a go. Apparently, it's received some excellent reviews."

Lara could only nod as Ray picked up where his wife left off. "Yes, it's good to finally have some time to ourselves, and this place certainly lives up to its reputation. Are you two here on holidays or have you moved to Sydney?"

This time Adam answered. "No, we're heading back to Brisbane next week. We've been down here on business for a short ti—"

Without warning, Anne cut in, addressing both of them with a beaming smile. "Oh, *that's* right. You've been starring in *My Fair Lady*. I saw something about the two of you in the paper a few weeks ago."

"Yes, we are," Lara replied cautiously.

"How exciting! I think I told you about it, Ray. Such a shame we missed out on seeing it, but things get hectic with three young ones underfoot. Gosh, I wish we'd given you our number before leaving Austria. Then you could've rung and come over for a meal. It would've been lovely to catch up – much better than trying to chat over a busy dining table like last time."

Lara kept the forced smile on her face, while inside her heart was pounding. Adam could sense how nervous she was and furtively pressed a reassuring foot against hers.

"Oh, thank you, how kind," she finally forced through her dry throat. "We've actually been extremely busy every night and on weekends too, so I doubt we would've found the time. Still, it's nice of you to think of us."

Ray's eyes lit up. "Of course, I remember now. I think Annie even mentioned something about catching a show." His wife grinned and nodded enthusiastically as he turned to Adam again. "Oh well, time gets away so quickly, and from the sound of it, the season is nearly over. I had no idea you'd given up architecture."

"Oh, I still keep my hand in, even if it has to take a backseat when there's a new production on the go. We finish next Sunday and then I'll be getting back into designing for a while."

"Oh, that's a relief – can't have such a great talent going to waste." He looked at his wife again. "Maybe we could make a date of it next weekend then, Annie – before it closes."

She turned to her husband, "Oh I'd love to! Imagine that, people we know starring in one of the most popular shows in town! The papers were raving about how fabulous you are, Lara. Oh honey, we really must try to get there!" Her excitement was obvious, even to those seated at nearby tables.

Lara and Adam were flattered by her enthusiasm, while at the same time dismayed at the coincidence of choosing this place for dinner. The last thing they needed was for others to see them together, especially anyone from the media.

Glancing around, he noticed countless strangers were now peering at them from all around the room.

"Well, that's settled then! We'll definitely be there to see you next week." Ray added.

"Great, let's hope you enjoy it," Adam nodded, glancing again at Lara.

"And how's your little girl ... Nikki wasn't it?" Anne went on, plucking the name from her recollections of that night.

"Goodness, what a great memory!" Lara answered in surprise, not wanting to be rude despite all the attention they were getting. "And she's doing fine. Growing like a weed and keeping us on our toes."

"So are our three. I can't get over how quickly they grow up!"

Lara was just about to respond when the waiter returned with the receipt for the Sydneysiders' bill.

Once again, Ray put out his hand and Adam took it. "Well, it was good to see you again and sorry for the intrusion. Now we'd better leave you to enjoy the rest of your meal in peace ... and I look forward to seeing you on stage next weekend. Goodnight."

After bidding each other farewell and watching the others disappear into the lift, Lara let out a huge sigh of relief. "Oh, I can't believe it ... of *all* the people to run into! Now what are we going to do?"

"Nothing, sweetheart, don't worry. Everything'll be okay, you'll see. It's not as though we're in Brisbane to cross paths with them all the time."

"But they're coming to the show! They'll see our surnames are different on the billboards and programme."

"They already have if they saw it in the paper, but that's okay. Married actresses often use their maiden names so it won't matter. And besides, I'm sure they'll just come to see us perform and then rush straight home to the kids rather than hang around afterwards."

"I hope so," she replied, concern still showing in her eyes.

The unexpected encounter had put a dampener on their evening. After hurrying through the main course, Adam suggested they leave rather than wait for dessert and coffee.

He could see she was too nervous to enjoy herself and they made sure not to touch or exchange any looks that may reveal their true feelings to all those other eyes that kept glancing their way – his well-intentioned plans for a special private celebration now swept away through the chance meeting.

§

The final weekend rolled around much quicker than expected. The Ashworths flew down early Friday afternoon and their son and Lara, along with an excited little girl, were at the airport to meet them. Elizabeth was determined to support

161

them through this trying time, knowing how hard it would be to say goodbye to these roles, not to mention the added sadness of being forced apart again when it was all over. Charles had an underlying reason for making the journey, although he hadn't mentioned anything to his wife.

While the others left for the theatre around five to prepare for the evening performance, the visitors were happy to look after Nikki and catch up on all her news. It also gave Helen her first Friday night off since the opening. After several stories were read, far too many turns of *Hide and Seek* to count, as well as a load of piggyback rides before bedtime, they were exhausted when the little girl finally dropped off to sleep around eight.

"This grandparenting thing certainly brings a lot of joy, but it's sure tiring too," Charles exclaimed with a groan, plonking himself down on the sofa and pulling Elizabeth down with him. "Just as well there's only one of her!"

When the others arrived home, Elizabeth rushed to put the kettle on, and they spent the next little while chatting over a late cuppa before retiring to their separate suites. It had been a long day and all four of them were looking forward to a good night's sleep.

The sun was shining brightly when they woke, so a visit to Bronte Beach seemed the perfect way to pass the morning. Nikki was in her element, chasing seagulls and paddling in the wave runoff while the adults looked on.

Adam couldn't resist and ran over to join in, grabbing the little girl and throwing her into the air. Her squeals of delight brought smiles to the faces of several others enjoying a day out on a glorious spring day. Afterwards, he took her by the hand and the pair of them had a great time jumping over countless rows of waves flowing to the shore. It wasn't long before they both ended up drenched from the waist down with small patches of foam clinging to her bathers and his once pristine shorts and shirt. Several big blobs dangled from the ends of her long plaits and she used them to tickle his nose and chin, which left him looking like a bedraggled Santa Claus.

Exhausted though still laughing, they hunkered down above the waterline to build another sandcastle; this time in the shape of a mermaid with long strands of seaweed for hair. His artistic skills came to the fore and soon a small crowd gathered around as Adam and his little helper added a few finishes touches to the sweeping tail. The detail was incredible with rows of fish-like scales fashioned from the tiny shells Nikki had scavenged along the shore and among a few rock pools. It truly was a masterpiece and Lara quickly whipped out her camera to remember the special day. Several onlookers did the same, taking photos from all different angles. Thankfully, the stars were too hard to recognise out of costume, but they still made sure none of those shots pictured them together.

It had been a relaxing few hours until Adam looked at his watch and noticed it was just coming up to two o'clock. They needed to get back to the hotel for a rest before preparing for the night's performance. With remnants from the picnic lunch now packed away, the family wandered up the street to hail a taxi.

Elizabeth sensed Lara's sadness and deliberately slowed her pace, linking arms with her 'almost daughter' and offering a caring smile. Adam and Charles went on ahead, swinging Nikki between them with her giggles keeping them company.

"My dearest girl, I'm so sorry this special time is coming to an end. It's easy to tell how much fun you've all had and I love seeing my boy so relaxed and enjoying life for a change. I just wish there was something I could do to make things easier."

"No good at hiding it, am I?" Lara grimaced with a look of resignation on her face. "Don't worry, I'll be okay. I knew this was coming – we both did – and at least we can be grateful for these last four months."

"You're an amazing young woman with an incredible attitude. I'm so proud of you."

"Oh, I don't know about that, but thanks, Elizabeth. It means so much to have your support."

"It does my heart good knowing you've had this time together. You've been such a blessing to him and I'm truly grateful."

"Oh, it's so easy to love him - I'm the one who's blessed. We've shared so much and had the best time ... far better than most ever get to experience in an entire lifetime. I'm dreading going home, but I have to remember to look on the bright side. It just means going back to accepting we can only share small snatches of time, but it's not like we'll never see each other again. Even when we're away for different shows, I'm sure we'll find ways to catch-up somehow. The love we share will never change."

Elizabeth's heart was breaking as she watched the subject of their conversation chatting to her husband up ahead.

"Sometimes I could just shake that boy. He's had to put up with so much over the years but still won't leave her. If I didn't love him so much, I'd kick him in the backside and tell him to wake up to himself!" She shrugged forlornly. "Still, I know what he's like once he's made a commitment to something – even if it is one-sided – and he won't break his word, no matter how much he wants to. I'm just so sorry you're the one getting hurt in the meantime. You don't deserve this."

Lara tried hard to smile through the sadness. "But I wouldn't change him for the world and that's exactly what drew me to him in the first place. Men like Adam are few and far between. From the moment he opened up about his life, my heart was his – and I haven't been the same since. And I knew what I was getting into, so I can't blame him" —her voice caught as she went on— "but I can't stop loving him either ... he's as much a part of me as I am."

Elizabeth squeezed the young woman's arm against her side, knowing there was nothing more she could say to ease her pain. They had to work it out between them while she and Charles remained in the background, always ready to offer whatever support was necessary.

"Well, just remember I'm always here for you. Charles and I will do everything in our power to provide a safe haven where you can both be together, even if it is only for a few hours when you're both free. We'll never forsake you, no matter what happens – you're the daughter I always longed for, and I love you very, very much."

Lara's eyes welled with tears as she leaned into the other one's shoulder. "I love you too, dear friend, and I'm so grateful to have you in my life. Thank you."

§

Everyone was feeling weary when they arrived back at the hotel.

"I'm off for a short kip," Charles announced, "this old man could do with some shut-eye after a certain little cutie wore me out chasing seagulls!"

"Yeah, I could do with one myself. She wore me out too and I need to get out of these wet things, the little humbug!" Adam growled, pointing to his grubby shorts before chasing the culprit around the room.

Both of them ended up on the floor in a heap, arms and legs going everywhere as he tickled her tummy until they were puffing with exhaustion.

"Okay, Missy Tuppence, it's time you went for a nap too. Come on, say goodbye to everyone," Lara said, picking the little girl up and carting her off to the smaller bedroom.

Nikki was fast asleep only a few minutes after her head hit the pillow – and Lara was much the same. Adam couldn't sleep thinking about the week ahead and having to return to his former life. He lay on his side watching her sleep and offering up a prayer of thanks for being given the opportunity to share the last few months with the woman he loved with all his heart.

Later that afternoon, the family gathered in Lara's living room for a chat over a hot cuppa. Nikki perched between Adam and her mother on one couch, doodling away in a colouring book, while his parents sat opposite.

It was a welcome chance to relax for a few minutes before heading off to the furore of costumes, wigs and makeup. Both the mother and daughter had their heads together, jointly colouring in a picture of Cinderella fleeing from the ball as the others chatted quietly in the background.

The drawing reminded Lara of a night at a gala dinner when she was dressed similarly to the character in the picture. She could still hear Nikki's warning not to stay out late in case she lost her shoe and Uncle Adam couldn't find her. And now the image seemed to be pointing her to this moment in time – their ball was about to come to an end, and it was nearly time for Lara to flee, leaving her prince behind to cope on his own. So many parallels wrapped up in a silly old fairy-tale.

"Mummy, why are you crying?" a little voice piped up as Lara's finger dashed away a drop of moisture when it fell on the page.

"Don't be silly, I'm not crying, that was just some water dripping from the ceiling," Lara responded, ducking her head even lower and pretending to add a few finishing touches to the glass slipper.

"Yes, you are. Your eyes are all shiny and your nose is—"

"Come with me, young lady. I think it's time we washed your hands and I helped you get ready for bed before Helen arrives," Elizabeth interrupted kindly, sending Adam a knowing look. With the little girl's hand tightly ensconced in hers, they headed to the bathroom.

Moving tactfully to a far window, Charles looked out to the harbour expanse, though he was oblivious to the eye-catching panorama. Without saying a word, Adam reached out and gently stroked Lara's hand, fighting back the tears himself. She turned away as another trickled down her cheek. A sudden rush of guilt hit him, knowing his indecisive actions were the cause of all her suffering. With a look of helplessness, all he could do was brush the tear away, pull her head firmly into his shoulder and hold her close.

Charles understood the young man's despair and his spirit dropped. What he had to tell them would only to add to the heartache. It was the reason he had put off the inevitable for as long as possible ... and a way to give them these last few hours before their dreams came crashing down all over again.

§

Just minutes before they were due to walk out the door, the phone rang. It was Helen apologising and saying she was feeling sick and wouldn't be able to look after Nikki. Elizabeth offered to stay behind – at least she could still attend the final performance the next day. Charles decided to stay behind with her. There were a few pressing overseas business calls in need of his attention and the timing was perfect with the time differences.

"Just go and enjoy yourselves and don't be in any rush to get back. We don't mind staying up late to look after our favourite little Poppet. You could even spend an hour or two afterwards at a nice little café to have some time to yourselves," Elizabeth suggested as they said their farewells. She was still worried about Lara and knew this would be their last opportunity to spend time in a public arena before that secret life had to rear its head again.

"Thanks, Mum," Adam said, blowing her a kiss as he closed the door.

The taxi was already waiting, so they slid into the backseat and he tucked Lara's hand in his. "I can't believe we only get two more chances to do this. I'll miss waking up beside you, knowing we have the whole day ahead of us."

The moment the words left his mouth, he wanted to slap himself. With the memory of her tears fresh in his mind, how could he have been so stupid to bring it all up again. Sighing in unison, their fingers took up that usual slow dance across each other's palm as the full realisation of his words sank in.

Suddenly, like a butterfly breaking free of its chrysalis prison, Lara shook her shoulders. "Okay, that's it! I'm not wasting one more minute thinking about next week. You and I are going to enjoy every single second we have left and just thank God for giving us these last few months. Instead of feeling sad, we should be celebrating, so that's just what we're going to do!"

Looking into his eyes, she smiled and planted a firm kiss on his cheek. "And *Professa 'iggins*, jus' so ya know, ya've made me da 'appiest womin in da world, ya 'av, an' ay takes me 'at off t' ya. An' ay ain't gunna be sad no more. Wiv you in me loif, it's bin righ' rosy n' 'appy, so I ain't gunna waste me toim worryin' 'bout tomorra."

It was the perfect pick-me-up, and Adam split his sides laughing, putting on a face only the stuffy professor would wear.

"Well, just you look here, young *Eliza*," he responded in a very prim English gentleman's voice, "I will have you know too much enjoyment of anything can lead to deep smile lines and fierce palpitations of the heart, which is *definitely* no way for any good, self-respecting young woman to behave!"

He wagged his finger and looked her deep in the eyes. "And, in addition, my dear *Miss Doolittle*, if you are not careful, you will become so relaxed I will never be able to turn you into the prim and proper young lady you were meant to become, and we certainly cannot have that now, can we? Rollicking frivolity is for the less-fortunate, not the well-to-do."

"Well, *Professa*, if tha's wot's gunna 'appen, ay don' fink ay wanna become a propa laydee *af'er* all! Ay fink ay'm gonna stay a poor flah-gil, ay do. Ay don' wanna become all 'oity-toity loik dem mis'rble tarts in posh ol' Mayfair who couldna smile even if ya tickled 'em on dere bloomin' arses!"

Even the taxi driver let out a loud chortle as he dropped them off at Stage Door. Their playfulness had changed the mood inside the car dramatically, and a much happier couple walked through the entrance, determined to focus on the task at hand rather than a bleak future.

§

Their performances that evening were as good as any over the eight-week run and Brad felt Lara's depiction of the wretched *Eliza* would be worthy of a Tony Award had she been appearing on Broadway. With the range of accents delivered perfectly, and the way she and Adam played off each other for the entire two acts, the audience went away totally satisfied. The price of a ticket was well worth this amusing night of entertainment.

Remembering Elizabeth's last-minute assurances, they decided to team up with a few from the cast for a late-night supper before going back to the hotel. Most had made friends easily because of their mutual love of music and theatre, and none of them was looking forward to saying final goodbyes the following day, although the luxury of being home in their own beds was a great incentive for most.

Just as they were about to leave through the back door, Paul and Max appeared in front of them. The director and agent had travelled down together to catch the final two shows after several glowing reviews had made their way into the local Brisbane papers. Their hometown was proud of its local stars, so they wanted to see for themselves how far the show had metamorphosed over its short run.

The young couple was thrilled to see their familiar faces and Adam immediately invited the two men to join them as they made their way to a little-known French café only a block or two away. It had become a regular hangout for most of the cast after shedding those restrictive costumes and resuming the normality of everyday life.

Max had met a couple from the ensemble during other productions and they were quick to make him feel welcome. The atmosphere around the large table was relaxed just swapping stories and enjoying each other's company. He even tried to entice one of the young supporting actors into joining his stable of clients by offering him a tempting deal.

"I appreciate the offer, Max, but I've already been offered the role of *Julian March* from *42nd Street,* so I'll be heading to Melbourne next month, and my agent has a few other things in the pipeline after that."

"Oh well, that's a shame. I could've done with you in my line-up. Not to worry, all the best with the new show."

He turned to Lara and Adam with a broad smile. "Well, he may not want me, but I've got some good news for you two. Apart from the obvious, there's another reason I wanted to see you tonight. I've recently had a phone call from the producers of *My Fair Lady,* and they want to offer you the leads in Rodgers and Hammerstein's *The Sound of Music,* which is due to open in Melbourne in April. They're most impressed by the way you both work together, so we've been in discussions for a couple of weeks."

Lara and Adam looked at each other in astonishment.

"Can you imagine Nikki's face when we tell her?" He caught Max's puzzled expression. "Oh sorry, *The Sound of Music* is Lara's daughter's favourite show and she'll be beside herself knowing her mother's playing *Maria.*"

"Well, there's no way I'll be saying anything until we start rehearsals ... that's if I agree to the part," Lara answered. "I couldn't bear all her nagging or the thought of watching that video over and over again while she makes sure I get my lines right!"

Max looked at her in astonishment. "What do you mean *if* you agree? Of course, you'll agree – you'd be mad not to. It's one of the hottest numbers around."

"Oh yeah, I realise that. I just don't want to be too presumptuous until my name's on the contract, or at least 'til I've heard all the details. Besides, Nikki's been away from home for long enough, so I need to make sure it's the right thing to do for her as well."

"Well, I can give you the details as I know them. Rehearsals are due to begin the second week of February, and it's playing at the historic *Princess Theatre*, which has just undergone a huge renovation. The opening's set down for the middle of April with a run of six weeks. Again, they're prepared to provide full care and tutoring for Nikki, and you'll be staying in a suite similar to the one you're in now with a full kitchen and separate bedrooms. There's really no need to worry."

Adam reached under the table to squeeze Lara's hand. He understood fully why she wanted to put the little girl first, but he was still hoping with every part of him they would get the chance to share another stage, especially so soon after this one.

"It does sound good, but—"

The agent wasn't prepared to give up just yet, knowing what a coup it was to have two from his clientele chosen for one of the most popular productions ever.

"It's mid-November now, so that means you'll have three months from when this finishes to the start of rehearsals – more than enough time, I should imagine, for everything to be organised before heading down south. So what do you say, Lara? Can I tell them yes?"

"It sounds fantastic, Max, and *Maria* is certainly every actress' dream, but I'd still like a few days to think it over as it means Nikki would have to miss a lot of school again and it's right at the beginning of a new school year."

"Sure, I understand, and I didn't expect you to sign off on it tonight. I just want you to know what's on offer. How about you, Adam, are you in?"

"It sure sounds promising with the schedule and everything. I'll just need a bit of time to think it over, too. How about I get back to you next week when I'm back in Brisbane and can look at what's happening at the office?"

His only motivation for delaying an answer was because he didn't want to contemplate travelling interstate and leaving Lara and Nikki behind if she turned it down.

Placing a friendly but persuasive arm around their shoulders, Max responded, "Well, I'll look forward to hearing from both of you *and* with affirmative answers." He sent a playful glower Lara's way before breaking into another smile. "Now tell me everything that's been going on with *My Fair Lady*. The reviews have been fantastic and Brad's rung a few times singing your praises."

After a conversation that steered clear of the earlier discussion, Paul leaned in between them and whispered so Max couldn't hear, "I think you'd be crazy not to take these new roles, but if you decided not to, there's always a little theatre in Brisbane that would gladly welcome you back."

§

An hour or so later they made their way to the hotel, tiptoeing into Lara's suite in case Elizabeth had nodded off. There was no need to worry. She was curled up on the sofa watching the end of a late-night movie and greeted them with an affectionate smile.

"So how was your night? I want to hear all about it, but how about I go and put the kettle on first for a nice hot cuppa before bed."

With cups in hand and relaxing in the soft glow of two lamps, they told her Max's news. Naturally, she was delighted and excited for them both.

"Of *course* you'll take it," came the quick reply as she bustled over to give Adam's broad shoulders a hug from behind. Looking down at Lara with a huge grin on her face, she implored, "How could you resist being leading lady again to *this* gorgeous man!"

Lara laughed at her blatant attempt at persuasion. "Well, when you put it like that..."

It was the perfect way to end the night. Draining the last dregs from her cup, Elizabeth bid them a fond goodnight before crossing the hall to Adam's suite where she and Charles were staying. Her husband was still up after just finishing the last of his business calls. Excitedly, she relayed the news, but couldn't help noticing his sudden look of concern despite trying to hide it by burying his nose in a briefcase lying on the desk.

"What was that look for, darling? Aren't you happy for them? I thought you'd be thrilled."

"I am, sweetheart. It's a wonderful opportunity. Maybe I'm just tired," he mumbled in an effort to dodge her questions. "Let's just go to bed for now and then we can talk about it in the morning."

Snuggling up in each other's arms, he went to turn out the light when his wife ran the back of her finger softly down his cheek. "I'm so glad we have each other. I can't imagine my life without you."

"Then it's just as well you'll never have to find out," he purred, moving closer to claim her mouth with his.

"Oh, Charles, I thought you said you were tired..."

"Never too tired for you, my Bessie."

169

§

Lara and Adam were too wound up to sleep after the excitement of Max's offer. Stretching out along the couch, they watched the lights of the cars streaming back and forth across the famous bridge. It was a beautiful balmy night and the French doors were open to catch the breeze. She leaned back in his arms while his hands painted a delicate pattern across her stomach and then over and around her breasts as they discussed the pros and cons of taking the roles. There was no question about this being a dream opportunity. The concerned mother simply had a few misgivings for her daughter's sake.

"I think we need to get together in Max's office to really nut out everything and then you can decide. What do you think, Baby?" Adam suggested, nibbling at her ear as his hands continued this sensuous form of art.

"*I* think we need to go to bed right now and I'll show you just how much *Maria* wants *Georg*," Lara replied with a saucy grin, turning around to run a pair of teasing lips all over his neck. "Then we can decide whether we're *really* suited for those roles!"

The look in her eye made him burst out laughing, and with one firm swoop, he had her in his arms. Carrying her into the bedroom, his foot kicked the door closed with a firm bang.

Chapter 13

Dappled sunlight playing across the curtains summoned Lara and Adam from a deep sleep. It was easy to take it as an optimistic omen the finale would be the perfect culmination to a fantastic run. Their bed offered a peaceful interlude before having to face the reality of what this day meant, especially with Suzie and Lucy and their respective partners expected to arrive later in the day. These few quiet moments would most likely be their only chance to be alone.

A pair of silky lips trailed over her eyelids as he brushed a loose strand of hair from her face. "The best part of any day is waking up next to you, beautiful lady."

Lara could hear the smile in his voice before she even caught a glimpse of his face. With their lives about to take a dramatic turn, Adam was determined to take advantage of this day and everything it held.

"And there's no place I'd rather be," she assured him, reading the poignancy behind his words. Her expression reflected all he was feeling and the trust emanating from her eyes as she looked up at him made him catch his breath.

After losing his parents so tragically, Charles and Elizabeth had more than made up for their absence by offering him their unconditional love from the moment he turned up on their doorstep. Sadly, because of his youthful stubbornness and determination in thinking he knew best, the young man's heart had taken a battering by the woman he called his wife.

It was only in Lara's arms he had found the love of a true soulmate and the contentment that comes from being with that one person who makes you whole. She didn't have to do anything to make him feel he had the whole world at his feet except look at him as she was now ... and his greatest wish was to wake up like this every day for the rest of his life.

Bold fingertips danced a sensuous cadence as she ran them through his hair. The intimate contact caused a deep stirring to ripple through her every pore and Lara could feel all her senses come awake as she tenaciously massaged his scalp and neck. Adam couldn't hold back a loud moan as delicious shivers ran up and down his spine and his response drove her on even further.

Soon her teeth joined in, teasing him relentlessly by nibbling around his chin like a caterpillar chewing on a leaf. The sensation awoke even more torturous tingling and his moans went from ecstasy to agony within the space of a few seconds.

His vain attempts to hold it all together meant Lara relaxed her guard. Keen to gain the upper hand, Adam ducked his head to escape this impish form of torment, and now it was his turn to become the provocateur as his mouth sought out her neck and a ravenous tongue traced the curves of her tempting earlobe.

The room suddenly filled with a mixture of groans and giggles as Lara tried to evade her lover's indomitable assault. Just as quickly and much to his delight, she was back at it again, kneading his head and neck with fingers conveying just how much she yearned for him with every touch.

And all the while, they devoured each other with their eyes.

Times like these were part of what made their relationship so special and unique – their lovemaking wasn't only confined to a burning unbridled passion. Often it took on a form of playfulness and spontaneity, adding a wonderful other dimension to so many of their intimate interludes.

Her eyes sparkled, just like the sunbeams dancing across the coverlet, and he couldn't help smothering her in kisses as his heart swelled with a welcome sense of wholeness. No matter how often they made love, each time it became a new journey to their own form of paradise.

Her lips responded instantly and that earlier frivolity returned. Once again, she gnawed at his jaw-line, and it wasn't long before her hungry mouth crept across his neck, leaving a damp trail in its wake. Finally, she focussed all her attention on one vulnerable spot just to the side of the protruding bump in his throat – the one bearing his name.

Letting out an astonished chuckle, he pulled away again, this time holding her wrists firmly against the pillows. "Don't you *dare* bite me, you little vixen! I can't go on stage this afternoon with red marks all over my neck! The old professor would *never* have allowed *Eliza* to get close enough to do that."

"And that's *exactly* where his problem lay!" Lara retorted, chortling and wriggling beneath his grip. "If he'd actually *let* himself fall in love with her, then he would've treated her more like a woman than a project. *And* he might've actually *enjoyed* life instead of merely analysing it all the time. Thank goodness you're nothing like him!"

"You'd better believe it," came a determined growl as he now sought to get his fill by chewing on an exposed slice of stomach peeking out from beneath the sheets.

Adam's lips were well-experienced with all her vulnerable spots, and this new foray caused all sorts of sensations – from desire through to agony – to the point where Lara wasn't quite sure just how much more she could take.

Out of breath and weak from trying to break free, she pushed his face away with a loud, "Teddy, *stop!*"

"Oh, so now you *don't* want me! Make up your mind, woman!"

His demand was accompanied by a mock scowl, though it didn't last for long. Soon he was laughing along with her as she struggled to take in some much-needed oxygen between chuckles. Thoroughly exhausted, they both collapsed next to each other, gasping hard – but even that wasn't enough to diminish their simmering need.

Seeing her so relaxed and vulnerable made the temptation even harder to resist. He raised himself on one elbow as sultry, passion-filled eyes sent a message filled with both desire and need. She read him perfectly and bit down gently on her bottom lip while still holding his gaze. Unable to fight this new form of lure, Adam's free hand glided over Lara's bare shoulders and then across her breasts. Her chest heaved and heart raced under his loving ministrations as waves of desire surged through her veins.

This was their secret place ... a private space free of care where they could become the centre of each other's universe.

She reached up and inched her mouth across his neck again ... this time with no sign of that earlier playfulness. Instead, her lips began a slow waltz, beginning from his chin then moving around to first one ear and then the other, each touch like a butterfly's wing flitting across an open flower.

He succeeded in staying motionless for as long as possible until eventually, this new form of enticement became unbearable. In one fluid movement, he caught her up in a crushing embrace as his mouth possessed those tempting lips ... and his straining body pressed hard against the one it would always hunger for.

Like a she-bear, Lara emitted another loud groan – not because of the weight of him ... purely from the current of craving flowing through her veins. She matched the depth of his kiss with a passion that drove both of them nearer and nearer the edge. Neither one could get enough of their mate – the power of longing was like an unquenchable thirst. The more they drank, the more they wanted – even their eyes seemed to consume one another, while fingertips became instruments of pleasure in masterful hands, taking both of them to the point of no return.

Soft moans rose from deep down in her core as she began moving her body in a rhythm to match his ... until at last they were able to satisfy the other's deepest yearning. This was their time – an exclusive moment when all their senses aligned and everything else faded away. Nothing else mattered except a desire to be all their beloved needed right at this moment ... and time seemed to stand still as two became one flesh.

This was perfection in its rawest form – the way the Creator of the universe always intended love-making to be … absolute oneness leading to a wholeness of body, mind and soul.

§

And still that illustrious golden thread continued on its purposeful journey.

§

Half an hour later, Lara was in the bathroom putting the finishing touches to her make-up and sending a satisfied smile to her reflection, when Adam heard a tiny voice outside the door.

"Mummy, Annabelle's getting hungry! I think it's time for breakfast."

With a dramatic flourish, he opened the door and swept the little girl up in a tight hug. "I'm getting hungry too, Annabelle's mummy. So how about we grab *your* mummy and then we can go and join the others downstairs?"

"I think that's a *very* good idea," she nodded solemnly … until he tickled her tummy and a burst of uncontrollable giggles filled the room. As a cheeky form of payback, she started playing with his eyebrows as though trying to turn his eyelids inside out.

"You're just a little scallywag! Now go and fetch your mother so we can get something to eat," he laughed, putting her down and affectionately swatting her on the backside as she ran off to the bathroom.

Pulling on his shoes, Adam eavesdropped on their happy mother/daughter chatter, and he was convinced life couldn't get any better.

They found his parents seated at a corner table of the hotel dining room. It was perfectly positioned to give uninterrupted views of the harbour. As Adam helped Lara to her seat, Elizabeth couldn't help smiling at how well suited they were as a couple. It was obvious from their shared expressions and the way Lara's hand ran along the inside of his forearm their relationship was growing stronger every day. Her son had never looked so contented, and it did her mother-heart good to know he had found the love of his life, even though there was one major obstacle in the way. God willing, he would be able to remedy that soon.

Charles also caught the loving gestures, but unlike his wife, his heart was heavy.

The conversation centred on the upcoming family reunion with Suzie and Ben, as well as a long-awaited catch-up with Lucy and Jeff. Their plane was due around eleven, in plenty of time to ensure they were there for the final performance. Adding Paul and Max into the mix, and with Adam's parents already in residence, it was going to be a lively group to help carry them through this difficult time.

Nikki couldn't keep still. She was impatient to see Aunty Suzie again and her constant chatter managed to distract Lara from noticing the heaviness in Charles' demeanour. It was a different story with Adam. He kept glancing at his father, wondering what could possibly be wrong. Elizabeth put it down to her husband just being tired after their intimate interlude the night before.

With breakfast over, the troubled father knew he couldn't put the news off any longer. Tossing a soiled napkin onto his plate, he leaned over to whisper into Adam's ear. "Son, there's something we need to discuss. How about you and I go for a walk along the waterfront while we chat?"

Adam didn't like the sound of this. "Sure, Dad, is everything okay?"

Charles rose from the table. His only response was a slight shrug of his shoulders and a worried frown. As he turned around, all the women saw was a loving smile.

"Excuse us, ladies. I need to borrow this one for a little while. It's too nice a day to waste just sitting inside and I could do with a walk."

Lara had witnessed the exchange between the two men and she looked quizzically towards Adam. All he could do was shrug his shoulders and drop a quick kiss on her forehead before following his father outside. The two women watched through the picture window as their men walked slowly along the boardwalk, hands plunged deep in their pockets and Charles' head bowed low.

"Do *you* know what's going on, Elizabeth?"

The older woman shook her head as a frown creased her brow. She knew her husband far too well to believe his sole motivation was the need for a morning walk.

§

"What's up, Dad? You look like someone's died or something."

Oh, Adam, if you only knew ... quite possibly the death of all your dreams.

Charles didn't say anything for a moment as he searched for the words to begin ... then he took a deep breath.

"I received a phone call a couple of weeks ago." He pulled in another lungful of air before continuing. "It was Trina and at first I didn't recognise her ... she sounded so different."

Adam's heart was racing. For Charles to be so reticent meant it had to be something significant and the younger man was unsure just how much he wanted to hear. Swallowing hard, he stared across the water, not game enough to look into his father's eyes.

"She's moved back into the house ... nearly two months ago – while we were down here for opening night, as it turns out. Apparently, Judith did all she could to entice her into drinking again, even taunting her by saying she's far too boring to be around when she's sober. It all came to a head when Judith went on a long binge and turned abusive. From the sounds of it, that was just the 'wake-up call' she needed, as Trina put it. Anyway, she hasn't touched a drop since you've been

175

away and hasn't seen Judith at all in the last seven weeks."

Adam was in a state of shock and not really sure how he should be feeling. When he eventually summoned up an answer, his tone was cold. "What's she been doing with herself, then? We all know she can't stand being alone for any length of time without a drink in her hand. And who's been preparing her meals and looking after the house? I let the cleaner go before we came away because she was staying with Judith."

Charles could only imagine the range of emotions his son was wrestling with as their slow tread followed the harbour wall. "You probably won't believe this, but she's been taking cooking lessons, and the house is spotless ... she's even spending time in the garden, so the whole place looks immaculate. I went over last week – I didn't want to say anything without seeing for myself just in case it was all a ploy – but, as much as I hate to admit it, I'm really starting to believe she's a changed woman."

The other man could only stare at the ground with his mouth set as Charles continued.

"It's over a year since her time in rehab and she was quick to assure me there's only been that one slip-up at Christmas time. From what she says – and I must say she sounded convincing – not a single drop has touched her lips since then."

Adam started raking his hands through his hair, unable and unwilling to believe everything he was hearing. The fear in his eyes was almost tangible ... and yet lingering on the border of this avalanche of mistrust, Charles could also detect a faint glimmer of optimism.

The older man well knew how much his son wanted Trina to change, even now when there was no love left – not for the sake of their relationship, but for the sake of her future. He could never wish harm on his wife in any form. It was the main reason Adam had stayed with her all these years – until Lara came along and now fear for her and Nikki's safety was the only thing holding him there.

Charles paused for a moment, staring at the dark watery depths below their feet, almost as though he suspected something menacing lurked there ... and then he took another deep breath.

"And I'm afraid there's something else you need to know." Once again, he paused, loath to utter the words held in harness for weeks. "Trina's insisting she's going to do everything in her power to become the wife you've always wanted ... and she can't wait for you to come home so she can prove it to you."

Adam looked at him in disbelief, before letting out a mournful groan. "*Nooo!* I'm don't want that – she hasn't been my wife for years, other than in name only. And it's never been my home – it's just a house we both live in. Lara's the only one I want to make a home with. I couldn't do it to her ... not after last time." He shook his head from side to side, pleading with his father.

"I understand, son, and I'm not expecting you to believe her – but at least hear her out. Then make a decision."

"No, Dad! I can't ... I *won't* go back to being a husband the way she wants. How could she possibly expect me just to pick up where we left off seven years ago? She had her chance!" he flung out bitterly, kicking hard at the brick barrier fronting the boardwalk.

"I understand, son, truly I do, and I hate having to be the one to tell you. Don't forget, I'm only the messenger. I just felt it was best coming from me so you know what to expect ... and now ... there's one more thing you need to know..." He paused once more, and this time it was for much longer, dreading the reaction sure to follow.

Adam stopped dead in his tracks, standing motionless and holding his breath. His voice was cold. "What?"

"She's coming to the show this afternoon. There was a review in *The Sunday Mail* raving about how powerful your rapport is on stage, so she knows Lara's down here too and figures she's your leading-lady in every sense of the word. She said she wants to talk to both of you. Of course, I haven't mentioned a word about your relationship. Still, it didn't take much for her to figure it out herself."

Adam shook his head in anger and his face was a picture of despair as he imagined the scene. "I won't let her! She's not coming anywhere near either of us – especially not Lara. I'll just tell the doorman he's not to let her in. She's not going to ruin my life again!"

Charles grabbed him by the arm. "Adam, *listen* to yourself! You can't stop her from coming to the theatre. I understand what you're saying, but you need to look at this sensibly. The last thing you want is to cause a scene. You know what Trina can be like if you get her riled up. Besides, she actually admitted to understanding why you would turn to Lara after the way she's treated you over the years. And, as unbelievable as it sounds, I think she means it. I hate saying this, but you really need to talk to her ... but of course it's up to you."

It broke Charles' heart to see his beloved boy on the brink of true happiness about to have it snatched away again – and not only any possible future with Lara and Nikki further down the track, but also for his onstage career. He knew if Trina caused a scene in front of everyone, it could be disastrous for both his and Lara's future career paths, not to mention how mortified she would be to have their relationship dragged through the mud.

The urgent tone in his father's voice penetrated Adam's anguish and a semblance of wisdom squirrelled its way through the gloomy depths of the shocking news. All he could do was nod dejectedly and drawl, "Okay ... you're right. I do have to talk to her, but I *must* protect Lara. I don't want Trina speaking to her at all, so I'll need your help to shield her, Dad."

"I'll do my best, son. Still, I can't promise anything. It's not like before where I could access backstage. If I do see Trina, I'll try to keep her occupied, but you're the one who'll have to be there for Lara, both before and after the show." He placed a caring arm around his son's shoulders and shook his head. "I'm sorry to have to break all this bad news, today of all days, but I needed to warn you about what to expect this afternoon. Now, come on, we'd better go back before the others start to worry and send out a search party."

Adam turned to his father with a sceptical frown. "It's a bit late now after the way you looked during breakfast. I knew something was going on and I'm sure they did too." Like before, he ran his hands through his hair, frustrated and angry and in no way ready to face the truth about the changes in his wife. "*Grrr*, I don't *believe* this! I just wish I'd left when I had the chance ... while she was still in rehab. Why was I so *stupid!*"

They retraced their steps with Charles' hand resting on his son's shoulder, doing all he could to convey his support and concern.

With her eyes still glued to the window, Lara couldn't help noticing the expression on Adam's face when he came into view. She knew instantly something terrible had happened. The only other time she had seen him this upset was in the aftermath of the pantomime. Her heart dropped, and she stood up as the men entered the room, deep worry lines masking those beautiful features.

"Darling, what's wro—"

Before she could finish, Adam took her face in his hands, and his lips claimed hers in a deep kiss that left her breathless, almost as though he was trying to draw her into the deepest part of his soul ... and hide her there. The dining room was crowded, but he didn't care who saw them together – nothing mattered any more except Lara and assuring her of his love.

"What's going on, Charles? What's happened?" Elizabeth demanded, just as concerned as her young friend. Pushing the chair back, she clutched at her husband's arm as she got up.

Lara broke away and turned anxious eyes from Adam to his father, hoping he would enlighten them.

"Come and sit down, my dear, and I'll tell you." Charles' first concern was for the state of his wife's weak heart as he helped her back to her seat. Sending a sorrowful glance across to the young woman waiting anxiously to hear what was going on, he mouthed the words, "I'm so sorry."

Adam cared too deeply to put his father through such an ordeal. The news that would inevitably break Lara's heart needed to come from him alone, even if she hated him afterwards. Similar to Charles' concern for Elizabeth, he helped her back to her seat, then dropped into his own as her worried eyes searched his face.

With her hand tucked securely in his, he took a deep breath. Then…

"Darling … Trina knows … there was a review in the paper back home a few weeks ago. Dad's fairly certain she'll be at the theatre this afternoon – apparently, she wants to talk to both of us. I'm so sorry, sweetheart. I hate to think what she's going to do, or the ugly scene that's bound to follow. Unfortunately, there's nothing I can do to stop her. Dad feels it's best if I speak to her, and as much as I hate to admit it, maybe he's right. But no matter what, she needs to know I won't have her coming anywhere near you and Nikki – I'd never let that woman do anything to hurt either one of you."

Adam had given no thought as to what this would mean for his life. His only focus was on Lara and wanting to protect the woman and child he loved with all his heart.

She was crestfallen, knowing what this would mean for him. No matter how hard he tried to fight it, deep down he was still committed to his wife. Lara had no doubt he loved her – but she also knew his heart and what effect this would have on his mental state. Whichever way he turned, the guilt would eat him up. More than anything, he needed her reassurance far above her fear or anger.

"It's okay, sweetheart, don't worry. Everything'll be all right. No matter what happens, she'll never be able to destroy the way we feel about each other."

The anguish in his eyes was enough to break the strongest heart. With a strangled sob, she wrapped her arms around him, brushing gentle lips against his ashen cheek and whispering words of comfort. The tears flowed, though she was unaware of them – more concerned about him and the demons he faced as his mind and soul wrestled each other. His dark, haunted eyes spoke more than words ever could.

"Adam," she begged. "Look at me."

This time it was Lara holding his face between her hands, but she couldn't stop them from trembling at what this could mean. The look on her face implored him to believe everything she was about to say.

"We'll go to the theatre … and play out our roles better than ever before – we have to for Brad and Max's sakes. And then we'll face her together if that's what she wants. I'm not ashamed of the way I feel … and I won't let her threaten or browbeat you again."

Elizabeth and Charles had been listening on quietly, but now he groaned inwardly. Lara had no idea how much Trina had changed, nor how determined she was to make a go of their marriage. The men traded glances and Adam knew he had to tell Lara everything.

Ruefully, he repeated everything his father had told him, with Charles adding pieces Adam himself wasn't aware of yet – about how Trina was sorry for everything she had ever put him through, and how she wanted to make up for it by becoming a better wife. Like any father, Charles hated being the bearer of all this devastating news. Even so, it was better they heard it here from him instead of later at the theatre where all their colleagues could witness what she had to say. Trina had never been one to hold back if she was upset and he needed to prepare them beforehand.

As the full impact of his words sank in, Lara found it difficult to catch her breath. This seemed far different from those earlier revelations and she had no idea how to respond. If Trina had changed to this extent, then it made all the difference in the world. This was everything Adam had always dreamed for his marriage – at least until the night they shared that first kiss in the shadows of the old theatre.

Oh Lord, please help us get through this. Give Adam the wisdom he needs to know what to do.

Her heart wanted him to choose a new life with her, not daring to even contemplate how she would ever endure another round of the heartbreak of last time. Deep down, her conscience knew his torment would last forever if he left and Trina ended up hurting herself, or worse. That fear had always been at the back of his mind. From out of all these conflicting thoughts, another was able to worm its way into her subconscious, clinging on tenaciously as a reminder of what she knew was right.

Adam could tell how upset she was wrestling with her own desires ... although that other one deep down in her conscience, was far beyond his scope of understanding.

"It's okay, Baby, don't worry. We'll get through this – and always together."

His tone was absolute and she wasn't brave enough to challenge him. With the help of a deep sigh, she nodded and even managed to rustle up a tentative smile.

Charles called the waiter over to order a pot of coffee, hoping the strong brew would help to gather their thoughts before it was time to get ready. Wisely, he understood they needed a bit of breathing space to put everything back into perspective in order to perform to their full potential later.

They were a very subdued group trying to wash away their sorrows while attempting to make light conversation for Nikki's sake. With the wisdom of her years, Elizabeth had been able to distract the little girl with a suggestion she stand by the window and watch a large ocean liner dock at a nearby wharf. With boredom starting to take over, counting seagulls became her next form of entertainment. Thankfully, it managed to keep her occupied for another few minutes as the others tried to process the news.

When Adam noticed it was getting close to eleven, he drained his cup and everyone else followed suit. They left the dining room both concerned and mindful it was almost time for their friends and family to arrive and for the two stars to leave for the theatre.

At least this time there was no need to change into formal wear beforehand. This was no red-carpet gala opening of a new show – but it could be the opening of a whole new way of life neither of them wanted to visit. Brad had organised the usual wrap-up party afterwards, although none of them felt in the mood any more ... especially if Trina was expecting an invitation.

§

Adam was cleaning his teeth and Lara running a last-minute brush through her hair when she went to answer a knock on the door. Exuberant hugs and calls of congratulations were the perfect welcome as four of her favourite people elbowed each other out of the way to be the first to greet her.

Lucy was ecstatic to spend time with her best friend after such a long time – the pair hadn't seen each other for over four months and she was dying to catch up on all the goss. Phone calls had been a nightmare to coordinate between working at opposite ends of the day and having time off that rarely overlapped. Jeff managed to land a quick hello peck on Lara's cheek when his girlfriend wrapped her in a bearhug.

Suzie was just as excited and didn't want to be left out, cuddling both her sister and Lucy together, while all Ben could squeeze in was a friendly wave between the sea of heads. All three women began talking at once, leaving the men shaking their heads and sharing looks of bewilderment at how any of them could hear anything, let alone carry on a conversation.

Charles and Elizabeth arrived with a little girl in tow in the middle of this jumble of greetings. Nikki let out a happy squeal at the sight of her aunt and squeezed in the middle of the happy trio, adding her two bits worth in much the same fashion.

Like the women, Jeff and Adam were pleased to catch up again after so long. Ben was as well, despite feeling a little reticent being more of a newcomer still to the group. He pulled back a little as the two best mates exchanged manly hugs, and then broke into a loud chuckle when Adam looked Jeff up and down and slapped him on the back.

"Hey, check *you* out, buddy, looking good! Obviously, our wonderful Lucy's been taking good care of you. Looks like you're finally putting on some muscle – or is that just fat from all her good cooking!"

"Hey, watch it!" Jeff parried, landing a light punch on the other man's arm.

Lucy blushed and sent her boyfriend a shy smile, and he was quick to respond with a loud smooch on her cheek that had everyone laughing.

"*Jeff!*" she retorted, pushing him away and rolling her eyes.

"What? It's true, you're a *fabulous* cook."

He reached over again, and they shared a light kiss, while the other two let out a couple of wolf whistles.

Once the frivolity started to die down, Jeff turned to Adam again.

"Anyway, what's this I hear? Brisbane's all abuzz with Australia's new Michael Crawford! I can't see you ever treading the boards in our little theatre again after all the rave reviews I've been reading..."

"Don't be ridiculous!" Adam scoffed, meting out a friendly backhand to Jeff's bicep. "I'm still me, and there's no way I'll ever aspire to Mr Crawford's famous shoes ... though I'm flattered you should think so – and I'll pay you later!" he added with a cheeky wink.

The two friends sparred playfully as several protested Adam's self-putdown and were quick to back up Jeff's take on his level of talent.

The fun-filled catch-up was a welcome respite from the earlier news and Charles and Elizabeth exchanged relieved smiles.

"You should've seen how many people were coming up for autographs the last time we were here," Suzie boasted to Lucy, stretching out her hands. "Da-dah ... my little sister, the soon-to-be-famous Broadway star!"

Lara turned a deep shade of pink and picked Nikki up, trying unsuccessfully to hide behind her thick hair. Unfortunately, the ploy didn't work when the proud little miss joined in the playful banter.

"And every time we go out *anywhere,* people are *always* pointing to Mummy. And most of them come up to say hello talking like *Eliza,* but when I do it everybody laughs."

Adam patted her back with an affectionate smile. "*That's* because you're so clever and sound just like a Cockney flower-seller yourself. One day you'll be the one up on stage and everybody'll be coming to see you."

"Will *you* come and see me, Uncle Adam?"

"*Course* I will, Poppet. You're my *second* favourite girl in the whole wide world!"

Lara was watching them and the look on her face broke his heart. He guessed what was going through her mind and quickly took control, grabbing her hand before the tears started and their visitors realised something was wrong.

"Listen up, everyone – this beautiful lady and I need to get going. But as soon as the show's over we'll catch up some more – and just maybe you'll change your minds about those reviews when I fluff my lines this afternoon," he finished with a happy chuckle, hoping to make her smile again.

Sadly, the ploy didn't work. Loud scoffs came from the new arrivals, though none from Lara and his parents. They were more concerned his words might well become prophetic with what lay ahead. Charles and Elizabeth could only hope they would be able to concentrate and block all this mess out for the few hours they were on stage.

With hasty goodbyes, the stars slipped away before anyone noticed Lara's worried frown.

§

The taxi arrived at the theatre long before either of them was ready. It was a sombre journey with neither one wanting to give rise to the fear skulking in the darkest chambers of their hearts. The only evidence that anything was amiss was a wayward tear Lara was too slow to blink away. Fortunately, she did manage to catch it from under her lash before Adam noticed. Brad was counting on them to finish the show on a high note and she was determined not to let him down.

Thankfully, they were able to enter Stage Door without running into anyone. He grasped her hand while negotiating the rabbit warren of corridors and wouldn't let go, checking several times that she was okay. Most of their peers had already arrived and Lara was grateful she had a dressing room to herself so she didn't have to explain the fear in her eyes. Adam followed her inside, and as soon as the door closed, he took her in his arms.

"We can do this, Baby. Even if she's out there watching our every move, I'm not going to hide how I feel any more. I've had to pretend for far too long. But I do need you to promise you'll be careful, and if she tries anything, just walk away and come and get me."

"I'll do my best, but I don't want you risking everything, Teddy. You've put in too much hard work to have it all taken away."

"I don't care. You're all that matters now – you and Nikki – and I'm not going to let anything come between us ever again."

Suddenly there was a sharp knock on the door. They looked at each other, terrified of who might be waiting on the other side ... until a voice called, "Makeup's waiting, Ms Jennings."

Lara let out a loud sigh of relief and mouthed the words "I love you," before planting a firm kiss on his lips. She turned to leave, but Adam wasn't letting her go that easily.

He pulled her into his arms once more, searching her face for reassurance. "I love you too, Baby, and I need you to hold my promise in your heart. I won't let *anything* happen to us, you hear!"

She could only nod ... while that persistent worm of conscience pressed forward to make its presence felt once again, only this time much stronger. As before, she pushed it down to concentrate on the man she loved with all her heart.

They shared one last lingering kiss and the silent reassurance she read in his eyes gave her the courage needed for whatever lay ahead. Then they were off down the hallway to hair and makeup, with none of their cohorts having any idea about the drama playing out in the shadows of their hearts. No matter what was happening in their private lives, it was time to focus on the job at hand.

From then until the curtain rose, backstage was a hive of activity. During all of his normal preparations, Adam's eyes kept darting to and fro, just in case Trina managed to get past security. As the seconds crept away, he was able to relax a bit ... except for the usual pre-show jitters all actors experience before a show.

Lara was in her dressing room ready to go on when there was another knock on the door. Shaking off the constant feeling of dread, she opened it to find Adam standing there continuing what had become a pre-closing night ritual.

A huge bouquet of sunflowers greeted her and the look on his face melted away any of her fears.

"I think it's about time I put a bit of sunshine back in your life – I haven't managed to do that at all today ... hopefully, these will make up for it."

"Oh, Teddy, they're beautiful, thank you!" With a dazzling smile, she kissed him soundly on the lips. "But you always manage to put sunshine in my life – you *are* my sun, every single day ... from the moment I wake up until I close my eyes at night. And don't forget all those smiles you put on my face first thing this morning!"

The welcome reminder took them both back to her bed, where they had given themselves wholly to one another and in the way only they knew best.

Wrapping her arms around his neck, she planted another resounding kiss on the mouth she knew so well – one that now held a slight tremor. This was the part of him that only ever tried to offer words of hope ... and always brought her to life by their touch.

This time he was the one having to blink away a stray tear. "I will always love you and I'll never *ever* let you go. I want to smother you in sunshine every day for the rest of our lives."

Lara smoothed away the shimmering droplet hanging like a diamond from Adam's lower eyelash and her words of reassurance fell into his soul. "Oh darling, you already do. No one will ever touch my life as you have, nor make me smile so often ... or feel so loved."

"Five minutes everyone."

The words echoed through the halls before he could answer ... and suddenly the wheels were in motion...

With shoulders touching, they walked the brightly lit corridor ... not speaking and yet completely in tune with one another. They took their places, exchanging those token signals that had been the prelude to every one of their performances since an opening in Brisbane over a year earlier.

It was time.

§

Adam went straight to Lara's dressing room as soon as the house lights came on for interval. She was already there peeling herself out of a body-hugging silver ball gown and he turned his back when the dresser unlaced the tight-fighting corset. The last thing he wanted to do was embarrass her in front of the young woman.

As soon as they were alone, Lara turned to him. "Is she here?"

"I don't know. It was too hard to see beyond the front row so I can't say for sure."

"Well, don't worry, you were perfect. No one'd ever guess the strain you're under."

"Pure adrenaline, that's all. I nearly forgot my lines in a couple of places ... thank goodness, they came back just in time. How are you doing, Baby? I'm so sorry to put you through this."

"Don't worry about me, I'm okay. I've had to concentrate harder than usual, but as long as I stay focused, then I'm all right. What should I do when we finish – stay close to you or would it be better if I just go and find Suzie and the others?"

"I don't want her getting anywhere near you so just go and join the others and I'll come as soon as I can. And she's not invited to the party afterwards ... no matter what she thinks."

On cue, the dresser returned to assist Lara into her outfit for the study scene. Thankfully, it didn't require a corset so the change didn't take long and the five-minute call came soon after. With a quick check to make certain all was in place, they scurried to the backstage area for the last time.

Out of the blue, Adam pulled her close, and their lips met for one final kiss in the wing's shadows. He gave no thought as to what would happen to their makeup – all he could think about was how much she mattered to him. She was surprised after so many months of taking care not to be seen, and yet somehow the contact helped to calm the nerves and assure them everything would be fine.

Moments later and following one tight squeeze of their hands, *Eliza* moved to centre stage. The toss of her head and jaunty angle of her chin were so out of character from the woman Adam knew and loved, for a moment his face clouded over with fear. Despite having witnessed this same transformation on countless other occasions, today was different – this time a threat hung over their heads.

Watching the Lara he knew and loved seemingly disappear into the shadows, all Adam could do was pray it was only his imagination and not a sign of things to come.

"Please don't ever leave me," he breathed into the darkness.

Chapter 14

The audience leapt to their feet and Brad was clapping loudest of all. The whole season had been a triumph and he couldn't have asked for anything more from any of his actors or crew. Today was the culmination of many months of hard work. Despite the huge sense of relief knowing everything had gone off without a hitch, he was still sad to let it go.

Called back for three curtain calls, the evening concluded with the full cast lifting their voices one final time for a rousing rendition of *The Rain in Spain*. Everyone in the theatre joined in, even the backstage crew singing at the top of their lungs. It was a triumphant finish to a brilliant run. And then, with a sweeping bow and several faces awash with tears, the troupe received one last round of applause from their adoring fans.

When all of the greasepaint, wigs and costumes had been packed away, cast mates reverted to everyday folk with no trace left of the prim or coarse English accents they had mastered so well. People were bustling here and there, calling out to one another as some went to join family and friends in the foyer instead of disappearing through Stage Door.

Adam left Lara with a squeeze of his hand, along with reassurances of joining her as soon as possible. Her gaze didn't wane as he walked away. It was horrible seeing him go off alone, although she understood his need to have her safe with the rest of the family. Peering cautiously through a small doorway, she saw Suzie peering this way and that and then waving madly once she caught sight of her. Lara waved back and began making her way between the jostling crowds to join her sister and the others.

Nikki came running over and threw her arms around Lara before she had even made it halfway. "Mummy, Mummy, you looked so *pretty* in that long ball gown, but when you were sitting on the stairs with all that dirt on your face, I didn't even know it was you. I wouldn't be 'llowed to go out with all my clothes torn and dirty like that or with those yucky smudges all over my face, would I?"

Lara gave a stern shake of her head and replied, "No, Missy Tuppence, you certainly wouldn't."

The little girl screwed up her nose. "Well how come *Eliza* was 'llowed to?"

Holding the little girl's hand tightly in hers, they walked towards the others with Lara explaining the tattered and grubby garments were all *Eliza* had to wear as a flower-girl because of being so poor.

Nikki was horrified. "We'd better go home then and get my piggy bank. That way I can buy her a new dress. She's a really nice lady, and I feel sorry for her, 'speshly when that horrible man made her feel sad. I *never* want to see him again, and I'm glad Uncle Adam doesn't talk to *you* with a naughty voice like that."

Touched by her daughter's generosity, as well as amused by her innocence to suppose the two characters were actually real people now waiting somewhere backstage, Lara bent down and hugged her close.

"Oh, sweetie, *Eliza's* gone away now, but I know she'd say thank you if she could. That's a really lovely thing to want to do. I'm very proud that you'd give up your money for someone who doesn't have all the nice things we do."

As always, the little girl had managed to lift Lara's spirits and make her heart swell with gratitude to have her in her life.

Adam was watching from the sidelines, too scared to approach in case Trina decided to make a move. Even though there was no sign of his wife, he felt certain she was waiting somewhere, if only to embarrass him. His eyes kept darting from one side of the room to the other, hoping to intercept her before she could do anything.

As soon as Lara and Nikki joined the family, Lucy threw her arms around her best friend. "You were wonderful and I was so proud of you! I wanted to shout from the rooftops that we once shared a dressing room, but then I figured it probably wouldn't be quite the proper thing to do in this setting!"

"Oh, you're gorgeous, thanks for being here!" Lara laughed, thrilled to have her there to share this emotional time and help ease the tension. She hugged her back just as energetically, all the while looking over her shoulder to see if she could spot Adam in amongst the crowd ... but with no luck.

Suzie noticed Lara's eyes darting to-and-fro and moved in to offer a reassuring sisterly hug. "That was wonderful, but are you okay? Charles told us everything on the way here. I can't believe this is happening all over again."

"Thanks, Suze. Yeah, don't worry, I'll be fine. I'm just concerned about Adam. I can't see him anywhere. I don't suppose you've seen him?"

"No, there's been no sign of him so far. I hope he's alright."

The rest of the family gathered around to offer their congratulations and rave about the show, and to ensure Lara was sheltered between them.

Eventually, Adam came up from behind, a worried frown masking those good looks. "I can't see her anywhere. Maybe she decided not to come after all."

His father looked just as concerned. He was almost certain Trina would make good on her threat.

Mustering up a forced smile, Adam quickly changed the subject. He didn't want Lara worrying any further unless she had good reason. "Okay, let's hear the worst. I hope that pause when I nearly forgot my lines wasn't too noticeable. I couldn't get over how they just disappeared like that – just proves I'd better not become too complacent, or they'll never ask me to work in this business again. So much for good reviews!"

Those standing nearby were quick to reiterate no one had even noticed. Nevertheless, a few exchanged anxious glances. It was an understandable near miss with the amount of pressure he was under.

Just as they were getting ready to leave, a woman's voice floated over Adam's shoulder.

"*There* you are – I've been scouring this place looking for you everywhere!"

Everyone froze ... until they turned and saw it wasn't Trina, but an attractive woman with a handsome man standing by her side. Both wore beaming smiles and the man had a programme tucked under his arm.

Adam had to drag in a deep breath and let it out again as he put on a welcoming smile. "Oh Anne, Ray, you made it after all! It's nice to see you again ... thanks for coming."

Lara's whole body was trembling as she introduced them to the rest of the group. Apart from everything else, she now had the added worry of Nikki possibly blurting out that she and Adam weren't actually husband and wife.

"And this must be Nikki. Oh, she's adorable," Anne enthused, smiling down at the little girl and stroking her cheek. "Your mummy and daddy couldn't stop talking about you when we were at a special dinner in Salzburg, and they said you visited all the places the *Von Trapp* children danced and had so much fun."

The little girl's eyes lit up at the thought of her favourite place. Thankfully, it was the perfect topic to ensure she missed the glaring slip-up about Adam, although it still made Lara wince. Everyone else caught it too, but they weren't bothered, and Lucy rubbed Lara's arm as an assurance she didn't have to worry.

Nikki jumped up and down as she answered. "Yes, I did – *every ... single ... one* and we danced around the fountain and up the stairs and *even* had a race down the long tunnel of trees in the park. I had the *best* time ... it was sooo much fun. Were you there, too?"

Ray joined in. "Yes, we were, and I was there when he gave his special talks to all those important men. He's a really clever man and you're a very lucky young lady."

"I *know* I am and I love him with *all* my heart," she replied with a twinkle in her eye. "And he and my mummy are *famous* now! Did you know she's got *heaps* of different names sometimes and tonight she was *Eliza?* She even talks funny every now and then and that makes me laugh lots and lots!"

Everyone burst into easy chuckles as the little girl boasted about her mother – all except Lara, who still turned pink with embarrassment whenever she was on the receiving end of any form of attention away from the stage.

Anne took Ray's arm. "Well, I can see you have family here so we won't take up any more of your time. It was lovely catching up again and you both were terrific tonight – best version I've ever seen on a stage. Oh, and if ever you're in Sydney again, please look us up. We'd love to have all three of you over for a meal. Our kids would enjoy spending time with this little one."

She seemed such a genuine and kind-hearted person, Lara felt awful for being so cool and reticent about getting to know them at their initial meeting during the conference.

"Thanks, Anne, that would be lovely. We'll be sure to call if ever we're down this way again. And thanks for coming out to see us tonight. We certainly appreciate your support and kind words."

"You're most welcome – Ray and I thoroughly enjoyed ourselves. Oh, honey, do you have the programme? I wanted to ask if Lara and Adam would sign it before we go." She turned once again to the young woman. "I hope you don't mind."

"Of course not, it's a pleasure," Lara replied, taking the proffered pen and booklet from his hands.

Both stars signed their bio pages, adding a personal message of thanks. Then with a quick, "Thanks again," and a friendly wave, the couple was gone.

Everyone turned to each other with looks of relief as Adam took Lara's hand. "Come on, let's get out of here."

The crowds were starting to disperse. Just as the small group made their way to the entrance, another more determined voice caught their attention.

"Hello, Adam."

This time there was good reason for the frozen silence and everyone stopped in their tracks – even those who had never met Trina knew exactly who she was.

Only one was oblivious and she went straight over and tugged on Trina's hand. "Hello. My name's Nikki and my mummy's famous! Did you see her tonight? She was *Eliza* and she was *great!* I can ask her to sign your programme if you want. She wouldn't mind ... she always does."

"Come on, Munchkin. Let's go and see what's over there. I'm sure there are a couple of Clancy's friends you'd like to say hello to." Lucy and Jeff quickly took a hand each, leading her over to a pair of life-sized Ascot racehorse cut-outs positioned on either side of the entrance doors.

Adam had let go of Lara's hand and turned around as soon as he recognised her voice. With Nikki now out of earshot, he looked his wife straight in the eye.

"Hello, Trina. Dad mentioned you might be here."

"Can we talk, please?"

Her voice had changed, so much softer than he had ever heard it before and there was no drunken slur, nor any bitterness behind her words.

"Look, I don't want a scene – and definitely not here. How about you come to my hotel tomorrow after breakfast when all this is over? We can talk then..."

"I don't want a scene either, Adam. I just want to talk to you and Ms Jennings alone. And from what I just overheard, it's obvious there's a lot more to this than I realised. Nobody mentioned you'd *all* gone to Austria – *that* must've been a nice little bonus." A slight touch of that old cutting tone was back, although there was still a measure of control and none of her usual angry outbursts.

Lara was mortified and felt far too much guilt to look the other woman in the eye. The last thing she wanted was for Trina to learn about their holiday here in front of her family and friends.

Adam was becoming angry listening to her veiled sarcasm at Lara's expense and quickly took his wife by the arm, leading her to a private corner away from where the excited youngster was still admiring the horses. He was determined Trina wasn't going to upset her as well. Nikki was an innocent party and he wanted to shield her as much as possible.

His tone was serious and the message loud and clear. "I'm not discussing *anything* with you tonight. I know you're upset, but this is *our* night – Lara's and mine – and you're not going to do anything to hurt her. What happened is just between you and me. I want us to be able to act like adults, discussing things calmly and rationally away from everyone else. Please just leave now and we can talk tomorrow. And I'm warning you – you're not to go *anywhere* near Lara ... *ever!* Do I make myself clear?"

She reached out to touch his hand, but he quickly pulled away, flinching at her audacity after only ever giving him years of coldness and contempt.

"I don't want to upset you, Adam ... I don't even want to upset her. I only came down because I read so many reviews praising your performance. You're still my husband and I wanted to show my support – even though I've let you down badly in the past. There's a lot we need to talk about."

He was shocked at the change in her. Once upon a time she would have been ranting and raving – especially when she heard Lara had accompanied him to Europe – but this woman was so different to the Trina of old and he wasn't quite sure how to respond.

"Please just go now and we'll talk in the morning." Reaching into his pocket, he drew out a pen and paper, quickly jotting down the name and address of the hotel before handing it to her. "This is where I'm staying."

She took it with a nod. "All right, I'll leave it for now, but I'll see you around nine-thirty."

With one long last look at her rival, Trina turned on her heel and walked out the door.

§

The wrap-up gala was held in the famous Centrepoint Tower, a landmark skyscraper with breathtaking views across the harbour and beyond. The producers had booked the entire Sky Venue – the highest event space in the southern hemisphere – and it was decked out in festive splendour for the private function. Those involved, along with their families, were in party mood – all except for Adam, Lara and their small group. Trina's appearance had put a dampener on everyone's frame of mind.

Charles wanted to do something to lift their spirits, so he hoisted Nikki onto his shoulders and started dancing to one of ABBA's popular songs. The little girl really felt like she was a 'dancing queen' and kept giggling and waving to her mother. It was the perfect antidote, and soon they were all up on the dance floor, bent on having a good time.

Adam grabbed Lara's hand and twirled her around and around. For the first time since the disastrous morning walk, a smile lit up his eyes. "You look beautiful, my lovely. No one can hold a candle to you. I'm the luckiest man alive."

This was their night, just as he had told Trina, and nothing or no one was going to steal it away. Though her heart was heavy, Lara made sure to wear a smile on her face.

If you can pretend everything's okay, my darling, then I can do the same.

As they twirled around the room, everything else faded away. Adam's only thought was a strong desire to melt inside her and leave the world behind.

The meal was delicious and served around a huge round table. With Paul and Max making up the numbers, it was big enough to hold all eleven of them. Talk soon centred on the exciting future awaiting the new celebrities. When Max mentioned the offer of both leads in *The Sound of Music,* Nikki was so excited, she knocked over a glass of water and it nearly toppled onto the floor.

Lara was quick to rescue the downed item and mopped at the puddle on the tablecloth and a few drops that had splattered on her daughter's dress.

"Hang on, Poppet. Mummy's not sure whether she'll be able to play *Maria* just yet. We'll have to see what's happening at my old work and also see what your teacher thinks. It may be too soon to go away for another four months."

As the little girl's bottom lip dropped, Suzie turned to her sister with a puzzled frown. "What do you mean you won't be able to do it? Surely, David knew you'd be in demand once this was over. I thought he made it down for one of your shows."

"He did. He was in Sydney for business and we caught up a few weeks ago."

"Well, he must realise how popular you've become and know your future's about to take a major turn. Surely he wouldn't expec—"

Lara's steely glare made the other woman stop in her tracks. Leaning close, she muttered through clenched teeth, "Stop it, Suze. I don't know what's going to happen now that Trina knows about Adam and me. If he chooses to stay with her, there's no way we can work together again. She'd be furious and I couldn't handle seeing him everyd—"

"Of *course* he's not going to choose her," the other one broke in with a forced whisper. "He *loves* you ... anyone with two eyes can see that."

"That's not the problem. I know he loves me, but he's still committed to her in his heart and I dare not get my hopes up."

"Well, he'll have *me* to reckon with if he chooses her! I may love him heaps, but that won't stop me from telling him what a fool he is if he lets you go."

Suzie's eyes were blazing and Lara could see she needed to change the subject if they were to get through the night without falling into the doldrums of before.

Her answer was loud enough for the young child to hear. "Well, we'll just have to wait and see. Hopefully, I'll be offered another chance to play *Maria* if I don't take it this time. And besides, Nikki needs me more than the theatre world does, don't you, Poppet?"

A loud whine came from the neighbouring chair. "But *Mummy*—"

Lara cut her off with a raised finger and a stare to prove she wasn't joking. "That's enough, young lady. We'll talk about this when we get home, alright?"

"*Alll*right," the little girl clicked her tongue and grumbled, pushing her fork dejectedly around the plate and sending her a sullen look.

For the rest of the evening, Nikki kept glancing across at both her mother and Adam with eyes that should have melted the hardest heart. Despite this blatant form of coercion, Lara wasn't about to let them influence her. She had a lot to think about and everything depended on what happened the next day.

Over the next couple of hours, both she and Adam managed to put on happy faces in an attempt to enjoy themselves with those they loved the most. Jeff and Lucy rallied around their best friends, confident everything would be okay. They knew how much they loved each other and couldn't imagine them ever being apart again.

Lucy had no trouble remembering the heartbreak Lara had gone through last time after comforting her over and over throughout *Oklahoma's* rehearsals, and then again while helping each other get dressed before a performance. She dreading thinking how devastated Lara would be if Trina got her way.

Finally, with sore feet from all the dancing and Nikki barely able to keep her eyes open any longer, Lara signalled to Adam it might be time to leave. She hated saying goodbye to their fellow co-stars after forming close friendships with a few, but with a big day looming and an uncertain outcome, they needed to grab a good night's sleep before it was time for him to face his wife. Exchanging promises to keep in touch and assurances of catching up somewhere down the track, those in their small party slid into two waiting taxis.

The ride to the hotel was quite subdued, and after bidding everyone goodnight in the foyer of the hotel, Lucy and Ben slipped away to give the family time alone. When they reached the door to Adam's suite, Charles and Elizabeth's expressions gave away their concern.

"Don't worry, we'll be okay. Everything's going to be fine," their son assured them, and Lara did the same as she hugged them goodnight.

The sisters strolled on ahead with the men following, while Nikki was sound asleep on Adam's shoulder. Their footsteps slowed when they approached Ben and Suzie's room a little way down the hall.

The older sibling turned with a sad smile and placed a caring arm around her baby sister. "If you need me, you know where I am. Don't hesitate to ring and I'll come straight away."

She was mainly worried about Lara's state of mind. Apart from Nikki, there were no other family members left, and they had always vowed to protect one another.

"Thanks, sis, I'm so glad you're here. I'll try to ring when I know what's going on. Sleep well and please don't fret. I'll be fine, truly."

With one final hug and another concerned look, Suzie followed Ben into their room as Lara and Adam made their way to the privacy of her suite.

The nightly ritual of tucking Nikki into bed was even more important tonight. Dropping a tender kiss on the brow of the child he loved like a daughter, Adam stared at the photo sitting on the bedside table. His eyes filled as a melancholy finger traced the image of a man and a young child laughing into the camera as they stood proudly beside a sandcastle on a perfect winter morning.

§

Sleep eluded him for most of the night, while Lara eventually managed to drift off in the small hours, completely spent after all the emotion and worry of the day. With soft moonlight highlighting her features, Adam made a solemn vow never to let her go.

Following what felt like hours, and being careful not to disturb her, he slipped out of bed and went and stood by the window where the lights of the Harbour Bridge and the Opera House shimmered across the dark expanse of water. But the eye-catching vista was lost on him. All he could picture was another image – one of Trina lying naked and comatose in a pool of putrid bodily fluids ... barely breathing on the kitchen floor.

Oh God, please help me to stay strong. I'm never going back to that nightmare again.

Crawling back into bed, he carefully positioned his arm under Lara's head, and she snuggled sleepily against him. Loving lips brushed along her forehead as his laboured breath stirred a few wisps of chestnut-coloured hair. For the rest of the night, he simply lay there looking down at her, filling a need to savour these final few hours of what had been such a special time ... just in case...

Stop it, you idiot! You're not going to abandon Lara – it's Trina who's going to have to find a new life for herself.

He was horrified to think his thoughts were taking him down paths where could be Lara left behind. The realisation made him even more resolute their love story would last 'til the end of time.

Lifting his eyes, Adam's spirit sent out a plea to the Heavens.

Please don't let me cave in like before. Give me the strength to tell Trina she's the one who needs to make a new life for herself, not Lara and Nikki.

It was natural to include the young child in his musings.

Just after seven, Lara woke to find herself burrowed into his side and those eyes she always got lost in gazing down at her. Stretching lazily, she sent him a dazzling smile, unaware he had been too scared to move for most of the night for fear of disturbing her. With a smile to match hers, he stretched out his arm, hoping to dislodge the numbness that had been keeping him company for the last hour or more.

While Lara slept, that worm of conscience had no one to pester. Suddenly it was back, crawling through the chambers of her mind to keep her company once again. Similar to an arrow piercing her heart, the significance of the day all came flooding back. Her eyes immediately closed as though seeking to quell reality, but she couldn't stop a despairing groan from slipping through her lips.

Adam had no trouble guessing what she was thinking and his response was immediate. "Hey, gorgeous girl! Where's my morning smile? I thought you realised I can't function without it." His lips moved down her neck and along her jaw-line, nibbling and teasing in an effort to push away those awful blues.

Somehow, she managed a half-hearted chuckle, even though it was clearly only to please him. Pressing his face into her hair, he snuggled up close, wrapping his arms and legs around her as though creating a private cocoon for the two of them, far away from everything else.

For the first time since arriving in the southern capital, there was no passionate awakening to greet the new day.

Their hearts were too heavy...

Chapter 15

Nikki's usual sunny greeting was the perfect pick me up for Lara and Adam when she landed on their bed with a running leap. Her giggles brought a much-needed respite from the earlier sombre mood. For the next little while, they kept her entertained with a few rounds of Humpty Dumpty that sent her tumbling headfirst onto the bed with a loud squeal over and over again.

Unfortunately, the clock on the bedside table ticked away much too fast for their liking and it was soon time to shoo her away to get dressed while they prepared for a confrontation neither of them wanted. Hand-in-hand, the trio made their way to the dining room where the others were already waiting with sombre faces and concern in their greetings.

"'Morning all. Isn't this a glorious day, and what about that magnificent city out there – just look at that view! Gosh, I'm starving! Scoot on over, you two, and stop hogging all the space!" Lara was determined nothing was going to spoil their last day here as a family as she squeezed in between Suzie and Lucy.

Following her lead, the table soon resonated with everyday chatter as orders were taken and appetites sated from the extensive choices on offer. The others tried to pretend they didn't notice when she would suddenly stop mid-sentence and glance over to the door whenever it opened ... or when Adam followed suit.

Most already had their bags packed ready to fly out in the afternoon, while Lara had done the bulk of hers and Nikki's over the last few days. Only the basics were still to be done – toiletries and a few last-minute toys a little girl needed to keep her company for these last few hours. She planned to take care of them once breakfast was over, while Adam met with Trina. They were all taking the same flight out, and with the limo due to arrive after lunch, there was still plenty of time.

With their plates scraped empty, Lucy and Jeff invited Suzie and Ben to join them for a walk along the waterfront. Neither couple wanted to get in the way of the pre-arranged meeting, so they left the table with promises to meet up again for lunch around midday.

Elizabeth and Charles offered to keep Nikki amused by taking her to watch the yachts sailing on the harbour. Lara sent them a grateful smile and got up to leave after Adam's stern warning she wasn't to be around when his wife arrived. He was worried the old Trina would resurface and Lara would be on the receiving end of her latest threat. Despite what his father had said about how much she had changed, he still wasn't prepared to take any chances.

"Well, I'd better get upstairs and finish off before the cleaners arrive. Are you sure you don't want me to wait with you?"

He stood up too. "No, I want you right away from here. You never know how she'll be from one day to the next." His piercing look confirmed he meant what he said.

"But your dad said she's changed ... nothing like the old Trina."

Adam could read the fear in Lara's eyes as her mind ticked over. It wasn't hard to figure out she was thinking back to that first conversation in the café at Spring Hill when he had mentioned something along the lines of hoping his marriage could get better if he hung in there. Now with Charles' recent revelations from about how much Trina had changed, it wasn't surprising she was worried he may want to give his wife another chance. After all, he had buckled under that same pressure many times before.

He stroked her arm. "Baby, there's no need to worry. You and I are going to be together forever! Nothing she says can change how I feel. I didn't say anything before because I wanted it to be a surprise, but her turning up like this has forced my hand. The first thing I'm going to do when we get back to Brisbane is tell her I'm leaving. I'm not even going to unpack. Mum and Dad won't mind me staying with them 'til I can find somewhere small, and then once the divorce is through, you and I can get married."

Lara's heart skipped a beat listening to the words she had waited so long to hear ... but still there was that nagging check in her spirit making its presence known.

"You know how much I've dreamed about us being together, but please don't do anything rash 'til you've really thought this all through." She gripped his hand and looked at him anxiously. "You may feel differently once you've spoken to her."

He couldn't believe his ears. "*What?* That's *crazy!* I *have* thought it all through and there's only one thing I want. Don't you realise how much our time down here has meant to me? This is the start of a whole new life for us."

His answer came out far harsher than intended and she flinched. Straightaway a barrel load of regret hit him hard in the chest. Cupping her face with both hands, he pressed his mouth hard against hers.

"Oh, Baby, I'm so sorry. I didn't mean to snap at you like that. Oh, I *hate* this and I *don't* want to see her. I know how stubborn she can be. I just want everything all over and done with so we can get on with our lives!"

Her lips dripped with forgiveness when she touched them to his again. "It's okay, I know you didn't mean to." She stroked his face and tried to summon up a smile. "Everything's going to be fine, Teddy – don't worry."

"It's going to be *more* than fine. *I'm* taking control for once." He glanced tensely at the clock on the wall and sucked in a deep breath. "Okay, I need you to get out of here before she arrives."

"Fair enough. I should be finished packing in about an hour or so. There's not much left to be done. And hey … please be careful."

"I will and if everything goes to plan, I'll be up long before then – this is only going to be short and she's going to listen to me for a change."

He kissed her hard one last time and then pushed her away, anxious to get all the unpleasantness behind them and start their new lives. His eyes followed her as she made her way across the room.

She reached the door and paused to look back. Neither of them was able to disguise their true feelings … nor the hope in their hearts as she pushed that nagging moral compass down into a locked chamber in her heart.

How could I ever survive if I had to let you go, my darling? Trina doesn't deserve you anymore.

The foyer was crowded and people were milling about as Lara waited for the lift. The door started to open when she heard a timid voice come from behind.

"Ms Jennings, can we talk … please?"

Her heart was racing when she turned to find Trina standing only a few feet away. From the look on her face, it was obvious she was upset.

"*Trina!* Oh … I didn't expect to run into you! Look … umm … we can't … sorry, I - I have to go. Adam's waiting for you in the dining room and I'm just on my way upstairs. He doesn't want us to speak to each other."

The look of despair in the other woman's eyes was that of someone who had nowhere else to turn – as though she already knew what her husband had decided.

A trembling hand reached out. "Please wait and hear me out. I wanted to talk to you before I see him – just you and me … two women in love with the same man. Please…"

To Lara's dismay – and horror – she actually felt sorry for her. Sober, Trina was just like anyone else, frantically trying to hold onto all that was familiar before it slipped away. She sounded nothing like the woman who had yelled down the phone in the early hours of the morning almost a year ago.

Out of the corner of her eye, Lara spotted an alcove with two armchairs. Against her better judgement, she signalled for Trina to follow so they could talk in private.

Warily the two rivals sat opposite each other, both perched on the edge of their seats. Lara took a deep breath, needing to get everything out in one desperate plea.

"Look, I understand how you feel, honestly I do, but you must know how much you've hurt Adam in the past. He can't take any more. All he wants is the love and support of a proper family – something you've never been willing to give him. You've even taken away his only hope of having a child."

Seeing an instant look of regret flood Trina's eyes when she realised Adam must have told her everything, Lara's tone grew softer. "I'm sorry, the last thing I want to do is upset you, but surely you must realise it's no use. He needs me ... and he needs Nikki, my daughter ... and we both need him more than you could possibly imagine."

Regardless of Lara's gut-wrenching appeal, Trina wasn't about to give up, wringing her hands while the tears rolled down her cheeks. "But you have your *own* family – I saw how they shielded you last night. It's obvious even his parents are on your side ... but if he leaves me, I'll have *no* one. Mine couldn't give a stuff anymore ... I haven't seen them for ... oh, I don't know how long. You may *think* I deserve everything that's happened, but I'm begging you, *please* let him go. *I* need him more tha—"

"But what about *him?* What does *Adam* need?" Lara implored, regretting her earlier apology as a storm cloud of anger built up because of the other woman's lack of compassion for the man she professed to love.

There was no reply. Trina knew the answer, but she wasn't brave enough to give voice to it ... if she did, her rival would never let him go.

Lara's tone grew more urgent. "I *love* him, Trina – I have since the moment we first met ... and he loves me too ... you *know* he does."

Desperation was the other woman's driving force and she reached out, grabbing Lara's arm so hard her fingernails turned white. "But I can *make* him love me. We loved each other once ... I *know* we can do it again. I've changed, Lara – I'm not the woman he once knew. I'm never going to touch another drop of alcohol as long as I live, and that's what tore us apart in the first place. I was so stupid and had no idea what I was doing to him – to us."

It took every bit of willpower for Lara not to shrug her hand away and walk out the door. She didn't want to hear any more, but that frantic grip grew even stronger.

"He *adored* me when we first got married and I can make him feel like that again – we were so happy back then. Besides, you know as well as I do he still feels committed to me ... and he always will, otherwise he would've left years ago. Deep down, we *both* know he still cares. *Pleeaase* let him go, Lara, I have nowhere else to turn!"

With haunted green eyes now sunken and searching, Trina had the look of a drowning woman. As hard as she tried to fight it, Lara remembered back to what that felt like – she had been there herself, many times.

Firstly, through years of heartbreak when Tom, the man she married in good faith, played musical beds with any young starlet who caught his eye ... until that horrendous night when he had walked out, leaving her with a tiny baby and not much else ... except for wounds that went soul deep. Then there was the terrible grief of her parents passing and losing the two people she counted on more than any other.

And only last Christmas, this same woman now sitting in front of her begging for another chance, had forced the man Lara loved more than life itself to walk away, never to see them again so she and Nikki would be safe from her threats. No one in their right mind could expect anyone to endure all that again.

I can't, Trina ... don't ask me to.

And yet, when she looked into those desolate eyes, against all reason an overwhelming sense of compassion leeched into her soul. How could she deliberately put anyone else through that amount of heartache – even someone she loathed with every part of her being?

And even more compelling – beyond the wretched woman's pleas – out of the depths of Lara's innermost conscience emerged a certainty she could no longer ignore. The man she loved more than life itself had been living with a relentless sense of guilt that skulked into every moment of his day, no matter how hard he tried to ignore it. And all stemming because he was in love with a woman who could only be his by abandoning the wife he had once adored.

She had seen glimpses of it in his eyes, and most often after they had made love and he was about to leave her bed to go back to that other life. Not guilt for having loved her – the guilt of knowing he had broken the vows he made to stay true to the woman he had married for better or for worse. No relationship could endure under those circumstances – not even one offering more happiness than either of them had ever known before.

Like a thief coming in the night to snatch away all she held dear, Lara realised there was only one choice left to her ... but not here, not now. The inadvertent Good Samaritan recognised such a momentous decision needed to wait until she was home again – on familiar territory where she could frame the words with a clear head. And somehow, she had to talk to Adam's parents first without him finding out. It was the only way.

Bowing her head from the weight of so much heartbreak, and as her eyes filled with tears, Lara muttered, "Go ... go to him, but don't you *dare* say *anything* about talking to me. He must never *ever* find out."

Through a heart-wrenching sob coming from deep in her soul, she bolted from the chair and ran to the lifts, blinded by the tears now coursing down her cheeks as her heart shattered into tiny pieces.

Oh, God, what've I done? Please help him forgive me...

§

Trina had to take a deep breath before she made her way towards the dining room. Adam was in plain view when she came through the door and just the sight of him was enough to make her feet falter. Pressing her back against the frame, she needed to pluck up the courage to approach. From the set of his shoulders, she could tell he was uptight. The last thing she wanted was to get into another fight. There had been far too many over the years.

She straightened her spine and fought down a feeling of nausea as the echo of Lara's final declaration resounded in her head.

Did she really mean what she intimated?

Adam spied her out of the corner of his eye. Automatically, he pushed back his chair and held out the empty one opposite. It didn't matter about their differences or quarrels; he couldn't ignore his upbringing or the words of his parents to treat everyone with respect and courtesy.

"H-hello, Adam ... thanks for agreeing t-to meet with me." Her voice was shaky, and she was reluctant to look him in the eye, knowing he had every reason to be upset ... but she was fighting for her life and prepared to say or do anything to win him back.

After enduring more than twenty minutes wait since Lara had gone up to the room, and mulling over everything this meeting would entail, he was ready for whatever she wanted to throw at him.

"Hello, Trina. Look, before we even start, you need to understand, I'm not happy to see you ... but I won't ignore you either. Just say what you have to and then please leave – I've got a plane to catch." His manner was cold and distant.

"I do understand." Seeing him glance down at her trembling hands, she clenched them tight, feeling nervous and swallowing hard. "I suppose your father told you he came to see me."

He nodded tersely, watching her through a frosty stare from beneath dark furrowed brows.

With her eyes lowered and a tone so different from the one he remembered, the words came out gently ... almost pleading.

"Adam, I've changed. Much more than you realise. I haven't touched even a drop of alcohol since last Christmas, and I never will again. I haven't been to a club or party in months and I'm not having anything more to do with Judith either. She was always trying to ply me with drinks to keep her company, but when I said I wasn't interested, she just laughed in my face. I thought she was my friend..."

Unwittingly, Adam inched his chair away – almost as though he was subconsciously afraid what she was saying would make a difference to his steely determination to ignore any of her pleas. She didn't even notice – her sense of desperation meant the words just kept pouring out.

For the first time, she looked up at him, and their eyes met. "I'm sorry I've treated you so badly. I know you didn't deserve it ... but we can start again. I'm willing to become whatever you want me to be. Charles must've mentioned how much I've changed."

"Well, he did mention something about you *saying* you're different and that you've stopped drinking ... but that doesn't change a thing, Trina. It's too late for us. There's too much water under the bridge."

His stare seemed to cut right through her and there was no emotion at all in his voice. All Adam could think about was the despair he had seen in Lara's eyes when Trina had forced them apart last time, and he would never desert her again. Back then, it had been agony. Trying to live through it now was more than anyone should ever have to endure and he knew there would be no more second chances if he didn't make a clean break this time.

Like a drowning woman, she grabbed at his arm. "Adam, *please* listen to me and give me another chance! I *have* changed. I'm even volunteering in the children's ward at the hospital several times a week. It's brought new meaning into my life instead of that never-ending conga line of drunken parties. When you come home I'll *prove* it to you ... you won't recognise me ... or the house. I've even put in a veggie garden. I promise to take care of you this time and we can have a proper marriage again."

She smiled wistfully, as though recognising a faraway time. "I *know* we can be good for each other. Remember how it used to be? We were madly in love at the beginning – life was wonderful back then, and we can be like that again ... I'm sure of it."

As she was speaking, a shimmer of light filtered through the sheer curtains just to the side of her head. Those harsh features he had grown accustomed to appeared to soften in its subtle glow.

From a long-forgotten place he had no idea even existed anymore, Adam felt a slight softening on the fringe of his soul when he caught a glimpse of the effervescent young woman he had once fallen in love with. There was that same sparkle shining in her eyes, along with a hint of the carefree attitude that had once captivated his heart. Hearing the desperation underlying her words, coupled with the pleading tone in her voice, gave birth to a semblance of compassion he had never thought possible again.

Disgusted with himself, he shrugged off these long-forgotten sentiments – along with her hand. It was Lara he loved ... Trina had already been given far too many chances – and then thrown them all away.

"I *can't*, Trina, and I'm not going to discuss it any more – this isn't the time or the place. When I get back to Brisbane, we can sit down and talk about a divorce settlement." He looked at his watch. "Now look, I'm sorry, but I need to get going. There's still heaps that needs doing before the plane leaves. Please just go and I'll drop by the house tomorrow sometime."

He had already made up his mind to stay overnight at his parents' home. Adam was determined not to give his wife any further ammunition to use against him or Lara, including living together while waiting for the divorce.

There was nothing more to say, so he pushed back his chair and stood up.

Her eyes searched his face, brimming with optimism and hope, even after listening to his cold, parting words. It was almost as though she was trying to seek out the man she once knew and offer him the life once promised.

She picked up her bag. "Okay, it's time I went too, but please … at least think about what I've said and try to imagine what our marriage could be like again." For a moment she paused to look him straight in the eyes. Then with a tender expression he hadn't seen for years, she couldn't resist trying one more time. "You loved me once…"

Again, the image of a carefree young woman with red hair scurried across his mind, but he quickly flicked it away. "Yes, I did, very much … but you threw it back in my face once too often."

"You're still committed to our marriage, Adam – otherwise you would've gone years ago. And that's purely because you can't forget what we once had."

He couldn't answer, but he didn't need to. Trina could tell he had gone back to those days for a brief second. She looked at him intently as the makings of a hopeful smile played across her lips and touched her eyes.

See, I knew you still cared…

Adam was horrified at himself and waves of both disgust and betrayal washed over him. With a hastily thrown away, "Goodbye," he hurried away without looking back, berating himself all the way up in the lift.

What are you doing, you idiot! Don't encourage her! How could you do that to Lara…

§

The door burst open just as Lara was closing the lid on the last suitcase. She looked up, her body trembling with fear because of what she might find in his eyes. While her conscience dictated there was only one choice left to make, her heart longed to sweep the three of them away from the bleak and heartless reality that suddenly had control of their world.

Striding purposefully across the room, he swept her into his arms and pressed her body hard against his. With one hand splayed across her back and the other pressing her head into his shoulder, his need to protect Lara from all that had just happened was his only priority.

"It's okay, Baby, she gone and won't be coming back. It's all over … I told her I'd meet her at the house tomorrow to discuss the divorce. And she didn't even make much of a scene, thank goodness. I'm so thankful you were up here and didn't have to face her."

Lara could only nod into his shoulder. Since the encounter with his wife, her heart had been in turmoil. She was certain he would hear it in her voice and the last thing she wanted was to tell an outright lie.

He could feel the tension in her shoulders and grasped the tops of her arms, holding her away from him as he searched her face. "What is it, sweetheart? Everything's good now, there's no need to worry anymore."

Concern clouded his eyes as he tried to reassure her and she tried her hardest to rustle up a convincing smile. Pushing away long strands of hair, he pressed his lips against her forehead and a slight tremor pulsed through her veins as she leaned heavily against him.

The sensation brought with it a mass of goosebumps and he pulled her close again, running his hands firmly up and down her spine. "Oh, Baby, everything's going to be fine. We don't have to worry anymore. I've told her it's too late for us – now it's our turn. I'll ask Mum and Dad if I can stay with them tonight and then go over to the house first thing in the morning to pack my things and tell her I'm leaving for good. Once that's done, she's sure to get the message and realise it's really over."

Still there was no answer. How could she when the only thing he wanted to hear would need to be a lie. Knowing the reality of what lay ahead, the heavy beat of her heart was like a death knell ringing out the end of their love story.

Swallowing deeply, she finally managed, "Was she upset when you left?"

Much to his disgust, he remembered that tiny glimmer of hope in Trina's eyes right at the end, but he quickly pushed it aside. "Let me put it this way … I left her in no doubt our marriage is over, even if she didn't want to believe me."

Lara held his gaze as the back of her fingers caressed the line of his jaw. Out of her heart poured the truest words she would ever form, rising from the smouldering ashes of their dreams. She didn't even realise her eyes were glimmering with unshed tears – and neither did he as her words fed his soul.

"Well, my darling, I want you to believe this. From the very first moment we met, my life has been touched with the most beautiful light – those gentle life-giving rays flowing from your spirit. From the moment I wake up every morning, I've felt the warmth of your love and its gentle glow ... and then every night when darkness falls, a trail of stars has led me to your heart ... it's the one place I know I can rest easy."

A small droplet escaped and tricked down her cheek. He reached out and touched it with the tip of his finger, his own eyes glistening as she went on, completely oblivious to the underlying pathos underpinning every sentiment.

"Whenever you touch me with these loving, gentle hands" —she picked one up and touched his palm with her lips and then pressed it against her cheek— "it's as though the strains of the symphony playing in your soul blends with mine. Even when we're apart, I can feel you in my spirit, and it keeps me going until the next time we're together. I will love you, Teddy, until the last breath leaves my body ... and even then, my love will continue into eternity. Above all ... my greatest wish is for you to be happy every single day of your life. No one has ever touched my heart the way you do ... or ever will again ... you are my hope and all my joy."

Adam could see the truth of every word shining in her eyes. He knew each one was absolute ... and without her, his life would be a never-ending void.

Feeling overwhelmed by the sincerity of her promise, all he could do was hold her close and breathe out a long sigh of relief ... while she breathed in that familiar beloved scent that was his alone deep into her spirit – over and over and over...

He was looking with hope into a longed-for future ... all she could see was a bleak tundra plain of emptiness, with only memories to keep them company through the loneliness.

These last few hours were all they had left now – a treasure trove of moments to savour and to cherish – and wrapped in a cry from her heart that would need to sustain them both for the long, lonely road ahead.

§

And out in that other universe, masterful hands painstakingly tended a magnificent canvas artwork. Among the richer blends, several strands of a more-muted hue began making a crisscross pattern through the thick backing.

This new work of art took on the form of a watermark behind the other images ... of a tall, strong oak with roots buried deep inside the fertile earth of two hearts that would always beat as one.

Chapter 16

The porter had already taken their bags when Lara and Adam went to leave her suite. For a moment she hesitated, looking back over her shoulder to catch a final glimpse of the place where they had shared so many happy memories. This little haven had been their home for many months and the changes about to be set in motion from the simple act of closing the door weighed heavily on her mind.

"Are you okay, Baby?"

"Mmm ... just a bit sad to be leaving..."

"Hey, don't forget what lies ahead!" he answered with a glowing smile.

Such an innocent response and yet it cut deep into her soul. Ducking her head behind a long strand of hair, she closed her eyes, trying hard to hold the broken pieces of her heart in place for another few hours.

He took her hand as they made their way to the downstairs lobby where the others waited anxiously for news of his meeting.

Charles spoke for all of them. "How did it go, son?"

"As expected, but at least she knows how I feel."

Before he could go on, his mother cut in. "Did she cause a scene?"

"No, surprisingly she was quite rational, although I must admit we didn't talk for very long." He didn't want to go into too many details in such a public place, nor did he want to worry Lara by mentioning Trina's expectation of being able to salvage their marriage.

His father sent him a look of concern. Despite the changes Charles had seen during his own talks with her, he was surprised to hear she had taken the news so calmly. Adam tried to brush his unspoken questions away with a casual shrug. Elizabeth could only chew on her bottom lip, praying the disastrous marriage could be disposed of once and for all.

Both Suzie and Lucy took turns in giving Lara a hug, relieved it went so well after the threats of last time. As usual, Nikki regaled them with descriptive tales of everything she had seen on her walk, including one about a rogue seagull that tried to steal her ice-cream cone. Lara was grateful for the distraction as it helped to push the harsh reality down into the deepest recesses of her mind. Nothing was allowed to spoil what little time they had left.

Lunch was a relaxed affair at an authentic Italian café in the Darling Harbour precinct. The table was covered with all manner of pasta dishes, each one tossed through with lashings of fresh seafood, spicy chorizo or other ingredients to tickle their taste buds. The variety of sauces smothering each one made their mouths water and the hungry tribe were soon tucking in with gusto.

The conversation centred mainly on the exciting new projects most had planned for the next few weeks. Lucy and Jeff had been offered the leads in Paul's new production of *Mary Poppins,* with Charles taking the role of *Mr Banks*. Suzie and Ben had booked a relaxing week on one of the tropical islands of the Whitsundays in The Great Barrier Reef. These recent Sydney weekend sojourns had whetted their appetites for a real break. Lara and Adam joined in as much as possible, although too many other things were already rolling around in their brains to take everything in – and both at opposite ends of the spectrum.

It wasn't until they were settling into their seats on the flight home that Lara figured out the only possible solution for what she needed to do. Both she and Adam were in First Class – one of the conditions Max had insisted on in their *My Fair Lady* contract – and his parents were seated only two rows further back. The rest of the group travelled in the economy section, with Nikki in a vacant seat beside her aunt. Suzie missed seeing the little girl each week and suggested the change of plans to give Lara and Adam a brief respite from her never-ending questions. It was the ideal solution and Lara was quick to agree.

As the plane taxied out, her foot tapped an impatient beat, while a hand kept fidgeting with the crease of Adam's trouser leg and left a damp impression.

It was natural to presume it was all due to excitement and he pressed his mouth against her cheek with a reassuring smile. "Not long now, Baby!"

Lara tried hard to smile back, but once the seatbelt sign was switched off she leaned in to whisper, "Would you mind if I swapped seats with your dad for a little while? It'd be nice to have a chat with Elizabeth and this is probably my only chance before going back to work."

"Sure, just so long as you don't stay away too long… I'm getting quite partial to having you by my side."

She didn't dare let those words land in her heart, too afraid they would tempt her back from what her spirit had already decided was the only right thing to do.

"I'll be back soon," she promised, leaving him with a warm peck on the cheek and eyes that were too afraid to meet his.

Adam was happy to spend time with his father. It would be the perfect opportunity to ask about staying with them until he could find a place of his own.

Much to Lara's relief, Charles was just as happy to swap places. He was still worried about what had occurred at the meeting and hoped his son might open up a bit more. Elizabeth was pleased to have an opportunity to catch up until Lara sat down and the deep set of worry lines creasing her brow gave away something major was going on.

For what seemed like forever, the young woman tried to gather her thoughts, swallowing hard and nibbling at her bottom lip. The last few days had been worrying times for all of them, so Elizabeth waited patiently, reluctant to press her unexpected travel companion until she was ready. Lara tentatively glanced sideways and opened her mouth to say what was on her mind ... then just as quickly closed it again. Dropping her eyes, she fiddled with her thumbnail while still chewing steadily on that lip.

Adam's mother was finding it much too difficult to act as though nothing was going on. Taking the other woman's nervous hand in hers, she rubbed it gently as her brow creased with worry. "What is it, my dear? You can tell me."

"Oh, Elizabeth..." —Lara swallowed hard— "I have the biggest favour to ask ... I'm just not sure where to begin. But you have to promise to hear me out before saying anything."

"Of course, you know you can ask me anything." She squeezed Lara's hand and smiled kindly. "And don't worry, take your time. We've more than an hour before landing."

Lara held on like a child who had lost its mother and then found her again.

The words came slowly ... with long, drawn-out pauses as she formed each one in her mind before giving them substance. "Thanks, you're so lovely ... but I'm afraid ... you're not going to like ... what I have to tell you."

Elizabeth couldn't miss the troubled look in her eyes. She was suddenly filled with an ominous foreboding, similar to one from the year before. Having given her promise, she waited patiently for Lara to go on, although somewhat dreading what else was coming after those first few halting phrases.

Lara drew in a very deep breath and then let it out slowly. "As you already know, Adam spoke to Trina this morning." Still fighting to get the words out, her gaze remained fixed on their joined hands. "What you don't know is ... in the middle of the night ... he made up his mind to leave her ... and now he's going to demand she give him a divorce."

Elizabeth's eyes lit up and she gripped Lara's hand with excitement without registering just how damp it was. "Oh, Lara, this is *wonderful* news!"

When she saw the other woman's downcast expression, all of that joy soon evaporated and the rest of what she wanted to say fell away like Scrabble tiles scattering across the floor. "What is it, my dear? What's happened?"

Lara's tone was strained and Elizabeth had to concentrate hard to catch each word. "He wants to stay with you ... at least until he can find somewhere else to live ... and I shouldn't be pre-empting him by telling you all this ... but I have to because there's something else you need to hear."

"Of course he can, and it's about time!" burst from her lips, though the tone underpinning everything made her stop short.

Lara paused again to take another deep breath. Eventually, she managed to croak out the rest, only this time the dialogue came fast and intense, similar to a freight train on a collision course. It was the only way she could get everything out without falling apart.

"The other thing you don't know is that Trina had a private talk with me before she went to see Adam – and he doesn't know about this, so I need you to *promise* never *ever* to say anything to him."

Hearing Elizabeth's sharp intake of breath was the catalyst for Lara to finally look into her eyes. The expression on her face was one of pure misery.

"It was awful – she begged me to let him go ... said she has no one else to turn to. None of her family care, so Adam is all she has left. She kept telling me over and over again how much she's changed and never wants to go back to her old ways. Deep down, she knows he still cares about her, and I know that's true ... he told me the same thing when he first opened up about his marriage."

Having to whisper so Adam couldn't hear only seemed to magnify her anguish. Lara bowed her head, so wretched and heartbroken she didn't even feel the soft splash of tears onto their coupled hands.

Elizabeth clicked her tongue. "But, Lara, that's her own fault. He doesn—"

"No, please don't say anything. I know exactly what you're thinking, but if I don't say this now, I never will ... and I *have* to." With a strangled cry, the distraught young woman uttered words that once upon a time would have seemed impossible. "I ... I have to let him go ... even though it br...eaks my h...heart."

Elizabeth's mouth fell open and the cry came from the deepest part of her soul. "*Nooo.*"

Lara could only shake her head and push on, composing herself enough so the terrible pronouncement was audible through a rush of choked sobs.

"I *have* to if they're to have any chance at all. She was his first love ... his *only* love until I came along. Charles said she's changed and it's true, she was so sad and full of remorse. There were no demands or threats anymore ... just a broken, lonely woman. I honestly believe she meant what she said."

Elizabeth let out an exasperated groan, gripping Lara's hand hard with the force of her words, and having difficulty trying to keep her voice down so it didn't carry further down the plane. "*Nooo*, Lara. You *mustn't* believe her. She's even hoodwinked my beloved, naive husband. Trina's just a conniving wicked woman who'll say or do anything to keep Adam as her meal ticket. She always has."

"I understand how you feel, truly I do ... but if you could've seen the look of desperation in her eyes and heard the despair in her voice, I'm sure you'd feel the same. I can't help feeling sorry for her."

"Feeling sorry for her is one thing ... breaking his heart is another! My dear girl, think about *Adam!* If you leave, it'll *destroy* him. These last few months with you – and those in Europe last year – are the only snippets of happiness he's known since they married. Don't forget how heartbroken he was all those months you were apart. Please don't do this to him ... not if you love him ... *pleeaase,* Lara!"

The tears coursed down the young woman's cheeks as she listened to her pleas, but still she couldn't forget the look in those haunted green eyes earlier.

"I *am* thinking of him, honestly! That's all I *have* been doing, and because I love him so much, this is the only right thing to do. Deep in his heart, Adam's still committed to her ... even though he tries to deny it. He always has been ... you know that ... or he would've left years ago."

"But Lara, that was before you cam—"

"No, it's true. Remember when she was sent to rehab – it was the ideal time, but still he couldn't leave, not even after she came home, and that only goes to prove what I'm saying is true. I love him too much to blame him or get angry ... and I couldn't bear to see the guilt slowly eating away at him either – and it will. I've seen it in his eyes and know him too well to believe he'll ever forget the vows they made – and he'll never be able to forgive himself if any harm comes to her. They need to at least have a chance to see if the marriage can work this time. She's different and he's sure to see it too when they're together again. I don't have any other choice – I have to let him go..." Her voice tapered off at the finality of what this would mean.

"Lara, *listen* to me!" It was as if a fire blazed behind Elizabeth's glare and her whisper turned into an exasperated hiss. "He won't forgive himself if he *loses* you. *You're* what he needs more than anything! Trina's had more chances than she deserves and blown it every time. This is *your* time – yours and his. You two are perfect for each other ... you know that as well as I do. I don't understand how you could even consider doing this, not when he's finally made up his mind."

"And that's exactly why I *have* to. He only made his mind up *after* finding out Trina knew about us – she forced his hand – it wasn't his decision really. He's only doing it for my sake and I can't let him. Yes, he thinks it's the right thing to do at the moment, but it'll continually eat away at him – and forever at the back of his mind will be the question, 'What if...?', especially if Trina does anything to harm herself or decides to turn to alcohol again. I love him too much to let that happen."

They gripped each other's hands with the force of their words and two sets of fingernails bit into the soft flesh of their palms, though neither of them noticed. Both were too determined to get their individual points across to care.

Just then, the steward came by offering refreshments. Shaking their heads, they waved him away.

Determined to make her friend see reason, Elizabeth turned fully in her seat, still grasping Lara's hand firmly and holding her gaze. "But that's *her* decision – she still has free will. It doesn't mean you have to give up *your* dreams."

Lara shook her head in desperation, oblivious to any other pain except the one in her heart. "And what sort of person would I be to achieve my dreams and destroy someone else's? I can't do that – no matter how much I love—"

But you'll be destroying Adam's dream if—"

"Adam's dream was always to have the Trina he fell in love with sharing his life again. Yesterday I caught a glimpse of that woman he once loved. I just *can't*, I'm sorry – I can't do it to *either* of them."

"But what about Nikki? How's *she* going to understand what's going on, and who's going to explain why he's suddenly disappeared from your lives again?"

Lara broke into a sob, pushing away the scenario Elizabeth's words created. "Please don't! I can't think about that. I've no idea how I'm going to tell her ... but we have each other, so we'll just have to get through it together. I *have* to do this, Elizabeth, please understand. As soon as I saw that look on her face – one of fear and absolute despair – I had no other choice. I know what that *feels* like – I've been there myself ... so many times – and there's no way I can deliberately put someone else through that living hell ... not even her."

Realising she wasn't going to change her mind using Adam or Nikki as a form of persuasion, Elizabeth tried another tack, determined to use any means to make her see sense. "Well, what about you? How are *you* going to cope? Don't forget, I saw how broken you were last time – and that was only for a few months ... this would be for the rest of your life!"

A long sigh escaped, and Lara's voice shook, though her gaze remained steady. "I'll just have to learn how. I know what you're thinking, but it won't change my mind, Elizabeth ... no matter what you say or how much I love him. I need to let him go so they can have their chance. Until I came along, being in a happy marriage with Trina was all he wanted. And isn't that what true love really means? Putting the other person's needs first."

Adam's bewildered mother would never have thought Lara could be so unyielding, even though it was obvious her heart was breaking. All she could do was shake her head sadly. "Well, my darling girl, you're making the biggest mistake of your life ... but unfortunately, I can't force you to change your mind."

Hearing her sudden capitulation, Lara's chin dropped onto her chest.

Elizabeth drew the battle-worn woman into her arms and rocked her gently.

"Oh, my dear, this is so so wrong, but no matter what happens or where life takes you, I'll *always* be here for you and Nikki. Never forget that."

"Thank you, that means everything – I'm just so sorry I had to hurt you, too."

"You have, I won't pretend any different, but you're like my own daughter, and I can't stop loving you, even though this is going to break my boy's heart."

Lara raised tear-filled eyes. "I know, but this is the only right thing to do – it's the only way they'll get a chance to put things back together. If I stay in the picture, he'll always be torn two ways, and it'll end up ripping him – and possibly us – apart."

"Oh, *Lara*—"

Now it was Elizabeth with tears spilling down her cheeks as any further response caught in her throat. Lara reached over to wipe them away and brushed away her own at the same time.

"To be honest, I have no idea how I'm going to let him go ... I just know I have to." She took a deep breath. "And that brings me to another favour..."

Elizabeth looked at her in dread, wondering what else was coming, and the one making the request could almost feel her despair.

"When Adam tells you his plans, please don't let him talk to Trina until I've had a chance to speak to him first. I'll ring first thing in the morning to tell him I'm coming over. That way we can at least have tonight..."

Lara had already decided not to say anything until the following day, knowing full well Adam would do everything in his power to make her change her mind. She had no doubt it would cause a terrible argument, and to make matters worse, this would be their first and only fight. Even though it would make saying goodbye that much easier, she didn't want memories of their final few hours filled with anger and harsh words.

Elizabeth could only nod despondently and let out a deep sigh. "All right, I'll do my best ... just don't leave it too late. Knowing Adam, he'll want to go over there as soon as possible to get everything over and done with."

"I won't, I'll ring as soon as I've taken Nikki to school and then come over straight away. But I need your solemn promise never to tell him what happened between Trina and me."

She nodded sadly. "As much as I'm going to regret this, I do promise, but I know without a doubt you're making the biggest mistake of your life."

With a stifled whimper, Lara put her arms around her heartbroken friend – not only to offer comfort, but also to show her gratitude for all the care and compassion she had offered, despite disagreeing with every part of her plan.

Deep in her spirit, she offered up a prayer for Adam's heart to mend quickly once he saw how much Trina had changed. The final plea tacked on the end was for him to eventually come to understand why she had chosen this path ... and then be able to forgive her. His happiness was paramount, and she truly believed it was the only right thing to do ... but she didn't dare think of a future without him. Nothing or no one would ever be able to take his place.

Elizabeth could see by the look in her eye there was nothing more she could say to make her change her mind. All she had left were arms offering forgiveness and a silent prayer Lara wouldn't come to regret this unexpected and dreadful decision. Deep down, she harboured a secret hope the poor girl would come to her senses and set about rectifying everything before it was too late. Heaven only knew how either of them would cope otherwise.

"I'd better get back to him before he sends out a search party," Lara said, wiping her eyes and making sure her mascara was still intact.

Using the wet towel from the airline's complimentary toiletry bag, Elizabeth used it to help with the hurried repairs. "Of course. But Lara, please take some time to reconsider everything. This is so wrong in every respect."

"I know you think so, but I have to do what's right ... and I truly believe this is the *only* right thing to do. But I am very very sorry."

Lara reached over, gave her grieving friend one final hug of gratitude, and then summoned up a smile so Adam wouldn't suspect anything.

Charles was more than happy to give up his temporary seat, squeezing Lara's arm with an excited grin as they changed places. It was obvious the men's conversation was far happier than the one she had just been a part of.

"Are you okay, Baby?"

"Sure, I'm fine. Sorry I took so long. Your mum and I just had heaps to talk about."

"All good, I hope," he smirked.

She nodded, pressing her cheek against his. "Absolutely, and mostly about how wonderful your future's going to be!"

"*Our* future," he corrected, planting a quick peck on the end of her nose.

Lara's throat was raw from unloading so many heart-wrenching revelations – as well as trying to hold the tears in check – so she could only nod again. For the rest of the flight, her head rested against his shoulder, and loving fingertips picked up a soulful dance as she tried to imprint his touch on her skin.

When the pilot announced they were coming in to land, Adam gripped her hand, and his smile was huge. "Oh, I almost forgot, Dad's thrilled to bits with the news and invited me to stay for as long as necessary. He reckons they've waited far too long for their wayward son to come to his senses!"

It took everything within her to muster up a smile. "I figured you must've told him by the huge grin on his face when we swapped places."

"Pretty obvious, hey! So straight after breakfast I'll pop around to the house and tell her I'm leaving. But how about tonight we grab a taxi and spend a few hours at your place – just the three of us. And once Nikki's asleep, I want to spend a few quality hours with her gorgeous mother!" Those alluring dark eyes twinkled as he placed her fingers against his lips, raining a shower of kisses on each one. "After everything that's happened today, I think we deserve some time alone. And soon we'll get to spend the rest of our lives together – *nothing's* going to keep us apart anymore!"

Blinking back the tears, she quickly looked out to the vacant sky, while he sat beside her, humming happily under his breath.

A short time later at the baggage carousel, they met up with the others to wait for the luggage to arrive. Lara was careful to avoid Elizabeth's searching gaze. Instead, she chatted with her sister and Lucy, slapping on a cheery smile as they talked about the exciting possibilities about to open up in her career and personal life. Not too far away, it was obvious how excited Adam was as he sparred with Jeff and Ben in a playful bout of shadow boxing. Nikki did her best to protect her favourite uncle, willingly taking on his opponents with her small fist raised. In the middle of all the commotion, a bottle of fruit juice slipped from her other hand and spilled all over his shoes.

"Oh, pumpkin, now look what you've done," Suzie laughed as Adam started shaking his foot to get any of the sticky residue off.

Lara pulled a handful of clean tissues from her bag and helped her sister mop it up as best they could, grateful for another excuse to ignore those sad, pleading eyes.

Unfortunately, her ploy didn't work. Just as they were about to hop into a waiting taxi, Elizabeth rushed over and took Lara in her arms. "Please don't do this," she whispered into her ear. "You'll break his heart and everyone else's."

"I have to – please forgive me," came the raspy reply before Lara scrambled into the back seat and deliberately kept her eyes fastened on the road ahead.

§

As soon as the taxi pulled into the driveway, Nikki raced from the car and scrambled up the stairs.

"We're home, Annabelle, we're home!" she yelled, hopping up and down on the veranda as her mother searched for the key. Adam was still paying the driver and helping with the luggage.

"Hang on, Poppet; just let me open the door."

"Quickly, Mummy, I can hear all my toys calling out to me!"

Before the key was even out of the lock, the excited youngster burst inside, running off to her bedroom with a loud squeal of delight.

Adam dropped their suitcases in the middle of the living room floor and pulled Lara into his arms with a beaming smile. She soon found her mouth being smothered by a passion-fuelled kiss that made her go weak at the knees.

Coming up for air, he declared, "Welcome home, my lovely. Sydney was fabulous, but now we're about to begin an even better chapter in our lives, and this little place is going to see *loads* of good lovin'!"

His enthusiastic grin broke her heart all over again. Plastering on a happy face, she pretended to be just as excited ... while inside she was slowly dying.

The reality of the momentous decision suddenly hit her like a ton of bricks – there was no way she would be able to break the news to his face. His look of hope was so plain to see it felt as though a knife had sliced open her soul; how could she possibly say the words while looking into those trusting eyes? The only way was by making sure several miles separated them; otherwise, she wouldn't have the strength to go through with it.

His lips touched the tip of her nose again – it was one of those affectionate gestures he always used whenever he was truly happy. "Well, my love. Seeing there's nothing in the fridge, how about we grab some Chinese takeaway and take it up to our favourite lookout for a picnic dinner to really celebrate our homecoming?"

Without realising, Adam had chosen the only place worthy to share their final meal ... tonight needed to be perfect before the fairy-tale had to end. If nothing else, Lara would always have memories of spending it beneath the stars where so many other special memories had been made. She only hoped Adam would one day feel the same and not hate her for what she was about to do.

But then again, she reasoned, maybe it would be for the best if he was to have any chance of moving on with his life.

§

Nikki sang at the top of her voice the whole way up Mt Coot-tha's steep incline and the happy sound almost broke her mother's resolve. She couldn't deny that whenever Adam was with them, the little girl was happier than at any other time.

Lara looked across at her beloved soulmate as he lifted his voice to join in.

Oh God, please let me be doing the right thing. Nikki adores him, and he's my life ... the very reason I breathe. Please don't let me regret this.

Adam reached over and grabbed her hand, resting it on his knee as they drove along. All of a sudden, the thought of never seeing that gorgeous smile again was like a sharp dagger piercing her heart – until she remembered all of those long lonely hours spent waiting at home for an unfaithful husband. No matter how conflicted she felt, there was only one morally right thing to do.

"I can't wait 'til tomorrow, Baby! In just a few hours we'll be starting our brand-new lives together and with no fear of what Trina can do to us! If I'd realised we were going to be this happy, I would've left her the night we met!"

Lara wanted to place her hand over his mouth to stop the words that were making her heart ache even more. All she could do was hold onto this moment and be grateful for all those they had already shared.

Her eyes brimmed with unshed tears. "These last few months with you have been the happiest ever. I'm so thankful you came into my life and I'll hold our memories safe in my heart forever." She almost choked on the words.

He had no reason to think they were anything but happy tears and sent her a loving wink. "And there'll be many more, just you wait and see."

Ever so gently, he moved his hand so it was cradling her cheek. She leant against it with her eyes closed ... until a car flew past beeping its horn and he had to grab the wheel again.

All the way up the mountainside, Lara had to keep reminding herself, *Think of Trina ... remember the look in her eyes ... she needs him more than you do.*

She didn't dare contemplate how much Adam needed both her and Nikki.

And then that reminder into a plea. *Father God, please let time stand still ... just for tonight ... somehow.*

It was a fruitless prayer, but she needed to ask.

With that dark cloud looming, she was even more determined to make the most of every one of these last few hours. And more than anything she hoped that one day, no matter how much distance separated them, they would both be able to look back and remember how happy they had been right to the very end.

§

They made their way to the grassy patch at the edge of the lookout. Nikki skipped on ahead, searching out small skinks as they basked in the final rays of sunlight before scurrying off to their rock homes for the night.

Adam laid out a blanket, and it wasn't long before the trio were tucking into two containers of tasty Asian stir-fries and then soaking up the last dregs of sauce with tiny balls of rice. Well, maybe the other two tucked in; Lara had to force every mouthful down. Just as well she could fall back on her acting skills.

Afterwards, they settled back to watch the first stars come out. Tiny pinprick glimmers peppered the late afternoon sky as it turned into a dusky pink and later a slow-changing purple canvas. Lara looked up, and she felt her heart sigh; this really was the perfect setting for making memories needed to last a lifetime. She stretched out on the blanket and rested her head in his lap, while Nikki's lively chatter brought some much-needed light-hearted entertainment.

To any onlookers, they were just your typical happy family enjoying the late spring twilight hours ... while out on an unseen horizon, dark storm clouds hovered over all of their tomorrows, building like a tsunami before readying themselves to wash all of those longed-for dreams out to an endless sea.

Looking up at him from under cover of a dark pair of lashes, Lara's heart ached. This was the last time she would ever know the intimacy of being with the man she loved. She couldn't imagine ever being with anyone else like this.

215

Similar to having their very own troubadour, Nikki trilled the well-known lullaby about a twinkling star as she curled up in a ball beside them, trying to make out the different constellations. Lara ran soothing fingers through her long silky mane and it wasn't long before the singing ceased and the little girl drifted off. After all the excitement of the flight and rediscovering her much-loved toys, the warm night air was the last inducement to lull her to sleep.

The lights of the city provided an enchanting luminous carpet spread out before them, while the final glow of an amber and lilac sunset painted a glorious hue across their skin.

"Have I mentioned lately just how much I love you?" Adam murmured, wiping a tiny grain of rice from the corner of Lara's mouth and then bending down to inch his tongue over the sticky residue left behind.

"Mmm," she whispered, licking her lips. "Not nearly enough ... but if you keep that up, I'm pretty sure I'll forgive you!"

Under cover of the gathering darkness, he moved her head from his lap to the rug and then lay facing her. Sidling closer so their bodies were just touching, he rested his head on one hand as a pair of dark expressive eyes held hers. That familiar pulsing drum thumped a rapid refrain in Lara's chest and she couldn't look away.

Ever so slowly, Adam stroked her face with his free hand as his lips explored her mouth, eyelids and cheeks – bit by bit and with infinite care. The tip of his tongue followed the same path, and it was as though whatever nourishment had been missing from the meal was now being sought from the very pores of her skin ... and his touch left her breathless.

Lara lay completely still with her eyes closed ... drinking in every exquisite sensation. Her only response was the almost indiscernible whimpers escaping from her aching throat. She needed to relish every brushstroke, every emotion ... desperate to believe that by staying completely still, time would follow suit and her earlier wish would come true.

Long minutes later, she opened her eyes only to find them held captive once again by his unwavering stare. As though mesmerised, their hands sought out every contour of exposed flesh, soothing and caressing with the delicacy of a feather. Fingers took on the impression of tiny caterpillars, inching their way across supple skin and then seemingly metamorphosing into glorious butterflies as this new intricate melody grew into a stirring symphony.

Music was as much a part of their lives as the love they shared, and when both elements combined, their hands became the perfect instruments to play the soulful piece ... and every movement became part of a loving composition.

The rousing orchestration created the perfect mood for tendrils of desire to entwine like grapevines around two parallel souls. As their fingers continued this slow dance, Adam gazed into Lara's eyes. "How about I take you home?"

Reaching up, she placed her lips on his as a controlled whisper and glistening blue eyes joined him in their sultry persuasion. "Mmm, I think you'd better."

The electricity flowing between them was like a sparkler lighting up the darkness.

Adam wrapped the sleeping child in the blanket and carried her over one shoulder. Using his free arm, he pulled Lara close. With one last lingering glance over her shoulder to the world below, her last thought was wondering how she would ever learn to live down there without him.

§

Soft candlelight bathed every corner of the bedroom, casting shimmering reflections against the walls as two figures sank slowly onto the bed. Their eyes mirrored that warm glow as the woman's hands gently undid the top few buttons of the man's shirt to reveal an alluring glimpse of the chest she knew so intimately. Her actions seemed bittersweet and she savoured each one as every touch served to reinforce the totality of how much she would miss him.

Lara gazed down at the man she adored, her chin resting on the hand spread across his chest. Amorous fingers strummed a slow ballad through his thick, wavy hair and lingered for several seconds on that much-loved silver fingerprint. All the while, her eyes feasted on the image of him stretched out on her bed. She wanted to imprint this moment on her heart and in her mind so she could take it with her every day for the rest of her life.

From Adam's perspective, all he could think about was the woman he loved with all his heart looking down at him with a look of complete contentment … too caught up in the moment to discern the infinite sadness lurking behind her intense blue gaze.

With a sense of being pulled into those unsuspecting dark pools, she whispered, "I just want to stay here for the rest of my life and never close my eyes again. You're the joy of my heart and no one has ever touched my life like you. Thank you for offering every part of yourself to me – I feel like we were once two halves who merged to become one kindred spirit. You've given me a lifetime of happiness in these past fifteen months ... even the long lonely weeks we were apart mean more to me than anything in those years before we met."

He was unable to speak over the lump in his throat and could only look into her eyes, basking in the knowledge of having found everything he could ever need in this special woman who spoke from the innermost parts of her soul. And yet there were so many more keepsakes she still needed to share with him stored away in her heart's treasure house...

"I remember lying right here in this bed alone every night imagining these beautiful eyes gazing into mine. And even though I missed you more than life itself, you were always right here with me – as if my heart lived inside yours … just as it will forevermore." She brushed a gentle finger across his lips. "And memories of this gorgeous smile provided so much comfort – like a faithful friend helping me make it through another day."

His eyes travelled all over her face and hair before coming to rest on her mouth. Raising his head a little, he touched her lips with his, then as he lay back down again, a gentle finger traced along the edge of her cheek. The message conveyed in his expression was both earnest and sincere, but when he tried to speak, nothing would come – how could he possibly compete with prose that seemed to stem from the heart of life itself? Instead, he spoke to her through a gentle touch and Lara pressed her cheek into his palm, breathing in his presence for what she wished could be an eternity.

A solitary tear trickled down her cheek and landed in among the curly tendrils on Adam's chest. Instinctively he caught it up and rubbed it lightly between his fingers. Watching his every move, she was held mesmerised when he performed the most intimate and touching gesture she could ever imagine. With infinite care, he lifted the salty residue to his lips and touched it with the tip of his tongue.

Their eyes held as Lara's teeth caught the fleshy part of her bottom lip and the love and commitment she read in his made her heart ache.

How will I ever learn to live without you, my love?

With exquisite tenderness, she trailed her lips and tongue over that same spot, tasting the damp remnant left behind as her fingers revealed more hidden morsels of this man who had stolen her heart. Adam felt a distinct tremor in the pit of his stomach and the subsequent sensations created by her gentle ministrations made him yearn to melt inside her warmth and never come up for air.

This was love in its purest form, with no hidden agendas ... just the unfathomable adoration of a man and a woman wholly at one with each other.

Still she continued this soulful dance, trailing delicate kisses in swirling patterns across the length and breadth of his chest ... while those alluring blue eyes never left his.

Torturous shivers ran up and down his spine … but he could no longer just lie there without tending to her need as well. Sweeping her into his arms, now it was his eyes and mouth bringing their own form of excruciating pleasure.

Their lovemaking took on the form of any of the great love scenes created for the silver screen – only these were real flesh and blood lovers conveying the raw passion arising from their most secret yearnings ... not actors performing choreographed actions with memorised lines. There were no cameras lurking in the foreground to capture their every move – just one lonesome spider still hiding in the darkened recess high above their heads ... the only witness to this total abandonment to desire.

Every rise and fall of their bodies were a reflection of their breathing and took them to heights never scaled before. He became an extension of her flesh, while she was the very embodiment of his spirit ... and together they soared to the stars so a rainbow arch of iridescent colours burst across their own private skyscape.

With backs arching and mouths gasping as though each breath was their last, these two – now one – clasped hands as the heat raced through their veins ... flying to their own slice of perfection as a single cry burst from parched throats.

Chests heaving with their bodies still melded together and that deep-seated need spent at last, they lay sprawled across one another, legs and fingers entwined ... quiet now, nothing left to give ... simply bathing in that delicious glow of fulfilment.

§

With Nikki's bedroom located on the other side of the house, there had been no need for either restraint or any other agenda except to give of themselves entirely. Adam luxuriated in the belief this was the beginning of their new life together ... and with no further mantle of guilt weighing him down.

Lara's reality was at the other end of the spectrum. This heartfelt act was her secret swan song – a tribute to the love of her life ... and in the darkness, a lone tear nestled on another of the soft tendrils covering his chest.

This time Adam didn't notice – he was still too caught up in the wonder of having found his true soulmate – one who was about to make his life complete.

Thankfully, he didn't have the ability to look into the future or else he would have seen the only world he had ever longed for begin to topple off its axis and tumble into a void of heartache and despair.

As though uttered as a prophecy, the emotion-laden monologue spoken from her heart just before their bodies became one floated into their spirits and took up residence there, waiting in readiness to offer comfort for all their tomorrows.

And on dark and lonely nights when the heartbreak closed in, images from this night and her heartfelt expressions would become vital lifelines in a world seemingly spinning out of control.

§

Time was moving far too rapidly ... the grandmother clock in the living room became Lara's greatest enemy when she heard its hourly chime.

Adam noticed it too. "Baby, I'll have to go – I don't have a key, so Dad's probably waiting up for me."

He placed a gentle kiss on her forehead and pulled her close for one last cuddle. Glancing over his shoulder, it seemed even the beautiful Venetian mask hanging on the wall shared her heartache. The intricate pattern on those porcelain cheeks resembled a trail of tears.

When he went to throw the covers off, she flung herself on top of him and pressed her body hard against his, dreading the thought of what was to come.

Thinking it was just a playful ploy to keep him there, he let out a loud chuckle. "Whoa, what's all this? I *can't* make love to you anymore. You've worn me out, you little wench!" He kissed her soundly and then nuzzled into her neck, expecting to raise a laugh.

Instead, she took a deep breath – really a sentimental attempt to inhale more of him into her spirit – and peeled herself away with a rueful smile. "Sorry ... but you can't blame a girl for wanting to steal a few more minutes with her favourite man!"

He snuggled in close and pulled her head even closer so that it rested under his chin. The fingers on his other hand stroked along the silky trail of hair covering her arm. "I can stay a bit longer if you really want. Dad won't mind."

Oh, my darling, if you only knew.

"No, you can't do that; he'll only worry. I'll be okay. I'm just being stupid – after all, it's been more than four months since I slept on my own, so it's going to be strange not having you curled up beside me."

An affectionate smooch landed on her nose and he gave a cheeky smirk. "Well, don't get *too* used to it! As soon as this divorce is through, you're never going to be sleeping on your own again."

If they were giving out Oscars, Lara would have received the top gong for her acting ability.

Mustering everything within her, she managed to plaster a big smile on her face. "I know and I can't wait! You're the only person I *ever* want sharing my bed. But you'd better go quickly, or I really *won't* be able to let you go."

The emphasis was a natural addition to what she knew lay ahead. Giving him a gentle shove, she tried to hold back the tears.

Her heart was breaking as he phoned for a taxi and it ached even more knowing this was the last time they would ever see each other in the glow of a candle's flame.

As they walked hand-in-hand through the living room, Lara realised there was one more thing he needed to do – for his sake more than anything else.

"Come with me," she whispered, opening Nikki's door as quietly as possible. "You'd better say goodbye to this one. She won't know, but it'd mean the world to me. Do you mind?"

He missed the deliberate choice of that one forbidden word. "Course not. You know how much I enjoy saying goodnight to our little Munchkin. I'm just sorry she fell asleep before I could do it properly. Not to worry, this'll do for now."

They tiptoed to the edge of the bed and stood looking down at the sleeping child who meant so much to both of them. Nikki seemed to be even tinier curled up in a tight ball when he bent down to kiss her cheek.

For some inexplicable reason, he kept stroking her hair as a spontaneous benediction rose from his heart. "'Night, little one, I love you more than you'll ever know and I'm so glad you came into my life. Sweet dreams, precious girl, and may God keep you safe until we can be a proper family. But hey, don't grow up too much before that happens – I don't want to miss any more of your life."

The woman standing beside him felt her heart shatter into tiny pieces and she had to will herself not to break down completely.

For a few seconds more, his hand rested lightly against Nikki's cheek. Then he turned to Lara with a heartbreaking smile and pulled her into his arms. "Thanks for sharing her with me. I love her as though she were my own, and once it's the three of us, I'll have more than I could ever need or want."

Lara couldn't answer as a bucket-load of tears bubbled up inside and she tried frantically to get rid of the huge lump in her throat. Tucking her head under his chin, they left the room with their arms wrapped tightly around one another. He pulled the door shut with a soft click and the thought that had been plaguing her all day long returned for another assault. *And there's another 'last'.* An innocuous everyday gesture that closed another door – one leading to a future he and the little girl were meant to share.

Instead of going outside to wait for the taxi, he pulled Lara into his arms again, nuzzling into her hair as though sensing she was in need of some extra form of comfort. Standing in the shadows, the only sounds were the beat of two hearts and a soft rustle of clothing as loving fingers stroked one another's back.

"Don't be sad, Baby," he said, breaking the silence when he felt her shoulders tremble. I'll only be staying with Mum and Dad for a little while. Then we'll be together forever. The divorce won't take too long – Trina and I have been living separate lives for years now so we won't have to wait the usual twelve months."

His words cut like a knife, but she forced herself to look up at him with an encouraging smile. "Mmm, that's right … but just don't forget how much I love you in the meantime, okay?"

Those compelling eyes gleamed. "How could I *ever* forget that! You showed me just how much tonight!"

"*Adam*, I *mean* it! It's *more* than just making love to you – I love you with *every* part of me."

He was surprised to hear so much passion in her voice, and pressed his mouth against hers, hoping to bring back the smile he adored. "I'm sorry. I know you do. I love you, too, with all my heart. You're my hope, and my sunshine, and I want to be the same for you. I promise to make you happy for the rest of your life."

"You already have – more than you'll ever know."

Almost forcefully, he pressed her hard against his side as they waited for the taxi to arrive.

He had no way of knowing this conversation would come back to haunt him over and over, or that in just a few short hours he would be questioning whether either one of them would ever know true happiness again. But with each new dawn, the only thing able to keep him going was convincing himself she truly was ... or else he wouldn't have been able to make it through another day.

But those dark days were part of their future ... now was all they had left.

Lara placed his hand in hers – palm upwards – and her fingers took on the persona of a lone ballerina, performing one final solo act in the dance begun so long ago. Like gossamer wings, they ran across every crevice and contour ... flitting this way and that ... leaving an indelible imprint wherever they touched.

Throughout this meaningful expression, she prayed he would store away the memory for all the long lonely hours that stretched away forever. And those dark eyes glowed as she seemingly mesmerised all of his body with her fingertips.

As the dance reached its conclusion, his hands cradled her face, running his mouth along porcelain-like eyelids then inching down to cover her lips. It was as though he was leaving his personal imprint to ensure she would always be his ... with no clue as to the heartbreaking realisation at just how little time they had left.

Before another sob could give her away, Lara captured his mouth again and her tongue caught his in a different form of dance routine. This was much stronger – desperate even – as if she was seeking out a way to entangle her spirit with his. Being on the receiving end of such a strong outpouring of desire when they had only just left her bed came as a surprise, although his rapid breathing betrayed his own rising need when the kiss went on for several minutes.

Adam's whole body yearned for her again and she could feel the heat in his hands. Struggling to breathe, he dragged his mouth away, and the expression in his eyes set her heart aflame ... until the beep of a car horn shook them out of this passion-driven state.

"Phew, if you keep that up I'll *never* leave!"

"Maybe I don't want you to," she whispered against his lips.

"Little vixen!" he smirked, still breathing hard.

Another short, sharp toot sounded. She threw him one more heartfelt smile before they hurried down the stairs.

"See you tomorrow, Baby – when it's all over. Dream only sweet dreams ... and remember, *I* may not be in your bed but my thoughts certainly will."

Oh, Teddy, stop it! You're making this far too hard.

Somehow, she mumbled, "Mmm, I know, and mine are always with you – forever and always ... I love you more than anything ... I always will..."

"That's all that's kept me going. I love you too, with every beat of my heart."

He stole another kiss, and she couldn't resist dragging him into her arms again, for one last memory of when he was hers alone ... though it was over much too soon when the cabbie mumbled something about having other fares waiting.

Adam rolled his eyes and dropped a kiss on her nose before climbing into the backseat. Their last physical contact was when Lara reached through the window and brushed her hand against his. Looking into one another's eyes, he sent her that unique gesture she knew so well – a subtle reminder of the depth of his love. Mustering up every ounce of strength she could find, Lara managed to return it with the one offering that same message – the one he alone knew ... and his farewell smile tore her world apart.

§

While in another dimension unseen by anyone, a thread of gold stayed steady and true to its course along the centre of a magnificent tapestry – a unique strand celebrating the unity of kindred spirits. And just as its Maker intended, this slender piece of fibre never once deviated from his original blueprint as it formed a silhouette of clasped hands entwined by a ribbon of musical notes in front of a setting sun.

Although lacking the brilliant hues of earlier images, this was more detailed and powerful in its meaning. And despite a barrage of menacing obstacles all waiting to consume the parallel lives playing out on the planet below, its silken course remained strong – though the fullness of its beauty faded away from their only reality to reside in dreams of a lost and precious time.

Without warning, a stiff breeze sprang up and a sudden shower of leaves fell from the branches of a sturdy oak – the same tree standing as a lasting foundation behind all of those other images. The small, teardrop shapes were carried along in the wind ... all except for one still clinging tenaciously to the thickest limb. The starkness of the tree's bare form seemed so out of place to what had come before – and yet that tiny sliver held on with all its might, determined to outlast whatever life in this much colder world may bring.

With the greatest of care, the Artisan carefully reached into his workbox and chose a strand of the finest silk dyed a vivid amaranth purple. It was enhanced with a pure gold thread – the same one used in so many of those other images when the two had become one.

Using a delicate touch along the slender spine of this solitary leaf, he wrote a single word in ancient script. Four simple letters carrying the theme begun in a melody created several vignettes earlier ... and one that would endure as long as those loving soulmates took breath ... *Hope* ...

Chapter 17

Lara hardly slept at all. Lying in gloomy silence with the constant pounding of her heartbeat like a battering ram out to destroy all of their dreams, her mind was a jumbled mess trying to compose what to say in the dreaded morning call – convincing phrases to prove to Adam he was better off with his wife. Like before, her pillow collected the multitude of tears running down her cheeks.

When the sun's first rays seeped over the top of the thick curtains, she struggled out of bed rubbing at her sore, red eyes. Clutching a much-needed mug of coffee to help sustain her, she wandered out to the veranda. For over an hour, Lara contemplated the morning ahead as the city slowly came to life ... until Nikki's cheerful chatter wafted through the window as she greeted her dolls.

Breakfast was quite a subdued affair. The little girl kept watching her mother with the makings of a frown marring her brow until Lara was able to reassure her she was just tired from the flight. Thankfully, David wasn't expecting her back at work until the following day. It was too hard to contemplate having to face anyone once the fateful call was done – especially not her astute boss – and she was grateful for the small reprieve.

"I get to see all my friends today!" Nikki announced, clapping her hands with glee as she ran off to get ready. "I can't wait ... yippee!"

Her bubbly demeanour managed to summon up a smile and it was just the wakeup call Lara needed. No matter what else was going on, her daughter's needs must come first. It would be hard enough losing Adam from her life without then having to watch her mother retreat into a bleak, dark world where nothing could penetrate.

§

The atmosphere was exactly the opposite in a guest bedroom of the Ashworth home. Like Lara, Adam had hardly slept, only for vastly different reasons as he envisioned spending the rest of his life with the woman who had given him back a future laden with anticipation and joy. His cheerful whistle as he skipped down the stairs made his mother groan and send a worried look her husband's way. What excuse could they think up to detain him until Lara's call? She was in no doubt he would be suspicious, but somehow they needed to convince him.

She and Charles were standing on the terrace when he came out to join them.

"'Morning, Mum, Dad, isn't this a glorious day! No wonder I love living in Brizzie when she puts on a display like this," he chirped, arms spread wide to emphasise the glistening sunlight where it danced on the surface of the river. The scene was made even more noteworthy by a few dusky rays filtering through a stand of tall gums lining the bank on the other side.

A long time had passed since the trio had shared breakfast in the family home. On any other day, it would be a welcome change. Unfortunately, the events about to unfold made for an entirely different scenario.

His father's greeting held its usual warmth, while Elizabeth found it too difficult to look directly at her son. All she could offer was a motherly hug, along with a mumbled, "Morning." Bustling from one to the other, she kept busy pouring cups of coffee and glancing at her husband, hoping he would be the one to bring up the dreaded subject. She had neither the heart nor the strength.

Claiming the chair beside her boy, she rested a loving hand on his arm in a silent act of support. He leaned across and kissed her cheek, and his carefree smile made her heart ache. Charles' eyes filled with compassion looking across at his family. Knowing how much Adam loved Lara, he was dreading what this day would bring and all the pain in store for his beloved son. He caught the anxious look Elizabeth sent his way and nodded sadly.

Taking a deep breath, he plunged straight in. "Adam ... son ... before you leave to go and see Trina, there's something I just need your help with, if you don't mind. It won't take too long."

The other man frowned as he looked up from buttering his toast. "But Dad, I wanted to get everything over and done with straight away as soon breakfast's over. Lara doesn't start work 'til tomorrow, so I want to spend the rest of the day with her afterwards. Can't we put it off until later?" He looked across at his mother. Surely, she knew how important it was to get the unpleasant task out of the way as soon as possible.

Elizabeth hated lying to him. Flicking her wrist, she tried to make light of it. "Oh Adam, just relax and enjoy your breakfast. I'm sure it won't take long to help your father and then you can be on your way. Trina's not going anywhere and Lara'll understand if you're a few minutes late."

He wasn't expecting this and an even bigger frown creased his brow. It took him a few seconds to reply. "Oh ... mmm ... yeah, okay. Just let me wash this down with a quick cup of coffee. But I hope you don't expect me to change clothes for whatever it is – I really need to get over there as soon as possible."

He finished spreading the toast with a clump of marmalade and bit off a large chunk – nothing like his usual good table manners – and was even more surprised when his mother plied him with another piece and filled his cup to the brim again.

"Hey, no more. I'm full as it is!"

"Oh, go on, it'll keep your strength up … I made it 'specially," Elizabeth stressed, glancing at her watch. *Nikki must be at school by now. Hurry up and ring, Lara…*

Suddenly, the sharp trill of the phone pierced the air. Charles quickly shovelled a spoonful of cereal into his mouth just as the pot in Elizabeth's hand hit the ground with a crash. It shattered into tiny pieces and spilled its contents all over the tiled floor.

"Oh, *now* look what I've done!" she exclaimed, dropping to her knees and mopping at the mess with her napkin.

"Careful you don't cut yourself, Bessie. Here, let me help," her husband garbled through the gluggy mouthful as he bent down to lend a hand.

With a bemused smirk, Adam pushed back his chair and hurried inside, calling over his shoulder, "Don't worry, I'll get it! If I didn't know better, I'd swear this was a set-up and you just don't want to answer it." He had already reached the kitchen and missed the look passing between his parents.

"Ashworth residence. Hello?"

Lara had been holding her breath as she dialled the number, and nearly hung up twice before he picked up. The sound of that beloved voice made all of those carefully rehearsed lines fly out the window.

"Teddy ... it's me." Her mouth was so dry she could hardly form the words, so they came out in a nervous whisper.

Instant panic set in – this was nothing like the voice he knew so intimately. *"Darling!* Where are you? You sound miles away. Are you okay?"

"Yeah ... I'm fine ... just got home from taking Nikki to school."

"Is she alright?"

"Yeah, she's fine, too." She couldn't mistake his loud sigh of relief.

"Well, *this* is a nice surprise. Couldn't wait to hear my voice, hey! It's lucky you caught me. I'm just about to finish breakfast and then Dad wants my help with something before going over to the house. Hopefully, it'll be all over in a couple of hours, and we can go out to celebrate. I thought we could head down to Miami for the day – just you and me and this glorious sunshine?" When she didn't answer, he felt a faint stirring of fear in his stomach. "Are you *sure* everything's okay?" This wasn't the usual bubbly person he recognised.

There was a blanket of silence ... then...

"Adam ... I have to tell you something ... and you need to listen carefully ... please..." The last word came out with a soft plea before dropping away.

"Sure, but what's going on, sweetheart?" More echoes of nothingness greeted him and he really started to panic. "Something must've happened, Baby – I can hear it in your voice." The silence was deafening and his face turned ashen. Dropping heavily into a nearby chair, he gripped the phone 'til his knuckles turned white. "What *is* it, Lara? *Tell* me ... *pleeeaaase.*"

All sorts of images flooded his mind – the worst being that Trina had found out where Lara lived and paid her a visit.

The anxiety in his voice made it so much harder. She took a deep breath to help gather her thoughts. *Lord, please help me.* Then...

"Teddy ... my love" —her voice broke, but she had to go on— "this is so hard" —she needed to swallow— "but I have to ask you to do something for me ... and I *need* you to understand. I've thought this all through and I know it's for the best. Don't say anything 'til I'm finished ... pleeaase..." She faltered, trying desperately to push through the tears.

Adam's heart was pounding in his chest and this time he was the one holding his breath. Her voice had never sounded so measured or underpinned with so much anguish. He suddenly had a horrible feeling his entire world was about to crumble away and his tone dropped to nervous stammer.

"Lara ... what – what's going on? I don't – I – *please* tell me ... I'm really starting to worry." When she didn't answer, he added in desperation, "Okay, that's it. I'm hanging up and coming straight over – I'll be there in a jiffy."

"No ... Adam, wait!"

Having to face him was the last thing she wanted. She would never be able to get the words out if he was standing in front of her looking into her eyes. He needed to hear it now while she was still strong enough to go through with it.

"You *need* to listen to me!" She had to pause again to fight down the lump in her throat. "Sweethea—" The loving endearment turned into a sob when she realised it would only make things harder for him. "Adam, I can't do this anymore. It's too hard – and it's wrong. You have to let me go ... I *need* you to let me go. This might be your only chance to make a new life with Trina. And if you're truly honest, deep down that's what you've always wanted."

Everything was a lie, but Trina's desperation was her driving force, and she knew Adam too well to tell the truth. She had to make him believe this was her decision alone. It was the only way her scheme could work. Anything else and he would see through her heartache and realise this was all his wife's doing.

"What! Lara, *nooo!* How can you *say* that when I'm just about to leave? It's *you* I want, not *her!* You *know* that ... what are you *talking* about? This is what we've *both* been waiting for..."

His anguish spiralled down the telephone line and landed with a thud in her heart. Hearing his distress nearly broke her resolve, but she couldn't let it take up residence ... she had to keep going. As much as it was going to break both their hearts, somehow she had to convince him he needed Trina more.

"No, Adam! I *need* you to listen to me." Her resolute tone was nothing like the Lara he knew and loved, but knowing this was the only way to convince him,

she ploughed on. "If we were really meant to be together, you would've come to me last Christmas. Deep down, we both know Trina's the one you should be with. You never stopped loving her – not rea—" she gasped on the word and had to cover her mouth to keep from crying out.

He couldn't believe what he was hearing. This wasn't the woman he had made love to the night before – revelling in the love they shared and looking forward to a bright future.

What's happened to make you like this?

He wracked his brain looking for an answer, but could only shake his head while she shattered all of their dreams. It was almost impossible to believe what he was hearing – and yet that steadfast tone confirmed her words.

Choking back a sob she continued, feeling as though she was back on stage reciting words belonging to someone else – and nothing she said was the truth, even though she did her best to make him believe her. It was the only way to help him move on.

"I don't want you coming around to see us anymore. It's not going to work ... not at the expense of someone else's happiness. Go to Trina ... make a life with her ... and forget about us. You *have* to, for *all* our sakes. *Pleeaase*, Adam, promise me you won't try to contact us again!"

"I *can't* promise *that! You're my life!* I *need* you..." His voice dropped and she could almost taste the surge of desolation coming through the phone line. "I thought you needed me, too ... I don't understand ... what about what happened last night – not just the lovemaking ... everything we said from our hearts?"

Elizabeth had followed him into the house. She couldn't stomach the idea of her son having to face this heartbreaking news alone. Listening to the despair in his voice and seeing the look of disbelief in his eyes, she slumped against the doorjamb with tears pouring from her eyes.

Charles had come in too. He went straight over to rest a comforting hand on the broken man's shoulder. When Adam's head dropped fighting to understand what was happening, that hand tightened his grip. But the poor man was too distraught and bewildered to register his father was even there and just shrugged it away. The older one understood and left him alone, going instead to provide some form of comfort to his distressed wife. All they could do was hold each other close and listen as their son's world came crashing down.

Lara knew she had to be brutal if Adam was to work on rebuilding his marriage and forget about her. "*Please* understand. *Everything* I said I meant with all my heart, but I've been thinking about this all night long. You *have* to get on with your life and leave me in the past." Her voice fell as she uttered the next plea. "And you mustn't ring me ever again ... I need you to let me go."

He was in a state of total shock trying to take it all in. Nothing could convince him what she was saying was true, but she was so adamant he could only respond in the agony of defeat. "I don't understand why you're doing *any* of this. I *love* you and I *know* you love me..."

Lara couldn't answer – unable to comprehend any of it herself – except for the echo of a wretched plea from a desperate woman.

With her silence, he felt his heart shatter into what felt like a million pieces. How could he possibly believe anything she was saying? He knew without a doubt she still loved him – last night proved that – but he had no wish to fight with her either. He had to believe she would come to her senses as soon as they hung up.

"If that's what you *really* want, then..." He couldn't bring himself to add any words of capitulation, and yet he did manage to choke back a sob and vow, "But I will never *ever* give up hope that one day we'll be together forever. I *can't*. Don't make me..."

Her voice broke as she whispered the phrase they had sworn never to say. "Goodbye, my love..."

The last thing he heard was an anguished cry, along with the faint whisper, "I'm *sooo* sorry, Teddy, please forgive me," and then the line went dead.

Like a robot, Adam placed the receiver in its cradle, then sobbed as though his heart was breaking ... head bowed down over his knees as he rocked backwards and forwards.

"Nooo ... *nooo! Whyyy...*"

Elizabeth rushed over and took him in her arms, rocking him like a baby as she crooned, "Oh, my darling boy, I'm so sorry. I knew this would break your heart, but there was nothing I could say that would make her change her mind."

Adam's head shot up as if he had been stung. He looked at his mother, eyes blazing with shock as the tears streamed down his cheeks. "Did you *know?*" When she offered a tentative nod, he pushed her away and sprang to his feet, pacing the floor with arms outstretched and shaking his head. He couldn't comprehend this added avalanche of betrayal. "Why didn't you *tell* me? I could have *stopped* her ... this is *crazy!* I was all set to leave. How could she have *done* this? How could *you* have *let* her..." His voice fell away.

"Don't go getting upset with your mother, young man," Charles chastened. As much as he hated seeing his son in so much pain, Elizabeth's wellbeing would always be his first concern. "She hasn't done *anything* except love you! *And* tried everything she could think of to talk Lara out of taking this path. For some reason that poor young woman was determined to go through with it, no matter how much Mum begged her not to."

"So *you* knew, too – *both* of you..." A loud rush of air escaped as he shook his head in disbelief. "And that means Lara knew before we left Sydney..."

Elizabeth couldn't deny anything. Somehow, she had to make him understand without breaking the promise she had made never to divulge the truth behind Lara's decision.

Grasping his arms with strong, caring hands, she looked him straight in the eye. "Adam, it's *not* her fault. It's no one's. Lara told me in confidence what she had to do and I couldn't break my word. Yes, it's too hard to understand, but she knew you would always feel obligated to Trina – she's sure you still care deep down – and in her mind, this was the only right thing to do ... for the sake of your marriage and to erase any guilt at having betrayed your vows. Of course, you feel devastated – deceived even – but she never meant it like that, truly ... you *must* believe me. She was thinking of you all the time – never herself."

He kept shaking his head to fend off the truth. Nothing anyone could say would convince him this was what Lara truly wanted – not even her own pleas.

Still his mother continued, though it was breaking her heart. "My darling, *darling* boy ... I don't want to say this ... but I have to. You *need* to let Lara go ... and if you truly do love her, you'll do as she asks and never try to contact her again. It's be*cause* she loves you so much this has happened – not because it's what she wants. But you need to promise to leave her be ... for *her* sake."

His head kept moving back and forth as he mumbled, "No ... no ... *no*..." but she wouldn't give up until he understood.

"Think how hard this has been on her when she loves you so much. *Don't* make it any harder – she can't change her mind, even though it seems wrong."

Frantic fingers ploughed thick tracks through his hair as the tears flowed. He was unable to respond with the answer she wanted when the one pounding in his heart was the only truth. *How can I possibly agree to never see her again?*

After long moments of denial, he offered a crestfallen nod and then fell into her arms clinging on like a drowning child. "I can't believe *any* of this ... it's crazy – it's just *wrong!*"

With a heavy sigh of defeat, he raised his head and the look of despair pouring from his eyes was every mother's heartbreak.

"If Lara thinks this is what she *really* wants then I have to go along with it ... but only for her sake, but I'll never *ever* stop loving her ... not even when I take my last breath. My love for her will go on and on until the end of time."

§

Out in that other invisible world, a long trail of musical notes floating across a detailed tapestry suddenly shivered as a cold blast of air rose from the Weaver's throat. His broken sob then lifted them from the staves of a symphony and blew them away on the wind...

A Father's Heart fractured into tiny pieces, just like those other two...

PART TWO

Brisbane, Australia

November 1989 to July 1990

Chapter 18

Reeling from the call that had just shattered all of his dreams into slivers of nothingness, Adam couldn't even stomach the idea of talking to his wife, let alone contemplate picking up the pieces of their marriage. There was no use anymore. Not even Lara's final pleas were enough to convince him. He couldn't bear the thought of sharing his life with anyone else, especially not the woman who had brought him so much misery.

Both Charles and Elizabeth tried to comfort their son after his reluctant surrender to do as Lara asked, but all he wanted was to be left alone with his thoughts. Similar to those first few months when he was a grieving teenager, he took himself off to the stable and Clancy was the one he turned to for solace.

At Elizabeth's urging, her husband found him there an hour later, sitting hunched up on the hay-strewn floor with the pony anxiously nuzzling into his neck as though trying to console him. Adam looked a picture of dejection with both arms wrapped tightly around his knees and his head resting against them, and Charles' heart broke at the sight.

Clancy raised his head, giving a gentle whinny as he patted the distraught man's shoulder. "Come on, son. It's time you came back to the house. Your mother's getting worried."

Shrugging the hand away, Adam spat out, "If Mum was *so* worried she should've told me what was going on instead of letting me find out so cruelly!" The bitter words came from a wounded spirit that felt betrayed by the one person he should have been able to trust more than anyone.

Charles had no wish to add to his pain, and so his tone was kind. "You know she couldn't say anything, son. She gave Lara her word."

Hearing her name, Adam felt as if a sword had pierced him through – nothing else could inflict this much hurt. *How will I ever get through this?*

The two men ambled back to the house, Adam with his head down and brushing at his eyes as Elizabeth watched from the doorway, worry lines riddling the fair skin of her face. From behind the fence, the faithful pony sniffed the air as they walked away, almost as if to make sure his old friend was okay.

"I'm so sorry, Mum."

Wrapping heavy arms around her neck, Adam held on as though his very survival depended on her strength. They stayed like that for several minutes, her loving contact bringing a small measure of comfort to the heartbreak wracking his soul. When they eventually broke apart, she pressed gentle lips against his cheek. There were no words necessary – only a mother's love evident in her forgiving gaze.

For another hour he closeted himself away in his old room, lying on top of the bed with his ankles crossed and a forearm hiding his eyes. Over and over he kept rehashing every minute of the gut-wrenching call. He still couldn't believe she meant all those things – not after the night they had just shared. With her adamant declarations still echoing in his ear, along with that previously outlawed parting word, the tears flowed as he turned on his side and curled up in a ball.

Lara, my only love, I won't ever say goodbye to you – I can't, was the mantra flowing through his mind.

Afterwards, he made his way downstairs, wandering out to where his parents sat forlornly at the kitchen bench looking just as distressed as him.

Elizabeth made each of them a mug of strong coffee, but no one was in the mood to make small talk as they perched on a row of barstools nestled beneath the window ledge looking out ... to nothingness. Draining the last of his cup, Charles glanced at his son and decided it was time one of them broke the silence.

"Listen, my boy, Trina's sure to be waiting and wondering what's going on. It's time you went over there to at least tell her what you've decided."

"There's no point anymore ... besides, I didn't get a chance to decide *anything*. And I'm not going back there to live – she'll only rub my nose in it when she finds out Lara's dumped me."

"*Adam!*" his mother interjected, sending him a frustrated glare. "She *didn't* dump you. Lara was thinking more of you than herself."

He stared glumly into his mug. "Well, she might as well have. She made it very clear she doesn't want to be with me anymore."

His parents looked at each other over their son's bowed head. They both knew who the real influence was behind her decision and Charles felt he owed it to Lara to ensure Adam at least made some sort of effort to do as she asked. After all, the distraught young woman was just as heartbroken and suffering from a massive amount of guilt for having put him through this, even though he was in the dark as to the reason why.

"I still think you should go over there to explain what's going on – you owe it to Lara," Charles insisted, wanting at least some semblance of good to come from this heartbreaking situation. "Besides I think you should at least see what Trina's done around the house and garden – you might be surprised at her new attitude. She's really trying, and as much as I hate to admit it, I truly think she's a changed woman. And yes, I know that doesn't make up for everything but..."

The men's eyes met, and Charles could see the cynicism behind Adam's gaze, but he decided to push a little bit harder. "Go on, it won't hurt. At least then you can work out what you're going to do. I know you're hurting, and she's the last person you want to see at the moment; but even so, I really think you should make some sort of effort."

His wife didn't agree at all. She was still angry with Trina for having the audacity to approach Lara in the first place, but Charles' warning frown, when she went to add her bit, made Elizabeth bite her tongue.

With a gentle squeeze of Adam's shoulder, he urged, "Just go on over for a little while. That way you'll see what I mean and can decide then."

Having nothing better to do with his time now, the wretched man let out a heavy sigh and shrugged his shoulders. "Alright, I suppose I could ... but I definitely *won't* be staying."

Elizabeth went and put her arms around his shoulders, squeezing tight as she kissed the top of his head. "You know you're always welcome to stay here for as long as you need. You don't have to decide anything at the moment."

"Thanks, Mum. I really appreciate it."

Charles walked him out to the car. "Just be gentle with her, Adam. I know you're upset, but don't go taking it out on her. She may not deserve your trust, or even your time, nevertheless she's obviously been working hard to change over the last few months. The least you can do is be civil."

"I'm not going to do anything stupid if that's what you're thinking. But I'm not moving back in with her – I have to believe Lara'll come to her senses and give us another chance."

"Fair enough, I understand, and that's what Mum and I are hoping for too. But just make sure you think before you speak. You're extremely vulnerable at the moment and it would be very easy to lash out at the slightest thing." Being so out of character, the earlier outburst had taken Charles completely by surprise, though he really couldn't blame him.

Adam could only nod, acknowledging the wisdom behind his father's words.

§

The meeting with Trina went better than expected, almost as if she knew her husband was hurting deep down. She didn't push at all. Instead, she simply allowed him to lead the conversation.

They met beside the lake on their property, around a table already laid out with a light lunch. Needless to say, Adam had no desire for food – he was still reeling from the effects of Lara's call.

Absentmindedly, he watched a family of ducks swimming between the waterlilies as the mother protected her brood from an overly inquisitive swamp hen. It reminded him of Lara and the way she always watched over Nikki. His eyes grew glassy and a lump formed in his throat as he imagined the two of them walking along the beach at Miami without him.

Trina noticed his reaction and guessed at the reason. *I owe you so much, Lara. You're a far better woman than I'll ever be. It's not hard to understand why he fell in love with you.* She was positive Adam wouldn't be there except to pack his things and tell her the marriage was over if the other woman hadn't followed through with her unspoken promise.

She told him all about the volunteer work she was involved with at the hospital and how she enjoyed getting her hands dirty in the garden – even pointing out the salad they were eating included an array of vegetables freshly dug from the veggie patch earlier that morning. Glancing around, Adam could see her handiwork throughout all corners of the vast estate, but he still had no desire to live there again. He wasn't ready to take up even where they had left off four months ago, let alone going back to sharing a bed again. His pain was too raw to contemplate anything of that nature, no matter how convincing Lara's plea might have been.

Almost begrudgingly, he realised his father was right. Trina did appear to have come full circle. This was no longer the conniving bitter woman who had shared his life for so long. Instead, she seemed to have found a purpose for living and was enjoying life without the constant need for a drink in her hand.

The conversation only skimmed the surface about him deciding to stay at his parents' home. There was neither any mention of Lara nor the state of their relationship. He couldn't bear to form the words, especially not to her – it would feel like he was betraying everything he believed in. Then again, he didn't have to – she could see the vacant look of loss in his eyes whenever he broke off mid-sentence and stared off into the distance. Several times she had to remind him what he had been saying.

Albeit reluctantly, he promised to come over a couple of times a week to keep up with the paperwork needed to run such a large estate and to see how she was faring. He felt he owed her that much for all the changes she was making – both in herself and to the property. His wife knew she couldn't push him at all and was prepared to take things one step at a time. In her mind at least, Trina felt as though she had a chance now that her rival appeared to be out of the picture.

When Adam got up to leave, she did too, walking alongside him while he made sure there was a significant amount of daylight between them. He was quick to jump straight in as soon as they reached the car and closed the door with a distinct bang, unable to stomach the thought of any lingering farewell.

Lowering the window, he glanced up at her. "I'll give you a ring in a few days, once I'm settled back into work."

All she could do was nod, feeling the coldness in his whole demeanour. While he was distracted turning the key, she suddenly leaned in and pressed her mouth against his cheek. "Okay. I'll look forward to hearing from you soon. Take care … and don't forget, your home is here – it's where you belong."

The contact was only momentary, but it was enough for him to feel repulsed. Even so, he gave no response, nor did he pull away – it wasn't in his nature to be heartless, despite the fact he was numb with longing for another woman.

But he did ignore the sentiment behind her words, instead simply mumbling, "I'll drop by in a few days, goodbye."

There was no tender caressing of hands, nor any long looks of regret to be leaving – he didn't want them. They were gestures belonging to only one person and no one would ever take her place in his heart.

As Adam was driving away, the irony of what had just happened suddenly dawned on him – he had shown no compunction whatsoever in using that forbidden parting word when it came time to bid farewell to his wife.

Trina strolled back to the house deep in thought, picturing the same broken expression in two pairs of eyes over the same amount of days – one belonging to a young woman … the other to her husband.

It's not hard to tell how much you still love her … and in some ways, I can't blame you. She must be an amazing woman – not many people would do what she did, especially when it was plain to see how much she loved you. From the looks of it, the affair must be over, so it's too late for me to do anything to reverse what's happened. And even though I may never have your heart the way she does, I'm still your wife no matter how you feel … and now it's my turn...

All the way to his parents' place, Lara's parting words kept going around and around in his mind. Outwardly, he may be assuming an impression of having accepted her decision; deep down he couldn't imagine ever letting her go.

For most of the way, tears streamed from his eyes blurring the road ahead, and he had to keep dashing them away. When an oncoming semitrailer veered close to his lane, for the space of a few milliseconds the thought crossed his mind maybe this was the only solution to make all of that excruciating pain go away. Common-sense returned as it screamed past, and he knew he could never do anything so cruel to his parents ... and especially not to a beloved woman or her precious little girl.

§

For the next couple of weeks, apart from the familiarity of work and slotting back into their roles, Lara and Adam's worlds changed into places they barely recognised. Everything around them seemed to have lost any form of clarity. Nothing mattered and their whole existence seemed an endless gaping void.

Everything that is, except for Nikki. She was the only joy in Lara's life now.

Until one day when the constant pestering became all too much...

"Mummy, *where's* Uncle *Adam* gone? Why won't you *tell* me? I've asked you over and over. He hasn't been to see us for *ages!* I miss his hugs and I want to go back to the beach to make another sandcastle."

Lara's heart dropped again. It was finally time to face the inevitable. Pulling the little girl onto her lap, she took a deep breath and then uttered the words she had been putting off for many days.

"Well, little Munchkin ... it turns out, Uncle Adam can't come to visit us anymore. He has to go to his other work every day, and he's got his big house to look after on weekends – and that makes him very very busy. So that means we just have to try to do things without him now."

"*Nooo*, I *have* to see him – he's my *friend* and he needs to come and watch me ride *Clancy!* Can't we ring him, *pleeeaaase?*"

Flinging Lara's arms away, she scrambled off her lap and slumped miserably into the back of the sofa, crossing her arms and wearing the biggest pout her mother had ever seen.

"We can't, Poppet, I'm sorry..."

"But *why* can't we? You can help me find his number and then I can tell him how much I miss him. He needs to come over and make us laugh again – I like it when he tickles you 'n me and we get sore tummies. He's *lotsa* fun!"

"Oh, sweetie, we can't rin—"

"But *whyyyy?* He *always* used to come over, 'sept when he was *really* busy helping that sick person" —a frustrated sigh pushed through the pout— "but I *know* he'll come over if I tell him 'cause he loves us and we love him."

"And he'll *always* love you just like we'll *always* love him. I know it's very hard to understand, but he can't come to see us anymore. There's some... someone else who needs him more than we do."

"But you always said we're s'posed to share – why can't they share him with *us* then?" She looked up and her eyes were swimming with tears.

The sad young woman pulled the little tot onto her lap again, unable to reply through the thick lump that was nearly choking her.

Those big brown eyes looked up in earnest. "Maybe he's cross 'cause I spilt my drink on his shoes at the airport."

Lara's heart ached as she stroked her daughter's tear-stained cheek and a soft whimper accompanied the reply. "Awww... no, he's not, Poppet, promise."

But no matter how hard Lara tried to reassure her, she kept blaming herself.

Small hiccups accompanied her next cry. "But he *mu...st* be ve...ry cranky with me 'cau...se he didn't even say ... good...bye. Now he wo...n't know how much ... I'm going to mi...ss him."

To see the full impact her fateful decision had made on the little girl broke

Lara's heart all over again. Regardless of Elizabeth's warning, she had never anticipated the breakup would upset her young daughter this deeply.

She crooned into her hair, "Uncle Adam's not cranky with you at *all*, Munchkin. He loves you very very *very* much. He just has to be with his friend more than us. And he *did* say goodbye – he even gave you a great big kiss ... but you were fast asleep and didn't feel it."

"But why didn't he wake me up if he knew we couldn't go to the beach again or come and visit us anymore? I would've asked him to send me a postcard – at least *then* I'd know where he was. Maybe *we* could go and visit *him*."

For a heart already laden with grief, Nikki's pleas were almost too much to bear. Lara hugged the little form close, trying to explain through her own broken dialogue while struggling to contain the tears.

"He didn't know back then ... but now he's had some really sad news ... and that means he can't come over to say a proper good...bye. He *knows* how unhappy we are ... but he just can't help it ... and I'm sure he's ve...ry sad, too."

Two large teardrops slowly trickled out of those deep black pools that reminded Lara so much of another pair ... until finally, Nikki's bottom lip dropped as she struggled with her own grief and burrowed into her mother.

"Oh, my precious little Poppet," Lara crooned, rocking the tiny form as their tears flowed simultaneously. "We're going to be o...kay. I...I...I promise."

With damp cheeks resting against one another, Nikki looked up through a blurry film. "You're crying too, Mummy. Are you sad like me?" A tiny finger reached up to wipe Lara's cheek.

"I am, little one ... very, *very* sad. Mummy misses him very much, just like you do."

"Well, can't we go around to Aunty Elizabeth's house? He might even *be* there right *now* ... and if he's not there, I bet *she* knows where he is."

Oh God, please help me. "No, we'd better not, Munchkin ... as much as we want to. He's going to be *really* busy for a long, long time." Lara tenderly wiped the smudges from Nikki's face and looked deep into her eyes. "But maybe we'll be able to do fun things together like we used to – just you and me."

Musing over her mother's words, Nikki began twirling Lara's ring around and around – the one that hadn't left her finger since Adam had placed it there nearly a year ago.

Then a small voice whined, "But you don't make sandcastles like Uncle Adam does. He's the *bestest* sandcastle makerer *ever!*"

Lara couldn't answer. The lump had grown bigger and swallowed up anything more ... except for a heartfelt whimper – the kind that once upon a time made Adam's heart race. The strangled sound rose out of her grief as the mother and daughter hugged each other tightly, trying their best to obliterate the pain.

§

As time passed, questions from the little girl grew less in number, although at least once a day – and often out of nowhere – she somehow managed to wheedle him into a conversation. Lara struggled to answer in whatever way she could, thinking up all manner of things to make Nikki understand he was never coming back.

Every now and then, she thought she had actually succeeded – until the next day, and often the next, the man who meant so much to both of them was once again the main topic of conversation for a few minutes.

Over breakfast one morning, there he was again...

"It's been a very *very* long time now, Mummy," the little mite reasoned, recalling her mother's words from two weeks before. "Uncle Adam *must* be back from holidays *now!*"

"He's not on holidays, little one. Remember I told you he just can't come over to our house anymore."

"But *why?*"

"'Cause he's busy and has to look after that friend I told you about – and he has lots of other important things to do."

"*I'm* 'portant!" came the determined answer. "He told me I'm his *bestest* little girl and you're his faborite *big* one!"

Another blade pierced Lara's heart as the reminders of those days assailed her once again. "And he meant it too, sweetie, still..."

How could she explain the reasoning behind what she had done to a small child with no understanding of the truth behind Adam's homelife, especially when she was having a hard enough time trying to deal with the consequences herself? Once again, that now habitual whirlpool of despair sucked her into its murky depths.

For the first time, Lara fully understood why the doctors felt her father may have died of a broken heart – the unbearable pain was a constant reminder of all she had lost. She longed to be able to curl up into a tiny dust-ball and have the wind blow her away ... far from this deep-seated ache that had become her Siamese twin.

Her only salvation was having Nikki there to help keep her busy. And every morning, when that wriggly little body jumped onto her bed wearing the smile Lara adored, she knew she had to go on ... no matter what. She just had to ... for her beloved daughter's sake.

§

Work became their lifesaver – it helped to fill in the time and made the daylight hours pass just that little bit faster.

Night time was an entirely different story. Missing the comfort of familiar warm bodies curled up beside them, the lonely pair tossed and turned for hours at a time. Sleep was an elusive thing – like an annoying acquaintance you can never truly rely on. Those small portions they did manage to fall into contained images of dancing hands and dazzling eyes twinkling in the moonlight. When they eventually woke from a fitful few hours, it was back to the reality of that dismal loneliness latching onto their souls and never letting go.

David was pleased to welcome Lara back on deck, and for her, it was a blessing in disguise. Even though her passion now lay in the footlights, she had always enjoyed sitting at her flatbed. She savoured the thrill that came from putting all the pieces of a jigsaw puzzle together and then watching it come to life beneath her skilled hands. Over the years, filmmakers had come to trust her instincts as she manipulated the footage and brought out the essence of their storyline by melding all the different elements together. When word spread she was back, the phone rang hot with directors eager to offer his company their latest project.

"You're good for business, Lara," her boss chuckled. "Don't go off treading those boards too often or I'll go broke!"

His words carried both good and bad connotations. On the one hand, the surety of a regular income while waiting what could be up to several months for another production to come along was a welcome relief. On the other, always lurking in the shadows was the offer from Max and the thought of having to turn down the role of *Maria* when she eventually caught up with him in the next week or so. There was no way she could do it with all the longing and emotion involved in that classic storyline if Adam was playing *Georg*. Being in his arms just once would be hard enough without having to suppress her feelings night after night.

Adam's bosses were thrilled to have him back on board again. They had utilised all of the drawings and projects he had stockpiled before leaving and now were in urgent need of more of his creative ideas to put to clients. Throughout the recent Sydney sojourn, he had taken time during their regular daytime wanderings to observe many of the new architectural practices southern firms were adopting. Putting pen to paper became the perfect way to make those hands move around the clockface sitting above his desk.

Nearly a month had passed since that terrible morning and Adam was still living with his parents. After inspecting a couple of apartments close to the office, none had really grabbed his attention. Charles and Elizabeth were more than happy having him around and so they encouraged him to stay – it was also a subtle way of checking to see how he was coping with everything that had happened.

The sprawling home was large enough to ensure they weren't always in each other's pockets. Besides, Adam's work often kept him out late, so there was no fear of him intruding on their privacy. Twice a week he visited the country estate for a couple of hours, honouring his promise to Trina and to grab anything he may need ... and somewhat comply with Lara's plea.

Any lasting relationship between the husband and wife was still out of the question as far as he was concerned. Even so, the more time he spent in Trina's company, the more he was able to recognise changes in her attitude and demeanour. Although mildly surprised, it didn't change his ability to trust her in any way. Most times when he was leaving, she made sure to give him a hug. He returned the gesture, but there was no warmth in his touch, nor any desire to remain there. And always when he drove away, a huge sense of betrayal clutched at his heart and a thick mantle of melancholy accompanied him all the way home. Lara was still as much a part of his thoughts as always – though now there were only bittersweet memories to sustain him.

Often while trying to find that elusive thing called sleep, he would pour through the two albums she had put together with so much care. For the next nostalgic hour or so, he got lost inside a much warmer world, reflecting on the best times of his life. Sadly, one was missing, and he often wondered if Lara had ever ended up making another chronicling their stay in Sydney. Now he would never know.

Thank goodness, I remembered to take my camera down to at least have photo memories from those special months – but I do miss reading your quirky comments and beautiful prose, Baby.

A silver photo frame stood on his bedside table. It showed a small girl grinning broadly at the camera as she posed beside a sandcastle in the shape of a mermaid. Next to it was a similar keepsake, this time of a stunning woman whose expression was bright enough to light up the gloomiest heart.

Lara's curvaceous figure and long shiny hair were silhouetted by soft lamplight as she stood beneath a huge arched entrance leading to a quaint hilltop town in Tuscany. Her laughing image seemed to reach out to him and every night it was the last thing he looked at before turning out the lamp. So often, the tips of his fingers would linger on the glass for a moment, in a vain attempt to feel her close. Then lying in the darkness, images would replay over-and-over in his mind of that wonderful night when they had made love for the very first time. And for these few precious hours, he was back in those times – when hope was strong and life was filled with beauty.

Time was passing for both of them ... while the depth of their yearning never did.

Chapter 19

Christmas was just over a week away and Lara couldn't put off the dreaded appointment any longer. Her feet dragged as she made her way up the hill to Max's agency. For the last few days, there was always a new message waiting on the answering machine as she walked through the door. Knowing full well what his reaction would be, it was easier to ignore them rather than ringing back.

Since his initial offer, she had vacillated between responses. *Maria* was every actor's dream role and being able to spend time with Adam, even if only on a stage, was almost too great a temptation as the loneliness gnawed away at her. Following her initial resolve to pass up the part, tiny voices in the midnight hours kept urging Lara to change her mind, but as dawn crept in, sensibility quickly followed. It would be too cruel on everyone if she were to play opposite him night after night, and this had been the catalyst for her final decision.

To begin with, it wouldn't be fair on Trina after her promise to walk away. Next, there was Nikki's reaction if she happened to find out Lara was spending time with Adam when he hadn't been to see her. Above all, she couldn't put him through all that pain again, not after everything he had already endured from both Trina and herself. Underlying everything was what it would do to her heart ... and her resolve. Lara's greatest fear was being tempted to go back on her word as soon as she looked into his eyes.

There was only one thing left to do. Sucking in a deep breath, she opened the door to the agency.

§

"Lara, you can't *possibly* turn this down! What are you thinking?" Max retorted, reacting just as she had predicted.

He remembered her throwaway comment about having to think about it when the offer was first made, but it was natural to assume she was joking. He never would have dreamt she actually meant it.

"I just can't, Max. I have my reasons, but I'm not going into them. Please give my sincerest apologies to the producers – I truly am sorry." *More than you or anyone else will ever realise.*

He was determined to make her change her mind and went in with both guns blazing. "Well, what am I going to tell them? They deliberately offered those roles to the two of you because of the outstanding rapport you bring to a stage. What you both share is one of a kind and that's the whole reason they wanted you for this iconic piece in the first place – and again *without* an audition, I might add."

Lara's stare was resolute, despite her heart beating a heavy rhythm in her chest. "I *can't,* Max. As much as I understand why you're so upset, nothing will make me change my mind. I told you at the outset Nikki's been away from school for far too long – it's time she was home with her friends for a while."

He flicked his hand dismissively. "Oh, yes, I know all that, but there has to be a deeper reason. This is the opportunity of a *lifetime*. People would give their *eye-teeth* for this role." He shook his head in frustration and pleaded as much with hand gestures as through the reasons given. "Is it the *money?* Weren't you happy with the clauses written into the last contract for her?" He fought on, unwilling to let his latest recruit off without giving it all he had.

"No, it has nothing to do with money *or* the contract. My reasons are personal and I don't feel comfortable discussing them with you or anyone else. I'm honoured they want me so much ... but I just can't do it, I'm sorry."

He was astounded at her obstinacy after the easy compliance of their first meeting. "Well, have you spoken to Adam about your decision? How does he feel? He must be upset ... it's clear there's a strong connection between you."

Despite the distance now separating them, she still knew his heart better than anyone. Her thoughts returned to the last time they had spoken and the devastation in his voice. *More than you realise on both counts, Max.*

"No, we haven't spoken for a while and it's probably better coming from you." The flippant reply gave no clue to her true feelings.

This wasn't at all what Max was expecting, especially after witnessing their close bond during the last weekend of the Sydney show.

What aren't you telling me, young lady? It takes an extraordinary amount of courage to turn down an offer like this on the brink of a career that's just taking off, especially after the way Sydney audiences responded. As much as I admire your convictions, there must be a lot more to this than you're letting on.

His silent scrutiny caused Lara to lower her eyes and he noticed her hands were trembling where they lay in her lap. The change in her demeanour seemed underpinned by an unfathomable sadness and he was almost certain it had everything to do with her co-star.

Despite her obstinance, he couldn't let her go without a warning. "All right, I won't push it anymore, but I do think you're making a terrible mistake. This could've been the springboard to a great many productions down the track. I just hope other producers want to put their trust in you when more big roles come along. This can be a fickle business, I'm afraid."

"I understand, Max, but it's just something I need to do. I never meant to upset anyone..."

All the way back to the office, she replayed over and over that heady rush of euphoria experienced the last time she had trodden this path. Now her only hope was not coming to regret such a momentous decision further down the track.

§

When Adam arrived at Max's suite the next day to sign the new contract, he was totally unprepared for the agent's reaction.

"Okay, what's going on, mate? I've just heard Lara wants to pull out of *The Sound of Music*. Have you said or done anything to bring this about?"

Any morsel of hope Adam had been holding onto immediately vanished and he found himself being sucked even further into that never-ending vortex of gloom. *Oh no, so you really did go through with it.*

"No way. I was looking forward to working with her again. The last thing I wanted was to have her turn it down. We haven't been in touch for weeks so I had no idea what she was thinking, but believe me, I'm just as devastated as you are."

Deep down he had been holding onto a faint spark of hope they would be able to share the footlights once again. Maybe then he could convince her just how wrong it was to have thrown all their dreams away. This latest news only confirmed she really didn't want to have anything more to do with him.

Oh Baby, why are you doing this to us? Surely, you know by now we belong together. Haven't these last few weeks been the same endless nightmare for you? I miss you so much...

"Well, I hope *you* don't have any little surprises up your sleeve – like pulling out too."

"No, I'm in all the way. I wouldn't do that to you!"

"Good!" I don't want them having to look for a new leading man as well. I'm going to have a hard enough job as it is trying to convince any other producers to put their faith and money in Lara when she's only been in the big playing field for a short length of time, let alone two of you."

Despite his forced smile, Adam felt another nail pierce his heart. How would he ever come to terms with the fact she really was distancing herself from all aspects of his life? Broken-hearted, he signed the contract while putting on that now familiar pretence of everything being okay.

He was becoming quite the expert at subterfuge ... at least it was good practice for the upcoming role.

§

As the Yuletide festivities drew near, both Lara and Adam were reminded of the contrasting emotions of the last one – special times celebrating both the festive season and Nikki's birthday with his parents, and then the heartbreak of the second pantomime with its horrible aftermath. As much as she wanted to believe leaving him was the right thing to do, Lara would have given anything to be able to steal a few moments alone with the man who would always be her other half – simply to feel alive again.

A few days prior to Nikki's sixth birthday, Elizabeth rang Lara asking if the mother and daughter would like to spend the Saturday before Christmas with her and Charles at their place. She felt it would be the perfect way to celebrate both occasions together and exchange gifts at the same time.

This was the first time they had caught up since those sad goodbyes at the airport almost five weeks earlier, even though Elizabeth had been ringing faithfully each week to make sure they were okay. Whenever the offer of a meal or even a catch-up at a local café was extended, Lara always found an excuse of some kind – usually one simply snatched in passing. She well knew how persuasive Adam's mother could be and didn't trust her still hurting heart.

Any fears she had been harbouring for the upcoming reunion resurfaced when she drove through the wrought iron gates. Her gaze took in the gracious sandstone mansion with its formal gardens leading out to acres of lush green paddocks. Every niche and corner contained memories that had been sitting in a locked corner of her heart, and with a rush, they all came flooding back.

The smiling couple waiting at the top of the marble stairs brought back other reminders of former visits. For the space of a moment, Lara was tempted to put the car in reverse and run away from all the questions and searching looks she felt certain would accompany their visit.

Her eyes inevitably swept the grounds for any sign of the big silver Mercedes, convinced the invitation had been a ploy to bring them back together again. Seeing his usual spot was empty put paid to any of those thoughts, and her mood swung between welcome relief and bitter disappointment.

She approached the steps somewhat cautiously. Clasping Nikki's hand firmly in hers, she was uncertain what sort of welcome would be on offer after the way she had treated their son.

Elizabeth stepped forward first, though there was no sign of that usual verve. "My dear girl, it's so lovely to see you again. Thank you for agreeing to come today – we've missed you."

The formality of her greeting proved she was feeling just as reticent, although a gentle smile and warm hug were welcome reminders of previous visits.

Lara returned the gestures, yet her tone still betrayed a slight wariness. "Hello, Elizabeth – thank you for inviting us."

"It's always a pleasure," came the cautious reply before she turned to the little girl. It was clear Nikki was trying to wriggle free of her mother's firm hold. "Hello, little one! My goodness, just look how much you've grown!"

Even the child could feel the tension, although being on the receiving end of one of Elizabeth's hugs helped to overcome any misgivings. She wrapped her arms around the much-loved grandmotherly figure and kissed her on the cheek with a loud smooch that made the others chortle softly. The sound helped to break the ice a little.

Charles was just as careful when it came his turn to greet the visitors … until he noticed the degree of hesitancy in Lara's eyes.

"Come here, young lady," he said, and a pair of strong fatherly arms pulled her close. "It's so good to have you visit us again – as my darling Bessie just said, we missed you ... welcome back."

There were no accusatory expressions in either his or Elizabeth's eyes – simply the relief of having special friendships renewed after worrying whether the young woman would ever feel comfortable being there again.

Her arms encircled his waist as she relaxed against him, peering over his shoulder to include his wife. "It's lovely to be here; I'm sorry it's been so l—"

Elizabeth was first to respond. "Oh, don't worry about that. We understand – these last few weeks can't have been easy."

"That's right," Charles added. "We're just thrilled to have you here."

Their kindly smiles eased the last of her fears and she reached out to include Elizabeth in the embrace. Nikki was tickled pink to have things back to normal and clapped her hands with glee.

Charles opened his arms to include her too. "And here's our favourite little miss – my, I think you're a foot taller than the last time we saw you. Come and give your old uncle and aunty a cuddle, we've missed you heaps and heaps."

She rushed into the huddle with a ready giggle, and it was the perfect way to push down any remaining barriers.

Following warm bearhugs from her wannabe grandparents, and being made a fuss of for several minutes, the next item on Nikki's agenda was to lug a bagful of treats out to Clancy. Five months had passed since their last visit, far too long in a young child's mind.

With a loud whinny and a quick toss of his long creamy mane, the little pony cantered to the gate when he heard his name being bellowed across the lawn.

The others laughed as Charles shook his head and exclaimed, "Heavens, for a little tacker she's sure got a big voice!"

Nikki and her favourite fur friend shared a wonderful reunion, and watching them together brought a ready smile to Lara's face for the first time in weeks. For the next hour, Clancy happily trotted around the paddock with his pint-sized fan bouncing along on his back under Charles' watchful eye, while the two women chatted in a matching pair of luxurious lounge chairs on the terrace.

Elizabeth couldn't hide her concern as she looked into a pair of eyes that had lost their usual sparkle and now sported large dark circles beneath those thick, dark lashes. More than anything, she was worried about how thin the young woman had become over the last few weeks. Usually, her figure was one most women would give their eye teeth for, but it was obvious she had lost a considerable amount of weight since the last time they were together.

Lara couldn't ignore the probing stare and worried looks coming her away, so she tried putting Elizabeth's mind at ease with amusing snippets of everything Nikki had been up to. But there was no point trying to fool her. Elizabeth could tell she was missing Adam as much as he was missing her.

Eventually, she broached the subject both had been skirting. "I'm worried about you, my darling girl. Are you eating and sleeping properly?"

Pulling a wry smile, Lara shrugged. "Oh, yeah, I suppose. Having Nikki around means I need to cook, so I get my share."

"But are you actually *eating* anything? I know it's none of my business, but you certainly don't look like it."

"Don't worry, I'm just getting ready for any new roles that may happen to come my way – can't have me getting too fat for the costumes and clumping around like an elephant on stage!"

Her cynical attempt at humour wasn't fooling anyone, especially not a worried mother-figure. "Oh Lara, you really need to eat regularly to keep your strength up if you want to keep up with that little one," she stressed, inclining her head to where the little girl's laughter wafted across the paddock.

Another small shrug was the only answer. Hoping to change the subject, Lara leaned back and took in the peaceful scene. Out of the corner of her eye, she couldn't help noticing a pair of familiar chinos and a few recognisable shirts swinging on the clothesline at the side of the house. And there it was again, that tell-tale ache in her heart.

She turned to her friend with eyes veiled in a cloak of sorrow. Her voice was so soft Elizabeth had to lean in close to catch what was said. "So, he's still living with you...

A sad nod was the only answer.

"Why hasn't he gone home to her?"

Because he still loves you with all his heart – time hasn't brought any form of healing to either one of you, his mother wanted to plead.

Instead, she tempered her answer with a gentle whisper and intonations dripping with pathos. "Because he can't – that house means nothing to him anymore – the only place he wants to be is with yo—"

"But he *has* to. *Please* make him see he needs to try again ... otherwise, all this misery has been in va—" Lara broke off, realising just how much she was about to give away.

"Yes, that's *exactly* right. It *is* all in vain and *both* of you are miserable."

"But you *have* to tell him he needs to go back to her. He'll listen to you, even if he won't listen to me."

"Lara, he listened ... he just doesn't know how to. My beloved boy is still *very* much in love with you. If he went back, it would mean betraying everything you mean to him ... along with all the memories stored away in his heart."

All Lara could do was gaze across the river as the tears gathered in her eyes. She was aware of a caring hand reaching over to take hers and then squeeze it tenderly as another passed over a box of tissues. There was nothing either one of them could add to make things any easier.

Elizabeth didn't have the heart to confess Adam was actually at the large house in Brookfield helping his wife trim the Christmas tree.

Hoping to make amends for her former bad behaviour, Trina had invited both him and his parents around to spend Christmas lunch with her. This would be the first time Adam's entire family had come together for any form of celebration in many years.

At first, Elizabeth had put her foot down, refusing to even consider such an idea, until Charles managed to talk her around. Her preference had been to spend this time with Lara and Nikki and then have a quiet celebration with her two favourite men at home on Christmas Day instead. Eventually, Charles was able to convince her Adam's peace of mind was more important than making a fuss.

And just as Lara had no clue where he was, Adam had no idea she and Nikki were with his parents. If he had, Elizabeth was certain he would have found some excuse to hang around ... it wasn't hard to tell how much he still missed them. She had almost given into the temptation to say something before he went out, but it was important to honour Lara's decree never to see him again.

Lunch was the usual fare of a variety of dishes to make any mouth water. The Ashworths exchanged worried frowns as Lara picked at her food, even though she pressed Nikki to finish everything on her plate. All they could do was bite their tongues, though it didn't lessen their concerns.

Afterwards, they all congregated in the living room where a colourful array of presents waited under the stunning tree. Similar to last year, the room and staircase displayed all manner of birthday paraphernalia interspersed with a host of elegant Christmas ornaments. It didn't take much imagination to picture Santa Claus climbing down the chimney. Nikki's wide-eyed wonder as she tore away the wrapping paper brought delighted smiles from those watching on.

Naturally, there were a host of reminders from the previous year when someone else had joined in all the excitement ... except no one was brave enough to say anything. Elizabeth and Charles exchanged sad looks when Lara's fingers kept seeking out the sapphire and diamond treble clef hanging around her neck.

As the sun started sinking lower in the sky, Lara began gathering up all the paper scraps. "Come on, Missy Tuppence. We'd better go home before we wear out our welcome! How about you help me pick up all this rubbish and then thank Aunty Elizabeth and Uncle Charles for a lovely day."

"Oh, don't worry about that," he protested, grabbing the little girl and tossing her high in the air. "You've got *much* better things to do than tidy up *this* old place. Like giving me a kiss and telling me you'll be back to see us *very* soon!"

The birthday girl giggled as she flew into the air and a large kiss landed on his cheek when she fell safely back into his arms. "I will, I *promise!* I always want to come and see you and Clancy – it's lots of fun here!"

Carrying the wriggle worm out to the car, more happy giggles accompanied his footsteps when he blew loud raspberries into her neck. The women followed along behind, walking slowly and not looking forward to saying goodbye.

Before Lara could open the driver's door, Elizabeth wrapped her in a comforting hug. She was still convinced this 'almost-daughter' had made the wrong decision ... the battle scars were still visible in her son's eyes whenever he came down for breakfast, and then again across the dinner table after another busy day at the office. It was obvious Lara's reflected that same silent agony and she wished something could be done to change the situation.

"Make sure you come back to see us more often, okay? We miss you."

"We will, and we miss you too. Thanks for a lovely time. The turkey was delicious and my new earrings are beautiful – thank you. And remember, no matter what else has happened, I'll always love you."

"I know, and I love you too. And thank you for that wonderful album of memorabilia and photos from your time in Sydney" —she sent her a meaningful look— "I'm pretty sure it was really meant for someone else, but Charles and I will treasure it forever – it's plain to see all three of you had a fabulous time..." The rest of the sentence fell away as she glanced tellingly at the other woman.

Lara swallowed hard. "We did ... but he's not allowed to see it..."

"He won't. You made that very clear, but I do wish you'd change your mind." She sighed heavily. "Anyway, take care of yourself ... go to bed early and promise me you'll eat properly!" A gentle hand reached out to caress Lara's cheek ... a touching reminder of her own mother's loving concern so long ago.

The young woman nodded. After one last hug, she climbed in behind the wheel while Charles strapped Nikki in the booster seat and kissed her goodbye.

"Make sure *you* come back very soon, young lady. Then you can ride Clancy again. He's getting *much* too fat because he's not getting enough exercise!"

"I will, Uncle Charles, I promise. And thanks for my new saddle – it's *sooo* pretty." Looking up at him with those big brown eyes, she implored, "And *pleeaase* give Uncle Adam a really, *really* big hug from me and tell him I hope he has a Merry Christmas. He's gone away somewhere and we don't see him anymore so you'll have to tell him for me instead, okay?"

All day long they had deliberately avoided saying his name. Even during the discussion as to why Adam was still living with his parents, both women had made sure not to mention him by name. Lara gasped audibly, closing her eyes as the awful reality of all she had let go assaulted her yet again. All Charles could offer was a sad nod of affirmation and Lara didn't dare look at either of them. Instead, she went to drive off ... until Nikki let out a sudden squeal and started scrambling around in the backpack she had insisted on bringing with her.

"*Wait*, Mummy, I forgot Uncle Adam's present!" After a few seconds, she pulled out a tightly folded wad of paper and passed the unexpected token through the window to Charles with a sad smile. "Can you please tell him I made this 'speshly 'cause I miss him *sooo* much. He'll always be my *bestest* boyfriend and I don't want him to forget about me."

Lara had to swallow a sob and Charles and Elizabeth exchanged heartfelt looks as he placed the gift in his pocket. Fighting against a big lump in his throat, he reached in and stroked Nikki's cheek. "Of course I will, Poppet, and I'm sure he'd send you a big kiss and cuddle to say thank you because you'll always be his bestest *little* girlfriend." The look he sent Lara pierced her heart. She had no trouble whatsoever deciphering the meaning behind the accentuated adjective.

With one final wave as a blur of tears filled everyone's eyes, Lara took off down the driveway, to a home that no longer held the promise of nights overflowing with tender loving or a future filled with hope. Along the way, she reminisced over all the long hours of hard work she had put in to ensure not one keepsake or image was missing from the pages of the album now safe in his parent's keeping. Regardless of insisting Adam must never see it, a small part of her hoped he might stumble upon it one day and realise just how much she truly did love him, despite her cruel declarations during that terrible phone call.

§

For the last week or so a new form of guilt had crept in to catch Adam off guard. No matter how often he tried to push the notion aside, it still kept him company at least once a day.

Tunnelling out of the deep recesses of his conscience came annoying niggles telling him he should at least be making some kind of effort to spend more time with Trina. And echoing behind them was a beloved voice, sounding nothing like the one he knew as it implored him to go back to his wife and make a new life with her.

He still had trouble believing Lara's phone call had even happened, though as each new day dawned without any form of communication from her, it was evident she truly did mean everything she had said. As much as he hated to admit it, he really did owe it to her when she had set aside her own dreams to offer them another chance. But he still couldn't quite take that final step to move back into the house – not now ... not yet ... not when those captivating sapphire blue eyes still kept him company every waking moment.

During the week before Christmas, Adam dropped by the estate twice after work and then again on Saturday – the day of Nikki's party. There was no need for him to be reminded of what that particular date represented. Every moment of every single day she and her mother still invaded his thoughts, which is why he intentionally chose to spend the afternoon doing something menial over at his former home rather than just moping around his parents' place wondering where they were and what they were up to. It would have been a far different outcome had he known the truth of what was going on...

The only thing bringing any form of happiness to his Christmas season was being able to lay out the welcome mat for Charles and Elizabeth in the house he had designed a few years earlier. In all that time, his wife had insisted she didn't want anything to do with his parents, despite being the only family he had left. Usually, they only popped by once or twice a year after learning she was away with Judith for the weekend. Consequently, this year's event was a major celebration.

Adam joined them for the local Christmas service, singing loudly and trying not to think about another one happening in a similar venue only a few suburbs away. He was positive Lara and Nikki would be attending the little church they used to frequent when he was a part of their lives.

Afterwards, he drove his parents to the estate on the city outskirts where Trina was busy preparing the festive meal. The difference in her attitude and social habits had become more noticeable with every visit, and Adam was starting to let his guard down that little bit further whenever he dropped by.

"Merry Christmas, Elizabeth, Charles ... and you too, Adam," she greeted them at the door, pressing a light kiss on the cheek of each one. "I'm so glad you were able to come today."

"Merry Christmas to you too, Trina," Elizabeth responded, returning her greeting in a similar manner. "Thank you for the invitation, it was very nice of you to think of us."

Both men offered their own form of seasonal greeting, along with a tentative peck on their host's cheek.

"Lunch is nearly ready. Come in and make yourselves at home while I finish off in the kitchen. Adam, would you mind getting the drinks, please?"

His parents glanced at each other in astonishment, exchanging raised eyebrows at the warmer than usual response as they followed her inside.

"Can I help with anything?"

"Oh no, everything's fine thanks, Elizabeth. I'm almost finished, then Adam only has to carve the turkey."

The aromas coming from the kitchen soon made their mouths water and Charles caught his wife's look of amazement. This was vastly different to any of their previous visits.

The turkey looked exactly as it should with a crisp coating of brown skin. Piled high on a large silver platter was a steaming array of roasted vegetables, and next to it was a jug of rich homemade gravy as well as one filled with cranberry sauce fresh from the stove. The table looked spectacular with a garland of brand-new Christmas adornments as the centrepiece and a small bowl of fresh flowers from the garden at either end.

"Dad, would you mind offering up a prayer of thanks for us?"

Trina looked up sharply, surprised by the sudden request from her husband.

"Sure, son. Let's pray."

The three guests bowed their heads. Trina bit her lip nervously, peering around the table as the others sat with their eyes closed. The ritual had always been part of his parents' meal times. Since moving back in with them, Adam had come to appreciate the sense of peace and thankfulness that settled over him when prefacing a meal in this fashion.

"Dear Lord, thank you for this food and for the goodness of your blessings on our lives. Bless the hands that prepared it, and we ask your protection on family and friends, both near and far, as they celebrate your birth."

"Amen," everyone chorused, even Trina with a more quizzical tone when she realised this was actually a nice way to start a meal instead of everyone just tucking into their food without giving a thought to anything else. Hearing Charles' reference to all her hard work was a nice bonus.

Once upon a time, Adam had wanted nothing more than to see his wife make his parents feel welcome like this. Now as he carved up the turkey, his thoughts were a long way away – especially following the petition his father had made for those near and far.

He missed a little girl's excited giggles as she opened her presents ... and seeing her delighted smiles as she discovered what was in each one. Pictures of a snow-globe flashed into his mind and he wondered if the keepsake still crooned her to sleep. Maybe she was so angry at him for leaving without even a word of goodbye, it now sat dusty and forgotten in a dark corner of her toybox.

He wasn't game enough to conjure up images of a woman with laughing eyes and a smile that always set his pulse racing. As well as needing to guard his heart, Elizabeth and Charles didn't deserve having their Christmas spoilt because of his ongoing misery.

The afternoon turned into a subdued time for all. Even though the food was both hearty and delicious after Trina's extensive culinary lessons, and despite their best efforts to find common things to talk about to bring a bit of Christmas cheer, it was far from the celebration any of them either wanted or needed.

Trina's greatest wish was for Adam to move back in with her, especially with all the effort she had put in to make amends. His sombre mood was a telling reminder of exactly where his thoughts lay ... nothing she said or did seemed to make any difference.

He couldn't even contemplate taking such a drastic step, despite his growing certainty Lara was gone forever. How could anyone possibly pretend their marriage was okay when they were still carrying this much love in their heart for another? As the afternoon wore on, that earlier resolution to try to honour Lara's wishes dissolved away when his thoughts crossed the miles to another home filled with love and laughter...

Charles and Elizabeth kept imagining a little girl who missed having a father figure in her life, coupled with thoughts of a young mother whose face now carried a haunted look instead of the usual effervescence that drew others in. Their greatest wish was to find a way to turn back the clock, or at least be able to convince Lara to change her mind. Even so, with the current state of affairs, it was imperative they at least make an effort if Adam and Trina were to have any chance at all ... anything to make it easier on their son and hear him laugh again.

Farewells were polite and extended with cool graciousness, though there were no warm hugs or promises to catch up again in the near future. Instead, a few perfunctory kisses were exchanged and then Trina watched from the veranda as the car drove away.

Later that night, while Adam and his parents sat around the kitchen table partaking of a few leftovers Trina had sent home with them, Charles suddenly remembered something and went over to the sideboard. Exchanging knowing glances with his wife, he opened the top drawer and pulled out a thick wad of paper folded over and over on itself. Without saying a word, he slipped it beside Adam's plate before taking his place again.

The young man picked it up with a puzzled expression. "What's this, Dad? Did you win Lotto and this is my share of the winnings?"

"Just open it, son. Someone asked me to deliver this to you the other day, but as it's actually a Christmas present, I felt it was better to wait until now."

Adam glanced from one to the other, though neither Charles nor Elizabeth would give anything away. The look of sadness in her eyes was enough to make him wary. With great care, he unfolded the heavy paper and then sat motionless when the unexpected offering was spread out before him. He blinked hard and then had to bite his lips to stop them from trembling. His breath was so laboured, the others could hear it from across the table.

Decorating the edges of the work of art were colourful, childlike drawings depicting reindeer, angels and Christmas stockings. Carefully printed inside the festive imagery was a message that tore at his heart.

MERY CRISSMUS UNKAL ADAM.

I MISS U but im beeing VERRY brave jus like mummy told me. i wos in my play at skool and i wos the crissmus angel so i patended to be U cos U sing like 1.

An image of the drawing a little girl had made only a year earlier flashed into his mind as he read the rest of her heart-breaking screed.

Mummy krys sumtyms – i heer her wen shes in her room with the daw shut. I think shes VERRY sad cos she missus U but she trys to patend shes ok. When i heer her i cry to but i dont let her see me cos that makes her sader. My teecher said my riting is geting beta and thats why I mayd this speshly for U. Plees cum bak and see mummy an me. WE MISS U I LUV U NIKKI XOXOXO XOXOXOXOXOXOXOXOXOXOXOXOXOXOXOXOXOXOXOX

Blinking rapidly, he slumped against the table with one hand cradling his forehead, trying hard to swallow. When he eventually found the courage to look up, the pain in his eyes was unbearable. "When did you get this?"

His father answered and it was easy to see how difficult it was for him having to break the news. "They came over last Saturday and we celebrated Christmas and Nikki's birthday at the same time." At Adam's sharp intake of breath, he quickly went on. "We didn't say anything because it would only have made things harder for you. Nikki gave it to me just as they were leaving."

With tears slowly rolling down his cheeks, Adam passed the gift across the table. Their hearts broke in a similar fashion as they read the heartfelt words.

Again, his forehead dropped dejectedly into his hands as the words rushed out. "How can she *do* this to all of us? It's obvious none of us are happy – not if what Nikki says is true. For the life of me, I don't understand why she did it."

With a sudden resolute growl, he fished the car keys out of his pocket. "*Aarrgghh* ... I'm going around there right now to *make* her change her mind."

Elizabeth nearly knocked over the chair as she rushed to her feet, grabbing his arm when he went to push the table away. "Adam, you *can't*. I understand where you're coming from – believe me, if it were up to me, I'd have you back together in an instant – but she's made up her mind and you *have* to live with it, just as she is. Lara can't control what Nikki says ... in fact, she didn't even know about the note. This is just a little girl writing from her heart ... you have to let them get on with their lives. You owe them that much."

"How can you *say* that, Mum? She's even given up the role of *Maria,* and I know it's because she can't face me – because she still cares. On the last night we were together I could see it in her eyes – she wasn't faking *that. This* is the fake – this *farce* we're now living – *all* of us!"

He tried to break free, but still she clutched at his arm.

"And that's *exactly* why you have to stay away. We *all* know how much she loves you" —his mother looked at him with compassion flowing from her eyes— "but sometimes love just isn't enough. Even though her love for you will never die, she cares too much to see you trying to live with the guilt of being unfai—"

"But *Mum*—"

"*No,* son, *listen* to me! You need to understand she also cares about Trina in a roundabout kind of way. Lara can never forget the heartache she went through when Tom left her for another woman, and she doesn't want to be the reason for someone else having to cope with that awful feeling of abandonment.

She brushed his cheek to soften the blow of what was to come. *"That's* why she broke it off – because of the guilt she saw in *your* eyes and the guilt *she* carried for Trina. And now it's up to her to decide if she wants to start all over again. But while ever Trina needs you, nothing will make her change her mind."

It broke Elizabeth's heart having to speak so harshly, yet she knew it was the only way to get through to him – and thankfully, she still hadn't betrayed her promise not to implicate Trina in Lara's decision.

Adam slumped back heavily in his chair. He wanted to fight against everything she was saying, even though deep down he knew she was right.

"Lara knows you're still living here – she saw your clothes hanging on the line the other day – but when I tried to explain, she cut me off and wouldn't let me answer. She honestly thought you'd be back with Trina by now – she even begged me to make you try again. And as much as I hate to admit it, I think you need to honour her wishes. You know I've never liked Trina, but I have to admit, after today's efforts, she definitely appears to be trying to make amends."

His head snapped up, startled to hear his mother's changing loyalties as she stood up for his wife. But she hadn't finished.

"It's obvious Trina's trying hard to prove how much she's changed. Now it's time you tried a bit harder yourself."

"But Mum, I *have* tried."

"I know you have, better than anyone, but do this for Lara's sake if not your own. Then see how things go. If it doesn't work out – and I have to be honest, that's what I want too – at least you can say you gave it your best shot and Lara will know she did the right thing."

"Your mother's right, son," Charles pitched in, reaching out to place a caring hand on Adam's shoulder. "Just think about all she's said and go from there."

As much as he hated to admit it, deep in his heart, Adam knew what they said made sense. He remembered seeing the pain in Lara's eyes as she told him all she had gone through when Tom had abandoned her with a tiny baby and not much else. The circumstances surrounding this separation were very different; even so, his wife was virtually all alone in the world. When he really considered her circumstances, it wasn't hard to understand how isolated she must feel. At least he had the love of his parents to tide him over. Trina had no one.

That night as he lay in bed with Nikki's letter tucked away in a back compartment of his wallet, Adam pondered everything his mother had said. He tried to imagine what it would be like returning to his own home and at least attempt to make another go of their marriage.

After several sleepless hours, he reached a reluctant conclusion. With the obvious changes he had noticed recently in both Trina's lifestyle and attitude, if she could be trusted to fulfil her promise to stay away from anything alcoholic, then maybe – just maybe – their marriage might stand a chance.

Pushing back the sheet, he went over to the window and looked out to the lights of the city glowing in the distance. He knew Lara was asleep somewhere out there ... or at least trying to if she was still crying over him as Nikki had innocently confided.

A heartfelt whisper floated across the treetops. "My dearest love ... don't ask me how I'm ever going to do this" —he had to pause to take a deep breath— "but because I love you with every part of me, I'm willing to try my hardest to give my marriage one more go." He shook his head at the irony of this blatant oxymoron. "But *only* because you asked me to ... not for *any* other reason."

With a very loud sigh, he pressed two fingers against his pursed lips. Then with the gentlest of breaths, he blew across their surface out into the night.

"Merry Christmas, Baby ... no matter how much time goes by or what may come to pass, my life will never be the same without you."

§

Standing in a building only a few streets down from her place, reminded Lara of being there at the same time last year. Her local church was all decked out with Christmas decorations as parishioners raised their voices to sing the old carols. And just like her soulmate visiting his parents' church not too far away, she tried to join in while pushing away feelings that were just as miserable as those experienced last year – when circumstances had dictated they spend the festive day apart. At least back then they were still a couple.

Almost as though of its own choosing, her hand started playing with the eye-catching pendant lying just below the small indentation in her throat. At the same time, the intricate setting of a stunning ring brushed against a bare patch of skin – both poignant reminders of this time last year.

Traces of their past were everywhere.

Afterwards, she and Nikki spent the day with Suzie and Ben, sharing stories and gifts around the dining room table while trying to pretend everything was okay. Deep down, all four were dealing with the fact someone they loved was missing ... and would never be joining them again.

For Nikki's sake, the adults decided to all pull together and make the day as cheerful as possible. Apart from one sad whisper tacked onto the end of the Christmas blessing before the family started eating— "And please make sure Uncle Adam has a happy Christmas, too," —Lara managed to get through the day relatively unscathed.

The chimes of midnight, then one o'clock, and two, echoed through the quiet cottage. Before the next hour ticked over, she got up to go and sit out on the veranda. Looking up at the stars, she wondered what her soulmate was doing. It was natural for her thoughts to turn to him – they did every night once silence reigned.

There was one thing she needed to believe in and it was like a gift offering to herself ... as long as she felt something inside, even if it were only this dull constant ache, a tiny part of Adam would always be with her. The pain of losing him had taken on the form of a beloved enemy – an awful reminder of all she had lost, along with the never-ending certainty he would forever live in her heart.

"Merry Christmas, Teddy ... no matter how much you think what I asked of you is impossible, it's time to let me go. You need to go back to Trina and fulfil those vows you made to each other so long ago. It's time, for *all* our sakes.

"We'll never ever stop loving one another – we can't ... you and I are kindred spirits – but we both know this is the only right thing to do."

Oh Lord, just keep him safe always...

§

Once again, their spirits were in perfect harmony with prayers offered straight from their hearts. And that intricate tapestry fashioned in another realm, added a few more vignettes – this time using more sombre-coloured threads as the brighter skeins that once upon a time created images of a stirring symphony suddenly ran out. All that was left was a rich and harmonious musical score lying fractured and unfinished...

Chapter 20

The new year crept in ... similar to the pace of those tiny caterpillars Lara had once envisioned when two hands composed a closing encore and waltzed around their own imaginary ballroom at a lookout in the sky. Memories of that special time still brought a measure of comfort on a lonely night, though the missing was still raw.

The thought of an entire year stretching ahead for what seemed to be forever meant Lara wanted to ensure any time spent with Nikki produced similar keepsakes to fill the scrapbooks of her mind. It was far better than that constant numbing emptiness.

Adam's midnight musings still kept him company as he wondered whether Lara had ever made a record of their time in Sydney. Most nights were spent going through all the photos he had taken himself, but he missed the special touches she added that brought them to life in all their fullness.

He had no way of knowing that tucked inside her bookcase, alongside two others honouring similar happy times, was the duplicate of the one she had just presented to his parents for Christmas. And just like them, this one was filled with treasured anecdotes and hundreds of snapshots from those carefree months.

After Lara's world had fallen apart, and with all those never-ending evenings stretching on forever, most of December had been taken up with her recording each of their memories from those days, despite being bombarded with painful reminders of all she had let go. Apart from Nikki, she had nothing else to look forward to – everything good now lived in the past.

Once hers was finished, a voice in her head compelled her to make another for Adam, even though she had no intention of actually giving it to him ... she had no wish to jeopardise his new life with Trina by reminding him of those days. It was while she was wondering what to give his parents for Christmas that the idea came to her – offering them his was an ideal way to ensure someone in his family had a visual reminder of that special time. Now she just had to trust Elizabeth to keep her word never to show it to him.

§

Between the satisfaction that came from bringing other peoples' stories to life on a screen and spending time with her young daughter, Lara was learning to be content – though she still ached for him all the time. It was impossible to imagine ever wanting to share her life with another man. Apart from feeling she would be betraying Adam's memory, she didn't want to waste anyone else's time ... and certainly not her own.

By the time February rolled around, she and Nikki had visited his parents' palatial riverside home on five more occasions. Without fail, as soon as they sat down to a leisurely Saturday breakfast, Nikki begged to give Aunty Elizabeth a call so she could ride Clancy and break in the new saddle. Lara found it was the perfect excuse to make good on her friend's kind invitation.

Charles and Elizabeth always looked forward to these times, invariably extending an invitation for lunch as the visitors always brought some much-needed laughter back into their lives. From a shady nook on the terrace, the husband and wife exchanged affectionate smiles as they listened to Nikki's chuckles carry across the grassy expanse fronting the river when Lara chased the pony and his besotted young jockey around the paddock.

As much as the young mother tried to hide it, Elizabeth frequently caught her wistful expression whenever she glanced towards one of the upstairs windows. Mostly, she was relieved her son already had plans for the day, although in some ways it might have been better if he was there. Maybe then they could all go back to those blissful times again.

On Saturday afternoon of the second weekend in February, the women found themselves in their usual spot. Nikki's loud giggles echoed in the distance as she bounced along on Clancy's back with Charles keeping a watchful eye on them.

Elizabeth was privy to a secret that had been eating her up inside for days. With a certain amount of trepidation, she reached out and cradled Lara's hand in hers. "My dear, there's something I need to tell you – something I think you should know ... and sooner rather than later."

The melodious trill from a resident magpie and the whisper of the wind in a nearby gum tree added a gentle accompaniment to her melancholy tone. Lara guessed what was coming and she could feel her heartbeat accelerating. The loud repetitive thump added another layer to nature's impromptu concert.

Elizabeth couldn't hide her sadness, and she dreaded having to break the news. Seeing the trust in those understanding blue eyes gave her the courage to press on. "Last week Adam moved back to the house in Brookfield." She couldn't bring herself to include that final nail: *He and Trina are back together.*

Lara squeezed the hand still holding hers. "It's okay. I've been expecting it. Besides, he knew this is what I wanted."

In a strange way, she actually felt a sense of relief. As long as Adam was still living with his parents, the lure was always there for her to run back into his arms. Now it was too late ... he had moved on.

Reaching this momentous decision was one of the hardest things he had ever done in his life. Regardless of that firm declaration made on Christmas night, it had taken him several weeks to follow through on his vow. While ever he was busy at work, his resolve strengthened and his mind would start to tick over planning all the necessary steps to move out the following day. But in the sleepless hours, when thoughts of Lara were more potent, he couldn't envisage beginning a new life and losing all hope of making her his again. Once the commitment was made, there would be no going back.

The poor man couldn't count how many times he had picked up the phone and punched out her number before the echoes of her heartfelt plea once again rang in his ears. And every single time he went to press that last digit, the mantra, *Leave her alone. Hasn't all your previous inaction hurt her enough? After everything she's given up for you, the least you can do is to follow through on her request,* sent out its persistent call and he dropped the receiver back its cradle with a heavy thud.

Elizabeth had been dismayed when Adam came to her on the Wednesday evening to say he was going back to his wife over the coming weekend. Despite having insisted he needed to honour Lara's wishes, it still came as a terrible blow.

For the next three days, she wrestled with begging him to change his mind and simply burying the sorrow deep in her heart – to her, it felt like a death in the family or at least the death of his future happiness. Once his bags were packed and she saw the determination in his eyes to 'do this', as he put it, she knew it was too late.

Adam's sole reasoning for going down this path was all about timing. Rehearsals were about to begin in Melbourne and Trina had hinted she wanted to go with him, so this seemed the most advantageous window of opportunity if their marriage was to stand any chance. The added benefit was being so far away from any reminders of the past – he and Lara had never spent any time together in the Victorian capital city.

Deep down, his mother still questioned Lara's insistence about him being better off without her, especially when she noticed the faraway looks in both of their eyes at unguarded moments. It wasn't hard to guess they were back visiting memories once shared with their beloved soulmate.

While they were sitting there, and with Lara willing to talking about him openly for the first time since the breakup, she had to ask one more time. "Is it *really* okay, Lara? Can you say that in all honesty?"

"It's what Trina needs ... and it's what *he* wanted for so many years."

"But is it truly what *you* want?"

"There's only one thing I want..."

The slight hint of hesitation made Elizabeth's heart beat with hope renewed until Lara's sad pronouncement continued.

"...but unfortunately, I'm not the only person involved here, and I don't want to be responsible for breaking a marriage apart. As I've already said – I know what it feels like knowing your husband is with someone else. I couldn't bear trying to live with the guilt of having stolen another woman's husband. I know he denies it, but I'm certain it was eating Adam up as well. It was there whenever it came time for him to leave – that small glimmer of shame for what he was doing to both Trina *and* to me. And having to hide all the time is no good for any relationship – no matter how much you love each other. In Europe, and then again in Sydney, we were far enough away to pretend she didn't exist. But when she was standing right there in front of me with that haunted look, memories of all those lonely nights wondering where my husband was came flooding back."

Adam's mother sat wordlessly, all hope once again plummeting as the young woman's confession poured forth like a cathartic salve to ease the underlying sadness of having made such a painful decision in the first place.

Lara opened her hands and shrugged her shoulders in resignation. "One thing I've learned through all of this ... people can't do the wrong thing without paying the price somehow. Adam and I love each other with everything within us, except it's at the expense of someone else's happiness. I have to believe this is the right thing to do – for all our sakes – especially with Trina now doing everything she can to become the wife he's needed and wanted all of their married life."

Unfortunately – though in reality, it was more a blessing they had no idea – neither woman was privy to one dismal fact. On the solitary night Adam and Trina had come together as husband and wife, his sole focus had been on the pictures filling his mind, images highlighting a pair of bright blue eyes looking into his. And the only way he could complete the act was by having his eyes pressed tightly shut. The next morning, deep feelings of betrayal for the woman he still loved brought with them a certainty her spirit would always be with him.

Since that night, whenever his wife went to kiss him, Adam made sure her lips landed on his cheek instead of his mouth. It was a terrible blow to her ego, though she never said a word. Just having him back in her life was enough for now, and having to do without any romantic overtures was a small price to pay.

For the first time, Trina understood just how close she had come to losing her husband. She wasn't prepared to risk anything like that ever happening again.

§

The next time Lara came to visit, she took Elizabeth aside to a quiet corner.

"I need you to do something for me, please. I know you'll think it's strange, but it's really important – I wouldn't ask otherwise."

Elizabeth had been worrying all week about how the other woman was coping, so her answer came quickly. "Of course, dear, I'm happy to do anything to help, and in whatever way I can."

"Thank you … umm … this is hard."

"It's okay, I can wait. Take your time…"

"Well … I really want – I-I need you to tell me how Adam's doing – and not just today ... whenever we get together."

"*What!* Oh, Lara, I *can't* do that. Surely, it's hard enough for you already without hearing the details of his new life – besides, how can you expect me to betray his trust?"

"Oh, I'm sorry, that's not what I meant. I don't want you to tell me *everything*. I just need to be sure he's okay and getting on with life. Please ... if I know he's happy, then hopefully I'll be able to move on with mine."

Elizabeth visibly relaxed; it wasn't hard to understand why his happiness meant so much to her – after all, his well-being was the catalyst for Lara taking such drastic action in the first place.

Initially, she had done so with a certain amount of trepidation, but Lara was true to her word and never asked for anything more whenever she dropped by. The only thing the weekly visitor had no idea about was how often his mother exaggerated the truth to help her move on – Elizabeth knew her son too well to believe his forced smile was a true indication of this new life he was leading.

And everyone was oblivious to how often Lara still woke up crying in the night after reaching for him in her sleep, only to find the bed cold and empty. Her mind had let him go ... sadly, her heart was another matter.

§

Despite his concerns about Lara having jeopardised her musical career, Max soon had other offers coming in. At the beginning of April, she was about to commence rehearsals in a new production of *The Phantom of the Opera* – the epic musical by Andrew Lloyd Webber now wowing theatre audiences around the world. She topped the auditions for the lead role of *Christine,* so her agent soon had another signed contract in his files.

"You sound in fine form – audiences are going to be wowed in their seats," her boss said with a grin, popping his head around the corner of her editing booth.

All of her lunch breaks were being taken up with running through a mass of scales and singing along to the backing tracks as she practised the difficult score.

"*Aarrghh,*" came the reply, along with a nervous grimace. "This is one of the most daunting roles of all – for me, it's more a massive fear fest!"

"Don't worry – you'll shoe it in! Bet my bottom dollar."

"Hope so, now just to remember all these lines ... *and* reach all those high notes!"

§

While Lara was struggling with the new repertoire, Adam already had his numbers down pat with *The Sound of Music* about to open in Melbourne. Trina had accompanied him when rehearsals began in mid-February and they were staying in a modern hotel close to the Princess Theatre. If the reviews were favourable, there was every possibility the musical might then move to Sydney. All those from the cosmopolitan city's theatre world who had caught a glimpse of dress rehearsals were convinced this would be the case.

Each Wednesday after dinner, Adam rang his parents to fill them in on any news. Two weeks before opening night he rang them again, and they picked up both house phones at the same time.

After the usual pleasantries, his mother's first question was to ask how he was coping. She worried about him every day. Also, at the back of her mind, was a query from a certain young woman who was just as anxious to hear how he was doing.

"Everything's going fine, Mum. Trina's out shopping most days or enjoying all the restaurants on offer with some of the other cast members' wives, and I'm getting on really well with the rest of the team. Jessica's doing a great job as *Maria,* so the producers are saying it's sure to be a rousing success."

His father cut in. "That's wonderful news, son. Mum and I will definitely be down for the big night – we can't wait to see you. You're sounding good ... obviously, Melbourne's treating you well."

"Yeah, it's not too bad – apart from the weather, but what else is new for this place – four seasons in a day is certainly true for most of them! All in all though, things are working out okay."

Charles and Elizabeth were relieved to hear some life back in their son's voice. His leading lady hailed from Sydney and she had already made a name for herself. Even though they hadn't seen her work before, Adam was able to assure them the director was more than satisfied with their pairing.

Originally, the executives had been bitterly disappointed when Max announced Lara was pulling out. They were concerned the production wouldn't be up to the standard first envisaged. Now those earlier fears were proving to be unfounded.

When Nikki first learned her mother had turned down the role, she burst into tears.

"But I want *you* to be *Maria,*" she begged between heart-wrenching sobs. "Then *I* could be *Gretl* and we could go back to Saltburg with Uncle Adam and practise all those pretty songs again. *Pleeeaaase,* Mummy!"

Even her continuing and endearing mispronunciation of the Austrian city's name wasn't enough to convince Lara to change her mind. If she didn't put her foot down fast, Nikki would keep pestering her for weeks on end. It took several attempts, but finally, the message got through.

Between sad little hiccups, she turned pleading eyes to her mother once more. "Well, can we go and *watch* Un...cle Adam then? I really want to see him blo...w the whistle – *and* sing in the pretty glass hou...se again ... even if you're mea...n and won't sing with him."

Lara ached inside as she placed a caring arm around the little trembling body, gently breaking the news about how it wasn't plausible as he was much too far away. Again, the little girl cried as if her heart was breaking.

On their next visit to the Ashworth home, Charles heard how upset she was and took Lara aside out of Nikki's earshot.

"I realise it's pointless asking if you'll be there for the opening in Melbourne."

She nodded and the sadness in her eyes betrayed how much even the thought of not being there hurt. In a caring fatherly manner, he placed an arm around her shoulders and leaned in close.

"Well, Elizabeth and I were wondering if you would mind if we took Nikki down with us? We all know how much she loves that musical and I'd hate for her to miss out, especially as it could be years before it comes up this way."

"Oh, that's a lovely offer, Charles, but I couldn't let her go all that way without me, even if it was only for a few days."

"But we'd be thrilled to have her, and it will only be for two nights as I have to be back Monday afternoon. Besides, I think it would do you good to have a break. Think about it, my dear. She'll never get another opportunity like this."

Elizabeth was just passing by to check a pot on the stove when she overheard her husband's last few remarks. Placing a motherly arm around Lara's waist to match Charles on the other side, she whispered into her hair, "And it's a way for him to say a proper goodbye ... even if she won't really understand."

Their eyes met and the sentiment behind the statement hung heavy in the air.

With a pensive nod, Lara murmured, "Let me think about it."

For the next few days, she mulled it over. On their next regular Saturday visit, as usual, Charles and Elizabeth came out to greet them, waving madly and with smiles bright enough to lighten the gloomiest heart. This was the highpoint of their week and the fridge was stacked with bowlfuls of delicious fare.

As soon as the car came to a stop, Nikki scrambled out and flung her arms around both of them at the same time. They broke into delighted chuckles to find themselves on the receiving end of such a hearty reception and cuddled the miniature whirlwind in the tightest of bearhugs.

"Hello there, little Poppet!" Charles said, pressing his lips to her forehead. "We've been waiting *all* week to see you!" His eyes twinkled across Nikki's shiny crown of hair and Lara returned his caring smile with one of her own.

"That we have," Elizabeth concurred, planting a firm kiss on the little girl's chubby cheek and then wrapped welcoming arms around Lara to include her in the boisterous embrace. "And how are you, my dear girl? You've been in our thoughts and prayers all week, but I'm sure you know that already."

Her voice conveyed undertones of the love and concern held for this woman she regarded as a beloved daughter. Elizabeth had learned to read Lara's moods from one visit to the next, which meant she was becoming quite privy to her attempts at pretending everything was okay. Those keen powers of observation frequently caught a glimpse of the veil of sadness behind the young woman's smile, and also noticed when a stray finger stroked the fabric of the chair he always favoured whenever she went past. Often that same hand appeared to grasp a fistful of the air floating across its surface before pressing it against her breast ... almost as though she was trying to capture a trace of him to take home with her. Elizabeth's heart was breaking, but all she could do was trust God to help ease her friend's pain.

Lara hugged her hard, grateful for all the words of support. "I'm okay, and you're a sweetheart – thanks for your prayers ... they mean the world to me. It's been a hectic week at work finishing off the last of my projects before rehearsals start for *Phantom.* To be honest, I haven't really had time to think about anything else."

She had never been more thankful to have something to keep her mind and hands occupied, though nights were still peppered with loneliness and longing.

As usual, the foursome gravitated to their favourite spot outside, and Lara told them everything she could about the new role. Charles and Elizabeth were just as relieved this had come along to fill up the hours and take her mind off the other one she had turned down.

Once the empty plates from another of Elizabeth's mouth-watering lunches were set aside, Charles was just about to suggest he take Nikki over to see Clancy when he felt Lara's hand rest against his forearm.

"Would you mind waiting a moment? There's something I want to talk to you about, and Nikki needs to hear it too."

He was intrigued. "Mmm, of course, but how about we sample something at the same time. I'd be interested in your opinion on a new blend we've just put on the market." Sending her a friendly wink, he grabbed a large bunch of keys from behind the kitchen door and went off to the nearby cellar built into the side of a small rise at the far end of the house.

The little girl screwed up her face at having to wait for the long-awaited ride until Elizabeth pulled her onto her lap with a grandmotherly kiss. "Hey, what's that look for, *National Velvet?* You'll get your turn soon enough, I'm sure."

"Who's *Nat...ional Velvet?*" She stumbled over the unusual moniker.

"She was a *very* famous horse rider, and she could jump *anything!*"

The frown soon disappeared as she pictured herself and Clancy flying over a row of colourful jumps. "*Ooohhh*, then that's going to be *my* name when I grow up and ride Clancy in lots of shows!"

"What are you all laughing about?" Charles asked with an amused smile when he returned with an unopened bottle of wine cradled under his arm. He settled back into the chair next to Lara, ready to hear her news as he popped the cork.

"Oh, just the imagination of a very cute little girl," his wife responded with another kiss on that thick dark fringe.

Similar to their son, Lara had gotten into the habit of sampling a small glass of one of the new vintages from their Gold Coast hinterland winery. With a connoisseur's flamboyant touch, he soon had three tall crystal flutes ready for the taste test. Minuscule bursts of colour sparkled in the sunshine as the bubbles rose to the surface.

With Nikki perched in her usual spot on Elizabeth's lap and happily doodling in a colouring book, Lara smiled as she took in the picture they made. "You know the offer you put to me the other week about a certain someone accompanying you to Melbourne?"

While the adults' faces lit up with broad smiles, the subject of their conversation was so absorbed in her drawing she had no idea what was going on until Charles leant over and nudged her elbow. "Hey, I think you might be coming on an aeroplane with us, young lady!"

Her head jerked up and she turned to her mother, eyes aglow and mouth wide open.

Lara's eye's twinkled just like her daughter's. "Well ... I was wondering how you'd feel about taking a little person we all know on an adventure to visit *Gretl* and *Leisl* and *Marta* and some other children who're staying down there at the moment?"

Nikki let out a shriek and scrambled down from Elizabeth's lap, running around the table and squealing with delight. Even Clancy looked up from grazing in the far-off paddock to see what all the commotion was about.

"I guess that means I have to say 'yes'," Charles replied with a delighted smile, reaching across to give Lara's arm a gentle squeeze. He knew exactly what this would mean for the young woman, and his wife soon followed suit by bestowing a concerned kiss on her cheek.

In normal circumstances, Lara would have given anything to go with them, to be able to support the man she still yearned for every single day, but she cared too much to put either Adam or herself – and especially not Trina – through such an ordeal. After all, his wife was the very reason she had made the sacrifice in the first place.

Comments about the crisp, sweet spumante intermingled with working out details for the trip and Nikki made sure she wasn't going to be left out, happily adding her tuppence-worth whenever she had the chance.

She spent the next exhilarating hour riding the little pony around the paddock and trilling, "I'm going to Melll...bourne! I'm going to see *Gretl* and *Maria* and Uncle Aaa...dam!" as well as singing many of the much-loved songs while bouncing along on Clancy's back. His thick creamy tail flicked away any pesky flies and made for a pretty picture of two best friends enjoying each other's company.

As the sun dipped lower in the western sky, Lara and Elizabeth strolled alongside each other as they made their way out to the driveway. Charles had Nikki perched on his shoulders, making trumpeting noises and pretending to be an elephant, much to her delight.

Slowing her pace so the women's steps matched, Lara needed to clear up one more thing. "Are you sure about taking Nikki away with you? She can be quite a handful and you're not used to having a little girl wake up at the crack of dawn every morning. I don't want your time away spoilt because of her." Even though Elizabeth had experienced no ongoing problems with her heart since the initial attack years ago, Lara was still mindful of her condition.

"Of *course* we are! Don't worry; we'll get a kick out of taking her with us." Dropping her voice, she squeezed Lara's waist and a hint of sadness cloaked the next sentence. "And I know Adam will be thrilled to see his little mate," while her spirit whispered, *I just wish you could come too.*

Lara felt the familiar twinge of longing when she heard that beloved name. Just for a moment, her eyelids dropped and chest rose as she struggled to draw in the next breath. No matter how often she heard it, the reaction was always the same.

With a quick shrug of her shoulders, she pulled herself together again, and Elizabeth caught the glimmer of a pensive smile. "She'll be so excited to see him! She still misses him terribly, despite it being nearly five months now. Almost every day there's something she wants to tell him about school."

The other woman's heart grew heavy and there was nothing she could add to make either of them feel any better.

After exchanging caring hugs along with heartfelt kisses – and with Nikki waving and calling from the back seat, "See you next week – I can't *wait!*" – the mother and daughter drove home to their cosy little retreat on the hill.

§

For the rest of the week, Nikki nearly sent Lara crazy rambling on and on about everything she would see and do on the surprise trip. The happy little miss had no idea where Melbourne was – all she cared about was that her Uncle Adam was there and she would see the *Von Trapp* children at last.

When Adam received the phone call with news of what Charles had planned, his initial response was one of both excitement and anticipation. Then reality hit. How would he cope with seeing Nikki again, especially knowing the flood of memories it would dredge up? Deep down his soul groaned with both sadness and dread.

His mother knew instantly what was going on when she took the phone. "Adam, darling, I understand why you're worried, but please think about this carefully. That little girl still misses you dreadfully, and I think it's important you take this opportunity to tell her what's going on. Lara's done her best, but she needs to hear it directly from you ... and she needs to be given the chance to say goodbye properly."

"But what do I *say*, Mum? I can't *lie* to her." The plea in his voice was unmistakable.

"Tell her the truth, just don't go into detail. She's old enough to understand that sometimes people have to go away ... her own father, for instance. We've all tried to explain how much you still love her and how much you hate being away, but in her little mind, all she can come up with is that she's done something wrong and you don't want to see her anymore. She even told Lara it's because she spilt that juice on your shoes at the airport. She still brings it up every now and then."

He groaned loudly. "Oooh, the poor little mite. I didn't mean to hurt her like this..."

And then reality hit him all over again. His stupid indecision had broken the hearts of a host of people he cared about, and resulted in a tragic situation where there could be no true winners. And now it was too late to turn back the clock.

"Oh, my precious boy, don't beat yourself up. All I ask is that you think about it. This could actually be a blessing in disguise – it might even help to pave the way for the three of you to be able to let go once and for all."

Elizabeth well knew he was still pining for the child, while the youngster's many references to Adam confirmed she still expected him to come back into their lives somewhere down the track. Lara didn't have to say anything – the loss in her eyes still spoke volumes whenever they were together.

"Okay, you're probably right. And it will be fantastic to see her again. Tell Dad to book the flights; I'll organise a room for you at our hotel."

Much to his surprise, Trina made no objection when he mentioned what was going on. Her sole motivation was to keep him happy, whatever it took, as long as he remained committed to their marriage. The only thing she did baulk at was the thought of having Lara's daughter stay with them. She was agreeable to put up with the inconvenience of having her around for a few days if the child slept in the same room as his parents. Like them, Trina had seen the yearning in Adam's eyes whenever other children were around. She could only hope this would help put the past behind them once and for all.

During another call later in the week, Charles and Adam conspired together over a surprise for the little visitor. Neither one could wait to see her reaction.

§

Saying goodbye at the airport was one of the saddest things Elizabeth had ever done. She could see the brokenness in Lara's eyes as she farewelled her young daughter with a big hug, trying hard to blink away a host of tears. The older woman knew it wasn't simply saying goodbye to her only offspring that had brought about this reaction, and yet there was nothing she could do to make the situation any easier except wrap the still-grieving woman in her arms and offer her assurances she would take care of her precious little girl.

When the trio touched down at Tullamarine Airport, Adam was there to greet them with Trina by his side. Over the past few months, their relationship had changed, and those earlier vicious attacks had become just horrible nightmares best left in the past. Even so, Adam couldn't imagine them ever sharing the same closeness he and Lara had known. Elizabeth and Charles exchanged surprised glances at the level of warmth in their responses to one another, despite there being no evidence of the spontaneous caresses or caring gestures a couple truly in love couldn't help displaying.

Elizabeth had been concerned about Nikki's reaction when she first saw Adam and Trina together after Lara stressed her daughter mustn't learn that he was married. She was worried the little girl might blurt out something about him wanting to marry her or how Nikki thought of him as her daddy. During the flight down, his mother had tried to prepare her small charge in a roundabout way, explaining Trina was a special friend from a long time ago who hadn't been well and he needed to take care of her. Thankfully, she had no reason to worry. As soon as Nikki spied Adam crouched down with both arms spread wide, she rushed headlong into them with no thought for anything else.

"Uncle Adam, Uncle Adam, I *came!* I'm *here!* I missed you *sooo* much!" her voice carried across the arrival hall as she threw her arms around his neck.

"Hello, gorgeous girl, I've missed you, too." He hugged her just as hard, inhaling the fresh talcum powder smell he recognised so well.

Other travellers smiled as they passed by, moved by the touching reunion, but Nikki didn't notice. She was more interested in prattling into his ear about all the things the hostess had organised to keep her amused on the plane.

"*Whoa,* hang on there, Tiger, let me have a look at you first. Who's *this* big girl and what happened to my little Munchkin? Is she hiding in here?" He pulled a handful of long, thick hair aside to peer into her ear and then under her jacket as a playful hand tickled her ribs. She burst into a spray of giggles and clung to his neck again.

Dark eyes met Elizabeth's over the little girl's shoulder, and there it was again – that forlorn look of loss behind his gaze. She had hoped the wretched blanket of misery would have lifted by now, but it appeared he had simply become an expert at burying the hurt.

Every now and then, as though brought to life by a marionette's strings, a multitude of emotions pushed through the numbness and claimed his heart all over again, leading him down well-remembered and longed-for pathways. Mustering up every skerrick of willpower, he somehow managed to lay them to rest once again to pursue this new life the way Lara had begged.

§

Everything about the weekend was a resounding success.

When Trina saw how Nikki raced into Adam's arms, it was easy to tell they shared a close bond. She also couldn't miss the instant rush of love in his eyes when he first saw the little girl – nor the potent look that passed between the mother and son. In a strange way, it actually served to reinforce how important it was to make this visit a pleasant one for everyone.

While observing them together, for the first time she fully understood what a wonderful father Adam would have made had she chosen not to have the abortion or demanded he have the vasectomy. The reminder was too close to home and she pushed the bothersome thought away. But there was one thing she couldn't ignore. Lurking on the fringe of her conscience was a question she already knew the answer to. Had she really done the right thing by coercing her husband away from the two people who would have given him everything he longed for?

Well, there's nothing I can do about it now ... besides, he was mine first...

Initially, Nikki was cautious around 'Uncle Adam's special friend', however she soon came around when Trina started humming a few lines from *My Favourite Things* following lunch on the first day.

"Oh, *I* know that song! It's my *fabourite!*" the little girl exclaimed, joining in quite happily.

By the last line, Nikki had sidled over to lean against her knee, looking up with a smile as Trina placed a hesitant arm around her small shoulders. The scene was almost a replica of one from the movie when *Gretl* presented the *Baroness* with a posy of flowers at their first meeting. The others looked on in astonishment, between subtle sighs of relief. This definitely wasn't the Trina of old.

It turned out to be the perfect icebreaker and made the rest of the stay easy for everyone. Trina's acceptance of the little girl had been Charles and

Elizabeth's only concern in bringing her with them. As it turned out, they needn't have worried.

With the promise of a very special surprise the next day, Nikki was quite happy to stay in the care of the hotel's resident babysitter while the others went off to the red-carpet gala performance. Just like any opening, the glittering night was guaranteed to run late. Having the little girl safe in bed would give Elizabeth and Charles the chance to relax rather than having to constantly keep an eye on her among the throng of people at the after-party.

Nikki's bottom lip started to quiver just as they were leaving until Elizabeth assured her the *Von Trapp* children would be far too exhausted to stop and chat afterwards. In the end, she climbed happily into bed after spending the afternoon playing games and chasing her uncle along the banks of the Yarra River during what was supposed to be a leisurely walk and catch-up.

As the whole ensemble sang the final note while the *Von Trapps* climbed the mountain to safety, thunderous applause from all around the theatre was a guarantee for a sell-out season. The two stars received a standing ovation and were then coaxed into three additional curtain calls before the audience made a move to leave. Afterwards, the celebrations were a rowdy affair, held in a top-class restaurant right in the centre of the cosmopolitan city.

It was long after midnight when the family bid farewell to each other in the hotel corridor. Adam longed to join his folks when they went in to check on his favourite little girl, but rather than risk upsetting his wife, he left them with warm hugs and sincere thanks for being there to support him.

Nikki was fast asleep with Annabelle tucked into the crook of her arm when Charles and Elizabeth tiptoed in. Placing a gentle kiss on the child's forehead, she shared a wistful smile with her husband at the sight of the treasured doll.

The following day, just as Lara had predicted, an excited little girl was up with the proverbial birds. Just in time, she remembered her mother's warning about letting her aunt and uncle sleep-in. Between muffled whispers and muted giggles, she and Annabelle shared a make-believe tea party under the covers until a cheery voice called out, "Is our favourite little Munchkin awake yet?"

Much to the Ashworth's delight, she scampered onto their bed, delivering sloppy kisses and asking all sorts of questions about the afternoon to come. Adam had been a gangling teenager when he came to live with them, so this was the first time they had known the joy of sharing early waking hours with an exuberant little person.

"Wow, this is the best start to a morning I've ever had!" Charles exclaimed, grabbing the wriggly worm and blowing a series of loud raspberries into her neck and down her arm.

Loud squeals filled the room, and it was easy to see from their exchanged smiles his suggestion to bring her with them had been an excellent decision.

Similar to the previous day, Trina and Nikki were relaxed in each other's company. She even had Nikki giggling with glee at some of the stories from her charity work on the children's ward. Over the months, Adam had been surprised by all the changes he saw in his wife, and this was just another example. Similar to his parents, he had been concerned as to how Trina would handle the unexpected visit. Seeing all the effort she was putting in to make Lara's daughter feel welcome went a long way in pushing those fears aside.

He missed spending time with the little girl and had organised to set aside a few hours just for the two of them. With no formal plans for the morning or early afternoon, he decided to take her exploring around the quaint alleyways and stylish arcades of the city precincts. Elizabeth almost had to become a contortionist trying to squeeze Nikki into a pink polka dot dress and then braid her thick tresses as she squirmed and jumped up and down with excitement.

Adam and his little shadow held hands as she skipped along blissfully by his side. It felt just like old times and both wore huge smiles as they peered into all manner of shops and cafés along the way, often drooling over the contents. Everyone they passed could see they were having a wonderful time.

A fashionable glass roof set above the spectacular Royal Arcade had Nikki staring in open-mouthed wonder, especially when she spotted the striking Gog and Magog figurines positioned on either side of the two half-dome entrances. The maze of chequerboard tiles lining the walkway was too much of a temptation for the energetic miss, and she happily played a short game of hopscotch as Adam watched on like a proud father.

When her legs grew too tired to explore any further, Adam spied a charming laneway café off the popular Degraves Street. She looked around with excitement, feeling like a real celebrity mingling with the 'trendy folk' enjoying cosy lunches for two.

A green, white, and red flag hung from a flagpole above the entrance and Nikki recognised the familiar banner. Feeding her love for the colourful language, Adam read out the menu items in an exaggerated Italian accent. Her eyes lit up as she tried to mimic all the choices. They had a fun time sampling each other's dishes, although he felt a little pang in his heart when he went to wipe a few splotches of rich tomato sauce from her chin. He was suddenly taken back to watching her mother do much the same thing in a pretty villa in Tuscany when laughter had filled their days.

Nikki was elated to be treated like a grown-up and her happy smile as she bit down on her bottom lip tugged at his heartstrings. It was so like the gesture her mother made whenever she was enjoying herself, for a moment he allowed himself to dream Lara was sitting opposite him ... but he quickly shrugged it away before any of that old gloominess could put a dampener on the meal.

In one of the smaller arcades close to their hotel, they passed a tiny jewellery store. Draped on a stand in the centre of the window display, Adam spied a child-sized 18-carat gold necklace with three miniature hearts intertwined. It was the perfect gift for a little girl and he couldn't resist taking Nikki's hand to lead her inside. With the piece fastened securely around her neck, his secret hope was that Lara would recognise the significance of the design and realise he still hadn't let go of his belief the three of them belonged together.

All the way back to the hotel, Nikki kept babbling on and on about the unexpected gift. "I *love* my new necklace, Uncle Adam. Do you know what? I'm going to wear it all the time just like my mummy does. She's still got that pretty music thing you gave her and she never *ever* takes it off 'sept when she's singing sometimes in a show. But she always wears it to bed *every single night!*"

And yet another verbal missile landed in his heart. Pulling his emotions in check, he touched her nose with the tip of his finger. "I'm glad your mummy still wears it, Munchkin – it's a very special necklace just like yours. Maybe you can wear them together, and then maybe you'll remember how much I love you."

"Okay, I will, and I'll tell Mummy too."

With one hand tucked securely in his, she kept grinning up at him, while the fingers on the other one kept checking to make sure the new keepsake was safe. And just like before, an innocent little gesture brought back memories of her mother doing the same thing one Christmas Day.

"*Here* you are! I thought you must have gotten lost." Elizabeth greeted them with warm kisses and open arms.

"Look what *I* got, Aunty Elizabeth! Isn't it *pretty?* Uncle Adam bought it 'speshly for me!" she announced proudly, showing off the new trinket.

"It *is* pretty, sweetheart, and he must love you very *very* much."

She looked meaningfully at her son, but he carefully avoided her gaze, making a hurried aside about needing to get changed for the theatre. Elizabeth had no trouble recognising the message behind the symbolic setting and could only pray Trina wouldn't notice.

With Adam gone, she realised time was getting away and quickly bundled her small charge off to the bathroom. Between bathing and getting changed into fresh clothes, Nikki chatted on and on about everything they had seen and done, and continually checked the new necklace to make sure it hadn't fallen off.

A little while later she ran out to show Charles, looking like a ballerina dressed in a candy-pink organza dress with multiple layers of net petticoats. Lara had purchased the pretty ensemble specifically for the special occasion. The skirt billowed out whenever she did a twirl and waves of long dark hair floated around her like a parasol. As she spun around, the shiny gold necklace sparkled whenever the light caught it, while pink ballet shoes completed the image of a fairy princess ready for a special outing. Her face shone with anticipation and Charles and Elizabeth smiled at each other like any proud grandparents.

Nikki had no idea Adam had organised an informal dinner with the younger cast members and their families afterwards. The children had even offered to stay in character as an added surprise and he couldn't wait to see her reaction.

§

The pint-sized ballerina sat spellbound throughout the entire first act. Whenever the children sang the familiar songs, Elizabeth could hear a faint hum coming from the seat next to her. She nudged her husband's arm and they exchanged happy smiles. It was an honour to be entrusted with the little girl's care and she was delighted Charles had suggested they bring her with them.

Even the second act with its dark history interspersed throughout the storyline couldn't diminish the excitement on Nikki's face. Her mother still censored that part of the movie, however with Charles' whispered assurances about the family escaping from the mean soldiers, the wartime sequences were soon forgotten as the *Von Trapp* children performed a whole repertoire of new songs set within the never-before-seen ending – at least for a little girl lost in wonderland.

Adam came straight out to join them as soon as the curtain call was over – still wearing the mountaineer costume from the final few scenes.

His special little guest burst into giggles when she saw him. "Uncle Adam, you look *sooo* silly in those funny looking clothes ... and that's a strange looking hat!" she declared, screwing up her nose as she tweaked the brim and checked out the small feather tucked in the side when he lifted her into his arms.

"Well, that's a fine greeting I must say! Don't you think I look handsome? I stayed in them 'specially for you."

"I think you're *very* handsome ... but you still *look* silly," she retorted with a chortle when he hoisted her onto his shoulders.

From her lofty lookout, it was easy to spot the seven children still dressed in their mountain clothes – the boys in Lederhosen and the girls wearing thick woollen dresses to keep out the winter chill. She struggled to get down and Adam helped untangle her from his neck before she took off at a run. Soon the talented children, with Nikki standing right in the centre, put on a wonderful show pretending they were the real *Von Trapps* to keep the story alive for their audience of one.

The youngest two offered to teach her a few of their lines until Nikki proved she could recite each one just as well as they could. With a smile, the pretty teenager playing the part of *Leisl* took their newest fan onto her lap and soon the little girl was singing *Edelweiss* along with them, word perfect.

Watching from the sidelines, Adam and his parents were tickled pink at how the surprise had turned out. Trina had decided to stay around the hotel for the afternoon, thinking it would be better for the family to have a few hours by themselves. Because of how accepting she had been of Nikki, he tried to talk her around, but she was quick to reassure him she didn't mind in the least. Charles and Elizabeth were just as amazed, although they enjoyed having their son to themselves for a change. Even more so, it did their hearts good to see how happy he and Nikki were without the need for any restrictions.

It wasn't hard to recognise the pride and love in his eyes as Adam watched the little girl and her new 'best friends' sitting at a corner table in the Green Room. All eight were laughing and chatting over each other as they tucked into a light dinner.

Elizabeth sidled over and whispered so only he could hear, "I know a certain someone who would've given almost anything to be here to see this..."

The sentiment tugged at his heartstrings and he draped a caring arm across his mother's shoulders, pulling her close so her head nestled under his chin. "I know, Mum. Believe me, there's nothing I wanted more than to be in this show with her ... well, except for one other thing..."

She reached up to brush her lips across his cheek and felt a slight trace of moisture on his skin. With a mother's loving touch, she gently wiped the tear away with her thumb and then burrowed into his shoulder with a resigned sigh.

Adam had to shut his eyes as he murmured into her hair, "Nothing's the same without her. Nothing..."

§

On their way back to the hotel, Nikki rambled on and on about meeting the children. By the time they pulled into the entrance, she was yawning and finding it hard to keep her eyes open.

"Come on, Poppet, I think we'd better get you to bed. You've had a very big day and now it's time for dreamland," Adam said, carrying her upstairs.

Without Trina there, he was free to do what he had been longing to the night before. After tucking his little charge snugly under the covers in a fresh set of pyjamas, Adam plonked himself on the edge of the bed all set to hear her nightly prayer. Seeing her eyes closed tightly and hands folded neatly in front of her chin, he couldn't help smiling at the cute picture she made.

"Thanks, God, for letting me sing with all *Maria's* kids today and for helping them get away from those mean soldier men so we could all have dinner. And thanks for all the fun I had with Uncle Adam, 'speshly the yummy lunch in that 'Talian café and the pretty love hearts he bought for me."

His tender expression quickly turned to one tinged with sadness as the prayer continued.

"And please look after my mummy and don't let her be too sad just 'cause

I'm so far away ... and help her not to cry too much anymore 'cause it makes *me* very sad, too. I hope you're happy in Heaven and that you get to sing about your faborite things up there, just like I did today. Amen."

Thankfully, the final pronouncement managed to put the makings of another smile on his face as he gently kissed her goodnight ... but the rest of the prayer stayed with him all night long as he lay in the dark beside his wife, pretending to sleep.

Much to his relief, the next day was a rest day so it didn't matter about the dark circles under his eyes.

§

The following morning, a most subdued little visitor kissed Adam goodbye at the airport. Looking deep into his eyes with a pair of chubby hands pressed hard up against his cheeks and her face only inches away, she said many of the sentiments he had bottled up inside but was too afraid to speak aloud.

"I don't like not seeing you anymore. Why can't you 'n me 'n Mummy go back to Saltburg and stay there forever so we never *ever* have to say goodbye? I miss your tickles and your big warm hugs and all the fun times we had – 'speshly making sandcastles ... and I know my mummy does too. She's always touching the picture of you next to her bed, and she always keeps that pretty blue scarf you gave her in Sydney under her pillow, but it's a secret so you can't tell her I told you." She pressed a rigid forefinger against her lips with a whispered, "Shhh."

It was just as well Trina had made a hairdresser's appointment weeks ago, so she wasn't there to hear this forlorn speech ... or witness the look on his face. Charles and Elizabeth were, and the looks they exchanged reflected everything he was feeling.

Adam had to blink back the tears as he brushed hers away. "Oh, my precious little Munchkin, I don't like being away from you either. And I promise I won't tell. I miss you and your mummy very much, too, and it would be fabulous if we could all to go back to Saltburg again – and stay there forever. I wish you were my little girl so we could see each other all the time."

Nikki gently rubbed along his lips with the same chubby finger, as though in her own innocent way she was trying to feel the emotion behind his words.

He swallowed hard to get the rest out. "But sometimes we can't always have what we want, no matter how many wishes we make." Out of the recesses of his heart, he repeated the line she had said to him after their holiday ... the same one Lara used on the night she first opened up about her daughter and their lives ... and he knew this was the perfect time to reinforce it. Hopefully, she would remember. "Promise me you'll always remember I love you as big as the sky."

Two large tears wobbled in the corner of her eyes as she nodded. Then she quickly swiped them away with the back of her hands and sniffed loudly.

It broke his heart watching her desperate efforts to stay strong. Ever so gently, he placed his hand over her heart and pressed firmly. "And I will *always* live inside you right here, just like you live inside me. Don't you ever forget that, okay?" Then picking up her tiny palm, he placed it against his chest, and she could feel the steady rhythm. "See?"

She nodded solemnly and said, "Yes, I really *can* feel me in there – that's my heart beating with yours, and that's why it's thumping so loud."

He fought down a sob as a sudden realisation hit him. This was possibly the last time they would ever see each other. Biting down firmly on his bottom lip to hold in a gut-wrenching sob, Adam gathered the child he loved as a daughter into his arms and pressed her hard against his chest. Then for one final time, he breathed in the talcum powder scent he would miss so much.

And in a similar manner, she seemed to recognise the significance of the moment, clinging onto his neck for several minutes while trying to hold back the sobs. The hardest thing Adam had to face in many months was needing to pull her arms away when an announcement came over the loudspeaker for those with young children to get ready to board the plane. The sudden pain in his chest made it almost impossible to breathe ... and it had nothing to do with how much air was in his lungs.

After giving him one last hug, along with a firm kiss planted on his cheek, and a look that would make the toughest man cry, she took his parents' hands. Then with hesitant steps, the trio walked toward the boarding gate. As she reached the end of the corridor, Nikki turned back to blow him a kiss and offer one last forlorn wave ... before the gaping hole in the plane swallowed her up.

Goodbye, my precious little one. May God always keep you safe wherever you go – be strong and always follow your dreams. And please look after your mummy for me. She needs you very much ... almost as much as I need her.

Bowing his head, and with one hand buried deep in his pocket, he stumbled from the terminal ... brushing away the tears still blurring his vision before anyone noticed.

And with a leaden heart, he knew his life would never be the same again.

Chapter 21

The first thing Nikki did when she got off the plane was race into her mother's arms and declare just how much she had missed her. The second thing was to fish out the beautiful necklace from under her jumper and show it off proudly. It only took one glance for Lara to understand the message behind the piece.

"I'm never *ever* going to take it off, Mummy, just like you don't take your pretty necklace off 'sept when you're on stage and you *have* to! It's my 'speshel present, and it's got all our love hearts on it. *See?*" Without any prompting, even a young child could recognise its significance.

Lara had to hold her daughter close to hide the tears as she swallowed hard. Apart from wanting to give the little girl something she could treasure forever, it was obvious this was also Adam's secret message to the woman he still carried in his heart.

Oh, Teddy, what've you done! Don't you realise the only way I'm getting through this is by believing you're moving on? Why did you have to give me that sign, my darling?

"It's beautiful, Munchkin, but you'd better not wear it all the time 'cause you might lose it in the playground at school. How about you only wear it on special occasions – then it'll always be safe. It would be very sad if you lost it, don't you think?"

The little girl frowned before nodded solemnly. "Okay, I won't wear it *all* the time." She ran her finger across the intricate detail. "But it's *very* 'speshel just like yours is, and I want to keep it for*ever!*"

And you probably will, my sweet angel. Gosh, you remind me so much of me.

"And Uncle Adam said we could wear them at the same time because it can make us benember that he loves us."

"Oh, Munchkin, when did he tell you that?"

"When I told him you still wear your music necklace all the time. And do you know what else he told me?"

Her brow furrowed as she tried to remember everything he had said and Lara glanced over to Charles and Elizabeth. Their expressions told their own story, wondering what other painful tales she might tell.

"No, I don't. What else did he tell you, sweetheart?" She waited with her heart in her mouth.

"That he misses you and me very *very* much and that he wishes we all lived in Saltburg and that I was his own little girl, but he told me I live inside his heart and he lives inside mine. But when I was on the plane, I tried *really* hard to feel him in there but I couldn't. Do *you* think he lives inside my heart, Mummy? 'Cause if he does, then I won't ever have to be scared again."

Lara had to close her eyes for a moment at the images all these innocent revelations conjured up. Then she took a deep breath. "I'm sure he lives inside your heart, Poppet. Uncle Adam would *never* tell you a lie. If he said that, then it must be true. And if I know Uncle Adam, he's probably tucked a tiny little piece of himself right down deep inside just to make sure it can never get away."

"I hope so 'cause that way he can live in there with you, 'cause I *always* know you're with me, even when I'm a *long* way away. I could feel you inside me all the time I was in Melbourne," she whispered, kissing her mother's cheek.

"That's *exactly* right, and I could feel you inside me too."

The conversation was becoming far too close to home for everyone. Elizabeth and Charles had to look away before they broke down.

In an effort to bring some lightness back into the conversation, Lara kissed her daughter soundly on both cheeks while blowing raspberries at the same time. "And do you know what else, Missy Poppet? I'm *sooo* glad you came home to me 'cause I missed you *this* much."

She threw her arms out wide and Nikki responded by throwing hers around Lara's neck. The ensuing flurry of sloppy kisses and hugs nearly squeezed the life out of both of them and was just the tonic they all needed. Thankfully, the delightful sound of a little girl's giggles pushed any remaining grey clouds away.

And with that saturating deep sadness once again relegated to a dark chamber in Lara's soul, she plastered on a happy face as they picked up the suitcases and made their way home.

Fortunately, no one would ever know how difficult the weekend had been for the young mum. Every second had dragged by as she rustled up images of what her two favourite people might be doing while she was so far away. Lara had spent every spare moment either pouring through the albums or watching movies with tragic endings as stark reminders of all she had thrown away ... and as a twisted form of solace, to offer a sense of reassurance she wasn't alone in her sorrow.

Knowing Nikki and Adam had made memories they could cherish forever was her only consolation ... and she would never begrudge either of them those memorable few days.

§

The following weekend it was Lara's turn to tread the boards again ... only this time there would be no familiar eyes to follow her around or furtive caresses exchanged when passing in the wings. It entailed another move to Sydney with a cast of actors she had never met before, and meant there would be no form of support for those times she needed some good old-fashioned company to help keep the blues at bay. Neither would she have any other pairs of ears and wise advice offered to help with any decision-making sure to come her way. Most of all, there would be no warmth of a beloved body when she craved some loving affection. Even though she was accustomed to being a single mum with the sole responsibility of a small child, it was another matter being in a large city without family or friends nearby.

Her sister promised to come down as often as possible, as did Elizabeth and Charles. They understood the huge risk she was taking by moving so far away from everything familiar, especially with a young one in tow. Even so, they were fully encouraging, believing this could be a major step forward in helping her get on with life. At least this time it would be less than four months until she was home again.

The contract had all the same stipulations as the previous one, including the welcome bonus of having Helen come on board again. She was the same caring nanny and tutor who had looked after Nikki during *My Fair Lady's* run. It was a major worry off Lara's mind knowing the little girl would be with someone she already knew and loved.

Their plane landed in Sydney on a Saturday morning with Lara wanting to settle in before rehearsals commenced on the Monday. It came as no surprise to find the hard work began the moment she stepped foot inside the studio.

The role of *Christine Daaé* was certainly a demanding one, requiring a vocal ability few performers could aspire to. Lara's clarity and range soon had the producers confident they were onto a winner when she grasped every note with ease. Each session brought broad smiles all round as the cast and crew put everything into it. As far as cast rehearsals were concerned, the production was complete from the opening bar to the last note within a matter of weeks. Now the only thing left was the normal final polishing and two weeks of intensive work with a full orchestra to bring it all together to full production standard ready for opening night.

Lara was relieved to find the hotel chosen by the agency was a different one than last time. She wasn't sure how she would have coped having to walk the same corridors and nearby streets again. Being down here brought back far too many memories as it was; if she wasn't careful, she could easily slip into a deep hole of self-inflicted depression in no time at all.

Even the venue was different from the last one. The State Theatre was a magnificent architectural wonder built in the late nineteen-twenties and located right in the heart of the business district. The ornate red, green and gold marble interior with its spectacular dome and large crystal chandelier was a breathtaking panorama for anyone walking through its doors.

As soon as they entered its lavish Grand Assembly area, even before climbing the wide sweeping staircases on either side, patrons found themselves transported back to a bygone era where elegant women floated along in stylish ball-gowns, while men, looking most dashing decked out in tuxedos and tails, paraded them on their arms.

Lara stood in awe for several minutes the first time she went inside, unable to believe now it was her turn to grace the stage of this stunning location.

She and Nikki were ecstatic when Suzie and Ben popped down for a weekend in the middle of rehearsals. It was a welcome break from the busyness of learning lines and practising all the numbers, along with the constancy of the little girl's lessons.

Lara got on well with the rest of the cast. On some weekends, the mother and daughter duo mixed socially with a few others whose children had also accompanied them, though nothing compared to spending time with loved ones after weeks apart.

The family of four wandered the streets around Darling Harbour, checking out the variety of yachts and launches resting at anchor beside the boardwalk. The area was a mecca for tourists with a host of attractions set amidst fine eating-houses with views across the water. It wasn't long before they stumbled across the tranquil Chinese Garden of Friendship. This leafy oasis was a welcome break from the bustling city centre. They ate lunch at a table overlooking a large pond dotted with waterlilies, and Nikki spent most of the time trying to coax a few large koi to the surface with titbits of bread.

That evening, Ben offered to babysit while the women went out for a night on the town. Many years had passed since the sisters had done anything like this, and it wasn't hard to tell how excited they were from the amount of laughter floating under the door while working on each other's hair and makeup.

"I think my mummy's pretty excited!" Nikki grinned when she heard another loud chuckle, and Ben nodded enthusiastically.

The women ended up in a small bar overlooking the waterfront at pretty Cockle Bay. The music was soulful so they could still hear each other speak at a table in one of the quieter corner alcoves. Located only a few streets from the hotel, it was unlikely they would lose their way home even though this was unfamiliar territory. Neither of them indulged very often, but this time they decided to splash out on a bottle of *Brown Brothers'* finest Chardonnay Brut to celebrate Lara's new venture as they took in the panorama of lights reflecting off the water. The younger one was determined to wheedle out everything going on with her big sister's love life. Though she really liked Ben, she wanted to make sure he wasn't taking advantage of Suzie's good nature.

"You're such a nosey-parker, Lara-Lu! That's it, I'm not telling you anything more," Suzie chided with a determined click of her tongue after being bombarded with questions for the best part of an hour.

"Well, why hasn't he asked you to marry him yet? What's *wrong* with the man! I'll have a stern word in his ear when I get back – he needs to make an honest woman of you!"

Suzie was secretly horrified. She knew how direct her sister could be when it came to matters of the heart. But she needn't have worried. Lara's only concern was to ensure Suzie wasn't left broken-hearted again after losing her fiancée in an horrific motorbike accident a few years earlier.

For over two hours there was lots of playful banter lobbed back and forth, but halfway through a rare second bottle of wine, Lara suddenly turned quiet. Suzie watched her sister playing with the stem of the glass as she gazed out across the dark waters of the bay. As far as she was aware, it was years since Lara had drunk this amount of alcohol, but she recognised that look – it had been her constant companion the year before when she and Adam were apart for all those months. The alcohol may be to blame to a certain extent, but it was obvious Lara wasn't as okay as she made out.

"Are you okay, hon? How about we get outta here and go somewhere fun to dance? That'll cheer us up instead of listening to this mournful old stuff!"

Lara shook her head. "If you don't mind, I'd rather not – I'm not really in the mood."

Her thoughts turned to a night when she and Adam danced around a bedroom in Cortona – the romantic prelude to them making love for the first time – along with tender memories of being in his arms while waltzing around a glass pavilion in Salzburg. Now all she could picture was Adam holding a new *Maria* in his arms. There were so many reminders that crept up on her when she was least expecting them. No matter how much time passed, the hurt was just as raw as when she first said goodbye.

Suzie wanted to kick herself for being so stupid. Dancing was probably the last thing her sister felt like doing when it was obvious she was thinking about a certain man. "I'm so sorry, Lara-Lu. I wanted tonight to be fun ... not bring back any painful reminders..."

"I know you didn't, Suze ... and neither did I. Sometimes they just come out of the blue and for a few seconds I dare to dream again ... and then reality hits and I can't believe I let him go."

The pain in Lara's eyes broke the other woman's heart and her reply was underpinned with a wave of concern. "I can't even to begin to imagine how hard it's been for you trying to cope all these months, but it was blatantly obvious to me how much you loved him. I didn't want to say anything, but I've been really worried – especially knowing you were down here without any support."

For the first time since the breakup, Lara let down the barriers and spoke in a whisper from a hidden place in her heart. "I still love him ... as much as I ever did ... and I always will. I've just learned to bury it away so it doesn't hurt so much." An anguished cry tore through her soul and her head dropped into her hands. "Ooh, Suze, he was the other half of my heart. Now it's as if mine keeps missing a beat – his beat – like I'm only half-alive. I'm so sick of pretending all the time ... but I have to ... for Nikki's sake."

With a sad cry, Suzie pulled Lara into her arms, stroking that long thick hair as a way to offer some form of comfort. Her tone was soothing as she gently rocked the distraught woman. "Oh, you poor thing, I didn't realise it was still so hard. I hoped things were getting better and you were on your way to getting over him."

Lara raised grief-stricken eyes. "I'll *never* get over him. We shared an unbreakable bond ... whatever he was going through, I felt it too – he didn't have to tell me, it was just there, always in my spirit." Her eyes filled with unshed tears and the longing in her voice caused the other woman's heart to ache. "And he was the same ... even when we were miles apart, we always felt each other. We were kindred spirits who thought and responded as one. I'll never know anything like that again ... no one else will ever touch my heart like he did..."

The younger one sobbed as though her heart was breaking, burrowing into her sibling's shoulder while Suzie softly stroked her back and crooned into her hair ... bringing succour to a shattered spirit. Once long ago, during the terrible period following their parents' deaths, the girls had been one another's lifelines ... now only one of them needed that same measure of comfort to bring her back from the brink.

Eventually, the sobs turned to tiny gasps and Suzie stroked Lara's cheek. "Come on, let's go home and I'll make you a nice cuppa. I think we've had enough wine to do us for a while."

Walking back to the hotel, the sad cry of a night bird drifted from a nest in a nearby bush and matched the cry in Lara's heart. She remembered hearing a similar call on another night long ago when Adam was by her side. Why did she have to hear that mournful song again ... and tonight of all nights? Once again, her soul was invaded by memories of a man whose dark eyes still haunted her every moment.

§

When it came time for Suzie and Ben to fly back to Brisbane, the sisters held each other close.

"Are you sure you're going to be okay? I'm worried about you and it's not good being so far away from home with only Nikki for company."

"I'll be fine, sis, truly. And I'm sorry about last night. I don't know what got into me."

"No need to apologise ... it's only natural after all you've been through."

"Well, you don't have to worry – I'm okay. I've got the Munchkin and work to keep me busy *and* out of mischief – or at least the doldrums! Anyway, you'll be down in a few weeks for the opening so it won't be long 'til we're together again."

"Yes!" Suzie raised her fist and shook it in excitement. "And I can't wait to see you in that gorgeous old theatre. Who'd have thought a few years ago you'd be playing that coveted role! And I read somewhere that Mark Sinclair is over in Adelaide playing *Phantom* for some other big company – bet his leading lady is nowhere near as good as you. Pity he wasn't free ... I know how much you admire him, so to have him as your leading man would be a dream come true!"

As soon as the words left her mouth, Suzie could have kicked herself. She knew too well Lara only carried one dream for a leading man – in all facets of her life – and the last thing she needed was another reminder, especially after the heartbreak of the night before.

"It's okay, don't worry, I knew exactly what you meant. Besides, I'm well used to dealing with your prowess with that old 'foot-in-mouth' disease!" came a quick reassurance as Lara sent a wry smirk Suzie's way. "But I have to admit I'm a little bit jealous of the woman playing opposite him. As much as I love this cast, if I'd had the pick of Mark as my leading man, I sure wouldn't have complained! But I'm not in their league, so I'll just have to settle for this one."

She wasn't brave enough to pursue the idea of Adam playing the role ... just the thought of having him crooning all those beautiful love songs was enough to send her heart racing, without fantasising about having his smouldering eyes follow her for the length of an entire show.

"You'll knock 'em dead, kiddo! And I bet one day you'll be Mark's leading lady – mark my words – oh, and pardon the pun!"

Lara's answering grin was a nice way to finish the visit. Exchanging hugs all round, Suzie and Ben then make their way down the corridor to the plane.

Watching them walk away arm-in-arm, and even sneak a loving smooch when they thought no one was looking, Lara felt a slight twinge of envy. But just as quickly, she shook the feeling away. Nothing was going to steal away the thrill of seeing her sister in love and enjoying life again.

You'd better marry her, Benny Boy, or you'll have me to answer to!

Chapter 22

The Melbourne season of *The Sound of Music* was a huge success and producers were able to lock in a six-week run at Sydney's Theatre Royal. Adam wondered if he was ready to face that place again after performing there with Lara the last time he was in the harbour city. Having to tread those boards again would bring up painful memories, and his heart was still raw when it came to revisiting places and recalling things they shared. Not surprisingly, this was often the price actors paid in this close-knit business.

His show was due to open on the third Saturday in June following a two-week hiatus. Once the Sydney run was over, the whole production was then moving to The Lyric in Brisbane. Ticket sales had been phenomenal, and QPAC had an unexpected gap in their schedule, so producers were keen to send it north.

Ironically, this meant the Sydney season overlapped with *The Phantom of the Opera*. As much as he tried to fight it, Adam was secretly thrilled to be working in the same city as the woman who still invaded his dreams. After her numbing phone call, he was in no doubt Lara had no wish to see him, but just knowing she would be near was enough to set his heart racing and make him feel alive again.

The unseen communication line running from one stage show to the next had been working in overdrive when news came of the two productions opening within weeks of each other.

Lara was one of the first to hear when Max rang to give her the heads-up. When she had agreed to relocate to Sydney for this new role, he realised those earlier excuses of not wanting Nikki away from school so soon after her last stint in the southern capital had obviously just been an excuse not to work with Adam again. Without knowing all the details, the agent guessed something had caused a rift between them and he felt it was only fair to prepare his new star for this unexpected turn of events.

Most of her castmates were aware she and Adam had already worked together and several were eager to fill her in on any gossip. The only recourse left was to keep her mind deliberately focussed on her commitments and stay away from wondering how she would cope having him in the same city for such a long period of time.

§

The coinciding of their working lives brought about another major event – one that was invisible to earthly eyes.

A Master Craftsman stood before an elaborate half-finished tapestry. Using glorious threads of the finest silk, he set about fashioning a series of intricate outlines that depicted a duo of parallel lives.

Delicate stitches formed a reflection representing the *Windows to Two Thirsty Souls*. The backwash was cloaked in purply-grey hues, portraying the suffocating sadness buried in a pair of lonely hearts. On the left of this particular portion of the canvas, a man's piercing black eyes stared out to a distant dream. On the other side, their feminine counterparts sparkled blue as a vast ocean bathed in sunlight. This pair seemed to be peering over their guardian's shoulder, determined to remember every memory of shared moments – once the meeting place of two inseparable kindred spirits.

With the greatest of care, the Creator's imaginative fingers blended and mingled these two forms into one silken vignette, ensuring the safekeeping of that missing half of themselves. And with an unblinking gaze, these newly interlocked features settled on a lone leaf holding fast to a stately oak rooted in the centre of the canvas – a tenacious quiver of hope in their ongoing despair.

§

The first weekend in June was like 'old home week' when Lara's usual band of avid supporters arrived from Brisbane two days before the big opening. Much to her embarrassment, the enthusiastic bunch broke into a rousing ovation when they spotted her excited grin just inside the terminal's entrance. Charles and Elizabeth led the way, thrilled to be able to support her debut in the acclaimed production. Suzie and Lucy, along with their respective partners, were just as eager to be there for the special occasion and set about elbowing one another out of the way to get to her first.

Nikki was just as excited to see everyone, scrambling from one to the other with detailed stories of what she had been up to and anxious to hear how Clancy was getting on without her. Lara had been able to organise a few hours off between rehearsals, which meant they were able to spend the afternoon tripping from one picturesque part of the harbour city to another. The newcomers kept her so busy enquiring about the show and relating all they had been up to, she could almost forget there was one other missing from their midst. Almost...

Thankfully, Adam's troupe wasn't due to arrive for bump-in until the Tuesday following her opening – those few hectic days when the crew erect sets, set lighting and work out how to adjust everything for a different sized stage. It also gave the cast an opportunity to learn how to negotiate a vastly different space without falling all over each other or the relocated props. With his arrival occurring that little bit later, there could be no conflict of interest for the visitors' loyalty ... or for her heart.

Lara held the Sydney audience spellbound with her portrayal of *Christine* ... from the moment she stepped onto the stage as a shy chorus girl, until the very end as the shattered *Phantom* faded into oblivion when she left with his rival. It was as though the rising new star actually embodied the character when her expressive tonal qualities catapulted them into the mystical labyrinth hidden beneath the Parisienne Opera House. And just as *Christine's* beauty and talent bewitched her furtive admirer, Lara's stage presence did the same to those watching in the crowd.

When the last note faded away, the entire audience rose simultaneously to their feet with a rousing burst of applause as the deserving actress came to the front of the stage. Though her heart overflowed with gratitude, no matter how hard Lara tried to control her thoughts, just as potent was a secret wish to look out and see the love and pride in a certain person's eyes. Tenaciously, she pushed that impossible dream aside before it took hold and drove her crazy. She had no other choice if she wanted to get through the next six weeks.

The opulence of the State Theatre had always impressed patrons. One of its unique features was a matching pair of private viewing boxes on either side of the stage, high above the main auditorium. Both were draped with thick curtains, and once upon a time VIPs or important city officials and their guests had the privilege of watching a performance from the shadowy confines of these small, intimate alcoves. Due to workplace health and safety regulations, the boxes had been off-limits to the public for many years.

Gaston Leroux's enthralling novel told the tragic tale of how a *Phantom's* eyes continually followed his young protégé either from behind carefully placed two-way mirrors or from up in the rafters of the Opera House in Paris. Years later, Andrew Lloyd Webber masterfully adapted the story for musical theatre.

While the disfigured suitor's heartbreak played out on a stage for all to see, another pair of watchful eyes pierced the darkness formed by the thick curtains surrounding one of these private boxes. Mesmerised, they followed every move the lead actress made as the auditorium resonated with her clear sweet voice. And in every one of Lara's scenes, those keen dark pools overflowed with the same amount of pride and desire as his on-stage counterpart ... along with the identical heart-wrenching culmination of having to watch her leave at the end, albeit alone instead of with a newfound lover.

This silent onlooker knew he couldn't have borne the pain of watching his soulmate run off with someone else. That deep void in his spirit was never-ending, no matter how hard he tried to put her out of his mind.

Long after the echoes of applause faded away and silence was his only companion, this solitary figure slowly trudged down the elegant staircase, lost in thought as his heart ached to go back in time to a place where once upon a time she had sung to him with that same degree of longing. And if any stragglers happened to catch a glimpse of his expression, they might have believed *The Phantom* now haunted these halls instead of those in a make-believe Parisienne opera house, still searching for his lost soulmate.

§

For days Adam had wrestled with the sensibility of staying away. In the end, he couldn't resist the lure of opening night and flew up a few days earlier than the rest of his *The Sound of Music* colleagues. Trina already had manicure and hair appointments booked with one of Melbourne's top stylists on the Wednesday so she would join him later in the week. During one of their regular calls, Charles had unwittingly let slip that he and the others had booked flights for Lara's big night. Knowing his family was already in residence would be too much of an inducement to drop by her hotel if there was time to spare, so he had deliberately booked a flight due to arrive less than two hours before curtain-up.

The fact they were no longer together didn't matter – Adam wanted to support the woman he still loved, even though she had no idea. With his name becoming so well known in theatrical circles, it was easy to persuade the manager to allow him exclusive use of one of the private boxes. It also meant he was able to savour everything as if her performance was for his eyes alone.

§

With *The Sound of Music* about to hit town, Lara had been fretting over how she would cope when Adam was performing only two blocks away ... or if she could even trust herself to stay away. To ensure her vocal cords were given short respites during the challenging role, the director had organised for her to have every Thursday off. Her understudy was happy as this meant she got to play *Maria* on a regular basis. Unfortunately, it also meant that now it was Lara's turn to battle temptation. With no flight schedule quandaries, nor any pre-arranged appointment to keep her busy, there was nothing to prevent her from slipping into one of his shows to witness for herself what all the review columnists were raving about.

As the weeks passed, her mind and heart waged a constant battle.

Adding to the turmoil, if Nikki ever found out, her pester power would be almost impossible to resist. Trying to dodge the many posters scattered around the city centre became a feat in itself. The oblivious little miss saw it as a fun game when her mother would suddenly grab her hand and take off in a different direction with a hurried, "Hey, let's go see what's down here, Munchkin," or something in a similar vein. Lara was becoming most adept at playing Sherlock Holmes while keeping a constant lookout for the prominent signage.

Five weeks after *Phantom* opened, they were in the final stretch. The mother and daughter were due to return home following the Sunday matinee, and Lara was feeling quite pleased with herself. She had managed to keep busy on her weekly night off, either by taking Nikki to early movie screenings or on all sorts of adventures around the waterfront close to their hotel.

Tonight was the last show-free night to get through before her final four performances. Once those commitments were done and dusted, they would be on a plane for home ... far away from that constant lure to slip into the Theatre Royal. By some miracle, she had even managed to prevent Nikki from learning that *The Sound of Music* was in town.

The two of them were just finishing lunch at one of the many alfresco cafés lining Darling Harbour's boardwalk when, without warning, the little girl let out a shriek of delight and took off at a run. Lara knew there was only one person who could make her daughter react that way and her heart started pounding so hard she could scarcely breathe.

Barely daring to turn around but knowing she had to, Lara came face-to-face with those captivating warm brown eyes – the same ones that were always able to draw her in ... and hold her safe. Nikki was already in Adam's arms with hers wrapped tightly around his neck. It meant he was able to focus entirely on the woman standing in front of him. Neither one of them was even aware when he put the child down again.

"Hello, Lara."

That voice was the same ... tearing down all the barricades when she heard her name fall from his lips.

When he saw how fast her chest rose and fell, and watched as a trembling hand covered her mouth to keep from crying out, for the first time Adam had a clear answer to the question that had been plaguing him constantly over the last eight months. She hadn't stopped loving him after all, no matter how many times he tried to convince himself she would have moved on. Confirming his thoughts even more was seeing those sapphire-coloured eyes glistening with unshed tears.

Just like the first time their eyes met, they tugged at his soul and dragged him into her heart. And there it was again – a need to physically restrain himself from reaching out and touching the air surrounding her, as though her spirit actually radiated into the atmosphere. A pair of clenched fists was proof of his longing, but as long as that penetrating gaze held her hostage, she didn't even notice.

Lara couldn't speak ... uttering even one syllable was all it would take for those long-withheld emotions to spill out. She had no idea of the picture she made biting down on her bottom lip as though having to bite back the words waiting in readiness. All it took was a small glimpse of that well-remembered gesture for his heart to do cartwheels.

The effort she was making to hide how much she still loved him did nothing to aid his futile attempts at restraint. Surrendering to his need, instinctively he reached out and drew her against his chest ... craving just one more chance to breathe her into his spirit.

Following his lead, Lara's arms seemed to have a will of their own as they wrapped themselves around his waist. All she could do was cling on like a person drowning. Neither of them could subdue what was clearly an overwhelming urge after keeping their feelings in check for so long. She melted into his embrace, savouring her soulmate's familiar man-fragrance and touch.

For several minutes, this rediscovered world seemed to stand still ... until the passing eyes of a few strangers drew them apart – though not too far, just enough to enable them to look into their beloved's eyes once more. The months flew away when their hands met, holding on tight with no thought for anything else. Lara was so aware of his skin against hers, the enticement to pick up the ballet where they left off was almost too hard to ignore ... and yet she knew she couldn't go there. He wasn't hers anymore ... but even so, these few precious moments would always be theirs to savour over and over.

Eventually, she found her voice.

"Hello, Adam."

There was so much she wanted to say to reverse the outcome of that heartbreaking conversation ... but she couldn't ... and he knew it. Steady gazes reflected the agony like an unspoken testament to all the endless hours of yearning and loneliness. Nothing had changed, despite that awful reality of no longer being together – except for the passing of time since that fateful morning – but it was clear their bond was just as strong. Being here like this was simply a fleeting and cherished gift for two hearts forever bound together.

"How have you been?" Normal, everyday words blurted out before he could think clearly, along with a painful but necessary attempt to cover what he really wanted to say.

Stupid question, he chided himself. *I can see how you are. We're the same ... one-half of a single entity in desperate need of their mate.*

"I miss us," she whispered, those expressive sapphire eyes now open windows to a lonely soul.

He knew exactly what she meant. Three insignificant little words when put together could just as easily have come from his heart. One phrase encapsulating everything he had been going through and with the same amount of grief. They had always been an 'us' – from that very first meeting. No longer two solo individuals walking this earth alone. Instead, two halves of a whole and no amount of time would ever change that truth.

Lara didn't have the strength to move to a safer refuge for her heart – nor did she want to. "I found me when I was with you ... and now I still look for you wherever I go – it's the only way I can ever feel complete anymore."

He couldn't believe she was actually standing in front of him. It was easy to empathise fully with all she was saying, and he had to swallow deeply to keep a sudden rush of emotions in check.

Using touch as eloquently as words, she reached up to stroke his cheek and then fleetingly brushed the back of her forefinger across those lips she knew so well. "I know I can never be truly whole without you ... and as strange as it may sound, I honestly don't mind. As long as I miss us, I'm still able to feel ... and as long as I have that, then I can get through another day."

Her truthfulness broke his heart ... but he understood it wasn't said to bring about a different ending to their situation. She wasn't asking him to come back into her life ... just confirming what he had always known deep down. And now he understood – her coping mechanism was identical to his, and any attempt to believe she was over him had been the musings of a fool ... and yet it had been the only option left to him if he was ever to find a way to live with her decision.

Adam's hand still gripped hers firmly, as if he was afraid to feel the cold wind of reality blowing across his naked palm. Reaching out, he took her other hand and pressed it against his lips before resting it over his heart. "Oh, Baby, I miss us, too ... every single day ... all day long." Dark eyes bored deep into hers and neither one could look away. "But somehow, I'm learning to live with the missing ... and like you, sometimes I've found it's become a welcome friend."

In the end, nothing had changed – their emotions were still in perfect harmony. So long as that craving remained, along with it came the knowledge their love was everlasting ... no matter how much distance separated them. For both, the gnawing pain had become more welcome than the relentless numbness of those first few months.

Lara had to ask ... she had wondered every day. "Are you happy, Teddy?"

At first, he faltered – too afraid to answer ... until those trusting eyes reminded him of all the goodness contained within her soul.

Almost imperceptibly, he nodded and a hesitant, "Mmm," slipped through his lips. He couldn't lie – not to her – but neither was there even a hint of a smile, as though its very presence would disparage his true feelings. "I never thought I would *ever* be able to admit this ... but yeah ... some of the time I am. Not ecstatically so – not even to the point of liking what my life entails now – but every day I try to make the most of what I've been dealt."

His eyes never left her face, as if he was trying to imprint every part of her on his memory and imploring her to understand what he was trying to say. Eventually, the tender smile she recognised more than any other lit up those truth-telling windows.

"A beautiful woman I once knew taught me that – and I have to remind myself every morning when I get out of bed ... although with each new day it's getting just that tiny bit easier ... especially when I remember. After all, I've been loved so much more than most."

Lara's smile matched his, though her eyes once again shimmered with unshed tears. "So have I ... and I'm truly glad you're happy. I want you to be ... I *need* you to be – that's why I had to do what I did."

For the briefest of moments he hesitated, and then the raw honesty behind his gaze made her catch her breath as he whispered poignantly, "But it doesn't take away the longing ... nor the love..."

He squeezed the hand still lying against his chest. As though drawn there, they both looked down to where their other hands were still joined. Ever so gently and in perfect unison, the former lovers picked up the rhythm of a symphony – one that had been lying fractured and neglected for more than half a year. And with flawless synchronisation, a secret ballet once again danced across their skin.

Plucking up the courage, he dared to ask, "What about you, sweet lady, are *you* truly happy?" That intense gaze drew her eyes back to his again and the battle scars were clearly visible in their depths.

She stayed lost there for several seconds and then looked across to the little girl who was watching everything from only a few feet away – for once seemingly aware they needed this time without any interruptions.

And just like him, Lara couldn't lie. Instead, she slowly nodded her head. "Mmm ... mostly ... a certain young miss makes sure of that." Her gaze travelled back to his face, and Adam had no trouble recognising that smile – he had witnessed it many times before when she talked about her precious daughter – full of love and with a hint of wonder. "She always gives me a reason to smile, and I thank God every day for entrusting her to my care. Without Nikki, I honestly don't know how I would've coped ... she always seems to rustle up the sunshine whenever those dark clouds start to roll in."

He dragged his gaze away to look across at the little girl he would always think of as his own. Her serious expression was proof she was taking in every cue and reaction. Seeing the uncertain look in those big brown eyes so similar to his became another huge stumbling block for Adam's willpower.

As a way to see her smile again, he surrendered Lara's hands with a reassuring squeeze, and then scooped Nikki up to hold her at eye-level. "I've missed you too, my little Munchkin," he murmured softly.

"I've missed you as well, but I've been very brave just like you told me. And now my mummy'll smile more 'cause you're friends again."

Two sets of eyes met over her head, clearly distressed by this reminder of how their choices had affected someone so young and innocent.

Adam's voice was no more than a whisper as it struggled through the lump in his throat. "You *are* a very brave girl, and I'm so proud of you. I love seeing Mummy's smile again, and yours too, Missy Tuppence."

She rubbed her cheek against the whiskers on his chin and then burst into a spate of giggles when he tried to tickle her neck with them. And just as Lara had said, a small child's sunny disposition was able to blow the bleak clouds away, and they found themselves laughing along with her as she struggled to get down.

Neither of them wanted to be the one to break the spell ... after more than eight months of silence, they had barely spent more than ten minutes together. But suddenly everything came crashing back to earth when he glanced at his watch. She recognised the familiar Swiss timepiece ... but kept silent ... as did he – though their hearts knew.

This unexpected yearned-for reality was now about to be snatched away again by their worst enemy – the need to say 'goodbye'. No matter how much they longed to stop time, there was no getting away from its irritating little nudges any longer. And yet, despite having matinee performances due to start in less two hours, still they waited in silence – stealing whatever extra minutes they could ... needing them as sustenance for the dreaded act of walking away.

Lara felt the tips of his fingers caress the length of her forearm, and her heart skipped several beats as she watched him swallow hard. This was his last opportunity to speak from the innermost core of his soul.

"Seeing you again has been a wonderful and most unexpected gift – one I never ever thought possible. You look just as beautiful as that first time I saw you, and everything I remember from all our special times – they will always be ours, nothing and no one can ever take them away. But I still can't believe I ran into you like this" —he squeezed her hand again— "and knowing you're okay – and happy – has made my day." He shook his head and gave a pensive smile. "No ... not just my day ... my year! You're still the same woman I fell in love with ... with the kindest of hearts and such a loving spirit – rest assured, my feelings will never change, no matter what happens in the future."

The poignancy of her smile matched the vulnerability in his and any attempt to gain some semblance of restraint to simply walk away disappeared as she looked into his eyes.

"You've made mine too, Teddy ... more than you'll ever know. Meeting you like this has been a true blessing – one I'll cherish because now I know for sure you're okay. And like you, my love will never change or wane – it will just live on in a special place in my heart – a secret chamber reserved only for you. You taught me how to trust again, and even though our time together had to come to an end, I will always be grateful and treasure what we had. To be honest, I wasn't sure how I'd cope if we ever saw each other again ... but I'm so thankful we had this chance to talk ... thank you."

"The pleasure's all mine, believe me. I haven't felt like this in months."

"Me either" —the back of her forefinger reached out and lightly brushed along the hairs on his forearm— "and thank you for forgiving me."

He had to swallow hard as a sprinkle of goosebumps scurried across his skin. "I'm the one who needs forgiveness. I'm just so sorry I hurt you. I was too gutless to choose what I really wanted..."

She reached out fully and a caring hand stroked along his cheek. "No, you weren't – you chose what was right. You just needed clarity to set you on that path…"

"Oh, Baby, I don't deser—"

"No, Teddy, it's true. But I want you to hold onto the memories, so when the missing becomes too much, you can be assured I will never *ever* regret loving you – you've given me far more than anyone ever has … or ever will. And you still do – every little reminder becomes another reason to keep going."

The corners of his mouth lifted in a sad but grateful smile as he nodded in understanding. "And so have you, sweet lady ... so have you. I know exactly what you mean ... all of those precious keepsakes have become a form of sustenance ... every single day..."

With the greatest of care, she reached out so her hand touched the patch of material covering his heart. "And please take good care of this – it's the most beautiful one I know."

He pressed his hand against hers and whispered, "The best part of it still belongs to you – and always will."

A broken sob was her only answer as she blinked hard.

Time had gotten away again, but still he hesitated, trying to find the appropriate words of farewell without actually saying goodbye.

"Lara..." he pleaded, grasping her hand again. She searched his face during the silence, and then those familiar dark eyes revealed a twinkle of pride. "Just before you go, I need to tell you something ... you make a wonderful *Christine. Phantom* is the luckiest man in the world being able to love you night after night ... even if it is always in secret. I know exactly how he feels."

She gasped.

Stealing one more heartfelt squeeze of her hand to tide him over for an unforeseeable future, and then sending her one of those meaningful winks she knew so well, he kissed the top of Nikki's head and turned to walk away ... but not before being rewarded with the corresponding tweak of her nose.

Her gaze followed him all the way to the corner. Then with one last lingering wave, he turned and disappeared from their lives all over again.

§

As Lara was getting into character only a little while later, her heart beat a furious rhythm as she pondered his parting words.

What did he mean? Was he just presuming? Had he actually been there?

Keeping company with the numbing sense of loss she felt after watching him walk away was a tiny shiver of delight. Every part of her wanted to believe he had been to one of her performances.

During the matinee, her voice took on a more mature tone and she seemed to be projecting it even further than normal. The director came over as soon as the first act was over.

"That was fabulous, Lara! I don't know what's happened, but whatever it is just keep doing it. Not that I'm complaining about any of your other performances, but somehow today's offering surpasses all the rest. Well done!"

Her heart was bursting with joy. The reason was obvious, but all she could manage was a self-conscious smile followed by a stammered word of thanks. It had taken only fifteen minutes with Adam to bring the spark back into her whole demeanour and its effect had obviously carried through into today's show.

For the rest of the week, as she waited for the curtain to rise, his final words resounded deep in Lara's soul, spurring her on each time. On stage, she felt like she was soaring, while those in the auditorium were spellbound by the depth of emotion underpinning each number.

§

It was closing night and backstage echoed with the usual pre-show excitement as the cast headed to their dressing rooms. Underlying those pesky nerves, each one was feeling somewhat subdued now that another magical period of their lives was about to come to an end. It had been a sell-out season and none of them wanted to put their character to bed just yet.

The Webber musical was a recent addition to the musical stage and no matter where it played around the world, theatre lovers were in the grip of 'Phantom Fever'. Not surprisingly, Sydney was no exception. The cast and creative team had done a marvellous job, so it was expected the show would receive rave reviews. To the disappointment of theatregoers elsewhere around the country, all of the larger complexes in every major city had bookings for other runs, which meant no extension or opportunity to take it on tour was possible.

Tonight the house was full long before the usual cut-off time for ticket sales. The air of expectancy, as well as the buzz on everyone's lips, filled those waiting backstage with an even greater sense of excitement than usual.

At the ten-minute call, Lara heard a sharp rap on her door.

"These just came for you, Ms Jennings. There's a card attached," the Stage Door Security Officer said when she opened it. He was wearing a beaming smile when he handed over a vase filled with bright yellow daffodils. Intermingled amongst them were a dozen or so deep red tulips, and the entire arrangement was accentuated by delicate white baby's breath.

"Thanks, Joe," she replied quizzically, wondering who had sent them.

"Fit for a star, I reckon! Some fan knows you're up there with the best o' them," he added with a proud wink and touched the tip of his forefinger to the brim of his cap.

"Oh, get off with you," she returned with an embarrassed laugh.

Probably Suzie and Ben, just to cheer me up, she thought, closing the door.

Her sister had phoned earlier saying how disappointed she and Ben were at not being there to support her. Suzie's boss was working on an important case and he needed her help over the weekend. Lara opened the envelope with her name typed across the front, and one eyebrow lifted when she noticed the logo of a prestigious florist engraved in the corner.

Whoa, you must've won the lotto, sis!

The front of the enclosed card showed an eagle in full flight, soaring across the face of a snow-clad mountain peak bathed in the last rays of sunlight. It reminded her of the Italian Dolomites, those breathtaking mountains that had held her mesmerised as dusk fell. Emblazoned across the bottom in an old-style flowing script she read:

Wherever the music takes you, I pray God's Spirit lifts you higher…

Soaring across the mountains as that magnificent voice takes flight…

To any keen observer, it was obvious the sender had personally inscribed the touching message. When the card fell open, Lara instantly recognised the familiar penmanship. She held her breath as tears welled in her eyes.

> *Darling Lara, my inspiration … beloved angel who helped unfurl my own set of wings,*
>
> *Tonight as you soar to those same glorious heights I witnessed on opening night – yes, I was there, Baby, I couldn't stay away – instead of thinking of this as a chapter closing, I'm certain it's just the beginning of many new and exciting adventures for you. Even though I won't be with you physically, be assured I'll always be cheering you on in my heart – the one that's a mirror of yours – wherever you are … but most especially tonight.*
>
> *And every now and then when you pause for a moment, I*

pray you can feel me ... just as I always feel you. We both know our spirits still fly together...

Go gently through this world, my darling – I have to believe you'll always be safe and happy.

Forever and always ... Your Adam xo

P.S. Please don't be angry. I just had to do this once more for old time's sake xx

She clasped the card to her breast while a duo of tears spilled down her cheeks. *How could I ever be angry with you, my darling darling man?*

In what had become a treasured tradition, Adam had once again presented her with a spectacular bouquet just before going on for a final performance.

It took a few minutes for Lara to compose herself as she re-read the words that had poured from the deepest part of his heart. Before resting the card beside the crystal vase, her lips pressed against his name. She knew he would be with her in spirit when she stepped onto the stage ... just as he promised.

§

Both the fans and producers were euphoric when Lara came to stand beside the actor who had played *Phantom* at the conclusion of another successful show – one that rounded out a completely sold-out season. Long waves of applause flowed over them, though all she longed to see was Adam's beloved face smiling back at her after dedicating the moving performance to him just prior to going on.

Her eyes shone as she left the stage. Some were tears of happiness at the success of the show ... most were because tonight signified the culmination of two soulmates physically leaving one another behind as their lives inevitably moved in different directions.

§

And across that infinite expanse of space and time, in a corner of the Master-Weaver's work of art, divine fingers fashioned a tiny butterfly. With gauzy wings extended to catch the sun's rays, its dainty feet settled on the inner core of a strong golden daffodil – drawing life from the very centre of both sources.

Once satiated, the creature appeared to settle among the petals ... as though waiting for an event unseen to the human eye to set it on its path again.

Chapter 23

On the spur of the moment, Lara decided to stay in Sydney a few days longer. She became quite adept at making all sorts of excuses to convince herself it was only so she and Nikki could spend a few more days in the fast-paced city before heading home to their old routines. It was only in times of solitude she found the courage to confess – delaying their return meant Adam stayed physically closer just that tiny bit longer ... but nothing else.

After watching him walk away ten days earlier, she had closed her heart to thinking she would ever see him again. There was no way she was going to open herself up to believing they had a future together or any chance of even one more reunion once she knew for a certainty he was getting on with his new life with Trina. After all, this was the exact reason she had said goodbye in the first place.

So of course, there was no way she was ever going to act upon the thought trying hard to keep her company in a big, lonely hotel bed over the next few ensuing nights – the niggling one that kept prodding her to buy a ticket to the other show currently playing in town ... the one everyone was raving about.

Stay away from the phone ... and the Theatre Royal became her new mantra.

Adding to the frustration was an even stronger notion trying hard to knock aside that staunch resolve ... if she missed out on seeing it this time after refusing to fly down for Melbourne's opening, it was inevitable she would come to regret it years down the track.

The constant barrage eventually managed to kick loose a few panels making up that sturdy wall of willpower – and being a caring mother with a generous heart towards her young offspring didn't help either.

Well, on the off chance I did decide to take a look, I'd only be returning the favour of an old friend – surely, there'd be no harm in that. Besides, Nikki hardly ever gets to see any shows unless it's something I'm in. Anyway, The Sound of Music *is her favourite ... all the rest are usually out of her depth. It'd be a shame if she missed out.*

Somehow, it was quite convenient to forget the little girl had already seen it with Adam's parents.

All these conflicting thoughts kept racing around and around in her head and nearly drove her crazy.

Each morning as soon as she woke up, Lara was able to convince herself it was a stupid idea. Then over the course of a new day, tendrils of temptation would slowly rise again. By Wednesday afternoon, one voice had gained supremacy over the other, and she quickly dialled the ticket office before common-sense made her change her mind again.

At first, the operator apologised, announcing tickets had already sold out.

There you go, it just wasn't meant to be – and that's a good thing!

As a way to help, he offered, "Of course, I'm happy to put your name down for any cancellations – we usually get one or two so you might be lucky."

"Oh, no, it's okay. Besides, I need two together – one for myself and another for my young daughter."

"Well something might come up, and I'd hate you to miss out ... besides, you've got nothing to lose..."

Except for my heart again...

"Thanks anyway, but no, I won't worry."

"Look, why don't you just leave your name and number and I'll only call if two tickets become available next to each other."

Surely no one'll cancel this late in the day ... and even if they do, I can always say no.

"Mmm ... oh – yeah, alright. You can reserve them under the name of Lara Jennings, but they must be two tickets together, please – and not too close to the front if possible. I'm staying at th—"

"Certainly, just one moment, please. I'll just have to grab a pen," he said, pressing the hold button and hurrying into the manager's office.

Conrad Blane was thrilled to learn the same star who had brought so many patrons to his theatre the year before because of her magnificent portrayal of *Eliza Doolittle* now wished to attend a performance of its latest production.

It wasn't long before the operator was back. "Ms Jennings, I've just spoken with the manager, and he's arranged for two complimentary tickets to the best seats in the house. They'll be waiting for you at the box office tonight."

Lara groaned on the inside. "Oh, please tell him not to go to any trouble. I was just hoping my little girl could see it before we leave for Brisbane tomorrow. I'd be more than happy with seats at the back of the stalls. We certainly don't expect any special treatment."

"It's no trouble. He's already set them aside. I have them right here so you can just drop by as soon as you arrive."

My Fair Lady had made huge profits for the theatre when Lara was in the title role, so it was only natural for Conrad to be more than happy to seize this chance to repay her.

She was overwhelmed by his kind offer, though it also meant there was no chance to back out now even if she wanted to. "Well, please thank him for me – my daughter will be tickled pink."

"Of course, and it's our pleasure. Oh, and Mr Blane trusts you have an enjoyable evening."

"I'm sure we will, and thank you for your efforts, too. We'll be there in plenty of time before the curtain rises."

Just as predicted, Nikki was beside herself with excitement to learn what her mother had planned ... until a stern warning pulled her up quick smart.

"We're only going to see the show and then coming straight back here, so don't go getting your hopes up about meeting the children again ... *or* spending any time with Uncle Adam! *Understand?"*

A quivering lip and sad eyes made no difference to Lara's tough stand, and the little mite soon realised she wasn't going to change that immovable stance of what mum says goes.

"Hey, young lady, I remember someone coming home from Melbourne all excited after seeing her favourite show. Now instead of all this nonsense, think about how lucky you are to be seeing it all again!"

"*Allll*right ... I'll *try*," she muttered with the makings of a smirk replacing the pout.

"*That's* better!"

With a sudden lunge, Lara tried to grab hold of the little foot peeking out from beneath Nikki's jeans to tickle between her toes, but the little girl quickly dashed away, dancing around and singing at the top of her voice, *"Doe a deer, a female deer ... Ray, a drop of golden sun..."*

Phew! Got outta that one! Lara let out a relieved sigh ... until another thought quickly replaced it. *What have I done? Me and my fickle double-crossing heart!*

As they were getting ready later that night, Lara stood in front of the closet rifling through a rack filled with formal gowns. The last thing she wanted or needed was to draw attention to herself. More than anything, she didn't want Adam having even the slightest hint she was there.

After trying on several outfits and quickly discarding them as either too colourful, too ornate or revealing far too much flesh, she eventually settled on a dusky rose floor-length gown made of silk chiffon. The supple cloth hugged her full bust and then fell to the floor in soft folds. The neckline finished in a tight V just at the crease of her cleavage, with a thin layer of lace in the same hue encasing the entire bodice.

A hidden clasp on top of her head held those long chestnut tresses in a loose knot, while several wispy strands caught the light where they floated over her shoulders. Her only adornments were a beautiful Ceylon sapphire and diamond treble clef pendant nestling just beneath the hollow in her throat and a stunning ring set with the same dazzling stones on her right hand.

Her intention was for the simplicity of the outfit to ensure she blended in with the crowd, though it wasn't long before all those well-laid plans got shot down in pieces. When she stepped out of the taxi, those waiting outside found their eyes drawn to a woman who could easily have been mistaken for an elegant Hollywood movie star from the 50s about to walk the red carpet. Several recognised Lara from the recent posters for another show that had just finished its run and a few shared knowing nudges and excited whispers between themselves.

The mother and daughter duo made for a striking picture as they hurried into the building. Nikki felt like a ballerina frocked out in the same candy-pink dress she had worn to the show in Melbourne. All afternoon she had been pestering her mother that the cream one already laid out on the bed wasn't ''speshel' enough for Uncle Adam. In the end, Lara gave in. She was too worried about other things to argue over anything so trivial.

As soon as she gave her name to the young woman at the ticket office, a tall suave-looking man dressed in a dinner suit came out of a nearby office with his hand extended.

"Good evening, Ms Jennings. You may not remember me. Conrad Blane, manager of this fine establishment. It's an honour to have you join us tonight."

"Thank you, Conrad. Of course I remember you – it's a pleasure to see you again."

"And you. Now, I've commandeered the best seats in the house for your exclusive use – my own private box just above the stage to the right. A champagne cocktail and canapés will be delivered during interval, along with a suitable treat for the young lady. It's always a privilege to have one of our own grace us with their presence."

It was obvious from both his manner and the extended offerings, Conrad had personally organised only the best for his special guests. Lara was astounded ... and dismayed. Her only thought had been to slip surreptitiously into the back of the theatre, see the performance and leave. She had no wish to receive such lavish treatment ... nevertheless, she didn't want to be rude either, not after all the lengths he had clearly taken to ensure they would be comfortable.

"What a lovely surprise! Thank you so much, though you really didn't have to go to so much trouble. Did you hear that, Nikki? We're going to be sitting way above everyone else, so you'll see *everything* that's going on!"

"Yippee!" She jumped up and down, clapping her hands with glee.

"But what do you say?"

"Thank you, Mr Ticketman."

Lara may have looked calm and graceful on the outside. Inside she was a bundle of nerves, sending up a quick prayer that their seats were in the shadows so no one either on stage or in the audience would be able to identify them. The last thing she wanted was for Adam to see her. Even worse would be for Trina to be there and recognise them.

With a gentle pat on Nikki's head and another warm smile extended to his special guest, the manager led them through a concealed doorway then up an ornate staircase to his private box.

When Lara went to sit on the plush lounge chair set aside for her exclusive use, she found a long-stemmed deep red rose with a small card attached. On a child-sized matching chaise lounge – obviously designed for small children who may get sleepy before a show finished – Nikki discovered a Swiss chocolate box wrapped in transparent pink cellophane with tiny hearts embossed in gold velvet thread.

Conrad couldn't hide an affectionate grin as he watched the inquisitive little girl pick up the gift and examine it thoroughly with a curious frown.

"Uncle Adam said to tell you he's thrilled you've come to see him, and he can't wait to say hello afterwards."

Nikki's face lit up ... Lara's was filled with dismay.

Oh nooo, I knew we should've stayed away! Why do I keep putting myself through this all the time? We can't see each other again, Adam ... it hurts too much when it's time to leave. Why couldn't you just let me do what you did and slip away afterwards?

"Okay, I'll leave you to get settled. I trust you're comfortable and please let me know if there's anything else we can do ... oh, and please enjoy yourselves."

"Thank you, Conrad. This is so lovely and so unexpected. Goodnight."

She couldn't be angry with the manager. It was entirely plausible he may have caught a glimpse of how close she and Adam were during *My Fair Lady's* run and naturally assume he was doing her a favour. There was now no way she could deprive Nikki of seeing him one last time – especially when she knew he would be waiting for them afterwards.

But this is definitely the last time, she muttered determinedly under her breath once Conrad closed the door.

Lara's heart was thumping hard as she inhaled the spicy fragrance of the rose and then drew the heavy linen card from the small envelope. A blur of tears filled her eyes as she read the message it contained.

I prayed you would come ... see, He always listens...

Thank you, sweet lady x

She slipped the heartfelt message into her purse with a tremulous smile ... then brushed the tell-tale drops of moisture from beneath her eyelids.

The show was all she had imagined – and more – so much more. Seeing him in the iconic role brought with it so many conflicting emotions – firstly, feelings of joy just to witness him on a stage again, but also deep ones filled with envy for the woman playing the role that originally had been hers.

From the moment he first walked onstage, when he was being so callous and cold towards *Maria,* her eyes followed him wherever he went. Knowing it could have been her standing next to him made the longing so much harder. Then as the two main characters danced the *Ländler* on a moonlit terrace, memories came flooding back of a sensual waltz performed before a flickering fireplace in Cortona just prior to Adam taking her to his bed for the very first time.

Much later in the second act, the two leads broke into the moving *Something Good* after denying their true feelings for so long. Lara could feel her heart pounding and she needed to take slow, shallow breaths in through her nose and out through her mouth to ensure she didn't break down completely. In her spirit, she was back in the real pavilion in Salzburg where they had sung that same song with him looking down at her as a message of love poured from his eyes.

As *Maria* sang one of her lines and *Georg* leaned in to press his lips against her forehead, the angle Lara was on meant she was in Adam's direct line of sight. For the space of a millisecond, he was able to send an almost indiscernible wink her way. While everyone else was too far away to detect the secret form of communication, she couldn't miss the significance of the gesture. Before she could blink them away, two columns of tears flowed down her cheeks.

Lara felt as though her heart was in her mouth during every second of the performance. Watching him on stage again carried her back to some of the most thrilling times of her life. But always at the back of her mind was the knowledge he was expecting to speak to her when it was over. As the ending drew near, she fluctuated between rapture over his performance and the fear of being within close proximity of him again.

For the entire three hours Nikki had been sitting cross-legged in the special chair, her eyes riveted on the children she had already met starring in her favourite story once again. Seeing Uncle Adam as *Georg* was simply the icing on the cake for an adoring little girl. Apart from humming most of the songs under her breath while swaying to the music, there hadn't been a peep from her the whole time.

The moment the children moved forward to accept their applause, she jumped to her feet and started clapping loudly. Lara was quick to pull the excited little bundle of energy onto her lap, anxious to keep their presence hidden from any stray eyes in the audience.

When Adam's turn came to receive his well-deserved acclaim, she felt more tears trickle down her cheeks. With so many memories wrapped up in similar shared moments, she could do nothing to stem the tidal wave of emotions. Moving to the edge of the stage, he raised his eyes carefully and inclined his head just slightly towards her box. His eyes were twinkling with the glimmer of a loving smile. The gesture only lasted for the space of a moment, and yet it was long enough for Lara to realise she didn't dare meet with him afterwards. How could she ever look into those eyes again and walk away with her heart still intact?

As soon as the curtain dropped, she grabbed Nikki by the hand and slipped down the stairs, pressing a finger over her lips with a whispered, "Shhh." Her only priority was to slip out without him noticing, preferring to be on the receiving end of her daughter's disappointment rather than the agony of being in his presence again. Thankfully, she was already well acquainted with the maze of corridors leading to an obscure back exit. They scurried around the final corner with Nikki thinking it was all a new and exciting game to find her uncle.

Just as she went to turn the handle, Lara heard that beloved voice whisper her name ... and so did her small replica. Nikki swivelled around with a delighted shout and jumped straight into Adam's waiting arms.

"Uncle Adam, we *came* and it was *great!* We saw *everything* from a secret hidey-hole right over everybody's head. I even had a 'speshel seat just for me! Oh, and thanks for my chocolates, they were yummy."

"Hello, my precious little Poppet. What a lovely surprise to find you here! I'm so glad you came to see me, and I'm *really* glad you liked the chocolates. And don't you look gorgeous," came out automatically as two pairs of eyes met above the little one's head.

Lara found herself being swept into those dark liquid pools all over again. The change in her resolve was instantaneous, and she was suddenly more than willing to dive into that exquisite feeling of drowning in their depths once more.

Before either of them was able to exchange any further form of greeting, Nikki recognised the voices of the children playing the *Von Trapp* children floating around the corner. The excitement of being able to catch up with them again was something she hadn't been expecting. Letting out a happy squeal, she struggled to get down. As though running on autopilot, Adam lowered her to the floor, still keeping his gaze firmly fixed on the woman standing in front of him. Like a shot she was off, leaving them alone in the dimly lit corridor.

"And where were you off to, young lady? Just as well I thought to come this way," he teased, with a telling smirk and caring look. Deep down, Adam had already guessed she might choose the easy way out.

Glistening blue eyes reflected her pain and he had to strain hard to hear the heartfelt plea. "You know where. This is the last time, Adam. We can't keep doing this to each other. I wanted to get away quickly and quietly – just like you did when you came to see me in *Phantom*. It hurts too much thinking I'll never see you again, only to have you come back into my life for a few fleeting moments ... and then have to watch you walk away all over again. It's not fair on either of us ... and it's *definitely* not fair on Nikki."

A shadow crossed his face and he went to take her hand. Then just as quickly he pulled back, too afraid to add to her misery. "I know ... and I'm truly sorry ... I just didn't want to miss out on the opportunity of being with you one last time when Conrad mentioned you were coming tonight. I really do understand you don't want to see me anymore, so I promise never to do anything like this again. I know it's best for all of us and it's what you truly want and need in order to move on – even though just the thought of never seeing you again breaks my heart. Just put it all down to pure selfishness on my part, along with a whole lot of self-indulgence. Who knows when we'll be in the same city again..."

His eyes implored her to take him at his word ... deep down she didn't want to, even though it was the only way either of them could move on.

How am I ever going to say another goodbye to the very reason I live and laugh and feel whole again? she mused as that familiar ache rose in her heart.

She remembered once upon a time in this very city lying in his arms while watching the movie *Doctor Zhivago* on the small screen. They had both been heartbroken when *Yuri* asked *Lara*, the woman he adored, if she believed he was truly leaving and never coming back. Knowing it was the answer he needed, the distraught woman had nodded slowly. Then, with tears filling her eyes, she forlornly turned the gesture into its negative counterpart, unable to fathom her lover would ever willingly leave her behind.

The parallel storyline had touched Lara's heart in a way she had never thought possible for a fictional tale, only this time she was the one having to deal with an equally terrible admission. Just like her namesake in the movie, she didn't want to contemplate the truth behind Adam's promise ... and yet, if she was being completely honest, a similar dilemma had been with her every single day since telling him he must go back to his wife. In that secret place in her heart, when the missing became too much, she still wrestled with whether she had truly meant it ... and so often her hand wanted to pick up the phone.

Oh, Teddy, how could you ever have believed me when I said I didn't want to see you again after everything we meant to each other? I only went through with it for you and Trina ... never because it's what I wanted.

Now it was too late ... nothing could erase the past. The only way to save herself from the incredible hold he still had over her was by turning the conversation around to something far less precarious.

"Anyway, congratulations! You played a thoroughly convincing *Georg*. I was so proud of you. It's no wonder the producers are taking the show all around the country when originally it was only booked for Melbourne."

"Thank you." He couldn't ignore the mix of emotions playing across her face, and it was almost his undoing. Those caring eyes caressed hers as he murmured, "Although I could've done a far better job if I'd only had the chance..."

The subliminal message was plain to decipher, but she couldn't drag her eyes away ... nor did she dare give voice to her heart's deepest longing.

Instead, her inner voice's cry was, *Please don't do this!*

Still he searched her face. "...it's the only thing I'm certain of – if you'd been my *Maria,* there would be no need for all that play-acting."

Catching at the sob trying to bubble out of her throat, she peered around the corner as though looking for Nikki. In reality, she was seeking out a way to dash aside a few stray tears before he noticed.

Oh, my darling, why do you keep doing this to me? I'm always an emotional wreck whenever you're near. Come on, you stupid woman, pull yourself together!

With her eyes intact once more, she turned back, but could only whisper, "Adam, don't ... you know I couldn't. As much as I wanted to be standing there beside you with all my heart ... I couldn't do that to Trina..."

"I know, and I understand ... but it doesn't change how much I miss having you by my side." His words flowed over her, soft and tender ... watering a parched spirit like dew falling from Heaven. "During every single performance, all I've been able to imagine is you standing there with me ... and whenever we get to *Something Good* and that sweet aftermath, I'm instantly back in Salzburg. Only they're not your eyes ... nor your lips ... no matter how much I try to pretend they are."

All her resistance fell away. Like a kitten brushing up against its mother in a symbol of ownership, Lara's fingers bestowed a gentle caress across the hand resting by his side. "Oh, Teddy, I was going through the same thing during that scene. Our time in Salzburg was one of the happiest periods of my life and sometimes I have dreams about us all being still over there."

All he could manage was, "Oh, Lara..."

Helpless to change the inevitable, they both knew tonight was the last time. They couldn't keep putting each other through this agony any more. As though in slow motion, he raised her hand to his lips and pressed them into her palm.

Their matching expressions conveyed all the regret and love lying deep in their souls – a mixture of both bitter and sweet nectar – and a necessary companion to sustain them for whatever was to come.

And like so many times before and with just as much meaning, Adam wrapped her fingers around the tiny impression left behind. "Keep this safe ... as a symbol of all the others stored in my heart that belong only to you."

With infinite care, his thumb then rubbed against the spectacular sapphire and diamond ring given with another kiss so long ago.

She caught the murmur of a heartfelt sigh as his gaze held her captive and he spoke straight from the heart. "Only *one* thing keeps me going now."

Lara looked into those gentle chocolate-coloured depths and lost all will to fight the heavy onslaught of emotion. "What, Teddy?"

The faint murmur of her special name for him filled his senses. He reached out to touch a fingertip to her lips – but only for the space of a few seconds before his hand fell again, just in case the temptation to do anything more was too great.

"Hope ... that's all I have left now. I *have* to believe that one day it will be our turn."

His heartfelt entreaty fell into her ears and landed in her heart ... then floated into the eternity of her soul.

Lara pressed a hand against her breast, as though she was actually sensing his plea now rested inside the very core of herself ... and everything within her wanted to keep it safe for all time.

"Oh, Adam ... I'm *sooo* sorry ... I thought I was doing the right thing when I said goodb—"

Her voice broke when she saw his hand come up to stop her and he pleaded, "*Nooo, pleeeaaase* don't say it again…"

The sorrow hovering between them became so intense she had to drag her gaze away. To stay any longer would only prolong the agony.

Poking her head around the corner, she saw Nikki playing with several of the children, totally oblivious to the drama playing out in their little corner.

"Come on, Munchkin. It's time to go. Uncle Adam needs to get home."

Sending a cheery wave to the others, the little girl skipped on over and wrapped her arms around his waist as far as they could go. "You looked so handsome singing with that other lady in the beautiful glass house – almost as much as you did when you sang that song with my mummy – do you benember?"

He nodded sombrely, his eyes reflecting a time long gone. "Yes, I do, little one. I remember every moment ... and how we danced around the fountain singing *Do Re Mi*. They were fun times. I'm glad I was able to share them with you and your mummy."

"They *were* fun, and I'm going to go back there again one day and do all those things again. Will you come, too ... *pleeeaaase?*"

Unable to control the catch in his voice he tried hard to smile through the sadness. "I'd love to, little one, but I'm not too sure if I can. How about whenever you hear those songs, you try to remember all the exciting things we did together

... and if you wish really *really* hard, maybe *one* day it'll come true."

She nodded and whispered, "Okay, I will – every single time I listen to my pretty snow globe when it plays to me. It will help me to benember..."

"Good girl," he said, touching his lips with two fingertips, then pressing them onto her cheek, grateful he now knew the answer to that internal question of what had happened to the Christmas gift bought in Salzburg so long ago.

Sensing Lara was fighting to keep control, he looked directly into her eyes, giving voice to a phrase that made her heart break all over again. "I will always love you, my darling ... and I will never *ever* give up hope."

Her body felt as though it had no strength left due to the weight of longing crushing her soul. Seeing her grief-stricken expression almost tore his heart apart.

All she could manage was, "And I'll always love you too, Teddy ... forever and ever. God bless you, my darling." With one last fleeting caress across the back of his fingers, she took Nikki by the hand. Then turning abruptly, she hurried away ... only this time without looking back.

She couldn't ... otherwise, she would have run back into his arms and never let go.

§

Back in her hotel room, a single red rose joined the bouquet of daffodils and tulips already gracing the nightstand beside the bed. Lying in bed a short time later, Lara fixed her gaze on a silhouette of the colourful blooms against the opposite wall. Streams of tears ran into her hair and soaked into the pillow long after the light went out.

While off in an unseen dimension, a matching set of slender threads – the same ones originally depicting a pair of intertwined hands as the centrepiece of a beautiful tapestry – started swirling around and around each other, almost as though in a soulful farewell dance. Then with one final seemingly reluctant bow, the strands separated ... dipping and swaying along paths running parallel to one another while picking up the pieces of two former lonely lives.

The image left behind from this moving display was of a half-opened rosebud nestled in the small gap left between both hands – a perfect replica of the one now gracing a woman's bedroom, chosen by the man who would always carry her in his heart, no matter where life might take him.

And in that earthly realm, two hearts broke into tiny shards as they whispered final goodbyes lying in their own dark night of the soul ... so very far apart.

PART THREE

Brisbane, Australia

August 1995 to December 2000

Chapter 24

It was the middle of August and five years had passed. Opening night for The Queensland Theatre Company's latest production was about to get underway. Backstage, The Playhouse was a hive of activity as make-up artists and hairstylists were busy at their craft, while over in a few quiet corners, actors practised their lines. This intimate venue was part of Brisbane's main theatre complex at Queensland Performing Arts Centre, or QPAC as it was more affectionately known around town.

In a private dressing room away from all the chaos, a man's index finger travelled slowly across a laminated childlike drawing of an angel taped to one corner of the large mirror. His gaze moved across to a silver frame hanging from the other corner. Inside was a snapshot of the young artist standing proudly beside a sandcastle. Moments later, his eyes lingered on the much larger photograph mounted beside it. This one captured a beautiful woman laughing at the camera while standing beneath an ancient archway in the Tuscan Hills. Once upon a time, both photos graced the bedside table beside his bed at his parents' home where he had sought sanctuary for a few months. Because of his more recent living arrangements, they were now safely ensconced here, away from prying eyes.

In a ritual orchestrated before every performance, he kissed the pad of his thumb then brushed it across the woman's smiling mouth ... the one he still hungered for every moment of every day.

The three keepsakes had followed him from show to show and were his main source of inspiration whenever he stood in that pin-drop silence while waiting for another curtain to rise. These made up the bulk of his most precious possessions. The others were a matching pair of photo journals secreted away in the safe of his bedroom in a large house on the outskirts of Brisbane, and lastly, an expensive watch that could always be found on his wrist, except when he was impersonating another character.

"God bless you, my lovelies ... wherever you are," Adam whispered before hurrying off to wait in the wings for his cue, wishing with every skerrick inside that he would have the chance to catch a glimpse of them smiling back at him from somewhere in the waiting audience.

§

Only a hundred or so metres away, the woman depicted in the photograph stood in the foyer of the much larger Lyric Theatre. Both venues were part of the same complex so the place was bustling with patrons eager to find their seats. *The Secret Garden* was just finishing its Brisbane season and Lara had been looking forward to seeing it for weeks. Tonight, was her first free Saturday since *Kiss Me Kate* had wrapped up its southern run. Having a free night to see the well-loved story come to life in a new way had been one of her top priorities since leaving behind the fiery title role. *The Secret Garden* had received a host of glowing reviews and word around town said it was one of the best productions currently playing anywhere in the country.

Earlier in the day, she had spent a few hours with Elizabeth and Charles. They were still a major part of her life and Lara always made sure to find time to drop by their home between work commitments and catch-ups with her sister or Lucy.

Over a lunch filled with the usual tasty treats fresh from Elizabeth's kitchen, talk turned to what Lara's plans were before any further upcoming roles took her away again. She mentioned about going to The Lyric later that evening after receiving a personal ticket from the director herself. The husband and wife team looked at each other cautiously and Elizabeth sent him a resigned nod. She didn't want to be the one breaking the news.

Charles' voice was soft and dripped with concern. "I'm not sure if you realise, my dear, but just to prepare you … Adam's new show is opening at The Playhouse tonight."

Lara had been too busy to read the newspapers and so she was oblivious to his whereabouts. And as always, her heart did its usual somersault the moment his name floated into her ears.

The look on her face and a quick intake of breath were dead giveaways to her ongoing fear of accidentally running into him. "Oh no, I had no idea. Well, in that case, I'll have to stay home. I can't risk—"

Elizabeth cut in with the gentlest of tones. "My darling girl, don't you think it's been more than long enough now? You can't let his presence keep dictating your social life ... besides, he'll be at the other end of the complex; the odds of you two running into each other are almost non-existent."

Images of this very scenario had been a huge part of Lara's life since that last sad meeting. She hadn't been brave enough to place herself in a position where it could actually happen again. "But what if—"

"No 'buts', young lady," Charles interrupted with a father's tender look of concern. "Elizabeth's right, you can't keep avoiding each other all the time – running into him one day is bound to happen, especially in this business ... it's something you'll just have to deal with when the time comes. Besides, it would be rude to back out now when the director personally sent you a premium ticket."

Lara knew they were right, but it didn't make the reality any easier. She wasn't game enough to contemplate what the outcome might have been if she'd heard he was performing and the ticket from Susan hadn't arrived. It would have left her with the night free to do as she pleased and she had always been afraid of what might happen if ever they found themselves in the same city under those circumstances. The temptation to see Adam perform had never dissipated. Over the years, she had just learnt to bury it beneath a thick layer of determination.

The Secret Garden's American director had first met Lara in New York City the year before, when the Aussie actress' name had been put forward for an upcoming production about to hit Broadway. Much to her surprise, she was granted an audition for Susan's latest musical and flew out for a whirlwind week of nail-biting auditions, as well as the chance to visit a few landmarks in the city that never sleeps. Unfortunately for both of them, due to a last-minute International Equity ban, the role went to an American. Since then, the two women had become close friends and they kept in touch on a regular basis.

Within a few weeks of arriving in Brisbane, Susan had phoned her Aussie friend to offer her a complimentary ticket to this latest body of work. Lara was both surprised and honoured, and eager to see the renowned Anthony Warlow in the lead role after several papers had posted glowing reviews for this latest performance.

As she parked her car in the theatre carpark, she knew there was no going back. The staccato click of her high heels on the polished concrete beat out a strict warning: *Just stay away from Stage Door.* The back entrance was where all cast members entered or left the building. Even so, on her way inside, she couldn't resist stopping to look at a poster showing off that brilliant smile she knew so well. Her heart beat just a little bit faster as she walked up the thickly carpeted staircase, knowing Adam was so near and yet still so far away.

With Lucy Simon's award-winning score filling the auditorium, Lara sat spellbound as Anthony's incomparable voice blended perfectly with the orchestra. He brought an extraordinary stage presence to any venue and tonight's audience was completely mesmerised. Watching the story unfold, it came as no surprise she experienced faint traces of envy wishing she had been cast as the female lead. After all, every Australian actress dreamed of being given the chance to star opposite him.

Lara was just leaving through the main entrance, well away from Stage Door, when she heard the director call, "Lara, wait up!"

The two women embraced warmly, excited to have the chance to catch up after so long, and the rapport they shared was obvious for all to see.

"Susan! Gosh, it's wonderful to see you again – and here in my home town of all places!"

"I *know!* Isn't it fabulous! Wow, you look great, and that *hair* – just gorgeous! *Love* your dress too…"

"Thanks, and you look *amazing* – stunning as always! Love that style on you *and* the colour. Oh, and thanks heaps for the ticket. When I tried, they were all sold out."

The director tapped her nose and raised her perfectly tapered eyebrows with a smile. "It's who you know. Besides, I didn't want one of my favourite Aussies missing out."

"Well, it was fabulous so I'm really grateful. I would've been so disappointed not to have seen it – and what a brilliant cast!"

"Aren't they! But what did you think of the show itself?"

"Just superb! *Everything* was fantastic – congratulations! What an achievement!" She gave her friend another hug, this time purely to offer some well-deserved praise.

"Yeah, we're all thrilled with the way it's been received up here in Brizzie. Let's hope it does as well when we take it around the country. Anyway, how come you were slipping out so soon? Were you trying to avoid me?"

"No, of *course* not! I just didn't want to bother you with all the excitement going on, especially knowing there were sure to be others wanting to speak to you. But I *am* glad you caught me in time."

"Me too – I would've been so disappointed to miss out on catching up with you. It's been way too long."

"Yeah, and who knows when the next time will be. Anyway, that production couldn't have been more perfect! The score is so stirring, and Anthony's voice is simply divine."

"Isn't it! The best in the business according to the pundits. Things have been a bit of a whirlwind bringing it 'Down Under', but it's all been super exciting too!"

"I'm sure – you must be thrilled to bits. And it's bound to get the same response from our southern neighbours. I heard whispers around the corridors that Ms Simon flew over for the opening – is that true?"

"Yeah, she did – Lucy wasn't going to miss it for anything and she had a ball seeing how Australian audiences have taken to her baby."

"The cast must've been ecstatic having the famous composer fly all this way … and from your hometown no less!"

"I know, and she loved how the whole thing played out. Apparently, Anthony's voice blew her away. I heard a whisper she wants to create a brand-new musical and is now considering him for the lead after seeing how well he performed in this one – but don't say anything to anyone just yet!

"Sure, Mum's the word." Both women giggled as they each pressed forefingers against their lips.

"And she's keen to write a score to suit his voice – it's from some famous novel written years ago and she wants to adapt it for the stage. I think it's ... umm ... ooohhh ... no, I can't remember the name of it now – a Russian epic of some sort. All I know is, it has a strange name and they made a movie about it back in the sixties or seventies, from what I can recall."

"Well, that's exciting! What an honour, although I'm not surprised with that incredible range of his. Talk about sending shivers down your spine."

"Yeah, and like her, he blew me away the first time I heard him sing. Anyway, here's hoping it won't be too long 'til the score's done. I'd certainly be interested in directing that one. I love her work – she's a brilliant composer from a talented family – and she's a real joy to work with as well. Back in the '60s and '70s, she and her sister, Carly, were known as *The Simon Sisters*."

"Oh, that's right, and I remember when I was a kid listening to my mother singing along whenever Carly's hit *You're So Vain* came on the radio. She was always trilling away to something ... it was a popular number and still is today with a lot of musos. Anyway, that's fabulous news about Anthony. He certainly deserves it."

"He sure does. Australia has some of the best talent around, between him and the superb ability of your old acting buddy, Adam Peters – and let's not forget the talented Mark Sinclair – along with a certain friend of mine with a magnificent voice!"

The director's encouraging smile helped Lara deal with hearing his name trip so easily off her tongue. Before auditioning for the Broadway part, Susan had read all the write-ups highlighting the pair's connection onstage, so it was only natural to assume they still kept in touch.

She was embarrassed by the compliment and did her best to brush it off. "Thanks, Susan, but I'm only doing what I love. Please tell Anthony the next time you see him, I thought his portrayal of *Archie* was wonderful."

"Of course, I'm actually having lunch with him tomorrow, so I'll be sure to mention it. Hey, I've just had an idea. Mark was here tonight and I promised to meet him for a glass or two of bubbly afterwards to celebrate our upcoming show. He's the leading man in a new musical I'm putting together in Sydney before leaving for the States again, and we were going to discuss a few of the finer details. Why don't you come along too? I'm sure he wouldn't mind."

"Oh, I couldn't do that ... the last thing you need is having me intrude on such an important meeting."

"You wouldn't be ... honestly ... come on, it'll be fun. Besides, don't you already know each other?" She caught sight of Mark on the other side of the foyer and beckoned him over. "Oh, there he is now…"

Lara recognised the roguishly handsome actor as he waved back and threaded his way through the crowd. "Oh, I just met him briefly at a concert in Sydney years ago … he probably wouldn't even remember. I really don't think I made that much of an impression."

"Hi, Susan … hey, Lara, it's great to see you again!"

A pair of twinkling green eyes greeted her with the same degree of enthusiasm as his cheery welcome, and she was caught a little off-guard to feel the friendly touch of his lips brush against both of her cheeks.

"Oh … uuummm … hi, Mark!" she giggled nervously. "It's nice to see you again, too." Her awkward response proved how surprised she was to find he recognised her from the previous encounter.

Opening his arms wide, he accosted Susan in much the same manner. "Hello, you gorgeous creature! What a great job you've done with this show, but I had no idea you two knew each other. And don't you both look stunning!"

He looked them up and down with a teasing smirk, along with a raised eyebrow. Lara and Susan grinned at each other, shaking their heads and rolling their eyes at his cheeky display of flattery.

"You haven't changed one bit, Mark Sinclair … still as naughty and flirtatious as ever," came the director's amused reply. "I was just asking Lara if she'd like to join us for a drink. Would you mind if she came along too?"

"No, not at all. Who wouldn't want *two* beautiful women on his arm? I'll be the envy of all the men here tonight. Besides, Lara and I are old mates from way back – I remember a certain Sydney gala concert back in the early '90s. You performed *I Dreamed a Dream* from *Les Mis,* and it was absolutely breathtaking. Pity you couldn't have been there too, Susan – she was perfect!"

Lara was staggered at his good memory, and it took her back in time. Drawing on her acting skills, she sent him a big smile. "Oh, stop it! That's kind of you to say, but it was just one song. But how on earth did you ever remember? It was such a long time ago I'd forgotten what I sang."

The last phrase was a lie. She would never forget performing those poignant lyrics only a few months after that gut-wrenching final goodbye in a back corridor of a Sydney theatre. Much to her dismay, Lara's eyes blurred as memories of a song containing lyrics similar to one of the darkest periods of her life hit her full force in the heart all over again. She had put everything into that performance, and unwittingly brought out into the open those dagger-like shafts of pain normally buried deep in the hidden vaults of her heart. The emotion she had displayed touched everyone who witnessed it. Now a stray tear threatened to fall, but she was quick to blink it away.

I'm not going down those paths again ... I promised myself not to think of him tonight – but when will it end...

Any efforts to mask her emotional state were in vain. Both Mark and Susan glimpsed the sheen of moisture bathing her eyes and guessed there was a lot more to her story than she was letting on.

"No one who witnessed it could ever forget that performance – it was exquisite in every way! Now come on, let's go and grab that drink so we can tell you all about our new gig."

Hoping to chase her blues away, he linked arms with both women and did a little jig as they exited the theatre, much to the amusement of his companions and a few others standing nearby.

The happy trio made their way along a leafy path wending its way beneath a maze of steel and wire that formed a long bower adorned with masses of bougainvillea. The trail led to one of the many alfresco cafés and bars making up South Bank's busy precinct. Along the way, they passed a poster advertising Adam's new show. Lara felt her eyes being drawn to the eye-catching image staring back at her.

As usual, she felt a heavy tattoo thumping away inside her chest as soon as her thoughts turned to him. Reluctant to alert the others or have him invade her thoughts while still on a high from *The Secret Garden*, she dragged her eyes away and tried to focus on the conversation.

For the next hour, both Mark and Susan regaled her with stories of their new project while catching up on each other's news. At around midnight, the busy New Yorker picked up her bag. She had an early appointment in the morning and needed to grab a few hours shut-eye beforehand.

A bottle of Moët sitting lopsidedly in an ice bucket in the centre of the table still held a couple of inches of the heady stuff. Ever the gallant host, Mark had insisted it was his shout when they first sat down. After partaking of one small drink, Lara was quick to place a hand over her glass whenever another round was on offer. She still had terrible memories of a night on her front veranda when alcohol was supposed to be the perfect anaesthetic for the pain in her heart, along with another in Sydney when her sister had come to visit during *Phantom's* run.

Susan leaned in to kiss her cheek. "I'm so glad we had the chance to catch up again, Lara. I'll send you a ticket to our new show when it opens next year."

"Thanks, Susan, it was great to see you again too. If I'm free, I'll definitely be there. And thanks again for tonight – I had a wonderful time."

"My pleasure! It was good you were free to join us." As she went to kiss Mark, a warning scowl was sent his way. "And just you listen to me, my good-lookin' friend ... don't you dare keep this gorgeous woman out too late! I know she's hard to resist ... but just remember she has rehearsals in the morning."

Lara's face turned pink with embarrassment, while a few loud protests of innocence came from Mark's corner. With last minute farewell hugs accompanied by promises to keep in touch, Susan scurried across the road to her hotel, waving and laughing as she went.

The two left behind just looked at each other and smiled ruefully as they shook their heads.

"Don't worry, I have every intention of behaving," he assured her, breaking into a full-blown grin. Picking up the champagne bottle, he held it up to the light. "Good, there's just enough for one more small glass each. Are you up to helping me finish it before we go?"

The look she sent his way was veiled with a hint of cautious intent. "Mmm ... yeah, okay ... but that's all. I really should be getting home soon."

His gaze was steady. "Is there a Mr Right waiting there for you?"

She shook her head with the hint of a smile. "Well, actually it's *Miss* Right – my eleven-year-old daughter – and hopefully she's sound asleep in bed, but my sister is and probably wondering where I am."

"Well, that's no fun. Come on, you can tell me ... Susan was right, you're gorgeous *and* talented – there must be *some*one..." The statement was flippant, though there was also a question in his eyes.

Lara's smile disappeared and her expression turned pensive as she shook her head again. "No, there hasn't been a Mr Right for a very long time – and sadly, it turns out he wasn't quite as right for me as I'd hoped ... although it wasn't his fault – just a sad set of circumstances."

"Then he's stupid for letting you get away." Mark's attractive and heavily pregnant wife was happily waiting for him at home, and he would never do anything to jeopardise their relationship. Nonetheless, it still didn't stop him from recognising a desirable woman when he saw one. "But if that's the case, I've got a couple of good lookin' mates who're dying to meet you..."

"Whoa there!" Lara let out a chuckle and raised both hands like stop signs. "Thanks, but no thanks. Been there, done that. I'm very happy with my life just as it is, thanks very much!"

His eyes never left her face for the entire time it took to empty the last dregs of champagne into their glasses. They were intense and green ... and taking in everything she wasn't saying. He was positive there was a lot more to her story than just an eleven-year-old daughter waiting at home. Even so, he had no desire to press the issue and possibly be the cause of reviving any of that earlier sadness she tried so hard to hide. Instead, the conversation turned to the excitement of being first-time parents. Lara was happy to share a few pointers on how to cope with the big changes in store for both him and his wife.

When their glasses were empty, they got up at the same time.

"Listen, I'm parked in the theatre car park, but I'm happy to walk you to your car first," he said.

"Oh, thanks. Mine's down there anyway, so it's not out of your way."

They sauntered along the path again, chatting about their next projects. All of a sudden, Mark heard Lara's voice drop and noticed her steps falter. Stealing a glance, he caught her staring at a large poster near the entrance to QPAC's main building. Her full breasts rose slightly, and he caught the whisper of a soft sigh.

"Are you okay?"

"Yeah, I'm fine," she nodded, dragging her eyes away with a wry grimace.

He stopped dead in front of the eye-catching display. "I presume you know Adam Peters. If not, I can always introduce you some time – we've done a few gigs together over the years."

"It's okay; I've already met him ... a long time ago. We've done a few shows together, too."

"Oh, that's right – I'd forgotten the two of you worked together – that *was* a long time ago. Pity you haven't been given the chance to work with him lately – your voices would complement each other perfectly."

Lara tried to make her reply as casual as possible, while inside she was back traversing those wonderful months. "Yeah, it was eons ago; we haven't crossed paths for ages. Most of the time we're at different ends of the country."

"Oh, that's a shame – he's a really nice bloke."

"Yeah, he is, I remember well." She was looking at the poster again, and a tiny smile touched the corners of her mouth. "I'd forgotten how good looking he is – kind eyes, too. We shared a few good times over those shows..."

He didn't bother responding. It was obvious she was far away in the past and he had no wish to disturb her. Even though Mark was more than happy with their relationship, he wouldn't have minded if his wife looked at him like that every now and then.

For a few moments more she was lost in reflection, and then her whole body gave a shiver and she turned to him with a grimace. "Whoops. Sorry about that. I don't know where I was ... off with the fairies obviously."

I think you know very well, Lara Jennings. "That's okay, you're probably just tired – it's getting rather late."

"Mmm, you're probably right." *Tired of always wanting to be with him...*

An easy silence accompanied their footsteps as they took the stairs to the underground carpark, both lost in their own thoughts. Eventually, she came to a halt beside a sporty blue Toyota Corolla hatchback – quite modest compared to a lot of the racier European models, though obviously new from the gleaming paintwork and shiny numberplate.

To her dismay, the old maroon hatchback needed to be replaced only a few months earlier. It had been quite distressing having to say goodbye to the faithful old car. Adam's words on the night they met had always stayed with her, especially his teasing comment about the sunroof. Despite having the means to purchase a new one years earlier, Lara's sentimental streak always came to the fore until the vehicle had become far too expensive to run and spare parts were harder to come by. Her biggest regret was having yet another link to him broken. She had asked Suzie to go along with her, and the older sibling wasn't at all surprised to find Lara wanted to trade the old Corolla in on the latest model.

Lara took out her keys. "Well, it's been nice to meet up with you again, and it was great to hear the exciting news about the baby. I hope everything goes well with the birth, and all the best with this new project."

"Thanks – it's been good meeting up with you again, too. Don't be surprised to find me waiting outside Stage Door when your next show is underway – it's bound to be a cracker with you at the helm! Then I can drink *your* champagne and continue this conversation!"

The blush in her cheeks was a tell-tale sign she wasn't quite sure whether he meant talking about Adam or discussing her next role, so she tried to dismiss his connotations. "Goodness, you must have better things to do with your time..."

His smile put her at ease again. "It's okay, I only meant talking about your next project ... I'm already a fan. I bought your album a couple of years ago *and* listen to it quite often – it's great company on those long, lonely drives between gigs."

"You're kidding! There weren't *that* many cut. I'm surprised you actually found a copy!"

"Why? Your voice is amazing, and I bought one as soon as it hit the shelves. Though I must say, I was disappointed when you didn't win the Aria ... pipped at the post if you ask me. Anyway, there must've been thousands sold for you to have even been nominated." Like a flash, a grin lit up his face that made his eyes gleam. "Hey, I just had an idea – we should get together sometime and maybe put on our own show! What do you say? I'd enjoy sharing a stage with you."

She was astonished someone of his renown actually had her album in his collection, let alone wanted to join voices with her in the footlights. "Wow ... ummm ... yeah, I'd love to – sounds exciting!"

"Right, you're on! Leave it with me..."

"Okay, I'm in if you're up to it! And I've really enjoyed tonight, thanks. Now I'd better let you get home to that lovely wife of yours. And all the best with the new bub – you're going to love being a dad!"

He grimaced through a smile. "Hope so ... I'm really looking forward to it, although it is quite daunting – and thanks for the advice! See you next time." He kissed her warmly on the cheek and then waved as she drove away.

A goofy grin kept her company the whole way home as she recalled their friendly interaction. It felt quite nice having actually enjoyed being in another man's company for a change. Usually, she avoided spending time alone with anyone from the opposite sex. Somehow, it always felt as though she was betraying another time in her life.

It was only when she was walking upstairs that it dawned on her she hadn't been tempted to linger for a glimpse of Adam at Stage Door. She was astonished and felt quite proud of herself. Maybe her long ago retort to his quip had been right ... maybe he would have a bit of competition if Mark was around. Just as quickly she shook the thought away, knowing there was no substance to it. They were just a couple of actor/musicians sharing stories about their lives and the work they both enjoyed.

Suzie knew something was going on the moment her younger sibling sidled through the front door. Lara spent the next half-hour fielding a barrage of probing questions, especially when the other one learned she had actually indulged in two glasses of champagne in the company of an attractive man. Mark was renowned for his flirtatious manner and women everywhere swooned over his good looks. Hearing her sister had spent the last half hour alone with him sparked another spate of interest ... until Lara casually mentioned he was happily married with a new baby on the way.

Drat! One day, I'm going to find you the perfect man, but don't you dare fall in love with another married one ... I couldn't handle seeing you go through all that again.

Despite this newfound friendship, it was dark eyes and a pair of soft lips Lara dreamed about when she finally drifted off to sleep.

§

Only three months later Mark was able to make good on his promise.

This time it was Lara's turn to appear at The Lyric in Brisbane. She was just getting changed into street clothes at the conclusion of another show when there was a light tap on her dressing room door. Pulling it open, she expected to find someone from the cast offering her an invitation to join them for a late-night supper. Instead, a familiar pair of twinkling green eyes greeted her, and a large bouquet of red roses landed in her arms.

"Hey, good lookin'! Thought I'd better drop these off and offer my congratulations on an outstanding performance. You had me spellbound the whole time!"

"Mark! Goodness, what a lovely surprise! Thank you, kind sir." She glanced across to the tiny refrigerator standing in the corner before turning back to him with a cheeky grin. "I'm pretty sure there's a bottle of champagne on ice somewhere around here. Come on in, it's payback time!"

"Yay! Now that's my kinda payback! But I'm warning you, I can't stay too long – a tiny baby girl arrived just on eight weeks ago and I'm dead tired from all the broken nights!"

She threw her arms around his neck with a happy squeal. "Oh, that's *wonderful* news! How exciting! Nothing in the world beats having a little one come along to share your life. Congratulations, Mark, and well done! Okay, show me photos…"

Over a couple of glasses of champagne – a recent gift from the director and just perfect for this unexpected visitor, as well as wet the baby's head – they spent the next half hour goo-ing and gaa-ing over a brag book of adorable images he pulled from his pocket, discussed all the challenges that come with a tiny baby, chatted about her show and his next project, and then shared some of the usual gossip about what a couple of mutual friends from the theatre were up to. The easy banter and flowing conversations were proof of their growing friendship and mutual respect for each other.

When he was leaving, Lara was quick to offer a few words of reassurance. "Don't worry, they don't break, and I promise they *do* sleep all night long … eventually!"

"Oh, thanks. That's comforting news! Julia and I were starting to think a full night's sleep was just an impossible dream." He broke into the well-known song and the walls resounded with a fabulous blending of voices when she joined in.

A few of her castmates were just passing by and popped their heads around the door. Sending the duo a big thumbs-up, one called out, "Hey, you two should sing together more often – that was amazing!"

"See, I told you, and I meant what I said. We should get together sometime – we'd make *great* music together!"

Despite his response sounding like a double entendre, she knew better and laughed, "Okay, you're on!" while still feeling quite sceptical about actually being offered a chance to sing on a stage with one of her idols.

"Come on, one more before I have to go," he said with a wink.

Breaking into *Man of La Mancha,* she joined in with just as much gusto. Then with a friendly hug and a farewell kiss on her cheek, he winked and walked away.

A few minutes later she picked up the magnificent bouquet and wandered down to the carpark, humming as she went. A mischievous smile kept her company all the way home as she pictured the look on her sister's face when she learned who the flowers were from and about his recent proposal.

§

Lara popped her head around the double entrance doors with a warm smile as soon as they opened.

"Hello!" she greeted the woman on the other side, taking in the picture she made as the soft morning light highlighted her gentle features. "Gee, that colour suits you *and* you look just as beautiful now as you did on the day we first met." An affectionate kiss landed on the cheek of the woman she still thought of as a mother figure.

With a sceptical laugh, Elizabeth returned the gesture and the smile. "Oh, get off with you, Lara! You always say that. And *you* can talk – you're the one who looks fabulous. Obviously, life's treating you well."

Lara nodded as their eyes met and understanding looks were exchanged – proof of a special friendship that had grown even stronger over the past few years.

Elizabeth then turned to the pretty, young girl standing in her friend's shadow. Loving hands cradled Nikki's face, as she called her by the nickname most members of the family had adopted at one time or another.

"And happy twelfth birthday to you, Missy Tuppence! My goodness, look how tall you've grown – it won't be long till you're towering over me ... it seems you're turning into a young lady before my eyes."

"Thanks, Aunty Elizabeth," Nikki giggled, wrapping the woman she had only ever thought of as a grandmother in a tight spontaneous hug. She was just at that awkward stage – too old to be treated like a child, yet too young to be fully at ease in a world of adults – nevertheless, surrounded by family she quickly reverted to the easy-going youngster they all loved dearly.

Elizabeth's eyes glowed when she ushered them inside. "Come on in. I know someone else who's dying to see you both."

"Ah, now here's the birthday girl!" Charles exclaimed as Nikki ran across the room to greet him. He pulled her into one of his usual bearhugs and her feet left the floor as he twirled her around and around. Once the hug was over, a firm kiss landed on her cheek. "Still as pretty as a picture and swatting the boys away with a stick, I'll bet." His eyes twinkled as he looked across at Lara. "Or your mother is, I'm sure!" She nodded her head vigorously in agreement.

Well used to his teasing ways, Nikki burst out laughing. She was the only grandchild they would ever know, and the Ashworths always looked forward to these visits. Seeing them both was the highlight of their week whenever the mother and daughter were in town.

Today was extra special. Every year at this time, the family celebrated both Nikki's birthday and Christmas Day around a table laden with all manner of festive fare. Afterwards, they gathered beside the dazzling Christmas tree, exchanging gifts and sharing exclamations of delight as the paper came off. It was one of the most anticipated celebrations of the year for all of them.

§

Over the years, Elizabeth and Charles had secretly cherished seeing the subtle changes occurring in the lives of the other two members of their family – Lara's gracious maturity as she approached her thirty-third year, and Nikki's childish antics replaced with the delightful confidence of a girl growing up in a home where love and laughter were an everyday occurrence. With no blood children of their own, having these two in their lives had brought them more joy than either one had ever dreamed possible.

From their very first meeting, Lara had struck them as a woman with abounding grace and poise. As the years passed, their respect for her had only increased, especially when her musical career soared higher than even their initial expectations. She had risen to the highest echelons in theatrical circles, was in demand constantly and single-mindedly met every challenge asked of her for every role. Despite all of this well-deserved adulation, none of the acclaim had gone to her head or changed her in any way – except to make her even more grateful for the extraordinary opportunities coming her way. Even so, as much as she revelled in her work, Nikki always had top priority.

A few years earlier when her acting roles had increased and national tours were on the agenda several times each year, she had reached the sad conclusion that resigning from her editing position was the only sensible thing to do. She hated letting David down, though much to her relief he had been fully supportive when she handed in her notice, even going so far as to reassure her the position was always hers if ever she wanted to return.

Deep down he was sad to let her go, knowing full well it would be difficult to find anyone as proficient at their craft. Three years had passed since then, and Lara still missed the thrill of feeling the celluloid run through her fingers. Nevertheless, her life had been far too busy to even contemplate his ongoing offer. They still kept in touch regularly, and her boss usually went along at least once during each of her Brisbane runs.

Nikki had matured far quicker than usual for a child of her tender years – an offshoot of growing up in a single-parent family where they were each other's only company most of the time. She also had the added benefit of following Lara from place to place when a new show took off. The schoolgirl's classroom was usually the streets of whatever city they found themselves in and her knowledge of history and geography was way beyond her years. The private Brisbane college had been a godsend, with the principal more than willing to fit in with Lara's demanding schedule by allowing Nikki to return to class between out-of-town productions.

Whenever they were on tour, Lara's contracts continued to include a clause ensuring a tutor was made available. Naturally, Helen always put her hand up to continue in the role. Lara never took for granted how fortunate they were to have found the retired teacher, especially when she was more than willing to accompany them around the countryside as the actress' busy performing schedule demanded. The rapport between them was more like family, and the arrangement suited everyone.

Lara and Nikki's relationship was often the envy of all their friends, while to them it was just the norm. They were used to life on the road. It meant, as well as being mother and daughter, they were usually one another's only real companion in each new place. Helen always travelled with them, however on her free days she usually went off exploring by herself. She had no wish to intrude twenty-four hours a day, and this was the best way to ensure they had time for themselves, as well as having some much-needed alone time herself. In the end, the balance suited everyone.

Lara trusted her daughter above anyone, and she couldn't have been more proud at how well she was doing, both with her schoolwork and socially. Report cards always contained glowing accounts of her scholastic achievements, along with her behaviour and character. She was a delight to be around and Lara gave thanks every day for the joy and privilege of raising such an easy-going child.

§

Adam's parents found it was a definite bonus having Nikki's birthday fall so close to Christmas. It usually meant she and Lara were home to celebrate both occasions during the theatre world's hiatus and this year was no exception.

With the two women bustling around bringing out the food, Charles placed a grandfatherly arm around the birthday girl's shoulders. "Come on, Missy. It's time to fill your stomach before Jasper drives us all crazy wanting to sample more of those tasty titbits you always have squirrelled away in your pocket. He's been champing at the bit all week since I told him you were coming over."

"I can't *wait* to see him! It's been ages and I miss him so much when we're away."

Nikki's eyes turned to the striking gelding pacing up and down in the far paddock as they wandered onto the terrace to a table laden with all sorts of delicious treats.

"Doesn't he look grand!" she declared. Putting her fingers between her teeth, a shrill whistle soon penetrated the air and a loud whinny carried back on the wind. "And he still remembers his mother!" she finished with a grin.

"Where did she learn to do that?" Charles exclaimed, turning to Lara and shaking his head in astonishment.

"You'll never believe it ... one of the set decorators on *Oliver* taught her. I swear, growing up around theatre folk means she's learning to master things most kids her age wouldn't have a clue about. She can scale ladders so high it would make a fireman cringe, all to ferry things across to the lighting guys perched high in the rigs as they adjust the spots."

Seeing the look of horror on Elizabeth's face, she added quickly, "Yeah, I worried too to begin with, believe me, but they take good care of her and always make sure she has a cable line attached. Just don't tell anyone or we'll all be in trouble! Oh, and the other day she was madly sewing sequins onto costumes after one of the wardrobe assistants broke her ankle just hours before a show."

"*And* I pricked my finger umpteen times in the process! They're *sooo* fiddly, and it takes *sooo* long..."

Her foster grandparents commiserated when she showed off a series of war wounds.

To everyone's dismay, Charles had found Clancy lying cold and still in his home paddock nearly sixteen months earlier. After examining him thoroughly, the vet decided his heart had just given out at the ripe old age of twenty-three. The cherished pony had lived a fortunate life, first with Adam and then Nikki as his devoted carers. Even now, the family still found it hard to believe he was gone.

Because of their sporadic lifestyle, Clancy had been one of the only constants in the young horse-lover's life, and the pair shared a special bond. She had been inconsolable when Charles rang with the news, and her mother worried what effect his death may cause in the long term. Lara was convinced it had a lot to do with the common thread Nikki shared with Adam – Clancy had been his best mate when he first arrived on the Ashworths' doorstep as a grieving teenager, and now another link connecting them was gone.

Adam was just as heartbroken when his father phoned. One of his earliest memories since coming to live at his new foster home was of the many hours he and the pony had spent in each other's company while trying to deal with the loss of his parents. Entrusting his beloved ally to Nikki had forged an unbreakable bond between them. When the news came, he could easily imagine how badly it was affecting her.

As a surprise eleventh birthday present, the Ashworths and Lara had all put in to purchase Jasper as a combined gift. The magnificent horse was a few hands taller than Clancy to ensure the youngster wouldn't outgrow him when she was shooting up so fast herself. His coat was a striking liver chestnut in colour, with a flaxen mane and tail. Apart from his lighter overall shade, Jasper reminded the birthday girl of Clancy, with both horses sharing many of the same features, including two snowy white socks.

Unbeknown to either Lara or Nikki, after many weeks of searching, Adam had been the one to discover the new horse. He was determined to find a mount suited to his former protégé's riding style and capabilities, and Jasper met all of those strict requirements. A stern warning was soon issued to his parents never to disclose how he had contributed more than half the asking price.

The eye-catching Arab had strong bloodlines. Lara would never have been able to afford her full share as a single mum, not with private school fees added to all the expenses involved with her profession. At first, Charles was prepared to pay the difference, however after a long discussion with Elizabeth and knowing how much it meant to their son, they soon were happy to include him in the pot. In a way, they were glad he and Nikki still had this form of connection. It meant he could maintain a small role in the young girl's life, especially when there was no possibility of him ever being a part of Lara's again.

Charles and Elizabeth kept him abreast of what the other two were up to, although rather reluctantly at first as they hated jeopardising Lara's trust. Similar to what she had requested following the breakup, he simply needed to know they were okay for his own peace of mind. Realising it would help to set his mind at ease, they agreed to fill him in on the broader aspects of their lives. It was a given Adam would always have first priority when it came to their loyalty; however, Lara and Nikki ran a very close second and his parents were determined to shelter them from any more heartache.

All during lunch, Nikki had been wolfing down her food and trying hard to hoodwink Uncle Charles into doing the same.

"Nikki, slow *down,* you'll make yourself sick eating like that," Lara scolded, watching as another huge forkful disappeared into her daughter's mouth.

"But *Muuum,* I can't *wait* to see Jasper. Come *on,* Uncle Charles, race ya," came the almost unintelligible reply, as yet another mouthful joined the last.

Elizabeth and Lara shook their heads and exchanged expressions of feigned exasperation as he tried to keep up. It wasn't long before the two women burst out laughing as they watched the doting grandfather-figure and his impatient little shadow race each other to the paddock when another shrill whinny floated out to greet them.

Jasper pranced along the fence-line watching them approach, his blond tail swishing back and forth as that proud head and mane tossed with impatience. Nikki held out the sweet pieces of carrot he had come to expect and was in her own version of Heaven when the gelding's big soft lips nuzzled her palm. She rubbed her cheek against his, cooing in contentment as he grazed from her hand.

"Gidday, old fella, aren't you a gorgeous boy! Gee, I've missed you."

His gentle snickers and ticklish whiskers soon had her giggling like the four-year-old Charles remembered from her very first visit with Clancy. Once the treats were gone, the Arab pressed his forelock hard against her cheek. For the next few minutes, she offered him affectionate head rubs while they blew softly into one another's noses. The pretty horse tossed his head up and down when Nikki's breath tickled his nostrils, but he was soon back for more and she willingly obliged. The pair shared a unique connection and seeing them together always brought a satisfied smile to Charles' face.

Elizabeth and Lara sipped from tall glasses filled with fresh pineapple and coconut juice as they gazed across to where Nikki and Jasper were going through their paces. Both the horse and rider synchronised perfectly while completing a few rounds of the complicated jump formation Charles had set up in a nearby paddock. As Jasper's hooves pounded across the grassy expanse, the duo's matching long manes bobbed up and down with each landing. Between loud groans of disappointment when a rail hit the ground or excited cheers when they cleared a difficult combination, the women's friendly chatter focussed on their busy lifestyles.

For the first time in a long time, Lara felt apprehensive with Adam's mother. She wasn't exactly sure how to broach what had been playing on her mind all week. Once their regular news was out of the way, she paused and looked across at her loyal friend. Then with a deep breath, she ventured in – though not all the way ... she needed to test the waters first.

"So, how's Adam doing?"

The young woman would never admit to anyone how much she savoured the taste of his name on her lips. Just the feel of it brought him close and being with his family was the only place she felt safe to indulge.

Elizabeth's expression was tender, although it also contained a trace of uncertainty. "Mmm ... I'm not really sure, to be honest – that boy of mine has become a bit of a closed book when it comes to sharing his feelings lately. What I do know is that he's been offered the title role for *The Phantom of the Opera* in Perth at the beginning of next year. His fans on the west coast have been waiting years to see him perform, and from what I can tell, he's pretty excited."

She watched closely for Lara's reaction. Over the years, Elizabeth had observed many different emotions cross her face whenever she or Charles mentioned his name. Sometimes it seemed she was moving on as they calmly discussed what he was up to ... at others, the sadness in her eyes was almost tangible, staring off into the distance as though she longed to hurtle back in time.

The younger one nodded, and a wistful expression accompanied her gesture. "Yeah, Max mentioned what he was up to a few weeks ago. Actually ... they offered me the role of *Christine* at the same time. I know the director quite well – he was at the helm when I played her in Sydney, and apparently someone showed him the reviews from when Adam and I were involved in *My Fair Lady*. From what I heard, he was hoping to team us together again."

"And?" Elizabeth's eagle eyes held Lara's. Her son had already mentioned how many offers had been put forward over the years to have them play the leads in a variety of productions. She also knew Lara always turned them down.

"I can't, Elizabeth, you know that ... better than anyone."

"Somehow I already guessed that would be the case ... but I can always hope. I thought things might be getting easier as time passes."

Lara shook her head slowly. "It never gets easier ... I've just learned to live with the emptiness and all the 'what ifs?'."

With an understanding nod and a gentle caress along her friend's bare forearm, Elizabeth knew there was nothing more to add. Over on her side of the table, Lara fought the nagging reminder she still hadn't relayed the major news.

Their eyes followed Nikki and Jasper tackling another round of complicated jumps. Again, the pair moved in perfect unison and Elizabeth smiled pensively, wishing her son could be there to see the talented young rider on the purebred steed. After all the effort he had put in to find Jasper, she could think of nothing better than to have him witness the look of pure delight on her face.

Instead, she let out a small sigh and turned the conversation around to what she anticipated would be happier things. "So how are things going for you? What other great roles are in the pipeline?"

Lara swallowed hard, even though she couldn't have asked for a more ideal segue to break the news.

"You're not going to like this but ... there aren't any ... I've decided to give the theatre away next year."

Elizabeth leaned forward with her mouth agape. The talented actress/singer had made a huge name for herself and was in demand all across the country. "*What!* Why would you even consider doing that? You're one of the most popular female leads Australia has. Patrons purchase tickets specifically because your name is on the billboards ... they don't care what show it is."

"I can't help it. I've been thinking about this for quite some time, and I know it's the right thing to do. Nikki starts high school next year, so I can't keep dragging her all over the country – it's not fair. She needs a stable environment for these last important school years. When she was young it was okay, and Helen's been marvellous, but now I have to put her needs first and settle down in one city, at least during term time."

"What are you going to do then for finances? Not go back to editing?" When the other woman nodded, Elizabeth cried, "Lara, you *can't* just leave it all behind and waste that God-given gift of a voice!"

"I have to. My daughter's future is far more important than having me simply entertaining people night after night. Don't worry, Max has already tried everything he can think of to make me change my mind ... but I won't budge, so he's finally given up. Now he's looking around to see what other options are out there. The latest is just taking on one-night shows or short stints in different venues up here and on the Gold Coast. That way I can still perform to some degree and Nikki can stay in school all year round."

"But my dear girl, you're *far* too in demand to just play the smaller venues Brisbane and the Coast have to offer. A voice like yours was made to be showcased – and not only to Australian audiences but overseas as well. Nikki's been doing so well with Helen ... every report card attests to that. Surely she could incorporate high school subjects into their lessons."

She still couldn't believe Lara was willing to give up such an illustrious career, even if it was for the sake of her precious daughter.

"Max says I can still get into the Concert Hall at QPAC for one-off concerts etc, and I've agreed to travel to the southern capitals a couple of times a year, but only for a week at a time and mostly during school holidays. If something irresistible does come up during a school term, Suzie's offered to have Nikki stay with her, but I'll only take on things of a short duration. Mostly I want to be in Brisbane – my little girl needs me more than the world does at the moment."

Elizabeth had heard the same amount of determination in Lara's tone before. She knew it was virtually impossible to get her to change her mind once it was made up – she had tried without success on one other momentous occasion. As far as Lara was concerned, this was just as important.

"Alright, I understand how you feel. Even so, I do know you'll be depriving the rest of the world of an incredible experience if you're only based up here." Her mind drifted back to two years earlier when Lara was nominated for an Aria Award in the Best Female Artist category for her debut album featuring popular show tunes. Although someone else had taken home the award, it was a huge honour just to be in the list of nominees and proved the quality of her exceptional voice.

"I can't help it. As much as I love the theatre, Nikki will always be my first priority until she's able to take care of herself." Before Elizabeth could add anything further, Lara sent her a caring albeit determined smile and pushed back her chair. Offering a gentle squeeze of her friend's shoulder, she added, "Now, how about I go and make us a nice cuppa before you try to change my mind again..."

The family spent the rest of the afternoon opening presents and playing board games. As usual, Nikki came out the victor every time, much to her delight and their good-natured frustration.

Dusk was falling when Lara started gathering up their things. Elizabeth came over and took her hand, a touch of loving concern in her expression. "I truly do understand, and Charles and I want to be here for you as much as we can."

"I know – you always have been and I appreciate everything you've done to make our lives easier over the years. Both of you mean the world to us. I'm so grateful to have you in our lives – and thanks for not judging me too harshly." They exchanged affectionate smiles. "I'll be in touch in the new year – Merry

Christmas." She leaned over and softly kissed the other woman's cheek. "And next time you see a certain person, please pass this on from me – just don't tell him who it's from, okay..."

Elizabeth squeezed Lara's hand as her eyes welled up with sorrow for this caring young woman who still adored her son. "Oh, my precious girl, of course I will … just like always..."

No matter how much time had passed, Lara still needed some form of connection to her soulmate ... even if it was only second-hand. It was the only avenue left to her where she could leave an imprint on his skin ... even though he would never know. Little did she realise, Elizabeth was the bearer of similar tokens from him whenever the mother and daughter visited. And it broke her heart every single time knowing there was nothing she could do to change the sad situation.

All the way home, Nikki chatted on and on about how Jasper was clearing nearly every jump now and how she couldn't wait to take him to 'The Ekka' to compete against the best in the State. The August carnival was a popular event for locals and others from further afield as they wandered through exhibits and enjoyed the thrill of colourful sideshow alley with its plethora of rides and garish stalls. Crop farmers and stockbreeders from near and far submitted their produce or livestock for judging, while equestrian events and daring feats of skills were the major drawcards in the main arena.

"That's great, Poppet, but maybe you should wait a couple more years 'til you're a little bit older. Then you'll blitz them for sure!"

With the steady drone of Nikki's voice prattling on and on in the background, Lara's thoughts were on the man who still made her heart ache whenever she left his parents' home. Even now, his presence inhabited every corner of every room, despite the fact he hadn't lived there for many years.

Glancing across to the western hills, her heart cried, *I still miss you, Teddy.*

§

Christmas morning dawned bright and clear. An assortment of decorations on the tree twinkled in the early morning light as it filtered through the living room curtains. Lara and Nikki sat cross-legged on the sofa, with torn wrapping paper littering the floor and presents scattered in cumbersome piles around them. A soft breeze drifted through the window and blew against the fir branches, causing one of the shiny gold baubles to shiver and spin. The sudden burst of light triggered by the sun's rays hitting it caught Lara's attention.

Her gaze settled on three crystal ornaments with eighteen-carat gold filigree hanging in pride of place at the front of the tree. For eleven months of the year, these delicate keepsakes nestled in a beautiful velvet-lined box crafted specifically to keep them safe. Then for thirty-one special days and nights, they were on display for all to see.

Hanging from one branch was a delicate crystal reindeer sporting a striking set of antlers made of gold. On another, an elaborate nativity scene with a gold star hovering just above the stable seemed to shiver as a puff of wind caught it. A magnificent angel crowned the top branch, its outstretched wings made of spun gold. Adam had purchased the set as a surprise while wandering the streets of Salzburg seven years earlier. For a few moments, she was back in those glorious days, remembering the fun they had exploring so many of southern Europe's picturesque cities and villages. Looking out the window to the horizon, her usual Christmas blessing floated off into the atmosphere.

It doesn't matter how many years have come and gone, my darling, this old heart still reaches out to you. Have a wonderful Christmas, Teddy. I pray you're truly happy.

Suzie and Ben joined them for the early church service. Afterwards, she and Nikki spent the rest of the day at their place, tucking into a roast dinner and opening a stack of presents piled under the tree. This was Jack's first Christmas so it was extra special. At ten months old, he was the delight of the whole family, especially Nikki who was thrilled to have a little cousin to spoil. The happy couple had married nearly four years earlier and, following several failed attempts to fall pregnant, eventually, their beloved son had arrived.

Nikki had just turned eleven when he joined the family, and her constant pleas to give the little boy a bottle or take him for walks in the pram were welcomed by her grateful aunt. Now that the young girl had a real baby to play with, her tribe of dolls had been relegated to a cardboard box at the back of the cupboard ... all except for Annabelle. Lara still found the ragdoll tucked beneath the covers beside her daughter when she went in to say goodnight. The treasured gift from her forever 'faborite uncle' also took up pride of place on top of the pillow when Nikki made her bed each morning.

The adults spent the next several minutes watching Nikki help her small cousin rip open his stack of presents. A little while later, they were kept just as entertained by his loud squeals of delight tearing up the colourful paper strewn across the floor. Following a few rowdy games of Pictionary while Jack had his afternoon nap, the family finished off the lunch leftovers before it was time for the visitors to leave for home.

§

It was late on Christmas night when Adam tiptoed down the staircase of his home in Brookfield. He and Trina had spent the day at his parents' home, and now she was fast asleep while he had been lying wide awake beside her for the past few hours. Resigning himself to the fact sleep was still a long way off, he decided to sneak out of bed and settle back in his study rather than risk waking her.

331

With soft music as his only company, he sat in the dark, reflecting on the news his mother had shared when the pair of them strolled over to visit Jasper earlier in the day.

Feeling full from Elizabeth's usual banquet-style lunch, Charles and Trina chose to stay behind. The terrace sofa was the perfect place to take advantage of wafting breezes from the river and the shady trees overhead, both welcome respites from the stifling summer heat. Adam's father also had another reason to stay behind ... he knew his wife wanted a quiet word with their son.

"How is she, Mum?"

There was no need to ask who Adam was referring to. Hooking an arm through his as a way to delay the inevitable, Elizabeth searched for the right words to soften the blow. It was an unspoken truth that her precious boy still held onto the slim hope of one day sharing another stage with the talented actress.

Despite his ongoing optimistic need, she knew full well Lara wouldn't even consider the notion ... her love went too deep to open herself up to that kind of pain and longing again. His feelings were just as strong, although hidden the majority of the time, while she was more inclined to wear hers on her sleeve.

Elizabeth had never been brave enough to tell him just how deeply Lara still cared – nor how often she noticed her stray fingertip brush across the display of family photos on the side table during her regular visits. Seeing the look of despondency usually accompanying the loving gesture always made her heart ache. Telling him would only add to his.

Even though Adam and Trina had certainly done their best to make a go of their marriage, she could tell they weren't as happy as he tried to make out. There was no sign of the spark he and Lara once shared, and her motherly instincts noticed how often his eyes turned to the west where Mt Coot-tha's outline filled the horizon ... and the hint of wistfulness accompanying each look.

They negotiated a grassy path weaving between an array of colourful hibiscus bushes and bottlebrush shrubs. The noisy sparring of a pair of lorikeets fighting over a bud brimming with nectar muted their voices.

"She's doing okay, son. I suppose you heard she was offered the part of *Christine* when your *Phantom* goes to Perth."

"Yeah, I did ... and I also heard she turned it down. Max mentioned it the other day while I was signing the contract." He sighed heavily and the hand draped through his arm gave it a gentle squeeze.

"Did he mention anything else?"

"No, not really ... just something about how she couldn't do it because of Nikki." Thinking about the comment now, it suddenly dawned on him there could be something far more sinister lurking behind Max's announcement. At the time, all he had been able to concentrate on was his own disappointment. His pace slowed as he looked across at his mother with a worried frown. "Is Nikki okay? Has something happened?"

This time she patted his arm with a reassuring smile. "No, don't worry, she's fine. Growing like a weed, nearly as tall as me and starting high school next year! I don't know where that time has gone – it wasn't too long ago she was just a little tot."

"I do," he murmured softly.

He had missed out on so many family occasions and special events over the years. Thankfully, his father took photos to commemorate each one and Adam always asked to see them on his next visit. There was one regular date he kept each year, though sometimes even that was too painful and the desperate man wondered why he kept putting himself through such agony. Until the next time … and there he was again, tearing his heart out with that constant craving. Only Charles and Elizabeth knew his secret, and they had been faithful confidants.

The temptation to purchase tickets to all of Lara's shows had never left him – sometimes he was even offered one gratis from a mate who was also appearing in the cast line-up. But at the last minute, he always backed down … but only because of a promise made. It didn't matter how powerful the yearning was, Adam couldn't go back on his word – even when he was accosted with posters showing off a pair of sapphire eyes that still make his heart race.

But he had made no such vow when it came to that other annual event.

Elizabeth pressed his arm again, and her footsteps were slow and measured. "My darling boy, there's a reason Max would've said what he did … you'll hear about it eventually, so it's probably best if the news comes from me."

She swallowed hard. He caught the sound and waited for what could only be ominous news.

"Lara's decided to give the theatre away, at least until Nikki's out of school." She didn't even have to pause for his reaction.

As if a cold bit attached to a leather bridle suddenly reigned him in, Adam stopped dead in his tracks, only this time with a look of bewilderment. "*What?* She can't do *that* … Lara's adored all around the country! Why would she throw her career away when her shows sell out weeks in advance? What's going on?"

His mother waited patiently, listening unflinchingly to this unsurprising rant. When she did get the chance to respond, her answer was soft and filled with wisdom. "I understand why you feel that way – I felt the same at first – but when you really think about it, I can see her point. In her mind, Nikki's schooling is far more important, especially now when she's about to start high school. She wants her settled in a proper school with all of her peers rather than travelling all over the country. You know she's always put that little girl first."

"Yes, but to put her career on hold for at least five years is just ludicrous!

Surely, there's another way. I thought Helen was still tutoring Nikki whenever she's on tour?"

"She has been, only now Lara feels high school is too diverse for Helen to be able to do justice to all the subjects. So ... she's decided to stay in Brisbane and just play some one-off shows and the like to keep her hand in for the next five years at least."

He shook his head sadly, thinking what a waste of her unique gift. A loving arm reached around his waist and pulled him close. The mother and son looked at each other with thoughts united for a few moments. Then they took up the pace again, wandering along arm-in-arm with their heads bowed.

"I *can* understand where she's coming from" —his tone was resigned— "of course Nikki's education is important, so it's only natural she feels like that. But her fans are going to miss her ... and so will the majority of her peers..."

Elizabeth could only nod. She had no comforting words to offer as they neared the fence and the waiting horse – only a prayer of hope for two special people. Her hand reached out and gently stroked Jasper's strong flat cheek. The gelding had been watching their approach and nuzzled around their clothes for the scent of any treats that might be stashed away somewhere.

"Sorry, old boy, I didn't think to bring you anything today," Adam said, absentmindedly scratching under Jasper's long forelock then running his hand along the glossy neck, all the while imagining a woman with laughing eyes and long chestnut hair of a similar colour to the Arab's striking coat.

Another blow came when Adam realised his chances of accidentally bumping into her in theatre circles would now be almost negligible. For all these years, he had carried the faint hope of at least catching a glimpse of her at one of the many gala functions they both received invitations to. She rarely attended any, still preferring anonymity rather than the spotlight away from the stage, but he had never let go of the dream.

They spent several minutes as Jasper enjoyed a few vague gestures of affection while the mother and son took time to ponder the recent conversation. When they went to leave, Adam spotted a healthy thistle growing near his feet. He bent down to pick the purple flowerhead for the spirited animal to munch on while taking care to leave the thorny bud-case behind. That classic Arabian spoon-like profile bobbed up and down as the horse downed one of his favourite treats and Adam couldn't help admiring the stunning picture he made.

With one final pat, he added gloomily, "Well at least you'll get to see them more often, old fella."

Elizabeth had to bite her bottom lip to stop it from trembling as she took his arm again. Slowly the pair wandered back to where their spouses were still waiting in the shady nook overlooking the river.

While they were still out of earshot, she looked at Adam with concern in her eyes. "How's everything between you and Trina? Is she still keeping away from that dreadful drink?"

He nodded and sent her a loving smile. "Yeah, Mum, you don't have to worry ... she never goes near the stuff anymore. I'm really quite proud of all the effort she's made. Sometimes I even have trouble remembering how bad things were."

At least something good has come out of all this heartache, Elizabeth mused before answering. "And to give her credit, she's been most kind and welcoming towards your father and me." Her voice dropped. "I just wish *you* were happier. I miss hearing your laughter the way it was when—"

She broke off quickly. Adding the obvious would only make things harder.

He understood and left it alone to take another tack instead. "Thanks, Mum. Actually, we're not doing too badly ... at least better than a lot of others I know. Don't worry about me. I'll be okay." Leaning over, he brushed his lips against her cheek then playfully tickled her side as a way to bring back that usual ready smile. "Come on, the others are waiting."

§

Sitting in the darkness all those hours later, reflecting on the news, Adam remembered his first glimpse of the woman who still lived in a secret place in his heart. The sight of Lara rushing through an old theatre door on a cold winter's night was an image etched into his memory forever. Only a little bit later on that same evening, her crystal-clear voice and gentle spirit had drawn him in from the moment she opened her mouth – long before his father introduced them.

The theatre world is sure going to miss you, my precious love ... but not half as much as I do. Merry Christmas, sweet lady.

§

Unseen by anyone except its Creator, one of the slender silken threads on an unfinished canvas made a slight deviation. Ever so carefully, it took up the weave lying half-finished on another image – one that was familiar and comfortable, and found wrapped around a large film spool ... but without the bright splash of a footlight's hue.

Chapter 25

The air outside had turned quite chilly ... it was July and the middle of another Brisbane winter. There was a crisp wind blowing up from the valley, so Charles and Adam chose to sit inside their favourite Paddington haunt, despite the warmish rays of sunshine bathing their usual table of choice outside.

With his musical career leaping from one new production to the next, Adam's architectural work had taken a backseat for the last few years. The partners still kept his name on the company letterhead, although it was more a token gesture due to his reputation and innovative ideas. Whenever there was a decent break between appearances he still dabbled in his craft, however, any hours actually spent in the office were becoming fewer and farther between.

The intensity of playing eight massive shows a week for months on end drained even the most physical of performers. Because of this, Adam found he accomplished more from his home study as the mood took him rather than in the bustling walls of the city office. He certainly didn't need the money, even so, it was a handy hobby to keep him occupied before the next offer came along. Trina was out for most of the day with her charity work, so the house was usually quiet.

"Now listen, son, what's this I read in the papers about you being invited to give a series of lectures in Salzburg again?"

"Oh, so you saw that..."

"Mmm-hmm – and so did your mother. Another great feather in your cap!"

"Ha, don't know about that! According to the organisers' letter, it seems they've taken an interest in my ideas on this new form of digital design. I was surprised, especially seeing I've only been making a token effort for so long."

"I'm not – they appeared to be excellent ideas on those last drawings you showed me. So, have you agreed?"

"Not yet ... I'm not so sure I'm ready to walk those streets again." His reply dripped with nostalgia for another time.

The other man offered a sympathetic nod. "I can understand. Even so, it might do you good to get away for a while." As much as he was thankful for the change in Trina's attitude, Charles could still sense an underlying restlessness in her, and it made him uneasy. And from what he could tell, their rare displays of affection seemed more superficial than genuine.

"Well, I haven't given them my final answer yet, but if I do agree, I thought I might combine it with a quick visit to the vineyard to see Claudia and Antonio before they retire."

Every night as he lay in bed contemplating whether to accept the offer, Adam had mulled over whether he should add the side trip. He figured it was going to be hard enough anyway, and the fun-loving Italian couple would bring a bit of cheer to an otherwise poignant jaunt if he did decide in the affirmative.

"I think that's a *marvellous* idea – they're always asking after you. I told you Antonio's training up his grandson to take over the management."

"Mmm, you did, and it sounds like he'll do a great job. Mum said you're happy with his innovations for the new sparkling varieties, so he obviously knows what he's doing."

"Yes, I'm very pleased, and I've told Antonio and Claudia they can stay on if they like – more as overseers just to keep an eye on things. They're welcome to keep on living in the cottage for as long as they want, while Marius and his young family can take over one wing of the villa – it's certainly big enough and vacant most of the time so they might as well make good use of it. I can't see your mother and I getting over there again – at least not in the foreseeable future."

"That's a great idea. The vineyard's been Claudia and Antonio's home for so long now, and they've been such good friends to you and Mum. It'd be a shame if they had to leave for good."

"Well, it was your mother's idea originally, but of course I'm very happy for them to stay on. Anyway, back to your trip. Will Trina go with you?"

"I haven't asked, but I doubt it. Her charity work is taking up most of her time now, and I think she's attending some gala fundraising dinner for the hospital around the same time. Anyway, if I do go, it'll only be a flying visit. I'd spend a few days in Tuscany before flying up to Salzburg for the lectures and then come straight home again. I don't have the time to turn it into a holiday. Rehearsals for *The Pirates of Penzance* commence at the end of September, and I have heaps of work to do on a new building project before getting into that."

Besides, I haven't really enjoyed any holiday since then ... and it certainly won't be the same without a certain mother and daughter by my side.

"Oh, that's right – congratulations! It was a great coup to land that role over Mark Sinclair. I read he was desperate for it."

"Yeah, I was stoked actually! There's always been a bit of friendly rivalry between us."

"Don't worry, he's got nothing on you! Anyway, let Mum and I know if you both decide to go so we can keep an eye on the place."

"Okay thanks, that'd be great, Dad. I'll let you know either way."

For the next hour, their conversation centred on more mundane things until Charles looked at his watch. "Oops, it's time I got off home. We have visitors due shortly and I don't want to be late."

Adam instantly raised an eyebrow, but his father shook his head.

"No ... they're coming tomorrow after church."

The initial response was a pensive nod and then, "Well I'd better get going, as well."

Seeing the sadness in Adam's eyes made Charles' heart ache, although there was nothing he could do to make the situation any better. Pulling out behind the Mercedes a few minutes later, he wasn't at all surprised to see his son turn left instead of right at the bottom of the street.

Mmm, thought so. Still haven't really let her go, have you? Can't say I blame you, though ... I'd probably be the same. She's definitely one-of-a-kind...

Lara's gentle spirit had drawn Charles in as soon as they met, so it was easy to understand his son's continued devotion.

It was years since Adam had taken this route. Normally he stayed away, only today there seemed to be some unseen force drawing him back. The long silver car turned cautiously into Lara's street and cruised along slowly ... all the while those piercing dark eyes zeroed in on a neat little cottage about halfway along.

The Merc eventually pulled into an empty space beneath a silver wattle laden with bright yellow flowers, just a few houses back on the opposite side of the road. Its occupant sat motionless in the shadows, deep in thought ... picturing a little girl with long brown hair streaming out behind her as she rushed down those same stairs to greet him with a shout of glee and the tightest of hugs.

With a frustrated shake of his head, Adam berated himself. *Aaargghh, stop it! She's nearly thirteen years old and probably hasn't run down those stairs for years ... and besides, it's more than likely she's forgotten all about you by now.*

He stayed there unmoving for several minutes, both hands clasping the steering wheel with his chin resting against them and his gaze fixed ... until a new model, blue Toyota Corolla suddenly pulled into the driveway. His head snapped up, and his gaze fell on a pretty young girl as she jumped out of the passenger seat and ran up the stairs, laughing over her shoulder. He recognised that laugh and her happy-go-lucky gait, and had to swallow hard.

But it was a stunning woman with hair the colour of roasted chestnuts who captured his attention most when she stepped out from the driver's side. Those silky tresses were far shorter than he remembered – now reaching just below her shoulder blades – while the shapely figure still made his heart race just as it had always done all those years ago.

When she reached the top of the stairs, the woman's step faltered. Almost intuitively, she reached up and pressed a hand against her heart, as though it needed calming. Casting her eyes over one shoulder, a quizzical expression crossed her face, but the deep shadows from an overhanging tree thwarted her chances of recognising his car. For the space of a few seconds as she searched the street, her bottom lip caught in a gesture that still regularly visited him in his dreams. He could almost feel the noticeable shiver running through her shoulders and sat mesmerised when she turned to make her way inside. Before the door closed, and for another second or two, she glanced back once more.

Recognising all those well-loved characteristics caused a huge lump to form in his throat, along with a burning ache in the pit of his stomach. With a heavy heart, his chin dropped back onto a set of white knuckles as the door clicked shut.

I still feel you too, Baby ... every single day. And you're just as beautiful as that first time I saw you – nothing's changed ... well, nothing except for your hair. I can still feel it trailing over my body as we made love in the moonlight. Swept back in time, he let out a heartfelt sigh. *And obviously something else has been upgraded – my favourite old hatchback. I loved that little car – it was so like you in so many ways. But I suppose it was ridiculous to expect it to last forever ... but I wish I'd known – I would've bought it myself ... just to keep our memories safe.*

Unable to resist one final glimpse, simply to savour the memories wrapped up in those four white walls, he turned the key and then slowly drove away.

§

When Lara went inside, she paused again and had to lean against the door.

Why do I still feel you? Every now and then, it's as though I can almost hear you calling out to me ... but every newspaper and magazine portrays you as having a full and exciting life. All the photos show you as being happy ... which is exactly what I wanted. Oh, Teddy, I really hope you're not going through all this endless yearning that still manages to creep up on me out-of-the-blue.

Like Charles, she had seen the news article and been instantly dragged back in time to a picturesque country where the hills resounded with music and laughter and love ... so much love. She wondered if he was going through the same emotions while planning this trip. There was no question in her mind as to how much Adam had loved her, but she also understood he could never truly forget those vows once made to his wife. She couldn't blame him for staying, even after all this time ... but the pining was still a constant companion whenever she was alone with her thoughts.

Down through the years, society sections of the local papers often displayed pictures of him with the striking redhead on his arm. Usually, they were walking the red carpet to one of his opening nights or at an awards night where, more often than not, a statuette of some kind had his name engraved on it. Sometimes it was to attend a gala dinner to do with his wife's charities.

Anyone who knew Trina in the early days would have trouble recognising her now. She had lost the facial puffiness so often considered an alcoholic's trademark. Despite being six years older than her husband, she now looked years younger than before ... so different from the woman Lara had seen screaming at him in a hospital auditorium ... or the broken woman who had begged her to let him go.

Sometimes when Lara was reading a newspaper, there would be a sudden pang when she turned the page and their images stared back at her. Once upon a time, she had been the one walking into an elegant dining room with her arm through his, dressed in an eye-catching gown and feeling like Cinderella. These glimpses into his everyday life became all the more poignant when she remembered a little girl's plea about not losing her slipper in case he couldn't find her. In the end, they had lost each other, although it was nothing like the fairy-tale ... she still lived with the reality every day.

Yet, even now, Lara couldn't regret her long-ago decision, especially when the articles always portrayed a smiling couple who appeared to be blissfully happy ... after all, this was exactly what she had always wanted for him.

§

After mulling it over for days, Adam decided to take up the invitation to speak at the conference. Sharing ideas with his peers again was too great an honour to turn down. As expected, Trina was too busy to accompany him.

Antonio and Claudia's greetings were just as he remembered – warm, welcoming and peppered with cheeky retorts, and all able to bring an instant smile to his face. Similar to last time, the excitement of having the young man come to stay meant the Italians' speech was a mixture of both languages, adding a delightful flavour to the enjoyment of being together again.

"Adam! *Mio caro!* And as 'andsome as ever – Australia is *molto buono* for you!" Claudia took his face in her hands and kissed both cheeks soundly – the perfect Italian welcome for a man needing comfort after a long lonely flight and a drive filled with memories of another from what seemed a lifetime ago.

"*Ciao,* Claudia, still *una bella donna!* It *is* very good for me, and you've hardly changed since the last time I was here!"

"Oh, get away with you," she scoffed, pretending to swat his arm. "You 'ave not changed in your *complimenti* too. Not a *bella donna,* just *una donna anziana* – I am very old from the last time you came to visit," she laughed, remembering a similar greeting during his arrival on that occasion. Neither of them made mention of two others who were missing from back then.

"Come 'ere *il mio buon amico*." Antonio interrupted their laughter by slapping a pair of welcoming arms around the visitor. "Let me look at you. I thought you might be old and grey by now, but I am *molto felice* ... ummm ...

very 'appy to see you are still so good looking, but now you 'ave made me *geloso*. I am like an old man compared to you after all the years to 'ave flown away."

The two men were glad to see each other, so another round of laughter echoed around the courtyard until Antonio's eyes suddenly turned sad. "Are you truly alright, *il amico mio?* I remember 'ow 'appy you were last time, so I am *bene interessato e molto preoccupato* – aaahhh…" —he searched for the English equivalent— "*Si*, most interested but very worried for you to be coping okay."

Claudia threw her hands in the air and glared at her husband. "*Antonio, silenzio!* I told you not to say anything, *stupido vecchio!*" She was mortified to hear his blatant comments so soon after Adam's arrival.

"It's okay, Claudia. I understand. He only meant well, and after all these years I'm used to him saying how he feels." Grasping Antonio's still strong shoulder, he smiled at the older man to assure him all was well.

"*Si*, Adam, I knew you would understand. I remember the *molti momenti felici* we all had – truly 'appy times. *Sono molto molto triste* it not to work out for both of you … I want you to know that. You understand? … Eeh…" — Antonio paused as he tried to find the words and then— "…I am very very 'eartbroken," and he slapped both hands over his heart to emphasise the point.

"*Grazie, amico mio.* We did share some happy – *felice* – times and I'm very sad it didn't work out too. But as much as we try to avoid it, sometimes that's the way life goes. Anyway, I'm doing all right … most of the time."

"*Enough* sad talk!" Claudia interrupted, wringing her hands on her apron. She was desperate to change the subject for their special guest's sake. "I have your old room ready. Come, you will freshen up!" She bustled around behind Adam, pushing him into the house in a motherly fashion, completely oblivious to the expression on his face when he realised what she had just said.

Such an innocent statement … and with so much hidden in its depths. He had to close his eyes momentarily, readying himself to enter the room where they had made love for the very first time.

The trio scaled the impressive staircase leading from the living room to the floor above. Adam tried to help Antonio with his suitcase, but the old man wasn't having a bar of it – he was the host and that was how things had always been … a minor inconvenience like advancing age wasn't going to change anything to his way of thinking. As he looked around, Adam noticed nothing had really changed over the years … and it was easy to imagine a woman with love streaming from her eyes gliding down these same stairs to meet him.

Claudia led the way past a closed door at the top, and he was thankful to find those initial fears had been unfounded … though he couldn't help reaching out so an inquisitive thumb brushed across the handle in a vain attempt to feel her presence once more.

Maybe I should've said I wanted this room after all, Sweetheart – at least that way I'd be able to sense you lying beside me again.

§

Grey clouds were starting to roll in when he woke up in the bed used during his teenage years. Listening to the sounds of summer springing to life outside the window, he lay sprawled across the sheet for a little while longer as a few soft pigeon calls drifted from a dovecote in the courtyard below. If he concentrated hard enough, Adam wondered whether an echo of laughter might be heard from when he had chased Nikki out of this same bed to get ready for a memorable day trip to Florence. Letting out a heavy sigh, he eventually rose to get dressed, certain if he dawdled any longer the memories would become too maudlin and spoil the rest of his stay.

Over a hearty breakfast made up of a vast array of Tuscan delights, the three close friends relived memories from times spent there with his parents. Later, Adam made his way up the hill to Cortona and once again breathed in the enchanting ambience of his favourite little Etruscan town. He paused for a few moments beneath the same archway once captured in a certain photograph. It still accompanied him wherever he went and was even now sitting on the bedside table back at the villa. A host of years fell away as he pictured the wonder in Lara and Nikki's eyes entering these same gates for the very first time.

After years of practising energetic dance routines, and with the physical stamina needed to navigate countless raked stages, Adam easily scaled the steep, narrow streets. When his eyes took in the splendour of the fairy-tale hillside town, in some ways, it felt as if it was only yesterday since that last visit.

As always, the *piazza* bustled with tourists and townsfolk alike. He spotted a row of little tables with old men playing cards in the shadow of the imposing Town Hall – so similar to the last time he was there. Looking across, Adam caught sight of what he could only presume was the very same flower-seller tending her stall. Memories of Lara's reaction when presented with a pretty bouquet kept him company and brought a wistful smile to his face. One old man intercepted his look and gently tipped a worn beret with his knobbly finger. It was as though he understood the emotional journey the newcomer was on and this was his way of offering support. Adam acknowledged him by dipping his head, and the look they exchanged was the universal language of two souls quietly mourning the loss of a loved one.

A fine misty rain accompanied him to the top of the hill – up to the ancient abbey standing like a sentinel on a high ridge. In the shadow of the old basilica, he gazed out to the valleys below and couldn't believe how many years had passed since the last time he had stood on this exact spot. Back then, a little girl who always made him smile had been holding his hand. Contrasting that cute tiny tot with the almost teenager he had caught sight of only a few weeks earlier, Adam couldn't help grieving for all the lost years. This trip was becoming far more difficult than he ever imagined, and it hit home just how foolish he had been to let them go without a fight. It didn't matter how tolerable his marriage had become, being there highlighted the passage of years and all the things he had missed that made up their lives ... nothing could ever replace those times.

Whether it was because of the sanctity of the location or the flood of memories assaulting him simply by being there, he had no way of knowing. With no one to witness those deep feelings of regret, Adam fell to his knees and an anguished cry poured from his broken soul.

Oh, dear God ... why did I ever let Lara talk me into letting her go ... how am I going to do this for the rest of my life? It doesn't get any easier, no matter how much time passes. Please help me – I can't do it on my own anymore...

Rivers of tears mingled with the raindrops running down his cheeks, and the broken man tried to dash them away. Just then, a tiny butterfly settled on a flower clinging to a small patch of earth in a sheltered hollow near his feet. He watched its delicate wings being battered to and fro by the splash of droplets hitting the surrounding rocks. The courageous little insect clung to the fragile petals with all of its might, while the rocky outcrop provided protection from Mother Nature's full onslaught. Witnessing its steadfast tenacity helped to put into perspective all that had been happening in their lives. No matter what storms he and Lara faced, an invisible hand was always shielding them from the buffeting winds so they too could stand against whatever adversities may come their way.

Adam's sleep that night was fraught with images of a beautiful woman ducking and weaving around black storm clouds as she beckoned him to follow. Each time he was about to take hold of her outstretched hand, she suddenly disappeared ... only to reappear a little further on.

In the morning, he was mentally and emotionally exhausted and yet the image of the tenacious little butterfly remained lodged in his spirit – a pertinent reminder he could face whatever came his way.

§

Over breakfast, Claudia sent her husband a worried look when she noticed a film of sadness infusing Adam's eyes. It was easy to guess the reason for his subdued mood. Nevertheless, the sensitive duo felt it was better to keep their musings to themselves rather than add to his burden.

Antonio, along with his very knowledgeable grandson, filled the rest of Adam's visit with tours of the vineyard and a day trip to Florence only an hour's drive away. They wanted to introduce him to several restaurateurs interested in stocking their new range. The old vintner hoped Adam would be able to assure

Charles the business was thriving and convey how Marius was more than capable of taking his place at the helm. Even though his official retirement was still two years away, he was determined to ensure the changeover went smoothly.

On their way to the last appointment in the magnificent city, the three men had to cross the famous Ponte Vecchio Bridge. The carriageway stretched from one side of the River Arno to the other and was made up of several tiers. Each of these was lined with quaint old-fashioned stalls teeming with much-sought-after wares. From the reams of memories tucked away in the storehouse of his mind, Adam remembered a promise he had once made.

"Can you give me a moment *per favore*, Antonio? I won't be long ... there's just something small I need to do before we leave."

Ducking into one of dozens of tiny jewellery stalls, he glanced over several beautiful pieces until a dainty gold bracelet with a delicate butterfly as the centrepiece caught his eye. Its wings were made of finely spun gold and the whole piece shimmered with tiny pieces of blue and green opal, reminding him of a stained-glass window. Remembering his encounter with the butterfly on top of the hill and a special woman's fascination with old churches and their magnificent windows, it was obvious this would be the perfect gift for Lara.

Even though Adam had no clue if he would ever be able to deliver the bracelet to its intended owner, he still couldn't pass up what might be his only chance to fulfil that long-ago promise. He paid the jeweller and the black velvet pouch with its precious contents found a new home in his pocket.

§

On their last morning together, the three friends sat around a large table in the courtyard, drinking shots of aromatic espresso and trying to stay upbeat rather than dwell on the looming goodbye. They had just enjoyed another tasty meal from Claudia's kitchen when she turned to Adam with motherly concern.

"*Mio caro* Adam, it 'as been *molto bene* seeing you again and 'earing about your success on the stage, but I am so sorry it did not work out with *la tua bella* Larissa. She is *una signora speciale,* and I could see *il tuo amore* – you were so so 'appy together – *così felice*. I pray you will once more laugh with all that *libertà*." She shook her head and clicked her tongue, using a corner of her apron to wipe away a wayward tear.

"*Grazie*, Claudia." He reached over and squeezed her hand. "Lara certainly was *speciale,* and I am *così felice* you came to know and love her too." It was actually a relief hearing her name spoken as they had been avoiding any reference to her for the last three days. "And *grazie* for sharing your home with me. You and Antonio have always held a *speciale* place in my heart."

As they waved goodbye, Claudia wiped another tear from her eye and Antonio bent down to kiss her cheek. "*Ti adoro, mia cara,* and one day, Adam

344

will find 'is true *amore* again, for sure."

His wife could only nod sadly and hug him close, wanting to believe what he said was true. As they walked back into the villa, the faint echoes of a little girl's laughter wafted on the soft summer breeze.

And on that same gentle puff, and in a realm unseen, tiny fragments of a heart broken and bereft drifted into the air, anxious to seek out those left behind by its soulmate in Vienna many years earlier.

§

Flying into Salzburg, Adam peered through the window to a splendid vista of contrasts. Several of the mountains surrounding the Austrian city showed off summer's lush green foliage. Others were stark towering peaks with remnants of winter snowdrifts still lying in deep ravines on the highest reaches. A series of sparkling blue lakes surrounded the city, and the chain effect reminded him of a gleaming sapphire necklace. Instantly his mind's eye crossed the years and miles to one adorning a woman's neck, and somewhere down there was the store where he had purchased it.

Stop it, he sighed, while his soul whispered, *Better get used it around here.*

When the plane banked over the centre of town before coming into land, it appeared as though the spires on many of the buildings were stretching out their tall stone fingers to greet him.

At least you seem to be glad I'm back...

During the limo ride to the hotel, each new corner revealed spectacular buildings in panoramic streetscapes. Adam's love of Baroque architecture received a good dose of nourishment – reminding him of his first visit as a teenager with Charles and Elizabeth. The Old Town hadn't changed at all. If anything, the elegant marble and sandstone buildings seemed to have become even more grandiose as he grew older and looked at them through more astute eyes. He marvelled at the workmanship of the early architects and stonemasons over the centuries and found his eyes kept gravitating between them and the spectacular backdrop of mountains fashioned by the Master Creator himself.

Once again, his accommodation was the Hotel Bristol, right in the heart of town. The conference organisers had chosen the same exclusive hotel for all the guest speakers and Klaus, the Head Concierge for many years, greeted Adam as he entered the grand foyer. As before, he was dressed in an immaculate dark suit and displayed the impeccable manners expected of someone in his position.

"Mr Peters, it is a delight to see you again. Welcome back to our elegant hotel."

"Thank you, Klaus. It's a pleasure, especially to find you're still here."

"Thank you – you are most kind, sir. I have organised the same suite for your comfort. You may remember it looks over the Mirabell Gardens and has our best aspect. We want our guests to feel right at home, so please feel free to ask if there is anything you require." He glanced behind Adam and then back at him with a quizzical smile. "But where are your charming wife and delightful little girl? If I remember correctly, she was most excited to be visiting our city – I seem to recall her always trilling songs from that famous movie."

Adam was amazed at his recollection. Unfortunately, the innocent blunder also meant a well-known ache came back for a visit. "No, regrettably I'm on my own this time."

"Oh, I am so very sorry to hear that. We all enjoyed having *das kleine Mädchen* here, although I would imagine she is all grown up by now."

Picturing the slender pre-teen from only a few weeks ago, he was able to answer truthfully. "Yes, she is, and I'm sure you would have a hard time recognising her. Nikki's becoming a real young lady and I'm so proud of her."

"I'm sure you are. Please give them my warmest regards and tell them I look forward to seeing all of you together again on your next visit."

"Thank you, Klaus, I'll be sure to pass on your greetings when I see them."

"*Sehr gut*. Now, let me get you settled into your suite. You may recall it is on the top floor."

"Yes, I do. Umm … but Klaus, because I'm on my own this time, there's really no need for anything too large or luxurious. I won't be offended if you offer me something smaller so another family can enjoy all of its comforts."

"Oh no, Mr Peters, there is no need. You are a most important visitor to our beautiful city, and we want you to have the best. Besides, the organisers insisted on our finest accommodation for their keynote speaker. Now please come with me and I will show you to your suite. Your bags should already have arrived."

There was no use resisting any further, so Adam followed him up to the lavish apartment-style accommodation.

As soon as he set foot over the threshold, it was as though he could feel Lara's spirit there. Every corner seemed to exude a blending of fragrances that reminded him of her natural fresh scent after a bath. The bedroom was straight ahead through a pair of open double doors and he couldn't resist sweeping his gaze across the spacious room as though seeking her out. This was the first time he had been in a room where they had made love since that last night in her home and all the memories came flooding back. During his time in Cortona, he had deliberately avoided opening the door to the room they had shared there, not sure how he would handle seeing the bed where they had first become one. Now those feelings assailed him, and his whole spirit seemed to groan.

Klaus noticed him falter and immediately moved to his side. "Are you alright, Mr Peters? Perhaps you are exhausted from your journey. Is there anything I can do for you?"

"No, I'll be fine, I'm sure. But you're probably right ... a rest will help. Thanks for your concern."

Relieved to see his guest appeared to have recovered, the concierge moved to the double entrance doors. "Well, I'll leave you to get settled. Enjoy your stay and please don't hesitate to ask if you require anything at all. And please enjoy sampling our finest champagne." He gestured to a small bottle resting in an ice-bucket on the bureau and then swept out, closing the doors firmly behind him.

Adam took his time wandering around the familiar surroundings, occasionally brushing a hand across the expensive furnishings until at last he stood at the window looking down to the Mirabell Gardens. He could see the statue of the winged horse way off in the distance and could picture the excitement on Nikki's face when she saw it for the first time.

Stop it, you idiot! You've come to work, and that's all. It's been nearly eight years since they were here, so pull yourself together and concentrate on what you came to do instead.

Going through the conference compendium already laid out on the coffee table, he noticed all of his lectures were set down for the next three days. He made a mental note to keep busy for the rest of the time to ensure there was no chance of falling into that lurking pit of depression. The way he was feeling at present, it was something that could easily happen if he didn't take drastic steps.

After freshening up, Adam made his way downstairs to where some of the other speakers were already gathered in a stateroom just off the lobby. They recognised him immediately and beckoned him over, introducing themselves as soon as he joined them.

Late into the night, despite feeling exhausted, he was still wide awake ... surrounded by images of the woman who had once lain beside him in this very bed, with soft rays of early morning sunlight caressing her glossy hair.

No matter how much time passes, you'll always be the other half of my heart.

§

The daylight hours passed quickly enough because Adam made sure to keep busy at the other workshops on offer whenever his were done for the day. Last time, he couldn't wait to get back to their suite and showed no interest whatsoever in mingling with his colleagues. Now it was a godsend to have them occupy his time. He was relieved to note neither Elliot's nor Ray Carter's names were in the register, so there was no need to avoid any awkward questions.

Apart from dining at nearby restaurants with a few other lecturers, he spent the rest of the time within the hotel's confines. Loneliness was eating him up, and he couldn't bear the thought of having to deal with the heartbreak of passing by many of the landmarks they had visited together. Despite his best efforts, invariably he ended up standing before the floor length doors leading to the balcony as dusk fell, gazing across the river to the imposing white hilltop castle. For many minutes, he stared out to the many steeples and rooftops of the Old Town Lara had found so fascinating. Seeing it like this was hard enough; to actually walk the memory-filled pathways again would have been too much for the strongest of hearts, and his had been fragile for far too long.

His first night was the hardest. After tossing and turning for hours in the big lonely bed, he eventually drifted into a shallow slumber. Several times throughout the night his hand automatically reached out to touch the space beside him, almost as though expecting to feel her there. Each time it came away cold and empty, and all he could do was turn over and curl up in a ball. Ghostly images from an intimate ballet two hands had once performed only served to increase the longing to be back in her arms.

§

Three days later Adam's bags were packed and waiting in the lobby. Nothing could entice him to hang around for the final dinner – there were too many memories of another night, and he didn't want to open himself up to that degree of pain again. Having managed to get through his time there relatively unscathed, reliving something so close to his heart would be excruciating.

Klaus had already organised for the hotel limo to take him to the airport and he hurried over to bid Adam farewell just as the car swept into the entrance.

"Mr Peters, it was wonderful to see you again. I hope you enjoyed your time here and I trust everything was to your satisfaction."

"It was excellent, thank you, Klaus. All of your staff are exceptional, and as before, my suite was comfortable and well-appointed. I felt right at home."

"It was our pleasure," the Head Concierge assured him. "And please give my regards to your lovely wife and delightful daughter. I'm only sorry they were unable to join you."

"Of course, and so was I. Thank you once again."

The two men shook hands firmly before Adam slid into the back seat and the limo sped off to the airport. Pensively he looked out the window to the picturesque Baroque-style buildings rushing by. The effect reminded him of the rapid passage of time. As much as he craved being in the city where they had known so many magical times, far too many bittersweet memories lived there as well. He needed to get away and leave the past behind if he was to move on with the rest of his life.

For the very first time, he dared to give voice to that saddest of phrases.

"Goodbye, my dearest love."

Chapter 26

Nikki coped easily with the transition to high school with the private school catering to all year levels. This meant her circle of friends remained largely unchanged and they were able to share several classes. A competitive nature meant she excelled in all of her chosen subjects, which often made her the envy of others in her year level. It also meant report card writing was an easy task for her teachers. She was one of the first in line to join the choir and drama group, as well as participate in the school band. Adding in all the hours spent with Jasper on weekends, the teenager's life was busy with a host of activities, and so there was no time to miss the theatre world's gypsy lifestyle.

Lara found herself spending most Saturday mornings with Charles and Elizabeth as Nikki took her best friend off for a session at the local pony club just down the road. The keen horsewoman revelled in the different riding disciplines while putting the beloved horse through his paces. It didn't take long before the talented duo was making quite a name for themselves in the equestrian world.

For the next two years, they competed at 'The Ekka' – something both of them had been working up to since the spirited Arab had come into her care. The pair made a striking picture sailing over the jumps, even managing to pick up several ribbons on their last outing. Now one of her bedroom walls was covered with the colourful awards.

A celluloid doll dressed in a sequinned tutu-style dress still hung in pride of place amongst these new additions. It was the one Adam had purchased on her first visit to the annual Brisbane carnival when she was an exuberant four-year-old. The sparkling costume was faded now and the cupid-style face had lost its sheen, but she didn't have the heart to part with the cherished memento, even though a few close friends made fun of her with typical adolescent teasing. The old doll held too many fond memories of special times with the only father she had ever known to merely toss it away in the bin.

Lara had been just as fortunate when it came time to transition back into her previous career. All it took was a quick visit to David's office to explain her plans of cutting back on performing for the position to be hers again. Much to her relief, he even agreed to the same part-time hours, along with extra time off when the need arose to travel interstate to meet any short-term singing commitments.

She was in demand at several of the more famous clubs and venues around the city, often with bookings made several months ahead. Most gigs only ran on Friday and Saturday nights and fitted in perfectly with her editing workload, along with any time spent with Nikki. When word got around she was now based in Brisbane, several of the larger clubs on the Gold and Sunshine Coasts, including the glitzy Jupiters Casino, soon came calling. This meant loyal fans still enjoyed easy access to her talent.

Throughout the years, Max had been able to organise one-off concerts ... sometimes at interstate venues but more regularly in QPAC's Concert Hall, one of the most sought-after locations in the vast theatre complex. She enjoyed the thrill of standing once again on a stage in a first-class auditorium with its exceptional acoustics highlighting her exquisite voice. Lara had no regrets for having made the decision to give up touring, although whenever her one-woman show was booked in any of the smaller clubs, she missed the captivating atmosphere of working with the best orchestras. They offered that certain thrill only possible when a gamut of finely tuned instruments brought forth their unique sound.

Local papers and theatre magazines often displayed her picture when advertising any of these events and Adam had a subscription to each one as a way to fulfil his hunger to keep abreast with all her activities. Just the sight of them brought back that unquenchable longing ... but he didn't mind. They were the only times he felt truly alive. Even a small glimpse of her smile fed his starved spirit ... though he still kept true to that long-ago vow and stayed far away from the venues themselves.

Lucy had become her rock over the years and their friendship was as strong as ever. With Lara now living permanently in Brisbane, the friends were able to spend a lot more time together, and Lucy was a regular at all of Lara's shows. In an effort to turn matchmaker, whenever she could talk Jeff into coming along too, he soon found himself being badgered into bringing along a single mate. Much to his wife's disappointment – and frustration – Lara never gave any of these would-be-suitors the slightest hint of encouragement. Her heart still belonged to another and she knew it would be unfair to string anyone along.

Two years had passed since Jeff had asked Lucy to marry him. A few months later, they chose the City Botanical Gardens for the moving ceremony, with Lara and Nikki in the roles of matron-of-honour and junior bridesmaid. The mother and daughter were ecstatic to be included in the celebration. To Jeff's immense relief, Adam was involved in a big show interstate at the time, so there was no need to ask him to take on the role of best man. The busy star had always kept his vow to stay away from Lara, although the bride-to-be still gave her fiancé strict instructions not to give his best friend even a hint about who was in the bridal party. She was worried the temptation may have been too great for Adam to have his understudy take over for the weekend. The two men were still close friends, and Jeff always made sure any of their social interaction was far removed from wherever Lara might be.

The newlyweds were heavily involved in the same small theatre group. If her busy calendar permitted, Lara made sure she rocked up to the latest opening night to support them. Paul still maintained his directing mantle, and both he and the rest of the original cast were quick to welcome her back into their midst at any of the after-parties.

The two women shared loads of common interests, as well as an intimate secret close to both their hearts, although Lara had forbidden Lucy to ever raise that subject. Just the sound of his name was enough to bring back that old familiar ache. Her earlier unquenchable hunger for even the slightest whisper during those first few lonely years had been replaced with a determined effort to keep him out of any conversation.

The pain had never gone away. Instead, it lay dormant ... persistently lurking deep within her spirit. As soon as something reminded her of days overflowing with laughter and nights filled with sensual lovemaking, waves of memories came rushing in too ... and so would the longing.

Despite all of Lara's protests, Lucy still found every now and then it was almost as though she needed to feed her misery – like a drug continually drawing her back. Whenever these melancholy moods crept in, Lucy's phone would inevitably ring with an invitation to drop by. Then, with a box of tissues stuffed between them, the best friends curled up on either end of the sofa, watching videos of old movies with rivers of tears streaming down their cheeks. Most of the storylines were centred around heartbroken lovers, and Lucy would often glance across and catch a look of wretchedness in the other one's eyes ... and yet, in spite of this self-inflicted agony, Lara still came back for more. *Casablanca* and *Gone with the Wind* were two of her favourites, along with a few others she seemed drawn to several times each year.

During the winter of Nikki's second last year of high school, the teenager was away at a school camp when Lara felt that old maudlin feeling coming on. A telephone in a nearby suburb was answered on the third ring.

"Hey, Luce, the Munchkin's away for the weekend so how about a movie night?"

"Sure, I can grab a couple on the way to save you going out. Anything special you want to see?"

"Nuh, I'll leave it up to you. Just make sure they have *lots* of romance and the hero's good looking!"

"Okey-dokey, I'll be there shortly. And have the popcorn ready! I only had a light dinner 'cause Jeff's out."

It wasn't long before they were curled up in their usual spots on the sofa, a big bowl of buttery popcorn balancing between them and two cups of steaming hot chocolate in their hands.

"So which ones did you choose? They'd better be good, 'cause I'm in the mood for something soppy."

"Well, *what* a surprise! Don't worry, I brought a few – I can always come back tomorrow if we don't finish them all tonight," Lucy laughed, handing over a pile of four videos.

Lara glanced through the offerings. "*While You Were Sleeping* – yep, great movie, and the best scene ever around a dinner table – cracks me up every time! *Sleepless in Seattle* – yeah, I like that one. Reminds me of another old favourite and a bit of a tearjerker, though I'm really in the mood for something more tragic..."

Lucy rolled her eyes and shook her head in amusement. "Keep looking, I was pretty sure you'd want some sort of heartbreak so the other two'll probably suit you better."

"Oh, *An Affair To Remember* – there you go! One of my all-time favourites – great actors with a shipboard romance *and* a tragedy ... and..." With a quick glance, she tossed the next video onto the coffee table, making sure it landed face down. "Nuh, don't wanna watch that one..."

Lara felt as if her heart had stopped cold ... then it started up again, thumping so loudly she was sure her best mate could hear.

"What's the matter? Come on, Lars, this is *exactly* your kinda film – spectacular scenery, a good-looking hero with the softest of hearts and a heroine even sporting *your* name ... plus the reviews all say the ending's one of the saddest of all! It's just our cup o' tea!"

"No, I still don't want to see it." There was a rigid determination in her friend's voice, and Lucy was puzzled.

"Ooohhh, come on! I've always wanted to see this one. It's Omar *Sharif* – who'd pass up an opportunity to see him gracing the screen ... those gorgeous brown eyes just make me melt. Besides, I heard Julie Christie's absolutely perfect as his lover!"

But Lara wouldn't budge. "No, Luce, I told you I don't want to see it. Come on. Let's watch *An Affair to Remember* again. I know you like Cary Grant."

Lucy had no idea her friend had already seen the tragic story, which in so many ways mirrored her own. Lara's mind went back to a hotel suite in Sydney lying in the arms of the man she adored. Nothing could persuade her to face that level of heartbreak again. Having to watch *Yury Zhivago* frantically reaching out to his beloved after so many years apart, only to have him collapse on a frost-laden Moscow street, was something she couldn't even contemplate. Doing so would evoke too many memories of the times she had longed to reach out to Adam and then had to stop herself. She still cared too much to risk almost destroying his marriage again because of her selfish desires.

Though she would never admit it, deep down there was one more reason she vowed never to see him again – she was actually too scared to jeopardise his life in case the fiction became real and he was taken from her forever.

They ended up watching *Sleepless in Seattle* and finished with *An Affair to Remember,* despite Lucy trying several times to change her mind.

"Thanks for tonight, Lars, and I'll be back tomorrow arvo to watch the other *two!*" she emphasised, tossing another soggy tissue onto the pile already heaped in the wastepaper bin wedged between them.

Lara's only response was a mumbled, "We'll see," as she blew her nose and saw her friend to the door.

The moment Lucy's red taillights disappeared down the street, Lara locked herself in the bedroom. Then, as though cauterising a festering wound, she took out the well-worn albums of those never-forgotten times ... her fingers lingering on the image of a man whose much-loved smile once again brought light into her world.

And a little while later, those same laughing eyes became part of her dreams.

They never did get around to watching *Doctor Zhivago* when Lucy dropped by the next day. At the video store on her way home, only three movies found their way into the returns box. Later that night and with tears pouring down her cheeks, Lucy finally understood why her best friend couldn't stomach revisiting the tragic storyline.

§

The dawning of the new millennium passed without any of the disasters experts predicted – no critical computers crashed and the world was still intact. Lara and Nikki joined Suzie and Ben when they flew to Sydney, eager to take part in the once-in-a-lifetime celebrations for this memorable anniversary. Their apartment was right on the waterfront, overlooking the Harbour Bridge and Opera House where most of the festivities were to occur.

Just before midnight, the family group was out on the balcony, sipping flutes of champagne and looking out to the harbour now swarming with small craft. Even Nikki was allowed to partake in a small glass, though most of its contents were pure orange juice after her mother's strict warning this was definitely a one-off seeing she had just turned sixteen. Every vantage point around the shoreline swarmed with hundreds of thousands of people waiting for the show to begin.

Then the chant rang out, "Ten, nine, eight, seven, six, five, four, three, two, one..."

To the accompaniment of a loud burst of music, the prominent bridge came to life with a dazzling display of lights. At first, a large smiling face was the centrepiece, until the word *Eternity* took its place as thousands of colourful fireworks filled the night sky from all corners of the cityscape. The music medley blared across the water, adding an extra dimension of excitement to the blazing scene. The pyrotechnics were so loud they almost had to put their hands over their ears, still the thrill of being there more than compensated for the discomfort. The dark expanse of water glimmered with multi-coloured reflections and the dappled hues stained the onlookers' faces, giving the impression they were off to a fabulous masked ball.

Cries of "Happy New Year" echoed from every corner of the watery arena. As Lara looked up into the sky beyond the spectacle, she spied the distinctive shape of a half-moon. A lopsided grin gave the impression it was smiling down on her alone. Everyone else was so involved with the celebrations, they didn't even notice its silvery glow.

With her eyes firmly fixed on this intermittent visitor, the distinctive silhouette reminded Lara of her own life. The finest half – her guiding light – was hidden somewhere in the earth's shadow ... and similar to this half-formed entity, her smile had a large portion missing.

From the treasure-trove locked away in her heart, a silent message went out to the heavens.

Happy New Year, Teddy ... wherever you are. Somewhere out there this half-faced fellow is shining down on you, too. I'm not so sure I want to say goodbye to the twentieth century ... it's where we once belonged, even if it was only for a brief space of time. I really don't want to go into a new century where there will be no memories of us...

Two small tears rolled down her cheeks. As if on cue, a blaze of red fireworks lit up the night sky. The reflections touched her face and made it appear as though she was crying tears of blood. They matched her mood as her heart broke into tiny pieces all over again.

Oh, Lord, I really need your help to face another new year alone. If it's at all possible, please make the yearning go away. I'm not sure how much longer I can ignore this constant ache. And please keep him safe as he walks this earth...

Later, while lying in bed and hearing the clock chime three, Lara wondered whether Adam had thought to look back into the past to remember what they had once shared ... or if, out of necessity, he had been able to put her out of his heart once and for all.

§

In a hotel room on the other side of the country, the man dominating Lara's thoughts stood at the window looking out over the Swan River. With daylight saving and the two-hour time difference, Perth was three hours behind the Sydney celebrations.

As midnight ticked over, a chorus of chimes rang out from the brand-new glass bell tower built especially for this momentous occasion. The reverberating sound matched the pounding of his heart as it beat a requiem for all he had lost.

While Lara was contemplating whether she had been relegated to his past, Adam's spirit was looking off into the future – picturing her by his side. This was the only way he could face walking into the new millennium, and the only dream left to him if he was to live with the loneliness.

I'll never give up this endless hope, Father, no matter how impossible it may seem. Somehow, I have to trust you to see us through all this until she's mine again. I love her too much to let her go completely. Until then, please take care of her for me.

§

While out in a realm too far removed from human understanding, a pair of gentle hands gathered in the silken whispers of those heartfelt kindred pleas, spinning them into strands that then entwined around one another, until eventually they blended as one.

Reaching into a jewel-encrusted treasure-chest sitting beside a well-worn workbench, with intricate care these Instruments of Creativity selected a small shuttle and started to wrap the thread over and under, over and under, over and under for safekeeping until they formed a perfect spool.

Then with infinite care, the Master Craftsman placed the tiny gilt frame with its precious cargo back inside, where it lay nestled in a secret holding chamber.

Sending a tender smile out into Infinity, he formed a whisper, "All things are possible to those who believe..."

Chapter 27

By the end of January, Nikki was about to commence her final year of high school. Lara had never regretted her decision to virtually put her career on hold to settle in Brisbane for this vital period of her daughter's education.

Ever since their holiday in Italy when she was a four-year-old, the Latin mannerisms and culture had been in the young girl's blood. When Italian was offered as one of the language choices in Year Eight, her mother wasn't at all surprised to find the expressive vernacular at the top of Nikki's subject list. One other must-have course was drama, and she had consistently won lead roles in the plays and musicals that were a regular part of the school's extra-curricular activities. Sometimes she was able to combine both subjects and Lara was a willing witness to many an impromptu performance while she practised her parts.

Nikki's inaugural language lesson during her first year of high school was one of the more memorable events from those early days. The following morning Lara was in the kitchen making breakfast when the bubbly young teenager rushed from her bedroom, still struggling to fasten the compulsory school tie as she dropped a quick kiss on her mother's cheek.

"*Buongiorno, mamma, sei bellissima!*"

"And *buongiorno* to you, my little Italian *principessa* ... and you look *bellissima*, too!" Catching the surprised look on her daughter's face, Lara added with a fond smile, "Don't forget I've been there, too. Even though I may not be able to remember much Italian, there are some words I haven't forgotten!"

Out of the mists of time, she had a flash of another occasion when this same little girl had pronounced the word of greeting so carefully. Nikki's cute retort had sent both Adam and her into astonished chuckles – but that was a long time ago, and Lara had promised herself not to revisit any of those places anymore.

You'd better get used to this for the next few years, she warned herself tersely.

So the first year flew by ... then another and another. Soon the Italian phrases became far too complicated for Lara to decipher. Even so, she enjoyed hearing the progress her daughter was making in the language she loved so much.

§

When the second semester rolled around for Nikki's final year, two of her teachers recommended she represent the school on an Italian drama exchange program for six weeks. Every report card showed she was excelling at both the passionate lingo and her drama classes, so when the offer for the most deserving student came up, her name was the natural choice.

At first, Lara was reluctant to grant her permission as it seemed such a long way away and too long a time for an impressionable sixteen-year-old girl to travel to a foreign country virtually on her own. Then a call came from the principal with assurances Nikki would always have someone with her. After many hours of soul searching, she finally gave her blessing – although, for the entire visit, a host of petitions were sent Heavenwards for her daughter's safety.

A family in Rome agreed to billet the teenager so she could attend the famous *Accademia Nazionale Di Arte Drammatica* in the inner north of the city. There she would learn all the necessary elements of musical and dramatic theatre while gaining an even better understanding of the romantic language. When news came that the hosts' eighteen-year-old daughter attended the same academy, it helped to ease the anxious mother's concerns.

At the airport, Nikki couldn't keep still. Lara was just as excited thinking of all the fabulous opportunities this could open up for her talented offspring ... until it came time to say goodbye and the realisation hit just how much she would miss having her around and how lonely it would be living by herself for six long weeks. Making a determined effort, she ensured a beaming smile was the last thing Nikki saw before boarding the plane.

Every day she was away, Nikki filled reams of pages in her journal, detailing every moment of the exciting adventure. It was only natural she had picked up many of her mother's hobbies and traits over time, and this was one of them.

Whenever she and Lucia weren't at the academy, the two young women explored the streets of the fascinating city – visiting many of the places Nikki had only read about in history lessons. The Colosseum sent her heart racing when they climbed the steep stone staircases then looked out over the vast arena where so much bloodshed had occurred. She was astounded and even morbidly fascinated by the size of the chambers that had once housed hundreds of animals, gladiators and Christians as they awaited their fate. Yet the truth of their destiny was also a sobering reminder of the barbaric practices humankind could sometimes inflict on one another – often in the name of sport.

The impressive Roman Forum just across the way was a fascinating journey through the ages. During the course of her stay, the girls returned many times to spend hours wandering its ancient paths. On a few occasions, they even gave spontaneous mini-performances of their most recent class assignments under the imposing Arch of Titus, much to the amusement of other tourists. Some even threw a few coins for their trouble, and both Nikki and Lucia gave appreciative bows to these new and enthusiastic supporters.

As a going-away present, Charles had presented his would-be granddaughter with one of the new digital cameras beginning to flood the market, and this became another trusty companion wherever she went. Her daily journal was soon filled with images from each of these jaunts.

On her last weekend in the historic city, the now good friends made their way to the breathtaking Trevi Fountain. Nikki's coin soon joined a carpet of others on the watery floor of the magnificent work of art as she offered up the customary wish of coming back again one day. The famous site had been on her list of must-dos right from the start, however with daily lessons and other places to explore, it was the first time she had found time to visit this section of the city.

As she turned to go, an image of a man popped into her mind from when she was a little girl. It brought with it a flood of memories of a sad farewell at a theatre in Melbourne after watching her favourite show come to life on a stage for the first time.

Well, I did get the chance to visit Europe again, Uncle Adam, but only to Italy instead of Austria the way I'd hoped. I just wish you and Mum could've come along to share it all with me. She still thinks about you all the time, even though she never mentions your name ... and her eyes give away how much she still cares whenever she looks at that old picture of you taken under the arch at Cortona. I still miss the way you always made me laugh. I really hope you're enjoying life with Trina – you certainly deserve it after the great times you gave us. I just wish I knew what we did to make you leave...

Now it was starting to make sense why his answer had been so obscure. Back then, she had been too young to realise why they couldn't return to Salzburg together. It wasn't until a few years after the visit to Melbourne with his parents that she first learned he and Trina were married – she had seen their photos along with detailed captions in several of her mother's magazines. Nikki could also recall a memory of Aunty Elizabeth saying something about Trina being a sick friend he had to look after when they flew down to see him in the iconic musical.

Surprisingly, the young woman felt a sudden pang in her heart, realising just how much she still missed him. For the first time, she was able to grasp a little of just how heartbreaking it must have been for her mother. Lara had never told her the whole story, except to say something had happened and it meant they couldn't see him anymore even though Adam loved them both very much.

Nikki still caught glimpses of an unexplained sadness lurking in her mother's eyes whenever she thought no one was looking, and she still couldn't fathom why he had ended up marrying Trina instead of her. It was obvious from their responses during those two accidental meetings in Sydney just how much they still loved each other. Thinking back, she felt certain there was far more to their story than her mother had ever let on.

One day I'm going to find out...

§

Within a few short months, the beginning of December rolled around. The little cottage was abuzz with excitement as the mother and daughter prepared to celebrate Nikki's final Awards Night. Earlier in the week, a letter had arrived from the principal's office suggesting Lara should invite family and close friends along, with the added proviso Nikki wasn't to know anything about the strange request. Of course, Elizabeth and Charles wouldn't have missed it – they had been to every major event in her young life and clapped louder than anyone whenever her name was read out for some form of recognition. Hurried phone calls were made to Suzie and Lucy. In turn, promises were given they would be there to lend their support, and with Ben and Jeff in tow. Everyone was intrigued to find out what was going on.

Nikki donned her school uniform for the final time. When she came out of her bedroom, Lara's eyes filled with tears ... both from a heart filled with pride and sadness at saying goodbye to this phase of her life. Her little girl had grown into a highly accomplished young woman, and she couldn't help wondering where all the years had gone. Nearly twelve years prior, another round of tears had fallen when it was necessary to leave her young child at a school gate to face a new chapter in her life. Now they were about to face even bigger challenges.

Due to the high grades she always achieved in her Speech and Drama course, Nikki had just received word of her acceptance into the National Institute of Dramatic Arts, one of the most prestigious performing arts institutes in the country. This meant she would be taking off for Sydney in February for three years of intense study. Her pure sweet voice had been a significant factor in the offer of a place at NIDA and Lara couldn't have been prouder. Only those in the top echelon of their field from around the country were ever accepted.

The only drawback was it also meant her precious daughter was about to leave home. After that, their only chance to see each other would be during semester breaks or if Lara visited the southern city for a concert or short weekend away. It would be lonely not having the bubbly teenager around, and she wasn't looking forward to trying to find ways to fill up any spare time by herself when the pair had always done things together.

Nikki's biggest regret was leaving her beloved Jasper behind. The institute was located near the centre of the city, and she was staying at a boarding house nearby. With land at a premium, it meant there was nowhere close enough to stable a horse. Charles promised to take good care of him, while she vowed to keep up their training whenever she could find time to fly home for the weekend.

The mother and daughter were just about to leave for the ceremony when

Lara couldn't resist and pulled her only child into a tight motherly hug.

"I'm so very proud of you, Munchkin. You've put in so much hard work over the years ... and without one complaint I might add, even when I had you traipsing all over the countryside *and* dragged you away from all your friends for months at a time. No mother could ever be prouder than I am tonight!"

Nikki ducked her head and burrowed in close. She was embarrassed to be on the receiving end of so much praise and turned a deep shade of pink. "Oh Mum, I never felt like I was missing out. It was so much fun being with you – look at all the incredible places we got to visit and all those talented people we met along the way. If it wasn't for your career, I don't think I would've worked so hard to get into acting school. From the moment I first saw you on stage in *Show Boat*, I knew that's what I wanted to do when I grew up."

"See, it's because of such a great attitude and determination you've been accepted into one of the finest acting schools in the country! You're a true champion, and I love you with all my heart."

Blushing profusely as the compliments kept coming, Nikki landed a quick peck on her mother's cheek with a bashful laugh. "Thanks, Mum, I love you too, but come on, we'd better get going ... the others'll be waiting."

Lara couldn't resist and quickly pulled her much-loved daughter into her arms again for one last 'schoolgirl' hug. She had always been sentimental and tonight was one of those momentous occasions they would never experience again. "Okay, but I want you to have a wonderful time tonight seeing this is your last one."

"I will! Now let's get outta here!"

"Okay, but hang on, have you got everything?"

Nikki looked around and then let out a frustrated groan, "Oh blast, I forgot my blazer!" She rushed back into the bedroom while Lara shook her head with a knowing smirk.

"How on earth are you going to get on in Sydney when you don't have me to look after you!"

"Ooohhh, Muuummm ... I'll be fine! Come on!"

§

Nikki was right. The others were waiting ... right in front of the entrance to the school auditorium. Mum and daughter were still a few metres away when Suzie ran up to them with her arms outstretched. Grabbing Nikki around the waist, she swung her in a big circle so the teenager's legs went flying in all directions, and so did her hair.

"Here's my favourite girl! We thought you were *never* coming."

"Aunty *Suze*, not *here!* Everyone's *watching! Gee,* you're as bad as Mum!" Nikki rolled her eyes in mock disgust and tried to squirm out from under her aunt's arms.

Several schoolmates standing nearby sniggered amongst themselves, although most were used to seeing such open displays of affection at these sorts of occasions whenever Nikki's family was around. Some were even a little jealous, only they would never admit it.

After warm hugs of congratulations and affirmations from the rest of Nikki's tight-knit supporters, similar to those offered by her mother before leaving home, the excited group made their way to the seating area reserved for parents and friends. Nikki's place was with the rest of her peers towards the front.

With one last kiss for her mother, along with a hurried, "Love you, see ya later," she hurried off to join her friends.

The auditorium resonated with excitement and rousing cheers as surprised recipients were called up to receive their awards. Only two large trophies remained on the table when the Head of Arts came to the stage.

Holding out the largest one so the entire assembly could see the gilt-encrusted mould of Comedy/Tragedy Masks recognised in theatrical circles, her face beamed as she readied herself for this important speech.

"Tonight is a very special occasion for one of our students. The recipient of this award has consistently received Very High Achievements for each of her assessments since joining my Drama class four years ago. She has been one of the major leads in all of our plays and musicals, along with a long-standing involvement with the school Concert Band since eighth grade. In addition, as lead vocalist in the School Choir, this young woman has performed countless solos and formed part of the smaller Vocal Ensemble."

Nikki started to slink down in her seat when she recognised the familiar activities and achievements, fervently wishing the teacher would stop ... but without any luck.

"Well-liked and respected in the school grounds by her peers, and an absolute pleasure to teach in the classroom, the college's inaugural *Outstanding Contribution to the Arts Award*, along with a cheque for six thousand dollars kindly donated by one of our major sponsors to be put towards her college fees at NIDA, is awarded to ... *Nikki Jennings!*"

Piercing whistles, loud cheers and rousing applause echoed around the large auditorium. All the while, the young recipient stayed slouched in her seat, too stunned to move. Nikki had no idea she was even up for an award, let alone one with so much prestige. Learning about the huge cheque accompanying the trophy was all too much for her to comprehend.

Several of her classmates had to physically push her out of the seat. She made her way to the stage, head down and her face the colour of a tomato. At any other time, she relished being in front of an audience ... but only when clad in another character's persona. Similar to her mother, without the safety of anonymity, Nikki was decidedly uncomfortable with this amount of attention in front of a large crowd.

Lara was already on her feet, applauding loudly with a beaming smile. Her face was awash with tears of pride when the rest of her family and friends jumped up to join in. Clutching the trophy in trembling hands, Nikki looked down through the sea of faces until her gaze alighted on her mother. Her self-conscious smile was worth all the sacrifices Lara had made to ensure she received the best education possible. Not once had she ever regretted putting Nikki's needs first, and her expression reflected the many years of joy the young girl had given her.

From out of the corner of her eye, Nikki noticed a tall dark-haired man standing at the back of the auditorium. He appeared to be clapping just as enthusiastically as those in her personal cheer squad. The encroaching shadows obscured his face, although there was something strangely familiar about his stance. It was too hard to make out any of the stranger's features, and with all the excitement he was soon forgotten when she went back to her seat for the presentation of *Dux of the School*.

As soon as the official ceremony was over Nikki made her way over to where Lara and the others were standing, the heavy trophy and envelope containing the cheque clasped tightly in her hands. So many people kept slapping her on the back or stopping to offer their congratulations, it took several minutes to reach the family.

Warm congratulatory hugs and excited words of encouragement soon swallowed the besieged teen up when she finally reached them. Lara was happy to wait her turn, watching on with pride oozing from her eyes as the new graduate received all this well-deserved acclaim from those she loved the most. After spending so many nights helping Nikki rehearse her lines for the many roles she had played over the years, to see all her hard work rewarded in this way was the best feeling of all.

Once they were face to face, no words were necessary. Lara wrapped her arms around her precious offspring who was a replica of herself at the same age – a young woman who adored singing and acting and horses in that order. Even their hair was of a similar length again, with Nikki recently having all her long tresses cut to just below her shoulders in the same casual style.

They held each other tightly. "Thanks, Mum ... for everything!"

"Oh sweetheart, I'm so very proud of you. You've been a thorough delight to raise, and I've had the greatest joy being your mum ... you've worked so hard for this – well done!" Her hands cradled Nikki's face as she kissed the tip of her nose ... while a loving smile conveyed every bit of emotion welling up inside.

Deep in the shadows at the rear of the hall, a pair of dark eyes followed every nuance and shared emotion during the tender exchange ... a father-like expression of pride laced with a twinge of longing reflected in their depths.

You did it, Munchkin! You're a star in the making. Just as your mother and I predicted whenever we heard you singing to Annabelle, even though you were only a little tot at the time. No father could ever be prouder!

Tonight's ceremony brought an end to all those annual pilgrimages, and his heart was heavy wondering if he would ever see her again, even if only from a distance. With a farewell dip of his head and a heartfelt grimace of regret, Adam slipped quietly out of a side door before anyone could recognise him ... though not without taking one last glance back to where the only future he had ever wanted stood with their arms wrapped tightly around one another.

Afterwards, Charles and Elizabeth threw a party at their home to celebrate the happy occasion. Standing on the porch while greeting their guests, the pair exchanged sorrowful looks. They were both picturing the shadow of their son standing up the back of the auditorium and then watching him leave alone. Their second greatest wish was to have him there sharing in this special celebration. Number one stayed locked away as always – in a pair of hearts that for years had beat in unison with the same desire to see two lovers reunited.

A host of Nikki's schoolmates were there too. The giggling bunch had a wonderful time dancing on the floodlit lawn to a local band, while their families stood around chatting on the terrace. It was the perfect way for the hardworking graduates to let their hair down and Nikki was a picture of happiness as she danced the night away. It did Lara's heart good to see her daughter enjoying herself before it was time to spread her wings and fly to a brand-new destiny.

§

The next day Lara went up to the school to pay any outstanding fees. There was a spring in her step as she made her way to the office, knowing one considerable ongoing payment would soon be gone for good.

The college had a fine reputation with excellent staff and teaching methods and was renowned as one of the best in town. Unfortunately, this also meant it incurred rather high fees. Because of this, Lara sometimes had to do a bit of a juggling act when other major bills arrived in the post. Good budgeting skills learned from her mother's example helped to pay them on time, especially when there had never been any support offered from Nikki's biological father.

The unexpected bonus from the previous night's ceremony meant any further worries about meeting her daughter's first two years of tuition fees in Sydney was no longer an issue. The scholarship was a godsend, and while she was up there paying off the final amount, Lara wanted to thank the Head of Arts for her generosity at the same time.

As fate would have it, Mrs Baker was just coming out of the principal's office when Lara arrived. This meant she was able to speak to her before proceeding to the bursar's window. The teacher had also been a major spokesperson in choosing Nikki for the study visit to Italy earlier in the year, so she wanted to thank her for that opportunity as well.

"Excuse me, Mrs Baker, could I have a quick chat with you, please?"

"Of course, Mrs Jennings," the teacher replied with a smile, gesturing to a quiet corner.

"I just wanted to thank you for all you've done to encourage Nikki's love of music and drama. If it wasn't for your input, I'm sure she would never have been accepted into NIDA."

"What a kind thing to say, but I can assure you it had nothing to do with me. Nikki did it all by herself. She's such a talented student, any teacher worth their salt would've done the same thing. It's been a pleasure having her in my class, and I'm certainly going to miss her."

"Well, it was your passion that helped to bring it out, I'm sure. Oh, and I also wanted to thank you for that generous cheque. You've no idea how much it means for her move to Sydney. I wasn't quite sure how I was going to afford the fees as well as all her accommodation and meals, along with everything else she'll need down there. Having this boost has taken a huge weight off my shoulders. I can't thank you enough for what it means to both of us."

The entire faculty knew Nikki was from a single-parent family. Though Lara was a successful singer, they were also aware she had walked away from a lucrative theatrical career to put her daughter first. Her salary as a part-time assistant editor was nothing compared to what she would have received had she remained on the stage, and any musical gigs didn't pay very much because of their irregular nature and smaller audiences. A fair chunk of her income went into paying for Nikki's schooling, along with a long list of singing, music and dance lessons, not to mention an ongoing mortgage payment on the cottage.

Mrs Baker patted Lara's arm affectionately. "You're very kind, but actually the school didn't contribute to the scholarship at all. It came from a major sponsor who heard about the award and wanted to give the recipient an incentive to continue with their preferred career path. I have no idea who it was – none of us does – only the Board. I'm so pleased it will help to ease the burden."

"Oh my goodness … how very generous of them! If you ever do find out who it is, please tell them how grateful I am."

"Of course, and I can't wait to hear about Nikki's accomplishments further down the track. Oh, and all the best as you continue with your career as well. Talent obviously runs in the family." She looked at her watch. "I'm sorry, but I have another appointment so I'll have to go. 'Bye, Mrs Jennings."

Lara offered one final smile and a grateful wave as the teacher hurried away.

Watching her go, she mulled over this unexpected news and then shrugged her shoulders. *Well, whoever you are, I sure owe you a big thank you.*

There was only one thing left to do so she made her way to the bursar's window. Taking a chequebook out of her bag, Lara peered through the gap. "'Morning, Mrs Campbell, I'm here to pay the last of Nikki's fees, please."

"Of course, Mrs Jennings, it's good to see you again. Oh, and I hear big congratulations are in order after last night!"

"Yes, it was all so exciting! I'm still a bit overwhelmed – but what a welcome surprise! And I can't believe after twelve years this is the last time I'll ever have to do this. Sorry I'm a bit late paying this last bill. With all the excitement of the formal and then Awards Night, it completely slipped my mind."

The bursar smiled. "Oh, that's fine. I knew you were good for it."

"Normally I just pop a cheque in the post, but today I thought I'd drop by to thank you in person seeing I won't be coming this way again."

"I'm glad you did. It's nice being able to say goodbye to our parents rather than just having them disappear from our lives. And I remember that same feeling when my youngest left school – it certainly takes a load off, doesn't it?"

"It sure does, except when I first enrolled her, I was under the impression the fees were going to be a lot higher. Rather than being a huge shock to the system, I've been pleasantly surprised when a new bill arrived at the end of each term. How *has* the school managed to keep them at such a manageable rate compared to other private schools for all these years, especially with the quality of education on offer?"

The bursar's brow furrowed. "Ummm … I'm not quite sure what you mean."

"Well, they've only ever gone up a small amount each year, and from the outset, each invoice has come as a pleasant surprise – far less than I was expecting when I first looked into sending her here. I understand the government offers a considerable grant each year, but I expected the fees would've increased a whole lot more by now. To be honest, if they'd gone up too much, there's no way I could've afforded to keep her here. This place has been a godsend and the staff so supportive – I'm so glad there was no need to enrol her elsewhere."

An even deeper frown accompanied the other woman's reply, and her tone was quizzical. "We *are* quite expensive compared to other schools, and there's always been an increase of a *certain* percentage each year. Of course, with you being away so often when Nikki was in primary school, the fees weren't too steep during that time – I remember we tried to keep them on a par with the amount of time she actually spent in class. Besides, Mr Peters has always been prompt with his payments, so we knew there was no need to worry about you paying the balance on time. To be honest, all of our accounting staff have been a little bit envious when his portion was always paid in full long before it was time to send out your invoice with the outstanding balance."

Lara's mouth fell open with both astonishment and despair. "What do you mean? I don't understand! *I've* always paid her fees, not Mr Peters."

The bursar gasped, and her hand flew to her mouth. "Oh, I'm so sorry, Mrs Jennings, I thought you knew! Mr Peters has been paying more than half of Nikki's account each term from when she first started school. I can still remember him coming in to see me on her very first day, explaining in detail how he wanted to help because of you being a single mum. In fact, he stressed we were to bill him first and only include the balance owing on the account we sent out to you. I remember thinking it was a bit of a strange request at the time ... but who was I to question him when it was obvious you were very close friends. When Nikki was little, she would often go on about the things you all got up to during that wonderful trip you took to Europe."

Lara was mortified, firstly over the news about the payments and now anticipating the entire school faculty had known about their story all this time. "Oh, I don't know what she told you but—"

"Oh, don't worry. We all guessed it was a business trip when she mentioned you and Mr Peters sang together in Salzburg – what an amazing experience! The concert halls over there are spectacular – they have the best acoustics from what I've heard. How exciting to be invited to perform!"

Lara was so shocked she couldn't answer. Both her knuckles and face had turned white as she tried to take everything in.

Mrs Campbell was dismayed to learn she had just let the cat out of the bag. "Oh, Mrs Jennings, I truly *am* sorry. I was sure you would've known what was going on." She placed her hand over Lara's and added with a light-hearted grin, "But half your luck. I wish I'd had someone willing to be so generous when my kids were here. I'd be a rich woman by now!"

Oh Adam, what have you done? Why didn't you tell me when we were in Sydney? If I'd known, I would've stopped you. Nikki wasn't supposed to be your responsibility ... she was mine!

All manner of thoughts kept tumbling over and over in Lara's mind.

Thank goodness, the staff thought we were there to sing professionally rather than realising how close we were back then. Nikki and her big mouth! They must've presumed she meant we put on actual performances rather than those impromptu ones!

Even so, it was the first piece of news that caused Lara the most distress. Her head shook in denial as she tried to take it all in.

"But that can't be right. How could you have agreed without consulting me?"

"I'm so sorry, I would've said something if I thought there was anything amiss. We honestly had no idea, but it might be best to look at it this way – the fact he wanted to help proves how much he cares about the two of you."

Her heart raced at the truth behind that innocent comment, but she couldn't dwell there. "Can I please see all the accounts then, to check the true figures?"

When the bursar turned the computer screen around, to Lara's dismay every third line of the running total had a large amount with the name *Adam Peters* in the payer column.

"*Heavens!* I had no *idea!* And you say he's been paying this since the very first semester?"

"Mmm, right from the outset."

"It's no wonder I couldn't understand when I received the first bill in the mail. I thought I must've read the fee structure wrong in the welcome package. I only wish you'd told me ... I would've asked him to stop."

"I truly am sorry ... I really thought you knew. Mr Peters was adamant you were close friends, and I was under the impression you were well aware of the arrangement. I just presumed it was a private agreement between the two of you, which is why I never mentioned it ... I didn't think it was any of my business."

Lara had recovered enough to respond with an apologetic smile. "It's not your fault – please don't feel bad. I just feel terrible having had the benefit of his generosity all these years without knowing anything about it."

She handed over the final cheque, wondering how she could ever make it up to him, and offering a last word of thanks as she stuffed the receipt in her bag.

All the way home, Lara kept going over everything the bursar had told her.

Oh, Teddy, no matter how many years pass, you still manage to knock the breath out of me over and over again.

Her eyes kept misting over, and she had to slow down to avoid a few close shaves with other cars or pedestrians on the busy roads. Fumbling with the front latch, she eventually burst through the door and quickly pulled the phone's handset from the wall. Frantic fingers punched out a well-known number.

There was no thought given to any of the usual pleasantries, and her first words were curt. "Did you know about the school fees, Elizabeth?"

The woman on the other end of the line felt her heart sink. Both she and Charles had breathed a huge sigh of relief only the day before, thinking they were finally home free after so many years of subterfuge.

Her answer was soft and filled with pain. "Yes, I did, my dear."

"Why didn't you *tell* me? Why did you let me go on believing all these years that he'd let us go and was getting on with his life? I don't believe it ... *you* of *all* people! I *trusted* you ... and now it's obvious you betrayed me all along."

Elizabeth was heartbroken to hear the harshness in Lara's tone, but she could understand why. In all probability, she would have felt the same. "I'm so so sorry. I hated having to deceive you but – oh, my darling girl, I'm truly sor—

"How *could* you?"

"Dear Lara, all three of us only ever had your best interests at heart. You know how much Adam loved Nikki."

Through a swallowed sob, Lara replied, "I-I ... know he did."

"Well, that love has *never* diminished. Adam feels exactly the same way now as he did when she was a little girl. After what happened on that horrible New Year's night, he knew you'd be far too embarrassed to let him do anything to help ... that's why he went about it this way. He didn't want those high fees weighing you down."

"But I would've managed – I knew it wasn't going to be easy, but we would've been okay."

"Lara, you know his heart better than anyone. He just wanted to help ease your burden a bit by making sure Nikki received the standard of education you always wanted for her without having to sacrifice other things. It was simply his way of still being a small part of her life ... and yours..."

Hearing it all spelt out made Lara feel even worse. This was all her fault. If she hadn't insisted on sending Nikki to the exclusive school, none of this would have happened. Not to mention the guilt she now felt for all the sacrifices he had made, along with the secrets he was obviously still keeping from Trina.

When she didn't answer, Elizabeth pleaded, "You *have* to forgive him. He didn't do it to hurt you. Adam would rather die himself than cause you any more suffering. And he'd be mortified to learn you know about it. Promise me you'll *never* tell him."

"But I never expected him to pay for her ... I *have* to pay him back. I must owe him tens of thousands of dollars!"

"He *knows* you didn't expect anything from him, and paying him back is the last thing he'd want. This was his secret gift to the two of you. Just accept it for how it was meant – from someone who'll always care and just wanted to make your life a little bit easier ... nothing more. He never expected anything from you in return ... believe me. Besides, you know he's always had a generous soul. It's such a shame you found out – he'd be devastated to learn you're so upset."

The truth behind those words resounded in Lara's spirit. She knew how generous he was ... very well. She had been on the receiving end over and over again. Her left hand immediately went to the exquisite pendant still hanging around her neck. Like an extra reminder, she could feel the band of the expensive ring encircling her finger as she held the phone to her ear.

Still reeling from the revelations, her guard remained up. "Alright, I understand what you're saying, and I won't try to make amends, but please don't let him try anything like that again. You have to convince him I'm okay financially and we don't need his help. Next time you see him, please tell him about the cheque Nikki received last night; then he'll know we're okay."

The other woman didn't respond, and Lara could sense a layer of uneasiness travelling down the line.

"What is it, Elizabeth? What aren't you telling me *this* time?"

"I can't ... there were other promises made," came the soft, reluctant reply.

Lara's voice rose again. "*What* promises? *What* can't you tell me?" The silence was thick and impenetrable. "*Elizabeth* ... what *else* are you hiding?"

"Oh, Lara ... my dear girl, he knows about—"

"*What* does he know?"

"The cheque ... and the award."

For the third time in just over an hour, the younger woman felt as though she had been run over by a bus. All the fight went out of her and the blood drained from her face.

"What are you talking about? I know you can't have seen him ... how could he have heard what happened?" There was another long silence on the other end of the phone so Lara pushed further. "Did you ring him afterwards?"

A very loud sigh came down the line, and it was obvious Elizabeth was thinking about her reply. "No ... I haven't seen him, nor did I ring." She tried to ignore the increasing throbbing in her chest. "Lara dear ... he was there last night ... he saw Nikki receive her award."

"*No,* he wasn't. He *couldn't* have been! He's in Sydney for his new show. I read about the opening only a few weeks ago."

"He flew in last night, arriving just before the ceremony, and then he took the last plane out." Her voice was a whisper. "Just as he has every year."

Lara's knees went weak, and she sagged against the nearest wall. When an answer did eventuate, her tone was hushed and unbelieving, as though trying to get her head around this other massive landslide of deception. "*What?* He's *always* been there for Nikki's awards nights?" The stress placed on those two faint words conveyed her utter bewilderment.

"Yes, my darling girl ... every year without fail ... no matter what city he's been working in at the time. There's a clause in each of his contracts stating that if Nikki's award ceremony falls on a performance night, he's to have the night off and the understudy is to fill in."

The news echoed through Lara's mind as she tried to grasp its implications. "Oh, Elizabeth, I had no idea ... but in a way, it's just as well ... I never would've been able to cope knowing he was in the same room." Her heart was racing and her tone incredulous, "What if I'd run *into* him? It would've been agony pretending he meant nothing and then have to walk away all over again! He *promised* he wouldn't try to see me again."

"And he kept that promise ... he never tried to see you – in fact, he was determined you wouldn't even know he was there."

Lara could picture the scenario in her mind. *I know exactly why you kept it a secret, Teddy. You knew I could never keep my promise to stay away.*

His mother's voice was gentle, hoping to soothe her fears. "That's why I never told you. I didn't want you going through all that misery time after time, only to have to say goodbye again ... until the next year. He was just as determined to keep his distance to ensure you weren't hurt again – that's why he always stayed in the shadows up the back. Then he would slip out as soon as Nikki received her awards. He made it a point to always be there because he was so proud of her."

Lara's silence was an ominous omen of her continuing shock and disbelief.

There was no use hiding anything anymore, so Elizabeth readied herself for another onslaught as she continued. "He was fully aware of how well she was doing – the school sent copies of her report cards every term, along with the receipt for his payment."

"You've *got* to be joking. How much *more* is there?"

Elizabeth didn't respond, but instead took a different tack. "You must admit he had a lot to be proud of – there has been a heap of awards over the years!"

For the first time in the conversation, a faint smile crossed Lara's face. She looked across at the cabinet full of trophies, both from Nikki's studies and the equestrian circuit, on display in the living room. "Well, that's true. She has done very well." A wave of remorse rose up in her soul. "Oh Elizabeth, I'm sorry I was so upset at you. I'll be okay, but this all came as such a terrible shock, especially finding out about him being there every year on top of paying the fees. I know it's not your fault ... I just didn't want to believe it." Her voice broke. "It must've been so hard for him..."

Elizabeth's tone echoed the emotion Lara was finding impossible to suppress. "You'll never know how much. My heart ached every time I caught a glimpse of him standing up the back of the room. The mixture of pain and pride in his eyes as he watched the two of you was excruciating ... but he couldn't stay away ... and that's exactly why I never wanted you to know."

The broken-hearted young woman could only imagine his ordeal. She had to cover her mouth when a tiny whimper crawled out of her throat, as though it needed to breathe of its own accord.

"Oh, my sweet girl, please don't cry ... it's going to be okay. The damage is done, and we can't change anything now. The best thing you can do from this point is just to thank him in secret and then leave everything in the past where it belongs, especially now that her schooling days are over."

How can I ever leave anything to do with him in the past? He's always in my heart. Not a day goes by when I don't think of him ... and he still invades my dreams.

The thoughts came from deep in her soul ... but still she kept silent. Uttering them wouldn't change the reality of their current situation.

Hoping to ease the hurt, Elizabeth turned the conversation around to the events of the night before, sprouting on about how proud she and Charles were of the new graduate. Her tactic worked when she heard the usual sparkle come back into Lara's voice. They finished the call with promises to catch up on the weekend when Nikki took Jasper on one of their many adventures.

For the next hour, Lara curled up on the veranda sofa, quietly reflecting on everything she had just learned from two totally different yet equally surprising conversations. All the while, her fingers subconsciously played with the pendant lying against her throat. As she gazed out to the city, all of a sudden, the Head of Art's throwaway comment echoed back at her, along with memories of Elizabeth's long pause in the middle of their conversation ... and her comment about other promises made – using the plural noun rather than the singular...

And surprise, surprise ... I don't think I need a soothsayer to guess who was the mysterious benefactor of the cheque. How could I ever have imagined you'd be able to stay away from her? Nikki was the daughter you always longed for ... I'm the one who whisked her away. Oh Lord, what have I done...

§

At the same time in a plush hotel room in Sydney, a good-looking man reached into a back compartment of his wallet. With infinite care, he pulled out a Christmas letter written with a child's hand and pressed it to his lips. The edges had become a little dog-eared in places from being hidden away all these years.

Miss you, little one, even though you're not so little any more. My, you've grown up ... and turned into a beautiful young woman with the whole world at your feet. I just wish I could tell you just how proud I was to see you last night.

He set his mouth pensively and looked out to the horizon.

I only hope your precious mother doesn't cry herself to sleep anymore. I want her to be happy ... enjoying a life filled with exciting adventures to make her smile and laugh out loud – that's all I've ever wanted for either of you. She certainly looked happy last night – you both did. May God bless and keep you safe every single day ... no matter how many years pass, you will always be the daughter I wanted to cherish and wish had truly been mine.

PART FOUR

Snowy Mountains, Australia

December 2000 to September 2004

Chapter 28

Lara's Christmas present to her daughter was a two-week horse-riding trek for the two of them just prior to Nikki's studies commencing at NIDA. This most likely would be the last opportunity they would have to share any quality time together for several months, and she thought it would be the perfect way to make some lasting memories.

It was Boxing Day, and they were heading to the Victorian High Country, a southern offshoot of the Snowy Mountains, and one of the most spectacular places to ride in all of Australia. It had always been a dream of theirs to slow-canter across the scenic mountain ranges where the famous movie *The Man from Snowy River* had been set. On the way home, Lara planned to drop Nikki off in Sydney before making her way north again.

Charles was happy to lend them his large four-wheel drive to pull the single horse-float with Jasper safely settled inside. To afford him some much-needed rest stops and exercise, the trip down lasted three days and reminded them both of when Nikki was a little girl sharing holiday road-trips together. Similar to back then, they filled the hours by singing songs, reminiscing over other special times, playing off each other with favourite characters' best lines or chattering away about their hopes and dreams.

Stumbling out of the vehicle at the end of a very long and tiring third day, they spent the first night of their back-to-nature adventure in a comfortable chalet near Mt Buller, a small alpine village in the Victorian Alps. The accommodation throughout the ride had been organised in rustic mountain cabins along the way, so this provided a nice degree of comfort before the hard work began. It certainly wouldn't be a luxurious vacation, though this was exactly the sort of holiday they relished ... spending time in the great outdoors together with their favourite four-legged friends.

The weather was beautiful – clear, sunny days exploring the high mountain ranges and with just the touch of a nip in the air each night as they sat around the campfire enjoying a hearty dinner. It was a popular holiday choice at this time of year with several other families having signed on for the ride as well. Nikki had been teamed with Shelly, a friendly young lass two years her junior who was there with her father. Mike was a widower, and Lara often found herself paired with him on the daily rides since the other adults all had their own partners for company. At night, they found themselves seated next to each other in the firelight, chatting about their lives back in the real world.

Mike hailed from Coffs Harbour, a pretty seaside town between Brisbane and Sydney, where he owned a local dive business. Raised on a dairy farm in the hills behind his new hometown, he enjoyed getting back into the country despite the ocean being his life now. He was a couple of years younger than Lara, with tousled blond hair and smoky green eyes, all rounded off with a smile able to bring admiring glances from more than one woman on the trip. Shelly was fifteen and lived with his parents as the dive business meant irregular hours for the busy father. Farm life provided her with more stability and close friends with similar interests living nearby.

Their third night out happened to fall on New Year's Eve. Sitting in a circle around the fire as the date clicked over, those still awake raised their glasses to welcome in the new year. Mike clicked his against Lara's, and there was a definite hint of something smouldering – and not only in the firepit's embers but also in his eyes. Sitting beside the easy-going man, she held his gaze for a few seconds, unsure exactly of how she was feeling, though not shying away from his admiring glances.

Back in the cabin, Lara laughed in disbelief when Nikki teased her about having a toy-boy happy to follow her every move. Secretly, the teenager was excited to see her mother enjoying the attentions of the handsome man with Nordic-like features. She couldn't ever remember seeing this side of Lara before – relaxed and mildly flirtatious – though she could vaguely remember catching glimpses of her and Uncle Adam stealing playful kisses when they thought she was busy playing.

She was only six years old the last time they were all together. The entire time her mother and Adam were seeing each other, they went out of their way to ensure the little girl was sheltered from the intensity of their romance. Any passionate gestures or exchanges were part of a private universe and not something to share with others – especially not a child too young to understand why they couldn't be together all the time. Since then, Lara had been out on a few dates, mainly to appease her sister or Lucy, but they were never anything serious.

Often through the long hours on horseback, the two girls and their parents raced each other up some of the long grassy stretches leading to a rocky ridge. The views from these outcrops gave amazing panoramas to the valleys below and then out across to even more blue-hazed mountains in the distance. Breathless and invigorated, the quartet often stood in their stirrups, taking in the incredible vistas and exchanging heady smiles. All the while, their trusty mounts snorted from the exertion, causing lengthy trails of steamy vapour to explode from their nostrils, which then added another unforgettable layer to the experience. Lara and Nikki were in their element – even saddle-sore butts from all those hours in the saddle were a minor discomfort compared to the exhilaration of simply being in this breathtaking expanse.

Day five found them exploring one of the most famous sites in the area – the iconic *Craig's Hut*. This modest timber structure had been purpose-built as a location for the much-loved movie set around a sweeping Australian ballad penned from the mind and heart of Banjo Patterson. Now day-trippers on foot or in four-wheel drives – or a lucky few on horseback – found their way to the same spot, often enjoying a picnic lunch while listening to fascinating tales about the characters who had once inhabited the district.

Those from their group sprawled out on a grassy patch, sharing fresh sandwiches and tales of the morning ride. Jasper was tethered with the other horses along a wooden fence, cropping on thick, lush grass and welcoming this well-earned respite. The mob of trusty beasts were exhausted after scaling several long stretches through thick bushy undergrowth, even though most were used to it. It was easy to tell the excitable Arab found it invigorating being out in the open country enjoying the freedom of a good hard gallop. His thick glossy coat twitched in anticipation as he gave a few soft snorts while sniffing the fresh mountain air. Everyone was happy to spend a couple of hours relaxing while taking in the magnificent scenery – it was definitely something worth bragging about once they arrived home.

Several large boulders were scattered around the grassy knoll, offering even better views of the spectacular countryside.

Nikki suddenly jumped up and dumped her empty sandwich wrapper in a nearby bin. "Come on, Mum, race ya!" she yelled, scurrying away.

"You're on – bet I win!"

With loud shouts and shrill squeals, the mother and daughter raced away to the largest one, scrambling up the rocky surface and fighting each other for better hand and footholds to gain more leverage. Puffing and panting, both were determined to be first to get an even better look across the statuesque snow gums dotting the hillside.

As expected, the views from the top were simply breathtaking. The duo stood with their arms around each other, gazing out to a series of long rolling hills that disappeared as far as the eye could see into the azure blue horizon. Visiting the famous landmark had been on their to-do list for many years so being there with horses as their only form of transport was the fulfilment of a dream come true.

When their guide called for everyone to saddle up for another arduous trek to the next campsite, the pair exchanged sad grimaces. The visit had been far too short for their liking. With one more glance around, Lara and Nikki made a vow to come back one day for a longer visit.

§

As each new day unfolded, the mother and daughter shared many memorable hours riding side-by-side through the high country.

On the afternoon following their *Craig's Hut* adventure, they chanced upon a large wombat slowly waddling along the trail. It was obvious he was in no hurry to get away and even pulled up to watch when Nikki dismounted for a better look. As soon as she came near, the chubby marsupial surprised the pair of them by heading straight towards her at an alarming rate. For such a heavy lumbering creature, he sure could get some speed up. Lara let out an amused chuckle when, fearing he was about to attack her, the inquisitive teen slid in the slippery terrain. He wasn't interested in her at all and scampered past before burrowing beneath a nearby bush, his furry backside sticking up in the air while his victim landed with a heavy thump on her less-cushioned one.

"Little blighter!" Nikki laughed self-consciously as she swatted her butt to brush a few clumps of mud and grass from her grubby jeans.

"Another one for the diary – pity I was too slow with the camera," Lara responded, still chuckling from her lofty perch. "And definitely something to tell Charles and Elizabeth when I get home! My brave daughter ... scared of a little wombat!"

"Hush-up, you! This has to stay between you 'n me. I don't want it getting around that I'm chicken!"

The amusing incident was another lovely keepsake from the special holiday.

§

Lara found she quite enjoyed Mike's company as they galloped alongside each other with the strong wind whipping up her hair. The rest of the group noticed how smitten the easy-going young widower was ... and no one could blame him. Lara was a stunning woman in her late thirties who looked years younger ... and with a laugh to brighten anyone's day.

Sometimes if they were lucky, a mob of mountain brumbies came into view, racing along a far-off ridge with manes and tails streaming in the wind as their loud hoofbeats echoed across the valleys. It was a thrilling sight and definitely worthy of another journal entry at the end of the day.

On the first night of the second week, the exhausted riders took up their usual spots, relaxing in an easy circle by the campfire and lifting their voices to croon a few well-known bush ballads. Flickering flame-fingers rose from the fire and were perfect to toast sticky marshmallow balls for a sweet treat to end the night.

When some of their trail mates made moves to go to their cabins, Mike looked across at Lara with his eyebrows raised, nodding inconspicuously towards the thin stand of snow gums silhouetted on the edge of the campsite.

Leaning in, he whispered cautiously so others couldn't hear, "Care to take a stroll for a few minutes before turning in? That moon looks stunning, and I'd really like to see what the stars look like from under true cover of darkness."

For the past week, Mike's admiring glances had become quite noticeable, and she had been half expecting something like this to happen. Even so, for some unexplained reason, she was more aware of a cautious check in her spirit.

Am I really ready for this? He seems nice. I'm just not sure I want to go to the next step, and the last thing I want to do is hurt him.

From across the way, Nikki observed the furtive exchange and Lara caught a glimpse of her cheeky smirk accompanied by raised eyebrows and an almost indiscernible nod.

Well, it's obvious you have a bit of support, Mike! Little humbug...

Sending a nervous grimace the would-be matchmaker's way, Lara turned back to him with a faint bob of her head. As casually as possible, the pair rose from their chairs, strolling towards the tree line with only a few inches separating them. The white trunks resembled ghostly figures in the moonlight, and a sudden burst of rustling leaves caused a shiver to run down her spine. Mike was quick to notice and immediately offered her his jacket.

"Thanks, but I'm okay. It's just this place – it's quite eerie with the trunks glowing like that and a little bit freaky not knowing what's lurking below. I'm just a silly city girl who's a wee bit scared of just about anything that crawls!" She gazed up at the moon peering back at her through the leafy rooftop. "Oh wow, that's what I call spectacular!"

Lara couldn't possibly recall how many times over the years her eyes had been drawn to the smiling face, ever conscious it was shining down on a certain person at the same time. Somehow, being there with Mike seemed the right time and place to try to erase that other image from her mind. Those memories belonged to a lifetime ago, and she was in the here-and-now with another man.

They ambled along in the faint light with two sets of hands deliberately pressed into back pockets, unintentionally mirroring each other. Measured footfalls crunching through crackling leaves or the sharp snap of a tree branch were the only intrusions to this quiet contemplation, intermingled with a variety of night-time sounds.

After several minutes of silence, Mike cleared his throat. "I don't mean to intrude or make you feel uncomfortable, but I'm curious about Nikki's father? Is he at home waiting for you?"

"It's alright, you're not intruding ... I'm not exactly sure where Tom is anymore. We haven't seen him since she was a tiny baby – our divorce went through just before she turned two."

"I'm sorry. I shouldn't have asked."

"No, it's fine. You weren't to know ... and besides, it was a long time ago..."

They walked on a bit farther until he found the suspense too much. "Is there anyone else in your life? There must be ... you're too attractive to be on your own."

Lara didn't even notice the compliment – her mind was already careening back to another place and time. She couldn't reply straight away, wondering how to answer truthfully. Leaning against a tree trunk with her hands behind her back, she appeared to be searching the far off inky blackness. She had no idea of the breathtaking picture she made as the moonlight filtered down and formed a shapely silhouette.

Eventually she turned to look at him and her expression was resolute. "No, there's no one. There used to be ... a very long time ago ... but I've been on my own for many years now. Work and Nikki have kept me busy, so I haven't had time for anyone else."

A sudden breeze came up, causing a thin strand of hair to blow across her mouth. A faint remnant of lip-gloss held it fast and Mike found his eyes drawn there. Placing one hand on the trunk just above her head, the other gently brushed the tress away with hesitant fingers and then faintly caressed the edge of her jaw.

His gaze moved upward and their eyes met and held. Ever so slowly, he leaned forward and touched tentative lips to hers. Lara couldn't move. Her eyes stayed fastened on his, as though searching for something she wasn't quite sure could be found again ... then her lips parted slightly.

It was all the encouragement Mike needed...

Drawing Lara away from the tree, he pulled her body firmly against his and the kiss turned into something far more passionate. She wasn't quite sure how she felt about this obvious sign of possession. He was certainly handsome and good company, but once upon a time someone else had held her like this – and when he did, she could scarcely breathe.

This unexpected act of intimacy made her heart skip a few beats for the space of several seconds. She enjoyed the sensation of strong arms holding her again, but despite everything else, the delicious feeling of a stomach full of butterflies was nowhere to be found. This was so vastly different from those other times. Whenever she and Adam had been together, it was as if they melted inside one another. She wasn't sure how easy it would be to settle for anything less.

From out of a sense of rightness, she realised how important it was to give Mike a chance. It would be unfair to compare him with someone who had become a flawless ghost from the past. Almost imperceptibly, the present seemed to nudge her away from that distant vision, and she reached up to wrap tentative arms around his shoulders. Then with her eyes closed, she got lost in his embrace ... well, almost...

The kiss continued for several minutes until Mike raised his head and softly brushed his nose along hers. Surprised by the affection contained in his gesture, she opened guarded eyes to muster up a faint smile. Her heart wasn't beating any faster, but even so, she did feel relaxed and comfortable in his arms.

"I enjoy being around you, Lara. It's a long time since I was interested in anyone." He searched her face for any reaction.

"I like being with you too, Mike. I'm just not too sure I want to rush into anything at this stage. I hope you're not upset."

"No, I understand. I'm not expecting anything you're not quite ready to give."

"Thanks. I don't want either of us to get hurt."

"Me neither," he whispered, bending his head to press his mouth against hers once more.

Their lips connected, though only for a few seconds when Lara felt the distinctive need to pull away – not enough to be rude ... she just wasn't ready to trust him quite yet ... nor deal with the guilt of betraying the only mouth she ever thought would touch hers like this.

Offering an understanding nod, Mike took her hand in his as they wandered back to the campsite – the smoky aroma and distant flickering flames their only guides through the thick undergrowth. A few stragglers were still enjoying the fire's warm glow, and some sent encouraging smiles their way at the sight of the connected hands.

§

Later that night, with Nikki snuggled up on a small camp bed breathing heavily on the other side of the cabin, Lara was still wide-awake staring out a small window to the distant treetops lit by the moon's soft glow. No matter how many times she tried to justify the kiss, it was as if she had just betrayed the only person who truly mattered.

Why do you still have such a hold on my heart, Teddy? It's been so long, but you're still here. I need to make a life for myself, darling. I can't keep going on like this forever.

When she finally dozed off in the early hours of the morning, instead of those dark brown eyes she was so familiar with, this time it was a pair of smoky green ones staring back at her ... but she didn't recognise them. An uneasy whimper became part of her dreams, and the sound emanated from her side of the small space several times until dawn's gentle rays touched the windowsill. The only eavesdroppers to these niggles of anxiety were a tiny pygmy possum and her baby, hiding quietly in the shadowy rafters overhead ... Nikki was too busy dreaming about a stage with actors on horseback and a musical score that sounded like clopping hooves after another hard day in the saddle.

§

The rest of the week contained more of the same – exhilarating days spent on horseback exploring lofty mountain ridges or hidden grassy valleys lined with mountain ash or snow gums, and evenings where a group of weary riders relaxed around a campfire. After sampling another flavoursome camp-oven dinner, a good-looking man with an attractive woman by his side wandered into the darkness, eager to spend the next hour or so getting to know one another in a secluded grove ... a few wary kisses their only form of intimate connection. Not surprisingly, the same pair then lay awake for several hours at either end of the campsite, wondering how the other one was feeling.

Nikki spent most of her days happily spying on them, making sure to follow along behind whenever the tentative twosome enjoyed an invigorating canter with both mounts keeping pace, or chatted easily between themselves while following well-worn mountain trails at a slow walk. Later, as she and her mother dressed for dinner in their most recent nightly shelter, a bombardment of endless questions would land in Lara's ears. Nervous laughter accompanied the constant barrage, but she was reluctant to open up – unsure what she was actually feeling and disinclined to have her daughter read anything more into it.

Lara remembered a little girl once being devastated when the man she had grown to love like a father suddenly disappeared from her life. Having to endure a similar emotional journey was the last thing a hormonal teenager needed. Though Nikki had just turned seventeen, she was still vulnerable when it came to relationships – no matter what form they took.

On their last night, Mike once again suggested they go off by themselves and Lara was more nervous than she had been in years. From the way he had been acting all day, it was clear he was hoping to make their relationship more permanent than just an innocent holiday romance. Her feelings were still indecipherable, and she wasn't exactly sure just how much she wanted things to change. Despite enjoying his company, none of those anticipated fireworks went off whenever they were alone together.

I don't want to take advantage of you ... then again, I don't want to miss out if this is meant to be. Oh, why don't relationships get any easier...

They walked wordlessly in the moonlight, each one lost in thought until their journey came to a halt at the edge of a cliff. Thick darkness stretched like a blanket in front of them, while distant hills showed pinpricks of tiny light speckles from the farmhouses and cabins scattered around the district. The air was so clear the sky was a canopy of stars, and wherever they turned the spectacular Milky Way showed off its broad dusky trail. Standing in each other's arms, his lips grazed her forehead when she leaned into them.

"I don't want this holiday to end, Lara. These have been some of the best days – and nights – of my life for a very long time. It won't be the same being back at work and not having a pair of pretty blue eyes looking up at me, putting my world back on kilter again."

He always managed to say just the right thing and Lara was willing to admit there was a chance she may be able to match his sentiments. Like him, the holiday had brought some of her happiest days for many years, and she enjoyed having an affectionate male in her life again. Even so, a quick nudge of harsh reality reminded her they lived four hundred kilometres apart.

To make it even harder, Lara's two vastly different and very demanding career paths would make it almost impossible for them to spend any quality time together to find out if what they felt was likely to last. She knew Mike didn't want to leave his hometown and there were no work opportunities in either of her fields in the seaside harbour town. Besides, his father was getting older and needed assistance around the farm on the days Mike didn't have tourists to ferry out to the reefs. And then there was Shelly, his young daughter ... so many obstacles.

"Mmm, I know what you mean. I'll miss these walks and the excitement of racing from one valley to the next when I'm sitting at that newfangled computerised video-editing equipment my boss purchased recently. It won't be much fun putting together boring docos or ads for car batteries, believe me!"

The digital age had replaced old flatbed editing equipment and she missed the thrill of working with celluloid film, along with the smell and sticky sensation of white grease pencil residue smearing her fingertips. Thankfully, a few directors and cinematographers still preferred the older stock movie cameras, so every now and then Lara still had the chance to run huge reels of visual footage and soundtracks through her fingers on the old Steenbeck. They were tangible and familiar and still far more real and exciting than just looking at an image on a small screen while manoeuvring everything with the click of a mouse.

"Or getting to meet famous actors in blockbuster movies and singing to hundreds of people in concert halls around the country!"

He smiled down at her and she grinned at his teasing tone. "Mmm, well that too!"

Catching the impish smirk gave him the confidence to run a gentle finger along her cheek. Inching closer, he bent forward just enough to claim her mouth with his. For the first time, she surrendered fully to that silent persuasion – letting her mouth join his in a new form of trust.

Lara's response set his heart racing, and he pulled her even closer. This was the first time she felt at ease with such intimacy and the wave of guilt that came over her on that first night now seemed less intrusive. Still unsure whether the conviction of betrayal would ever fully leave, tonight at least it seemed to have become easier to deal with. She understood Adam never expected her to remain faithful to him, but their love had been so all-consuming it had been a natural response. Until now, there had never been any temptation to seek fulfilment from anyone else.

The kiss lasted for several minutes, until Mike raised his head, sucked in a deep breath and then released it slowly. He looked her straight in the eyes, and she was in no doubt as to his sincerity. "I want to try and get up to Brisbane at least once a month – I need to see you again ... and soon."

"I'd like that too ... but if you can't make it, I understand. I'll try to get down to see you whenever there's a weekend free in my schedule, though I can't promise how often that'll be. I'm usually booked up for months in advance."

"Yeah, I figured as much. Don't worry, we can work something out. At least we'll be able to ring each other every now and then when things aren't too hectic."

An unbidden thought sprang to life from the ancient treasure chest buried deep in her heart. Despondently, she rested her chin on his shoulder, while empty blue eyes closed around another memory.

Once upon a time, one phone call a day seemed like a famine...

Just as quickly, she admonished herself. *Grrr – stop it! You're not being fair. That was another life, and you can never go back there.*

"Come on, we'd better go back. The others'll be waiting," he suggested, taking her hand in his, completely oblivious to the battle raging in her soul.

Lying in the dark a short time later, Lara's thoughts drifted to what might happen further down the track. Mike certainly came across as nice – someone she could trust. She liked spending time with him, and the girls certainly enjoyed each other's company ... but could she give her heart to another man, especially when that heady rush of excitement was still missing? The last thing she wanted to do was bring more pain to someone who had already lost so much with the unexpected passing of his childhood sweetheart.

§

The next morning, the posse was up early to ensure they arrived back at their original starting point in time for a quick lunch before going their separate ways. Both Lara and Mike and the two girls were quite subdued on the last leg. Nikki and Shelly were sad to be saying goodbye while their parents had a lot to contemplate. Over a bowl of tasty homemade beef and barley soup soaked up with big chunks of fresh buttery bread, the talk around the long trestle table was cheery enough to bring smiles back to their faces. Firm friendships had been forged between many of the holiday-makers and loads of memory-keepers would have them reminiscing long after arriving home.

While the girls led Jasper into the float and said their goodbyes, Lara spent several minutes offering thank you treats and one last rubdown to her temporary fur friend. Dandy had provided a heap of thrilling adventures through the vast wilderness landscape and she was sorry to leave him behind. A gentle snicker as her palm nuzzled his soft lips was a lovely way to conclude their partnership. Her glance fell on Mike waiting near the car, and she knew it was time to go. With one last grateful rub under the faithful beast's long forelock, she strolled over to meet him. He took her in his arms with a friendly smile, bestowing tender kisses and promises to ring sometime over the next week.

"Take care and drive safely," were his parting words as he pulled away to open her door.

"I will and you too," she responded.

Joining Nikki in the front seat, Lara opened the window to give him a final peck on the cheek while the girls shared a hug through the other window. Then with a wave, she drove down the long dusty road, back to the bustle of the real world.

She watched him through the side mirror as he climbed into his car, though there was no tug on her heartstrings nor that constant wondering when they would see each other next.

Will I ever feel that way again or am I just going to get used to this...

Chapter 29

Leaving Nikki behind was one of the hardest things Lara had ever done in her life. When the realisation hit that her entire life was about to change forever, it brought back memories of walking away from another beloved soulmate. Even though the pain was less intense, the pull on her heart was just as strong.

Standing with their arms wrapped tightly around one another, Lara found it especially difficult to let go. The longest they had ever been apart was when Nikki went to study in Italy and those few short weeks had seemed like a lifetime ... now three long and lonely years stretched into what seemed forever. Work would help to keep her busy and bring about a much-needed sense of satisfaction, however nothing could compare to the joy of listening to her daughter's laughter and lively chatter at the end of a day.

"Promise me you'll ring often and take good care of yourself ... and don't forget to eat properly!"

The young woman rolled her eyes and clicked her tongue. "Oh, *Muuummm* ... okay, I promise – at least twice a week. And don't *worry;* I'll be getting three meals a day with my room and board so I'll be fine."

"Well, make sure you don't stay up too late – and remember ... no going into the city at night unless someone's with you ... and make sure you stay away from King's Cross! Nikki, promise me!"

"*Muuummm, I promise* ... now get in the car and take Jasper home to his paddock! I'll be fine, don't worry," she managed to laugh through the sudden lump in her throat, giving her mother a gentle shove.

"Alright, my angel," Lara said with a self-conscious grimace, planting one last kiss on her precious girl's cheek. She looked into those big brown eyes again and just like any caring parent in a similar situation, her hand reached out to stroke her face one final time. "But I can't help it, I'm your mother and I do worry – it comes with the territory!"

With a deep sigh, she climbed into the car to begin the long journey north.

From the trailer, Jasper let out a loud whinny as his own form of farewell when Nikki waved them off. Two large tears rolled down the teenager's cheeks.

She would miss them both after being on the receiving end of their generous support while enjoying her two favourite pastimes ... performing on stage and exploring the open countryside. The mother and daughter's eyes stayed fixed on the rear-view mirror's reflection as the car drove away.

All the way up the long coast road, Lara kept envisioning Nikki and Jasper galloping across those spectacular mountain ranges with the wind blowing through their matching thick manes. The holiday had been the perfect way to conclude this chapter of their journey with memories to cherish forever.

She stopped overnight in the coastal town of Nambucca Heads, halfway between the two east-coast capital cities. It gave Jasper a much-needed break from the small confines of the float in the paddock adjoining the motel, and she could stretch her own cramped legs before grabbing a good night's sleep.

The sleepy village was a pretty place to wind down after spending so many hours behind the wheel. A secluded beach below the headlands was a nice spot to munch on a succulent piece of snapper fresh from the ocean. A fresh side salad with all the trimmings was the perfect accompaniment. For over an hour, Lara watched the waves breaking against the rocks ... and reflected on her future.

Her sleep was fitful being in another unfamiliar bed. Within an hour of the sun rising over the Pacific Ocean, she was back on the road again. Though never admitting it even to herself, thoughts of Nikki filled her mind far more than any of Mike. It was only when she was passing through Coffs Harbour – a mere three-quarters of an hour away – her thoughts turned to him. Twenty minutes later the realisation hit that she could easily have dropped by to say hello, or even stayed the night in a motel there instead of the earlier stopover.

That well-remembered sense of guilt kept her company the rest of the way home as she compared the all-consuming sensation of hers and Adam's first parting to what she was feeling now.

Oh, well, we can catch up soon and hopefully get to share more good times.

§

The following Monday she returned to work. David was happy to see her and pulled her into an enthusiastic hug the moment she walked through the door.

"Welcome back, and look at you – great tan, but you look like you've been put through a wringer! Bet that old aching body or yours is reminding you it isn't quite as supple as it used to be after being cast as the real *Annie Oakley*!"

"Hey, not so much of the *old*, you cheeky blighter! You're right though ... my butt sure let me know for the first few days. Thank goodness, I feel a lot better now. And thanks for letting me come in late – I sure needed a sleep-in."

She hadn't slept properly on either night following her arrival home, mainly due to missing Nikki and her happy chatter, but the extra couple of hours that morning did help.

"Well, you certainly look rested up and raring to go. How was the trip?"

"It was great, thanks. The mountains were just spectacular and seeing them on horseback was the perfect way to get around. We had a fabulous time, but it was horrible having to leave my girl behind. I'm going to miss her so bad."

"I'm not surprised after the exciting lives you two have led! After all, she's been your main focus for nearly two decades."

"Mmm, that she has and I've loved every minute. Thank goodness I have work to keep me busy!"

"Well, I'm glad you feel that way." There was a distinct guilty grimace accompanying his reply. "Sorry to do this to you as soon as you get back but we've just been given a rush job. I hope you've got your skates with you because I doubt you'll get much sleep for the next few weeks."

"Well, that's a lovely greeting... makes me feel sooo glad to be back!" Her retort contained a massive dose of sarcastic laughter.

There was a guarded look as he mumbled, "Just don't say you weren't warned..."

Her boss' tone was so unlike his normally easy-going manner, she stopped laughing and looked at him with a hint of scepticism.

"Just what are you up to? Come on ... spill the beans! You know I don't mind a bit of hard work."

His eyes dropped and he muttered like a naughty child. "I'm not exactly sure just how ready you are for this; hopefully you're in a forgiving mood."

She sized him up and down with a wary frown. "I didn't catch all that but what's this about forgiving you? Now you're really starting to have me worried. From that look, I don't think you're glad to see me after all. What's going on, Davey?"

"I *am* glad to have you back, honest. Work's been flat out since you've been gone and I haven't had time to scratch myself!" He paused and his eyes never left hers. "Hopefully you'll be willing to take on a new project – something you know a fair bit about."

Lara laughed. "Oh, is *that* all! *Course* I will, but what's with the face? There was more to your greeting than just a welcome home ... and what was that you mumbled before that forgiving mood business?"

Without saying another word, David pointed to the corner table where a large pile of silver film canisters was stacked and bound together with tight leather straps. The project had arrived only a few hours earlier. Plastered across the top was a distinctive white label announcing in big bold letters:

A NIGHT OF ENCHANTMENT – <u>URGENT!!</u>

If he hadn't already been in the middle of finishing off an info commercial due before the end of the day, he would have taken it on himself.

"Mmm, great title! I wouldn't mind a night of enchantment myself!"

Her flirty response brought an exasperated roll of his eyes as he passed her a torn envelope. "Hope you still feel that way when you read this."

Lara couldn't help noticing the worried expression behind his flippant response. Throwing him a puzzled look, she fished out the note tucked inside.

Dear David,

Thanks for agreeing to take on this project at such short notice. I'm pretty sure it will be a bit of a change from your usual action-packed blockbusters and docos. As I already mentioned, we're on a tight schedule to have it completed in time for the special going to air on 14 February 2001, though I have a feeling that talented assistant of yours will find it just up her alley.

I sincerely appreciate your help, and will owe you a good bottle of bubbly once it's in the can! Please let me know as soon as it's ready to receive the final okay.

I look forward to working with you on future productions.

Yours sincerely
Steven Atkins
Director, Night of Enchantment

The contents were intriguingly cryptic. Sending a quick glance her boss' way, an even deeper frown creased Lara's brow as she began undoing the thick straps binding the canisters together. "What is this, Davey? It certainly sounds intriguing, but gee, three weeks puts it on a really tight schedule. No wonder you're looking so worried."

"Uummm ... well, actually I've got a bit of a confession to make. I nearly turned it down, except I owe Steven a big favour. He's sent us heaps of work over the years and got me out of a slump many moons ago, so I didn't want to lose his business all because of this one." Subconsciously he gnawed at his top lip, seemingly awkward and unsure for the first time in all their years of working together.

Lara plonked herself down on a stool, and her eyes didn't leave his face. "Now you really have me intrigued. Come on ... spill! I won't bite, you know. What's so special about this one? Apart from being in celluloid rather than digital" —playfully she punched his arm trying to bring out a smile— "but that's a good thing – it means I can actually get my hands dirty. You know how much I enjoy the old ways compared to this new fandangled technology!"

Without saying another word, he pulled open the top canister, placed the heavy roll of film on the flatbed and wound the huge spools to take up the slack. When it was ready to go, he turned to her and his expression was grave.

"I think you'd better see what it is rather than me trying to explain ... maybe then you'll understand."

He flicked the switch.

The visualiser sprang to life and a large floodlit stage filled the screen. There was no sound, and yet the flickering images were enough to make Lara catch her breath. A solitary figure stood in front of a microphone ... it was clear the singer was waiting for his cue, while the audience sat spellbound from one end of a vast stadium to the other.

There was no need for any audio to send shivers up and down her spine. It was enough to see Adam standing on a stage seemingly looking into her very soul as he stared down the camera. She could practically sense a glimpse of concern behind his eyes, and she felt a sudden check in her spirit ... almost as though he knew what had been happening over the last couple of weeks and was querying where her loyalty lay.

A sudden film of moisture blurred her vision and she tried to blink it away. David caught her response and placed a gentle hand on her arm. "Are you okay? I'm so sorry. I had a feeling you still cared about him ... I just wasn't sure how much."

More than a decade had passed since the last time she had seen him getting ready to perform like this. Her quenched spirit drank in every frame as the vision continued. With her eyes still fixed on the small screen, she gave a miniscule shake of her head. "No, I'm okay. It's just the shock of seeing him on a stage after so long."

Oh, Teddy, I may not be able to hear you physically, but I know exactly how you sound in my spirit.

"Listen, I can do it instead if you like."

But she was in another world and couldn't answer.

Right from the start, her boss had always felt there was more to their story than Lara let on. It was only when he caught her sobbing at her desk while she was editing a film about lost love that she finally broke down and told him everything. It was many years ago, a few weeks after her arrival home from Sydney following *My Fair Lady's* run. Knowing what happened helped him to understand why work was so necessary to fill the yawning void in her life. Though they never mentioned it again, he always wondered whether she had truly gotten over her former co-star. Witnessing her reaction now only confirmed his suspicions.

He had to repeat his offer. "Hey, how about I do it instead? There are plenty of other things you can go on with."

"No, I want to do it – I *have* to. Now get outta here so I can get started," she implored, shooing him away.

"All right, just so long as you're sure ... and thanks. I owe you big time." At her silent nod, he slipped out the door, shutting it firmly behind him and leaving her alone with images that brought back all of the old loneliness and longing.

The darkness of the studio enfolded her in its fullness. Lara sat mesmerised as she ran every vision reel through without adding the audio. It was filming in the raw, footage of various lead-ins and takes running into each other, though all she could concentrate on was the man who seemed to be looking straight into her eyes. Even without the layer of sound to captivate her ears, she was an audience of one ... and he was the nourishment feeding her famished soul.

A few hours later, she heard a soft knock on the door.

"Come in, Davey."

He popped his head around the corner with a tentative grimace. "Are you still talking to me?"

To his immense relief, she smiled and beckoned him over as she dashed away a last stray tear. "Of course I am. Come right in. I won't bite your head off – promise!"

Phew!" he joked, pretending to wipe a film of sweat from his brow. Settling on the stool beside her, a gentle hand covered hers. "I fully understand if you can't do it. I'm just about finished an urgent job Channel 7 needs to air tonight, and then there's a kid's doco I was about to start after that. You've already done work for the director, so you know his foibles. How about we swap and I can take this on, that way big smears of mascara won't end up all over your face every day like they are at the moment!"

Grabbing a tissue from a box on the desk, he tried dabbing away the long messy streaks of black, but without much luck. They were drying and starting to cake her cheeks from running unchecked for so long.

What she had already seen of Adam's performance had left her hungering for more. There was no way she was going to let anyone else work on it – not even her boss. This was a gift made especially for her, and she could already envisage the finished product with fade-ins and some of the editing tricks she had learned from years of crafting the perfect final cut. Thankfully, three cameras had captured his image so she could manipulate the footage from various angles. With Adam as the subject matter, her job became that much easier. She was already familiar with all of his little nuances and knew his best angle to show off to a television audience.

"No, David, I really want to do it. I'm sure this was meant to be, especially after only just saying goodbye to Nikki. It's something I can really sink my teeth into, and because I don't have to get home early or be anywhere else for that matter, I've got all the time in the world..."

She didn't add the obvious, *Even though I've just met someone who could potentially fill the void in my life.* Lara wasn't sure she wanted anyone to know about Mike just yet.

"Fair enough. Well, I'm always here if you need help, or if it all becomes too much. After all, you're not superwoman, even if you do come close..."

She was already looking back at the screen to a close-up of Adam's face frozen in time. "I'll be fine ... now go away and leave me alone – I'd better get started if you want this finished on time."

§

For the next two weeks, Lara's small editing room resembled the back blocks of an old discarded movie studio. Half-open canisters and piles of reels took up every spare inch of space. There were thousands of metres of film stock to edit from the vast array of cameras angles required for the television special ... and she was in her element.

Every morning she sprang out of bed and hurried to the studio, usually working late into the night on the concert Adam had given for a charity in Melbourne. He had always been generous with his time and talent for a worthy cause, and one of the national television stations had won the rights to screen the special on Valentine's Day. The footage consisted mainly of show tunes with a romantic theme, so this was the perfect occasion for it to go to air. Working alone in the dark with his voice filling the small room, she could almost imagine he was singing every line to her alone. Making it even more real, the smooth feel of celluloid film running through her fingers took her back to the exquisite sensation of caressing his skin as though it was only yesterday.

§

On one of her hurried lunch breaks snatched between hours of sitting in front of the tiny screen, Lara popped down to Fortitude Valley to pick up a new gown she had ordered for her next show. Situated close to the city, the area had once been a seedy nightclub precinct. Recently, a flurry of trendy boutiques and eating-houses had sprung up along the tree-lined streets, bringing a new kind of customer to the district.

Dashing back to her car with the dress folded carefully in its carry box, she passed a little French boutique selling all sorts of chic items and apparel. As though drawn there, Lara happened to glance into the large display window. Tucked into a corner, she noticed an eye-catching pewter sculpture with the word *Hope* fashioned in elegant script and decorated with delicate filigree. It was about the length of her forearm in both height and width and could easily have been fashioned for her bedroom decor.

Her heart raced as she was transported back to the last time she and the man who still lived in a quiet corner of her heart had spoken. His heartfelt farewell that day had dripped with sentimental prose centred around this very word.

Without a moment's hesitation, she entered the store. Her emotions ran amok when a trembling hand reached out to touch the individual letters ... almost as though each one contained its own heartbeat waiting to spring to life in her hands. To come across this particular work of art centred around this precise sentiment after all these years, and just when she was in the middle of working on his concert, filled her heart with a new sense of hope ... God was still out there, and he still cared about the two of them.

A few minutes later, she walked out the door with the sculpture now wrapped in delicate tissue paper and carried as if it was made of the finest crystal.

Later that evening in the stillness of her bedroom, Lara carefully took the piece out of its wrapping. Almost reverently, she placed it on her nightstand beside the picture of a good-looking man standing beneath an archway outside a Tuscan town – a mirror image of the one Adam took with him around the country from show to show, except his depicted a woman with long chestnut hair.

That night and for all those to follow, whenever Lara turned out the bedside lamp, these were the last things she looked at. Then again in the morning, they were the first things she noticed when her eyelids opened ... and every single time she added her own prayer to his...

One day, please God ... more than anything, please keep that hope alive...

And on her regular dusting day, no longer was it only the photo and ornate Venetian mask hanging on the bedroom wall that felt the lingering touch of her fingers. The message matching the one from Adam's heart now formed part of this weekly ritual.

Though Lara's life had moved forward and another man seemed to be manoeuvering himself into a foot-lit corner of her life's stage, hiding in the wings a persistent flicker remained ... faintly illuminating the most vulnerable corners of her soul.

§

A few days later Lara arrived home following a stressful day where nothing she did seemed to go right. The tight deadline was looming, and she still had several major final touches to add to the project. For over an hour, she sat in the shadows of the cottage veranda, weighed down by the heaviness of all she had lost after experiencing the tenderness of having Adam sing to her day after day. In the middle of all these melancholy musings, the phone rang. Hoping it was Nikki or at least her sister with some cheery news, she hurried to answer it.

"Hello?"

"Hi Lara, I thought it was about time I gave you a buzz to see how you're doing."

"Mike! Goodness, this is a surprise! I wasn't expecting to hear your voice – it's been ages. I'm fine thanks ... how are you?"

Plonking herself down in the closest armchair, she kicked off her shoes and hung her legs over the armrest. After such a busy day, it was nice to settle down for a chat, though no matter how hard she tried, Lara couldn't quite remember whether his eyes were blue or green. For almost two weeks a pair of mesmerising brown ones had held her entire focus.

After offering an apology and explaining how flat out he had been, the conversation went on for nearly an hour, meandering between what they had been up to and working out when they would both be free at the same time.

Lara glanced at the calendar hanging on the wall close by. "Ummm, hang on, I'll just check ... mmm ... no, I can't next weekend – I'm off to Sydney for two shows ... but the next ... no, that's no good either – I'll be down at the Gold Coast for another two on Friday and Saturday nights ... then I'm up at the Sunshine Coast the weekend after that. I'm sorry."

"Wow, you really are busy!"

"Sure am. You know the old cliché, no rest for the wicked!"

He was disappointed, even though he understood her work had to take priority, at least while things were still new between them. If everything turned out the way he planned, her priorities would change and they should be able to get together more regularly.

What he had forgotten to take into consideration was that they each had working lives far from the norm. His diving trips were both weather and customer dependent, with most occurring on weekends and public holidays, while Lara's free time was sandwiched between project deadlines on weekdays – that often ran late into the night – and her music gigs on Friday and Saturday nights.

"Oh, well, maybe next month..."

"Okay. I'll see how my schedule's looking and get back to you. I really am sorry."

"That's fine, you can't help being popular! Anyway, how's Nikki doing?"

They related news about both their girls, but because of the earlier disappointment, neither one could think of anything uplifting to add that could turn the gloominess around. Lara hung up feeling just as despondent as before.

Afterwards, she wandered into the kitchen, hoping to rustle up a late-night snack to replace one of many missed dinners from staying late at work. When she fell into bed, her sleep was undisturbed for a change. She was far too exhausted after such a gruelling day and still couldn't remember exactly what Mike looked like to be able to transport him into her dreams. For once, even that other image was silent ... hovering in the shadows of her spirit instead of raising his voice with hers on a brightly-lit stage – something that had become a nightly occurrence since work began on the Valentine's Day concert.

§

A few minutes before three on Thursday afternoon, Lara leaned back in her chair, sighed loudly and wiped the last remnants of grease pencil from her fingers with a scrappy piece of rag. The final cut of *A Night of Enchantment* was complete. Though she was pleased with the outcome, there was also a deep sense of sadness keeping her company. While another unscaleable Everest loomed over her, Adam was completely oblivious to the fact that for the last two weeks he had been singing only to her. Now it was time to set him free again, only this time for the whole world to share. She had no idea when she would next see him on a stage – even if it was only one featuring on a small screen.

Before opening the studio door, she sent the image staring back at her a sombre, "It's time to say goodbye again, my love. It's been the most unexpected and wonderful gift having your voice in my ear over these past few weeks. Now I have to send you back out into the world again, but I'll always love you."

Pressing two fingertips against her lips, she gently touched the screen. Then with a distinct nod of farewell, she managed to summon up a smile before calling David in to have a look. He was eager to see her handiwork and pulled up a stool inside the cramped room that had almost become her home-away-from-home after so many late nights.

The title bar rolled while a single blue ray of light caught the image of a tall, handsome man projecting his remarkable voice to a rapt audience. Every scene was perfect, and the transition from one song to the next was even better than Lara herself had imagined during all those long hours of concentration. Her ability to manipulate thousands of metres of raw film stock into a passionate portrayal of the well-known pieces was a credit to her commitment and devotion.

David was totally enthralled. His knowledge of the process meant he could easily discern each of the almost imperceptible fingerprints left behind by a woman still in love with the man on screen. Only someone who knew Adam intimately could use each frame to portray him so flawlessly.

"Oh Lara, that was brilliant ... truly incredible! Steven's going to be ecstatic ... from the very first frame right through to the final credits. I knew you could do it, although I'm still amazed you were able to produce something of this quality in such a short space of time."

Deep down, she knew this was her best work, and his enthusiasm was just the boost she needed. "Thanks, boss! I'm pretty happy with it too! Now let's hope you're right about Steven's reaction."

"He'd *better* be ecstatic – I doubt anyone else could've topped what you've created here. And I know it mustn't have been easy, but you did an outstanding job. I'm really *really* proud of you."

She couldn't answer through the emotion welling up in her throat. Looking into her eyes, David could see what a toll it had taken on her heart.

He leant over and placed an affectionate arm across her shoulders. "Okay, my friend, get on outta here ... you deserve the rest of the afternoon off!"

"Thanks, Davey, you're a good sport. I could do with an early night..."

"But I need you back bright and early. Something else just turned up that you're sure to want to sink your teeth into ... but it can wait 'til tomorrow. Oh, and eat a proper dinner for a change!" he called from the door on his way out.

"Yes sir," she responded with a cheeky salute against her forehead.

Along with her bag, Lara picked up a beautifully bound leather box overlaid with images depicting scenes from the Italian countryside. Inside was a single film reel containing usable footage that hadn't made it to the final cut. These were some of the off-cuts normally only found inside scrap bins at the end of another long day. Instead, Lara had lovingly gathered these precious fragments from off the floor and spliced them together into her own personal concert. She couldn't have handled throwing away any of his images or reels of that wonderful voice. Although holding no meaning for anyone else, in her heart these were some of her most treasured possessions.

And on those long lonely nights when sleep was an elusive fugitive, fingers once used to create a symphony purely by touch, threaded the transparent film stock through a mini-projector positioned on the wall above her bedside table. Then for countless hours, Lara lay in the dark unable to look away from the flickering images dancing across the opposite wall ... while a beloved voice kept her company.

This was her Adam ... the one she would never have to share with anyone else.

§

Any phone calls between Lara and Mike had been quite erratic in the two months since the riding holiday, mainly because of their crazy schedules. Whenever he was free, she was normally working, and vice versa, which meant they usually only found time to ring every couple of weeks. Even though they were able to keep up with each other's news, without the benefit of really knowing how the other one felt, their conversation was often stilted and cool. He came across as rather shy over the phone and seemed reluctant to ask about her earlier life, while she was still unsure exactly where she wanted the relationship to go.

Another six weeks passed before they were finally able to see each other. His business was booming so there had been no time to get away and Lara had bookings in various clubs across every weekend, making it impossible for her to consider the ten-hour road trip there and back. She was exhausted by the time April came around, and David agreed to swap her days so she could add another one to the Easter break and drive down to Coffs Harbour without the need to rush back.

She left just after breakfast with the idea to stop by a beach somewhere along the way for an early lunch. The scenery was spectacular as the Corolla wove its way over green rolling hills, through thick eucalypt forests or followed the coastline in several places. The views could change within a few kilometres and made the journey even more interesting. Passing the sign for Byron Bay, her thoughts instantly flew back to a weekend spent in a luxurious B&B.

Stop it, you idiot! she chastised herself, trying vainly to put the image away. *Why do you put yourself through this! Those days are long gone, and it's more than time to move on.*

Even so, she couldn't resist and decided the seaside town was as good a place as any to stop for a bite to eat. Unfortunately, the hippy-like atmosphere of the main town area wasn't really her thing, so she grabbed a quick bite in a beachside café and then headed south again. As much as she was tempted, Lara didn't trust herself to drive past Watagos Beach where she and Adam had stayed without feeling that old sadness rise up again. Hoping to keep the blues away, she slipped one of Anne Murray's CDs into the slot and the popular singer's mellow voice kept her company for the rest of the way. Singing along to some of the numbers was able to lift her spirits somewhat and she looked forward to the weekend ahead.

It felt good to stretch her cramped legs and weary back when she pulled into the resort a couple of hours later – her home for the next few nights. Mike had suggested she stay at his place, but Lara wasn't quite ready to take things to the next level. In her mind, anything more than the present status quo meant a form of commitment she wasn't prepared to give just yet. It had taken months for her and Adam to go beyond anything more than breathless kisses. Sharing a bed with Mike at this stage of their relationship was something she couldn't even contemplate.

He was still out on the boat when she settled in. With the unpacking out of the way, the views from her balcony looked so inviting she scooped up her sunglasses and set off for a walk along the beach. The waves were gentle enough for her to wade shin-deep along the shoreline. Every now and then she absent-mindedly skimmed flat rocks in the calmer water or dug her toes in the sand seeking out any elusive pipi shells, all the while wondering where this brief stay would lead.

It wasn't long before she heard a voice calling her name. Looking up, Lara spotted Mike coming towards her. It wasn't hard to recognise his thick shock of blond hair and tanned skin from being in the sun so much. She sent him a friendly wave and his pace quickened, which meant he was breathless by the time they met.

"Hi! You made it – it's so good to see you."

"Hi! Yeah, I only got here a little while ago ... it's good to see you, too!"

More than three months had passed since the last time they were together, so neither one was exactly sure what form of greeting to expect. Before figuring out whether to offer a hug or not, the opportunity was long gone. Instead, they shuffled their feet and could only manage embarrassed smiles.

When he pointed out some rock pools on the other side of the resort, they strolled along side-by-side with hands thrust deep into the pockets of their shorts. Peering into the rocky crevasses for any form of fish-life helped to cover any nervousness as they chatted about her drive down and what was happening at work – topics of a personal nature were put on the backburner for later when hopefully the awkwardness would have disappeared.

When they eventually arrived at the door to her suite, she invited him in for a drink. Both chose chairs opposite each other on the balcony rather than the longer sofa until it was time to leave for dinner. Although their conversation was still a bit stilted, it wasn't enough to worry about. They figured things would get easier as the night evolved.

§

A few hours later, they were seated in a beachside restaurant with views out to the Pacific Ocean.

"So, tell me, how's the editing business going? Not as busy as it was after our holiday I hope." Mike's expression was mellow as he leaned back in his chair, thoroughly sated after a delicious meal of local seafood topped off with pavlova shells brimming with fresh bananas, strawberries and whipped cream. "You had a rush job on for a while if I remember correctly."

Instantly she back in the little editing suite and her gaze seemed to be searching the ocean. Thankfully, it appeared as though she was simply taking in the view of a trawler fleet heading out to sea for their nightly run.

Dragging her mind back to the present, Lara managed to fashion an answer. "My, you've got a good memory! Mmm, things've been a lot less hectic since then, thank goodness. Apart from the usual docos and the like, now it's an overabundance of singing gigs keeping me busy."

"I must try and get up to see you perform sometime soon. Finding time is the problem. Like you, I've been flat out for the last couple of months. The water's been pristine lately, which means business is booming. Lucky for me, tourists always want to take advantage of the clear conditions. By the way, have you ever dived, Lara?"

"No way! I've never been game enough to venture into the deep. Snorkelling is more than enough excitement for me. I don't think I could handle being metres under the water and not knowing what's lurking behind. Eerrgh..." She shivered, imagining the notorious great white sharks sometimes spotted off the coastline. Even the more harmless grey nurse variety was enough to put her off.

"Oh, rubbish! There are heaps more things to be scared of on land than what's out there. I can't wait to take you out – I hope you brought your bathers."

"Oh no, you don't," she retorted with a laugh. "Besides, it's way too cold to swim in the ocean ... and don't even think about getting me into one of those tight-fitting wetsuits – I don't want to look like a seal! Give me a heated pool any day."

"Don't tell me you're afraid of the ocean. Not when it's my life and livelihood."

"Yep, that's me – Nervous Nelly! I don't mind watching the waves all day as long as I'm somewhere safe like here. But as far as swimming where those large things with huge teeth are ... forget it. You can have that all on your own!"

Her answer disappointed him, but he didn't reply. His first wife had enjoyed exploring the deep, and he was hoping Lara would want to learn its secrets too. But there was no use forcing the issue ... the last thing he wanted to do was scare her away.

§

Mike had managed to organise a fill-in to take over the dive charters for the holiday weekend. This meant they were able to spend the entire four days walking along the beach or visiting his family's farm at the foot of a pretty waterfall about twenty kilometres west of the harbour town. Lara was in her element rounding up a mob of cattle over and around the rolling hills on the back of one of the family's working horses. He was by her side, and it was a delightful reminder of how they first met.

She enjoyed catching up with Shelly again, as well as spending time with his parents, though it was obvious they were cautious with the new woman in their son's life. She had no idea they were wary of letting her get too close in case Mike decided to pack up and move to the Gold Coast many miles north. The place was a well-known tourist destination able to provide far more dive business opportunities ... and it would mean he was a lot closer to Lara as well.

Each night when he drove her back to the resort, Lara invited him in for a nightcap. Usually, they sat next to each other on a long seat on the balcony with his arm draped casually across her shoulders, watching the waves roll in and talking about the day. Every now and then, he would lean across for a quick kiss before settling back into his corner again. These tokens were nothing like what she had been expecting after those deep lingering ones exchanged down south.

It was years since Lara had been swept off her feet and she missed the sensation of feeling that overwhelming rush of desire. Not that she wanted to take things any further at this point, but there was still an ever-present longing to experience that heady sense of craving again.

After Mike dropped her off on the final night, she lay in bed pondering the last few days. Lara knew she enjoyed his company, but there was still an element of doubt as to just how far she wanted their relationship to go.

It's just as well I haven't fallen head over heels ... at least for now. He lives too far away to be hankering after him all the time...

She turned over and one last uninvited thought crept in.

Last time was torture ... but I still miss every one of those glorious sensations.

§

When Tuesday morning rolled around, they managed to fit in one last stroll along the beach before it was time for her to leave. The duo walked along the wave residue near the shoreline in an easy companionable silence. Her hand rested comfortably in his and every now and then one of them playfully splashed up a flurry of water with a stray foot. It brought a bit of lighthearted frivolity and was a nice way to end her stay while trying to avoid the liquid onslaught.

"Thanks, Mike, I've really needed this" —Lara smiled up at him— "time away from the rat race to find myself again." She reached up to place a light kiss on his cheek before paddling through the shallow water again.

"Is this truly what you needed, Lara? I'm not too boring after your usual fast-paced life, not to mention the A-Listers you usually mix with?"

"Of course you're not boring. You're dependable, solid, trustworthy and without a massive ego, exactly what every woman with a life like mine needs."

And there they were again – similar words from long ago... *Oh, go away!*

"Sounds boring when you're used to the bright lights of the city and clubs. Maybe I should come up to see you next time and try to show you another side of me."

Lara shook her head. "I don't need another side of you. I like you just the way you are." She truly meant it. As much as she hankered for the butterflies and racing heart, she didn't want to be swept off her feet again ... in the end, it hurt too much. No, this was much safer for her heart.

By the time the car was packed, a steady rain was falling so their goodbye wasn't the lingering farewell she had been expecting. Following a quick kiss and a promise to ring when she arrived home safely, Mike rushed to get under a nearby awning while she hopped into the driver's seat. Pulling out of the driveway, she sent him one last farewell wave through a small opening in the window.

Lara made her way through the busy township, envisaging how it would have been if she had been saying goodbye to someone else. Not surprisingly, a very different scenario crossed her mind ... of two people standing with their arms wrapped tightly around one another, completely oblivious to a bit of bothersome rain.

Instead of pushing those images away this time, they were a welcome companion on the long drive home. No matter how much time passed or what circumstances she found herself in, her thoughts still returned to their true north.

§

Only one day earlier, on a terrace overlooking the Brisbane River, a woman in her early sixties sat chatting to a well-built man whose fortieth birthday had come and gone in June of the previous year. It was obvious from the look on her face he meant the world to her. When the autumn sun began to fade, a late afternoon breeze caused the temperature to drop quite rapidly.

With a sudden shiver, she rubbed the tops of her arms. "Oooh, it's starting to get chilly. I think we'll have to go inside soon."

Her companion got up quickly and then bent down to kiss her cheek. "Stay there and enjoy the sunset, Mum. I'll be back in a minute."

Elizabeth's eyes followed him fondly as he crossed the flagstones leading to the house.

It was years since Adam had been inside his parents' bedroom, but he still remembered exactly where she kept her favourite shawl. As he went to open the drawer, his gaze fell on a photograph standing in pride of place on the dresser. He could still recall his father snapping it many years ago – when a man and a woman, with a young child in tow, were about to leave for a life-changing European holiday. The image captured the moment perfectly as they smiled into each other's eyes, seemingly without a care in the world.

Instantly, he was back sharing those same adventures and having the time of his life. Vivid memories tore through his heart and mind. Seeing the picture positioned in a place where Elizabeth could look at it every single day of her life confirmed how much she still missed those special times too.

Adding another layer to this trip down memory lane was discovering a thick journal filled with photographs, descriptive prose and keepsakes tucked behind the photo. The cover displayed a large image of the same man and woman, this time with the young child sitting on the man's lap, all laughing into the camera lens and with the Sydney Opera House in plain view behind them. Across the top and fashioned in careful screed he read,

A Memorable Sydney Sojourn ... with a Special Man, a Precious Child and the Woman Who Will Love Them 'Til the End of Time

Adam's hands shook as he opened the pages. Realising he could no longer trust his legs to hold him, he found himself sinking down on the edge of the bed. For countless minutes, his eyes feasted on every morsel contained in its pages, brushing his fingers across each photo and piece of memorabilia. Every treasured keepsake from those four love-filled months came back in full-blown technicolour.

So, you did make one after all ... but why didn't you show me, Mum?

If he was brave enough to be truly honest with himself, he already knew the answer ... his mother knew full well he would have raced around to Lara's home, begging her to give him another chance.

Almost twenty minutes had passed by the time he joined her again. When she caught sight of the shawl in his hands, there was no need to ask what had taken him so long, especially when she noticed the melancholy shadow in his eyes. Before he reached her chair to drape the material across her shoulders, she rose to meet him. Without uttering a word, her arms folded him in a tight embrace.

He clung to her with an anguished cry, and his shoulders shook controllably when the realisation of everything he had lost overwhelmed him all over again.

Chapter 30

It was early May, less than a month later, and the leaves on the trees were beginning to fall. Lara was just sitting down to a solitary dinner when the phone rang.

"Hi, Lara!" She recognised the voice from years past. It belonged to her former director whose company was still based in a suburban theatre on the fringe of Spring Hill.

"Paul! What a lovely surprise! How are you?"

The conversation was a welcome bout of catching up, mostly about family happenings and life in general, along with their most recent projects. It took a while before he was able to get around to the main reason for his call.

"Now Lara, there's something I wanted to ask you."

"Sure. Fire away."

"I was wondering if you're starting to miss the theatre, or are all those one-off gigs and that lonely old editing career satisfying enough for you?"

"Oh, wow, I wasn't expecting this. Umm … I hadn't really thought about it. Both have been pretty full on lately, so that keeps me out of mischief. To be honest, sometimes I do wish I was back there – I miss the excitement and the camaraderie of a large troupe, and the close friends I've made. Are those talented old mates of mine treating you well and turned you into a millionaire yet?"

"I wish! But they're doing well – we've had full houses every night for the last three runs."

"Wow, that's great! Congratulations, but I'm not surprised. Luce did a fabulous job as *Calamity Jane* last time. Don't forget to send me the latest flyer so I can be there when the next one opens."

"Actually, that's the reason for my call. I was wondering if you'd be up to joining us for the next one?"

"What! Be part of a full musical again?" Her heart started thumping louder than it had in ages.

Despite her obvious interest, his manner turned almost sheepish. "Umm … yep … and I know you haven't been on a theatre stage for years, but I've just been given the opportunity to put on *Phantom,* and you're the only *Christine* who can do the part justice ... unless I want to pay a small fortune for Marina," he finished with a nervous chuckle.

She recognised the name of the well-known star who had made a name for herself as the first Australian to take on the demanding role. Lara had seen her in *The Secret Garden* over five years earlier and could still remember that beautiful voice blending beautifully with Anthony Warlow's. Appearance fees for someone of her calibre would be far more than a suburban director could possibly afford and she knew him too well to take offence at his comment.

There was, however, an ulterior motive for Paul's request. Recalling Lara's soft spot for a good cause, and also because of their earlier relationship, he was hoping she might be willing to do him a favour. "So, how about it? We'd all love to have you back."

Flattered by his offer, she was also mindful of her best friend. "But what about Lucy? She's been your leading lady for so long now. It wouldn't be fair to bring me in over the top of her."

"Don't worry. Lucy's the one who suggested I give you a call. Her voice is fabulous, but she knows her range isn't wide enough for such a demanding role. She's quite happy being cast as *Meg Giry,* so there's no need to worry. Now I know Max is sure to be furious when he finds out I've gone over his head, but I'm trying to raise much-needed funds for some new medical equipment at the kids' hospital. Having you top billing would be a great way to increase their coffers. The whole team would be honoured to have you back again ... so long as you can fit us into that busy schedule of yours."

Paul had always sported a generous heart, and this charity meant the world to him since his daughter underwent urgent surgery as a baby.

"Of course I will, and I'm the one who should feel honoured. After all, it's years since I've trodden any proper theatre boards. I'm probably rusty, so you'd be doing *me* a favour."

"You'll really do it?"

"Sure!"

"Oh thanks, sweetheart, you're a lifesaver! But you'd better check that calendar first. I don't want to put you out ... especially when I won't be able to pay any of those astronomical fees you're used to!"

"Don't worry about that – I'm happy to donate my time for such a great cause, and I can work my schedule around yours."

"I knew I could count on you!"

A sudden wave of conscience hit him. Once upon a time, Lara's contracts had ensured she was earning appearance fees similar to Marina. The last thing the director wanted was to take advantage of her good nature.

"Now listen, are you really sure about this? After all, paid bookings are much more important than this old charity case."

"Course I am! I happen to owe heaps to 'this old charity case'! And don't worry; I'm sure I'll be able to convince Max."

After everything Paul had done for her career in the early days, helping him out was far more important than any other bookings in the pipeline. If necessary, she was prepared to postpone them all to fit in with his needs.

Lara could hear the excitement in his voice as they went on to discuss the timetable for rehearsals and performance dates.

"You've no idea how much I appreciate your willingness to step in, especially at such short notice, and I'm sure you won't be disappointed. I promise to make it up to you with good advertising so all your fans will know you're back treading the boards."

"Oh, Paul, you don't have to worry about that!"

A hearty chuckle filled her ears. "Oh yes, I do! Then the biggest producers'll be back hounding Max to get you in their new productions, and he'll forget all about how mad he is at me for asking for a freebie! That way, we'll both be in his good books again!"

Her infectious laugh joined his hearty chuckle when she recognised this backhanded form of blackmail. "Fair enough and thanks again. I can't wait to get back into that old theatre, and I'll definitely be there when rehearsals begin."

They hung up and Lara couldn't control her smiles or the burst of adrenaline rushing through her veins. She hadn't realised how much she missed being part of a full musical production until it was once again within her grasp.

Only a minute later, the telephone was back in her hands.

"Hello, my gorgeous friend! How can I ever thank you enou—"

Lara had to hold the receiver several inches from her ear when Lucy's loud shriek came down the line.

"Yaaaay, you're going to *take* it! That's fantastic! I *knew* you'd say yes!"

When Paul had first put it to the company about producers being interested in putting *Phantom* on, Lucy knew straight away this was the perfect vehicle to bring her friend back to the stage. After discussing it with Charles, he quickly agreed and was willing to back her idea all the way. Lara was a popular club and concert singer, but everyone knew musical theatre was where her light truly shone. Their plan had worked, and she couldn't be happier.

"How could I ever say no to coming back, although you really should be the one playing *Christine*. After all, you're the principal female there now."

"Are you kidding me? I haven't the range, so I'm not upset at all. I'm just thrilled we're going to be working together again. Can you imagine how exciting it'll be to share another dressing room? I can't wait!"

The exhilaration in her tone was contagious, and Lara was carried along in the excitement as the conversation fired back and forth about the new project.

Down through the years, no matter how busy their lives had become, at least once a month the two women met up for either a quick coffee or a meal. When time permitted, sometimes a movie date was tacked on the end. During one of these girls' nights out, Lara had spilled the beans about the riding trip and holiday romance. Deep in her heart, Lucy sensed Lara was feeling conflicted in her loyalty to Adam, but she respected her friend too much to let on, especially when the relationship was still new and there was a chance he was just what she needed to help her move on. The last thing Lucy wanted was to cause her best friend any more heartache.

Before hanging up, Lucy felt it was only polite to ask. "So, how's Mike?"

"Mmm, he's good. I actually just got back from a few days in Coffs."

For the final few minutes, Lara filled her in about the recent visit. The only thing she left out was how often her thoughts still turned to another, despite a mountain-load of efforts to control them.

§

Lara was singing at the top of her voice as she hurriedly put a few last minute touches to her make-up before racing out the door. She couldn't wait to get to the theatre for the first rehearsal and had been watching the clock all afternoon.

Crossing the car park beside the familiar old hall, her gaze immediately swept across to a shadowy far corner. From out of the blue, an image emerged from deep in her spirit ... one that had been tucked away for many years. A rabble of butterflies suddenly played havoc in the pit of her stomach with the memory that this was the place where she and Adam had first sealed their love with a kiss.

She could almost taste his passionate mouth devouring hers again. Her recollections were from long ago, but even so, in many ways, it felt like only yesterday as she recalled every moment and each sensation. Her feet slowed as she stopped to gaze at the empty space. It was as though, similar to a time-traveller, she was being transported back in time ... and her heart would have given anything to go back there in reality.

"We never did get the chance to shout about our love to the world, Teddy," she breathed into the darkness ... sadly, the only reply was a shrill chirrup from a solitary cicada on his nightly prowl.

Voices from inside the theatre roused her from these forbidden thoughts. With one last heartfelt sigh, she whispered lovingly, "I still miss us, my darling."

Making her way into the familiar old hall, a sudden revelation hit home with full clarity. It had only taken one single thought for that exquisite rush of desire to flood her body in that old familiar way. Unfortunately, it was for the one person she would never have the chance to experience it with ever again.

§

The moment she walked through the door, a burst of rousing applause greeted her. It was just what Lara needed to lift her spirits out of a longed-for past.

Her old acting troupe had always been a tight-knit company. The majority enjoyed working with Paul so much it was a rare thing for anyone to leave. Having worked with most already, Lara felt right at home as she went to join those already gathered in clusters up on the stage.

Charles was standing almost in the exact same spot as the first time they had spoken. Back then, Lara had been a shy young woman just starting out. With a beaming smile she made a beeline to his side, greeting him with a warm hug and affectionate kiss on the cheek.

"Hello, my dear friend."

He held the top of her arms and looked down at her with a caring smile. "Welcome home, my beautiful girl. It's wonderful to have you join us again. It made my day when Paul rang to say you were coming back – even if it is only for one production."

"I'm so excited to be here. It's been so long, and yet it really does feel like I've come home. I couldn't believe it when he asked me, but this is just what I needed after being away so long. I'm really looking forward to working with everyone again..."

Her eyes suddenly clouded over ... there was no 'everyone' anymore.

All Charles could offer was a silent hug as he read her thoughts behind that sorrowful pause. Just then, a sudden shriek came from the entrance doors.

"Lars, you're here! Oh, I can't believe you're back."

Lucy rushed down the aisle and quickly raced up the stairs. Lara found herself nearly bowled over in all the excitement as she was pulled into the newcomer's welcoming arms. Charles grinned as he watched them together, thankful Lucy's bubbly personality had chased away that earlier hint of gloom.

"Hi, Luce, it's so good to see you – and being back here makes it even better! You sure know how to convince a person that saying yes to this new/old caper was the right thing to do!" Lara laughed, returning the hug with the same amount of enthusiasm. Under her breath, she sent up a silent prayer of thanks for special friends who understood.

"Of course it is – musical theatre is where you belong!"

Rehearsals went smoothly, and it wasn't long before those old wooden floorboards became a recognisable foundation for a pair of feet that had missed the fun and excitement of performing with an experienced band of triple threat performers – ones who could sing, dance and act. Paul was pleased with everyone's efforts, and they were a happy bunch exiting the theatre a couple of hours later.

All the way home, Lara's heart soared at the thrill of being back in a group situation rather than her usual solo act, even though those same feet now sported two fat blisters from the energetic dance routines after so many years' absence.

Be that as it may, lying in bed later that night a small part of her soul cried out for the one person who had always made her feel complete ... and for the first time in a long time her pillow soaked up a myriad number of tears.

§

The weeks flew by and the best part of Lara's week was time spent in rehearsals. Since Nikki had left home, she often found herself growing morose while roaming around the little cottage, looking for something – anything – to fill the vacant hours. Many evenings quickly disintegrated into memory-lane-blues, especially when she looked out her bedroom window and saw a special hilltop with its twinkling beacons in the distance. Sometimes when one of these dark moods descended, the lights on the four towers appeared to be winking at her, which then became another sad reminder of a man offering similar gestures to convey how much he loved her. Being back in the theatre was her saving grace. It was little wonder she was eager to get lost in the world of make-believe and music all over again.

The calls with Mike continued. Every ten days or so they found time to kick back with a steaming mug of coffee in one hand and the phone in the other, sharing news and funny anecdotes from their workdays. Chatting with him helped to break up the monotony of those evenings when the television was her only companion. On the nights he called, Lara also found her midnight musings were less torturous, and she fell asleep trying to recall the words they shared rather than those others from long ago.

§

Nikki was enjoying her time at NIDA, even though there was so much to learn. She soon made close friends with several other students, especially those living in the same boarding house. Sometimes on a free day, she managed to catch up with Matilda, her best friend and Helen's granddaughter from when they were youngsters. The two girls had always remained close since sharing sleepovers whenever Lara was on tour in Sydney. Now they were having a marvellous time exploring the city as grown-ups while reminiscing over recognised places and shared childhood secrets.

The constant demands of study kept her busy and helped to fill the void of missing her mother. On weekends, she and her mates often headed to the movies or just hung out in each other's rooms, jamming or learning their lines.

Being underage, any trendy clubs or bars were strictly off the agenda. Other first-year students often snuck into the Kings Cross nightclub scene, but Nikki wasn't going to let anything tarnish her reputation at the institute and possibly risk losing her place to someone else eager to get in. Overriding everything was a determination not to disappoint her mother, especially after all the sacrifices Lara had made to see her succeed. They rang one another every few days for a catch-up. Even though most calls only lasted a few minutes, it was enough for Lara to hear her precious daughter was happy and doing well at her studies.

§

"Hey, Mike."

"Hi, Lara, how's your week been?"

"Mmm, pretty good thanks, how about you?"

The two phone buddies shared their news, and after about twenty minutes the call ended with what had become their regular sign-off routine.

"Okay, better go, it's getting late. I've got an early start in the morning."

"Okey-dokey," he responded. "Glad to hear you're doing well. All the best with final rehearsals and I'll try to ring again next week. See ya."

"Sure, talk then. 'Night."

Sitting in the dark afterwards, she pondered her life and their relationship. Suddenly it dawned on her that nearly every one of their conversations was simply those of two casual friends killing a bit of time rather than the excitement of hearing the voice of that special someone you were eager to share everything with.

As much as she hated to hurt Mike, Lara realised her feelings would never be strong enough to consider settling down and making a life with him. He was a good friend, but she just couldn't envisage experiencing a desire so powerful it would have her yearning to make love to him with reckless abandon. In spite of experiencing deep feelings of trepidation about how to break the news, that night she went to bed as though a heavy weight had been lifted off her shoulders. She knew it was confirmation of her true feelings.

For the rest of the week, there was a distinct spring in her step. Even David commented when he heard her feet tapping along to one of the show tunes as it fell from her lips.

"That sounds more like the sidekick I recognise!"

"Mmm, I feel really good – the new show's about to open, and I have a great job! What could be better!"

He smiled to himself. *I think it's more than that. Maybe you've found yourself a new man. Hope so ... it's about time someone came along to sweep you off your feet.*

Lara found it helped not having to pretend to herself how she felt anymore, though this changed attitude hid a dark secret ... one she didn't want anyone else figuring out. With Mike now relegated to his rightful place in her life, a yawning emptiness grew in her soul as she once again contemplated a life spent alone.

The following week his regular call came and Lara's hand shook as she picked up the handset. How could she tell him what she was feeling without sounding callous and uncaring? His day had been filled with excitement from a large group of Americans taking in all the sights of the fascinating underwater world. He rambled on and on so much, it was hard to try and get a word in edgewise. In the end, she chickened out rather than putting a dampener on his day.

When they rang off, it was with their usual best wishes for a good week and his customary farewell line, "Talk to you sometime next week. See ya."

Only a few days later, Lara was driving along the southern motorway towards the city following another one-night gig on the Gold Coast. The day was perfect and without a cloud in the sky. When she topped a steep rise near the inner-city suburb of Tarragindi, off in the far distance the very tips of two rugged mountain peaks forming part of the majestic Glasshouse Mountains came into view.

The sight of them took her back to a day when a young couple with stars in their eyes had looked down from a lookout onto those same mountains. Memories came flooding back of Adam declaring he wanted to design and build a home for them right there – a place where they could hide away from the rest of the world. For a little while she was back in his arms again, feeling loved and desired as the hint of a poignant smile touched the corners of her mouth ... before that inevitable chasm of loss opened up again.

And then the truth finally hit home – something she hadn't wanted to face while contemplating sharing life with somebody else.

No matter where she was, her heart still searched for its soulmate – in the little everyday things that conjured up his form. All she had to do was reminisce over a long-cherished memory and a smile would instantly light up her eyes, like a match striking against flint. Then for those few precious minutes, a comforting glow warmed the empty chambers of her heart ... until the flame inevitably petered out and all that remained was the faint aroma from the spark – a solitary reminder of all that had once been. And like a bolt of lightning came the stark realisation – these were the only romantic memories she would ever want in her life.

Swallowing hard, Lara knew there was only one place she could turn to for comfort and strength.

Oh, Lord, please give me the courage to do this. Adam is and always will be the biggest part of my life. For the first time, I fully understand that neither Mike nor anyone else will ever be able to take his place in my heart. Please help me to stay strong...

Chapter 31

The last Saturday in June was opening night. Nikki flew up especially for her mother's much-anticipated comeback. It was six long years since Lara had set foot on a theatre stage and she was determined to be there to offer her support.

While Lara rested her voice on the morning of the big event, Nikki went over to visit Charles and Elizabeth and spend some quality time with Jasper. The last time they had been together was when she flew home to celebrate Mother's Day five weeks earlier. The Ashworths were on the terrace enjoying the heart-warming reunion when a series of loud whinnies carried across the lawn.

It was obvious the chestnut gelding had recognised his owner's cheery laugh. Seeing his head tossing back and forth as he sniffed the air, Nikki sent off a loud wolf-whistle. Offering up another whinny, Jasper started prancing along the fence-line, his flaxen tail swishing back and forth.

"Off you go and say hello ... he's been waiting ages to see you," Elizabeth said kindly, nudging Nikki's elbow with her own.

Grinning widely, the eager young horse fanatic offered her a grateful hug before taking off at a run, weaving around bushes and jumping small logs as the spirited animal paced even faster. Watching his best friend approach, Jasper blew in and out through those wide nostrils, trying to catch her scent.

For the next exhilarating few hours, she and the beloved horse explored the local area, rediscovering special haunts and lush paddocks filled with clover. In the afternoon, her mother joined them for a late lunch before she and Charles had to leave for the theatre.

A heavy schedule of balancing two careers meant there was rarely time for Lara to pop over as often as Adam's parents would have liked. Most of Elizabeth and Charles' Saturdays now consisted of simply pottering around the garden instead of the relaxed family time they all used to enjoy. Having the mother and daughter there was a rare and treasured treat.

Once Charles and Lara left to get ready for the opening, Elizabeth whipped up a fresh pot of coffee then took it out to the gazebo to share with her beloved granddaughter. Over the next hour, they savoured sitting in the warm winter sunshine while the lively teenager kept the other one entertained with stories from her new life in Sydney. Elizabeth missed her company far more than she cared to admit.

During a lapse in conversation, Adam's mother broached a subject that had been playing on her mind for quite some time.

"So how do you think your mum's coping on her own, sweetheart? I don't see enough of her anymore to know if she's really okay."

"Tell me about it! She's been so busy with everything that's going on, I'm having trouble keeping up with her myself, although we usually manage to fit in a couple of phone calls each week. I think she's doing okay, especially since rehearsals for *Phantom* started. She certainly sounds a lot happier than earlier in the year."

Elizabeth smiled kindly and leaned across to pat her hand. "I'm pretty sure we can put that down to missing you, young lady! It wasn't easy having to leave you behind in Sydney. You've been her life for so long, and she loves you more than words could ever convey. I'm glad she's gone back to the theatre – it's exactly what she needed to lift her spirits."

"Yeah, me too, although I really think there's more to it than that. Most of the time she sounds cheerful enough, but every now and then I can detect a sort of sadness in her voice ... almost as if something's troubling her. But whenever I ask her about it, she just brushes me off." She shrugged her shoulders. "Typical Mum ... doesn't like to worry anyone."

"She's been a bit like that with me, too. Do you know how the relationship with Mike's going? She never says much, and I didn't want to put her on the spot at lunch ... not when she has so much on her mind already with the opening tonight. Goodness, I even forgot to ask if he'll be there!"

"I'm not really sure how it's going, to be honest. I thought something was sure to happen when they first met in January ... she really seemed interested back then. You know she went down to see him at Easter, but I got the feeling she wasn't as enthusiastic when we spoke on the phone afterwards. From what Mum says, he must call fairly regularly. Still, I think it's more friendship than anything else. Oh, and he's not coming tonight – apparently, a busload of Americans chartered his boat for the weekend so he can't get away. I must say, she didn't sound too upset when we were talking about it."

"Mmm, that doesn't sound too promising." With a caring smile, Elizabeth leaned over and squeezed her arm. "Oh well, at least you'll be there to watch her perform, and I know that means more than anything. I can't believe that little mite who used to beg her Uncle Adam to take her down to see Clancy has grown into such an accomplished young woman. I'm very, very proud of you, my girl."

A bashful grin accompanied her reply. "Thanks, Aunty Elizabeth." Gazing across the river, Nikki's expression suddenly turned wistful, as though she was trying to focus on a shadowy film reel from ages past. "That was such a long time ago. How's he doing? I haven't seen him for so long. I suppose he's changed heaps since Mum and I bumped into him in Sydney when I was about seven or eight – oh, and I remember sitting in a private box above everyone else watching him play *Captain Von Trapp*. I was so excited and feeling so important to be up there – like a princess."

Elizabeth's expression mirrored the younger woman's as the faintest glimmer of a poignant smile touched the corners of her mouth. "Oh, that's right. He told us how excited he was to see you again – my, that was such a long time ago. Mmm, he's still the same deep down ... and I think he's doing okay ... at least that's what he tells us. Our boy lives such a hectic lifestyle these days, we don't get to see him as often as we'd like. Still, I suppose that's understandable. Producers all over the country are constantly trying to outdo each other to get him signed for their productions, and so that means he and Trina don't get home very often anymore. I've even heard there's talk of him being offered a show in London – on the West End no less!"

"Wow! That's *hugely* exciting ... every live performer's dream is to land a role in one of those famous theatres!"

"Mmm, one producer's been eager to get him over there for the last couple of years, though I'm not sure when it's all coming together." Her voice grew softer. "I'm not sure if your mother knows anything about it ... or how she'll feel knowing he's so far away."

"Well, she hasn't said anything to me ... then again, she never mentions him at all. I never understood why they broke up in the first place – to be honest, I haven't been game enough to ask what happened. His photo still sits on her bedside table, but all I can remember is hearing her crying in the night when I was little. I haven't wanted to bring up his name in case it upsets her again."

"Good, your poor mother's suffered enough." She paused as a misty sheen touched her eyes. "He loved both of you, far more than I think you realise ... and it broke his heart having to say goodbye. You probably don't remember that night, but I know he still carries a letter you wrote to him in his wallet..."

"*Really?*"

"Yes, really ... and do you remember that picture of an angel you once drew for him?"

Nikki frowned as she tried to recall the long-forgotten memory. Suddenly her face lit up. "Oh, yeah, I do remember. I think I made it for him in Sunday School, but I must've been only small."

"You were and just the cutest little button any of us had ever seen! You brought so much sunshine into all our lives. I know Adam couldn't have loved you more, even if you'd been his own flesh and blood. In fact, he still takes that drawing with him wherever he goes ... along with a photo of your mother."

"You're kidding!"

"No, I'm not kidding ... I've seen them. They're always taped to the top corners of his dressing-room mirror whenever he's touring with a show."

"But why?"

"Because he thinks of them as his good luck charms ... they've followed him from one production to the next no matter what city he's been performing in."

Nikki's eyes grew even wider. For the first time, the teenager was beginning to understand just how much she actually meant to him. "Does Mum know?"

That gentle smile suddenly turned into a determined stare. "No, and you have to promise me you'll never tell. It would break her heart even more."

Nikki nodded slowly, contemplating all she had just learned. "I won't, I promise ... but I still can't believe it. Sometimes I remember things we did together ... but it's been so long, I think I've forgotten a lot from back then. I can still remember how much he used to make me laugh, though ... and I know he was great at making sandcastles." She gave a shy smile. "I still have pictures of them on both bedside tables – one at home and the other in Sydney."

More blurred memories resurfaced, and she screwed up her nose as if trying to ferret them out of a shadowy past. "I still remember some of the things we did in Italy, especially when we were with Aunty Claudia and Uncle Antonio – we had so many fun times with them. I just wish I could've gone to see them during my visit to Rome last year. Things were so busy, I just didn't have time."

"Don't worry, they understood, but they have fond memories of you, too."

"I loved that big old house and all those scrumptious meals she and Mum and I rustled up to impress the men. I really want to go back there one day."

"I hope you get the chance to. They'd be thrilled to bits to see you again."

"Oh, and I remember the three of us dancing around the fountain in Salzburg. I'll never forget that day because I pretended to be *Gretl* and Uncle Adam acted just like *The Captain* ... I remember wishing so hard he was my dad – but somehow I don't think I ever told him."

Elizabeth's expression softened even more. "You would've made him the happiest man alive if he'd known."

Her young visitor's reaction was the exact opposite – Nikki's face clouded over as she recalled another image. "I missed him so much when he went away – I still do in some ways when I think about all the good times we shared. But when he didn't come back after so long, I figured he must've forgotten about me. I used to wish he'd come to my school awards nights. I remember every year seeing a man standing up the back watching everything that was going on, but whenever I tried to see his face it was always in shadow. He was never with anyone, so I used to pretend it was my father there to support me, but whoever it was always left before I had the chance to see him properly."

Elizabeth's heart broke seeing the sad look on her granddaughter's face. It was enough to have her break a firm resolve made many years ago.

Forgive me, Lara, but she needs to know the truth.

Clasping Nikki's hand in hers, and with eyes glistening from unshed tears, she began relating a story far too late in the telling.

"My sweet, sweet girl ... that *was* your Uncle Adam. He missed you too – very much so – and always made sure he was there to support you ... every year without fail. That precious son of mine never stopped loving you. Even now, whenever we find time to talk in private, he always wants to know how you are."

"Why would he do that? He went away before I even *started* school I think, and I never saw him again after that time in Sydney. Mum never told me the whole story, but I do remember her saying something about him having commitments, which meant he had to go away. I know he's married now, but why couldn't we be together back then? I always thought they should have gotten married..."

"So did we, believe me, but your mother was right. He did have commitments, though it broke his heart just the same." Elizabeth paused to take a deep breath, reluctant to disclose the whole truth. Even so, she felt Nikki was mature enough to learn what really went on. Squeezing her hand, she looked into those deep brown eyes. "Sweetheart, he was already married ... even back then."

"*What?*" Startled, she snatched her hand away, frantically searching her grandmother's face.

"Your mum never told you because of the massive sense of guilt she's been living with all this time, along with the heartache she continually has to bury deep down inside."

"You mean to tell me she had an *affair? That's* the word, isn't it, when someone sleeps with another woman's *husband!*" Disgusted, she spat the words out of a wounded heart.

Elizabeth's tone was soft. "Oh, Nikki ... sweetie, it wasn't like that. Yes, they did have an affair, only there was a lot more to their story than you realise."

"But he was *married!*"

"Yes, he was, but his home life was horrific. Back then, Trina was a violent alcoholic and his life was a living hell. The only joy he knew was spending time with you and your mother. That's why he loved you both so much and why he never really got over you."

"Well, why didn't he leave if things were so bad? He mustn't have loved us *that* much if he stayed with her."

"Oh, my dear girl, it's not my place to tell you everything, but rest assured he wanted to be with you more than anything. You have to believe me when I say they both paid dearly for loving one another. Both your Uncle Charles and I knew they belonged together, and yet your mother put her own needs aside to give Adam and Trina a chance to repair their relationship. He loved your mother more than life itself, and you were the daughter he always longed for."

Elizabeth could sense her explanation was beginning to soften Nikki's heart. Grasping the teenager's hand again, she looked her straight in the eye.

"Something terrible happened, and it meant he could never have children of his own. You were the closest thing he had to seeing that dream come true. That's why he always made the effort to come to your awards night every year – even if it could only be from a distance. He was always so proud of you."

"So why didn't Mum tell me he was there? I would've gone up and said hello, but she never mentioned anything at all."

"Because she had no idea either. They were both broken-hearted when she had to say goodbye." She squeezed the teenager's hand and looked at her sadly. "You need to understand something, sweetie – theirs wasn't a normal relationship breakdown where one person falls out of love and leaves. They loved each other more than any couple I've ever known. A sad set of circumstances drove them apart ... not because they wanted it to happen. Your mother's a remarkable woman after everything she's had to endure ... facing so many things alone while endeavouring to give you the best life possible. You'll never fully understand all the sacrifices she's made ... that's one of many reasons she means so much to me."

"Well I'm glad she's had you to lean on then."

Unable to bear the sadness any longer, Elizabeth got to her feet and pulled Nikki up with her, holding her close in a warm embrace. With gentle hands stroking those smooth, silky tresses, she whispered, "You need to forgive your precious mum, my darling girl, and don't ever blame her for falling in love with my son. She's gone through her own kind of living hell, but never once complained or neglected her responsibilities, even when her heart was breaking. And she loves you more than life itself."

"I had no idea. Thanks for telling me," Nikki whispered back as the other one kept stroking her hair. When they drew apart, their arms rested loosely around one another's waist. "Is that why Mum won't talk about him, and why she's never been interested in seeing anyone else before this?" When Elizabeth offered a thoughtful nod, she went on. "I always wondered ... lots of men have asked her out, but Mike's the first one she's ever really shown any interest in."

"Mmm, I'd say you're probably right. She hasn't talked about it for many years, but I've always known she still holds a candle for your uncle ... and maybe that's why she's not too upset about Mike not being there tonight." Elizabeth looked at her watch. "Anyway, young lady, we'd better go up and get ready. We don't want to be late ... I know she'd be most upset if *you're* not there. And please don't let this affect your relationship – your mother's already paid her dues – she couldn't bear to lose you, too."

"I won't, I promise," came the earnest response.

All the way to the theatre, Nikki mused over their conversation. So many things seemed to make sense now – the look in her mother's eyes whenever she trawled through the album containing keepsakes and photos from their European holiday. Then there were the other two depicting shows she and Adam had been in together. She recalled watching Lara's fingers brush across their pages as though they were caressing every image – similar to how she touched Nikki's face whenever they had been apart for any length of time. She remembered all the times she had caught a glimpse of tears forming for no apparent reason. Whenever she asked what was wrong, her mother made out it was only dust or the wind.

A short time later, as the eager audience waited impatiently for the curtain to open, another familiar image worked its way into her memories. So many times she had glimpsed her mother's fingers stroke the sapphire and diamond pendant as a tragic love story played out on the TV or in the cinema. The glittering piece had hung around Lara's neck for as long as she could remember. In fact, Nikki couldn't ever recall seeing her mother without it except when she was playing another character and it was inappropriate for the role. Even during Lara's own concerts, the treble clef always rested just above her heart.

And one guess who gave you that beautiful ring. I always thought it must've been from my father. Oh, Mum, why didn't you tell me? I'm sorry I've been so wrapped up in myself. I didn't realise how lonely and sad life has been for you.

Offering up a heartfelt prayer, Nikki promised to make it up to her somehow.

§

The opening was the success everyone had been hoping for. It was inevitable they would draw big crowds with Lara in the role of *Christine* and Jeff playing *The Phantom.*

This was one of Lara's favourite musicals. The score was so powerful it always sent shivers up and down her spine, beginning with those first few stirring bars following the opening scene at the auction. Patrons experienced a similar reaction wherever it played around the world, and this became one of the major drawcards that kept bringing them back.

From the moment she stepped into the footlights, the star of the show was back in her element. Lara's heart soared while singing the emotive numbers. It was obvious this was her true calling, and she made a decision during the interval to return to musical theatre full-time. She would miss working with David,

415

however music truly was her life and the theatre her life's blood. For the first time in many years, she felt fully alive again.

When the curtain came down on the final scene, the theatre erupted with loud acclamations for the two leads' superb portrayals of the tragic couple.

Over the ensuing days, tickets sold out within hours of them going on sale. Paul was ecstatic and quickly extended the season for another two weeks. Lara didn't miss one performance, and for once even her understudy didn't mind – Lucy was tickled pink to be treading the boards with her best friend again.

While waiting for her cue at the beginning of each performance, Lara's heart beat so hard she felt as though it would burst through her chest. The only dark cloud overshadowing these times was how much she missed playing opposite her soulmate on the stage where they had first laid eyes on each other.

And just as she had never forgotten the loving gesture he always sent her way prior to the curtain rising on another performance, when the last round of applause sounded at the end of the night, she could still picture him standing beside her with those captivating dark eyes of his overflowing with love and pride. And always with those images came a mad rush of memories of all the times he had pulled her around a dark corner to offer his own form of congratulations in that special way that was his alone.

It was only when she was back in her dressing room that reality hit full force and it felt like a small knife was turning in her heart. Her only saving grace was knowing if she could just make it through the next few hours her spirit would come to life all over again, even if only for a few short hours while standing within a spotlight's silvery beam.

§

Mike's calls continued during the show's run. As usual, his conversation was more friendly than romantic and Lara breathed a long sigh of relief each time. Her decision to end the relationship was just as strong as ever, however, rather than breaking the news of her true feelings over the phone, she decided to take a few days off once *Phantom* was finished. Then she could make a quick trip to Coffs Harbour and tell him to his face.

Four days before her final performance, he rang with an unexpected surprise.

"Guess what! I've managed to wrangle a day off this weekend. That means I can come and see you before the musical finishes."

After hearing the excitement in her voice as she talked about how magical it was to be back doing what she loved best, Mike figured it was high time he put in an appearance to see what all the fuss was about. Being a typical country boy who lived hundreds of kilometres from a major city, there hadn't been any opportunity to attend a major theatre event, so he wasn't sure what to expect.

"That's great." She tried to sound enthusiastic, despite a sudden sense of panic overriding everything else. "When are you planning on coming?"

"On Saturday – probably early afternoon after dropping by the farm to see the folks and Shelly beforehand. I figured I'd stay overnight if that's okay, then leave again around mid-morning to be back in time for a late afternoon dive. Sorry I can't stay longer, but it's the best I can do."

Lara's feeling of dread gave way to a sense of relief. Now she could tell him before he left, rather than having to make the trip herself the following week. "Don't worry, I understand, and thanks for making the effort ... but are you sure about coming all this way for such a short visit?"

"Oh yeah, I really want to see what you get up to, but you don't sound too excited about it. Is everything okay?"

"Sure, I'm fine, don't worry. I've just got a lot on my plate at present. Max's trying to sign me up for other productions, and I'm still finishing off a few last projects with David. I think I told you I'm going back to theatre full-ti—"

"Yeah, you did, and that's something I want to talk to you about."

He sounded upset so Lara asked what he meant.

"Oh, don't worry – it'll wait 'til we're together, then we can talk about it properly."

She wasn't quite sure she liked the sound of that, but with time getting away they rung off with a hurried, "Okay, see you next week," and "Yep, looking forward to it."

Afterwards, she sat in the dark for nearly an hour, pondering the unexpected visit and wondering how to break the news. It went against her nature to hurt anyone, but there was no use pretending they had any chance of a future together. Also at the back of her mind was a niggling worry...

Why was he so upset when I mentioned the theatre? I just hope he's on the same page as me...

§

Lara was on tenterhooks all day as she waited for Mike to arrive. She heard a car start to slow in the street just before the clock chimed four, only an hour or so before she had to leave for the theatre. A well-worn ute turned into the driveway and a loud honking of its horn brought her to the door.

She waved and called out, "Hi, I see you found the place okay." Plastering a smile on her face while walking down the stairs, Lara made sure she was standing on the other side of the open car door when he got out.

"Gidday, good lookin'. Gee, you look great. Sorry I'm a bit late – I was delayed at the farm and the traffic was horrendous. That's a heck of a long drive – it's nice to finally stretch the legs," he said, slamming the door behind him.

Before he could place his lips on hers, she turned her head so they landed against her cheek instead. With a quizzical frown, he offered her a quick peck,

417

deciding to let the casual greeting go for now rather than make a fuss. Hoping to make up for the unexpected sleight, she quickly wrapped him in a welcoming hug. It helped to ease his concerns a little, assuming she was probably just being cautious about catching a cold or something that may affect her voice for the show. He knew she couldn't risk coming down with anything on closing night.

"Come on up and bring your things," she called, scurrying up the stairs.

Grabbing a canvas duffle bag from the ute's back tray, he followed along behind, glancing around and finding the homey little cottage was just as she described.

As nonchalantly as possible, Lara called over her shoulder, "Nikki's room is all ready for you. It has a nice view and shouldn't be too cold as it gets the afternoon sun."

Again, his brow furrowed as an automatic response echoed in his head. *I thought you might be keeping me warm.*

Lara led the way inside to a room clearly meant for a teenage girl. There were photos of horses and rows of equestrian ribbons hanging from the picture-rail, along with a faded celluloid doll clearly the centrepiece as it stood in pride of place. Positioned in the centre of the bedside table was a frame with a faded photo of a man and child standing beside what looked to be a gigantic sandcastle.

Mmm, must be Nikki's father, I reckon.

Then he remembered Lara mentioning they hadn't seen him since Nikki was a baby. Glancing at the photo again, his mind formed the silent question, *So who are you and where do you fit into this family?*

Dropping his bag on the floor, with a tentative smile he turned to take her in his arms. This time she went into them more willingly, though continued to make sure their lips didn't touch.

"You should be comfy in here – the bed's fairly new, and there are extra blankets in the cupboard."

"This is fine just so long as Nikki doesn't mind," he whispered into her hair.

"Oh, she won't mind at all." After landing another peck on his cheek, she carefully extricated herself and led the way to the kitchen. "How about I make you a nice hot cuppa after that long drive?"

"Sure, that'd be great, thanks."

While she kept busy putting the kettle on and placing a few freshly baked brownies on a plate, Mike positioned his hands to spring onto the bench-top.

Before he could complete the manoeuvre, she quickly cut in with, "Oh, don't sit up there. I haven't had time to clean properly. Besides, you must be tired from such a long drive. Why don't you go and make yourself comfortable on the veranda while I finish up here. I won't be long."

Again he was puzzled as the surface looked spotless. But rather than making a fuss over anything so trivial, he shrugged his shoulders and called on his way out, "Okay, but don't be too long. I've come a long way to see you and I don't want to waste any more time."

Lara bustled around getting everything ready and then leaned back against the counter to gather her thoughts as the water slowly rose to the boil. An idle hand gently brushed the bench-top as she stared out the window to four tall television towers in the distance ... until the kettle's shrill whistle brought her back from these long-lost daydreams. With a determined shake of her head, she went back to focussing on the job at hand.

When she went to set their mugs on a small side table, a small sigh of relief slipped through her lips when she saw he had chosen one of the classic white rattan wingchairs instead of the longer couch. This gave her a small reprieve from any further intimate exchanges – at least for a little while.

She settled into the chair opposite with a friendly smile, deciding it was better not to say anything about her recent misgivings about their relationship until the following morning. The last thing she needed just before a show was any form of heavy discussion, especially when an unhappy outcome was more than likely.

Time passed quickly as they chatted about the drive, their latest work projects and family life, along with her excitement over the musical. Sipping on the honey-infused tea, Lara could feel herself starting to relax as they looked out to the city skyline. The soothing hot beverage was always her drink of choice before a performance.

After a while, Mike placed his mug down and both his tone and gaze were serious. "Okay, Lara, what's all this about you going back to the theatre full-time? I thought you enjoyed editing as a career."

"I do – it's been a fabulous part of my life, but since Nikki's moved away and I'm not tied down with other things, I can go back to committing to much larger productions that may entail travelling around the country. It's been six years since I gave it all away. Being back in those familiar settings means all my old hopes and dreams are starting to come alive again. I'm enjoying treading the boards in a full show ... I hadn't realised just how much I missed it until this."

Mike wasn't quite sure he liked the sound of her 'not tied down with other things' quip. Was he one of them? If so, where did that put their relationship? When Lara glanced at her watch with an anxious frown, he knew it was time to go and get ready. Rather than pursue the issue, he decided to wait until later to quiz her further.

"Well, I'll just have to wait to see how talented you are before deciding if it's a good thing or not," he teased, trying to steer the conversation into safer waters.

"I hope you won't be too disappointed seeing you haven't been to the theatre before. After all, tonight's show is only put on by a small suburban company. If ever you get to see a full-blown production on one of the country's major stages, I'm sure you'll understand why I feel the way I do."

"Maybe I will. Now, how about you scoot off and get ready while I clean up all this. Can't have you late for my debut!" he warned with a grin, taking their plates and mugs into the kitchen as Lara made a hurried dash to her bedroom.

As soon as she closed the door, her gaze fell on a word fashioned in pewter. The sculpture had been positioned carefully in front of a treasured photograph as a way to hide its image from prying eyes. All morning she had wrestled with putting the photo away in a drawer. Eventually, she couldn't bring herself to relegate it to that inky blackness. Despite knowing Mike might happen to see it, she was willing to take the risk. For far too long Adam had remained hidden away from everything else in her world. She was adamant it wasn't going to happen in the privacy of her own bedroom.

§

Mike sat in the second front row as the legendary tale unfolded, and he was surprised at how much the music and storyline affected him. Watching Lara put everything she had into her performance gave him an understanding as to why she was eager to get back into it again. Her voice was exceptional, and those in the audience were mesmerised at how she embodied the naive and enchanting young opera understudy caught in the spell of the *Phantom's* magnetic shadowy figure. As the crowd filed out, he couldn't wait to offer his congratulations and tell her just how much he had enjoyed himself.

In the privacy of their dressing room, the two best friends helped each other change for the after-party. Lucy couldn't help admiring Lara as she stepped from the white floaty wedding gown required in the final emotional scene into a raspberry-toned chiffon strapless gown. She looked absolutely breathtaking where it hugged her upper torso and then drifted down like a sunset-tinged cloud.

Nestled just below her firm, full breasts, a Swarovski crystal clip held fast a tiny handful of the sheer top layer which then flowed to her knees. The delicate skirt was fashioned into thin pinch pleats which floated across her hips and made her appear almost ethereal in the flowing fabric. Bejewelled high-heeled sandals in silver finished the outfit, while a chestnut swathe of shoulder-length hair swished around her bare shoulders.

When she came out to join him in the foyer, Mike let out a very loud wolf whistle. "Wow, don't you look a bit of alright!"

Blushing profusely, she responded with a bashful smile, "Thanks, Mike."

Oblivious to her coyness, he still hadn't finished, and the excitement in his voice drew a few amused looks from those standing nearby. "Crikey, Lara, you were fabulous up there! If this wasn't the last show, I'd willingly drive up next weekend to see you do it all over again!"

His enthusiasm managed to wipe away any embarrassment and soon had her laughing freely. "Well, I'm happy to hear you liked it so much. See, I told you it's not just for the hoity-toity rich folk!"

A ready chuckle joined hers as he took her arm and she didn't resist as they wandered out to the street.

The party was held in the large function room of the popular Gambaro Seafood Restaurant just around the corner – the same venue used to host another show's closing so many years ago. Rather than getting maudlin by a bombardment of memories, as soon as they arrived Lara dragged him over to meet Lucy and Jeff. Mike had been looking forward to meeting her friends after hearing glowing accounts of their various exploits while getting to know Lara on the riding holiday.

The two couples chatted for several minutes, making small talk and finding out about each other's lives and interests. Mike appeared to be happy and relaxed, while Lara could tell her best friend was carefully sizing him up and down, despite her friendly manner.

"So, Lucy, what's the story with this one?" he asked, inclining his head towards Lara who was now deep in conversation with Jeff several feet away. "How come she's still single when she looks like a goddess dressed like that? Give me all the goss ... there must be something she's not telling me."

The young woman waved her hand in the air. "Oh, there's no goss, I can assure you. Lars is always way too busy – it's been tough raising a child on her own all these years and work has kept her focussed the rest of the time."

"Oh, come *on!* Don't give me that when there's obviously a full stable of good-looking cohorts ready to sweep a knock-out like Lara off her feet! That young buck playing *Phantom's* rival seemed pretty taken with her." His expression was almost leering as he looked Lara up and down.

Lucy sent him a puzzled frown, not quite sure how to respond. "But everything on stage is all make-believe. Besides, he's married to the woman playing *Carlotta.* I can assure you, Lara isn't interested in any of her co-stars."

"But she's always mixing with showbiz personalities in both jobs – surely someone's taken an interest. Come on, you can trust me! There must be some deep, dark secrets in her past I should know about..."

His grilling put her on the spot. Lara was too far away to hear what they were discussing, but Lucy felt as though he was asking her to betray their friendship.

"Look, Mike, like I said, she's been far too busy with two careers on the go at once. Besides, Nikki's been her life for so long, she hasn't had time for anyone else ... until meeting you." As soon as she finished speaking, her eyes darted around the room.

"Well we haven't had much chance to see each other, and she's out a lot of the time when I'm free to call. Maybe one of her theatre buddies has managed to sweep her off her feet, especially with me living so far away unable to keep an eye on things. She certainly seems different since going back to the stage compared to the country gal I met a few months ago. Besides, she's far too beautiful not to be on somebody's radar."

Lara had just finished her conversation with Jeff and caught his final comment. "What are you two going on about? Whose radar? Don't you go giving away any of my secrets, Luce!"

She chuckled nervously while sending her best friend a mock frown, but a hint of concern in those piercing blue eyes betrayed her anxiety as to where the conversation was heading.

Grateful for the sudden reprieve, Lucy mustered up a relieved smile, though nestled behind her cheerfulness was a noticeable veil of unease. "I wouldn't dare. All your secrets are safe with me ... you know that." She elbowed her friend's arm playfully and threw a cheeky wink Mike's way, hoping to make light of their comments.

While he quizzed Lara, Lucy took advantage of the distraction. Once again, her eyes quickly scanned the room. Then, with a noticeable swallow of relief, she turned back to eavesdrop on their conversation.

Mike's attention was concentrated solely on Lara. "I was just wondering why someone hasn't whisked you away on a magnificent white steed and locked you up in a castle tower to keep you all to himself. I even thought of doing something similar when we were riding in the Snowies ... but just my luck, the only castles down there were old tin sheds." He returned Lucy's wink, joining in the teasing with no clue as to the effect his words were having on the other two.

She actually felt sorry for him. Apart from that earlier cross-examination and ogling look, he really did seem quite nice, and she could understand why Lara had been attracted to him in the first place ... but she also knew why her bestie wasn't as keen as someone else in her situation.

Lucy had always had a secret crush on Adam herself ... nothing serious enough to risk their friendship – or her marriage to Jeff – but if he had ever looked at her the way he did Lara, she wasn't sure she would have been able to resist his advances either. The possibility of being loved with that degree of passion was every woman's deepest desire. As much as she admired Lara for her integrity in doing what she thought was right, Lucy still believed it had been the biggest mistake of her life. Adam really was one in a million, despite the phrase being an over-used cliché. Unfortunately for Mike, there really was no comparison between the two men.

"Who needs a castle anyway?" Lara answered lightly. "They're far too overrated and cost the earth to maintain. I'd much rather my little home with all its memories any day, even if I am on my own most of the time."

And there I go again! Why does everything always end up coming back to him?

For the third time in almost as many minutes, Lucy's eyes cautiously perused the room. Lara wondered what was making her friend so edgy, but then decided to leave it alone rather than spoil the easy-going mood.

The place was filling rapidly as the cast along with their families and friends joined in. Lara spotted Charles and Elizabeth talking to someone on the other side of the room. A palm frond obscured most of the trio, and people kept crossing her line of vision so she couldn't make out who the other person was.

It was weeks since the two women had last seen each other and performance days had been far too hectic to find any time for a long chat with Charles. This seemed the perfect opportunity for a good catch up and the best way to introduce them to Mike. Even though it was unlikely they would ever see each other again, she didn't want to appear rude by leaving him alone with Lucy and Jeff while she was off socialising.

With her arm linked through his, she called over her shoulder, "Sorry, you two, I'm just going to borrow Mike for a bit. Won't be long..." She turned to him with a smile. "Come with me. There are a couple of very special people I want you to meet – they've been like grandparents and parents to Nikki and me over the years."

Straightaway, Lucy's worried gaze darted over to where Elizabeth and Charles were standing and then back to her husband. Jeff knew her too well and could sense she wasn't happy, especially when she elbowed him hard in the ribs. The others had left already and missed all of this silent interaction.

As she and Mike drew near, Lara noticed Adam's parents were now standing on their own. The person they were talking to earlier had obviously moved on. Both still had their backs to the newcomers and were completely unaware of their approach, until Lara gently touched Elizabeth on the shoulder.

Letting out a sudden gasp, the older woman turned around and immediately clutched at her heart. "Oh, Lara, you gave me such a fright!"

Expecting her usual welcoming smile, the newcomer was concerned by Elizabeth's reaction and reached out to take her arm. "I'm so sorry ... I didn't mean to startle you."

"Well, you did – I-I hate being surprised like that!" the older woman stammered.

"Oh Elizabeth, I *am* sorry. I just wanted to introduce you to a friend of mine. Mike, this is Elizabeth, one of the dearest people in my life."

"It's okay, I just wasn't expecting to see you." Her hand still rested over her heart as she turned to the young man. "I'm sorry ... hello ... Mike, is it?"

Even more perplexed by her cryptic response, Lara cut in before Mike could reply. "What do you mean you weren't expecting to see me? Of course I wanted to say hi to my favourite fan!" It was clear something was bothering the other woman and then she remembered Elizabeth's former heart condition. "Oh dear, are you feeling alright? How about we go and sit down while we talk."

"No, I'm fine, don't fuss! I don't know what I was thinking. Now let me start again." Hastily she put out her hand, attempting her normal warm smile. "Hello, Mike, it's nice to meet you at last. Lara has told us all about that wonderful holiday and how you two met."

"It's nice to meet you too, Elizabeth. She hasn't stopped singing your praises since then either!"

The gentle woman blushed and waved a dismissive hand. "Oh my, but then she was probably exaggerating! Here, let me introduce you to my husband. Charles, this is Mike, Lara's friend," she added hastily, anxious to get the focus away from herself.

A momentary look of panic shadowed Elizabeth's eyes when she turned to her other half, though she managed to bring it under control at the sight of his concerned frown. Lara was surprised to find her acting so out of character and couldn't fathom what was going on.

As a way to put everyone at ease, Charles extended his hand. "So, you're the Mike we've been hearing about. It's nice to meet you at last."

Before the other man could respond, a deep voice could be heard coming from behind Elizabeth, "Here you go, Mum. I was on my way out, but then I thought you could do with one of these ... lemon, lime and bitters for my favourite girl and a glass of bubbly for you, Dad."

That instantly recognisable tone had filled Lara's dreams for more than a decade and her heart began to race. Without even realising, she let out an audible gasp and quickly let go of Mike's arm.

Adam's eyes had already sought out Lara's when he heard the sharp intake of breath slip through her lips. Immediately, his gaze fell headlong into hers, and just as flint ignites a flame, it was as though her spirit sprang to life. But she wasn't able to say anything – her mouth was too dry and she couldn't trust herself to speak.

"Hello, Lara."

Tender and filled with the pent-up yearning of so many years apart, just two words were enough to feed her starved soul.

As if drawn there, his eyes moved to her neck, seeking out the glittering musical symbol. Next, they travelled down to her right hand, and the glimmer of a reflective smile touched his lips when he caught sight of the pendant's mate ... until those matching blue eyes quickly drew him back into their depths.

Instinctively, Lara's fingertips stroked the sapphire and diamond-encrusted treble clef, and their silent message was plain and clear. *Yes, my darling, they still come everywhere with me.*

When she was finally able to swallow, a flurry of nervous dialogue fell from her lips.

"Adam! What a lovely surprise! You're looking good ... in fact, you've hardly changed at all."

She could have kicked herself. Such a stupid greeting after everything they had been through ... though she really didn't care. He was standing right in front of her, and that was all that mattered.

Oh, my darling, is it really you? ... It's true, you haven't changed ... well, not to me ... but you promised to stay away ... but I'm sooo glad you didn't ... Please don't look at me like that ... I can't bear to see the pain in your eyes ... Oh, Teddy, have you any idea how much I still miss you ... how much I miss us? ... And do you still feel me the way I feel you? You've always been the best part of me.

From the very first moment that deep penetrating gaze found hers, similar thoughts had been flooding his mind ... and there was nothing he could do to stop them.

My sweet love, I tried to stay away, truly I did, but I had to see you again – just this once for your special night ... You look so beautiful ... you always have ... and I've missed having you in my life ... Please don't be angry ... I never meant to intrude ... I even made a promise to slip away quietly as soon as it was over ... but I couldn't, I needed to see you up close again just for a few minutes ... You were marvellous tonight, and I couldn't look away ... I still can't ... and I still feel you, my love, every single day.

Like entwined spirits, they responded silently to each other's despair through shared looks and silent reflection ... all the while drinking in the sight of their beloved soulmate after so long. Neither of them could control the thoughts swirling around in their hearts and minds. Both stood as though paralysed, unable to say another word – feasting on the sight of their other half.

Charles recognised their dilemma and immediately came to their rescue with a shaky laugh. "Goodness, son, you're still here. I thought you'd left already."

With his eyes still fastened on Lara, Adam mumbled, "I was about to ... but then I couldn't ... there was something I still needed to do..."

His father understood exactly what had brought him back and his heart ached for both of them. Elizabeth slipped a trembling hand into her husband's while pressing her other arm against Adam's back, making sure not to spill the recently acquired drink as she tried to bring a measure of comfort and support to the son she loved so much.

Her heart was pounding with anxiety. *Oh, my darling boy, why did you have to put both of you through this again ... you should've just left like you promised...*

Trying to gather his thoughts, Charles turned towards the out-of-town visitor. "Ummm, Mike, this is our son, Adam. Don't mind these two ... he's been working all around the country, so they haven't seen each other for several years. You may have read about him in the papers or seen him interviewed on television. We're all very proud of everything he's achieved." He was blabbering but needed to do something to draw the man's attention away from the other drama playing out in front of everyone.

Mike was watching Lara out of the corner of his eye when he replied. "No, I can't say I have, but then again Coffs Harbour's a pretty small town compared to Brizzie, so none of the larger shows are ever on its agenda."

"Oh well, that's understandable," Charles replied quickly, searching for another distraction.

When Elizabeth first learned her son had decided to come to the theatre that night, she tried everything in her power to dissuade him. When those pleas fell on deaf ears, a stern warning was issued to stay right away from the star of the show, especially once she learned Mike was going to be there too. The last thing Adam needed was to see them together. Determined to waylay any further heartache, she had begged him to leave when she noticed Lara on the other side of the room – now it was too late, and clearly all those valiant efforts had been in vain.

While Charles and the other man conversed, she put down her drink and clung to Adam's arm, as though restraining his hands from reaching out to the woman he still loved. She could feel the tension in his body and see the agony reflected in both their eyes, but there was nothing she could do to help either one.

Sensing the undercurrents growing even stronger between the reunited lovers, Charles turned back to his son, anxious to gain his attention. "Adam, I told you about Mike, remember? He's Lara's friend from down south."

This time his father's words registered and Adam had to drag his eyes away from the irresistible woman who still captured his heart with a single glance.

"Oh, that's right. Yeah, I do remember. Hello, Mike, it's good to meet you. How do you like our thriving city?"

He extended his hand and Mike took it as both men sized the other one up and down like two possessive lions about to do battle over a lone lioness.

Mike's eyes narrowed and he gave a terse nod. "Gidday, Adam ... I haven't seen much yet, but the place sure seems to have grown since last time. And to answer your old man's question, I'm pretty sure I do recognise you after all. I was in Nikki's room today and noticed a photo on her bedside table. At first, I thought it must've been her father ... now I know better." As if laying claim to his territory, he added quickly, "I'm staying with Lara for a few days."

Again, Adam's eyes sought out the woman standing between them – a host of unspoken questions falling into her soul.

Lara knew she had to answer and her voice dripped with emotion. "You're right, Mike, it is a picture of Adam. He and Nikki were very close when she was little, so she's always kept a photo of him in her room." Her reply may have been targeted to the other man, but her gaze didn't waver from her former lover's ... and neither did his. "There used to be two mounted right above her bed ... 'til she took the other one with her when she moved to Sydney."

Adam had to close his eyes for a moment as the implications of those words landed in his spirit. Then he caught her gaze again. Lara knew him so well she could see the torment of another question hanging between them. Anxious to heal his wounds, her tone now became matter of fact, like an informant in a courtroom's witness box, with no embellishments necessary to get her point across ... and still those eyes held his.

"I met Mike in Victoria at the beginning of the year. Nikki and I were on a riding holiday and he was there with his daughter. The girls clicked straight away, so we all became friends. Because he lives halfway between here and Sydney, we've only seen each other once since then, and he only drove up this afternoon to be here tonight. Then he heads back again tomorrow morning. I put him in Nikki's room – that's how come he saw your photo..."

She knew it was unfair for the other man to hear their relationship described so impersonally, and yet she couldn't do anything else after seeing the look on Adam's face.

During this whole exchange, Mike was watching every interaction with an ice-cold stare ... like a sentencing judge in that same courtroom while the undercurrents played out around him. More than anything, Lara's lack of emotion and detail confirmed there was something more to her and Adam's story. Her implication about them being simply friends surprised him, but he decided now wasn't the time to mount a challenge, although he did want Adam to know there was a lot more to their relationship.

Trying hard to push his simmering resentment down, he made one more effort to stake his claim. "Lara's right, we shared a fabulous holiday. And it was really hard watching her leave without me, but at least we're able to catch up regularly by phone. She came down to Coffs for five days recently so we could spend some quality time together. Mum and Dad really enjoyed getting to know her and my daughter was ecstatic having her around again. I wouldn't have missed tonight for the world. I thought she was fantastic!"

His underlying tension began to dissipate when he remembered how much he enjoyed seeing her on the stage. With a possessive flourish, Mike picked up her hand and placed his lips firmly against the delicate skin of her wrist. "And

I'm super proud of her."

"Oh, Mike!" she sniggered nervously, turning red with both shock embarrassment, and cautiously pulled away.

An urge to claim that same hand almost overpowered Adam ... but he drew back. He had no right – she was no longer his. With a sudden rush of envy at having to witness someone else touching the woman he had been yearning after for so many years, the hurting man blurted out the first thing that came into his head.

"Oh look, I think I just saw Jeff and Lucy. I'd better go over and say hello. It was good to meet you, Mike. Enjoy your stay." Unable to resist one more shared moment, he turned to Lara so she had his full attention without any distractions for these last few precious seconds. Glimpsing the misty sheen in her eyes was enough to make him swallow hard, and his voice was little more than a whisper. "It's been fabulous running into you after so long, sweet lady. I'm thrilled to see you back on a stage again – we've all missed having you up there. You know it's where you truly belong."

Their thoughts were united ... both knew where she truly belonged ... though the words hovered in that private space between them, entwined just as their hands had often been when creating a clandestine dance to their own symphony.

Her reply was tender, similar to his, and the endearment automatically fell from those lips he knew so well. "Thanks, Teddy. It's a huge thrill to be back and such a wonderful surprise to see you here tonight. Take care ... and please keep safe. We may not cross paths any more, but I often wonder how you are."

For the first time since setting eyes on each other, the makings of a true smile touched his mouth – and yet it was poignant and filled with something only she could decipher. And just like her, he couldn't help himself.

"Don't worry, I think of you just as often." Their eyes didn't deviate from this unexpected homecoming. "And you keep safe too, please Ba—" he managed to stop himself just in time "—old friend. Loads more fans than you realise need you back in their lives. And I hope you find true happiness wherever you go – the world's a far better place when you're in it to brighten things up."

A sudden dark shadow of despair clouded his eyes, and he had to seek refuge before a rush of overwhelming grief gave him away. Hurrying off to join Lucy and Jeff, he moved too swiftly to hear the catch in her throat as she whispered, "And I always wish that for you too..."

A pair of shimmering blue eyes followed him ... until she sensed Mike watching her with a sceptical sneer plastered on his face.

Lara turned to Adam's mother with a feigned grin, summoning all of her strength while struggling to get the words out. "Well, that was a nice surprise – he's looking good, just as I remember..."

The anguish in the other woman's expression matched the sadness in Lara's spirit. Being careful so Mike couldn't see, she squeezed her young friend's hand, though the only response was a faint glimmer of a smile – the huge lump lodged in Lara's throat prevented anything more.

As a way to give her some breathing space, both Elizabeth and Charles took turns steering the conversation into safer waters by asking Mike about his work. It didn't take long for his whole demeanour to change and he grew quite animated describing what it was like opening up the wonders of the sea to clients. That earlier intense scrutiny directed at Lara diminished with the conversation focussed solely on him, and it appeared their son had disappeared from his thoughts.

Not surprisingly, the same couldn't be said for her. Just being in Adam's presence had made those deeply buried feelings spring to life again and she was finding it almost impossible to concentrate on the conversation. After a few minutes, Lara excused herself, mumbling something about having to go to the ladies' room while really needing to regain some form of control over her emotions.

For several minutes she gripped the edge of the basin, looking at her reflection in the mirror, albeit seeing instead another pair of eyes filled with unbearable longing and pain. To have him so close had brought everything back in all its fullness – and yet it was useless ... he still belonged to someone else. Inhaling several deep breaths, she was eventually able to still the hammering in her heart. With her emotions finally under control, she walked out the door only to hear that same voice again.

"Lara, can we talk for a moment ... please?"

Her step faltered and she turned towards him, helpless to resist the pull he still had over her.

"Adam, I can't! It's too hard. Please just go..."

Waves of relief tumbled around those same protests. *Thank goodness, no one can see us or else they'd know exactly how much I still love you.*

"I never want to hurt you. I just need to give you something."

His anxious gaze didn't leave her face as he fumbled around in his pocket and then pulled out a black velvet pouch. It was crumpled and worn and looked like it had lived there for a very long time.

A concerned frown creased her forehead and he could sense her fear. With infinite care, he reached out and picked up her hand before placing the small bag on her open palm.

She was breathless at the touch of his skin on hers. "What's this?"

"Something I promised you a long time ago. I found it in a little jewellery shop on the Ponte Vecchio in Florence when I was there five years ago. I've carried it around with me ever since, hoping one day we'd run into each other..." His words drifted away regretfully when he had to let go of her hand.

Lara looked up at him with tears flooding her eyes as she remembered his promise. Reaching out once more, he carefully opened the pouch and slowly tipped its contents into her hand. She gasped when she saw the delicate gold butterfly inlaid with blue and green opal pieces, the centrepiece of an expensive gold link bracelet chosen especially with her in mind.

"Oh Teddy, it's beautiful..." For the briefest of moments, she touched the expensive keepsake with a hesitant finger ... then hurriedly pressed the item into his palm, willing him to take it back even though everything inside her cried out to hold it close to her heart. "But I can't accept this. You shouldn't have bought me anything. Give it to Trina ... she's your wife."

He heard the tiny catch in her voice and it broke his heart. "It doesn't belong to her ... I bought it for you, Lara. I can't take it back now. I fully understand if you don't want to wear it ... but at least keep it in a safe place as a way to remember me and what we once had."

She choked back the sob threatening to spill from her throat. *Remember you! I haven't forgotten one moment of our time together ... I don't need anything to help me remember. Sometimes I almost wish I could forget ... knowing we'll never be together again is becoming too painful.*

For another few seconds, Lara's finger traced the creature's intricate wings, and then she slid the bracelet back into its pouch. Holding his gaze and with an almost imperceptible nod, the unexpected gift dropped into her purse.

"Thank you," she whispered as a large tear rolled down her cheek.

Adam held his breath, and the beat of his heart increased when he reached out to wipe the shimmering droplet with a caring finger.

"Oh, my darling, please don't cry. I never meant to upset you." His voice betrayed his anguish, but he couldn't look away as the feel of her skin held him mesmerised. Then the tips of his fingers inched down, tracing the soft flesh of her lips for the tenderest of moments. "Why haven't you ever married, sweetheart? It's been so long. You're an incredibly desirable woman – there must've been a long line-up of men wanting to share your life over the years."

Her eyelids grew heavy with the emotion welling up inside from his caress. "Don't you realise, Teddy ... you ruined me for anyone else. I couldn't settle for anything less than wha—"

He cut in, and the torment in his tone broke her heart.

"Oh, Lara, I'm so sorry for putting you through all this. I never meant to hurt you."

"It was never you, my darling man. *I'm* the one who chose to walk away. But it's okay ... I've learned to be strong ... though I've never forgotten one moment..."

Lara stroked the hand still fondling her lips before resting her cheek against his open palm. For one sweet moment, he had to close his eyes from the exquisite sensation emanating from her touch ... until, loath to miss the reality of being able to look at her, she found her gaze captured within his once more.

"I need you to be assured of something ... in all these years, you're the only woman I've ever loved."

She could almost feel his heart reaching across the small space separating them. The loving smile she offered emerged out of the poignancy of the moment and drew his attention back to her mouth. "I started to suspect that was the case at the end of last year."

"What do you mean?"

"When I heard who's been paying the majority of Nikki's fees since she first started school ... and from what I can guess, that same generosity has paid for NIDA."

His frown turned to a look of concern overlaid with fear. "Did Mum tell you?"

"No, the school bursar did when I was paying her last lot of fees..."

"Are you angry?"

She shook her head, and her expression oozed with compassion. "No ... never angry ... but I was upset because she wasn't your responsibility. I felt terrible because of the dreadful risk you took." This time it was her forehead creased with worry. "What if Trina had found out?"

A glimmer of the stomach-churning smile she adored touched his lips. "I didn't care. It was simply my way of staying in Nikki's life – and yours – even if it was only from a distance. Besides, it wasn't much ... it just helped to make me feel like we were still connected – almost as if you still needed me, even though you had no idea. I was just being selfish ... I did it purely for my own gratification."

"Oh, my sweet love, you don't have a selfish bone in your body, though you do have the most generous heart I've ever known. I could never thank you properly ... just know for certain that you've always been a part of our lives – and in everything ... not only that. It's impossible to tell you how many times I've felt your presence with me when things have seemed insurmountable ... and I certainly couldn't have kept her at the school without your input ... even though I never even knew. I've always loved you – from that very first moment you put your hand in mine. Learning the truth and then hearing Elizabeth confirm you've been at her awards night every year proves your heart and reinforces what I felt right from that very first meeting. You've always been my soulmate..."

"And you will always be mine, sweetheart..."

As though drawn there, Lara's hand reached up to caress his face. Loving fingers ran along the strong jaw-line then moved across his cheek to outline the crease beneath one of those captivating dark eyes. Then that gossamer touch strayed across his strong forehead and over a set of thick eyebrows. Finally, they came to rest in the middle of his hairline, on a slightly larger patch of grey than the last time they had strayed there. It wasn't hard to imagine she was trying to inscribe herself on his flesh.

All of a sudden, Adam remembered the man waiting with his parents and his eyes clouded over. "What about Mike? Where does he fit into your life?"

Her expression begged him to believe her. "He's a friend – we met during a two-week holiday in January and found we had a lot in common. Then I went down to spend some time with him for the Easter weekend to see— "

Off in the distance, they heard Lucy calling her name, and she looked around anxiously.

"I have to go! I can't let any of them see us together. It wouldn't be fair, not after everything they've done to help me get through the pain of losing you."

But he couldn't let her go like this ... not after so long.

Reaching out as if seeking for a way to rebuff the aching void waiting to swallow him up again, Adam cradled her face with gentle hands then covered her mouth with a kiss that made both of them ache with desire. Lara responded with a heartfelt whimper, taking him back to long nights awash with a never-to-be-forgotten passion.

Waves of longing threatened to overwhelm him, and he couldn't control those deepening emotions any longer. Frantically, he pulled her into his arms and pressed his strong, taut body hard against hers. Just as fervently, she matched his craving and they became lost in each other's eyes while hungry mouths rediscovered every beloved contour for what seemed like an eternity after so many years apart. Lips moved perfectly in time as tongues tasted that sweet nectar of their soulmate's unique flavour. As though mesmerised, two sets of eyes stared into a longed-for future ... caught in one another's spell, unable to look away ... or even blink.

Then from out of a tiny semblance of coherent thought, Lara remembered Lucy's summons, and she pulled away with a mournful cry.

"Teddy, I'm sooo sorry ... I *have* to go. Please forgive me – and *please* take care of yourself." She reached up and touched his mouth with hers again ... just for a miniscule fraction of time ... stealing one last taste of her other half while a stray finger lovingly traced a well-defined eyebrow. "I need you to be happy – it's the only way I can do this. Promise me you'll make a worthwhile life for yourself ... and give Trina the chance to offer you that joy you so deserve – promise!" Grasping his hand, she implored him to answer as tears filled her eyes.

"But the only time I'm ever truly happy is when I think of you and what we shared during those few precious months." Lara's broken sob tore at his heart. "I've tried, but I can't help it. Baby, they were the best days of my life. I'll never give up hope that one day we'll have another chance. It's all I have to cling to. Take care, my darling. The only way I manage to get through each day is by believing you're safe..."

"I'll be careful, Teddy, and I'll never stop loving you."

She clutched at his hand and gave one last gesture of reassurance – the old familiar one formed with her nose. The pressure of their grip increased when he replied with a lingering wink offered through a film of tears.

Then before Lucy could find them together, and reminiscent of previous partings, their clasped hands fell apart as Lara walked out of his life once again – not daring to look back.

Adam's head bowed low due to the weight of the loss of all he had ever treasured ... and with an even greater cost than ever before. After tasting her on his lips and in his soul, how would he cope trying to live with that aching emptiness again?

A mournful cry came from the depths of his heart. *Oh God, I don't know how to let her go again! I need your help now more than ever before.*

§

And in that other dimension, hidden at the back of an intricately woven tapestry, two silver threads re-emerged to make their way to the centre of this magnificent work of art. With painstaking perfection, they formed the shape of another delicate butterfly – this time rising from a shiny, silver chrysalis.

For the next few weeks while Adam and Lara fed from the nourishment of their unexpected encounter and reminisced over all they had shared, those luminous strands continued to weave an elaborate dance as the beautiful creature flitted across the canvas from one detailed vignette of their former lives to another. Engraved into its wings were what appeared to be a bar of musical notes, which once upon a time had formed part of a glorious symphony accompanying two loving hands in another expressive dance.

Eventually, the reality of loneliness bit into the man and the woman's earthly flesh, and a yawning chasm opened up to snatch away that beloved dreamtime. This return to reality had another effect in the Heavens as those slender trails of silk wandered down two distinctly different paths again, continuing the story of two separated, though forever-interwoven lives.

Chapter 32

During the short drive back to Lara's place, a heavy blanket of silence hung over her car as she and Mike mused over the night's events. He sat ruminating over the swathe of undercurrents that seemed to underpin every conversation at the restaurant, while Lara wouldn't have changed one moment of the poignant exchange with Adam, despite feeling a deep sense of shame for having treated Mike so badly. Seeing him standing there had come as such a shock, everything else simply faded into the background, especially when those arresting dark eyes of his captured hers all over again.

He had hardly changed ... except now that easily recognisable ebony-tinged hair had touches of silver streaks joining what she still thought of as her own personal fingerprint above his brow. Somehow, the lighter tones only served to make him look more distinguished. He was still as handsome as the day they first met and so it was only natural for all of that old desire to rise to the surface. Mike's enthusiastic holiday kisses hadn't affected her nearly as much as the mere sight of her former lover suddenly materialising in front of her.

Echoes of his voice wafted through her musings – a thrilling timbre that always sent her heart racing. Hearing it again tonight, Lara had instantly been transported back to places belonging to a lifetime ago, when her life had been filled with laughter and love.

An unexpected thought sidled up to keep her company and resulted in a tiny smirk touching her lips, completely unbidden yet impossible to control.

Oh, my darling love, now I have a memory of us in this new century ... one I can keep with all my other treasures of you!

Such a small thing, although to her it was the most precious gift.

Pulling into the driveway, Lara felt a sharp niggle in her conscience. She realised it was time to store away the recent reunion for later and concentrate on the man sitting beside her. He deserved better, and her parents would have frowned at her behaviour. They had brought their children up to show respect and kindness; now she felt a deep sense of shame for ignoring him as soon as Adam appeared on the scene.

"Come inside and I'll make us both a hot drink – that'll warm us up," she said, mustering up a smile.

"I'd prefer something stronger if you don't mind. I'm not really a tea or coffee kinda guy."

"Oh, I'm sorry, I didn't realise."

Lara was surprised at his request when he had shown no interest in any of the alcoholic beverages on offer around the campfire during their riding getaway. She hadn't really been around anyone with a taste for strong alcohol since Tom's sudden departure, apart from the occasional beer Jeff and Ben consumed whenever they were all out together. It was no wonder she hadn't thought to offer him anything.

"I think I have a bottle of scotch somewhere – it was given to me ages ago by a client. I don't normally drink anything alcoholic, so you're more than welcome to have a glass. In fact, you might as well take it home with you when you go."

"Sure, thanks. I prefer beer, but a good drop of scotch'll do."

At the top of the stairs, Mike took her hand in his and she had to fight everything within her not to pull away. Lara had no desire for any form of romantic tryst because of what she had to tell him in the morning. Even more so, she didn't want to lose the imprint of Adam's hand still lingering on her skin. Her lips still tingled from their passionate kiss and she couldn't help running her tongue over them in an effort to taste him again.

Using the excuse of having to look for her keys, she managed to disentangle herself quite easily, all the while frantically hoping he was oblivious to the state of her heart. Much to her relief, he seemed happy to wait as she fumbled in the dim light. Unfortunately for her, it also meant she was totally obvious to the fact that this same cloak of darkness concealed just how intensely he was watching her every move.

When the door swung open, she threw out a nonchalant, "I'll just go change into something more relaxing – make yourself at home. I'll be back soon."

"Sure."

She came out a few minutes later, barefoot and wearing a cosy jumper over a casual pair of jeans. Nikki's door was closed, so she presumed he was changing too and hurried out to the kitchen to organise their drinks. When Mike eventually came out to join her, she was relaxing in one of the single lounge chairs with a steaming mug of tea in her hands. On a small table next to the seat positioned directly opposite hers, he noticed a crystal glass about a quarter full with the freshly opened bottle of scotch standing beside it.

"That feels better," he sighed, plonking himself down in the comfy chair and stretching out his legs with his feet crossed. He was dressed in a similar fashion and his blond hair was tousled and quite boyish-looking. "I'm not used to penguin suits, and I definitely haven't been to a party like that one before," he said, picking up the glass and taking a long sip.

"Mmm, this is far more comfortable without those cramped shoes," she said wearily. Curling up so her shapely legs wrapped to one side, Lara leaned back in the chair with her eyes half closed.

They sat in silence, concentrating on their drinks rather than foraging for something to say after all of those awkward moments at the party.

The constant tick of the grandmother clock seemed much louder than usual, almost as though it was trying to make some form of conversation to fill the emptiness. Lara knew something had to give ... and so did Mike ... both at the same time.

"Thanks for making the eff—"

"Lara, there's some—"

They both laughed nervously, and it helped to ease the tension.

"You go first," he offered, gesturing towards her.

"Sure. I was just going to say thanks for making the effort to be here tonight. I'm sorry I didn't get to spend as much time with you as I should've."

"Oh, don't worry, although I did wonder what was going on when you disappeared for so long. Anyway, not to worry; at least we get to catch up now."

She swallowed carefully and mumbled, "Mmm, it's been a bit full on since you arrived."

"Yeah, I suppose, but I must say I was pretty chuffed to find I actually enjoyed the show." At Lara's astonished chuckle, he realised just how pompous that must have sounded and laughed nervously. "Oops, I didn't mean it quite like that! What I should've said was that I wasn't sure it'd be my kind of thing, but the story was great and the music sure was stirring."

"Phew – that sounds better! I'm really glad you enjoyed it."

"I sure did, and your voice is definitely a cracker. Now I understand why you want to get back to the stage full-time. And from what the others were saying, it seems like you have their full backing – especially certain people."

She frowned for a moment and then decided to let the aside go rather than fuel what could be an awkward exchange. "Thanks, Mike. It really is where I belong. And yeah, they all seem happy for me. I'm so glad you enjoyed it – I must admit I was a bit nervous having you there."

"Why? I'm not *that* intimidating, am I?" He took a long sip from his glass and peered at her over the rim.

She tried to sound normal, though his steady gaze was quite off-putting. "No, not at all, but seeing this was your first show I didn't want to turn you off musicals for life by putting in a bad performance. There was a lot resting on my shoulders to impress a nice country boy like you!"

The compliment seemed to change his demeanour. Letting out a loud guffaw, he raised his glass. "Well, you certainly did that. Here's to you. And it was nice getting to meet your friends – I like Lucy and Jeff, and Charles and Elizabeth were real friendly. He filled me in about their vineyards on the Gold Coast and in Tuscany, and Elizabeth said you're like a daughter to them. While you were off in the ladies' room, she mentioned you'd been through some pretty tough times in the past – things you haven't told me."

His eyes suddenly narrowed again and he appeared to be watching her even more intently. Lara felt quite uncomfortable being scrutinised so thoroughly. Somehow, she managed to keep her face a picture of composure, even though inside her heart was racing.

Stop being stupid, Lara! It's just your imagination. He couldn't have seen what happened and Elizabeth wouldn't say anything about Adam.

Taking another mouthful of tea to moisten her suddenly very dry mouth, she tried to sound blasé. "Oh, it's been hard in some ways. Still, I've managed okay. What sort of things did she tell you?"

"Oh, just about your parents passing away and how your husband walked out when Nikki was little. She hinted about things being pretty tough both financially and emotionally for you for quite a few years." His glass was now empty, so he poured himself another much larger one. Slouching low in the chair, he continued staring at her while taking another long swallow.

She waved her hand and screwed up her nose. "Oh, I'm fine, don't worry. That all happened a long time ago and Elizabeth just likes to make sure I'm okay. She's always treated me like a daughter and worries more than she should. Anyway, I interrupted you. What were you going to say?"

It was obvious she didn't want to talk about those times, so he shifted in the seat then cleared his throat. "I'm not sure how to say this, especially after all the hoopla of closing night and the party afterwards..."

She looked at him with her heart in her mouth, too scared to try to imagine what was coming.

Another swig made its way down his throat. "Look, I don't think it's going to work between us. Don't get me wrong ... I really like you – you're beautiful and vivacious and every man's dreamboat – but I get the feeling you're no longer interested."

"Oh, Mike, I'm sorry if—"

He held up his hand, and his voice rose a little. "No, wait, just let me finish ... this is hard enough as it is. When we were together in January everything seemed great – I thought we were getting on really well and I enjoyed spending time with you. Then when you came down to see me in April, things seemed fine, although not as romantic as I would've liked. But since I've been up here, you're not the same girl I rode the mountain trails with. Here you're sophisticated and elegant and have friends in high places, while I'm just a dive boat captain helping his dad out around the farm on my days off ... and usually in scuba gear or jeans instead of penguin suits or fancy chinos."

His piercing stare was so unsettling, she moved uncomfortably in her seat. Dragging her legs out from under her, she leaned forward as he downed another large mouthful of the amber liquid.

"Hey, that shouldn't matter—"

"But it *does,* and I'm pretty sure there's a lot more to yours and Adam's story than anyone's letting on, even though Charles assured me the only reason you were fawning all over each other was because you hadn't seen one another for several years. *Anyone* watching the two of you tonight would have no trouble thinking you were long-lost lovers. I *saw* the way he was looking at you *and* how nervous you were around him!" He bent forward in his seat, arms resting along his strong upper legs with the glass dangling from his fingers.

Lara pressed back into her chair and gnawed away at her bottom lip, too scared to interrupt again when Mike's glassy stare bored into hers.

His voice rose with every sentence, and the staccato beat of inflections was proof of his frustration. "It's *obvious* he's in love with you, and I'm pretty sure you feel the same, *despite* Lucy telling me there hasn't been anyone in your life for years. It may be ages since you've seen each other, but there's definitely *some* sort of attraction going on, *especially* when you went off to the ladies' room and he *conveniently* disappeared a few minutes later..."

More waves of uneasiness rose up, before deep feelings of shame pushed them aside. She felt terrible at having deceived him, and yet, in some ways, it was a relief knowing their secret was finally out. It might help to clear the air and mean she wouldn't have to spend a restless night wondering how to break the news she was no longer interested in him romantically.

Despite his need to hear the truth, Lara still felt quite sad. Telling him could bring an end to what might have been a good friendship. Her eyes were downcast and tone remorseful as she spoke from the heart.

"I'm sorry, Mike. I never meant to deceive you ... but you're right. Once upon a time, Adam and I were very much in love ... although it was many, many years ago when Nikki was a little girl. In fact, we met on that same stage over thirteen years ago. No matter how hard we tried to resist, the chemistry was there from our very first meeting ... but we never meant to fall in love. And just so you know, there hasn't been anyone else since ... you're the first person I've been interested in since we broke up. I truly thought you and I could be good for each other ... but maybe you're right. Maybe our worlds are just too different."

Relieved to finally have everything off her chest, Lara let out a heavy sigh.

This was the first time she had told anyone outside of her immediate circle of friends and it felt almost cathartic.

Mike had been sitting stony-faced during her heartfelt confession. Now his eyes narrowed and he downed a third glass of scotch with one large swig. His voice grew even louder and a frown creased his forehead as everything started to register. "I thought he was *married!* I'm sure Charles said somethin' about his wife and how they got hitched when he was just out of uni."

A mixture of remorse and worry caused her to speak softly. "Yes, he is, but there's a long story behind their marriage and the circumstances that brought us together."

His expression turned cold and Lara could sense he was distancing himself even further.

"Well, I'm *sorry,* but in *my* world there's no excuse for cheatin', no matter *what* the circumstances. I'm just relieved I found out now before things went any further. If you treat marriage vows as though they mean nothin', how could I *ever* trust you?"

She understood his disdain – her moral compass had been the same before falling in love with Adam ... and it still was deep down. Even now, she couldn't condone what they had done. After all, Tom had cheated on her many times, and she vividly remembered that numbing feeling of betrayal. Watching Adam battle his continual feelings of guilt was one of the main reasons she had said goodbye – and why they stayed apart.

Now the hardest thing she had to deal with was remembering how desperately unhappy he had been and the difference being together had made to his life following all of those turbulent early years with Trina. As much as she knew it was wrong, the few short months they had shared were still the happiest in her life and she wouldn't have changed one bit – though she didn't dare open up that door when they had finally come to terms with never seeing each other again.

Shaking those thoughts away, she looked over at him and the regret in her voice was noticeable. "I don't blame you for feeling that way. I'm just sorry you had to find out like this. I had no idea he would be there tonight. Please believe me when I say I never meant to hurt you."

Letting out a loud expletive, he jumped up and strode across to the window, hands clutching menacingly at the glass as he peered into the darkness.

His words were slurred and filled with disgust. "*Course* ya di'n' – he was ya li'l *seeecret*. But it doesn' matter anymore, and it's probly jus' as well I foun' out now t' see the sort o' woman ya *reeally* are." He swivelled around to face her, swaying unsteadily on his feet. The anger in his eyes was plain to see as an accusing finger poked the air. "A blin' fella could see ya still in *love* with 'im ... ya couldn' take ya eyes *off* each other the whole time. An' I bet *he's* the one who gave ya those huge rocks tha' never leave ya neck or finga. Don' think I hadn' noticed."

Instinctively, she grasped the treble clef resting in the crook of her neck. The movement caused the ring on her finger to glitter in the glow from a nearby lamp.

Before she could say anything, he snarled, "Yeah, though' so ... see, I'm betta off withou' ya."

Lara was taken back by the rapid change in his demeanour. Hoping to give him time to calm down, she decided to take her cup into the kitchen. When a few drops of perspiration fell into his eyes, he rubbed at them with the heels of his hands. Straight away, she snatched up the now half-empty bottle of scotch and stashed it beneath her jumper. The last thing either of them needed was a nasty scene, and this one seemed to be hurtling in that direction.

His voice carried out to her, getting louder as he spat out the words. "An' o' *course* ya wouldn' wanna spoil ya *precious* closin' night by tellin' me *beforehan'* ya weren' *in'rested* anymore! Why didn' ya tell me on the *phone* 'stead o' wastin' me time drivin' all this way only t' be *insulted?* Oh, *tha's* righ' – li'l miss *performa* who always needs an audience, no matter *who* it is." Following her into the kitchen, he stumbled over to where she was standing facing the sink. "*Look a' me Lara, or haven' ya got the guts?*"

Mustering up all her courage, she turned around slowly and looked him straight in the eye. She wasn't going to be intimated so her voice was slow and steady. "I think you'd better go to bed, Mike. I understand you're upset, but I don't want to get into an argument. I really need you to calm down and a good night's sleep will probably help."

"*Don' tell me wha' t' do, ya slut!* I know wha' women like *you* ge' up t' – ya string a man 'long, then throw him in the dust when he doesn' fit all your expec– ex-pec-tashuns." He poked a long, accusing finger in the air while trying to get the word out. "I ain' ya la-de-da toff *Adam* with all o' his hoity-toity ways. Anyways, he's jus' a *scum-bag* for cheatin' on his wife with a whore ... ya both *deserve* each other!" An arm careened in the air close to her head and she quickly ducked out of the way.

Stunned at the venom in his tone, she was transported back to the days when Tom had arrived home drunk and itching for a fight. Keeping her voice calm, she tried to get him to listen to reason.

"Come on, Mike. You don't know what you're saying, and you've obviously had too much to drink."

She went to take his arm and lead him into Nikki's room, but he lashed out angrily, "*Ge' away from me, ya stinkin' slut!*" In the space of a split second, his closed fist struck Lara hard in the middle of her face.

The sight of blood pouring from her nose and lip and then dripping from her chin was enough to sober him up. Grabbing her by the shoulders, there was a look of sheer panic on his face.

"Oh, *hell!* I didn' *mean* to hi' ya. Here, le' me help ya ge' cleaned up."

He tried to wipe her mouth with a nearby tea-towel until she pulled away. Breathing heavily, she placed both hands hard over her mouth and nose in an effort to staunch the blood.

In shock, she glared at him and mumbled through her fingers, "Don't you *dare* touch me! Just get your things and leave ... *now!*"

She wasn't game enough to trust him to leave her alone and wanted him out of the house straight away. Tending her injuries could wait a few minutes more.

He backed away with both hands raised. "A'righ', I'm goin'. I really *am* sorry, Lara, I've never 'it a woman in me life before, and I didn' mean t' hurt ya ... but I can' believe ya lied t' me either."

"Just go. I've got nothing more to say to you."

With a look of regret, he turned and went into Nikki's room, gathering up his things while she waited in the living room. When he came out, all he could do was brush past her with his eyes downcast. At the front door, he turned back and mumbled, "I'll call ya tomorra t' see how ya doin'."

Lara could only nod, too scared to say anything more in case it provoked him even further. As soon as he started down the stairs, she raced to the door and turned the lock with trembling fingers. The look in his eyes reminded her of a night when another atrocity had occurred, and she sent a hurried prayer of thanks to the heavens for having him gone without inflicting any more damage. Hearing his car drive away, she let out a huge sigh of relief and slumped against the doorjamb. It took several seconds to register she needed to do something about her injuries.

Shaking uncontrollably, the injured woman stumbled to the bathroom mirror only to be confronted with a sight she never thought to see again. Large spatters of congealing blood covered the lower part of her face and her top lip had a fairly deep cut across it. Despite the ghastly mess, it was the damage to her nose that was her main concern. Grossly swollen with a trickle of blood still seeping from one of her nostrils, large dark bruises were beginning to form under each eye.

Thank heavens it was closing night tonight, she thought, wincing as she attempted to wash the thick, red globules away. *Paul would've been too happy having me turn up looking like this for a show ... I'd have had to borrow the* Phantom's *spare mask, and then there would've been two mysterious characters sharing a stage. Oh well, at least it might've given the show a whole new perspective!*

It was a relief to find something to joke about after such a frightening experience, though she couldn't stop her hands from shaking. Gingerly, she examined her nose and realised the damage inflicted may have affected her voice, depending on the extent of the injuries.

Great! Just when I've decided to give up my main form of income, the one thing that could guarantee me a decent wage looks like it might've just been snatched away!

Gingerly tucking a wad of tissues across her top lip and up inside her swollen nostrils, Lara sucked in mouthfuls of air through her damaged lips as she got into the car. Driving slowly, she made her way to the hospital emergency department where a doctor could assess her wounds.

The hands on the dash clock showed it was just past four o'clock when she finally made her way home. With thin strips of plaster adorning her nose and several tiny sutures puncturing her lip, along with a bottle of painkillers tucked away in her purse, she drove along the darkened streets. The doctor on call had provided her with a referral to an Ear, Nose and Throat specialist for an urgent appointment later in the day so the true damage could be assessed.

When asked if she wanted to press charges, Lara declined vehemently. It was enough to know her assailant lived far enough away so she wouldn't have to face him ever again.

§

Lara couldn't wait to get home. She needed the catharsis of a long hot shower to wash all traces of Mike from her life. Standing under the soothing water with her eyes closed, she let it run over her head and down her body until the water turned cool. After such an emotion-charged evening, she was exhausted and hardly had enough energy left even to dry herself. The soft, warm bed felt wonderful and she sank gratefully into its comfort and safety.

When she reached out to turn off the light, her gaze fell on the clutch purse lying on her bedside table. With utmost care, she took out the black velvet pouch and tipped its contents into her hand. The image of the delicate butterfly was all it took for a solitary tear to trickle down her cheek. After that earlier unexpected act of violence, this symbol of freedom and rebirth was a soothing balm to her wounded spirit. For Adam to have given it to her tonight of all nights was like a gift from Heaven in her hour of need.

Hungering for a sense of his presence, she pressed the butterfly against her heart and rubbed the smooth opal pieces across the skin covering the top of her breast. From out of the corner of her eye, she noticed the pewter sculpture seemingly glowing in the soft moonlight. Its message now held even more meaning after their brief encounter. Somehow it seemed fitting to hang the bracelet from the first letter. She didn't realise at the time, but this had become the beautiful trinket's new home whenever it wasn't surrounding her wrist.

Along with all of her other treasures, the keepsake formed another part of the miniature cosmos adorning her bedside table – each one a precious reminder of the man she still loved with all her heart.

A short time later, Lara fell asleep to the memory of gentle hands caressing her face ... and delicious warm kisses filled her dreams for the rest of the night – while those other angry images floated into nothingness.

§

When Lara went for her specialist appointment early in the afternoon, his diagnosis couldn't have been much worse. Her nose was broken in two places and she had a deviated septum. He warned that when a singer sustained this level of damage, it could result in major complications for their career because of the way it affected their breathing.

Being able to breathe correctly was vitally important for vocal projection, so the doctor recommended immediate surgery to correct the alignment. Stressing there was only a very small window of opportunity for the surgery to be beneficial, he told her it was imperative she have the procedure done right away. Thankfully, she had already remembered the emergency doctor's warning not to eat anything after breakfast. By the time she left the ENT's practice, her signature was on the consent form and the receptionist had booked the procedure for four o'clock that same day.

She arrived home to grab a few essentials for her hospital visit and found the message light blinking on the answering machine. As soon as Mike's voice echoed around the room, a series of shivers ran up and down her spine. Without even waiting to hear what he had to say, she deleted its contents with a flick of her finger.

Lara didn't owe him anything after his angry outburst, and she had no desire to speak to him ever again.

§

The surgery went well and she was out of hospital within a few days. Two very black eyes and thick wads of gauze dressings under her nose made Lara feel highly self-conscious. So much so, she refused to leave the house until the swelling and bruising had all but disappeared. David and Max received separate calls announcing she had a heavy bout of the flu and needed a couple of weeks off. Over the phone, the raspy nasal inflection made her story sound more than plausible. David commiserated and told her to take as much time as she needed, while Max wished her a speedy recovery and threw in a couple of true-blue remedies before hanging up.

By the end of the first week, she was able to have the sutures removed from her lip. The plastic surgeon who had repaired it on the night of the incident was confident there would be no visible scarring or adverse effects to her speech.

Suzie was a godsend, offering to look after her sister throughout the ordeal.

443

She was relieved Mike was out of the picture after hearing what had occurred. Despite the ghastly circumstances, the two siblings had a great time together, bringing back happy childhood memories of sharing a house for the first time in many years. Suzie even managed to bring some much-needed laughter back into Lara's life. Within a few days, the shocking event had been relegated to the past, never to be discussed again.

The only people she told about the attack were her sister and Ben. Initially, Lucy was going to be in on the secret, until Lara remembered Jeff and Adam were still best mates. It also meant she couldn't say anything to Charles and Elizabeth in case they accidentally let something slip. She knew if Adam ever found out, there was no telling what he might do. Remembering how the two men had sized one another up, the last thing she needed was for him to do something stupid to settle the score. Even though Adam had never shown any hint of violence, she wasn't prepared to take the risk after what had occurred.

Lara was just as determined for Nikki to be kept in the dark. She didn't want the teenager worrying about her living alone. Besides, she and Mike's daughter had been close during the holiday. She had no wish to sully her memories of their time together.

Once all signs of the cuts and bruising had disappeared, she invited Adam's parents and Jeff and Lucy over for afternoon tea. It seemed a good way to celebrate the success of the show, though her real reason was something far closer to her heart.

They were sitting on the veranda enjoying a hot pot of tea and a fresh apple and cinnamon cake straight from the oven when she nonchalantly broke the news.

"Just so you all know ... Mike and I are no longer seeing each other. We've decided there's way too much distance separating us and we're both far too busy with our careers to have time for a proper relationship."

No one was surprised or upset, although they did try to mask their true feelings.

"Well, he seemed quite nice, but I can understand why you feel that way," Lucy responded, giving her friend a caring hug. "Long distance romances are much too hard to maintain." She still remembered that leering look he had given Lara, along with all the probing questions, so she was relieved to hear the news.

Elizabeth was secretly pleased too, especially after witnessing the unspoken yearning passing between both her and Adam during the after-party. She knew Mike had no chance of a future with Lara as long as those long pent-up feelings remained.

The conversation still wasn't done and they were all surprised at her next request. "Now there's one thing I need you to promise me ... it may sound strange, but please don't say anything about the breakup to Adam. It's better for him to think I've moved on with my life ... that way he can get on with his."

"But, Lara, he needs to—"

"No, Elizabeth, I've caused him enough problems in the past and I don't want to do it again. I've thought about this a lot over the past few weeks. If he thinks Mike and I are together, hopefully, he'll be able to put what we had behind him."

Despite each of them wishing the outcome could be different, her explanation seemed reasonable – and probably for the best – so they all agreed to keep the secret. Sadly, they also knew her last statement was a total impossibility, though it might help a little in giving his marriage a chance to move forward.

§

Only a month later Lara left the editing suite for the last time. She had a clean bill of health from the ENT specialist, her vocal coach was pleased with her progress, and she had spent the last two weeks finalising any projects she was working on. Now it was time to say goodbye to her old career.

David had invited several directors she had worked with, along with some of her friends in the industry, to a farewell dinner in a private room of the local club. In his speech, her boss spoke glowingly of Lara's excellent work practices and praised her for the great reputation she had helped to make for his company. He was under no illusion ... without her attention to detail and creative eye, his business would never have been so successful or as busy. As David's speech drew to a close, it was obvious to everyone how much he was going to miss her.

"Lara, you've been a true friend, as well as a loyal worker. There's no way the company would've completed half the things it did on time without your commitment and hard work. I've enjoyed every single minute we've spent working on all our different projects."

Looking around the room at their colleagues and so many famous and not-so-famous directors, an animated smirk accompanied his next story.

"I've also been a willing spectator to many free concerts while being serenaded by that amazing voice of yours as you went about your work, not to mention spending oodles of hours having a good laugh over all those hilarious blooper reels you put together with that usual flair! And I'm sure many others here have done the same thing after being presented with their own copy once their latest project was in the can!"

The room resounded with raucous laughter, accompanied by several loud calls of acknowledgement before David inclined his head in a form of salute. "I wish you well on this exciting new road to becoming a famous Broadway star!"

She grinned and dropped her head in embarrassment while others called out, "Hear, hear!"

"Actually, I remember prophesying one day I'd be editing your work," he continued. "Now it looks like my prediction may come true. But if this new venture doesn't work out for any reason, there'll be a permanent home waiting for you back here whenever you want it."

With a beaming smile, he raised his glass, as did everyone around the room.

"To Lara!"

"To Lara!"

Her boss went over to give her a warm hug to the accompaniment of a few wolf whistles and a sheepish smile from the guest of honour.

Once he sat down, two well-known directors simultaneously took his place at the microphone. Much to Lara's embarrassment, the pair sang her praises in an amusing ditty they had written together. The room echoed with laughter until their speeches turned serious at the thought of having to work without her talented eyes and ears. Both had won Logie Awards for shows she had been involved in. Without her skills, it was unlikely either of them would have taken home the prestigious awards – and they were quick to acknowledge the fact.

Next, the director of a comedy series she had worked on for several months made his way to the microphone.

"Lara, it's no secret most of us in this room will never work with anyone as dedicated to their craft as you – whether it's editing one of our projects or the many times we've seen you gracing a stage over the years – you always put everything you have into all your endeavours. My wife continually hounds me to buy tickets whenever she spots an ad for one of your gigs, which means I've probably seen more of your shows than anyone else in Australia! Thank goodness, you'll only be in Brisbane a few times a year from now on. My bank balance will certainly look a lot healthier ... as long as I don't have to work interstate!"

Peals of laughter filled the room, along with sprinklings of applause.

"But I have to add, to be honest, I'm really going to miss working with you. I couldn't count how many hours we've spent haggling over what thirty seconds of multiple takes would best convey my message – and usually *you* won out, I might add, and all because of that outstanding ability of yours to envisage the end product – but I've enjoyed every minute! I've never seen you get angry, nor too tired to put in another hour whenever a deadline's looming, but I've certainly seen you nearly fall asleep sometimes when the clock's struck two in the morning and the rushes still haven't been finalised for the following day."

Lara grinned and nodded as she remembered lots of late nights fighting that dreaded thing called sleep.

"I wish you well, and I raise my glass to the best assistant film editor this director has ever worked with. To Lara!"

Around the room, glasses clinked together and again the words, "Hear, hear!"

or, "To Lara," came from every corner.

With the applause growing and cries of "Speech, speech!", Lara reluctantly took the microphone with a shy smile.

"I really don't know where to start in saying thank you for the amazing experiences you've all brought to my life over the years I've worked with David." She looked across to the man who, in the industry was her boss, yet in her heart was a wonderful friend. "Davey, I could never express how much your faith in me has meant since the first time I walked into that pint-sized editing suite and was offered a job – the best behind-the-scenes job in this crazy world of showbiz if you ask me!"

Everyone laughed, empathising with her words – show business in all of its many and varied forms definitely made for a crazy world, though none of them would change a thing ... once you had a taste for its fascination, it was in your blood forever.

"I'm going to miss you so much – all of you. Even though I can't wait to get back on a stage again, some of my most memorable times have been hunched over that old flatbed, being transported to places I could only ever imagine, and with characters who've made me laugh ... and cry ... and often at the same time!"

Again, there were smatterings of laughter coming from all around the room. Pausing for a moment, Lara recalled the hours and hours she had sat mesmerised while editing Adam's concert. A poignant smile caused her eyes to shine and a lump to form in her throat. Those discarded slices of film collected from the cutting room floor still came out on a regular basis – whenever she needed a good dose of his presence. As had occurred so often since those few precious weeks, Lara lifted a silent prayer of thanks for their studio being the one chosen for that particular program. The Valentine's Day special had offered her a priceless gift filled with footage of him that was for her eyes alone.

"In some ways, I really don't want to leave. I'll miss the magic of seeing countless hours of repeated takes become a finished product to enthral audiences around the country, as well as overseas ... and laughing at so many fluffed lines and faulty props ... or kids and animals doing the darnedest things!"

The entire guest list was familiar with that well-known showbiz cry never to work with either one. It was virtually impossible to fully control what could happen if one or the other were added to the mix. She had worked around some great examples of what should have been catastrophic scenarios during her time behind the old Steenbeck and then the newer digital equipment, but her skills had made them look like faultless takes. Seeing the twinkle in her eye brought a smile to everyone's face.

"And David, I *am* going to miss making up those blooper reels! Sometimes they were the best part of a project, like those exciting docos on the necessity of mealy bugs or what's the best way to cure constipation in farm animals – not that any of them were yours!" she added hastily, grinning at the many faces she had worked with over the years.

More loud laughter filled the place. Each of them understood not every project was riveting material, even though most pieces were at least a necessary evil.

"But I must say *Tessellation in Nature* was fascinating to put together – it's certainly given me a greater appreciation of this amazing world we live in. That one was my first job and I'm sure it played a big part in getting me hooked!"

Two very loud whistles split the air, this time from the cinematographer and soundman who had worked on the project.

She sent them a big grin as well as a cheeky wink before continuing on with her plaudits. "Seriously, I've been so blessed to be a part of this life, and I'm really going to miss each and every one of you. Thanks for the memories ... especially you Davey..."

Following an awkward bow, Lara made her way back to the vacant seat beside her boss, and he sent her an affectionate wink as she sat down. Afterwards, she was swamped by a crowd of well-wishers wanting to offer her a farewell hug and send her off with the familiar old Aussie, "Chookas".

§

As soon as the place was deserted, Lara started gathering up several bouquets of flowers when David wandered over. Much to her surprise, he pulled a beautifully wrapped box from behind his back and presented it to her with a touching smile.

"I wanted to give you this after the others had gone. I could never repay everything you've done for me and the business, but somehow, I think you'll get a kick out of the sentiment behind this. It's just a small token of my appreciation and something to remember me by."

With true sincerity, she replied, "I don't need anything to remind me of you, Davey. This party has been the perfect gift, so there was no need to buy me anything more. You're a super friend, and I'm so glad to have you in my life. Your friendship has kept me sane on many a long, lonely night."

Over the years, he had often noticed tears gathering in her eyes whenever a tragic love story blazed across the small flickering screen above her worktable. Afterwards, he had taken her out for a quick bite to eat, and he soon had her laughing again at his abysmal attempt at humour.

It was a well-known fact around the traps that whenever any of the movies she worked on with a romantic genre had its first screening in a cinema, the directors always came away delighted with the finished product and the audience's reaction. None of them had any clue as to just how much of her own heart and soul was contained in the effort she put in to make their films the best they could possibly be. Nevertheless, her boss was certain of one thing ... even though the greatest love of her life now belonged in the past, manipulating the footage to convey the best romantic storyline was her way of keeping him alive in the here and now.

Taking her in his arms, he whispered into her hair, "I still think he's a fool ... despite me being the one who benefited from his loss."

Her look was quizzical as she raised shimmering eyes to his.

"You never would've stayed if Adam was still in your life. I only wish you could've had both. You would've made two men very happy..."

She hugged him close, blinking away a sudden rush of tears and grateful for his thoughtful heart. Only a few knew of their story, and sometimes it was a relief to hear that beloved name mentioned aloud, even if it was only for a brief moment in time.

"Thanks, old friend," came the soft reply as she kissed his cheek.

Sending her a caring wink, he nudged her elbow with his. "Come on, enough of this soppy old stuff! Hurry up and open your present before we turn into a pair of blubbering idiots!"

The down-to-earth retort was the perfect pick-me-up, and she quickly ripped open the paper to discover a brand-new state of the art digital video camera. It was the best money could buy, and she gasped when she looked up at him.

"Now you can capture your own movies ... and hopefully get an opportunity to film your own blooper reels!"

"Oh David, you've always been so generous! This is perfect ... thank you so much. You've been an amazing boss and I'm so glad I had the chance to work with you."

"And don't you ever forget it, young lady," came his quick rejoinder.

"How could I possibly forget, especially when you willingly worked around my singing career when I first started out ... and then took me back when I'd been away for so long! You may not be my boss anymore ... but you'll always be my friend."

He wrapped her in another tight hug and then answered with a warm smile, "I'd better be! You're not going to get rid of me that easily. I'm going to be in the audience as often as I can, but I'll miss that fabulous voice serenading me every day."

Lara couldn't answer as her eyes filled with tears again. Offering him a final wave, she turned and walked away to a new life – one where the voice he was going to miss would once again be given the opportunity to soar to its rightful place.

Chapter 33

Adam had never lost that old yearning to see Lara treading another stage. It had become a daily battle trying to stay on track and just go about his business while this ever-present companion waited in readiness to rouse those smouldering desires all over again.

Down through the years, whenever their busy schedules had productions coinciding at the same time in the same city, he only managed to push the temptation away because of a promise already made. When he overheard his parents discussing Lara's comeback as *Christine*, the lure to catch a glimpse of her one more time plagued him every day of its six-week run.

On the morning of that fateful finale, an unwinnable battle had been raging in his heart, and it began from the moment he first opened his eyes. With Trina away at one of her interstate charity events, there was no need to hide his feelings. For more than an hour he tossed and turned in their bed, envisioning Lara's smiling mouth and the touch of her fingers on his skin. He remembered how perfect she was in the role during its Sydney run – to be able to see her in the original old theatre where they had first met made the idea even more irresistible.

All morning as he worked around the house, these thoughts kept him company. Over a steamy cup of coffee during a welcome break, came the niggly reminder this would be his last chance to see her perform the challenging role. His spirits grew even heavier knowing anyone else could see her whenever they wanted, while he had to pretend she meant nothing and ignore his heart's cry. Letting out a loud groan, all of those self-denials suddenly flew out the window, and he was overwhelmed with an impenetrable determination nothing was going to keep him away this time.

Following a lonely scratched-up lunch, Adam went for a long walk around the property, all the while schooling himself that he would only observe her from a distance and then leave as soon as it was over.

Later, as he donned his best suit, one solitary thought shadowed his every move. *I only want to see you on stage once more ... then I'll walk away ... nothing else, I promise.*

He didn't dare think about the butterfly bracelet still burning a hole in his coat pocket after so many years of waiting.

It was well before opening time when Adam left for the theatre. Along the way, he decided to drop by his former home to see if his mother would like to go with him in his car. Knowing his parents' habits well, he could imagine she would be getting ready for the big night, while his father would already be donning his costume in one of the backstage dressing rooms several miles away.

Elizabeth couldn't believe her eyes when her son pulled up dressed in a smart suit and with a ticket stashed in his pocket. Imagining a host of heartbreaking scenarios if Lara happened to run into him, she was quick to extract a firm promise that he would slip away quietly as soon as the curtain came down.

"Now listen to me, my boy. I don't even want you waiting around to congratulate your father. You'll see him at lunch tomorrow anyway."

With Charles playing one of the new managers of the Parisienne Opera House, he had another plausible excuse to attend the final performance.

"It's okay, Mum, she won't be able to see me. I deliberately chose a seat near the back. And I promise to leave as soon as the doors open when it's over. Don't worry, the last thing I want to do is hurt her any more than I already have."

All she could do was hug him close and pray Lara would be none the wiser.

With his heart racing, that earlier mantra to leave straight away stayed with him as the lights went down prior to the first act. Later during intermission, he remained in his seat, eyes glued to the thick velvet curtain with that firm vow still keeping him company. He was totally oblivious to the excited chatter of other patrons, focussing only on the earlier image of *Christine* standing in *Raoul's* arms during the final scene of Act I. Once upon a time Lara's own voice had whispered similar sentiments into his ear in the sanctuary of her bedroom...

Say you'll share with me one love, one lifetime ... say the word, and I will follow you...

Adam already knew every line by heart. Since making the decision to be in the audience, he was well aware how difficult it would be to hear those agonising words fall from her lips. But not surprisingly, for those few brief moments, he pretended she was once again crooning them to him.

Far too soon for his liking, the closing number was done and the outbreak of loud ovations faded away to nothingness. All he could concentrate on was knowing she was standing only a few feet away behind a flimsy velvet barrier...

It had never been his intention to hang around afterwards. Unfortunately, with reality came an overwhelming longing to catch a glimpse of her as the Lara he remembered, rather than simply playing a character hidden beneath layers of makeup and a coiffured wig. Suddenly the heartfelt promise made earlier to his mother turned into more of an annoying suggestion. From his seat in the twentieth row – selected on purpose to ensure he couldn't look into her eyes and be tempted further – witnessing her magnificent portrayal of *Christine* was over three hours of exquisite torture. The love-starved man could easily identify with his onstage counterpart aching for a woman who could never be his.

And neither Adam nor Elizabeth had factored in one other component that set off the domino effect for the night's events ... an innocent suggestion from a passerby that included the touching reunion, and then ended with Mike's sudden violent outburst and hurried departure.

It all started when the show's leading man ran into his best friend as he tried to sneak out a side door. Without thinking, Jeff immediately invited Adam to the after-party. Of course, his offer was too hard to resist – after all, there were sure to be dozens and dozens of people around so it would be a cinch for one person to get lost in the crowd. Besides, Adam was used to being careful – he had certainly put in enough practice through having to hide his true feelings.

If I stay far enough away, she won't even know I'm there. I just want to catch one more glimpse before she disappears from my life again.

Lucy was just coming down the same corridor to meet her husband when she overheard the invitation. While Adam hurried off to find his mother and fill her in on the sudden change of plans, she could only look at Jeff in bewilderment and biff him across one shoulder with a well-aimed backhand.

"Grrr, what on *earth* are you doing! Don't you realise Mike's going to be out there?" She shook her head in exasperation, and sent him her best glare. "I can't believe you just did that! And how's Lara going to cope if she sees him?"

All Jeff could do was shrug his shoulders and spread his hands, holding them up as though to ward off both the rebuke and the slap. "Ouch, don't hit me so hard! I couldn't help it. Didn't you see the look in his eyes? How could I just let him walk away – he still *loves* her..."

"Which is the *very* reason why you shouldn't have invited him! Men ... *aarrgh* ... no idea!" she declared, shaking her head once again.

I may love you dearly, but gee, you sure can be an idiot at times, my darling.

§

Ten long months had passed since that bittersweet night. Even so, Adam still couldn't stop thinking about those few stolen minutes in the restaurant's back corridor. It didn't take too much imagination to picture Lara in his arms again, or to taste her on his lips. And it was impossible to count how many times he had woken in the night dreaming of them making love. His only solution was to turn over with a heavy groan and curl up on his side of the bed, feeling as if a leaden weight was pressing against his heart.

During daylight hours, a pair of sapphire blue eyes kept him company wherever he went. When night fell, and there was nothing else clamouring for his time, memories of her touch and captivating smile filled his heart and mind.

One day, following a visit to his parents' vineyard near the Gold Coast, he felt drawn back to a spot that had always held a special place in his heart. Climbing the steep, rocky stairs to the lookout overlooking Miami Beach at Nobby's Head, he could picture a young mother and daughter chasing each other over the golden sands below as their long tresses danced in the sunshine.

Standing on the headland looking out to sea, memories of their last encounter at the old theatre came flooding back. Everything from that night was still a vivid memory. He could still remember thinking her voice had woken him from a deep sleep, almost as though she was crying out to him from across the miles. Startled, he had thrown back the covers to hurry to the window.

Then for several minutes, he had just stared into the darkness as his spirit implored, *Are you okay, Baby? What's going on? Oh Lord, I hate this!*

Back then, the sound of rustling leaves had been his only answer. He hadn't dared to ring her number knowing Mike was staying at the cottage, so the only option left to him was to offer up a prayer for her safety and then trust God.

As he slowly retraced his steps down the lookout's staircase, Adam once again wondered how she was and whether she was enjoying her new life with Mike by her side. No matter how many times he scoured the magazines or newspapers in different cities, there was never a mention of them as a couple. But then again, he wasn't surprised. Adam well knew how private she was and liked to keep her personal life away from the prying eyes of the public.

"Stay safe … and please take good care of her," he whispered on the wind.

§

Trina's volunteer work still kept her busy. For the last few years, whenever Adam was involved in an interstate production, it had become increasingly difficult for her to accompany him when his shows usually ran for several months at a time. As a compromise, every few weeks she tried to fly down for a few days. Then together they spent his off-time relaxing around the hotel or visiting some of the hospitals and children's wards her charity helped to raise funds for.

Life had become very different from those earlier turbulent years filled with disgust and despair. Now Adam was able to admire what his wife was doing, and he always made sure to mention how proud he felt knowing the difference she was making to so many lives. As time passed, the couple grew comfortable together, although emotionally they were still miles apart.

On the rare occasions both lives intersected, social activities mainly revolved around prestigious parties with hosts from the highest echelons of entertainment and business. Though the liquor flowed freely, Trina was no longer tempted since that ugly spate of incidents from years past. Now, when their paths met, they were able to partake in the lifestyle she had always hankered for.

Living alone for months at a time meant Adam found it easy to revert to the life of a solitary man following one of her flying visits. Most times, he welcomed the company of his own thoughts rather than mixing with others.

And that insatiable hunger for a woman with laughter in her eyes and hair the colour of roasted chestnuts never left him as he wandered the streets of many of the places she also frequented during similar sojourns for her career. Only the privileged few who knew his secret understood how his soul still searched for traces of her everywhere he went – though no one was game enough to say anything in case it reawakened that overwhelming urge to see her again.

§

No matter how much time had passed, Lucy and Lara still remained the closest of friends, and they were always up for a catch-up whenever the busy star happened to be back in Brisbane. Lucy had given up trying to find Lara a love match among Jeff's many acquaintances after the horrible outcome with Mike.

Contrary to her sister's stern directive, a few weeks after the shocking incident, Suzie made the crucial decision to tell Lucy what had fuelled Mike's sudden departure. In her mind, Lara needed as much support as possible to help her get over the attack, especially in the early days when the uncertainty of losing her ability to sing was hanging over her head.

Lucy was shocked at the news and vowed not to say anything to Jeff, knowing it was the only way to make sure Adam didn't find out. Although his name was never mentioned anymore in Lara's presence, both women knew how much she still loved Adam, and understood how pointless it was trying to encourage her to find someone else to take his place. Once she got the all clear from the doctor saying her vocal cords had sustained no permanent damaged, the three of them sent up a quick prayer of thanks.

§

Every show Lara was involved with became an instant hit. Max was continually fielding phone calls from producers wanting her for their next project. There was no time to miss her old job, although jetting from city to city with no one to share this exciting new life emphasised just how much she missed the fun-loving rapport she and David had known.

Being on the road turned out to be a lonely life at times. Having no close friends or family around to join in on an old-fashioned chinwag was what she missed most. Her ever-changing array of castmates were mostly friendly and easy-going, and she was often invited to join them for supper after a show. Sometimes, during their only regular day off, a few would band together to explore the local area. Unfortunately, due to the nature of showbiz, these shared lives were only of a few months' duration. Then a new production would come along with an entirely different cast and crew. And so the cycle continued.

Sunday mornings usually entailed a visit to the local church in whatever city she found herself. She sought comfort in the familiar old hymns, as well as a new breed of songs with a much livelier tempo. She enjoyed sitting in the pews listening to the pastor share insights from the Bible, and sometimes stayed behind for a cuppa and chat with the assortment of parishioners who had taken her under their wing. Even so, the gypsy-like nature of her work meant it was hard to make lasting friendships. Nothing was really stable in the life of a musical theatre star.

The only constant in this temporary world was a familiar display adorning each of her hotel suite bedrooms. Rubbing shoulders with a photograph of Nikki astride Jasper, and another of Adam smiling at the camera in Tuscany, was an ornate snow-globe of her favourite Austrian city – one a little girl had given her all because of the generosity of a special man. The centrepiece of this perpetual array was a pewter sculpture with a message that always managed to lift her spirits. And every night a dainty butterfly bracelet joined them. These were the last things she looked at before turning out the light. The ritual had become a touching conclusion to her day that sent her to sleep with traces of a wistful smile.

Following close on Brisbane's heels, Sydney became her next favourite place because it meant Nikki could stay with her both during rehearsals and while a new show ran its course. NIDA was only a short distance from the city centre so she could easily catch a bus there on lecture days. It was just like old times – watching the midday movie curled up like bookends on either end of the couch, or trawling the city's vibrant streets looking for new places to explore and seeking out places where hearty, homecooked meals were on offer.

They had a few favourite lunchtime haunts – usually out-of-the-way little places where Lara could maintain a degree of anonymity. Every now and then someone from her large group of followers spotted them sitting in a discreet corner. Even though she tried to appear inconspicuous, Lara's stunning looks and sparkling blue eyes made her instantly recognisable. Much to their delight, she was always willing to pose for photos and offer her autograph. They were her bread-and-butter, and so she was more than happy to spare a few minutes of her time. Apart from being graced with a fabulous voice, this was another reason she was so popular and why people continually flocked to see her perform.

§

It was May of 2002. From their seats in the front section of a vast Sydney auditorium, Nikki glanced across at her mother and her alluring brown eyes shone with excitement. Lara mustered up a nervous grimace and then sent a shy smile to a few of her colleagues as they offered excited thumbs-up gestures or whispered words of good luck as they went to their allocated seats. Tonight, the mother and daughter duo were part of the audience instead of treading a stage.

A few weeks earlier an embossed card had arrived in the mail, announcing Lara's nomination for a coveted Helpmann Award. It was a prestigious honour extended to those artists excelling in the live performance industry and only the second time the awards had been held. She felt humbled to be singled out this way. Except, as usual when it came to receiving any form of praise, she loathed being the centre of attention.

Stuffing the card back into its matching envelope, Lara quickly pushed it under a pile of papers on the kitchen bench. She had no intention whatsoever of attending, though her reasons had nothing to do with a fear of not winning – more the possibility that a certain someone may also be there. Adam often attended similar events with an attractive redhead on his arm.

As fate would have it, Nikki was home for Easter break and accidentally stumbled across the elegant envelope while rummaging around for a misplaced shopping list. Her mother was already elbow-deep in dishwashing water and had no chance of snatching it away before a pair of prying eyes saw what it contained.

"What's this?" the inquisitive teenager asked, fishing out the contents and perusing the invitation inside.

Lara tried to grab it from her hands. "Nothing important. Just something that arrived the other day. Please put it back. I was going to check it out later."

Letting out an excited yelp, Nikki instantly grabbed her mother by the waist and started twirling her around the kitchen. Soapy water streamed from Lara's hands, leaving droplets through her daughter's hair and down over her brand-new top, but the excited eighteen-year-old didn't even notice.

"*Muuum*, you've been nominated for a *Helpmann!* That's *fantastic!* I can't wait to see what you'll wear, let's go shopping this afternoon for a new dre—"

"Hang on, hang on, don't get too excited. I won't be going, so there's no need for a new dress – or anything else."

"*Whaat!* Don't be *ridiculous* ... are you *crazy!* Anyone'd give their eyeteeth to get an invitation to one of these things, let alone be nominated! Of *course* you're going and I'm coming with you – I'll be your date for the night!"

So often in the past, Nikki had seen how self-conscious her mother became whenever any sort of fuss was made over her. She well knew Lara hated being the centre of attention away from the stage, especially if it meant attending a function by herself. Not only that, Nikki had a feeling her reluctance had something to do with a certain man whose photo still sat on Lara's bedside table.

It took lots of persuasion and finally a bit of bribery with Nikki threatening to catch the first plane back to Sydney before Lara agreed. So, what had begun as a reluctant shopping trip soon turned into a light-hearted affair, with both of them trying on a huge array of dresses and having a fabulous time. The unexpected adventure finished with a soiree in their favourite café at South Bank Parklands, on the edge of the Performing Arts District.

When the two women walked the red carpet in Nikki's new hometown five weeks later, there was no dallying for photo opportunities or press interviews in the roped-off area near the entrance. Instead, the popular nominee hurried inside with her exasperated daughter following closely behind.

Lara felt like Cinderella at the ball when she looked out over the sea of faces representing so many different productions and genres ... unworthy to be there and, with a different twist, wishing the clock would hurry up and strike midnight so she could disappear.

Simply being nominated was enough of a surprise, but when Lara heard her name read out as the winner in her category, she could only sit there dumbfounded ... until Nikki threw her arms around her neck and then eagerly pushed the reluctant recipient towards the stage. The theatre erupted into thunderous applause as she made her way up the stairs with her head bowed and cheeks tinged with pink. Her one saving grace had been an earlier phone call from Elizabeth, conveying the news that Adam was stuck in Melbourne working out a new contract.

Phew, at least I don't have to worry about being caught in those eyes again.

For the next week, headlines in theatre magazines right around the country announced her win in full-blown headlines. It didn't take long for the phones in Max's office to start ringing hotter than before.

§

A year later on a brisk night in June 2003, Adam waited anxiously in the audience for a new musical to open. It was unusual for him to be out on a Saturday night in a city that wasn't his hometown. Normally he was on the first plane home to Brisbane once his latest show had finished its run. Only tonight was different. This was Lara's latest opening and, despite all of those previous declarations, it was an event he was determined not to miss.

Speaking together even for those few precious minutes two years earlier had rekindled the fire in his soul. Needless to say, the temptation to pop in to watch her from the confines of a dark theatre hall was always lurking just below the surface whenever she was appearing in a new production. He still found it a struggle to stay away whenever they were working in the same city, although that solemn vow always helped to keep him on track.

A Little Night Music was about to begin its new season in the stunning Capitol Theatre, a century-old venue restored to its former glory just a few years earlier. His latest venture had just finished its Sydney run, and with a small break until his next role, a delay in returning to his country estate in the northern capital for a few days would cause no harm.

There was one additional element to this new musical, and it was the reason Adam had reserved a premium seat for opening night. Long forgotten words rose out of a distant past the moment he spied two names displayed in bold letters on a new set of billboards dotted around the city. Seeing them took him back to the final performance of *Les Misérables* in Sydney when Lara was by his side. Her comment about him having a bit of competition if Anthony Warlow or Mark Sinclair were around had been given in jest, as was his teasing reply about dragging her back to his side if ever she was playing opposite either one.

Tonight, those words had come back to haunt him. Mark had top billing, and Lara was playing his former lover.

§

The female star's dressing room was somewhat more subdued than for a usual first night. Dragging the lavish costume over her head, Lara could feel the nerves starting to build, and it didn't help knowing what tonight signified. In theatre circles, most could think she had reached the pinnacle of her career – playing opposite Mark was every Australian actor's dream. In fact, a host of leading ladies around the world would do almost anything to see their name up in lights beside his. Even so, this wasn't the reason for her uneasiness.

Walking the red carpet only a short while earlier, Lara's hand had been firmly ensconced in her co-star's well-toned arm. Giving a soft chuckle, he bent close and whispered, "Well, lovely lady, we're finally here! I told you I wanted to sing with you one day. Hopefully, this is only the first of many, so we'd better knock their socks off tonight." He gave her hand an affectionate squeeze.

Lara's captivating blue eyes sparkled with expectation as they turned to meet his and Mark grinned when her infectious laugh fell into his ears. "Isn't it amazing and I still can't believe it! Nikki's over the moon knowing we're finally working together. It's all she's been able to talk about for weeks."

Mark and the excited teen had met during rehearsals when she dropped by to share lunch with Lara one day. Once her initial shyness subsided, the famous actor and the up-and-coming young actress spent quite a few minutes chatting over a cup of coffee while her mother went off to change. Mark was able to set her at ease talking about acting, horses and Italy – the three things Lara had mentioned were closest to Nikki's heart.

"I hope she's here tonight." His eyes swept across the swarm of heads.

"Of course she is! Somewhere out there in the crowd, although I haven't been able to spot her yet."

Thinking about Nikki, other family members came to mind, and her expression turned pensive. "I just wish my parents could be here tonight."

Mark already knew the tragic story behind their deaths, and he squeezed her hand in sympathy. "They'd be very proud, I'm sure," he said, with a friendly wink, hoping to lift her spirits. "Come on, where's that gorgeous smile gone? You and I are going to have a great time tonight, but you'd better smile for the cameras, or we'll be tomorrow's newspaper headlines for all the wrong reasons if they think I've upset you."

She knew he was right and quickly pulled out the smile she was famous for just as several flashbulbs lit up her eyes. The duo now looked exactly how they should – talented stars about to take centre-stage in front of a glittering crowd.

At the back of the throng of onlookers just out of their line of sight, a tall, dark and handsome man was carefully observing everything that was going on. Decked out in an immaculate dinner suit with a crisp white shirt and black bow tie, Adam wasn't upset, just desperately wishing he could make good on that old pledge to drag her back to his side.

Lara peered over her shoulder as they reached the entrance, trying hard to catch a glimpse of Nikki among the sea of faces. Those watching from the crowd noticed she suddenly seemed to falter and her whole body gave an involuntary shake, as though someone had run an unexpected finger down her spine.

"Ooohhh..." she groaned, pressing a hand over her heart.

It was an unnerving experience, and Mark both heard and felt her reaction. Straightaway, he placed an arm around her waist as a way to steady her. She leaned into his shoulder gratefully, struggling to take a breath.

"Lara, what's wrong?" Both a worried frown and her companion's tone conveyed his concern.

Again, she peered back into the waiting crowd, as though searching for something even she wasn't sure was actually there. For the briefest of moments, Lara pondered the strange sensation and then shook her head.

"I'm not sure. It was like ... umm ... I don't know really ... something familiar but sort of unnerving, all at the same time." Turning back to face him, she repeated his earlier direction. "Don't worry, I'll be okay. Come on, it's time we smiled for the cameras!"

Once again, a volley of flashbulbs lit up the area where they were standing.

Smiling patiently for the row of paparazzi to get their fill, somewhere out of the deepest recesses of her mind, Lara recalled a faint memory. Fleetingly, she closed her eyes as a rush of emotion brought with it words from a flippant promise made on another night many years ago.

Oh, darling, was that you I felt? Forget all this carry-on. I'd give anything to have you drag me away so we could spend just one more night together.

§

About an hour later in her recently renovated dressing room, Lara was just finishing buttoning up her costume when, for some unexplained reason, she felt another shiver run along her spine. The cast had recently come from a flawless run-through of some of the more difficult numbers, so it was nothing to do with being unprepared. *Oh, why can't I shake off whatever it is?* For the first time since returning to the stage, nerves began to get the better of her. It was nothing like that feeling of raw edginess just before a curtain opening, and she had no idea what could be causing such a reaction.

With another quick shake of her shoulders to push any uneasiness away, Lara hurried down to the backstage area to wait in readiness. The show was already several minutes in as *Desiree* wasn't needed until the storyline was well along.

"Are you okay, Ms Jennings? You don't look very well," the make-up girl commented as she made some last-minute touch-ups to the actress' lipstick.

Lara took a deep breath and let it out slowly. "I think I'll be okay. I just feel a bit strange ... as though something peculiar is going on."

"Better not say that too loud, or you'll put the spooks up everyone! Just keep taking deep breaths, and hopefully you'll be okay," Sally replied, nervously glancing around.

"I hope so, but I'm sure it's nothing. Oh well, here goes." Grasping the long skirt in one hand, Lara swept onto the stage with her voice ringing out clear and pure.

During her stint in front of the audience, those strange impressions continued – like someone had placed her under a microscope and was dissecting each fragment piece by piece. Adding to her confusion, the longer it continued, the more confident she became, almost as if some unseen hand was guiding her every move. Thankfully, throughout the whole process, her acting prowess was in fine form. All she could put it down to was having first-hand knowledge of the heartache and longing that comes with loving the husband of someone else.

Mark was the quintessential leading man, never trying to outshine his counterpart. Instead, he enhanced Lara's performance by subtly highlighting all of her strengths, skilfully showcasing the artiste everyone had come to see ... and all without missing a beat in his own role of *Fredrik*. Their perfect pairing grabbed the audience and held them spellbound, while the poignant tale carried many along a path of despair as *Desiree* watched the man she still loved – the father of her child – make a fool of himself over a much younger wife.

Sitting in the centre of the fourth row, lost in the shadows and far enough away so as not to be recognised by anyone on stage, a man with dark eyes followed Lara's every move. And mirroring a response from long ago, his hand – now clenched and white-knuckled – craved to reach out and touch the very air surrounding her. Even that tiny portion of space knew the sweet caress of her presence ... while all Adam had was this silent and ever-present ache.

§

Interval came and backstage was a hive of noise and activity as costumes were changed, replacement wigs anchored into place and makeup reapplied. Lara had only a few minutes to reflect on the strange sensations causing the heady attack. Sally from make-up dropped by her dressing room with a mild medication, hoping it may help to ease the earlier reaction. Lara was feeling much better and waved her away with a grateful smile. Strangely, the feeling actually brought with it a new sense of confidence and those watching from backstage had noticed a keener edge to her performance when Act I reached its conclusion.

Act II continued this sad tale of the poor besotted man and his ex-lover. Their lives had taken vastly different paths, and yet both shared the same outcome of lost dreams. Heartbroken and defeated, *Desiree* broke into the compelling *Send in the Clowns*, a well-known piece lamenting the fickle foolishness of love.

The tragic lyrics described the anguish that comes with bad timing and lost opportunities, and all the fools who miss them. The moment Lara raised her voice, that same tingling once again started in her spirit. Recognising the many parallels to her life, she figured it might just be a different expression of that old, deep-seated longing. And just like *Desiree*, she wondered if her last chance at happiness with the only man she would ever truly love was gone forever.

Only a few scenes later, *Fredrik* finally came to the realisation his former lover was the real love of his life. Wasting no time, he returned to *Desiree*, hoping to begin again. When Mark took his co-star in his arms while joining voices for the touching duet from the classic finale, their lips met and Lara's own past, present and longed-for future intertwined with the fictional story. Adam had always taken her to their own private paradise whenever they made love, and the only mouth she was able to envisage was the one belonging to her soulmate.

This emotional reawakening was so intense she was powerless to stop a tiny whimper from escaping – that never-forgotten longing to one day be with him again was back, and it drew her into its fullness. Lost in this seemingly unattainable goal, she forgot the microphone taped high on her forehead. It had the ability to pick up the slightest sound and carry it across the auditorium – even over the loud swell of music. Patrons with keen ears caught the cry from her heart, and several could be seen wiping away a few wayward tears.

Those earnest dark eyes following her every move from the fourth row now glistened with their own private grief. Like her, Adam was picturing them together in a scene similar to the one being played out onstage. And similar to *Fredrick,* he was confronted with an undeniable truth – Lara was the only woman for him and no amount of distance or time would ever change that fact.

Oh, Baby, so many times you made that same sound in my arms. Why didn't I fight harder for you? There's so much I want to tell you ... like waking up every morning with memories of us bringing my spirit to life again, and then at night it's as though your spirit falls asleep in my heart – and for those few brief hours, I dream you're safely home again. Inside, you're never far away...

And similar to one of *Fredrick's* lines, with this reality came a heartfelt wish: *Maybe one day we'll get the chance to experience a coherent existence after so many years of muddle...*

§

"You were *wonderful,* Lara! Did you hear all those sniffles and stifled coughs at the end? That's the true sign of a successful opening night, my friend!" With one arm resting lightly around her waist to guide her, Mark's green eyes shone with excitement as they made their way through a throng of actors on their way to a row of private dressing rooms located at one end of a long corridor. "I *told* you we'd be good together."

Though she was feeling absolutely mortified at the unfortunate slip up, Lara smiled along with him and gently nudged his shoulder. "Yes, you did, though at the time I never thought it would ever come to pass. Thanks for being such a sensational leading man. And I'm sorry if my imagination seemed to take on a life of its own at the end."

"Oh, don't worry. That little moan just made the scene more real!" he winked kindly, nudging her in return.

"I can't believe I did that! Please assure Julia she has nothing to worry about!"

He broke into friendly laughter. "It's okay; my wife's had to put up with watching me kiss loads of beautiful women over the years. Seeing you in my arms is all part and parcel of this business. She assured me years ago I could stop feeling guilty every night, though I'll be sure to pass on what you said."

"Phew ... thank you! And I promise not to be quite so vocal from now on. I don't know what I was thinking ... I'm so sorry."

Mark's green eyes caught her attention when a caring look took the place of his easy-going comments. "Oh, I think you do. There was a lot more to that kiss than you're letting on..."

His tone was soft – similar to Charles or Elizabeth whenever they felt her pain.

She blushed and closed her eyes for a moment, but wasn't game enough to respond.

Leaning close, he whispered so only she could hear, "It's okay. Everyone's allowed a secret or two. Men can tell when a woman has another man on her mind." At her quick gasp, he added with a light-hearted hug, "Hey, I adore Julia, and don't want anyone else, but I certainly wouldn't object if you feel the need to respond that way every time ... and I'm sure the audience won't either!"

It was just the pick-me-up she needed after that sudden momentary fear. Planting an affectionate kiss on his cheek, she hurried away to get ready for the after-party.

A little while later, a lone figure stood watching in the shadows as Mark took Lara's hand to help her into a waiting limo. Just then a much younger woman came over to join them, and he took her hand as she climbed in too. Turning back

462

for a moment, her anxious gaze swept the lingering crowd. When that silent witness' eyes met hers, Nikki's filled with tears. All he could do was incline his head sadly as a touching acknowledgement of her obvious concern.

Once Adam saw them pull away from the curb, he turned despondently and trudged down the street with hands plunged deep into his coat pockets. Wishing he had the courage to drag the woman he adored back to his side and run away with her forever, all he could do was steel himself to face the lonely hotel suite and another night on his own.

§

The celebrations went on into the early hours of the morning, and Lara was feeling quite weary when she and Nikki arrived back at their suite. Trying hard to stifle a yawn, she turned the key in the lock. The excitement of the opening, coupled with Mark's unexpected foresight, was starting to take its toll.

"Well, I'm off to bed. Sleep well, gorgeous girl, and thanks for coming tonight. It was fabulous having you there," she said, kissing her daughter's cheek and peeling off an expensive, midnight blue, shawl-style jacket with an Italian couturier label inside the collar. The elegant, woollen article was still her first choice for special occasions whenever the weather turned chilly.

"Mum ... before you go, can we have a chat for a minute?"

"Sure, Munchkin, what's up? I *think* I'm ready for you to deliver your take on my interpretation of *Desiree*..." she offered with a nervous grimace.

"Oh Mum, that's not what I meant, but for the record, you were fabulous as usual. Oh, and I still can't believe my mother actually got to work with Mr Sinclair! How *cool*, and everyone's sooo jealous at NIDA ... and me most of all. Working with him is on all of our bucket lists!" Nikki smirked as she plonked herself down on the sofa and snuggled into the cushions.

Lara burst out laughing and settled herself down in the chair opposite, still on a high at the thought of pulling off a good performance despite all of those earlier worries. "I can't believe girls of your age have bucket lists already – they're supposed to be for old people like me!"

"*Muuummm*, you're not old ... just mature!"

"What? Like old cheese! Thanks, Niks," came her flabbergasted retort as she tossed a well-aimed cushion at her only child.

After exchanging a few more light-hearted taunts, the teenager hunkered down in her seat and hugged the soft missile to her chest. Looking across at her mother, that beaming smile suddenly disappeared, and she took a deep breath hoping to find some last-minute courage.

The words came out hesitant and soft. "Mum ... um ... oh, heck..." Her face was a picture of sadness as she took another deep breath. "Well, here goes. Look, there's something I think you should know..."

463

Lara was surprised at the mantle of caution preceding Nikki's statement. She was used to her daughter being open and eager to share everything. It was more than obvious something was weighing heavily on her mind.

"Sure, sweetheart, what's up?"

"Mum—" she broke off again and began gnawing at her lip.

It was enough to make Lara really start to worry, and she leaned forward in her seat. "What's wrong, sweetheart? This isn't like you. What's going on?"

"Umm ... something happened tonight ... but I don't want to upset you." She paused again, hating having to bring her mother down from the recent high, but sensing what she had to say was important.

"Get on with it, young lady. I've already been feeling strange all night ... I don't need you giving me any more angst." Lara wasn't upset, just becoming even more frustrated and so her tone was sharp.

"Mum..."

"Yes!"

With one last swallow, the young woman dove straight in the deep end. "Uncle Adam was there tonight..."

Instinctively, Lara's hand flew to her mouth. *So it is true ... I do still feel you. Oh, my love, now I understand why it seemed as though someone was showing me the way. It was you. You always were that light guiding me home.*

Seeing the pain in her mother's eyes, and the shocked reaction followed by a quick intake of breath only confirmed everything Nikki had suspected all along. "You've never gotten over him, have you? Not really..." When there was no answer, she pounced. "I *knew* it!"

Lara's gaze was piercing. "I'm not getting into any of that now. Just tell me what happened ... where was he?"

"Sitting all by himself, right behind me in the fourth row ... and Mum, he looked so sad when it came time to go."

Lara automatically bit her lip as she tried to stop the ache in her heart from consuming her. Swallowing hard, she asked, "Did you get the chance to talk to him?"

"Of *course!* I *had* to. I couldn't just leave him sitting there looking so forlorn ... but when I called out his name, it was as if he didn't even recognise me."

"Well, I'm not surprised. You've turned into a beautiful young woman and dressed like that with your hair swept up, you're nothing like the cute little girl he once knew. But surely he must've responded somehow."

"Yeah, he did ... eventually. But I'll never forget the look in his eyes when he just sat there staring up at the curtain – it was as though he was willing it to rise again." She looked intently at her mother. "His eyes were all red like he'd been weeping ... Mum, it was heartbreaking, and I had no idea what to say."

Tears swam in Lara's eyes, and she listened without moving as her daughter went on.

"When he finally registered someone was calling out to him, and then realised who I was, it was obvious he was trying to act as though nothing was wrong. He did seem pleased to see me, but it was nothing like the Uncle Adam I remember ... so full of life and always trying to make me laugh. It's like he's just a shell of the man we once knew. Mum, I'm really worried about him."

Lara had to close her eyes as she pictured the scenario. She knew exactly what was the cause of his reaction.

Why did you have to come tonight, my darling? You must've known how much it would hurt to see Mark and me together after your old throwaway threat.

Nikki pressed on, needing to hear the truth. "Mum, what *really* happened between the two of you? You've never really told me, and he wouldn't say anything, except to ask if you were happy. In fact, he asked me twice, almost as if he had to be sure you really were okay."

She had to blink back the tears. "I hope you told him I was fine. I don't want him worrying. He's been through enough as it is."

"I did, but then he mentioned Mike and wanted to know if you were happy together. I was *astounded* and told him you'd broken up ages ago – just after *Phantom* finished its run."

"Oh, Nikki, you *didn't!*"

"Of *course* I did, and you should've seen the difference it made – it was like his whole demeanour changed and a light suddenly came back into his eyes. I don't understand. Why wouldn't Aunty Elizabeth have told him?"

Lara was shattered. *Oh, Teddy, I'm so, so sorry. I honestly thought it was for the best.*

Realising Nikki was old enough to handle the truth, she opened up about those few stolen moments on the night of her comeback – all except the final more intimate scene. Bringing everything up again made Lara realise just how foolish she had been for not telling him the truth about Mike and their relationship. Then she remembered Lucy's sudden interruption and her response dripped with regret at what had been left unsaid.

"I was never able to finish telling him that Mike and I would only ever be friends. Aunty Luce was calling out to me, so I had to rush away." Images of their parting kiss filled Lara's mind, and her heart ached at the memory.

Nikki's sombre brown eyes had been fixed on Lara the whole time she was opening up, and her tone was perplexed when she eventually responded. "But why didn't Aunty Elizabeth or Uncle Charles tell him you'd broken up? I really don't understand."

"Because I asked them not to. After what happened that night, I realised he needed to forget about me – about us. It was obvious he'd never be able to get on with his life otherwise ... I figured that was the best way."

"Mum, how *could* you? You must've known how hurtful it would be!"

Lara hung her head in shame, her face awash with tears as a mountain of grief crushed her heart. "It was all I could think of to help him get over me."

A gut-wrenching sob tore through her throat as she tried to imagine the amount of agony he had been dealing with all this time. Living with the knowledge that he and Trina were together had been a terrible burden to bear, but at least it had been her choice to walk away. This cruel deception had offered him no choice except to believe she had completely moved on, despite her promise never to give up hope that one day they would be together.

Nikki couldn't handle seeing her mother suffering from so much guilt. She rushed over and wrapped Lara in her arms, rocking her gently in a distinct reversal of roles.

"I'm so sorry, Mum, but honestly, you two are as bad as each other. Both of you are unhappy, it was *obvious* tonight, and Blind Freddie can see you belong together. It's about time the pair of you acknowledged that fact and did something about it. I just wish you could've seen the look of relief in his eyes when I told him about Mike."

Lara looked up sadly, into those dark eyes so like another pair she loved just as dearly, and stroked her daughter's hair with a trembling hand. "It's better I didn't. He's still with Trina, and that's where he belongs. Too much water has flowed under the bridge to go back now. We both need to just get on with our lives."

"But have you really ... either of you?" Nikki responded with more insight than her mother cared to admit.

Lara couldn't answer, and they just held each other while the clock ticked loudly on the wall.

Several minutes passed before Nikki kissed her mother's cheek and wiped away the residue of tears. "I love you, Mum."

"I love you too, sweetheart. More than you'll ever realise. Thanks for caring about me – about us."

"Of course I care! Remembering all the things we did together are some of my favourite memories," Nikki answered, wishing there was something more she could do.

"Mine too, sweetie ... mine, too..."

Chapter 34

In December the following year, Lara received an unexpected invitation to participate in Melbourne's popular *Carols by Candlelight*, a special event where families came together to celebrate the wonders of Christmas. Spectators brought along picnic blankets or fold-up chairs and set themselves up on a long grassy slope to watch all the proceedings on the large stage area situated at the bottom of the hill. A colourful display of lights from the city's heart created the perfect backdrop to the concert. Televised live across the nation every Christmas Eve, the carols had been a Melbourne tradition for decades. Receiving an invitation to participate was an honour all artists aspired to.

She picked up the phone to sign up straight away, thrilled to be included in the star-studded line-up, and looking forward to catching up with several of her colleagues who would also be performing on the night.

The concert was a spectacular occasion, and Lara soon had the audience eating out of her hand with her poignant rendition of *Silent Night*. The fluttering flames of thousands of candles lit up the hillside in front of her and added a fairylike dimension. Nikki had flown down specially to support her mother and jumped to her feet applauding loudly when the well-loved old carol ended. Lara felt as though she was in wonderland watching all the children's faces light up as their candles swayed in time to the music at the magical event.

§

In a Perth hotel room thousands of kilometres away, Adam had just finished eating a solitary dinner. Sprawled across the king-sized bed, he absentmindedly flicked the switch on the remote to see if anything was worth watching on television. First up was a game show, then a couple of children's Christmas movies, but nothing grabbed his attention. For the next little while, his thumb kept pressing the channel selector. All of a sudden, the room filled with the familiar strains of a much-loved Christmas Carol. Santa was standing on a brightly festooned stage with fairy lights scattered all around. A cluster of small children sat at his feet with a look of wonder on their faces.

Adam couldn't remember the last time he had watched *Carols by Candlelight*. Since reconciling with Trina, he deliberately avoided them. After all, they were mainly targeted at families with children – something he would never experience ... or at least, never again. Watching the youngsters' spellbound faces reminded him of another ... and it was just too painful.

Tonight was different though ... he was alone with his thoughts and feeling just a little melancholic. Nothing else was worth watching, so he left the television playing in the background while idly perusing the local paper. At least some of the performers were acquaintances, and they were much better company than the never-ending silence broken only by the crackle of turning pages.

He was due to fly home in a couple of days after performing in a charity pantomime. Being married to a well-respected philanthropist, he had also been asked to participate in a local telethon to help raise money for one of the major children's hospitals. Normally Trina attended this type of function, except this year she had commitments elsewhere. Being in the city already, Adam was happy to volunteer as her fill-in.

They hardly celebrated Christmas as an occasion any more ... his wife had never really been interested. For the last couple of years, she usually arranged to be busy with one of her charities over the holiday season rather than going to what she considered 'unnecessary bother' at home. She still looked forward to receiving any gifts doled out during the festivities, but couldn't see what all the fuss was about when it came to actually celebrating its true meaning.

Her attitude meant all the wonder had gone out of it for him as well.

Adam could still recall Christmases spent with his first parents and the three of them celebrating together. But that was before a terrible accident had left him orphaned. Memories still lingered of the family attending early services at the church down the street. Afterwards, a few close friends always came around to share the delicious meal his mother had taken hours to prepare. His job had been to hand out the pile of brightly wrapped parcels from beneath the huge Christmas tree, and it had always been fun watching everyone's reaction to their gifts. As a naïve teenager, Adam could never have imagined how much his life would change in the blink of an eye, and he still found it hard to think about all he had lost.

There was one other memory that burrowed out of Adam's past during these few days every year. Without fail, his thoughts drifted back to the best Christmas he had ever experienced – a special celebration at his foster parents' home with the woman and child he adored by his side. He could still picture them in the living room as Lara and Nikki opened a pair of snow-globes purchased in Salzburg. Their loud exclamations of delight still resounded in his ears and tugged at his heartstrings. And each time his heart grew heavy remembering the way her eyes had glowed with a tender look of thanks after finding the sapphire and diamond pendant in the shape of a treble clef nestled in its *Tiffany* giftbox.

Adam still celebrated with Charles and Elizabeth whenever he was home on the twenty-fifth. If work commitments took him out of town, a phone call was always his first priority on Christmas morning.

The television was still playing in the corner when his eyelids started to grow heavy. Pushing aside the newspaper, it didn't take long before he surrendered to the wave of tiredness and his breathing slowed. The soft string accompaniment to *Away in a Manger* was a gentle lullaby to soothe him to sleep as he burrowed deep into a feather pillow.

Dreams rose out of a long-ago past – of a beautiful woman with long flowing hair and a voice that was warm and sweet, and smooth as liquid chocolate. His subconscious was used to this welcome visitor, only tonight her intonations were clearer than usual, and the lyrics mentioned something about sleeping in Heaven.

Into these misty imaginings, came an earnest cry as he called out to her, "Oh, Lara, is Heaven the only place we'll ever be together?"

The echo of his plea was loud enough to wake him ... and somehow that beloved voice was still keeping him company.

Scrambling out from under the pillows, he swiped at his eyes and peered across to the flickering screen. And there she was – centre stage at the concert, wearing a spectacular long red gown that draped around her body perfectly. A trail of silky hair swathed her bare shoulders in a shimmering cascade as she looked straight down the camera lens and captured his gaze. It didn't take much imagination to pretend she was singing only to him.

Falling back against the pillows with his eyes fixed firmly on her face, Adam lay there enthralled for the rest of the song. Then when the final note drifted away, with a cheery wave and big smile to the audience, she wished everyone "Merry Christmas and God bless" before blowing a kiss to those viewers behind the camera as she floated off-stage.

His heart sank.

And now I have to watch you leave all over again. I still miss you so much...

His attention drifted down to where a hand lay across the coverlet. He could almost feel the caress of her fingers join his for one of their intimate dance routines.

Similar to a churning sea, a sudden surge of despair flooded his heart, pillaging every crevasse as though trying to wash away her memory. A loud cry filled the room when he punched the pillow with all the force he could muster.

"*Why* do we have to be apart forever? Haven't we suffered enough? I *know* she still loves me..." He looked up at the ceiling, anguish written all over his face. "And *why* can't you make a way for us to be together? I don't know where else to turn! Please, God, *tell* me what to do!"

The frustration continued, only this time resignation replaced that anguished despair, and he fell face first into the pillow's downy comfort.

"I *know* what we did was wrong, but she's my soulmate and the *only* woman I'll ever truly love. Why couldn't you *make* me listen to Dad right from the start – then we wouldn't be in this mess. Oh, why did I *ever* let her go?"

The more Adam berated himself, the deeper his heartache ... until he lay spent and beaten with deep, mournful sobs wracking his body.

A few hours later, his dreams once again contained visions of Lara. Only this time when her name fell from his lips, all he could do was watch in anguish as she drifted out of sight.

§

Because Lara and Nikki had never been to Melbourne together, they decided to stay on over Christmas. After feasting on a festive lunch with all the trimmings at the hotel, the mother and daughter spent the next few hours trawling the quaint, narrow laneways and sophisticated arcades of the city precincts.

The metropolitan city was renowned for its out-of-the-way cafés and elegant boutiques. Many were tucked into charming alleyways or part of sprawling emporiums found in the central shopping district. Wandering along a stylish arcade close to their hotel, Nikki was running her eyes over the displays when she recognised an unusual logo in the window of an exclusive jewellery store.

"Mum, quick! Come and look over here," she exclaimed, pulling on Lara's arm. "I'm pretty sure this is the same place Uncle Adam bought my necklace when I was a little girl."

Peering closer, Nikki recognised other pieces with the same centrepiece as hers – obviously the signature design of the specialty jeweller.

"It is! Look, they're exactly the same as mine." Nikki's hand went to her throat to touch the pendant lying in the small hollow. "I'll never forget that day and how special I felt being taken out to lunch by someone so important. When he fastened this around my neck, I felt like a princess."

The keepsake always came out for special occasions and watching her mother sing at *The Carols* was the perfect excuse to wear it again, especially as this was her first trip to Melbourne since that memorable weekend. As she grew bigger, the chain had become tighter and needed replacing with a new one, though the pendant itself still brought back fond memories of those few unforgettable days.

Lara hadn't seen the piece for several years, and the three entwined hearts took her back to the agony of that sad and lonely weekend when Nikki had flown down with Charles and Elizabeth to see Adam perform in *The Sound of Music*.

"Oh Mum, I'm so sorry. I didn't mean to upset you." Nikki could have kicked herself when she saw the veil of sadness over her mother's eyes.

"Don't worry, I'm fine," came the quick reply as Lara attempted to brush it off, hating herself for putting a dampener on their happy mood. *You stupid woman, stop reacting all the time just because something reminds you of him!* Grasping Nikki by the hand, she quipped, "It's time I got over him and cut out all this nonsense. Come on, there's something really special I want to show you, and it's not too far away."

Because of the holiday, Melbourne's streets were so much quieter than the usual hustle and bustle of a normal weekday as they wandered up to Fitzroy Gardens. Lara had stumbled across the parklands located just outside the city centre many years ago and wanted to show Nikki one of its famous features – the historic Captain Cook's Cottage. During the early nineteen hundreds, a large sailing vessel had ferried the eighteenth century stone dwelling brick-by-brick from the famous navigator's hometown in England. Now it stood in pride of place in the parklands. Captain James Cook was the British explorer who had discovered the east coast of Australia and claimed it for his homeland. He was a legendary figure studied by every Aussie child in primary school.

With the heritage cottage closed for Christmas, they could only peer through a series of small leadlight windows to the old-world furniture and knick-knacks dotted around the cramped downstairs area.

"Oh, I'd love to live in something like this! Modern houses have nothing on the architecture of olden days," Nikki announced, her eyes shining brightly when she saw the narrow staircase leading up to the attic-style bedrooms. "I remember all of the old stone cottages and villas in Italy with their roaring fireplaces and canopy beds. It was so romantic!"

And once again, invading Lara's thoughts came similar images ... of lovers lying naked on a rug in front of a crackling fire in that same country. And just like before, she quickly pushed the intruders aside, only this time with a muffled groan and frustrated shake of her head. Thankfully, her daughter was already peering through another window, too far away to notice.

Leaving the park, they crisscrossed a maze of streets, happily window-shopping and secretly coveting many of the enticing articles on display until darkness began to fall.

Still full from the generous Christmas lunch, dinner was a light affair. They sat upright with their backs against the headboard of one of two Queen-size beds, watching the original version of *Miracle on 34th Street* and picking at a simple platter of fruit and cheese. Before they were even halfway through, Lara heard the distinct sound of heavy breathing and noticed Nikki had fallen off to sleep. Smiling to herself, she reached over and pulled up a light blanket before kissing her creaseless forehead, just as she had done so many times when this fully-fledged young woman was an adorable little girl.

You may be all grown up, but you'll always be my precious little Munchkin.

These brief few days had been a delightful break from reality, but with the dawn of a new day would also come a stark reminder it was time to head back to their respective hometowns.

Crossing to the window, Lara looked out and spotted the faint outline of the new moon peeping through the trees. In a familiar ritual for this time of year, her heart sent off its usual message…

Merry Christmas, Teddy. May God bless and keep you safe always. Sleep well, my darling, wherever you are.

§

With the dawn of the new year, Nikki was now qualified to make a name for herself in the major theatres around the country. Her NIDA course was all done, and recent exam results showed she had passed with flying colours.

The new graduate was in a quandary as to where her future lay. Even though the majority of professional theatre work could be found in either Sydney or Melbourne, she felt the need to be closer to Lara now that her study days were over. Nikki had never forgotten a promise made following Elizabeth's revealing chat about her mother and Adam's relationship. Within a few days, the decision was made to move back to her old hometown. Plenty of college friends were renting flats in the southern capitals and had offered to put her up if she was lucky enough to gain a role in any productions down that way.

After all the excitement of having her precious girl home again, Lara soon fell back to earth when Nikki announced she wanted to rent something small in a neighbouring suburb. Despite being sympathetic to her need for independence after being on her own for so long, she had been looking forward to sharing the Paddington cottage again with her bubbly daughter.

Another reason for Nikki's move north was how much she missed putting Jasper through his paces. The faithful gelding had missed out on some much-needed attention while she was living down south, and it was vital to keep up his training if they wanted to stay on the competition circuit. The talented young rider couldn't wait to spend more quality time with her beloved horse.

Max was quick to impart some wise advice about putting her name down on the books of a few temping agencies in the city. He explained this option would best suit her new career by helping to keep the coffers full while working around auditions and roles, especially if she was granted one and had to perform out of town for any length of time.

Recalling a late-night conversation when Lara had opened up about her relationship with Adam was another excuse for wanting to move closer. She couldn't help noticing the sadness in her mother's eyes – it was obvious how much she still missed him.

Lara's own lifestyle had always been a bit of a whirlwind, so the separation wasn't as bad as she first envisaged. The popular star was always in demand by the more renowned companies, and she was continually being offered roles for new productions. These often ran back-to-back around the country, which meant there was hardly any time to miss having her daughter around.

Trina rarely accompanied Adam to his out-of-town productions any more. Her charity work had increased so much, hardly a week went by without an invitation arriving in the mail to some major function or fundraiser. Every now and then Lara noticed their picture gracing the pages of newspapers or magazines covering the gala events. And as usual, that slumbering niggle of yearning would once again raise its head to keep her company for the rest of the day.

Although she always enjoyed catching up with Charles and Elizabeth, for the last couple of years Lara had deliberately shied away from asking any questions about their son. It was too painful, and she always went home feeling depressed. At first, they were surprised after her earlier demands to find out how he was doing, however, both soon realised the wisdom of keeping his name out of any conversations during her visits. With his parents being her only link to him, and knowing they had the freedom to spend time together whenever he was in town, that old pain could always be seen in her eyes whenever his name was mentioned.

§

A few months later towards the end of March of 2004, Lara noticed an ad for a film airing at the local cinema. Reading the synopsis, she felt that familiar quickening in her heart. *Under the Tuscan Sun* was a movie set in Cortona, a little town in Italy she was already well acquainted with. Based on a book by an American author, it recalled her adventures restoring an old villa situated on a hill just below the old Tuscan town's fortified wall. It wasn't long before the phone was in her hand.

"Hi, sweetie, it's me. What are you up to this weekend?"

"Hi, Mum! Not much really. Training with Jasper on Saturday morning ... and then again on Sunday afternoon, but I'm pretty much free the rest of the time. What's up?"

"How about coming to the movies with me on Saturday afternoon then? I've just read there's a new one set in Cortona about to hit the big screens in the city."

"*Really!* Sure, count me in! I'd *love* to see my favourite old medieval town again, even if it is only secondhand."

Lara's keen ears detected a smidgen of sadness underpinning her daughter's enthusiasm. "Are you okay, Munchkin?"

"Yeah, although I just wish I'd been able to get back there when I was in Rome for my school exchange. It was so frustrating I ran out of time."

"Mmm, I can understand. I just wish I'd thought to send some extra cash so you could've caught the train up to see Claudia and Antonio at least for one weekend while you were over there. I'm sure they would've been thrilled to bits to have you bunk down with them for a couple of days."

"Don't worry. I would've loved to have stayed with them too, but the trip itself was already expensive so I understood ... besides I was getting homesick and couldn't wait to get home to you and Jasper."

"Oh, Niks, I missed you too ... still, it would've been nice."

"Yeah, but I've already promised myself to go back there one day. Anyway, when and where do you want to meet up for the movie?"

They worked out the details, and Lara smiled as she anticipated spending time with her favourite girl. It wasn't the same having Nikki living away from home. Still, at least she was close by, and that was a lot better than when she was living in the southern capital for those three long years.

Later that evening as she went to turn out the light, Lara's gaze settled on a fading photograph. It was still sitting in pride of place on the bedside table surrounded by other reminders of him.

'Night, Teddy ... love you...

§

The mother and daughter met outside the theatre. Lara was excited to think they would soon be walking those fascinating streets again, even if only from behind the lens of somebody else's camera.

The storyline was both romantic and sad, with enough touches of comedy to make them laugh out loud. So many scenes captured the lovable mannerisms and customs of the Italian way of life, along with a crazy trio of Polish renovators. The script brought back fond memories of Antonio and Claudia's endearing rapport.

Lara and Nikki sat mesmerised as so many familiar places appeared in huge dimensions on the screen in front of them. The gracious Town Hall built of ancient stones was prominent in many of the scenes. Lara pictured the three of them standing on the top of the stairs looking down over the *piazza*. She could even imagine the group of men playing cards at several small tables lining the square were the same ones who had flirted with her on that far-off Autumn day.

The beautiful old *Church of Santa Maria delle Grazie al Calcinaio* was also featured a couple of times. Lara could feel her eyes filling with tears as a wedding scene took place in the same location where she had once offered up a prayer of thanks for having Adam in her life.

Oh, I wish we were back there, my darling. I still miss you and the things we shared ... every single day.

For the first time, Nikki began to understand her mother's emotional journey, especially when she caught sight of so many long-forgotten places and the rush of memories accompanying each one. A long shot of Cortona came across the screen, and she glimpsed sections of a sprawling abbey standing on the crest of the hill. In a flash, she was back exploring that same area with Adam while her mother waited on the old church steps further down. A pensive smile kept her company as she recalled trying to match her tiny footsteps with his as they climbed the steep roadways.

More recollections burrowed out of that misty past. One in particular was of being hoisted onto his shoulders after she ran out of puff near the top. Faint twinges of sadness rose up to keep her company, along with a stark realisation of just how much they had all missed out on over the years. Reaching across under cover of darkness, Nikki brushed her hand lighting against Lara's and suddenly felt it being gripped tightly. Glancing cautiously out of the corner of her eye, she could see Lara was having an even harder time trying to deal with an avalanche of emotions while being confronted with a host of places that held so many poignant memories.

They left the cinema with red swollen eyes and hands gripping wads of soggy tissues. It wasn't hard for Niki to see how upset her mother still was. "Hey, how about I shout you a cup of coffee? There's a quiet little café just around the corner up there."

"Sure, that'd be lovely – I miss having you around so it'll be nice to have a chat. We should do this more often."

"Mmm, we should."

Lara had never been one to talk about her innermost feelings, so Nikki hadn't really understood just how much she still missed Adam, or how lonely her life had become. It was relaxing, albeit bittersweet, sitting in the shade of a poinciana tree, sipping on the hot brew and chatting about all the places they had recognised in the movie.

Her mother started reminiscing over Claudia and Antonio, and how much fun the old Italian couple were, especially his flirty ways and Claudia pretending she wasn't interested. As Lara talked, her face was glowing, and Nikki hadn't seen her looking so relaxed and happy for a very long time.

Before she was even halfway through another anecdote, Nikki put down her cup and leaned back with a gentle twinkle in her eye. "Mum, how would you feel if I moved back home?"

It was as though Lara's whole spirit sprang to life. She sat forward, eyes shining and grasped Nikki's hands. "Oh sweetie, I'd love it! That would be fabulous … but are you sure? What about you? I thought you liked having your own space."

"I do, but it's a bit stupid renting my own place when I'll probably be away for months at a time once I start getting regular theatre gigs. If I moved back in with you, then I could look after the cottage whenever you're away and help out around the yard. Besides, you're not getting any younger, so you'll probably need someone to take care of you soon!" she added with an impish snicker.

"You cheeky little monkey! I'm not that decrepit," her mother responded with a mock scowl, picking up the menu and swatting Nikki's arm.

"Hey, watch it! I won't be able to do *anything* around the house, let alone ride Jasper for weeks if you break something!" Ever the performer, Nikki made an over-the-top show of rubbing her arm as she sent her mother another big grin.

Lara's bright blue eyes grew round with excitement as she imagined having Nikki home again. The cottage had been deathly quiet without the bubbly youngster's enthusiastic chatter keeping her company between shows. More than three years had passed since the mother and daughter had shared a house. It would be a godsend having her noisy chatter and fun ways filling each room.

"Okay, okay, I'll be careful, promise. Gosh, I can't wait to have you home again! Your room's ready and waiting" —she peered over at her only offspring with concern in her eyes— "but are you sure you won't mind living back home after all this time?"

"Course I won't! We've always been good mates, Mum – today just proved that – and it's one of the things I missed most about Sydney. I love spending time with you, either at the movies or on our regular drives in the country – and we can play *Scrabble* or *Rummy,* and maybe I can beat you for a change! Besides, if I move back home, it means I won't have to eat takeaways all the time. Home cooked meals ... yum!" She rubbed her hands and licked her lips, laughing at Lara's open-mouthed gasp.

"No wonder you've never got any spare cash if you're eating out all the time. What about all those cooking lessons we shared when you were a little tot ... and the ones Claudia gave us both in Italy? That settles it. You're definitely coming home ... then I can at least make sure you eat properly!"

"As long as you promise to go easy on the carbs. I remember her pasta – it was full of them ... and all those yummy sauces! I have to be careful with all the competition out there ... after all, I know how filling your meals are."

"From the sounds of it you've been having lots of carbs anyway. I can't believe you eat takeaways all the time!"

"Not *all* the time ... just when I don't have time to rustle up a quick cup of tea and toast before heading out again!" She laughed and ducked away when another swipe from the menu came her way. "Anyway, I think it'll be great to be home again. We had so much fun together, and with both of us working, I doubt we'll get in each other's hair much at all. I'm up for it if you are."

"I'm definitely in!" Lara answered with a laugh, imagining evenings where she wouldn't be so lonely any more. "Come on. Let's go straight round to your place now so I can help you pack!"

Chapter 35

Only a few days later, Lara found an official-looking envelope sitting in her mailbox. A postmark with the word *Nederland* had been impressed across the corner stamp displaying a portrait of the Dutch Queen. Quizzically she turned it over and found an elegant crest embossed on the back flap.

It looked to be important, but for some inexplicable reason she couldn't quite bring herself to break the seal. Leaning back in one of the veranda wingchairs, her fingers idly turned the envelope over and over. A slight frown creased her forehead as she sipped on a glass of freshly squeezed orange juice topped with mango slivers and wondered who would be contacting her from the other side of the world. Even though autumn had only just begun, the weather had turned quite humid again. The refreshing drink along with a late afternoon breeze offered a welcome respite. Over the space of the next few minutes, the city lights started to flicker on and matched the flutters of anticipation in her stomach.

Peering closer at the crest, Lara could just make out the imprint of a violin with a rosebud lying diagonally across the bridge as though replicating a bow. With her curiosity finally getting the better of her and taking care not to damage the insignia, she broke open the seal. Tucked inside was a sheet of linen notepaper inscribed with a handwritten script that reeked of style and good taste.

Her interest was suddenly piqued when she scanned the contents.

Dear Ms Jennings

On a visit to Australia over Christmas, I had the pleasure of witnessing your performance of 'Silent Night' during the Carols by Candlelight concert in Melbourne. Your rendition was exceptional, and therefore I would like to request your presence to appear as my special guest for three exclusive concerts I will be conducting in Tuscany later this year.

Lara fell back against the chair, mouth open and eyes as big as saucers. "Special guest ... exclusive concerts ... *Tuscany!*" she cried out in astonishment.

Consequently, I am writing to invite you to join me in September in the beautiful town of Cortona for each of these events. I was honoured to conduct three other performances there last year for my loyal fans, along with the residents of that charming place, and so I have decided to once again include it in my schedule this year.

She couldn't believe her eyes ... how was it possible out of all the places in the world when that same little town already held so many wonderful memories. Lara had to pause for a moment and she gazed over the lights of the city below, imagining the enchanting township that had captured her heart so long ago. Shaking her head at such unbelievable timing when she had just watched a movie shot in that same location, she read the final few paragraphs.

It would be both a thrill and an honour to have you as my special guest. If you are happy to be included, Tineka, my P.A, will be in touch shortly to work out all the details with you over the telephone.

I trust you will grant us both this opportunity to make music together and I look forward to your response.

I remain, respectfully yours,
André Rieu
Maastricht, The Netherlands

Her eyes grew even wider. "You've got to be kidding! *The* André Rieu ... inviting me to be a part of his concerts ... and in *Cortona!* I don't believe it!"

She couldn't contain her excitement and so the words just tumbled out. Lara hadn't felt this excited in years – not since receiving the news she and Adam would be working together in Sydney for *My Fair Lady.*

When Nikki arrived home from rehearsals a little while later, she wondered what was going on. Her mother was standing at the top of the stairs waving something in the air with a huge smile on her face. Everything soon clicked into place once she blurted out the news.

"Oh Mum, I can't believe you're finally able to go back there! How *fantastic,* especially after just seeing *Under the Tuscan Sun* ... proves it's meant to be!" She grabbed her mother around the waist and began twirling her in circles.

"Hang on, hang on, I haven't agreed yet," Lara laughed, trying hard to put an end to the giddy dance. "How do I know this is even legitimate? Besides, he hasn't heard me in anything else so he might change his mind down the track."

Nikki rolled her eyes and pointed to the invitation. "Don't be *ridiculous,* of *course* it's legitimate – look at the postmark *and* the insignia on the envelope and notepaper! And he's probably heard your album, too. Of course you're going to agree. People'd give their eye teeth just to be in the audience, let alone be invited to be a part of it."

"But the concert's on the other side of the world! It's not exactly like flying to Sydney or Melbourne."

"And that's exactly why you have to say *yes!* You'll *never* get another chance like this. It's André *Rieu,* Mum! Think what that *means!* He's brilliant, conducts a world-class orchestra *and* is one of the leading violinists on the planet! An invitation to join him is the *hugest* honour. If you don't write back and say yes, then I will ... there's no way you're passing this up!"

While Nikki was emphatically ordering her about, Lara bit down hard on her bottom lip as she skimmed the letter again. She might be a well-known performer in Australia, but an invitation to participate in even one of his European concerts was way beyond her wildest dreams – to be in three of them was absolutely mind-blowing. Monstrous doubts started to flood in. After all, she had only ever sung in English before while continental audiences were sure to expect Italian or some other local language to entertain them. Besides, she had responsibilities to her Australian fans, not to mention her daughter...

She could think of dozens of reasons to turn down his offer.

Nikki rolled her eyes again as she watched the play of emotions cross her mother's face. Shaking her head in frustration, she suddenly made the decision for her. Grabbing the letter, she held it high in the air as Lara tried to snatch it back.

"Mum, stop it! You're going. I don't care what excuse you're trying to come up with. There's no way you're turning this down."

That steely determination was just what Lara needed. Raising her eyebrows in a clownish kind of way, she sent her daughter a cheesy smirk. Nikki let out a shrill shriek and grabbed her mother's hands. As they waltzed around the room, echoes of their laughter carried out the window and across the lawn.

A jogger on his nightly run peered in and let out a hearty chuckle at the happy picture they made through the big bay window before continuing on his way.

§

For the next couple of months, Tineka and Lara worked out the details through emails and regular phone calls. Plans were in place to rehearse with the maestro's full orchestra for a few days before the main event. In the meantime, backing tracks and sheet music arrived in the mail so she could become familiar with the chosen numbers.

One day she came home to find a parcel propped up against the front door.

Along with a booklet outlining Italian and French phrasing, there was a CD containing audio lessons for correct language pronunciation. Now there were no more valid excuses left to her to back out.

§

Only a week after the invitation arrived in Lara's Brisbane mailbox, a plane touched down at Heathrow Airport on the outskirts of London. Among the first-class passengers was a famous star of the Australian stage with an attractive redhead by his side.

Adam had just been chosen as the lead for a musical about to open on the West End. After being sent a host of reviews from one of his recent projects, the English producer boarded the next plane to Australia, eager to offer him the prime role for his new production.

Trina had been quick to say she wanted to accompany him. Her mind ticked over with all the high society events this could mean for her image. Once the show's anticipated five-month season had run its course, Adam felt a holiday on the continent for a few weeks would be a good way for them to reconnect. Between his heavy schedule of shows and her charity work, it had been impossible to find a block of time where both were free at the same time, so this would be the first holiday they had taken together in many years. Over the last several months, things had been so hectic their paths had hardly crossed. It seemed logical a decent getaway was vital if their relationship was to last the distance.

The years had been kind to both of them. Adam was just as handsome now as on their wedding day. The only obvious changes were a dignified maturity brought about by the passing of time, and the silver patch at the front of his hair had expanded even further as the years slowly marched on. Though he still thought of it as a blemish – thankfully, one able to be tucked beneath the many wigs required for the vast array of characters coming his way – every now and then he could almost sense Lara's fingers brush against it. Echoes from those days were always hovering in his sub-conscious, as though her fingerprint really did go with him wherever he went. Whenever a hairdresser suggested adding a touch of dark to the front portion, he quickly dismissed it as pure vanity, while the real reason was far more personal.

Women still swarmed Stage Door at the end of a performance, eager to catch a glimpse of their idol. Those brave enough to ask usually went away with an autograph or a quickly snapped photo as a memorable souvenir. Time hadn't altered Adam's willingness to give back to his devoted fans. He was always prepared to spend a few minutes mingling among the crush of bodies before rushing back to his hotel. A few true devotees had even followed him out from Australia and some he remembered by name, much to their delight.

More than fifteen years had passed since Trina had downed any form of alcohol. Though his wife was only a few months away from turning fifty, she looked years younger and a healthy glow enhanced her fair complexion. There was no sign of the former puffiness or bloodshot eyes from those ghastly hangovers and Adam felt proud to have her on his arm at public events.

For his fortieth birthday three years earlier, she had hosted a lavish party at one of Brisbane's top restaurants. Charles and Elizabeth joined in the celebrations, along with a good number of his colleagues from his two vastly different careers. The alcohol flowed freely, though his wife made no attempt to touch any. AA meetings had remained a regular timeslot on her calendar for quite some time until her charity work grew more demanding and they slowly petered away.

Adam was always grateful for the concerted efforts she put in to ensure no gossip or shame could besmirch his name. He was happy to encourage her with small gifts or a surprise meal at her favourite restaurant whenever he was home and she always thanked him with an affectionate hug and peck on the cheek. Although neither one of them could say they were 'in love', as time went by an easy companionship had formed and he was content with his lot after spending those first years trapped inside a hellish marriage. For her part, Trina had become more of a closed book, preferring to keep her true feelings to herself and just get on with life. Even so, she was always polite and willing to entertain his family and friends whenever the occasion demanded.

Once again, they had reverted to sleeping in separate bedrooms. With Adam often invited to join fellow cast-members at after-show suppers, it usually meant he arrived home in the small hours of the morning, and with Trina's presence often needed at early morning appointments, it had become less practical to share the same bed. While on tour, he always made sure to organise a large two-bedroom suite for those odd weekends she was able to join him.

As much as he still cared about her, Adam always experienced an overwhelming influx of guilt whenever they made love. For the last few years, this part of their relationship had slowly tapered off until it was only on rare occasions the couple visited each other's bed. As hard as he tried to ignore them, a pair of crystal blue eyes still invaded his thoughts whenever he went to kiss his wife. Even after all this time, as soon as he felt any stirring of desire, those flames soon died down with the realisation anything else would only ever be second best.

For the last several years during any of Adam's regular visits to his parents' home, the pain in his eyes and voice had grown more pronounced whenever Lara's name was mentioned. The day following the final performance of Paul's production of *The Phantom of the Opera* when their poignant meeting and passionate farewell kiss had occurred, he went to bring her name up in conversation again while chatting to his mother. Letting out a heartfelt sigh, Elizabeth dragged him across to the sofa and pulled him down next to her. She held his gaze and sent him a look that emphasised her concern as one hand gently stroked his.

"My darling boy, you can't keep doing this to yourself. I know you too well, and I can see how much it affects you talking about that precious girl. If you still care so deeply, then you need to do something about it ... or let her go completely."

"But, Mum, hearing about her from you is all I have lef—"

"No, Adam, I can't do this anymore. It's not fair on either one of you, and most especially now that she and Mike are seeing each other."

Even though it broke her heart having to inflict even more wounds, she knew it was for his own good. At first, anger and frustration had overridden common-sense, but over time Adam came to realise the wisdom in her decree ... at least as far as the outside world was concerned.

Since then, his mother hadn't mentioned anything about Lara or Nikki in his presence, though he still carried around an insatiable longing to hear her name again.

One thing he couldn't resist was scanning the papers whenever she was appearing in a new production. Behind closed doors, every article or photograph with even the smallest reference to her ended up in a leather-bound journal similar to the one she had made for him on their return from Italy. It was hidden away in a locked drawer of the rosewood desk in his study with the three Lara had given him. Late at night, all four albums would invariably come out to keep him company – usually when the hunger inside threatened to overwhelm him … and Trina was fast asleep.

Naturally, there were no cherished photos on display in the house ... only a snapshot of him, Lara and Nikki taken on one of their many adventures around Sydney. The edges were worn from the countless times careful fingers had slipped it out of a secret compartment in his wallet. The keepsake had been squirrelled away with the little girl's Christmas letter for more than a decade-and-a-half.

And wherever he went, two other much-loved pieces still adorned his dressing room mirror – they accompanied him from one show to the next all around the country. Between productions, both the photograph taken outside Cortona's main entrance gate and Nikki's drawing of an angel then joined the albums in the locked drawer, far away from prying eyes.

Adam's commitment to his marriage vows was as strong as ever, and he dreaded the thought of Trina stumbling across any reminders from those times

... but his heart would always long for its soulmate and he didn't have the heart to part with them.

§

In the middle of June, Lara flew down to Melbourne and went straight into rehearsals for her next role as *Anna* in *The King and I*. Because of the theatre's busy upcoming schedule, the show could only be booked for a short run. Closing night was set down for the middle of September. This meant she would be free to fly out to Italy straight afterwards.

Following her arrival in Cortona after a long flight and then a much shorter train trip from Rome, she faced four days of intense rehearsals with André and his orchestra. It would be a hectic few months, but she was looking forward to embarking on this new venture.

Melbourne was freezing at that time of year and icy cold rain often accompanied her as she dashed from the hotel to the theatre located just around the corner. The thought of glorious sunny days and crisp autumn nights in the Tuscan hills was an extra incentive, and she scoured the shops looking for appropriate clothing whenever she found some free time. It was the most excited Lara had been for a very long time and she couldn't wait to walk those streets again ... along with a much-anticipated catch up with Claudia and Antonio.

§

The concerts were drawing closer. Lara anxiously practised both numbers whenever she could find a few minutes away from her regular commitments. Only a month before she was due to fly out the maestro himself telephoned to ensure everything was going according to plan. She thanked him repeatedly for the honour of working beside him and André was quick to reassure her just how happy he was to have someone of her calibre on his team.

This was the first time Lara had the chance to tell him she had already holidayed in the charming town. They spent the next few minutes sharing stories about the friendly townsfolk and their recollections of all the eye-catching vistas and delightful customs pertinent to the region.

"I'm really looking forward to September and being part of your concerts, as well as seeing Cortona again. It just happens to be my favourite little town in all of Italy!" she enthused.

"I'm delighted to learn you have already visited one of my favourite places, Lara. Most people I talk to have never even heard of it, let alone had the chance to visit. I think this is even more confirmation our working together was meant to be," he assured her in his broad Dutch accent. It was easy for her to detect the smile accompanying his comments coming down the line.

§

By the end of June, Adam's show was receiving rave reviews in of London's tabloids. It was an enormous relief knowing the British theatrical fraternity had accepted him into their ranks. Several Aussie colleagues had warned that playing to a West End audience was much more demanding than anything he had experienced back home. With such a large choice of shows constantly playing in the famous district, theatre-goers were quite choosy when it came to spending their hard-earned money – and reviewers could be quite brutal in speaking their minds if they didn't like a performance.

Trina made friends with the wives and partners of several of Adam's fellow cast mates. She was often seen around town dining in one of the elegant restaurants or shopping in the more exclusive fashion houses scattered around London's busy high-end streets. Within a few weeks, she was receiving invitations to events starting mid-morning and continuing until well after Adam arrived home late at night. Her circle of friends was widening every day and newspapers often featured photos of her out-and-about with London's society elite.

With the adrenaline running rampant in their veins after another successful performance, once the houselights came up, Adam was regularly invited to join others from the cast for a late-night supper. Knowing his hotel suite would more than likely be cold and empty, he enjoyed this much-needed form of camaraderie to push other thoughts away.

His topsy-turvy working hours and a need to rest his voice or catch up on sleep, coupled with Trina's constant need for company, often meant their social paths were miles apart. It was only during his one full day off a week they actually found time to sit down and talk about everyday matters or wander the streets close to their hotel seeking an out-of-the-way café where they could share some quiet time. Adam was still with the same agent and Max had insisted the international contract had a clause reserving one of the plush suites of the Mandarin Oriental Hyde Park Hotel in Knightsbridge, positioned directly opposite the famous park, for the duration of their stay.

Location was most important as Adam was usually exhausted from the constant late nights, along with a growing fan base who continually accosted him in the streets as he became more widely recognisable. He didn't like to wander too far, and the quieter location meant he was able to leave the bustle of the main city behind.

On one of these lazy mornings spent relaxing around the hotel, Trina suddenly produced an invitation to a party in the country with one of her newfound friends.

"Oh, by the way, I was given this last night. I wouldn't be surprised if I'm invited to stay overnight rather than rushing back in the dead of night, especially if it's going to rain like the forecast says."

"Oh, okay, that seems logical. Sounds like you should have a nice time."

He was happy to see she was enjoying herself and starting to chill out after the rigorous demands of her charity work.

An hour or so later his wife came out toting a Dior travel case in one hand and a matching garment bag in the other. "I'll be off now. See you later," she called cheerily.

Peering around the newspaper he was reading at a small table in the bay window, Adam smiled and responded, "Okay, enjoy yourself. I'll see you tomorrow sometime. Hey, before you go, where are you staying just in case something comes up and I need to contact you?"

"Oh, I can't remember – some country estate just outside Oxford. Don't worry, I'll be in good hands," came the nonchalant reply before she rushed out the door.

Glancing out the window a few minutes later, he watched as she tossed both pieces of luggage into the boot of a bright red sports car before hopping in the front passenger seat. The hood was up so he was unable to see who was driving. With a casual shrug of his shoulders, Adam went back to reading his paper, the recent image of her laughing happily soon fading into the background.

§

Quite late the following afternoon, Trina burst into the room, obviously in a cheery mood. Adam was sitting in the same spot in the bay window with his nose buried deep in a book. There were a teapot and a half-finished cup of Earl Grey tea positioned on the table beside him.

She pulled up short. "Oh, you're still here ... I thought you might've left already."

"Hi, welcome back! No, I just wanted to finish this chapter. You look like you've been enjoying yourself." Placing the book face down on the table, he sent her a smile.

"Yeah, it was marvellous ... although I'm absolutely exhausted. Best thing I've done in a very long time!"

"That's great, I'm glad it turned out okay. What did you get up to?"

"Oh, nothing much, just mixing with the aristocracy," she answered, shaking a few droplets of rain from her thick, red hair before hurrying down the hallway to the bathroom. "I'm just going to have a nice long soak," she threw over her shoulder. "It was freezing up there, and I need to warm up. Brrr ... those old castles can be horribly draughty!"

"Who were you with exactly? I can't remember you mentioning it," Adam called after her in an effort to take an interest in this new lifestyle.

"Oh, just a few folk I met not long after we arrived ... it was when you were in the middle of rehearsals and I went along to Sotheby's for that charity auction.

I'm sure I told you..." There was a sudden bang as the bathroom door closed firmly behind her.

Adam recalled a vague reference to the famous auction house and figured it must have been when he was concentrating on learning his lines. If that was the case, it was more than likely their names were long gone from his memory. Without giving it another thought, he once again picked up the book – an intriguing murder mystery from a well-known author – and settled down to finish the chapter before it was time to leave for the night's performance.

§

A few days later Trina disappeared for the afternoon without really conveying where she was going or who she would be with. Once again, Adam wasn't too concerned. Tendrils of guilt had been plaguing him at the amount of time she had to spend on her own while he was out working. Having these new friends to keep her company meant she had something to occupy her time, so he was pleased for her.

Arriving back around midnight, it was obvious she had only just got in herself. He found her just slipping out of a very crumpled gown with a pair of bright red stilettos littering the living room floor.

"What happened to you? That dress looks like it's been caught in a tumble dryer!" he joked.

"Oh, I know. We ended up at this crazy nightclub and it was so crowded on the dance floor nearly everyone came away looking like this. I'll just send it to the dry-cleaners tomorrow. Don't worry, it'll be as good as new."

There was no reason to query her explanation so with a friendly, "Goodnight," he went off for a hot shower before retiring to his room on the other side of the hall.

Trina's afternoon outings became a regular occurrence, and Adam often came home around midnight to find their suite empty. Having her arrive home sober pushed away any niggles of concern, especially when she woke close to lunchtime always bright and cheerful – such a difference to her demeanour when drinking had been her constant companion.

After a few months, he noticed she started putting in an effort to spend an hour or two with him each day before another event beckoned, either lounging in their luxury suite reading and chatting, or sharing brisk walks in Hyde Park across the street. Following a late afternoon tea, she would soon be off again, while he made his way to the theatre around six. Even though their relationship wasn't idyllic, he was becoming used to this new way of life.

PART FIVE

Cortona, Italy

September 2004 to 26 December 2004

Chapter 36

A Boeing 747 from the Qantas fleet landed in Italy in the middle of September. Lara looked out of her First-Class window as the jet flew into *Aeroporto Leonardo da Vinci* late in the morning. With the airport situated near the coastline, and having the sun shining overhead, it was the ideal vantage point to take in the spectacular sight of the sparkling Mediterranean Sea below. Exiting the terminal an hour or so later, she hailed one of a host of taxis waiting outside before being spirited away to *Roma Termini* – the *Eternal City's* main railway station. Because she was due in Cortona that night, there was no time for any sightseeing.

She was disappointed not to have enough time to spend a few days beforehand in the Roman capital. Instead, she did the next best thing: feasting on the spectacle flashing past her window as the car wove in and out of a host of narrow streets until reaching the centre of the bustling metropolis. Rounding one corner, she caught sight of the magnificent dome topping St Peter's Basilica where it rose proudly above a multitude of other historical buildings.

Similar to her reaction the last time she was there, Lara's breath caught in her throat and she wished there was enough time to visit the holy cathedral's many monuments and treasures. Instead, the keen traveller promised herself a week to explore everything the ancient city had to offer before heading home. Flashes of the single night spent here with Adam brought back bittersweet memories, though she was quick to sweep them aside before that frequent melancholy visitor descended again. This was another time and place in her life and she had new memories to make.

The station was bustling with both resident commuters and foreign tourists. The loud hum of different languages added another thrill to her experience. It wasn't long before she was hopping on a train bound for the tiny village of Camucia, located in the valley below her final destination. She relished acting like a local by taking in the gorgeous countryside from the carriage of a train as it wound its way north. This option was much more pleasant than hurtling along a busy motorway in an unfamiliar car while trying to both drive and navigate from the wrong side of the road. Along the way, she savoured the lyrical language and pulse of her passionate fellow travellers.

Antonio had offered to send his grandson, Pietro, to pick her up, hoping she could pop in for a quick visit before continuing to the hotel in the centre of Cortona. Unfortunately, she had to turn down his kind offer. With the need to rest her voice before rehearsals began and concentrate all her attention on the real reason for the visit, she felt she owed it to André after his generous invitation. She was also reluctant to inconvenience Pietro with a long trip in the middle of busy grape-harvesting months.

As a way to make up for it, Lara had set aside four days to spend at the villa once the concerts were over. Claudia and Antonio were looking forward to a long catch-up and her pantry was stocked full of ingredients for every imaginable dish for their important visitor. Elizabeth had already rung before she left home, conveying how excited her old Italian friends were to receive two of the coveted free tickets on offer for the opening gala performance. The Aussie singer was looking forward to seeing their familiar faces in the crowd.

André's chauffeur was already waiting outside the station and soon had her luggage stored in the back. Making their way up the steep and winding country road to the small town perched on top of the hill, she felt like it was only yesterday instead of nearly sixteen years since her last visit. They drove under the same stone archway, then up the narrow cobblestone street leading to the centre of town. She couldn't help glancing behind, picturing Adam standing there looking after her with the adoring smile she remembered so well, just as she had captured him in the photograph that kept her company on the bedside table.

Her mind was awash with imagery from that memorable night and a lone tear gathered in the corner of her eye ... until she dashed it away.

You told yourself you weren't going to cry ... now stick to it!

The Hotel San Michele was a striking stone and stucco palace once belonging to a famous *Marquis* from the twelfth century. Tucked away on one of many steep roadways leading up to the main *piazza*, its impressive façade grabbed her attention as they drew closer. For some reason, the area seemed vaguely familiar. When the car pulled up, her gaze fell on a sign with the words *Ristorante Preludio* displayed in an ornate window on the neighbouring building.

Lara's heart skipped a beat. This was where she and Adam had shared a romantic and intimate dinner. Images of the following few hours – making love for the first time in the room Claudia had prepared so carefully and with so many thoughtful touches – flooded her mind and she had to remind herself to breathe. So many memories wrapped up in one small sign...

While the chauffeur gathered her bags, Lara couldn't resist running gentle fingers across the old grooved stonework forming the arched entrance to the dining room, almost as though they were seeking out a hidden doorway so she could be swept back in time.

Dispelling all these musings, André's charming accent caught her attention as he came out to greet her with both arms outstretched.

"Lara, my guest star, you have arrived at last! What a pleasure it is to meet you after all of our long-distance communications." He offered her a welcoming smile and kissed her on each cheek in the European way.

His bronze chiselled features would make anyone's heart race, and Lara's was no exception. She returned his smile, though her voice was timid as she returned his greeting.

"Hello, Mr Rieu, it's a pleasure to meet you, too."

"*Nee, nee, nee.* None of this 'Mr Rieu' – call me, André, please. It is much nicer to be friends than just colleagues, *ja?*"

Lara nodded, and her eyes sparkled to hear the famous conductor address her so freely. She had no thought of her own success but was mesmerised by his charming presence. "That sounds wonderful, thank you ... André..." She almost stammered, still not quite believing she was even there, let alone meeting the music legend in person.

"You are most welcome, my dear, and I am so glad you made it on time. I was hoping it would still be light enough for you to enjoy all these breathtaking views."

His expressive hand movements drew her attention to the four-storey ochre building adorned with colourful flags from various nations, then down again to the charm of the street. The roadway ran sharply down the hill and in the far distance, beyond the town walls, she could just make out a valley planted with olive trees. Turning back to look more closely at the hotel's facade, she could tell it was a stunning example of old-style architecture, with grey flagstones forming the arch around the entranceway as well as framing all the lower storey windows.

"Oh, everything is just spectacular! No wonder I adore this little town. Thank you again for inviting me."

"It is entirely my pleasure. *Und ja*, it is one of my favourites, too. I am delighted you could join us. Come, I want you to meet my talented musicians. We were just enjoying an aperitif on the rooftop terrace. Follow me, and I will introduce you."

As they made their way up the marble staircase, Lara was stunned at the opulence of the former *palazzo*. Her eyes kept darting to and fro trying to take it all in. The hotel was more boutique-style compared to others Lara had stayed in, although it was just as luxurious as those Adam had chosen during their visit to this charming country. Soft lighting and sumptuous furnishings brought a unique ambience to the interior. The views from the terrace took Lara's breath away as she looked down across multi-layered rooftops to green olive groves and rows of vineyards adorning a ridge of lower hills off in the distance. Even though her work had taken her to all manner of grand hotels and venues over the years, her enthusiasm for new places never waned, and she enjoyed taking in the beauty of this latest home-away-from-home.

For the next few hours, she mingled with members of his entourage, getting to know each one and sharing stories from their similar careers. Most seemed fascinated to have an Aussie join them, and she was soon fielding a barrage of questions about her homeland and the variety of unusual creatures to be found there.

§

Over the next four days, she spent most of her time in rehearsals or watching other artists practising their numbers. During lunch breaks, Lara took herself off to the *piazza*, sitting on the Town Hall's steep stone steps and feasting on a variety of Tuscan delights. It was a fascinating way to pass the time watching the hustle and bustle of townsfolk and visitors alike going about their business. The town had become a popular tourist destination since the movie *Under the Tuscan Sun* had been running in theatres around the world. Many were there specifically for the concerts after reading about them on the Cortona website.

In many ways, Lara felt as if she was stepping back in time. Clusters of tables were scattered around the perimeter of the square, each one playing host to old men deep in concentration as they enjoyed various games of chequers or chess. The scene was all so similar to the last time she was there. One had four friends hunched over a game of cards. Whenever a sudden breeze sprang up, there was a mad scramble to keep the cards on the table. The men's antics brought a constant stream of laughter from the many onlookers. Lara relished the atmosphere and felt grateful to have this opportunity, even though it brought back so many poignant memories.

At dinnertime, she and a few of her new muso friends wandered up the hill to mingle with the townsfolk in a variety of *trattorias* dotted along the streets. Over rich Italian dishes, they shared tales of their various homelands. Locals rocked with laughter and shook their heads at the newcomers' halting attempts to speak the native language. It was a lively group and they usually stayed late into the night over a few bottles of shared Chianti. Lara kept her share small, remembering an infamous and stupid attempt to drown her sorrows long ago.

Adding a more sombre tone to the experience were a couple of restaurants definitely out of bounds on her agenda. Memories from two romantic dinners were too close to her heart ever to contemplate setting foot inside either one. It was hard enough treading the same streets ... choosing to revisit them would be

491

far too painful.

At least twice a day she had to pass by the one boasting a magnificent stone archway – a mirror image of the one leading to her hotel. And every single time her stride slowed and gaze lingered on a handle that had once known Adam's touch. Sometimes, when her guard was down, Lara could almost feel his presence in the cramped niches and alleyways she passed while exploring further afield.

On the third day, one steep staircase caught her attention, and she stopped abruptly in the middle of the narrow thoroughfare. On a night long ago, she and Adam had kissed furtively in its shadows while Claudia and Antonio strolled on ahead with a little girl in tow, oblivious to the smouldering passion playing out behind them.

Memories were everywhere...

§

Nearly fifteen hundred kilometres away, Trina was still enjoying her merry forays out on the town every evening. That constant hankering for the bright lights had come back full force as Adam trod the boards singing and dancing his heart out night after night.

She had taken to arriving home later and later. Most nights he was already fast asleep by the time she stole through the door. Having a two-bedroom suite was a godsend as it meant he was left undisturbed when she crept into bed just as the sun came up most mornings. A full night's sleep was necessary to recoup all the energy he lost during a performance.

For some unexplained reason, she still hadn't introduced him to any of her newfound friends, even though he often suggested inviting them over for cocktails before heading off to their latest party or event. Her evasive behaviour was starting to play on his mind more and more, although it wasn't enough to warrant causing any friction while things were still okay between them.

As much as he enjoyed the excitement of London, Adam missed spending time with his parents or hanging out with Jeff and Lucy. Any communication between him and Trina had slowly evaporated since her life had turned into a constant round of dinner parties and weekend country outings. Apart from the absence of alcohol, her social life appeared to have metamorphosed into the habits of old. Adam tried to give her attention in whatever free time he had, but for some reason, it wasn't enough to satisfy her anymore.

For the last few weeks, things seemed to have deteriorated even further when she started sleeping long into the afternoon. As a consequence, even the few short hours they normally kept free to catch up on any news had gone by the wayside. The last straw was seeing her creep in three mornings in a row while he was having morning tea. As far as he was concerned, it was time things got back on kilter.

Arriving back from his daily walk the next afternoon, he found her sitting by the window busily filing her nails. Striding across to the telephone, he quickly dialled room service.

"Good afternoon. Could you please send a pot of coffee and a plate of sandwiches to Suite 143? Thank you."

Leaning down, he kissed the cheek she disinterestedly proffered his way. "Hi. You seem to be keeping busy lately. I hope you're not wearing yourself out too much."

"No, I'm okay. It's a nice change compared to hanging around by myself." She didn't even look up from her task as he took the seat opposite.

The grating rasp of the file was the only sound in the room as she got ready for her fifth major event that week. It was obvious she wasn't interested in any small talk, so he just gazed out the window, waiting for the food to arrive. Room Service didn't take long, and after signing the chit, Adam poured each of them a cup from the steaming pot. He placed hers on the table near her elbow, but all she could offer was a half-hearted mumble that wasn't even discernible.

"Trina, I've been thinking."

She glanced up, but it was only to brush away the nail dust from her skirt. It took all of his willpower to keep his voice steady as he went on.

"How would you feel about going across to Bath for a couple of days? I could probably wangle an extra day off along with my usual one – George, the understudy, has been itching to fill my shoes. We could take in the sights and relax in one of those famous spa hotels. I think it'd be good for us to get away, even if it is only for a short break."

"Oh, I really don't think I can find the time," she responded disinterestedly, painting her long tapering nails with a flaming red varnish. "I've been invited to several parties and a few balls over the next week or two. Oh, and there's a polo match in the country – it's the last of the season, so I don't want to miss it."

Adam was disappointed. He was exhausted and keen to get away, as well as hoping this would be a good way for them to reconnect. "Do you really have to go? We've hardly seen each other in the last few weeks and this is something I thought you'd enjoy. Bath has several good clubs from what I hear. Maybe they can make up for all you'll be missing out on by coming with me."

"I'm sorry, Adam, I couldn't possibly get away. There's so much to do right now in London ... besides, I've already said yes. But you go along if you want – I really wouldn't mind – and then I won't disturb you if I'm late getting home."

He looked over in surprise. For the first time, a few seeds of suspicion kept his cloak of disappointment company. Without uttering another word, he observed his wife over the rim of his cup while she continued with her preparations.

We already sleep apart so why would you think you're disturbing me? What are you up to?

Unsure of what else to say to get her to change her mind, he suddenly pushed back his chair and strode to the door, leaving the pile of untouched sandwiches growing soggy and unappealing on the table.

"Alright. Well, I'm just going out for a bit – I need a walk and the park looks inviting. Won't be long."

"I thought you only just got back from over there. Oh well, I'll probably be gone by the time you get back. See you tomorrow sometime," she replied nonchalantly without looking up as he rose from the table.

Wandering the shaded avenues weaving through Hyde Park with his hands buried deep in his coat pockets, Adam couldn't help thinking about another – the woman who would have jumped at the chance to go anywhere with him. Being together was all that mattered and whatever time they were able to share overflowed with the heady excitement of two people deeply in love. As happened so often, he wondered how different his life would have been if she hadn't made that heartbreaking phone call. With Trina's apparent disinterest in any form of conversation, Lara's memory became the recipient of all his hidden desires and reflections.

Oh, Baby, I'd give anything to turn back time. Life just isn't the same without you. We may not be as young as when we first fell in love, but just the thought of you still takes my breath away. I wish I knew where you were and what you're up to. Stay safe and just maybe, every now and then, you can still feel how much I need you. Not a day goes by that I haven't missed you.

Trudging back to the now empty hotel room, Adam would have given anything to hear her voice one more time. Keeping him company was the sad realisation it was highly unlikely they would ever see each other again, despite his earlier vow never to give up hope.

Reality dictated too much time had passed.

§

On a balmy night of that same month, the quaint little Etruscan township of Cortona was all aglow – not only with the glorious ambience of its old lamp stands, but also in anticipation of a special event about to take place in her streets. From every corner, people thronged up the steep, narrow roadways leading to the *piazza*. Several of her residents leaned out of the upper windows in their multi-storey homes, happily spying on the activity below and chatting animatedly to neighbours across the way as only the Italians know how. A couple of tabby cats perched high on a ledge abutting two of the dwellings were leisurely grooming themselves, showing no interest whatsoever in what was happening below.

The distorted tuning strains of a large orchestra floated over the ochre rooftops and down narrow staircases that tumbled into a maze of cobblestone thoroughfares. These then opened out onto the main *piazza* surrounded by houses and businesses – most three or four storeys high. Row-upon-row of chairs lined the square, while an expansive semi-circular stage was the main focus – stealing the limelight for a short time from the gracious Town Hall.

From above, it looked like a fascinating rabbit-warren of places and treasures to explore, but no one was interested in wandering further afield tonight.

Thirty minutes later, there were no empty seats to be seen. Even the grand stone staircase nestled in the shadow of the stately clock tower of that same Town Hall was hidden beneath a mass of people. The entire perimeter of the *Piazza della Repubblica* was standing room only as guests continued to stream in from the surrounding area. The pleasant night air was full of excited chatter as the crowd eagerly awaited the maestro's entrance. Then, with only a few minutes to go, a sudden swathe of floodlights bathed the scene in a variety of different hues, subtly changing colour every few seconds and turning each corner of the outdoor auditorium into what looked like a magical wonderland.

Standing on a tiny balcony slightly above and to the right of the main stage was Lara, completely mesmerised as she took in the spectacle below. Regardless of how many packed theatre halls she had performed in over the years, nothing could compare to the atmosphere rippling around this beautiful old town, or the look of enthralled anticipation on the faces filling the square. Each guest knew they were in for a fabulous spectacle – André was world-famous for enchanting legions of fans with his stage presence – and the Australian performer almost had to pinch herself into believing she was actually there.

From a duo of seats in the centre front row, Antonio and Claudia caught sight of their friend and started waving enthusiastically to gain her attention. Lara's eyes shone at the sight of their beaming faces, and she waved back with just as much fervour.

Seeing them so happy only added to her excitement and her stomach fluttered with what felt like a thousand butterflies waiting to be set free the moment she opened her mouth.

The Antonio-of-old blew several extravagant kisses her way. She blushed at his larger-than-life antics, while Claudia laughed loudly and clawed at his arms, trying hard to restrain her embarrassing spouse.

You haven't changed at all, my adorable old friend ... obviously still very much the flirt ... and Claudia still has trouble controlling you, I see!

When Lara first mentioned to André about her Italian friends being in the audience, he kindly offered them tickets for the best seats in the house to ensure they had an unhindered view of the entire show. His invitation also extended to the private after-party to be held in the Town Hall. She was taken back by his generosity and thanked him over and over. It would mean they could catch up afterwards without the worry of trying to find each other among the throng.

Over the enthusiastic buzz echoing around the main square, the orchestra struck up one sustained note. Straightaway and in unison, the audience rose to their feet and started applauding loudly. Almost as if this human drumbeat had summoned him, a tall, handsome man immaculately dressed in suave tails with a crisp white shirt and carrying a prized Stradivarius violin under his arm, emerged from the side of the stage and made his way to the front. The skip in his step made his shoulder-length locks seem to dance in the night air. With a warm and welcoming smile, he surveyed the sea of faces. This was the moment everyone had been waiting for.

The concert was everything Lara had imagined ... and so much more. The atmosphere was electric as piece after piece of rousing music wafted across the crowd, bringing spirits to life in a way many had never known before. André's elegant panache and showmanship sent shivers up and down her spine when his fingers made the priceless violin dance. Those in the audience sat as though mesmerised for over two breathtaking hours. Several times this huge sea of fans lifted their voices to sway in time to the music as their souls were fed. Glancing around the multitude of faces, she couldn't help noticing many had tears coursing down their cheeks, often left unchecked as the music held them in its spell.

Her turn came towards the middle of the second act, standing on the Juliet-style balcony as the maestro and his orchestra accompanied her. Every eye was riveted on the miniature dais as a single beam of light captured Lara's image when she crooned the haunting *Ave Maria*. For the songstress, it felt like she was floating on a cloud of candyfloss while being transported to a brand-new wonderland.

Throughout her performance, André played almost entirely to his guest artist, only turning sporadically to smile at the audience before those twinkling blue eyes returned to where Lara stood bathed in a rosy glow ... and all the while, his long dancing fingers cavorted along the instrument's slender neck as the bow swayed and dipped across the strings. It was the perfect setting. She knew nothing would ever be able to compare for sheer joy and beauty – nothing, except the possibility of being able to sing in the presence of a certain someone.

She had grown used to living with the longing, though it still didn't stem the dull ache in her heart. But even that never-ending numbness couldn't quash the exhilaration filling her spirit on this night-of-nights.

As the last note fell from her lips and his accompanying mastery on the seventeenth-century violin, rousing cheers and hearty applause filled the alfresco arena. It resounded from the walls of the surrounding buildings and through the streets flowing down the hill. Ever the flamboyant showman, André turned to Lara and blew her a kiss of gratitude, once again drawing the crowd's attention to the little balcony above their heads. Returning his gesture, she quickly offered an appreciative smile and wave to both him and the audience. Another round of fervent applause echoed around the *piazza*, confirming the talented duo had given the crowd exactly what they came for, just as André had envisaged when issuing the invitation. There was no trace of arrogance in either of their responses ... just the comforting knowledge of having satisfied a multitude of souls, including their own.

More numbers followed as the maestro and his entourage continued to bewitch the audience, with Lara joining in for one of the final pieces. Her magnificent voice reverberated across the stone facades during a solo verse, and every eye once again was fixed on the tiny podium overlooking the stage. Just as the concert reached its grand conclusion, he rounded off the evening with a rousing Italian composition that had everyone on their feet and clapping to the beat. Some even formed a conga line and Lara couldn't believe her eyes when she noticed Claudia and Antonio in the middle of the line-up, having the time of their lives. Despite both of them nearing seventy, their actions were those of a much younger couple out enjoying themselves with a night on the town.

§

At the after-party held in the Town Hall's temporarily transformed main reception area, Lara searched for her old friends. After several minutes, she eventually found them standing in the centre of the room chatting to the conductor himself. She was surprised to hear they had already met the year before, following his previous concert. André remembered Antonio for his mischievous antics while flirting with the conductor's attractive backing singers.

"And here she is – my newest star," her patron announced with a beaming smile, bestowing a grateful kiss on both her cheeks. "Lara, you were brilliant! I knew that marvellous voice of yours would be perfect in this arena with its exceptional acoustics."

"Oh, Maestro, how can I ever thank you!" she enthused as he placed a proud arm around her waist, similar to that of a doting father. "I've *never* performed in a more breathtaking setting than tonight. It's no wonder I fell in love with this gorgeous place all those years ago."

Antonio and Claudia exchanged knowing looks, which Lara couldn't help intercepting. There was no need for her to wonder what lay behind their sad expressions. All three were thinking of a certain someone ... and wishing he could have joined them for this once-in-a-lifetime event.

"It was my pleasure to have you as part of our brilliant team. Thank you for being willing to travel halfway around the world to join us. It was truly an honour to have you as my special guest."

"Well, I'm certainly honoured to be here. It's something I will never forget."

They chatted for a few minutes more until André politely excused himself to mingle with the other guests.

When it was just the three of them standing amongst the noisy crowd, any remnants of that former formality fell away. With generous hugs all round, the excited trio greeted each other like long-lost family ... and a mixture of both happy and sad tears fell from both women's eyes. It was years since they had all been together and so many memories came flooding back.

Claudia understood what lay behind Lara's emotional display and quickly dabbed at both their cheeks with an embroidered handkerchief laced with the popular Yves Saint Laurent's *Paris* perfume. When she was done, two large kisses landed on Lara's cheeks in the manner of all Italians and speaking with so much tenderness it reminded Lara of her mother.

"*Ciao amico mio bello, per favore,* do not cry or you will make my 'eart break with you."

"Oh, Claudia, *caro amico*, it's so good to see you after all this time. And I'm sorry if I made you sad. I really wanted to put a smile on your face tonight ... not tears."

"*Caro Larissa*, you did put a smile on my face with *la bella voce*. I am *molto* 'onoured to call you *amico mio* after you sang like an *angelo* tonight. Many of *miei altri amici* were 'ere, and it makes my 'eart glad to 'ave you sing to us in *mia bella città vecchia* – my beautiful old 'ometown."

The women hugged once more in a heart-warming display of the true affection they felt for each other. Lara was secretly pleased to hear Claudia use the European form of her name again after so long.

Not to be outdone and in his usual flirty manner, Antonio playfully nudged his wife away and pulled Lara into those thick, strong arms of his. "Now it's my turn to *congratulo con questa donna bellissima* and tell 'er 'ow she makes my 'eart race away! Lara, you were *magnifico ... grazie, grazie!*"

Lara couldn't help laughing at all the old familiar compliments. He hadn't changed one bit, and it did her heart good to be on the receiving end of his teasing again. Since the night had begun, she had been on the brink of tears, aching to have Adam by her side. Antonio's mischievous ways were a welcome respite.

They spent the rest of the evening together. The singer was proud to introduce her old friends to the new ones she had made in the orchestra, other guest artists and those from the backing group. Some had fond memories of his flirtatious overtures from the year before and soon they were on the receiving end of even more of his hilarious comments and cheeky winks.

When the old clock tower chimed midnight, Claudia once again kissed Lara on both cheeks.

"*Buonanotte Larissa*, it is late. We 'ad better let you go to bed, and it is time we were there, too" —her eyes instantly widened, and she shook her hands widely— "ah, but in our cottage – not yours!"

Lara couldn't help laughing, imagining the mayhem sure to follow if she ever found Antonio in her bed. Claudia soon joined in, though her cheeks were stained bright red.

"*Oh la la*, I am so sorry! You know what I mean!" She covered her mouth as another fit of laughter ensued, but they both soon sobered up with her next remark. "But I do not want 'Tonio driving us over the edge in the dark. The road, it is very very steep and winds like a *serpente* down the mountain. It can be most dangerous if you are not careful."

"Yes, I remember it well," came Lara's response as her eyes clouded over.

Seeing her thoughts start to wander down paths from years past, Claudia quickly cut in. "Anyway, enough of the worrying. Please come and join us for lunch tomorrow ... but only after a good, long sleep-in."

"I'd love to, Claudia. I've been looking forward to spending some proper time with you and catching up on all the family's news. I bet Amalia's two *bambini piccoli* have grown into *belle signorine!*" Lara well remembered how kind Claudia's niece had been to take care of her daughter while she and Adam explored the streets of Florence, and how much Nikki had enjoyed spending time with Marianna and Luca, who were of a similar age.

"*Si*, you wouldn't believe 'ow *bellissimo* they are now," Antonio replied with that familiar twinkle in his eyes. "Their *mamma* 'as to beat the boys away with a stick – just like you must over your *prezioso* Nikki. Is true, no?" They all laughed as he offered her the customary duo of farewell kisses.

"*Si, tis molto* true, Antonio! She's grown up way too fast, and far too many boys are interested for my liking! Now, drive safely, and I'll see you tomorrow," she replied, bestowing similar tokens on his cheeks before doing the same to Claudia.

Antonio took his wife's hand before starting down the hill, pressing it against his lips with a flourish, just as Lara remembered.

You haven't changed one bit, she thought, smiling at them affectionately as they sent her a farewell wave. She watched as they strolled down to where Antonio had parked the car beyond the town walls, still turning around every now and then to send her another wave until the darkness swallowed them up.

The last of the stragglers were getting ready to leave as a band of workmen finished packing up the chairs in the square. Lara sought out André to thank him again for offering her the opportunity to be part of this unique event. His warm smile confirmed how much he appreciated her contribution and how thrilled he was to have invited her to share his stage.

"Sleep well, my dear. You deserve an undisturbed night after all the hours you put in to help bring about such a magical evening. I will see you late in the afternoon for a quick rehearsal to ensure our performance tomorrow night is just as good. *Buonanotte*."

Similar to Antonio and Claudia, he kissed her on both cheeks, and she was quick to respond with a dazzling smile. The evening's celebration of music was something she would treasure forever.

§

Before retracing her steps to the hotel, Lara wandered around the now-deserted *piazza*, staring up at the small balcony where she had performed only a couple of hours earlier. She almost had to pinch herself to believe she really was back there, along with trying to get her head around the concert and all it entailed.

The streets were silent now. As so often happened whenever there was no-one else around, her thoughts turned to a man with love in his eyes. Adam had always been her inspiration, and nothing had changed, despite all the years and miles separating them. For a fleeting moment, she dared to pull down the barriers guarding her heart. Rather than going back to an empty room, she tried to imagine what it would be like to find him there waiting for her instead of that endless silence. Just as quickly, she brushed the thought aside before it had a chance to take hold and send her spirit spiralling into that sad and lonely place again.

Unfortunately, her strategy only worked for a short time. Reaching the top of the stairs leading to her suite, she could almost hear his gentle laughter and see the look of pride in his eyes when she went to turn the doorknob. Walking those streets again and finding reminders around every corner only emphasised how much was missing from her life without him being there to share it.

She tried hard to drift off to sleep, but kept tossing and turning for over an hour as a host of memories jostled on the fringe of her consciousness. Her emotions were too raw and she wasn't game enough to let them in. Instead, she deliberately pushed them away, longing instead for the blissful nothingness of a dreamless sleep.

§

Sunrise was still a few hours away when the sound of tiny whimpers floated around an elegantly decorated hotel suite. Lara lay curled beneath the covers of a large canopied bed. Every now and then her eyelids tremored and she moved her head from side to side as the shadowy images of the man whose memory had been following her for the last few days came to life in her dreams. Only this time, his eyes were full of laughter as he beckoned her to follow.

Much to her dismay, as soon as they were close enough to touch, he drifted away again. Panicking, she ran after him and around the next bend there he was, arms outstretched and his face lit up with the smile she knew so well. Laughing with pure abandonment, he pulled her close and their lips met in a kiss filled with both passion and tenderness ... she was home at last.

The scene was so real Lara let out a deep cry, loud enough to startle her from the dream. She woke to find every pore tingling with anticipation. Her heart raced as reality returned and she struggled to catch a breath, chest heaving with bitter disappointment at the realisation she was alone. Every part of her ached to go back into that other world.

Throwing the feather doona aside, she climbed out of bed to pour herself a cool glass of water. Wide-awake now, she settled into a niche in the top floor window recess, staring out at the sleepy township. The moon had only just started its new cycle. The only part visible was the crescent forming what looked like a crooked smile.

Letting out a long, sad sigh, she folded her arms along the windowsill and rested her chin against them for several minutes. Silent and reflective, she looked down over row upon row of rooftops fashioned from tiles the colour of burnt sienna that seemed to cascade into the panorama below. In the soft glow of the street lamps, they resembled a giant staircase leading down to the ancient wall surrounding the town.

Remnants of the evening's performance helped to lessen the sadness, while always lurking in the shadows was a painful and honest truth ... the happiest days of her life still belonged to Adam. Nothing or no-one would ever change that fact. It was a constant reality and tonight's celebration was just one of many she longed to share with him.

From out of a far-away place, Lara was reminded of something she had always held onto – a salve to help ease the hurt following that fateful phone call; those few short months together more than made up for all the long and lonely hours since. She would never regret their time together and wouldn't have traded one minute, not even if all the gold and silver in the world was offered in its place. And yet still those same memories often brought with them a mountain of pain and yearning, so much so, at times it had become almost too much to bear.

Absentmindedly, she picked up a pen from the writing desk and began leisurely scrawling his name in elaborate cursive script on a piece of the hotel's signature stationery. Two lines of teardrops trickled down her face as she outlined each letter over and over.

In the midst of all this sadness, Lara suddenly had to press a hand against her chest. She wasn't in pain so much as it was more like a tiny twinge of something she couldn't quite fathom trying to penetrate her soul. Whatever it was only made the missing stronger. In another realm unseen by human eyes, the tiny piece of her heart left behind while flying out of Vienna so many years ago now came home to rest, bringing with it fragments of another left behind in Cortona the last time Adam was there.

Rising from the core of these reunited kindred spirits, flowed words that seemed to have been waiting for this exact moment in time. Her fingers danced effortlessly across the paper ... similar to the many times a loving ballet had come to life through the melding of mirrored hands.

> *My Darling Adam,*
>
> *You've come to me as you always do – and in the only way you can now – in breathtaking dreams emerging from the depths of my heart ... that secret place where you alone dwell.*
>
> *Our time together was our own private place ... a fragment of space in the vastness of the universe ... and yet those glorious hours have touched my world every moment I've taken breath ... and nothing can erase you from my memory.*
>
> *I don't have the strength to regret the decision I made so long ago – I know if I did, I wouldn't be able to live with the pain ... but I will always long for you in that secret place ... the one I've made in my heart especially for you ... every day, until I am no more...*

With a torrent of emotions flooding her soul, this was Lara's personal atonement – her tribute to a lifetime filled with longing and remorse. In many ways, it was her swansong to him as well, even though he would never get to read it himself.

She put down the pen slowly and re-read each line. Then with a heartfelt sigh, carefully folded the delicate notepaper and slipped it into the back of her purse ... ready to join several other treasures when she arrived back home in a couple of weeks.

Chapter 37

Dappled sunlight spilled onto Lara's bed long before she was awake. When her eyes eventually did open, one glance at the clock on the nightstand showed it was nearly eleven o'clock.

"Oh, no!"

Claudia and Antonio were expecting her for lunch, and she still needed to buy something from one of the town's specialty shops to add to the meal. Springing out of bed, Lara rushed to the bathroom, berating herself loudly for not setting the alarm. She had been too exhausted to think clearly after climbing back into bed just as daybreak peeked over a far-off ridge.

Twenty minutes later she hurried into the *piazza*. A large round of ripe goat's cheese along with a bottle of homemade pesto from a speciality deli spotted on one of her earlier explorations were quickly paid for before she rushed back to the hotel.

Her first port of call was to the concierge's desk.

"*Scusa*, could you please order me a taxi straight away. I need to be at a friend's house near the old church below town within the next few minutes."

"*Mi scuso*, Ms Jennings, the only taxis in the district 'ave to come from Camucia, twenty minutes away, 'owever we do 'ave a car for guests to use if you need to be there sooner."

"Oh dear, I didn't realise. Well, I suppose that will have to do then. I'll be down shortly if you don't mind having it ready for me."

"*Certamente*, I will organise it myself."

"*Grazie*, I'll just get my things and be back soon."

"*Prego.*"

Despite never having driven on the right-hand side of the road before, or behind the wheel of a left-hand drive vehicle, Lara felt confident she would be okay for the short journey down the hill.

She was grateful the kind concierge had organised to have a compact Fiat waiting at the hotel entrance rather than trying to back it out of the narrow opening to the cavernous garage herself.

Thank goodness it's automatic and small! was her next thought as she turned the key and then buckled the seatbelt.

It was easy to remember where the entrance to the villa was because of the beautiful old church positioned only a few metres before Claudia and Antonio's driveway. It didn't take too long for Lara's confidence to return as she wound her way down the very steep and winding mountain road.

"Careful, you silly girl!" she warned herself loudly after taking a deceptively sharp bend way too fast. Claudia's words of caution about the treacherous road from the night before kept her company as she continued on her way.

Just as she rounded another corner, a sports car raced up behind. The driver pulled out as soon as the road straightened, speeding past before she even realised he had disappeared from her rear-view mirror.

Whoa! No wonder Italian men win all the Grand Prix if that's how they drive. Wide, open tracks with cars all going the same way are a breeze compared to these narrow two-way roads!

Lara shivered anxiously and then remembered uttering a similar phrase when Adam was behind the wheel as they were leaving Rome.

"Stop it! Just concentrate on driving..."

The sound of her own voice helped to settle the nerves, although she still held her breath as another bend loomed into view.

The unmistakable dome of the church was now only a few hundred metres away, and she sighed with relief as her car followed the line of the road. All of a sudden, a large truck loomed into view from the opposite direction at the exact same moment Lara realised she had underestimated the sharpness of the corner. The driver took up most of the road, so she turned the steering wheel frantically to get out of his way.

Hitting the brakes hard when she saw how close to the edge she was, two of the side tyres skidded in the soft gravel on the shoulder as she tried desperately to control the steering wheel. Just when she thought everything was under control again, the back fishtailed, causing it to spin in a large circle.

Everything happened in a horrible blur. Because the car was unfamiliar, Lara was unable to bring it under control quickly enough. With a loud bang, the rear end hit a steep bank in a narrow section of road that caused the whole body to shudder uncontrollably. The impact flipped the car onto its roof and sent it crashing through a low barrier before plunging over the edge and down the side of the steep hill. For what seemed like forever, the vehicle continued rolling over and over while making sickening crunching sounds with Lara still strapped inside.

The truck driver had already driven several metres around the corner when he glanced through his side mirror and noticed the car plummet over the edge. Slamming on his brakes, he pulled to the side and threw open the door, racing over to the edge of the cliff just in time to see the already mangled car slam into a tree about a hundred metres below. A broken barrier and the cloud of dust from its tumbling journey were the only signs of anything untoward happening. Frantic, he scrambled down the hillside, sending rocks and rubble flying from under his feet. He pulled a mobile phone from his pocket and managed to ring the emergency number while skidding on the rocky terrain.

Fifteen minutes later, two ambulance officers found him anxiously applying CPR to the body of a lifeless woman. What looked to be her blood coated his hands and clothes. It wasn't hard to guess the thick red liquid came from the gaping wounds riddling her arms and legs. A large open gash above her hairline continued to pour the precious fluid onto the ground. One officer quickly took over the lifesaving efforts as the other tried to staunch the rapid flow of blood.

"Do you know who she is?" one asked the dazed driver, but he could only shake his head from side to side. A look of despair and uncontrollable shaking were his only other responses.

Just then, a siren split the air as a police car screamed up the mountainside. One of the *poliziotti* soon clambered down to join them, slipping and sliding on the treacherous terrain. His partner stayed behind to investigate the scene and call for backup.

It took the rescuers another forty minutes to climb back up the hill, hindered by the weight of the unidentified woman lying unconscious on the stretcher they had balancing between them. Their only relief was knowing they had managed to get her breathing again, although each gasp was short and shallow. It was all too obvious the injured woman wasn't out of the woods yet.

As soon as the rescue team and truck driver climbed over the broken barrier, other police officers started questioning the distraught man, hoping to piece together what had occurred. One already had a small purse in his hands and was rifling through the contents for anything that might aid in identifying the woman. Unfortunately, because of her mad scramble to get ready, Lara had left her passport and papers behind in the hotel's safe. Their only clue was a glossy brochure from the concert that had taken place in Cortona the night before. It was only logical to deduce she was probably an out-of-town visitor who had been in the audience. At least now they had somewhere to begin. If any of them had bothered to look closely at the photographs inside, they might have recognised the attractive singer, although the amount of blood still seeping from her head would have hindered an easy identification.

With sirens once again piercing the still air, the ambulance sped off to the nearest hospital in Fratta-santa Caterina, a small township only ten kilometres away. Its only passenger lay lifeless and still as the blood continued to ooze from her wounds and soak into a wad of thick bandages, despite their best efforts to stem the flow.

§

Antonio and Claudia were starting to worry. Lara had been due for lunch around midday. Now it was nearly one, and there was still no sign of her.

When the clock chimed the quarter hour, Claudia began pacing the floor between the window and stove where a large pot of *Osso Bucco* had been turned down to a low simmer. She kept looking anxiously at her husband and wringing her hands.

"Maybe should you ring the 'otel? She would not be this late without letting us know."

Antonio spoke to the hotel clerk for several minutes. His face was creased with worry lines when he turned to his wife and shook his head. "*Il concierge* say she left over an 'our ago after borrowing the car of the 'otel. She was running late so 'ad no time to book a taxi from Camucia."

Her hands flew in the air. "She should 'ave rung us, and you could 'ave go to pick her up. *Mamma-mia*, where could she be?"

"*Si*, I was not thinking to say anything last night with all the excitement of the *concerto*. I do not understand where she would go. Lara does not know anyone else in Cortona apart from 'er friends in the orchestra, I am sure."

Claudia could only shake her head as her imagination raced ahead at a great rate of knots envisaging the worst possible scenario.

Her husband was looking just as worried. "Did you 'ear *le sirene* before? Something went past *in un grande* 'urry."

"*Si ... oh Dio mio*, do not let it be to do with our Larissa! We must 'ope she is just visiting *la chiesa* to say a prayer before coming to see us." There was one scenario she was too afraid to contemplate, but it kept niggling at her conscience.

"*Si,* you are probably right. But it seems a long time to be praying..."

Recognising the look on her husband's face, Claudia knew she had to say the words. "You 'ad better to ring the new *ospedale* in Fratta. 'Opefully, they will know nothing, and she is just sitting in a pew of *la chiesa* and forgotten the time it is."

§

It was nearly midnight when the phone rang in a large home on the banks of the Brisbane River.

"Oh Charles, *grazie a Dio*, it is me, Claudia. I 'ave been ringing for such many 'ours but you 'ave not answer." Barely able to speak from the shock of what they had just seen, her voice was almost unrecognisable.

Charles was surprised to hear from his manager's wife so late in the evening, so his response was cautious and concerned. "Claudia, is that really you? I'm sorry; we've been out with friends and only just got home. You sound worried.

Is everything alright? Has something happened to Antonio?"

"Oh, Charles, I – *o Dio, per favore* – eeh ... I do not know 'ow to say this – my English is not good for trouble times. It is your Larissa; she is in *Ospedale Santa Margherita* in Fratta-santa Caterina. Charles, she is *molto molto malato* – oh, 'ow ... eeh ... si, 'ow you say very very sick in the 'ospital."

The poor woman was having trouble trying to communicate in the unfamiliar tongue. Charles could easily detect the distress in her voice.

As soon as Elizabeth saw his expression she knew something was terribly wrong. Snatching up the other extension, she listened in on the conversation.

"Larissa – our *bella* Larissa, 'as being in *auto incidente* – she is *inconscio* – she will not wake up! 'Er family will have to come to Cortona, but we no know 'ow to find number for Nikki, so we 'ave to wait for you to come 'ome. We 'ave been ringing and ringing over and over...." Images of the little girl she remembered so well, along with all they had just witnessed, caused Claudia to break down. Her loud sobs echoed down the phone line.

Antonio took the phone from his wife's hand. His English wasn't much better, but thankfully he was more in control and able to fill them in on the details.

Both Charles and Elizabeth sank into some chairs close at hand, still clutching the receivers as the blood drained from their faces. Neither one was able to process the shocking news. They had been so excited when Lara received the invitation. Now they were in a state of shock trying to comprehend her lying in an intensive care ward all alone on the other side of the world.

"So what did the doctor say?" Elizabeth asked, dreading his answer.

"'E thinks she 'as maybe break 'er back, but it is too quick to say. She still 'as not woken up since they found 'er. But I not really *comprendere* what 'e was telling me, and they are still checking all of 'er when we leave to ring you."

Charles realised they wouldn't be able to find out what really happened without talking to the doctor himself. With a firm promise to get back to them, he hung up the phone and turned to his wife. She was absolutely devastated and slumped into his arms, sobbing on his shoulder. He wasn't much better and had to keep blinking the tears away.

Just over an hour later, following four phone calls – two to Italy and two others that were both hurried and vague – the persistent peal of chimes echoed throughout the house. It was obvious whoever it was had their finger pressed against the doorbell. Thankfully, after speaking to Lara's doctor on the other side of the world, he and Elizabeth were now armed with far more information about the extent of her injuries. Now they could tell the rest of the family exactly what was going on and what steps to take.

When Charles and his wife opened the door, both Suzie and Ben were standing there with their sleepy nine-year-old son leaning against his mother. Before Elizabeth could say anything or even escort the newcomers inside, a late-model Mazda screeched to a halt in the driveway. Nikki threw open the car door and raced towards them with a look of sheer panic on her face.

"What's happened, Uncle Charles? Why have you called us all here in the middle of the night?"

Elizabeth immediately took charge and put a loving arm around the young woman's shoulders. Leading her inside, she crooned softly, "Come and sit down, sweetheart. There's something Uncle Charles and I need to tell both you and Aunty Suzie."

The young woman stopped in her tracks. "What's *happened?*"

"I'm so sorry, sweetie ... there's been a – oh dear..." Despite her good intentions, Elizabeth had to bite her bottom lip to stop them from trembling. When she was back in control again, the words came out in a rush. "Nikki, your mum's been in a car accident ... just outside Cortona."

"*What?* Is she all right?" Those dark brown eyes darted between the older couple, unable to comprehend what she had just heard.

"Come into the living room so I can tell you everything we know."

Elizabeth led her distressed granddaughter across to the large sofa while Charles hurried out to the kitchen to make hot drinks for everyone. She had spoken to the doctor and knew a lot more of the details, while he preferred to keep busy as she filled them in.

Suzie was just as stunned at the news and sat on the other side of her niece, holding her close while the older one related everything she knew.

"Apparently your mum was on her way to visit Claudia and Antonio when a truck came towards her on one of the steep bends. Somehow her car ended up plunging down the side of a hill." Her tone grew softer as she went on and the others could only listen on in shock. "They're not exactly sure whose fault it was at this stage, but the car she was driving ended up wrapped around a tree."

"*That* can't be right. Mum would *never* have driven over there – she'd be too scared, especially on those narrow roads."

"They think she was running late and borrowed the hotel's car instead of waiting for a taxi." Elizabeth's brow furrowed and she had to take a deep breath while trying to remember everything. "The paramedics got to her fairly quickly" —she paused again, dreading having to finish the sentence— "but her heart had stopped by the time they arrived." The last phrase was punctuated with a choked sob.

Nikki gasped loudly and her eyes widened with fear. Trembling hands slammed against her gaping mouth, fully expecting to hear her mother hadn't made it. Suzie was just as devastated, trying hard not to picture the scene in her mind as the tears poured from her eyes.

Realising how final those concluding words must have sounded, Elizabeth pulled both women close and crooned, "Ssshhh, it's okay ... they were able to revive her in time, although the doctors say she has horrific injuries and a large cut to the top of her head."

The grandmotherly figure could only offer up soothing assurances, hoping to impart whatever measure of comfort she could with such limited information. Suzie was speechless, rocking senselessly as she tried to process the news. Ben hurried across to comfort her and she burrowed into his shoulder, crying softly.

Elizabeth glanced towards her husband as he came in with a tray of drinks and they shared another worried look. She had to take one more deep breath before breaking the rest of the news.

"Nikki, there's something else you need to know..."

The young woman peered up at her with renewed fear filling her eyes.

"Your mum's had to have a tube inserted into her throat to help her breathe, and they think she might also have a fractured skull. She's been put into an induced coma until the swelling goes down ... then they can assess if there's any other damage."

The news was getting worse by the minute and everyone was in shock. *How could this be happening?* was the question on all their lips, but apart from a few heart-wrenching sobs, no one could utter a sound.

Suzie was shaking badly, so Ben pulled her even closer. How could this be happening to her effervescent little sister? She shrugged away from her husband's hold and reached for Nikki and Elizabeth. The trio clung to each other while trying to take everything in. The men could only look on helplessly and shake their heads sadly. Thankfully, Jack was already fast asleep in the guest room, totally oblivious to the unfolding drama.

As the extent of what happened started to register, Nikki suddenly cried out, "Oh dear *God, noooo!* I *have* to go to her! She's all alone in a strange country..."

She tried to get up, but Suzie pulled her down again, gripping her shoulder tightly. "Hang on, pumpkin. We need to know exactly what's going on before we can do anything." The childhood endearment was an automatic reaction, and she pulled her niece closer, fearing she would race to the car and take off to who knows where. "What else did they say, Elizabeth?"

The older woman paused again, looking across at Charles and knowing the worst was still to come. She could tell he was fighting back the tears.

Squeezing Nikki's trembling hand, her voice was no more than a whisper, and she faltered every few words. "They think ... your mother may be ... oh Nikki, it looks like she's paralysed in both legs—"

The petrified young woman let out another loud gasp, and her expression was filled with horror as Elizabeth finished.

"—but they need to wait until she comes out of the coma to fully assess the damage."

Nikki couldn't sit still any longer. Jumping up, she paced the floor as her tone grew angry and disbelieving. "*Nooo, not that!* Mum *has* to be able to walk. She just *has* to. That's it; I'm flying over there. She *needs* me. I can't just sit around here wondering what's going on."

"We'll both go." Suzie went over to her distraught niece and wrapped tight arms around her shaking form. "I want you to come and stay with us tonight. Then I can book our tickets as soon as we get home."

Charles immediately turned to Ben and whispered, "Don't worry, we'll pay for everything – flights, accommodation, food, and whatever else is needed to get Lara well so they can bring her home."

When the younger man started to protest, Charles put his hand up to stop him. "Please don't argue. Lara will need every penny she has, and we have more than enough to cover everything. It's the least we can do – she's the daughter we never had, and Nikki is our only granddaughter ... and they both need Suzie there to support them."

Ben laid a grateful arm around the older man's shoulders, unable to put into words the depth of his relief. Neither he nor Suzie could afford the mounting expenses that were growing larger by the minute. Having the Ashworths' help meant his wife could accompany Nikki rather than letting the grief-stricken girl try to cope with everything on her own.

They spent the next hour in discussions about what still needed to be done to ensure their quick arrival. Elizabeth jotted down the hospital's address as well as the doctor's personal mobile number and slipped them into Suzie's hand, along with a few hundred dollars in cash. She didn't want them having to worry about how to pay for things along the way.

When Suzie tried to protest, she shook her head. "It's okay; you may need this – just take it, it's the least we can do. I just wish I could come with you."

Everyone was aware of Elizabeth's heart problems. It was unthinkable to even consider her making the long journey herself.

The family was subdued when it came time to leave. Nikki was heading straight home to pack and gather up whatever she thought Lara would need to make her stay as comfortable as possible. Afterwards, she planned to drive over to Suzie and Ben's and stay with them for the rest of the night.

Charles gathered them all together into a tight huddle at the door. He felt the need to offer up a prayer pleading for Lara's full recovery and safe travels for the other two. The family drew strength from his words and it was a welcome form of comfort for what lay ahead.

On her way home, Nikki sent up her own prayer that both she and her aunt would find seats on the first available plane.

Just as she went to close the suitcase, the young woman ran back into her mother's bedroom to pick up the pewter sculpture that had been sitting by Lara's bedside for several years.

If ever we needed hope, it's now ... you're coming with me.

There was a noticeable gap in the usual meticulous display – both photographs were missing, though it wasn't surprising. The same thing always occurred whenever her mother was away on tour. She gave a sad grimace trying to picture where they were now.

Don't worry, Mum, I'll be there soon – and I'm sure Uncle Adam's with you in spirit, even though he has no idea...

None of them was able to sleep at all that night. Ben managed to find a flight leaving first thing in the morning, even though it meant flying to Sydney to catch the next plane to Rome ... but it didn't matter. Nikki's only concern was getting to her mother's side as soon as possible.

§

It was nearly thirty-six hours later when two women – one in her early twenties and the other several years older – sped down the corridor of a brand-new hospital, searching frantically for the intensive care ward. A nurse approached and using her best attempts at English asked who they were looking for.

"Lara Jennings. She's my mother. We were told she arrived two days ago. She's been in a terrible car accident."

The kindly nurse now understood their distress and led them to a room located directly opposite the nurses' station. If she hadn't been there to point the patient out, neither one would have recognised the beautiful woman they knew and loved so well.

Several metres of snake-like tubing protruded from Lara's mouth and nose, as well as from beneath the bedclothes. Drip lines pierced both arms and the constant whoosh of a ventilator was frightening evidence she was only breathing with the help of a tracheal tube. There were deep purple bruises under Lara's eyes, which were both swollen shut, and another on her forehead that looked more like a large dark birthmark. Her face was almost double its usual size and most of her head was swathed in thick, white bandages hiding what used to be a crown of thick glossy chestnut hair. The only sounds were the constant beep of the heart monitor and the breathy rhythm of the machine now keeping her alive. She looked so small lying in the stark white bed, and Nikki was too scared to approach.

This can't be my mum. She's always full of life, but this person is just an empty shell. I don't even recognise her.

511

Suzie was clutching her niece's hand and could feel her fear and trepidation. "Come on, pumpkin. It'll be okay. I'm right here with you."

Slowly they approached the bed. That's when Nikki noticed a tiny scar on Lara's finger. Her mother had cut it on a barbed wire fence while attempting to rescue a snagged sugar glider during their riding holiday in the Snowy Mountains. The unusual mark, along with the magnificent sapphire ring peeking out from beneath the covers on her other hand, were all that was needed for the fearful young woman to recognise this unresponsive form really was her mother.

As gently as possible, Nikki picked up the hand lying closest to her. Pressing it softly against her cheek, she sobbing uncontrollably while sinking into a chair beside the bed. This was the first time she had been able to cry since learning what had happened and it was impossible to control the tears after so many hours of worry. With flights first to Sydney and then onto Rome, a train trip to Camucia – similar to the one Lara had taken only a few days earlier – and then the taxi ride to the hospital, she was exhausted and all the emotions held rigidly in check suddenly overflowed.

"M...um, it's m...e. You do...n't have to be scar...ed anym...ore. I'm h...ere ... and so is Aunty Su...ze. But d...on't you *dare* di...ie on me – I wo...n't let you..."

There was no response from the woman who had been Nikki's best friend all her life and the stark reality of the situation finally began to sink in. Her mother was gravely ill, and unless a miracle occurred, there was the distinct possibility she may not be coming come home except in a cold, wooden box.

§

Claudia and Antonio came up to the hospital late in the afternoon. Nikki flew into their arms as soon as she spied them coming through the door, remembering all the love and affection they had showered on her when she was a little girl.

"Oh, Nikki, I am so 'appy to see you but so sorry for what 'as 'appened to your *mamma*," Claudia crooned, rocking her in much the same manner as she used to all those years ago.

"*Grazie, Zia Claudia* and *grazie a Dio* you found out and were able to let us know. I don't know how we would've heard otherwise."

Antonio hugged both Nikki and his wife close, kissing the top of her hair and subconsciously registering how much shorter it was than the last time they were together. "*Ciao mia una preziosa*, it is *orribile* but we 'ave been praying for 'er every day in the *bella chiesa vecchia* on the 'ill near our 'ome."

"*Grazie, Zio Antonio,* I can only hope *Dio* has been listening to all of us. I've been praying non-stop since hearing the news. Oh, *mi scusi*, this is mum's sister, Suzie ... Aunty Suze, I want to introduce you to Uncle Antonio and Aunty Claudia," she added, dragging them over to where her aunt stood.

Suzie was surprised to find herself clasped in the same comforting embrace with her niece. She was grateful to have caring shoulders to lean on after trying to be strong for Nikki's sake since hearing the news.

The group of four huddled together in a silent cluster, finding comfort in each other while trying to take everything in. Eventually, Claudia cupped Suzie's face with her hands, struggling through the sadness to summon up a smile. "*Ciao*, Suzie. *Grazie a Dio* Nikki 'ad you with 'er for the journey ... it would 'ave been *una cosa terribile* for 'er to 'ave to come all this way on 'er own. I am *grato* you are 'ere with us."

"Mmm ... *ciao*, Claudia, and I'm grateful too. I couldn't let her just come on her own." Her smile was just as poignant as they both blinked away the tears.

Taking over from his wife, Antonio placed his hands around the top of Suzie's arms and kissed her on both cheeks. "*Ciao*, Suzie, it is very good for us to meet you at last. We are so sorry it 'as to be under these *terribile* circumstances, but we will 'elp in whatever way we can."

"*Grazie*, Antonio, it's a godsend you were here. I know my sister would be most grateful for your kindness."

"*Si, io adoro* Lara like she was my own."

"Well, it's wonderful to finally meet you. She has told me so many lovely things about their stay here. I just wish it didn't have to be this way."

Claudia nodded gravely as they all turned to look at the figure lying so still in the bed. Adding to her husband's sentiment, she said through a sob, "She is *molto speciale* – and so is this one ... since she was *una piccola bambina!*" Her lips touched Nikki's cheek as they all huddle together again while the tears flowed. "Now we just 'ave to wait for *un miracolo per la sua mamma!*"

They spent another hour beside Lara's bedside, whispering softly while the husband and wife shared news of both the concert and the accident, as well as wanting to hear how Elizabeth and Charles were faring. Claudia insisted the visitors stay with them, but Suzie and Nikki had already decided on a little bed and breakfast just around the corner from the hospital that Ben had found online. Neither of them wanted to hurt her feelings, but it seemed more practical and far easier to get to the hospital than from ten kilometres away, especially as the villa only had one car for everyday use. Neither did they realise at this early stage, their footsteps would soon carve an invisible path between the temporary home away from home and the hospital.

§

The following day, Nikki placed the pewter sculpture on her mother's bedside trolley. She wanted it to be the first thing Lara looked at when she woke up. Standing beside it was a beautiful arrangement of flowers and the card tucked in amongst the colourful heads read,

Best wishes, my glorious prima donna. Hurry up and get well. The music world needs you for many years to come. I will add my prayers to others every single day ... Godspeed, André Rieu

He and everyone involved in the concert had been shocked by the news. A few from his entourage dropped by in the first few days to see how she was faring, though they were only permitted to speak to the nurses on duty as Lara's visitor regime was strictly for family only. Two other concerts had been scheduled; the first on the night of the accident and another the following day. After some hasty changes to the programme, both shows were able to go ahead, with André making a special tribute to Lara before each one commenced. He even offered up a prayer for her healing on both occasions.

By the end of the first week, the performers had all left for their homes, leaving Nikki and Suzie with promises they would continue to pray for Lara's full recovery.

The maestro himself dropped by the hospital once more before flying out, and the strict visitor rule was waived away when the nursing staff recognised the famous composer. It was obvious he was visibly upset to see the beautiful and vibrant singer now rendered helpless and vulnerable. He remembered a stunning woman with flowing hair and captivating smile who bore no resemblance to the one lying unconscious on the bed in front of him.

When he turned to go, André wrapped a caring arm around Nikki's shoulders. "I will keep you and your mother in my thoughts and prayers, young lady, and please keep me informed of any news. She is an exceptional artist, so we have to believe that God hears our prayers."

"I will and thank you. I know Mum was absolutely thrilled and honoured to be a part of your concert. Thanks for including her. Aunt Claudia said she was so happy afterwards."

"It was entirely my pleasure, and she was marvellous. Now, remember, I want to hear how she is getting on, and don't forget to take care of yourself. She will need you when she wakes up, *ja?* Goodbye, my dear, and may God bless you all."

Just before leaving, he went over and shook Suzie's hand, offering final words of comfort to the worried sister. Then with a wave, he was gone.

§

Those on the nursing staff were always helpful, keeping Lara's family up-to-date with everything that was going on. She required surgery on three more occasions to help relieve the pressure on her brain, and they kept her in an induced coma as the neurologist grew more concerned when the swelling didn't abate. A physio came twice a day to exercise the patient's muscles and prevent them from wasting away. Nikki begged him to teach her the proper technique – she felt helpless just sitting beside her mother's bedside day after day with nothing to do. The rigorous workout helped to make the time go faster. It would also assist in aiding Lara's recovery once they were able to take her home. The determined young woman didn't dare contemplate any other outcome.

Twice during the first week, Suzie and Nikki caught a local taxi up to Antonio and Claudia's home at the vineyard for some much-needed respite from the intensity of hospital routines. It was also the perfect way to catch up with their concerned friends in a relaxed setting. Not surprisingly, whenever they caught sight of the twisted barrier beside the road, Nikki couldn't help shuddering as she pictured her mother plunging down the rocky hillside.

As soon as the owners of the B&B learned their guests were using taxis to get around, they immediately offered the use of their second car. It was easy to see how draining Lara's accident was on their Australian visitors and they wanted to help out in whatever way possible. Most of the residents of Fratta-Santa Caterina came to their aid in some form, several offering posies of flowers from their gardens for the invalid, while many put together tasty meals for the visitors to heat up after their daily hospital visits. Suzie and Nikki were overwhelmed at the town's generosity and knew they couldn't possibly repay everyone.

At the beginning of the second week, Nikki decided to visit the old *chiesa* around the corner from Claudia and Antonio's place. It had been quite a few years since she had gone to church – apart from the usual Christmas and Easter services – even though she had gone regularly with her mother as a young child and teenager. Lara still attended her local parish chapel, clinging steadfastly to her beliefs. Often her faith had been the only form of solace during those dark times. Now Nikki turned to the only place she knew that could bring about a much-needed miracle, along with offering herself a measure of that same comfort and trust.

Tiptoeing into the sacred building – the same one her mother had visited all those years ago – she immediately felt a sense of peace settle over her soul ... her first since receiving the awful news. She knelt before the altar and raised her face to the famous picture of the Madonna and Child located beneath the magnificent arch.

With her eyes tightly closed, the distressed petitioner prayed as she never had before – asking God to be merciful and bring healing to all the broken parts of her mother's body. It was eight days since the accident and Lara was still lying in a coma – unmoving and deathly pale. The heartbroken young woman was becoming more worried each day, fearing she would never wake up. There was still no response to any form of stimulation in either leg, giving the doctors even more reason for concern. Visiting the church was her last hope.

When the prayer ended, she felt an overwhelming urge to plead for her own sake. Opening her eyes, Nikki gazed up at the image of the Holy Mother and Baby through eyes filled with tears as she begged aloud from the depths of her spirit.

"Father God, you're the only one left I can turn to. I know I haven't been to church for ages, or even given you any of my time. I definitely don't deserve your mercy or even have you bother with me ... but Mum has, and she really needs a miracle. She's all I have and I need your help to make her better 'cause the doctors don't know what else to do. You know how strong her faith has always been ... please be merciful to her now. I'm begging you, more than I ever have before – I can't lose her ... I just *can't*." A loud sigh rose from her spirit as she added a heartfelt whisper. "Thanks for listening. In the name of the Father, and the Son and the Holy Spirit, Amen."

Following the ancient tradition, she touched her forehead and three points on her chest in the Sign of the Cross and then pressed the tips of her fingers to her mouth.

Almost instantaneously, an indescribable sense of peace came over the young woman. When she rose to her feet, a faint smile touched her lips. For some inexplicable reason, this unlikely pilgrim knew her prayer had been heard. She left the quiet sanctuary feeling just a tiny bit lighter instead of that heavy burden of worry weighing her down.

Although she had no idea what the outcome would be, Nikki's faith had grown stronger, and she was certain God's presence would be with them.

§

Over the next few days, the swelling in Lara's head appeared to be subsiding. It gave the doctors a faint degree of optimism that she may have turned a corner. As a result, they were able to slowly decrease the medication keeping her in the comatose state.

Each morning when Nikki stood by her mother's bedside, she noticed the bruising and swelling around her eyes seemed to be lessening. Remembering her recent chat with God in the local church, she quickly offered up a silent word of thanks. The large gashes in Lara's arms and legs were healing well; especially now all the stitches had been removed. Despite leaving raw and red wounds, the plastic surgeon had been able to do an excellent job to ensure there would be minimal scarring.

On the twelfth day while Suzie sat beside Lara's bed and Nikki was down at the cafeteria buying them both a much-needed coffee, the patient's eyelids began to flutter and her fingers started to twitch.

Rushing to the door, Suzie called out, "Quickly, get the doctor *per favore!*

Something's happening. I think she's waking up!"

Hearing her cry, several of the staff came running from all parts of the ward. Everyone had been praying for a miracle, so this was the hope they all needed. By the time Nikki came back with the coffee, five people were bending over her mother's bed.

"*Nooo!*" Both cups fell from her hands as she ran to see what was going on.

Two of the nurses stood aside when she fell beside the bed, grasping her mother's hand and burying her face into Lara's stomach, thinking she was gone forever. In the midst of all this anguish, Nikki felt a soft wisp of fingers touch her hair. She looked up with tears streaming down her cheeks. Those familiar blue eyes that always glowed with pride whenever they looked her way were once again fastened on Nikki's face, not twinkling like usual, but open and enquiring ... and the most welcome sight she had ever seen.

Still clutching Lara's hand, a relieved grin lit up her face as a few large droplets fell from her chin onto the coverlet.

Anxious to see her mother clearly, she swatted the wetness away with the back of her hand. "Mummy, you're back!" she exclaimed, resorting automatically to the childhood name. Sending a relieved smile Heavenwards, she mouthed a heartfelt, "Thank you..." and then sighed loudly as those loving eyes captured hers once more. "I *knew* you'd come back to me. I've been so worried and missed you so much."

With the trachea tube still protruding from deep in her neck, Lara could only smile faintly and try to mouth her daughter's name. It was all the encouragement the young woman needed for her spirits to soar. For the first time since answering her grandparents' cryptic phone call, she felt confident everything was going to be all right.

The doctor arrived a few minutes later and carefully removed the complicated apparatus so Lara could breathe on her own at last. Those standing around watched with their hearts in their mouths, until a rasping cough could be heard and she took her first unassisted breath in nearly two weeks. Though it sounded ghastly, everyone broke into huge grins and loud exclamations of relief. Minus that thick piece of tubing and with most of the bandages gone from her head, Lara now looked far more like the woman her family knew and loved. Nikki and Suzie could only hug each other in relief. The white wad of gauze dressing covering the gaping wound was a welcome sight after the horror of thinking she may never breathe on her own again.

"Your mum's going to be okay, Nikki, I just *know* it," the jubilant aunt laughed as she held her niece's face in her hands and kissed her soundly.

"I know, but I'm still having trouble believing it," Nikki responded, glancing down at the patient once more. She was so choked up, all she could do was squeeze Lara's hand when her mother reached out to her. No words were necessary. The strength of their grip conveyed exactly how the other one was feeling.

For the rest of the afternoon, Suzie and Nikki stayed by her bedside, explaining in detail everything that had been going on since the dreadful accident and subsequent phone call. Lara couldn't respond much except to offer a smile, a nod or to simply blink her eyes. The gaping hole in her throat prevented any form of oral communication. Even so, it was enough – they had their beloved mother and sister back.

That night, back at the B&B, Nikki dialled a familiar number. Charles and Elizabeth both picked up at the same time. She had been making regular calls to keep them up-to-date with what was happening, and they were ecstatic at the news.

"Does this mean she can come home soon?" Elizabeth asked.

"The doctors still can't say – they need to carry out a load of tests to check if there's any form of residual brain damage from the fracture, and there still hasn't been any movement in her legs. That's the major worry now. But it looks as if she'll at least be able to talk once her throat's fully healed. Thankfully, she's turned a major corner, and that's the best news yet!"

In a twisted form of unison, it hit them all at the same time what implications the trachea wound could have on Lara's vocal cords. There was still a distinct possibility she may never sing again. If there were to be any damage at all, it would inevitably mean the end of her career. Underlying all of this was the possibility she may never walk again.

Even though this sombre thought cast a pall over all the former good news, they were still in high spirits when it came time to hang up. Afterwards, and on opposite sides of the world, prayers of gratitude were said for having their beloved Lara back.

Wandering into their bedroom after enjoying the soothing effects of a long hot shower, Charles was just running a towel through his thick shock of grey hair when he found Elizabeth propped up in bed with a sad look on her face.

Stretching a loving hand out to him, she asked, "Isn't it time we made a phone call to England ... especially now that we have better news?"

With his expression matching hers, Charles shook his head and lay down beside her. Snuggling in close, he rested his cheek against her breast. "Not yet, my love. Not until we can ask Lara what she wants. It has to be her decision."

Recognising his wisdom, she nodded sadly and then reached down to softly kiss the only lips she had known intimately for nearly fifty years. "You're a wise man, Mr Ashworth; it's no wonder I love you so much."

A little while later as she lay in the darkness with the sound of heavy breathing coming from the other side of the bed, Elizabeth's heart ached for a man who was completely oblivious to everything that had been happening to the only woman he had ever truly loved.

§

The following day the doctors were even more optimistic when they noticed Lara was able to wiggle one of her toes slightly. There was no other movement in any other part of her legs, but at least this was a hopeful sign.

Nikki and Suzie arrived straight after breakfast and were greeted with her sunny smile and outstretched arms. The strips of gauze covering the wound in Lara's throat were a welcome sight after the scary breathing contraption she had been hooked up to yesterday. She still was unable to speak without a lot of difficulty and pain, so a thoughtful nurse had given her a small whiteboard and marker to relay anything she wanted to say. In typical Lara-fashion, her first thought was for her daughter – mainly concern for how she was coping and appreciation for her being there. Nikki was quick to reassure her she was much better now after all the worry of recent weeks.

The nurses warned they could only stay for a short while as the exertion of breathing on her own and the excitement of being able to communicate would soon wear the patient out. The visitors were thankful for whatever time they were offered, and Lara communicated via a series of messages using shaky scrawls or gestures to convey her love and gratitude. When her eyelids started to grow heavy, Suzie and Nikki nudged each other and got up to go. They left her with warm hugs, relieved smiles and promises to return later in the day.

Their first task was to make a visit to Antonio and Claudia's hillside villa. The excited Aussies were eager to fill them in on the wonderful news. Over the next couple of hours, the courtyard resounded with a flurry of happy chatter and loud exclamations over a spontaneous celebratory lunch their hosts were able to rustle up from the vineyard's veggie garden and well-stocked pantry. Nikki and Suzie left around two with a large bouquet of flowers gathered from the garden, along with firm promises for the patient that her Italian friends would drop by in a few days once her strength had returned.

Charles and Elizabeth put a call through to the hospital that night. With the two women acting as interpreters, Lara was able to answer all of their questions through her written words.

After a few minutes of excited banter back and forth on the speaker phone, Elizabeth cautiously broached the subject foremost on her mind ever since the accident.

"Lara, I really think Adam needs to be told what's happened. Would you be agreeable if we put a call through to London? Naturally, he'll be devastated, but it'd be far worse if he heard about your accident from another source."

Lara shook her head adamantly, despite the pain it caused. Her eyes were blazing as she wrote in big letters across the board:

"NO! NO! NO!"

Suzie's heart broke as she conveyed the message down the line, and all four tried whatever coercion they could think of to make her change her mind. Much to their dismay, the answer remained the same as she double underscored each word.

Charles took over from his wife. "But my dear girl, he's going to find out somehow. The local papers have published several articles about your accident. When he arrives home, someone's bound to tell him – besides, all the theatres are sure to be buzzing with the news. It's only a matter of time..."

But her decision was set in stone, and the pen moved swiftly across the board:

"Don't want him to <u>EVER</u> find out. He'll want to come but he MUSTN'T see me like this. DEVASTATE him <u>AND</u> wreck his MARRIAGE. <u>MUST NOT TELL!!!</u>"

She underlined the last three words over and over, determined to get her point across ... and nothing anyone could say would make her change her mind.

Despite this adamant refusal, the call ended on a happy note with both Charles and Elizabeth reiterating their joy at the news, and sending promises to call again the following day. A string of noisy kisses was blown down the line from their end, and Lara's face was beaming, though no audible sound could be heard when she attempted to send a similar form of farewell. Nikki quickly mimicked her mother's response with sound effects so her grandparents on the other side of the world could understand what was going on. They rung off with happy chuckles and loads of well wishes for a good night's sleep for everyone.

Talking to Elizabeth and Charles had been a huge emotional rollercoaster for the patient. The others recognised the signs of exhaustion in her eyes and got up to leave. Lara shook her head and smiled as she grasped Nikki's hand. Picking up the board again, she began writing another message to her daughter.

"I <u>love</u> you, precious girl. Thanks for not giving up on me – and for asking God to perform a miracle. See, I <u>know you too well</u>!"

Nikki grinned and nodded in confirmation, then blew her mother a kiss. Still Lara continued to write – this time more frantically and with steely determination.

Tears pooled in the young woman's eyes as she gave a heartfelt sigh and swallowed hard. It was obvious she had to do as her mother asked ... even though her heart was breaking.

"Alright ... I promise ... but I *know* you're wrong. He *really* needs to know, Mum."

Remembering the look on Adam's face the night they had talked following *A Little Night Music,* it was clear as crystal how much he still cared and would want to hear about the accident.

Oh, Mum, you need him ... now more than ever before. Why are you being so pigheaded and stubborn?

Deep down, she knew the reason. Lara would never want to burden Adam ... she still loved him too much to put him through this after everything else.

For the longest of moments, she continued searching Lara's eyes, imploring her to change her mind ... but that stare never wavered. Resigned to do as she was bid, with a sad smile Nikki bent down and gently kissed her mother's cheek instead. It had been a big day for all of them.

Even so, this determined young woman wasn't about to give up the fight. As she turned to leave, Nikki deliberately picked up the pewter statue and placed it directly in her mother's line of sight. Before following Suzie outside, she sent her one final long hard look. Lara's only response was to shake her head sadly.

A little while later and just before the sleeping pills kicked in, her weary gaze fell on the familiar work of art she had been avoiding all day. Closing her eyes to deaden the pain of knowing their long-held dream was now dead and gone, she quickly turned her face to the wall so no one could witness her heartache.

But her spirit still cried out to him.

Oh, Teddy, I know my precious girl means well, but any skerrick of hope is now long gone. I couldn't bear for you to see me like this – half a woman with no chance of anything else ... that's all I'll ever be now. You deserve so much more – you need so much more.

Goodbye again, my darling love ... and this time it has to be forever. Any hope for our future has disappeared. Stay safe and I pray your life will be filled with happiness, even though I'll never get to see that beautiful smile again...

Chapter 38

T he weather was turning bitterly cold as November rolled around. Suzie and Nikki stood beside a pile of suitcases as they said their goodbyes to the hosts of the B&B, their home for the last six weeks. The couple's hospitality had been a godsend with lots of little extras thrown in, including the use of their second motor vehicle.

A local taxi pulled up to take them to the train station. With one last wave, they were away, heading for home and the warmth of summertime *Down Under*.

It had been an arduous few weeks while Lara struggled to learn to talk again. Scar tissue from the tracheotomy had left her unable to speak at anything more than a whisper. Even so, it was a very small sacrifice after only being able to communicate via the whiteboard during the first two weeks following the coma.

The speech therapist was cautiously optimistic her voice would be back to normal within a few months, even going so far as to say he felt she would one day be able to sing again. Lara's radiant smile was more than enough thanks for all the hard work he had put in to bring her to this stage of the healing process. Much to his surprise, a generous money order had arrived through the hospital's postal system with the return address *C & E Ashworth, Jesmond Road, Fig Tree Pocket, Queensland, Australia* printed across the flap. Every staff member involved in her recovery had received a similar offering during her last week in hospital. Due to the beautifully worded albeit articulately adamant notes tucked inside each envelope, none of the recipients ever mentioned to the patient herself about their unexpected windfall.

The prognosis for Lara's paralysis was nowhere near as hopeful, despite her concerted efforts to at least be standing at the parallel bars when the all-clear came for her to return home. Movement in her toes was increasing marginally, though she still couldn't flex either of her ankles or knees. With only a slight sensation from just below her thighs showing up throughout the countless and rigorous daily tests, it was going to be a long and slow process. Regardless of all these unfortunate setbacks, she was determined to walk again no matter how long it took.

Having already graduated to a wheelchair, once Lara was able to show she could stay comfortably upright for a few hours at a time, the doctors willingly signed her discharge papers for the lengthy and arduous journey home. Nikki and Suzie were there when the doctor delivered the good news, and all those within earshot let out a loud cheer. They knew how taxing the whole process had been on their patient, and not only from being away from the rest of her family and friends for so long, but also having to deal with a foreign language as she tried to decipher whatever the medical staff were trying to convey. Thankfully, Nikki had been by her side for the entire time and able to interpret many of the unfamiliar medical terms.

Antonio and Claudia had visited nearly every afternoon, bringing all sorts of treats from her kitchen to help keep Lara's strength up. Even while she was lying flat on her back, Antonio continued his flirtatious ways. Several of the nursing staff looked for any excuse to drop by during his visits, hoping to be on the receiving end of some of his flattery. Lara's room became the life of the ward for a few hours every afternoon, which then turned out to be one of the best tonics to aid in her recovery.

On the eve of their departure, Lara and the family invited their Italian friends to join them beneath the spreading canopy of one of the region's oldest stone pines growing in the hospital's courtyard. Claudia had brought along a large saucepan filled to the brim with duck ravioli fresh from her kitchen. The dish had become one of Lara's favourites, so it was the ideal way to end her stay.

The hungry group was keen to savour the tasty fare and quickly took their places around a rustic wrought-iron table. Once Suzie made sure Lara's wheelchair was securely in place, they all joined hands as Antonio sent up a quick prayer of thanks. Much to everyone's amusement, once he pronounced the final amen, this always-amorous Latino leaned over and planted a firm kiss on his wife's cheek. Lara looked across at her daughter and sister, and the trio exchanged happy smirks – one definitive memory from their stay was observing the passionate and fun-loving relationship the Italian couple shared.

Glorious views out to rolling hills covered in vineyards and olive trees provided the perfect backdrop as they soaked up the last dribbles of creamy mushroom and white wine sauce with thick slices of home-baked bread.

The Aussies would miss the husband and wife duo more than any of them would admit. When it came time for goodbyes, it was no surprise the tears flowed freely. Despite her spritely gait and bustling manner, Claudia was now in her mid-seventies. Considering her age as well as Lara's injuries, both women realised this could very likely be the last time they would ever see each other. Saying goodbye was much harder than either one anticipated.

As a way to ease their sadness, Claudia set about giving Lara extra incentive to get back on her feet. "You must promise you will keep onto doing those exercises to get bigger and stronger. Then you walk well to meet me when we come for a visit to your country," she lectured as the tears continued. With both hands cradling her friend's cheeks and the hint of a smile to take away the sting, her voice shook as she went on. "I want to be 'earing how well you are becoming so I no need to worry anymore."

Lara tried to smile through watery eyes when she heard the emotion peppering the stilted speech. "Oh, *mia dolce amica*, I promise to do everything I'm told to get better. Then when you come for a visit I'll run to you, you'll see."

"*Splendido!*" Claudia clapped her hands. "I will make sure to come if you will do that. And you will make sure Elizabeth *telefoni* to me with 'ow well you are being."

"I'll tell her, I promise ... the minute I start walking again! You've been such a wonderful support and *un amico molto speciale* through all of this. *Grazie, bella signora!*"

"*Prego! Ti amo...*"

"I love you too, and I always will." They held each other tightly with neither one wanting the hug to end.

As Claudia was getting ready to leave, Antonio crouched down beside Lara's chair and pulled a small black box from his pocket.

"This is from Mamma and me to carry with you wherever you go."

Inside she found a tiny gold medallion lying on a bed of white satin with the form of a woman carved into its face.

"Oh, Antonio, it's beautiful, *gracie, amico mio.*"

"She is our *Blessed Margaret of Castello*, the patron saint for anyone with *una disabilità*. She lived very close to our town many centuries ago and was born with *una terribile afflizione*. Mamma and I believe she will watch over you and make you well, so we wish you to wear it on your watch or carry it in your purse so it goes everywhere you are. Then you will remember our Lord is with you always. And I know she will also be praying for you from *Paradiso*."

A huge lump formed in Lara's throat as she picked up the precious icon. Putting her arms around his shoulders, she planted a warm kiss on her dear friend's weathered cheek. "Oh, Antonio, this is so *bella e speciale,* and I promise to wear it always. *Grazie molto molto,* and you too, *cara* Claudia. Both of you are such generous people and have been so kind to our little family. I'll never forget either of you – ever," she said, reaching out her hand to include his wife.

Claudia bent down and the two women held each other tightly, although Lara was too choked up to say anything more. She knew how much their faith meant to them after Nikki relayed how often the pair visited the old church to pray for her healing, and then to give thanks afterwards once she was out of danger.

"Ah, Nikki," Antonio said with a sad twinkle in his eyes as he took the young woman in his arms. "Stay safe, *bambina*, and don't forget about your old *amico Italiano* when you find yourself a boyfriend back 'ome or I will be *molto geloso!*"

She laughed through her tears and hugged him tightly, relishing the times spent with the loving couple throughout all of the recent drama. "I won't, Uncle Antonio! At least now Aunty Claudia will have no need to be *geloso* of all the young nurses receiving your attention!"

"*Si,* Nikki! 'Tonio, you need to listen to this wise *signora giovane!* It is my turn now to 'ave you to myself!" his wife joined in, sweeping the young woman into her arms and planting extravagant kisses on both her cheeks.

Suzie looked on with affection. Since meeting the charming couple, she could easily understand the love her family had for them and was feeling just as sad saying goodbye.

Not wanting to miss out, Lara quickly wheeled herself over to be included in the embrace, pulling her sister along too so she was part of it as well. A bearhug encompassing all of them was the perfect way to end their stay.

Lara's heart felt as though it was breaking while waving her friends goodbye. She quickly had to wipe away a few stray tears as her gaze followed their progress out through the hospital grounds. The trio left behind were a subdued lot as Nikki wheeled her mother back inside. Suzie walked beside the chair, squeezing her sister's hand.

§

The following morning an ambulance pulled up outside the main entrance to the hospital. It was there to take Lara to Florence airport. A specially outfitted private jet used to transport patients with serious medical conditions was waiting for her on the tarmac. Charles had organised everything, including a nurse to accompany her all the way, and all was in readiness to ensure she had the best of care while in the air.

Nikki and Suzie had been allocated seats at the front of the plane. This flight would be far different from the one filled with panic and uncertainty when they first flew halfway around the world. Lara was prepared for a tiring ordeal, but she didn't mind. It was a relief to be leaving after enduring such a long stay in a foreign hospital. Her new home, at least for the next few months God-willing, would be a single room in a rehab centre. As long as she was in Brisbane with family and friends close by, she could deal with the rest.

At long last the singer was on her way home, still quite broken and with an uncertain future ahead. Despite having to face this horrible ordeal, she would never regret being part of an enchanting concert in a picturesque Tuscan town ... nor retracing her footsteps along the quaint streets once shared with her soulmate.

§

In another country a long way west of where the recent farewell occurred,

525

Adam's London season was coming to an end.

Following two months of rehearsals, the production had enjoyed a five-month run with every performance playing to a packed house. Now in its final week, he and Trina were about to spend two weeks together in the south of France. The popular actor had certainly made a name for himself in the busy cosmopolitan city and he enjoyed entertaining theatregoers, despite the continual run of late nights. Mixing with the crème de la crème of the acting fraternity was an added bonus that could open up other doors for the future. Following a miserably wet autumn, it was no wonder he was looking forward to relaxing on a warm beach and visiting the scenic Mediterranean townships scattered along the Riviera before heading back to the slower pace of home.

One thing he definitely wouldn't miss were the flocks of paparazzi continually hounding him every time he stepped foot outside the hotel. Even more importantly, he needed to get back to the warmth of his hometown. The colder weather always played havoc with his chest, something he couldn't risk when singing was his life, and one of England's bitter winters was on its way. The fact it was coming into a Brisbane summer suited him perfectly.

Trina's outlook was the polar opposite. After thriving on a busy social calendar with London's glamorous high-end of society, the thought of returning home to what she was now coming to regard as small-time charity fundraisers suddenly held no appeal. So much time had passed since anything worthwhile filled her days, she had lost sight of the people who were once her sole focus.

For seven fast-paced months, her life had centred around being out every night at some opening or gala function. Along the way, she had made a swarm of good-time friends who, despite their incredible wealth, seemed to live shallow existences. There was no sense of wanting to give back to society in any shape or form. Instead, most spent their days and nights reeling from one party to the next, taking advantage of whatever was on offer.

Two days before she and Adam were due to leave, Trina waltzed into their hotel suite with a smug grin on her face.

"Guess what! I've just been invited to join the gang on Lester's private launch, cruising along the French and Italian coastlines for a few weeks. There's even the possibility I can stay on longer if I want."

Her husband's look of disbelief did nothing to stem the flow.

Casually tossing her bag onto the table, she added, "And before you say anything, I've already said yes so don't try and talk me out of it." Shrugging off her jacket and flinging it haphazardly in a corner of the coat closet, she headed for the bathroom without waiting for his reply.

Adam was aware she had been spending a lot of time with 'the gang'. He just hadn't realised how chummy they had become. It never crossed his mind she would even consider holidaying with them, especially when plans were already in place to get away by themselves.

Well acquainted with his wife's stubborn streak, he knew there was no point trying to get her to change her mind, and he certainly had no desire to provoke her into a fight. It just wasn't worth it.

While she was off getting ready for what he could only presume was her next ritzy event, he settled into his usual chair located in the window alcove and looked out to the serene greenspace making up Hyde Park. His focus wasn't on anything in particular – more pondering a future that now seemed bleak and pointless. Shrugging his shoulders and letting out an audible sigh, Adam had finally come to a place where he was ready to face reality in all of its fullness.

To be honest, I don't even think I care anymore. If that's what you want, Trina, then go for it. It's easy to see I've never really made you happy.

Their relationship had grown further and further apart over the last couple of months. Nowadays, it had reached the point where even his free days were spent alone after she had made it obvious his company was far too boring and routine for her liking. And he couldn't really blame her. He was often invited to mix with producers and those who had major pulls in theatre circles, either at late night suppers or over fancy luncheons a couple of times a week. Another society bash was the last thing he was interested in on his one day off per week.

It was actually nice to be idle for a change. He found his own company far more preferable to the gossip she usually indulged in. It gave him a chance to reflect on those things that really mattered ... like two sapphire blue eyes that had once sent his pulse racing whenever they looked his way.

When Trina sauntered out nearly an hour later decked to the nines in a long flowing gown, he decided it was time to find out exactly what was going on.

"Before you head out again, I think it'd be a good idea for us to sit down for a few minutes and discuss what's happening in our future."

"Oh, Adam, I can't stop now. I'm about to meet up with a few friends downstairs. We've been invited to dinner with Lord and Lady Chamberlain, and then we're all off to the opera, so I can't be late. They own a fifteenth-century chateau near Paris; if I'm lucky, maybe I can wangle an invitation."

"I just wanted to find out what your plans are once this cruise you're supposedly going on is done ... and from that last comment, it sounds as though you're going to be busy for the next few weeks. We really need to sit down and talk, especially with my show finishing tomorrow and the fact you're due home in a few weeks for that charity fundraiser at the Stamford Plaza. After putting in so much work to make it a success before leaving home, you can't let them down now. I realise there's no point talking about our upcoming holiday – it's obviously slipped your mind ... or you don't care. One or the other."

"Oh, I'm not getting into that now. Ask me later when I have more time. Look, I really have to go. I won't be home 'til who knows when, so we can discuss it tomorrow sometime."

Watching her sweep out the door, clearly not at all concerned about anything to do with their marriage, it finally dawned on him how unimportant and unnecessary he was to her life ... and had been for a very long time if he was completely honest with himself. It didn't matter how long they had been together, their relationship had become more acquaintances than husband and wife. It seemed the only worthwhile thing staying together had brought either one of them was when they needed a partner for the next function, or having someone to pass the time of day with every now and then ... just so long as their calendars coincided.

What a waste of a lifetime, he couldn't help berating himself. *All these years together ... and for what? Sitting alone in a hotel room thousands of miles away from the only woman I've ever truly loved ... and not even having the guts to fight for her when I had the chance. You're a stupid, stupid idiot, Peters, and you deserve everything that's happened.*

Glancing out the window of their suite, his gaze fell on a young woman putting her horse through its paces around the designated riding arena in the park opposite. The pretty scene transported him back to his parents' home and a little girl having the time of her life on the back of their once-shared mountain pony.

I'm so sorry, my darling. I've been the king of fools.

Like a billowing curtain rising to open a brand-new play, he suddenly saw a whole new future of possibilities opening up before him. If Trina wanted to go off partying, then why should he worry? She still hadn't touched a drop of alcohol, and wasn't likely to after all this time ... he had no reason left to stay.

§

It was almost four o'clock the following afternoon when his wife slipped in the door, acting as though there was nothing unusual about coming home more than twelve hours later than expected. Adam had already changed into the clothes he wore for his usual walk to the theatre. With a few minutes to kill before setting out for his final West End performance, he was just finishing off a cup of tea at his favourite spot in the bay window.

Sashaying over to pour herself a cup, Trina plonked herself down in the chair opposite, yawning loudly and obviously exhausted. He didn't say anything, just watched her blatant display of indifference towards him and for being so late.

"I suppose you want to have that talk now," she remarked nonchalantly, taking a long sip and peering out the window.

"Yes, I think that's probably a good idea. It seems we have a lot to discuss, especially from what you were telling me yesterday."

"Mmm, I guess so. So, what do you want to know?"

"What your plans are, to begin with. I'd like to know when you intend coming home now that you've decided not to come with me to France. From all the invitations arriving in the mail lately, there are a host of Australian charities eager for your return, and I'm sure the hospital must be relieved to know you'll be back soon."

She brushed a dismissive hand in the air. "Oh, they're doing fine without me. I was on the phone to the hospital director only the other day and the woman filling in for me ... what's her name ... umm ... oh, I can't remember ... anyway, she has some excellent ideas, so they don't really need me anymore. Besides, it was only something to fill in my time while you were off touring with a show, or locked away in that damned study of yours scribbling away on one of those fancy skyscrapers."

He watched her intently, though she was more interested in the goings on outside. "You could've come with me, you know. And what about if I need *you*, or have I just been something to fill in your time, too?"

Taking another long sip, she took her time thinking about an answer. Determined to receive a response, his eyes didn't leave her face. Eventually, she met his gaze and her tone was cool and distant.

"Oh Adam, you haven't needed me for a long time. In fact, I don't think you ever did. I'm sure the only reason you're still with me is so you can feel good about yourself."

Shaking his head in disbelief, her husband's tone was low but firm. "How can you say that after all the sacrifices I've made for you over the years?"

Trina's teacup hit the saucer with a loud bang and her voice rose with every sentence. "Sacrifices! *What* sacrifices? You've never made *any* sacrifices for me. I've always had to follow you from show to show if we wanted to spend any quality time together. Why do you think I came over here?"

His voice remained steady, despite her angry outburst. "Don't be ridiculous, Trina. In the early days, all you wanted was to go out to parties and get drunk. Even when things got a bit better, you always did what you wanted, when you wanted. The only reason you came over here was because of the people you could meet. We've hardly laid eyes on each other in the last few months. To be honest, I don't think you ever really loved me at all ... just the life I could offer."

Her eyes blazed as she gritted her teeth. "I ... never ... loved ... *you? That's* a bit rich. Do you want to know why I *really* moved out of our bedroom again a decade ago? Every ... single ... frigging ... night ... you called out *her* name in your sleep – sometimes over and over until I couldn't *stand* it anymore."

She jabbed her finger at him as the accusations kept coming. "*And* I'm *so* stupid I even thought things might change once we came over here, away from any reminders of her ... obviously, it didn't make any difference at all. I still see that look in your eyes whenever you think I'm not watching and I know *exactly* who it is you're thinking about. *That's* why I don't care anymore *and* why I'm not going back with you!"

What she said shocked him to the core. Adam was ashamed to learn he had been calling out Lara's name in his sleep. He felt terrible for having hurt his wife so deeply, but the venom in her voice took him back to when she had screamed at Lara over the phone ... and it was the final straw. There was only one way for him to make amends, but he refused to react as she was. Dropping his eyes, his tone was filled with regret, along with a sense of resignation.

"Trina, I truly am sorry. I had no idea that was happening. Honestly, I never meant to hurt you. I really thought we could make a go of it, but now it's obvious we both want different things ... and have done so for a very long time if we're honest. I'll be leaving for home in two days – I can't be bothered going to France by myself. You do whatever you like – divorce me, live in England, marry someone who can make you happy – whatever it is you think you need. And as far as our assets are concerned; don't worry, I'll make sure you get your fair share. I'll ring the lawyers as soon as I get back to start the ball rolling."

His sense of relief at having finally uttered those words was like a heavy weight had suddenly lifted off his shoulders. He hadn't realised just how unhappy he really was until they came tumbling out of his mouth.

Trina could feel her anger abating and the reaction surprised her. Having spent years worrying about how she would manage coping on her own, suddenly she felt invigorated at the possibility of living the life she wanted without any need for restraint. There was no one in Australia she felt close to anymore – not since Judith had thrown her away like an unwanted piece of rag. During their stay in London, she had made a host of new friends. They would help to keep her occupied for many years to come.

She looked him in the eye and he could see her whole demeanour change. "Thank you. I mean that sincerely and I *am* sorry it didn't work out for us. I still believe we loved each other at the beginning – we shared some good times when we first got married ... but it's obvious we've grown too far apart to keep on pretending."

Adam was surprised at the look of acceptance in her eyes and this new level of compassion in her voice. Letting out a sad sigh, his eyes misted over thinking back to those days.

Trina knew there was one more thing she needed to say – something her husband needed to hear. For the first time in their marriage, she put him first. At first, she hesitated, unsure exactly how to phrase it. She swallowed hard before the words spilled out – all in a rush in case this rare display of courage ran out.

"I think it's about time you went home and talked to a certain person who has always been at the forefront of everything you've done ... a woman you've loved far more than me. We both know you should've been together all along."

Adam's head snapped up. He was struck dumb and his eyes were as big as saucers as he waited for the inevitable retraction of this unexpected declaration.

Trina shifting uncomfortably in her seat beneath his intense scrutiny, but she couldn't back down now. "I realised that fact a long time ago – especially after watching you and Nikki together when your parents brought her down for *The Sound of Music* tour..."

Her words took him back to that weekend in Melbourne. A momentary wistful smile touched the corners of his mouth as he remembered both the joy and sadness of those few short days. He had been tickled pink to see the little girl, despite how desperately he was missing her mother.

In amongst all these memory joggers, the reality of the here and now pushed everything else away. Focussing again on his wife, he sent her a quizzical look, determined to learn the truth behind what she had just revealed.

She nodded knowingly, albeit without any of the old malice. "See what I mean. You only have to think about them and it's written all over your face..."

Shamefaced, he offered a contrite, "I'm sorry," then his tone turned quizzical again as he met her gaze. "But hang on, are you saying we should've split u—"

Her hand came up like a stop sign, halting him in mid-sentence. There was a lot more needing to be said, but she had to pause for a moment. He heard her take a deep breath as if rustling up the courage. This time, she was the one dropping her eyes ... and then...

"I already knew long before that weekend ... I think it was just after I talked to her in Sydney – oh no, not then – ummm ... yeah, that's right. It was when you came around to see me the next day at the house..."

His whole demeanour was a picture of despair. Leaning forward in his chair, Adam almost shouted at her, but he managed to pull himself up in time. "What are you talking about? *When* did you talk to her in Sydney?"

She looked up at him and her eyes held his, though her voice was barely more than a whisper. "Lara and I ran into each other in the hotel lobby before we had our discussion in the dining room. I talked to her for about twenty minutes – about you and me and what was best for our marriage." Her manner turned desperate as she spread her hands. "I had to, Adam ... I was fighting for my life!"

Her husband could only shake his head in disbelief as a multitude of questions exploded in his brain. Scared of what he might say or do, he clenched his jaw, waiting for her to go on. Stark white fingers gripped the handle of his cup ... but he didn't even notice.

"I could tell straight away she was exactly the type of woman you needed –

caring and compassionate, as well as strong and courageous – and it was obvious how much she loved you. That's when I really understood why you loved her so much and why she made you so happy ... but I couldn't walk away – I needed you too, so I had to put up a fight. When I begged her to let you go, the pain in her eyes was indescribable, but I didn't know what else to do..."

A mournful groan came from the other side of the table. Adam slumped back in his seat, staring out to nothingness as this unexpected confession continued.

"After lots of pleading on my part, Lara agreed to walk away ... she could see how much I needed you. And I'm pretty sure she thought it was best for you too, even though it was the last thing she wanted. Her sacrifice sealed our fate, so I took a chance on winning you back. It was only when you came around to the house the next day that I knew your heart could never be mine again ... but the wheels were already set in motion and I'd promised never to say anything to you about our talk. To be honest, my pride wouldn't let me admit what I'd done."

She hung her head in shame when she saw the look of despair in his eyes. Her hand reached out to touch his knee, but then quickly fell away, knowing any form of contact would only be an intrusion. She had caused him enough hurt as it was.

"You probably won't believe this, but I truly *am* sorry for everything I've put you through ... both of you. I honestly believed I couldn't live without you – especially back then when I had nothing else. But that's no excuse ... not after everything else. I made your life a living hell in those early years; I'm ashamed of myself ... and regret everything that's happened."

She fell back in the chair, her face a canvas of remorse.

Adam couldn't believe his ears. Unable to sit still any longer, he jumped up and began pacing the floor. He raked his hands backwards and forwards through his hair while trying to take everything in. Her admissions had been like a hot iron searing his flesh ... and the pain went even deeper.

Why did you let us squander so much time if you knew it was all a mistake? Did you hate me that much?

The words stuck in his throat and he felt like strangling her for all the wasted years. Even so, he knew any form of revenge on his part wouldn't change the past. Those days were long gone; they could never get them back. He could only hope it wasn't too late to make a future with the woman who had always brought sunshine into his life – even from afar.

Once he was able to gather his thoughts, the anger subsided and a sense of sad resignation followed. As though compelled by an unseen hand, he reached out and drew her into his arms. Feelings of gratitude for her honesty and obvious regret replaced everything else. No matter what, he couldn't hate Trina, and he certainly never meant to hurt her so deeply.

She went into them and clung to him like a drowning child. Deep down Adam realised this embrace was also a farewell and most likely the last time either of them would ever see each other again. He wanted to make sure their last moments together would be something they could look back on with a hint of fondness rather than filled with hatred or blame.

Trina slumped in his arms and began weeping quietly into his shoulder. She recognised what this moment signified and could only hope she wouldn't come to regret her decision, especially now the truth of what she had done could never be retracted.

After a few minutes, he held her at arm's length. Looking into her eyes, his tone was kind.

"Thank you. You'll probably never understand just how much it means to hear you say you're sorry. And for your sake, I hope you find someone who'll love you just the way you need. I never meant to hurt you, so I'm sorry too." He pressed his lips against her forehead as a tear slowly trickled down her cheek. With a gentle fingertip, he wiped it away. "Goodbye, Trina. Be happy."

"You too, Adam ... and with Lara by your side. Goodbye."

Her last gesture of farewell was to press her lips against his cheek. Then she hurried away to her bedroom. There was nothing left to say.

Half an hour later, he let himself out of the hotel's grand entrance doors and set off for the theatre. Anyone who knew him well could easily detect the hint of a spring in his step. Deep down, there was also a touch of sadness tinging his soul at the passing of a marriage that had cost him so dearly. He had tried his best and paid the price, now his only hope was that Lara hadn't given up on him – or found someone else in the meantime.

As Adam reached Stage Door, for the first time in a long time, he could feel that welcome sense of hope building in his heart. An older couple strolling by noticed a handsome man in his mid-forties suddenly break into a wide grin. Their exchanged smiles turned into delighted chuckles when he punched the air with a closed fist and yelled at the top of his voice, "Yes!"

The theatre's regular security guard opened the door and tipped his hat with a welcoming smile. "Top of the evening to you, Mr Peters, you're looking mighty chipper tonight!"

"And you wouldn't believe just how much, William!" he beamed, with a friendly pat on the man's shoulder as he passed.

Chapter 39

Three days later, a taxi pulled into a long, sweeping driveway. As the driver passed through a set of ornate gates abutting a perfectly manicured hedge, his gaze fell on the silhouette of a stately two-storey home.

Whoa, welcome to the land of the rich and famous, rattled around in his private headspace. The dashboard clock showed it was coming up to midnight. He could tell his back-seat passenger was suffering from jetlag after observing him through the rear vision mirror trying to stifle several yawns along the way.

"Here you go. Keep the change," the man said, handing over a hundred-dollar bill.

"Oh gee, thanks, mate. Have a good night." The cabbie was happy to pocket more than a third of the fare, and he couldn't help noticing the excited glint in the other man's eyes when they exchanged nods.

"Thanks – you too. And hopefully, tomorrow will be even better. Drive safely."

It was already the second week of November and Adam had a long-awaited reunion to attend in the morning. Wanting to be refreshed and ready for the much-anticipated outcome, his first thought was to revive himself under a long steamy shower. Thirty minutes later he climbed into bed, his thoughts consumed with the woman who lived only a few suburbs away. Far too many months had passed since they had even been in the same country, let alone spent any time together. He couldn't wait for the sun to come up to see her again – and for the first time in his life, without that awful sense of guilt.

He was too excited to sleep. After tossing and turning for more than an hour, Adam decided to check the latest edition of *On Stage*, a national theatre magazine delivered to his door each month. His father had been collecting the mail each week and sorting them into various piles, so there was no need to search for long.

After feverishly scouring the pages and finding no references to Lara, he let out a huge sigh of relief. Hopefully, it meant she would be home when he knocked on her door. Just to be certain, he picked up the previous month's edition. Unfortunately, it was so badly water stained, all the pages were stuck together. Letting out a frustrated groan, he tossed it in the bin beside the bed.

Great ... typical Queensland downpour from the looks of it. Oh well, if I'm lucky, she's between shows.

If Adam had taken a few minutes to prise the first section apart, he would have come across the picture of a beautiful woman with chestnut hair in the bottom right-hand corner of page three. Accompanying it was a small headline with several paragraphs announcing the career of the famous musical theatre star had come to a sudden halt at the bottom of an Italian hillside.

Instead, he spent the next half hour rifling through earlier copies and found several references to Lara's performance in *The King and I* during its Melbourne run a few months ago. The September edition had a half-page spread about a concert soon to be held in Cortona's main *piazza*. In large letters, it stated she was to be the guest artist for André Rieu, the world-renowned composer and violinist. He devoured every word like a starved waif, trying to imagine the thrill of seeing her perform in the charming little town still so very close to his heart.

Oh, rats! Why didn't you tell me, Mum? Then he remembered her stern edict all those years ago. *Yeah, I know we agreed not to talk about her any more, but you could've made an exception just for this. I'd have given anything to take the night off and flown over to see her, even if it meant having to hide in the crowd. Crikey, I wish I'd been there...*

§

Just after eight the following morning, Adam bounded up the stairs of a familiar little cottage in Paddington that housed so many memories of a magical time in his life. In his arms, he cradled a large bouquet of yellow roses.

His heart was beating a rapid tattoo in his chest as he knocked on Lara's door. Waiting for her to answer, he looked around and noticed the garden seemed quite neglected and the windows shut tight – unusual for this time of year with summer already sharing her humid breath with all and sundry.

Oh no! I hope this doesn't mean you're away again, my darling – not now ... not when it's finally our time.

Adam could've kicked himself for not ringing first, but his main focus had been to see the look of surprise on her face rather than just hearing it in her voice. After waiting a few seconds more, he rapped loudly on the door again and tried peering through the curtains. Unfortunately, they were drawn tight, making it virtually impossible to see inside. He hurried around to the back of the house, thinking she might be hanging the washing out, but the side gate was locked tight, and there was no sign of a key.

Feeling frustrated and bitterly disappointed, he grabbed a pen and notebook from his pocket. For the next few minutes, his fingers raced across the page. With a heartfelt sigh, he pressed his lips against the fold and then tucked it securely in amongst the pretty array of blooms. As he trudged back to the car, Adam kept glancing back, hoping to catch sight of that beloved smile – but without any luck. He sent one more look up to the veranda as the powerful midnight blue Mercedes, purchased only the year before, pulled slowly out of the driveway. After ensuring the bouquet was leaning against the door with its bright splash of yellow in full view, he drove away.

When he arrived home, Adam started dialling his parents' number within seconds of walking into the kitchen. Elizabeth was thrilled to hear his voice, but her smiles soon turned to a look of despair when she learned Trina was staying in England and he was looking for Lara. Just then, her husband poked his head around the kitchen door. Anxiously, she signalled for him to pick up the other extension.

By the time Adam finished relating everything that had transpired, Charles and Elizabeth were sitting in stunned silence. Of all the times for this to happen, why now? After so many wasted years, their beloved son was finally free, while Lara was lying in a rehab centre, barely able to move. The silence was deafening, and he had no idea what was going on.

"Mum, are you still there? Why aren't you saying anything? I thought you'd be excited." He still had no idea his father was listening in on the conversation.

Remembering their promise not to say anything about the accident or even where Lara was, her reply was subdued and not at all what he was expecting. "Yes, son, I'm here. I'm just taking everything in. How are you feeling?"

He let out a long groan. "Ooh, how do you *think!* Relieved ... stunned ... sad for all the wasted years. Mostly ecstatic because it means I can finally go to Lara as a free man!"

She could hear the joy in his voice, and her heart ached.

Twice before, Elizabeth had lied by omission. This time the lie needed to be barefaced, even though it went entirely against her nature. Her thoughts were a jumbled mess as she tried to delay the inevitable for as long as possible. When she eventually managed to speak, her answer was evasive. So much so, she could easily have won an Academy Award trying to convince him ... and herself ... just how happy she was.

"That's wonderful, dear! It's what your father and I have been waiting for all these years. I just pray you'll be happy together."

"Well, you certainly won't have to worry about that! The only time I've ever been truly happy was when we were together. I can't wait to tell her what's happened ... except I have no idea where she is. I've just been around to the cottage, but there's no sign of either her or Nikki. The garden's all untidy too – it's as though nothing's been done to it in weeks."

Elizabeth grimaced at Charles who was watching her intently. His furrowed brow and despairing look made her heart ache even more. She bit her lip and tried to form a plausible answer. Then...

"Uuummm ... oh, that's right. Nikki mentioned something about being away for a few weeks ... something about helping a friend who's going through a tough time. I'm not exactly sure when she'll be back."

She grimaced again, praying he would believe her. Her gaze travelled across the ceiling to where Adam's former bedroom was located on the upper floor. The young woman's belongings were currently taking up room in the spacious walk-in robe. Instead of going home each night to the lonely little cottage after spending all day at the rehab centre, Elizabeth and Charles had kindly offered to have her stay with them.

"Well, what about Lara? Have you any idea where she is? From the looks of the place, she must've been away for a while. I've been through every *On Stage* magazine since going to London ... well most, except for one that was soaked through. There's no reference to anything she might be currently involved with, so I've got no idea where she could be. Oh, and by the way, please thank Dad for collecting the mail for me."

"Sure, son," she said with a sigh. At least she could respond to that truthfully.

"Well, have you heard anything? All I could find was a half-page article about the André Rieu concert in Cortona ... but that was a couple of months ago. I'd have thought she'd be back by now. How come you didn't tell me?"

Elizabeth's heart was in her mouth as another worried glance was sent Charles' way. "Tell you what?"

"About the *concert* – you must've known I'd be interested. Yeah, I know we agreed not to talk about her, but the least you could've done was tell me she was performing in my favourite little town. It's not like I could do anything from London." He didn't dare mention he would have flown over just to see her.

Charles knew he had to help his wife out and quickly cut in. "Hello, son, I've just been listening in on the other extension. First and foremost, from the little I heard about what's been going on between you and Trina ... it's about time! All I can say is, *thank goodness!* It's just a damned shame all this didn't happen a long time ago."

"Oh hi, Dad, I didn't realise you were there. Yeah, I know. It's wonderful news, though I could've strangled Trina when she first told me about her meeting with Lara ... still, there's nothing I can do about it now, and I sure can't turn back the clock ... as much as I want to."

"I wish you could, too – more than you know." Charles' voice was nearly breaking as he answered. *Even two months ... things could be so different.*

Sending him a worried stare, Elizabeth's finger flew to her lips, fearful he might blurt out about the accident. All her husband could do was raise his shoulders, shake his head sadly and roll his eyes in resignation.

"Well, do *you* know where Lara is? As I just said to Mum, I was sure she'd be back from Italy by now." The longing in the bewildered man's voice was obvious.

Once again his parents exchanged heartbroken looks. "Well, I heard she did decide to stay on for quite a bit longer afterwards..."

"Mmm, well that makes sense. Maybe she wanted to take a long holiday seeing the house is all closed up – I know she always wanted to go back there, but I hope she doesn't stay away too long. Anyway, what happened at the concert? How did it go? You *must* know something about that."

At last, they were onto a topic able to bring a smile to his mother's face. It didn't take long before she was singing Lara's praises. "Oh, apparently it was fabulous! Claudia and Antonio were in the front row and said she was *'Magnifica!'* I can just picture Antonio sprouting on and on with his usual flair! They were so proud to hear her sing in their hometown, and the three of them were able to catch up quite a lot before she left Tuscany."

Once again, the sadness returned to keep her company, remembering all those sombre phone calls when her Italian friends conveyed news of Lara's slow progress.

"So where is she *now?* You *must* know – she always keeps in touch with you and Dad. Lara wouldn't just disappear off the face of the earth."

Elizabeth's eyes filled with tears. She was picturing the beautiful though still badly broken woman wheeling herself out to their car to say goodbye following a visit to her new home only the day before.

His father's tone was grim as he tried to think of a credible excuse. "Mmm, maybe she's gone off on an extended vacation somewhere. From what we heard, she had a really busy time over in Italy. We spoke to her not long after the concert and she had decided to stay over there for a while longer; there was a heap of things on her agenda that would take a fair bit of time to get through."

He shrugged his shoulders at his wife – how else was he expected to dodge all their son's probing questions?

At her understanding nod, Charles continued. "I know the poor woman was exhausted by the time she arrived home a few days ago. I wouldn't be surprised if she's resting up for a while, far away from everything. You know how much she loves her privacy."

Adam was relieved to hear his father talk about her so freely. It was years since any of them had brought Lara's name up in conversation. He could picture her wandering around Rome, visiting all the sites he had promised to show her one day. It was natural to assume she would spend some time at the old villa and he wondered if Claudia had offered her the master suite or whether, like him, she had slept in the smaller one Nikki used.

"Well, just so long as she's okay. After what happened with Trina and me, maybe I could've joined her for a few days instead of coming straight home. I wish I'd known she was over there. Then the two of us could've explored all the places we missed out on last time, and spent time with Claudia and Antonio again. I bet she had a fabulous time, especially performing with André."

"I'm not really sure just how much exploring she was able to do..."

"Oh, I hope she was able to do at least a little bit – there's nothing like European architecture to stir the blood! I'll never forget our holiday there – especially staying in Cortona and then climbing up through the Duomo in Florence. That was the best holiday of my life!" He gave a hearty chuckle, realising the possibilities now opening up to them. "Hopefully we'll be able to do it again in the not too distant future ... just as soon as I can find out where she's hiding. I tell you – that woman's like an elusive butterfly at the moment..."

His mother couldn't stifle the cry rising out of her heart, quickly stammering something about a pot on the stove needing her attention. With a hand clamped over her mouth, she dropped the phone and ran from the room. No other love story had ever moved her like theirs. It was no wonder she couldn't handle hearing the hope in his voice knowing Lara had locked hers away forever.

"Is Mum okay, Dad? She sounded a bit strange just then."

Charles tried to sound upbeat. "Oh, she's fine, son. Just gone to check on our lunch, I think – it smells like something's burning. Sorry, I can't help you any more with finding out where Lara is ... rest assured I would if I could."

"Oh well, I'm sure Suzie knows. I'll give her a ring soon, but I'd better call Max first, just to let him know I'm home. He might even know where she is. Anyway, it's been great catching up ... I'm so glad to be home after so long."

"It's great to have you back too." He didn't dare reply to the other comments.

"Thanks, and I'll drop by to see you in the next day or two – once I get everything else sorted. Please give Mum my love, and take care of yourselves ... I've missed you."

"We've missed you, too. Take care ... and don't worry. I'm sure Lara will be okay."

Elizabeth was watching from the doorway when Charles hung up the phone. Seeing the anguish on her face was almost too painful to bear. All he could do was wrap her in his arms ... and together their hearts cried for two very special people who now had yet another Everest to conquer.

§

Adam tried ringing Suzie later that afternoon, then again at night. He started again first thing in the morning and persisted several times throughout the day. Much to his disappointment, there was never any answer.

Oh well, I'll try again tomorrow. Seems like everyone's out of town at the moment...

Lara's sister had been home all the time, forcing herself not to pick up the phone after Elizabeth warned of his impending call. Charles made the same phone call to Max. Between them, they managed to forewarn the few people who knew what had happened ... and it broke their hearts. The promise Lara had forced from everyone aware of her accident, as well as her decision to keep Adam at arm's length, was now a chain around all their necks. The only person with the key was Lara herself, and they all knew how stubborn she could be at times.

Two of their closest friends had no idea of Adam's frustration. Lucy and Jeff were currently holidaying in Europe, oblivious to the drama unfolding back home.

§

A few hours following what was supposed to be Adam's surprise visit to Lara, Nikki dropped by the cottage to check for any mail and water the plants. It was a ritual she kept every day after visiting her mother. Walking up the stairs, she couldn't help noticing a beautiful bouquet of yellow roses lying against the door. She picked them up to read the note attached, and her spirit plummeted.

Oooh nooo, not nooow! Oh, you poor man; she's never going to let you see her. I'm so sooo sorry.

She couldn't sleep and ended up tossing and turning for hours, worrying about Adam and what he was about to face. She kept glancing over at the vase and each time her heart sank. They were a constant reminder of a conversation she and her mother needed to have the following day.

§

Lara's eyes lit up as soon as she spied Nikki coming through the door with a spectacular display of yellow roses weighing down her arms.

"Oh darling, they're gorgeous! But you shouldn't be spending your hard-earned wages on me," she croaked in a breathy whisper.

Nikki took a deep breath as she wordlessly placed the arrangement on the hospital trolley directly in front of her mother.

Lara noticed her daughter's apprehensive expression. After sending her a quizzical frown, she buried her nose deep in the centre and inhaled the heady fragrance. A small card protruding from a plastic holder grazed her skin when she moved in closer. "Ouch!" Peering closer, she instantly recognised the distinctive handwriting. Nikki watched on helplessly when Lara closed her eyes and covered her mouth with a trembling hand in an effort to stifle a wretched cry.

"I'm so sorry, Mum. They were waiting on the veranda when I went home to collect the mail yesterday. Obviously, he's back in Australia."

Lara had to blink her eyes several times to decipher the words on the card.

To My Beautiful Lara — always the love of my life,

After all these years, now it's finally our turn! Eternity won't be long enough to play all the music that's been waiting in our souls … but let's start creating a symphony of love and laughter together right now…

Come away with me and I'll take care of you always … it doesn't matter what's happened in the past — we never have to be apart again.

All my love forever … Your Teddy xxoo

In shock, she clutched the card close to her breast. When Nikki saw her expression, it broke her heart.

"*Oooh, nooo!* How does he *know?* Did you tell him? What am I going to *do,* Niks? I don't want Adam thinking he has to take care of me!"

You don't know the half of it, Mum, the young woman's spirit whispered into infinity.

Nikki handed over a piece of notepaper that had been folded in half, her eyes brimming with unshed tears.

"Mum, don't worry. He doesn't know about the accident. This was with them, too … obviously written after he wrote that card. Promise me you'll read it with an open heart."

She squeezed in close on the bed beside her mother, resting a comforting arm around her shoulders as Lara devoured the words Adam had written.

12 November 2004

My Darling and Adorable and Sweetest Lara…

SWEETHEART, I'M FREE!

Yes, it's true — honestly!!! Trina's staying on in London and we're getting a divorce. At LAST, you and I can be together!!

I dropped by to see you today, but there was no one home. PLEASE ring me as soon as you get back — I have so much to tell you, and I'm already designing our new home overlooking the Glasshouse Mountains. Now we can spend the rest of our lives together! I hope you're as excited as I am!!

I CAN'T WAIT TO SEE YOU, BABY … THIS IS OUR TIME … FINALLY!

My love always and always and ALWAYS, Your Adam xoxo

The desperation in Lara's eyes was more than Nikki could bear. Shaking her head from side to side, the injured woman's cry was stifled by the scar tissue marring her throat, although it was just as gut-wrenching.

"Oh, no ... no ... *nooo!* Not *now!* I can't – there's no – oh, I just can't let him see me, Nikki, you know that. Oooh, why *now?* Why has this happened when my *stupid* legs won't work. We can't possibly have a future together ... I won't let him see me like this – I *can't* ... *nooo,* it's not *fair!*"

Pounding at her legs with clenched fists, Lara's mournful wail rose from a heart that had been shattered into tiny pieces once again.

Nikki grabbed her by the shoulders and looked straight into those tearful blue eyes. "But Mum, he *loves* you. He won't care what's happened! You know Uncle Adam ... he'll only want to help you as much as he can."

Lara couldn't answer. She just kept shaking her head from side to side as the tears flowed.

"Mum, look at me, please. Just think what it'll be like when he hears you've been going through all this alone. You know he's bound to find out. Don't you think it'd be better if you told him before somebody else does? You *have* to..."

Lara's husky whisper grew louder and even more desperate. "But I'm *not* alone ... I have you and Suzie and Charles and Elizabeth. I couldn't bear to see the pity in his eyes whenever he looks at me. Promise me, if you ever run into him, tell him I've moved interstate or something – anything to help him forget."

Shaking her mother by the shoulders, desperation made Nikki rougher than intended. "*Now* you're being *ridiculous! Think* about it. He *knows* you haven't moved – Aunty Elizabeth would've told him – so he'd *never* believe me. And how could he *possibly* forget now when he hasn't after all these years."

"But he *has* to! You can make up something – *anything*. Promise me, Nikki ... *promise!*"

The only answer was a tentative nod. Nikki was convinced her mother was making a terrible mistake. But knowing that stubborn streak, she figured it would be fruitless trying to convince Lara to change her mind.

Their eyes met and the look of relief in those sad blue ones knowing her wishes would be granted broke the other one's heart. When Lara caught sight of the pain in her daughter's eyes, she buried her face in her hands. Wracking sobs tore through her broken body as the full realisation of his message hit home.

All Nikki could do was cradle her close as waves of grief threatened to engulf them both.

Chapter 40

By the time December rolled around, Lara was growing more and more frustrated. No amount of exercise or determination would make her stupid legs respond the way she wanted them to.

Punching the top of her thighs as hard as she could, she cried out, "I'm so *sick* of this! I'm *never* going to walk again at this rate. I don't even know why I bother ... grrr..."

"Come on, Lara, five more and then we'll call it a day."

Josh, her ever-patient physio, wouldn't let her give up until the allotted hour was over, no matter how tired she was.

Summoning all of her energy to push shaky feet against the leg press was the hardest thing she had to do in the twice-daily routine. Her arms had already regained a lot of their strength from manoeuvring the wheelchair around the hospital corridors and along the many pathways in the park next door. Being forced to endure a heap of weight exercises, both in the morning and again in the afternoon, had been the greatest help to get her body back in top form – all except for 'these stubborn, useless pieces of meat forever dangling hideously off my body' as she was heard to moan on a regular basis. Whenever she tried to gain the slightest amount of traction against the apparatus they would start to spasm, which meant the press wouldn't budge more than a centimetre or two.

In the month since taking up residence in the rehab facility, Lara had been able to sense a slight amount of feeling along the entire length of both legs. Even her ankles were slowly regaining some movement. This turned out to be the best incentive for Josh to coax her into taking a few twisted steps, even though she had to cling for dear life to the parallel bars. Only this morning he had let out a loud "Woo-hoo" after she managed five clumsy shuffles before collapsing in a heap on the floor. With his usual patience, he dragged her back into the wheelchair while she died of embarrassment all over again. The health-care worker was excited at her progress ... but it was never enough for his patient.

Sometimes she was reduced to tears, furiously berating herself for giving up when the regime became too much. Then with some more gentle coaching and deep breathing exercises, he could usually lift her spirits enough to try and reach that elusive goal once more.

§

Four weeks earlier, on Lara's very first day in this new 'home away from home', Nikki was unpacking her mother's suitcase when she brought out the pewter piece with the word *Hope* fashioned in large fancy letters. With a determined flourish and a loud, "There you go, now do your stuff!" she placed the sculpture on the windowsill, directly in Lara's field of vision.

Unable to resist its pull, the patient found her eyes being drawn to the sentimental keepsake. And in an instant, all of that old pain came flooding back.

Blinking away the tears, she stated adamantly, "You might as well take that home again and shove it at the back of a drawer. I don't have the strength or the faith to trust what it says anymore."

All of that old hope of one day sharing a life with Adam was long gone. He deserved to be on the world's greatest stages making a name for himself, not hampered by an invalid. If she couldn't be a fully able-bodied wife walking proudly by his side, there was no place for her in his life. The love she felt ran too deep and she couldn't have borne seeing the pity in his eyes.

But Nikki wouldn't be swayed. The young woman was even more determined than her mother. Lara had certainly passed on her genes to the feisty almost twenty-one-year-old, especially when it came to stubbornness.

Confident Lara would one day walk again, she was quick to challenge the defeatist statement. "It's *not* coming home with me – I don't care what you say. I know you originally bought it for another reason, but at least for now it's going to be your incentive to get out of that chair and walk again. *I'm* not giving up hope, and neither are *you!*"

Her forceful attitude was exactly what Lara needed. Three days later she made a promise to herself and a bold sign was taped to the window just above the pewter piece. Seeing them together became her greatest motivations.

By Christmas, I'll be walking again.

I will never give up ... I will never give in.

I'm going to live in hope every day for the rest of my life.

§

Those on duty at the rehab centre would never forget the loud displays of emotion accompanying Charles and Elizabeth's first visit on the morning following the new patient's arrival. They were used to moving scenes from other similar encounters, but this one went much deeper, though none of them had any idea what lay behind it. Cries of joy underpinned with tinges of sadness wafted under the door to Lara's room.

The Ashworths were both shocked and distressed to see the frailty of her condition. Charles used all of his acting prowess to disguise his sorrow by plying her for news of the concert. His wife followed suit with questions about what was happening in the lives of their old Italian friends. Neither of them was brave enough to bring up Adam's name as they tried to come to terms with the reality of what Lara faced in the coming months.

Later that same night, the heartbroken couple wept openly over the impact this would have on all the family. They couldn't imagine that glorious voice being silenced forever, nor the thought of the talented singer losing her much-loved career if the partial paralysis was found to be permanent. The only silver lining was having Nikki back in Brisbane full-time. At least her presence should help to lift Lara's spirits.

Over the next week, Charles' Jaguar became a regular addition to the car park and the most touching visit of all occurred on Lara's third day as an inpatient.

The husband and wife team had quickly learned to put on happy faces before turning the corner into her room. Elizabeth's arms were laden with treats from her kitchen, while his juggled piles of reading material and DVDs to help fill in the long days and even longer nights ahead of the patient. One of the first things they noticed was a large arrangement of yellow roses sitting on the bedside table.

"Oh, aren't they lovely – I wonder who could've sent them," Elizabeth announced with a knowing look. Nikki had poured out the story of finding them on the porch, along with Lara's gut-wrenching reaction, over dinner the night before.

Lara didn't answer but waited in readiness – and dread – for the bombshell to fall. It wasn't long in coming, although Elizabeth tried to lessen the impact by offering a gentle caress along her arm. All the while those clear blue eyes pleaded for the son she loved so dearly.

"My darling girl, don't you think it's time you put all of us out of our misery and let Adam know what's happened."

Lara shook her head vehemently, her gaze unwavering as she pleaded just as hard through a raspy throat. "*No!* He must *never* find out! I don't want his pity."

"Oh sweetheart, he would never pity you – he *loves* you."

"Yes, he would – eventually – and I don't want him burdened down with a pathetic creature who can never be the woman he fell in love with."

The gentle caress stopped abruptly as Elizabeth grabbed Lara's hand and squeezed tight. "*Stop it!* You're *not* pathetic, and you'd *never* be a burden! He loves you too much. Please, Lara, it's heartbreaking watching how broken he is wondering where you are. *Please* give us your blessing to tell him..."

"I *can't!* He needs far more than I could ever give him now."

Charles lovingly stroked his wife's back as he took over. "But, my dear girl, he can help you get through this. You've always been his motivation. Elizabeth and I both know he wouldn't have made it this far if it wasn't for all those memories of you to keep him going. It's time you let him be yours. We've never seen him so upset. He's truly lost without you."

Her shoulders slumped. "Better to be lost than dealing with a hopeless future. His life's been hard enough as it is without having to put up with all this." She gestured to her legs as several large tears rolled down her cheeks.

"You're wrong, Lara. Any future you two shared would be bright and filled with hope – no matter what the outcome. He would *want* to help – you must know that."

For the next several minutes a frustrating discussion ensued. Their appeals grew even more persistent trying to persuade Lara to change her mind, but she wasn't going to budge, no matter how convincing an argument they put up. Unfortunately, the door was open, so several of the medical staff gathered around the nearby nurses' desk overheard everything. Most shook their heads sadly and exchanged knowing looks.

During rounds the night before the Ashworth's visit, two from their ranks had been privy to a long bout of sorrowful cries coming from her room – along with several heartfelt prayers for someone called Adam. To ensure those involved in the new patient's care were aware of just how vulnerable she was, a detailed note had been hastily added to her chart. Lara's midnight meltdown made it obvious she not only needed healing for her body but also for a broken heart.

With their pleas falling on deaf ears, Elizabeth and Charles left Lara about an hour later, with both a prayer for her recovery and two forced smiles, along with solemn promises to return. Much to her relief, the following day no mention was made of the touchy subject. Two days later they were up again with another appeal, but no matter how hard they pressed, she refused to change her mind.

The following Wednesday, Elizabeth tried another tack and came on her own. His roses were still sitting on the bedside locker – less vibrant and a little bit wilted – but it was obvious Lara didn't have the heart to throw them out.

Over a hot cuppa, she was given the exact details of Adam's marriage break-up and how excited he was to finally be free. His mother stressed how heartbroken he was not being able to find her and painted exciting word pictures of their life together in the house he was designing near the Glasshouse Mountains. She finished with, "I know it must be frustrating and scary not knowing what's going on, but you're still as beautiful as before, you're still the same person inside, and at least you could accompany him whenever he's on tour."

"I've already told you, Elizabeth, I won't see him – I *can't!* I made a vow way back when that all I wanted was for him to be happy. I know he loves me, but it'd break his heart to see me like this and I love *him* too much to put him through that. Besides, I couldn't go with him when he's performing out of town – my chair's far too cumbersome, and I don't want anyone's pity ... especially his. And even if I did manage to accompany him, there's no way I could keep up all the physio and speech therapy appointments, as well as everything else this stupid injury entails. I'm sorry, but I'm not going to change my mind."

"Well, what about them and them and them?" her visitor said, pointing to the roses and then the sculpture sitting on the windowsill before sliding up to the highlighted message pinned directly above it. "You know what yellow roses mean to him – he only ever wanted you to have sunshine in your life. All he has left *is* hope ... and obviously, it's what you're clinging to as well or else why have that still on display? We both know you made it for a purpose..."

"I *do* know, and they're beautiful – I love roses, especially them – but I can't let sentiment change my mind. The only form of hope I have left now is for Adam to be okay and me to get better ... nothing else. It's time you gave up."

When Elizabeth arrived home a short time later, her heart was heavy. Charles was sitting at the kitchen table when she walked through the door. Their eyes met, but all she could do was shake her head.

§

Three weeks had passed with no further mention of the taboo subject whenever Charles and Elizabeth dropped by for their regular visits. They had given up trying to persuade the headstrong woman to change her mind. Even so, before settling down to sleep each night, a heartfelt prayer asking God to somehow intervene became their last act of the day.

One afternoon only a few weeks before Christmas, Lara made her way back to her private room after another gruelling session with Josh. Rolling through the door, her gaze automatically went to the sign in the window with its direct link to the pewter sculpture.

She was still too wound up to register someone was sitting in a chair on the far side of the bed, though the visitor couldn't help noticing what had grabbed her best friend's attention. Lucy's first words were typical of the compassionate heart Lara knew so well.

"We're all in this together, my precious friend. None of us will ever let you give up, especially not me."

Lara's expression went from one of despondency to instant joy. "Luce! Oh wow, you're *back!* And don't you look *fabulous!*" she exclaimed with that usual gravelly croak. She wheeled herself expertly around the bed to give her old friend a welcoming hug.

Lucy had been really looking forward to this long-awaited catch-up, despite feeling somewhat anxious as to how she could possibly act normally after hearing the dreadful news. She and Jeff had only just arrived home from Europe after spending two months sightseeing, mostly as part of an organised tour. Like Adam's parents, she was heartbroken to see her friend now wheelchair-bound with both legs twisted awkwardly to the side. Fighting down the sadness, she made sure to plaster a big smile on her face.

"Hi, gorgeous girl, sorry I couldn't get here sooner ... we only just arrived home yesterday," she mumbled between strangling bearhugs and warm kisses.

Lara was so excited the husky words came out in a rush. "That's okay, I understood. I just can't believe you're finally home again. Oh, it's *sooo* good to see you – I've missed you heaps and heaps!"

"I've missed you even more than that – and that fabulous smile!"

"And look at you – just as stunning as always!"

"Oh, get outta here." Lucy blushed awkwardly and landed a friendly punch on Lara's arm. It was a good attempt at cover-up after witnessing firsthand the problems her former dressing room cohort was having with her speech. She was devastated thinking the singer's exquisite voice may never hold a tune again and couldn't bring herself to mention anything about the accident.

With typical canniness, Lara understood and made sure the conversation stayed focussed on the newcomer by blabbering on and on about the trip.

"So how was Europe and what did you get up to? I can't believe you spent a whole week in London, you *lucky* duck! *And* Salzburg! Oh, I love that place – it's my absolute favourite. I'd move there tomorrow if it weren't for this." She gestured towards her legs without thinking. Before Lucy could answer, she rushed on. "Didn't you just love Italy? That countryside is absolutely breathtaking! Thank heavens, *you* managed to get back in one piece ... unlike someone else we know! It's just a shame I turned into such a klutz on those narrow roads!"

Needing something to break the ice, Lara had deliberately thrown the last statement out there. Before Lucy could answer, she pulled her into another tight cuddle. The visitor returned the gesture with a tentative laugh at this morbid attempt at comedy, while breathing a huge sigh of relief to find she didn't have to act as though nothing had changed.

"Hang on, hang on ... one question at a time. Our trip was wonderful! We did heaps everywhere we went – far too much to remember straight off the bat. London was fabulous – so much to see and do – and Salzburg definitely was *my* favourite too. And ... ummm ... heck ... what was that other question?"

"Italy!"

"Oh, yeah! Italy was amazing and *sooo* old – no wonder you fell in love with it. Anyway, enough about me. Lars, you look great, much better than I anticipated, especially seeing how well you can get around in that nifty contraption. If I didn't know better, I'd think you went over that stupid cliff just to get all the attention." As soon as the words fell from her lips, Lucy wanted to sink into the floor. The look on her face gave away just how mortified she felt.

Lara grinned and squeezed her forearm. "It's okay, Luce. I don't want everyone thinking they have to walk on eggshells around me. This has been my new life for over two months now, so I'm getting used to all the awkward comments inadvertently coming my way. And besides, you're right; I'm even becoming an old hand at wheelchair races, so there's no need to feel bad!"

"I'm *sooo* sorry – I can't believe I just said that! You know me, most of the time I only open my mouth to change feet!"

"Yeah, I remember!" Lara said with a giggle.

Lucy screwed up her face, recalling other times when her unwieldy tongue had become her worst enemy.

"Hey, it's fine, truly!" the patient quickly assured her. "Besides, we both know they're so big you're always tripping over them. It's no wonder they make their way into your mouth so many times!"

Loud chuckles filled the room and echoed down the corridor. Falling back into their usual camaraderie was the best antidote for this sobering new reality.

Once the laughter faded away, Lucy down looked at Lara and her expression was filled with regret. "I'm so sorry we didn't get a chance to visit you in hospital over there – our tour schedule was full-on the whole time."

"Don't worry, I understood ... you couldn't have done anything anyway."

"Yeah but I still feel terrible. I'd already booked our tickets, and it was impossible to change them or even grab a flight out for a quick visit. We only had overnight stays in most places, and by the time we arrived in Florence, you were already home. Then we were off to Greece for the cruise and England for a month after that."

The long string of excuses made it obvious Lucy felt she had let her best mate down.

"Hey, it's okay. Besides, it wouldn't have been much fun seeing me stuck in a bed with tubes running all over the place! This is far better. At least I can finally speak to you ... even if I do sound like *Donald Duck!* Besides, your gorgeous bouquet arrived safely while I was over there. *And* the tray of Bowen mangoes – you're a treasure. Mangoes are my favourite fruit, and they were scrumptious! I still can't believe you had them shipped all the way from North Queensland, though."

"I'm just glad they arrived okay. I figured you'd need something to stop the homesickness and possibly give you a bit of a pick-me-up."

"They sure did, and all the staff begged for a taste. None of them had ever tried that variety before so it's just as well you sent a boxful! Thankfully, I did manage to save some for myself though. By the way, you really do look fantastic

... and putting on weight, I see – must be all that rich French and Italian food you've been hoeing into over there!"

Lara rubbed a small tell-tale bump on her friend's belly, and the look they exchanged was one of pure delight.

"I know! Far too many carbs and butter for my liking!" came the excited reply, followed by a teasing wink.

"Gosh, that's the best news. Talk about clever – my bestie about to become a mum!

"Well, Jeff had a bit to do with it too, and we're thrilled to bits! Can you believe it?"

"Hardly, but I'm super excited. Any more morning sickness?"

"No, thank goodness! That stopped just before we left Rome. Anyway, how about you and me get outta here for a while? We could go for a long walk in that pretty park next door. It's not too hot today, and there's so much to tell you." Too late she realised she had done it again. Lara wouldn't be walking anywhere. Her face turned bright pink as she groaned, "Ooh, I'm sorry. There I go again ... me and these stupid big feet!"

Lara was frustrated at how everyone felt it was necessary to be cautious around her all the time, so her answer was accompanied by a cheeky grin. "Don't worry, how about a drag race instead – you and that rapidly growing butt, and me in this old contraption on wheels! Maybe now I'll have a real chance of winning with you carrying all that extra weight around!"

The playful retort was perfect to bring back the smiles. She grabbed Lucy's hand and pulled. "Come on, Mrs Puddle Duck, I'd *love* to go for a walk in the park with you. I'm dying to hear about everything you got up to over there. I've missed you so much – can you believe it's been nearly three months! But don't you dare go away again for a while – I need you near to make me laugh!"

Lucy pulled her into a tight hug as they fell back into their usual camaraderie. It wasn't hard to recognise her friend of old – those brilliant blue eyes still sparkled with mischief, and that sassy fervour bubbled over simply by being together again. Nothing could dim Lara's spark, no matter what happened ... after all, Lucy had already seen her best mate rise from the ashes once before...

They spent the next couple of hours wandering through a maze of pathways. The newcomer became an expert at pushing the wheelchair while spilling the beans about all her overseas adventures. Along the way, they spotted a shaded garden seat on a peninsula jutting into a serene lake. She parked the chair carefully and made sure the brakes were on tight before plonking herself down to watch a family of ducks splashing and foraging amongst a mass of waterlilies.

Taking Lara by the hand, she gave it a hard squeeze. "As you can probably tell, we had a brilliant time, but I can't believe it's already over. One of my favourite parts was exploring all the side streets and out-of-the-way places in London. That place is incredible; there's so much to see and do. Oh, and you wouldn't believe how many shows play the West End. We even managed to get tickets for Ad—" she broke off and swallowed hard as her face turned red again.

Lara simply smiled and finished the sentence for her. "You got tickets for Adam's show ... he was brilliant ... and you were able to catch up with him at Stage Door ... and then go off to a quiet little place for supper afterwards!"

"Oh, gosh, I'm sooo sorry. What is it with these clumsy feet and why am I so *stupid!* How about you just take me out the back and put a gun to my head! That way you can put both of us out of our misery..."

"Hey, it's fine!" This time it was Lara squeezing Lucy's hand. "I'm tickled pink you went to see him. I'd have done the same thing myself if I'd been there – I just wouldn't have let him know..." She smiled wistfully for a moment and then shook her head and broke into another grin. "Besides, how many people can say one of their oldest friends is performing in that famous place?"

"You're right ... and thanks ... I just didn't want to upset you." Lucy remembered Lara's former strict instructions never to speak his name out loud.

"You didn't. I'm fine, truly. Anyway, for those last few weeks in hospital, a copy of *The Times* was delivered to my room each day. One had a write-up about the night Prince William and his girlfriend attended a performance. It was a great piece, and from the sounds of it, Adam deserves all the accolades.

"He certainly does – he was absolutely brilliant! And thankfully we made it just in time before the show closed."

"Well, *did* you manage to catch up with him?"

"No, worse luck, and Jeff and I were so disappointed. We tried, but there were so many people hanging around we couldn't get anywhere near Stage Door. Oh, and you wouldn't believe how many paparazzi were jostling to get the best photo – it's chaos over there for performers. We only just managed to spot him getting into a car as he was leaving. And there wasn't time to catch up later because our tour to the Lakes District left the next day."

Lara could picture the scene, and there was that old look of longing in her eyes. For the first time in ages, she wanted a full-blown description to put flesh on the images. "What did he look like? Is he still as handsome as ever?"

Nodding slowly, Lucy's gaze remained fixed on her best friend's face as she filled in the blanks. Her tone was soft as she reflected on the night. "Yeah, he is. A little greyer now, but it actually suits him – makes him look even more handsome if that's possible..." She paused, uncertain as to how much to reveal.

"Come on, what else? Don't keep me in suspense!" Lara leaned forward, and her eyes were shining with anticipation. Hearing about him after so long was like a tonic and she craved to know every detail – something she didn't dare do with

Elizabeth, knowing full well it would only start her pleading to tell Adam all over again.

Figuring it would probably do Lara good to learn he was happy, Lucy related what she remembered from that night. A faint smidgen of wistfulness peppered each word. "He looked wonderful. To be honest, it reminded me of what he looked like when he was younger … and so in love with you…"

Lara gazed across the water, picturing the look in his eyes when he had loving on his mind.

Lucy noticed a small pensive smile play across her friend's lips as she went on. "We were lucky enough to make it in time to see his last performance. After such a long run, I thought he'd be exhausted, but he was in fine voice, and the atmosphere was electric the moment he walked on stage. It's not surprising really when you think how popular he's become – not quite like the old days in our little theatre when we played to an audience of a few hundred."

She sent another worried glance Lara's way. But like before, there was no need to fret – her face was glowing imagining every second.

"In the tiny glimpse I caught of him afterwards, he was laughing and looked like he was having the time of his life." She reached over and caught Lara's hand in hers again. "He really *does* seem happy, Lars, just like you always wanted."

"Was Trina with him?" Lara couldn't help asking. Suddenly it dawned on her, Lucy hadn't been home long enough to hear news about the breakup.

"No, I didn't see her at all – just the woman playing his leading lady and a couple of others I presume were from the cast. It looked like they were off to the wrap-up party – there was lots of playful backchatting and laughing as they scrambled into a waiting taxi."

The best friends remembered nights from long ago when the pair of them, along with Adam and Jeff, went off to have a late-night supper following one of their shows ... but neither one was game enough to say anything.

Recalling what his parents had told her about all that had led up to the separation, Lara felt certain she knew what lay behind his carefree manner. The timeline fitted exactly with the afternoon of Trina's unexpected revelations.

"Luce, there's something I need to tell you ... but you have to promise not to give me a hard time afterwards."

"Mmm, this sounds intriguing, but I'm not promising anything until I know what's going on," she replied with a cautious smirk. "Knowing you, it could be a trap!"

"No, I need your promise first. I know *you* too well – besides, I'm an invalid, so you need to do as you're told in case I have a set-back!" Lara's expression was deadly serious even though there was a cheeky glint in her eye.

Lucy rolled her eyes at this blatant attempt at bribery. "Oh, alright, I promise

... whatever it is!"

"I doubt whether you've heard about it yet, but here goes." She had to take a deep breath and then… "Adam and Trina have separated; they're getting a divor—"

Lucy shot out of her seat with a jubilant cry. Grabbing Lara in a bearhug, she nearly knocked the wheelchair over and had to quickly right it again before her friend fell onto the ground.

She was so excited it was her turn to be the motor mouth. *"What!* That's *fantastic* news! Wait 'til I tell Jeff! It's about time that silly old fool came to his senses! I bet he rushed back from London to be with you. Oh, he must be over the moon – and so must *you!* Heavens, Lars, that's incredible; I'm thrilled to bits!"

"Luce, lis—"

Lucy cut her off when her face broke into a massive grin and she grabbed Lara by the shoulders. "How come you didn't tell me straight away? When are you two getting married? It'd better be soon – we've all waited long enough! Oh wow, I can just picture it! Suze and I can be your matrons-of-honour and Nikki chief bridesmaid ... and I can help with all the arrangements so you won't have to do anything except get better." Pulling Lara into her arms, she planted a resounding kiss on her cheek. "Oh, this is *sooo* exciting!"

Lara just sat there with a blank expression, while Lucy went to town. She knew her too well ... when she was wound up, there was no stopping her.

Suddenly it registered. "Lars, what's wrong? Why aren't you saying anything?"

"Because there isn't going to be a wedding..."

Dumbfounded, Lucy plonked herself down on the seat again, mouth agape and eyes wide open as she mouthed the word, *"What?"*

Before she could say anything more, Lara put up her hand.

"Listen, Luce ... and I'm not going to argue, so don't even try. Adam's never *ever* going to see me like this" —she pointed to her legs— "and I'm not about to change my mind, no matter what you say. I've had plenty of time to think it over these last few weeks; I don't want him knowing anything about the accident – it wouldn't be fair on him. So that means you're not to say anything ... *ever.*"

"What! Don't be *ridiculous* – he *has* to be told."

"No, he doesn't, and I need you to promise. I know he'll try to wheedle it out of you – he's been calling everyone he can think of, asking if they know where I am. He's rung his parents and Suzie umpteen times – but he must *never* find out! I need you to promise you'll never say one word about any of this."

"Lars—"

"No, I told you, I'm not changing my mind. You'd better get your head around it and understand this is the way it has to be. I'm not going to discuss it again." She sent a determined look her friend's way. "Come on, wheel me back to my room so I can make us a cuppa – at least I can still do that!"

The walk was made in silence, except for the rubber tyres crunching over leaves littering the path and the melodious warble of a sole magpie in a nearby tree. The happy little feathered critter mightn't have any cares, but Lucy's heart was breaking, picturing her husband's closest friend searching frantically for the woman he had never stopped loving.

§

Later that afternoon, after sending a heartfelt look of thanks to her friend as they waved goodbye, Lara settled back for a relaxing soak in the tub fitted with a hoist specially designed to lower patients into the water. After more than two months of humiliating sponge baths undertaken in her bed, this was the first time she had been strong enough to enjoy its benefits. The silky water felt wonderful where it caressed her skin. She could even stretch her fingers out far enough to reach down and wash her lower legs. It was a thrill to be able to experience the slight tingling sensation when only a few weeks ago she had felt nothing at all.

Maybe there's hope for us after all. You and I are going to work really hard, then one day we just might surprise everyone.

Leaning back with her head resting on an air cushion, she ran a bar of lavender soap lazily across her fingers and over her palms. Without warning, an image from long ago filled her mind, and a sudden stream of tears spilled from her eyes as she remembered a glorious ballet routine once performed on a stage made by two sets of hands.

Oh, Teddy, so many touching memories. I know you don't understand, but the past is all we have left now.

She glanced down at the sparkling ring that had never once left her finger since being placed there nearly sixteen years ago. The years hadn't tarnished it, nor had it lost its brilliant lustre. Pensively she rubbed her thumb across the setting.

From the midst of all those distant memories, she remembered a phrase he had once used for her, only this time she added her own spin to it.

At least in my heart, we'll always be together ... 'til the end of time.

§

Adam was labouring over his study worktable later that night and racking his brain. For the life of him, he couldn't figure out where on earth Lara and Nikki might be. After three weeks, he still hadn't been able to find out anything about either one of them. Whenever he rang her number, the call went to message bank ... and the same thing happened whenever he called her sister. It was almost as though Lara's entire family had disappeared from the face of the earth. Driving

554

by the cottage, it appeared to be always empty no matter what time of day it was. Max was off on an overseas holiday, so he wasn't contactable either. Even his own parents didn't know where they were. Having no idea where else to turn, he was becoming more and more frustrated and anxious.

The pencil drawings in front of him showed the almost completed images of a magnificent lowset home flowing around a resort-style swimming pool. In the top left-hand corner were sketches of what looked to be a stable or shed.

No matter how long it takes, Baby, I'm determined to find you. Then we can all live together in the home of our dreams.

Chapter 41

The Ashworths were still making daily visits to the hospital. Even though it was a heartbreaking situation, they made sure no mention was made of either their son or the flowers left at Lara's door. Elizabeth was aching to say something, but Charles was worried it may set back her recovery time.

Adam kept ringing or dropping by at least twice a week, desperate to hear if they had news of her whereabouts. His mother hated deceiving him all the time, especially when she had to continually witness the depth of loneliness and anxiety reflected in his eyes and voice. Unfortunately, there was nothing that could be done and her heart ached with grief.

Josh was hopeful Lara would be out of the wheelchair by the middle of the following year and eventually be able to walk without any form of aid. His encouragement was enough to ensure she worked her butt off each day. Even the slightest degree of improvement was incentive to spur her on.

A week after making that late-night silent vow to find her, Adam called on his parents with the finished plans for the new house. At least they could share in the surprise while he waited for the woman it was intended for to come out of hiding. He could think of no other way to describe her mysterious disappearance after spending hour upon hour combing through theatre mags and newspapers, not to mention the number of times he had asked around the traps if anyone knew anything. It was beyond his comprehension for someone so well-known just to disappear so easily. At least planning their new home helped to fill in the time.

The house was perfect – everything Lara could ever have dreamed of. Purely by coincidence, the layout catered ideally for someone with a disability, even down to being built on a single level and having a roomy open-plan design. This meant there were no awkward corridors for a wheelchair to navigate. Even though the entrance had two small steps leading up to a long wide flagstone terrace, adding a ramp would be an easy job. Any other changes could easily be adapted when the time came. The block of land now had a bare pad of concrete where the magnificent dwelling would soon stand. Located on a wide flat ridge, the views across to the Glasshouse Mountains were absolutely breathtaking.

All Adam's parents needed to do now was convince Lara to let them tell him where she was.

§

It was two days before Nikki's birthday and Christmas was just over a week away. Elizabeth had been bustling around in her kitchen all morning. A fresh batch of White Christmas squares and a tray of rum balls had been cooling on the bench for the last hour. Over in one corner, the large baker's oven emitted a hint of sweet aroma from a chocolate cake that was almost done. A little while later she rushed out the door with a tin of sweet treats tucked under her arm.

Hopefully, these will help to cheer you up, my precious girl.

Heading down to the patient's room, she bumped into Josh coming along the corridor. Always quick to sniff out her culinary delights, he bent close enough to savour this new batch of mouth-watering aromas. The physio had been on the receiving end of many of her home-baked offerings over the last couple of months, and he could often be seen lurking nearby when she was due for a visit.

"Hi, Mrs Ashworth, you're looking lovely today ... just like always!" He raised his eyebrows Groucho Marx style and offered her a cheeky smirk. "What are you smuggling in for my favourite patient today? Mmm ... smells great!"

His flattery worked. With a friendly grin, she removed the lid to offer him a choice. "Oh Josh, you're such a charmer. They're just some Christmas treats I made this morning. Here, have a taste."

"Lara'd kill me if she knew I was pinching more of her goodies. I was in big trouble last time ... she can turn pretty fierce when it comes to anything sweet!"

"Oh, go on. Promise I won't tell. I made plenty so she won't even notice," she responded with a conspiratorial smirk.

"Well ... they do look delicious," he capitulated with a knowing wink, helping himself to one of the small squares and popping it straight into his mouth.

"My goodness, gone already! Here, you'd better have another one then," she offered again, nudging his arm with hers. "Go on."

"No, my life wouldn't be worth living if I stole two!"

Once their chuckles faded away, Elizabeth's expression turned quite serious. "Now, let's get down to business ... how's Lara really doing? She won't tell me much, and I don't like to push. You know how hard she is on herself."

"Tell me about it – *and* she can be as stubborn as a mule at times – but she's doing really well. Both her physician and I are thrilled with her progress."

"Oh, that's excellent news, thank you."

"Isn't it, and it's my pleasure. I'm just as happy as you are. I've even had her walking the entire length of the parallel bars in the last few sessions, admittedly still holding on for all she's worth because of the twist in her ankles ... but when it comes to swimming, she's like a fish. The strength in her arms is increasing from the daily exercises, and that makes up for the lack of strength in her legs ... she's even managing to kick them a bit more than this time last week."

"See, she hasn't told me any of this. I think Lara's frustrated things aren't moving along as fast as she hoped. She always tends to keep the important stuff to herself."

"Well, sadly, she won't get her wish to walk by Christmas. Still, it shouldn't be much longer 'til we can get her up on a walking frame. Then eventually she'll be able to throw that old wheelchair away – at least for any outings close to home – and hopefully for good in the not too distant future."

Elizabeth was elated. She threw her arms around the young man, taking him completely by surprise.

"That's fantastic news! Thanks for all the hard work you're putting in. Charles and I sincerely appreciate your dedication to our precious girl."

He returned her hug with a happy chortle. "Don't thank me. Lara's the one doing it all. I've never had a patient push herself so much. She's one determined lady once her mind's set on something."

"She sure is. I've seen that trait in her *many* times. Now, what about her speech? Her voice seems to be getting that little bit stronger; it doesn't look as though she has to strain so much to be heard. Do you think she'll ever have it back fully, especially so she can sing again?"

"Mmm ... well, that's really not my area, although from what I've seen on her charts and also talking to her speech therapist, it appears Lara's vocal cords don't have the amount of scar tissue damage they originally feared. Her Italian surgeon did a wonderful job. Someone must've told him she was a vocalist because it seems he took extra care when he went in. In my personal opinion, I think she'll be back lighting up stages this time next year, at least as far as her range of movement is concerned if she continues to improve to the same extent." He gave a hopeful smile and raised both hands with two sets of fingers crossed on each one.

"Oh, that's fabulous news! Wait 'til I tell Charles! It means so much to all of us. You've given us hope ... something we haven't had much of lately."

And most especially for a man who doesn't even know what's happened, her heart whispered.

"Oh, Lara's one of our special ones. We care about all of our patients, of course, but there's always one you're inclined to put just that little bit more effort into just because they get inside your heart. She's definitely mine."

"And she is to us as well. Thanks again, Josh. Now I'd better get in there, or she'll be wondering where I am! Merry Christmas and I hope you have a lovely break."

"Thanks, Mrs Ashworth, I hope you have a Merry Christmas, too. Oh, and thanks for the slice, it was delicious."

"Well you'd better have another piece to keep you going," she said, sending him a cheeky wink. "It can be our little secret."

With an impish grin, the young man helped himself to one more portion – the biggest in the tin. Then sending her a cheery wave, he hurried off in the opposite direction, both cheeks bulging with the gooey treat.

Elizabeth was thrilled at all the positive things he had said and she couldn't resist indulging in a celebratory pirouette outside Lara's door. Just as quickly, she brushed at her dress and fixed a few stray tresses, hoping no one had witnessed a woman with a head full of silvery locks now almost camouflaging the strawberry blonde ones seemingly impersonating Ginger Rogers.

Seeing Elizabeth's grin when she popped her head around the door was a welcome surprise, and Lara couldn't help laughing at the mischievous expression accompanying it. "Now there's a look I probably should be worried about. Okay, spill the beans. What've you been up to?"

Elizabeth tried to act dumb as she placed the container of tasty morsels on the trolley beside the bed. Kissing the patient on the cheek, she tried unsuccessfully to conceal her joy. "Nothing at all. I just had a bit of exciting news, that's all. Here's a little something to help keep your strength up."

"I suppose I should thank you, but if they're anything like your normal offerings, I'll put on a stack of weight and won't be able to move. Then Josh'll be furious and I'll be in his bad books all day!"

"Oh don't worry about him – I've already softened him up on the way in!"

"Have you been giving away my treats again to that greedy boy?" Lara laughed through the pretence of a scowl as Elizabeth pulled an affirmative grimace. "I *knew* it – the little thief! Now, what's all this about exciting news?"

"Oh, I've just been hearing about a certain patient I love very dearly, who's now almost running the length of the parallel bars and swimming like a fish in the pool! Well done, my darling girl, I'm so so proud of you!"

"Pffft ... don't believe everything that one tells you ... he'd say anything just to sample your scrumptious cooking," Lara scoffed as her brow furrowed, though the twinkle in her eyes gave her away.

"Well, he's certainly singing your praises and says you should be back on stage this time next year. Now that's the best Christmas present an almost-mother could ever ask for."

In Elizabeth's heart, Lara had become the daughter she always longed for, and she enjoyed reminding her every now and then. Since the accident, the two women had grown even closer, and Lara had no idea how she would have coped without the other one's constant encouragement and support. She had intended keeping the news a secret until she was able to walk without tripping over her blasted twisted ankles. Knowing Elizabeth was in on the gossip, meant the younger woman was now beside herself with excitement.

"Isn't it wonderful? I can't believe it! I've still got a long way to go, but maybe my wish *will* come true after all."

"What wish? Walking ... or Adam?"

All it took was the sound of his name for her soul to sigh with yearning and she quickly had to close her eyes before composing an answer. Harnessing in all of that endless hunger before opening them again, the sadness behind Elizabeth's gaze was enough to cause Lara to utter a term usually reserved for his exclusive use. "You know how I feel, Mum ... and I can't go back on what I said."

In spite of the gloomy answer, Elizabeth's heart leapt to hear this new form of address and her reply oozed with tenderness. "Oh, Lara dear, thank you ... I've waited so many years to hear you call me that ... but I wish you'd realise just how much you need him ... *and* how much he needs you."

Lara ignored the second part to concentrate on the first, hoping it might send the conversation off on another tangent. "I should've started calling you by that name long ago. You've filled my mother's shoes in every way possible. She'd be so grateful for everything you've done for Nikki and me, especially lately."

"It's been an honour, my darling girl ... but what about my son – why can't you see how much you need each other?"

"Because his career is just starting to take off overseas and I'd only be a hindrance – and an embarrassment. I can't put him through that. Now more than ever, he needs to get on with his life."

"No you wouldn't, my dear – you'd be his hope for a better future after everything he's been through." Grasping Lara by the hand, she held her gaze and her eyes brimmed with tears. "He's a lost soul searching for his home. I wish you could see the despair in his eyes whenever he talks about you. He's on the phone all the time, trying to work out where you might be. He's even rung André, asking if you're in rehearsals for another concert together."

Lara looked at her with concern, afraid the Maestro's staff may have mentioned the accident, but Elizabeth shook her head. "Don't worry, all his PA would say was that they have no idea where you might be. Max even called the other day begging me to put him out of his misery – he can't stand hearing the pain in Adam's voice whenever they talk. *Please* let me tell him. I'm begging for *both* your sakes."

Streams of tears rolled down Lara's cheeks, but she could only shake her head as a pair of troubled eyes pleaded with the other one to understand.

Elizabeth gave a strangled cry and pulled her close, rocking gently as she crooned into her hair. "There, there. It'll be alright..."

When Lara eventually raised her head, she begged, "I know how hard this is on everyone – most especially him – but please understand ... I have to do this."

All the visitor could do was nod, conceding defeat in getting this stubborn new daughter to change her mind. The only sound for the next few moments was of both of them blowing their noses.

Lara tossed a sodden tissue in the bin and managed to drag up a smile, turning the conversation to something sure to lift their spirits. "Enough of all that. Did you hear Nikki's been offered the part of *Nancy* in *Oliver*? It's such a coup. No matter what the doctors say, I'm definitely going to be there for opening night!"

"We did, and it's fabulous news," Elizabeth managed to respond, wiping the last trace of moisture from her eyes and cheeks as she struggled to break out a smile. "She was telling us over dinner last night, and sounds so excited. Charles and I are both thrilled to bits, and we're so glad it's playing up here rather than in one of the other major cities as it means she can stay close to you."

"I know! It's wonderful; I couldn't be prouder. But I don't want her thinking she can't leave me if a role comes along somewhere else – I never want to be a burden to anyone, especially not her. She doesn't deserve the worry of having to look after a pathetic mother."

Elizabeth gave a deep groan of frustration and rolled her eyes. "*Aargh* ... as if she'd worry about *that!* You must realise how much she cares about you."

"I do, and that's exactly why I don't want to hold her back – she's young and has the whole world at her feet."

"I seem to remember someone who put their whole world on hold for a certain much-loved daughter, including giving up the theatre for many years." A tender smirk softened the hint of sarcasm.

"But that was different! I was her mother ... I don't want Nikki thinking she has to be mine."

With infinite tenderness, Elizabeth kissed away the frown marring Lara's brow. "She won't. She's a sensible young woman who just happens to love you, like the rest of us. So how about letting me take on that motherly role instead."

"Thank you," Lara whispered, overwhelmed at the love and acceptance Adam's mother had poured out on her ever since their first meeting.

They were sharing a warm embrace when there was a sudden rap on the door. As Lara called out, "Come in!" Mary, the centre's tea-lady, bustled in pushing a trolley laden down with cups and a large urn. It was the perfect interruption. They beckoned her closer with welcoming smiles and Elizabeth was quick to offer the newcomer a Christmas treat. Smiling in delight after sampling several others over the weeks, she tucked one into her apron pocket.

"I'll keep it for later, thank you!" she said, bobbing her head before pouring each of them a cup.

As soon as they were alone again, Elizabeth paused before taking a sip. "Now, about Nikki's twenty-first birthday—"

"Oooh, don't remind me! I can't believe in two days my little girl's going to be that old! Where's that time gone?"

"Exactly! And Christmas is coming up as well. Before leaving yesterday, I was able to have a word with your doctor. If you do well over the next few physio sessions, he'll happily give you a leave pass for all of Christmas Day..."

"*Really!* I can get out of here? You're kidding!" Lara blurted out, her eyes wide with excitement.

"No, I'm not! He thinks it's a great idea. In fact, he's told me it's just what you need."

"I'll go along with that," she chuckled, imagining being back in the outside world instead of cooped up inside these four cold walls or on one of her short sojourns to the park.

"Thought you would! Now, over dinner last night, I mentioned what he said to Nikki. She's decided Christmas Day would be perfect for the combined celebration rather than holding them both on her birthday like normal."

"But this is her twenty-first – it wouldn't be right holding her party on any other day. I was hoping to ask the family and her closest friends to come up here for a couple of hours to celebrate. I could host it in the garden and then she and her mates could go somewhere less sombre afterwards. Or maybe I could ask the doctor if it'd be okay for me to get out on her birthday instead. We could then have it at your place just like always, as long as you don't mind."

"Of course I don't, and I suggested the same thing, but he'd rather waited a few days more to get your strength up. Besides, Nikki assured me she's not a little girl anymore, so it doesn't really matter if it's not on the actual day. Apparently, her friends are getting together tomorrow night to celebrate with a bit of a shindig at your place ... she doesn't want to disturb us with the loud music. I'm sure she thinks Charles and I are turning into a pair of old fogies!"

"Oh, how dare she – that's just plain rude!"

A flurry of laughter filled the air until Lara spied the wheelchair standing in the corner. Just the sight of it sent her spirits plummeting back to earth. "Mmm, she did mention something about going out the other day. I feel terrible not being able to put on a proper party with all the trimmings. After all, I'm her mother so it should be me making all the fuss, especially for one this special."

"Don't worry, she understands. Besides, Suzie's asked Lucy and Jeff to join us all up here at noon on the actual day. She wants to organise a special lunch. You haven't forgotten she, Ben and Jack are leaving for the Gold Coast the next day."

"No, she mentioned about going off on a holiday to Burleigh Heads for a week. A break will do them good after all the mayhem and worry she put up with in Italy. It'll be strange not seeing them around for Christmas, but I've taken up enough of her time. They need time to themselves for a change."

"Yes, it'll do them good, and they're bound to have a lovely time ... it's a great spot. Now, back to Nikki's special day. All of us are bringing something to share for the birthday lunch – but no presents, according to your daughter."

"What? Why on earth not? It's her twenty-first – of course, she's getting presents!"

"Well, according to her, she'd rather wait until Christmas. That way we can open them all at the same time as we usually do. You know how much she loves celebrating around the tree, and she'd much rather wait until you're out of hospital."

"Oh, that's okay then. It's a shame Suzie and the others'll miss out, but I suppose it can't be helped."

"True, but don't worry; they'll probably bring her back something unique from one of those jazzy surf boutiques the coast is renowned for. And this means Nikki can celebrate with us 'oldies' on the proper day – after all, having you there is all that matters. A few months ago, it was touch and go whether you'd be around at all, so stop making things harder on yourself. She and the others will have a great time celebrating. Then you can make it up to her next year by kicking your heels up on the dance floor!"

Lara's face lit up as she imagined having all her old friends there for Nikki's milestone, even if it was only for a small lunch instead of a full-blown party. She also had the excitement of breaking free from her rehab room and celebrating Christmas at the Ashworths' spacious home to look forward to.

"Well, if my doctor says it's okay for me to get out of here in a week, that's fantastic! I don't believe it ... away from this miserable old place for a *whole* day! Bring ... on ... Christmas!"

"Mmm, I'll say and Charles and I are over the moon at the thought of having our favourite people join us on the actual day itself – it's been far too long!"

Lara's beaming smile suddenly disappeared and she glared at her friend, frozen with shock as deep worry lines creased her forehead.

"I won't be able to come ... not if Adam's going to be there!" Her head shook from side to side.

Elizabeth's heart sank and her chest rose and fell with a weary sigh. "Oh, my darling girl, do you really think I'd do that to you? Don't worry, it'll only be the two of us – oh, and Nikki of course. Adam flew down to Sydney yesterday and he won't be back 'til after the new year."

The question left Lara's mouth before she could stop it. "What's he doing down there?"

Despite all her refusals to see him, she hated the thought of him being so far away again ... even though deep down she knew it was for the best. Her only consolation was that it may help to take his mind off looking for her for a while.

"Don't worry. He has a meeting planned with the director of his next production. Then he wants to catch up with some old theatre friends for a week or two." Elizabeth didn't dare mention he was also in the southern capital trying to find out if anyone down there knew of Lara's whereabouts. "If he keeps to his usual practice, we'll get a phone call early Christmas morning – long before you arrive – and then we can all relax and enjoy our time together."

With a wry smile, Lara reached over and squeezed her hand. "Thanks, Mum, I really couldn't face him ... not when I look like this."

The two women glanced down to where Lara's legs stretched out awkwardly on the bed in front of her. Her feet were twisted and limp with no ability to right themselves. Embarrassed by their misshapen form, Lara reached down and quickly straightened them with her hands.

And then another problem raised its head. "But what about my chair? And how will I get to your place? I'm much too heavy for Charles to carry me."

"It's okay. Everything's already been taken care of. The centre has a mini-bus especially designed for wheelchairs. Your doctor said they're happy to drop you off, chair and all!"

"But even if I go around to the back of your place to save tackling the front stairs, there are still two steps to negotiate. Oh well ... I'll just have to drag myself up on my butt." She burst out laughing. "At least my arms are strong enough now, but it certainly won't make for a pretty picture! You'll just have to look away so I can keep my dignity!"

"Oh, don't worry about that ... Charles can work it all out. He's strong enough to carry you up two small steps. I can't wait to have you visit us again, and I've already worked out the menu!"

"And it's bound to be delicious as always – especially if it's anything like these." Lara quickly dropped another square of White Christmas onto her tongue. "I'm so excited to be getting out of here, even if it is only for one day. Thanks ... Mum."

Lara smiled affectionately as the unfamiliar term she had now used three times in the space of a few minutes slipped easily from her tongue.

Elizabeth rewarded her with one that was similar. "I *adore* hearing you call me that. Thank you."

"And I love using it," Lara replied, unintentionally screwing up her nose as she did so. It was the exact same gesture offered to Adam so many times as a symbol of her love. As always, it took her back in time and the memories made her heart ache for all those shared tokens from their distant past.

Oh, Teddy, I'm so sorry. I didn't mean to betray what was supposed to be ours alone.

As though her spirit still felt him, she had a sense of what his response would be.

You didn't betray us, sweetheart ... whenever you're with Mum, I'm right there too ... it's the only way I can be with you now...

With the faint stirrings of a thoughtful smile, Lara deliberately turned her focus back to the present. Dwelling too long in the past made the longing unbearable. She didn't dare think about what his life was like because of her decision.

Elizabeth caught the faraway look and knew exactly where Lara's thoughts had taken her, even without knowing the cause. Rather than letting their time together end on a sad note, she turned the conversation back to the upcoming outing. "Oh, before I forget, I've already booked your place on the bus for Christmas morning. Unfortunately, you won't be able to join us at church for the early morning service – it isn't feasible with so many other patients to ferry around."

"That's a shame, but it's understandable. I miss going to my usual church with its amazing acoustics, although they do hold a small service here in the community room on Sundays. This'll be the first Christmas service I've missed out on, but I suppose it can't be helped. I saw a notice saying they're holding mass here the night before so that will make up for it."

"Well, I'll be sure to say a prayer for you at ours on Christmas morning."

"Thanks, Mum. You're a darling."

They chatted for another hour until Elizabeth looked at her watch. With dinner to get sorted and things needing to be done to prepare for Nikki's birthday lunch in two days, it was high time she was on her way.

She hugged Lara close and kissed her cheek. "I'm so glad you can join in both occasions with us – and having them at our place is even better! I was worried you'd be stuck here all day ... although we would've brought Christmas to you if that was the case."

Lara smiled, returning her gestures of farewell with just as much gusto. "Thanks, Mum. I still can't believe they're letting me out of here! It'll be so nice to be in a normal house again. See you tomorrow, and please give my love to that good man of yours!"

Elizabeth smiled all the way home as the echo of Lara's new endearment swirled around in her mind and heart. She couldn't wait to start organising the double celebration ... and one other surprise she had planned.

Later that night she lamented, *And please let our boy forgive us, dear Lord...*

Chapter 42

Christmas Day dawned bright and clear. Lara woke to the happy chittering of a Willie Wagtail outside her window just as the sun broke over the horizon. She was excited at the thought of returning to the real world, even if it was only for one day. Nearly eight weeks had passed since her arrival at the rehab centre and almost six months since she had last visited Charles and Elizabeth's riverside home. Her short Melbourne run for *The King and I* and then the unexpected long sojourn in Tuscany had kept her away far longer than anticipated.

Wheeling herself down to the dining room, she sent cheery hellos to other housemates heading in the same direction. Their replies were just as upbeat. The majority were getting out for the day, or at least having visitors to help chase away those horrible blues most of them had to battle with at some time during a normal twenty-four-hour period.

Lara had made several friends during her stay. Each of them shared the common bond of having to cope with the loss of dignity that came from displaying their vulnerabilities for all and sundry to see, especially when carrying out daily exercises or relearning everyday tasks. The only good to come out of all this was sharing a unique rapport. Here at least inpatients were removed from the concerned albeit somewhat awkward glances often coming their way when mingling with the able-bodied.

By ten o'clock, Lara was dressed and ready for her outing. The cap-sleeved sapphire blue dress of crinkled chiffon was the perfect choice as the material shouldn't crush, even though she would be seated all day. The bodice was a V-necked crossover, tailored to fit just beneath her full bust line.

Elizabeth had been quick to offer her help in finding an outfit suitable for the special occasion. This particular design was ideal because it emphasised Lara's eye-catching curves while the full length ensured her legs were kept hidden. Consequently, only the toes of a pair of gold sandals peeped from beneath the floaty hemline. The colour matched her eyes and highlighted her thick crown of glossy hair.

Lara was feeling quite invigorated being able to dress up for a change after having to wear casual tracksuits or loose-fitting trousers most of the time. Unfortunately, they were a necessary evil to cater to her twice-daily exercise regime and constant shuffling in and out of a hospital bed.

Because of the rigorous routines, Lara's upper body was well toned and gave the appearance of her being fit and healthy. With her legs fully covered, it made it difficult to tell just how thin they had become. She looked exactly as she used to – vibrant and beautiful ... and ready to conquer the world.

Even the scars on her arms were starting to blend in with the healthy suntan she sported from being out in the sun on regular jaunts around the nearby park. It was fortunate a thick sweep of hair hid the nasty one on her forehead from inquisitive eyes. As it had done for many years, a stunning necklace still circled her neck. She was grateful the sapphire pendant fell across her recent surgical wound, shielding it from sight.

It took quite a bit of effort by an attendant to wheel her chair into the mini-bus. After a bit of manoeuvring, Lara eventually settled in and her eyes lit up at the thought of leaving this temporary home behind. Taking in the scenery, she noticed a little girl laughing merrily as she wobbled on a shiny pink bicycle. A man ran along behind, keeping a steady hand on the seat. Lara smiled as she watched his worried face and presumed him to be her father. Down another street, a young boy on a brand-new skateboard tried his best to balance on the teetering mode of transport as a frisky puppy gambolled around the wheels.

For the first time in many months, Lara felt truly alive again. Even the leaves on the trees seemed greener as they shivered in the soft morning breeze. Garden beds filled with long-stemmed flowers appeared to nod their colourful heads in a cheerful greeting when the bus drove by, while an avenue lined with frangipani trees gave off their sweet, heady fragrance. It brought back a myriad of recollections from other times when she and Adam had driven beneath this same yellow and pink corridor on their way to visit his parents.

Soon they turned down an even more familiar tree-lined street. Lara's heart started pounding when she recognised a stately stone fence bordering the spacious property at the end of the cul-de-sac. There were so many heart-wrenching memories bound up inside its borders and each one centred on a beloved man's glorious smile ... one that always made her heart race even with the smallest glimpse. Taking a couple of deep breaths as a way to keep her emotions in check, she managed to turn a sudden rush of yearning into a thankful though somewhat pensive smile.

A distinguished-looking man and two attractive women – one older and the other considerably younger – were already standing at the end of the driveway in front of a staircase leading up to an elegant two-storey sandstone home when the vehicle came to a halt only a few metres away. Their beaming smiles and hearty waves were all Lara needed to lift her spirits.

You're so fortunate, you silly girl. Don't you dare let any of those old longings spoil today, she warned herself.

In the short time it took for the attendant to unbuckle the wheelchair and roll her to the door, their excited greetings and cries of delight chased the last of those blues away. To everyone seated on the bus, it was obvious this was a long-awaited homecoming.

Before she was even halfway down the ramp, a whirlwind flew up to meet her, laughing and crying at the same time. Lara was soon swept into a tight hug that reminded her of when Nikki was a little girl. After the last few trying months, the young woman was having a hard time choking back the tears at the sight of her mother away from the sterile clinic. No one had any idea how many nights she had cried herself to sleep with worry. Nor did they realise how on her very first visit to the intensive care unit in Cortona she had wondered whether Lara would even survive the crash. To see her looking so well and able to share in the double celebration was all the gift she needed.

Through a beaming smile, Elizabeth wiped away a stream of tears from both hers and Lara's cheeks when she went to greet the special VIP. "Oh, my darling daughter, it's so wonderful to have you home at last!" Clasping Lara close, her welcome was the perfect motherly touch for the happy homecoming.

"Thanks, Mum. It's so great to be back here again," Lara said, smiling through the tears during the impromptu mop-up. Catching Charles' joyous reaction at this new form of address for his wife, her expression matched his.

"Welcome home, my dear girl, we've all missed you very much," he crooned, offering the visitor a warm hug. They exchanged a telling look at his subtle reference to Adam, knowing this was where her heart felt closest to him now.

Charles pushed the wheelchair across the paved driveway and onto the grassed area leading to the back of the house. Nikki and Elizabeth walked alongside clutching onto Lara's hands. She looked across and noticed Jasper with his neck stretched inquisitively over the paddock fence, taking in everything that was going on. There was the faint echo of a few gentle snickers as he smelt the air as a way to catch her familiar scent.

"Hello, old boy," she called as he tossed his head and paced up and down the boundary fence. It was clear he recognised her voice. "I've missed you too and God-willing one day soon I'll be able to come over and say hello properly."

Nikki squeezed the hand she was holding and smiled down at her mother. "I sure hope so, and *I've* missed you, too."

The look Lara bestowed on her only daughter spoke of everything in her heart. "Don't you *dare* make me cry, young lady. Not today!" It was her only defence to control all the emotions welling up inside, and Nikki understood.

When they reached the edge of the terrace, Charles scooped Lara up in one swift movement and carried her through to the living room where a recliner chair had already been set up to ensure she was comfortable. He deliberately left the wheelchair outside – it was too painful a reminder of just how close they had come to losing her. The last thing he wanted was for any memories of those dark days to mar this special occasion.

"There you are, my dear, a throne fit for a princess where we can spoil you all day long! I've designated myself as your slave, so I'm happy to transport you wherever you need." He smiled and placed a warm kiss on her forehead as a gentle finger chucked her chin.

"Thank you, but you'd better not go spoiling me too much or I might just get used to it. Then I'll never want to go back to that dreary old place again."

His reply was soft and only for her ears. "I'll spoil you as much as I want. I don't get many chances to do so anymore."

Lara's send him a loving smile as her eyes turned misty.

Nikki was busy looking for a comfy cushion to wedge behind her mother's back. "There you go," she trilled after making sure it was positioned just right. "Make yourself comfortable and I'll be back soon. I'd better go and help in the kitchen. We want to feed you up so you can come home for good." She left them with a beaming smile and a firm kiss planted on the special guest's cheek.

Lara and Charles glanced affectionately at her retreating back. Reaching down, he squeezed her hand. "It's wonderful to have you here again. Our two princesses back where they belong – what more could Mum and I ask for."

"I still can't believe I *am* actually here. It's so much nicer being with people I love rather than ones who only want to prod and poke at my legs all the time!"

His expression was tender as he looked into her eyes. "My dear, I have a very big favour to ask."

"What is it? You know you can ask me anything."

"It did this old heart of mine good to hear you call Elizabeth 'mum'. She's always thought of you as a daughter. Would it be asking too much to have you call me 'dad'?"

He was left in no doubt when he saw her huge smile. "I'd *love* to ... Dad. I can't think of anything nicer. Since our first meeting, you've always treated me like part of the family. I'm only sorry I didn't think of it long before all of this happened."

It was a solemn moment as they hugged each other ... and one that meant the world to both of them.

"Okay. Who wants an icy cold glass of tropical punch?" Nikki called from the other room.

"I'd love one," they chorused together and shared a surprised smile at the mirroring of their responses.

When the sound of the doorbell echoed throughout the house, Charles threw Lara a cheesy grin.

The sudden chime caused her heart to leap into her mouth. Her immediate thought was to wonder whether Elizabeth had been telling the truth the week before. Panic filled Lara's eyes and she felt sick to the stomach, frantically trying to cover her feet with the hem of the dress when he went to answer it.

Please don't let it be him... Please...

The prayer rose from the bottom of her heart. But as much as she tried not to, her gaze was fixed on the doorway leading to the foyer.

"Well, look who we have here! Come in, come in," Charles called out as he opened the front door.

A mini-tornado raced through the foyer and landed with a thud on the arm of Lara's chair. Then a pair of skinny arms wrapped themselves around her neck as a flurry of sloppy kisses landed hard on her cheek.

"*Oooh, Jack!* You gave me such a *fright!*" Lara laughed in relief as she gathered up her nine-year-old nephew with a smothering cuddle. "Where did *you* come from? I thought Mummy and Daddy were taking you for a holiday down the coast for the week."

"We're *still* on holidays, but we've been invited over as a special surprise for you. We couldn't miss Nikki's birthday *or* seeing you for Christmas! I've missed you heaps and *heaps*, Aunty Lara!"

The duo had always been close, even though her career entailed travelling from place to place for months on end. She had missed him during her time in Tuscany and subsequent sojourn in rehab. Suzie had received strict instructions not to bring Jack up to the hospital. Lara didn't want the sight of her injuries, along with all the paraphernalia associated with them, upsetting her young nephew. This was the first time they had seen each other for over four months. Despite that small hiccup when the doorbell sounded, Lara was thrilled to have the entire family there for Christmas.

"I missed you too, little mate. And *look at you!* My goodness, *sooo* handsome and I swear you're nearly as tall as your big cousin!"

She looked him up and down, ruffling the mop of curly dark hair then glowered playfully at her sister and brother-in-law. Their sheepish grins confirmed a lot of secret plotting had been going on to make her first outing extra special.

"Why didn't you say something about coming today when we were at Nikki's party?" Lara chided.

"Because we wanted to surprise you and it certainly looks like our plan worked!" Suzie replied, giving her sister an affectionate hug.

"It sure did, but I didn't hear you arrive – where's the car?"

"Ben came in the back way to make sure you didn't see or hear us drive in."

She glanced out the window. There was no sign of the large Toyota LandCruiser. "Well, your plan certainly worked. I had no idea who was at the door. But it's *so* good to see you ... now my day is perfect!"

"It's great to see you too, especially away from that cold hole!"

"It's nice to be out and about, believe me." Pulling her sister close again, Lara whispered into her ear, "Thank you."

"You're welcome." A tender smile and loving squeeze accompanied her response.

Suzie had witnessed Lara's reaction when Charles first opened the door. It hadn't been too hard to guess where her sister's thoughts had taken her. She hoped having the family there would help take her mind off someone else.

Just then the birthday girl waltzed in from the kitchen with an assortment of finger food on a large silver platter.

"Happy birthday, young lady!" her aunt exclaimed.

She grabbed Nikki around the waist and landed a warm kiss on her cheek just as Ben kissed her other one while throwing in a cheerful, "Happy birthday, beautiful!"

Not to be left out, Jack rushed over and threw his arms around his cousin, nearly knocking them all over in the process. "Happy birthday, Nikki! When can I ride Jasper? It's *ages* since I've seen him."

"Oh, Jack, be careful!" his father admonished, sending a worried look Lara's way. He was afraid they might all topple onto her from the excitement.

She was just as quick to respond that everything was okay. It was a real tonic being with all the family again and the last thing she wanted was to spoil the mood.

"So *can* I see Jasper? *Pleeaasse...*"

"After lunch, young man. First, come and help me bring all the presents in from the car."

Jack grimaced in frustration before grabbing Nikki by the hand. "Well, you'd better help too, 'cause there are heaps and heaps and the biggest one's for you!"

The two cousins followed Ben as he went to bring in the basket-load of gifts. The ornately adorned Christmas tree positioned in the curve of the long staircase was a sight to behold once their gifts joined the others piled beneath its branches. When everyone had settled into the two plush sofas in the living room with Lara in between, Jack was given the honour of playing Father Christmas.

Loud exclamations of delight and offerings of thanks filled the room as the large parade of gifts was passed from hand to hand. Not much later, it was Nikki's turn to be the centre of attention as she opened her birthday gifts.

Lara now understood why her daughter hadn't minded leaving her present opening until now. The celebration was just like old times, and having Suzie and the family there made the day even more special. Her gaze swept the room and then came to rest on Elizabeth. The older woman recognised the look of appreciation in their depths and blew her an acknowledging kiss.

Torn wrapping paper littered the floor and piles of gifts encircled the birthday girl until there was only one person left to hand out hers. Charles' face was beaming as he pulled out a noticeably heavy and unusually shaped parcel from behind the sofa.

Placing it on the floor in front of his beloved granddaughter, he announced with a tender smile, "And this one's from your mum..."

"Whoa, that's huge! What on earth can it be?" she responded with a puzzled frown, trying to sneak a look under each corner.

Her mother answered, "Well, you'd better open it up and see. I doubt it's going to open itself!"

Sending a grateful glance Charles and Elizabeth's way, Lara discreetly mouthed the words, "Thank you."

She had found it so discouraging trying to arrange Nikki's gift from the confines of the rehab centre. When the Ashworths offered to take care of all the details, she breathed a heavy sigh of relief and happily accepted their help. A telephone call was all that was needed for an order to be placed and the delivery organised. Charles and Elizabeth were just as happy to take on the wrapping as well as purchasing an appropriate card to save her the worry.

When Nikki ripped away the copious amounts of sticky tape, she gave an excited shout and turned to her mother. "Oh Mum, a *jumping* saddle! This is perfect! Thank you *sooo* so much!"

"You're welcome, my darling! Now, how about you bring it over here so I can test how it feels. I tried to pick out the best one from the catalogue to suit both you and your big, beautiful boy. His typical Arabian short, straight back narrowed the field, but this looked like the one you always wanted."

Nikki had been eyeing off the catalogue for several months, but the saddle had far too pricey for a young actress with limited funds.

Taking great care, she placed the awkward item on her mother's lap. It matched Jasper's chestnut coat perfectly, and the eager young rider couldn't wait to see it strapped around the magnificent gelding's girth. Together, their fingers traced the supple calfskin leather of the master craftsman's work, exploring every contour and dip to ensure its quality.

Recognising the renowned *Ascot Saddlery* brand embossed in elegant script across the bottom of both flaps, her eyes opened wide with astonishment. "This is *exactly* the one I wanted! But how could you organise everything when you've been stuck in hospital for so long?"

Lara's eyes sparkled as she nodded towards her newly-adopted parents. "Along with the catalogue and convenience of a telephone, I had some welcome help ... you'd better thank them as well!"

Nikki responded by throwing her arms around their shoulders. "Oh, it's the best! Thank you so much! You've both been wonderful to Mum and me. I'm not sure how we would've coped over the last few months without your help."

She was well aware of the amount of time, effort and money they had put into Lara's hospitalisation costs, as well as everything needed to fly her home from Italy by private jet. Added to that was the invitation to stay with them for the last two months.

"We love you both, so it was nothing really," Charles replied, thrilled at the reaction on the exuberant young woman's face. "Besides, you've outgrown that old saddle, so it was high time you had a new one."

"And I bet you and Jasper win a heap more ribbons with this little beauty," Elizabeth added, hugging her only granddaughter and planting a firm kiss on her cheek. "Your darling mother was determined to give you the best – she even had it especially tailor-made by asking the saddler to come out here and measure Jasper's back and girth to ensure everything was right."

Everyone marvelled over the superbly crafted piece as Lara watched on with love and pride in her eyes. Jack had them all in fits of laughter, pretending to be a cowboy and calling out a few "Yee-haws" as he straddled the new gift after Nikki draped it over one of the sofas' armrests. His mother had to physically pull him away when Elizabeth announced lunch was almost ready.

The festive meal was served in the formal dining room, both to honour Nikki's special day and to celebrate Lara's first visit after such a long time. Usually, they gravitated to the terrace. This year, however, Elizabeth insisted the two celebrations were worthy of the finer setting, including the addition of a guipure lace tablecloth. The table looked spectacular with its silver cutlery, crystal glasses and Royal Doulton dinnerware, all set off by a magnificent arrangement of colourful Christmas baubles perfectly arranged as the centrepiece in a crystal bowl.

Charles carried Lara over to the table and placed her carefully into a chair he had organised specifically for her needs. It had generous arms and extra cushions to make her feel more comfortable. She was seated directly beside Nikki, who had been promoted to pride of place at one end of the table. Elizabeth had happily given up her normal spot to sit between Lara and her husband for the significant event. Ben and Suzie sat opposite, with Jack seated in between.

Casting her eyes over the beautiful table setting, Lara could picture three exquisite crystal and eighteen-carat gold Christmas ornaments purchased especially for her in Salzburg. The set was currently tucked away in its own velvet-lined box in the bottom drawer of her dresser at home.

I haven't forgotten about you, and you're going to be back on display right in the centre where you belong this time next year, she vowed in her heart.

The parade of food Elizabeth and Suzie marched to the table was fit for the two princesses Charles had mentioned earlier. There was a cooked ham on the bone lavishly decorated with glazed pineapple and glacé cherries, a perfectly roasted turkey with crispy brown skin accompanied by a rich cranberry sauce, and enough trimmings and vegetables to feed a small army. The meal was accompanied by one of the new wine varieties from the family vineyard in the hills behind the Gold Coast.

Lara squeezed Elizabeth's hand. "It's easy to see you've been hard at work in the kitchen. Your Christmas dinners are always delicious – the best I've ever tasted – and as usual, this one looks amazing."

From his place at the head of the table, Charles took his wife's other hand with a proud smile. "She certainly has, and it's no wonder considering what a great occasion this is for all of us!"

Elizabeth blushed profusely. "Oh, get out of here – and besides, it wasn't all my doing. I had a willing helper." She looked across at the birthday girl, and she and Nikki exchanged grins.

"Well, you both deserve a medal from all these delicious smells!" Lara declared. "I can already tell I'm going to leave here much fatter. Then I'll be in trouble when it comes to doing all of those horrible exercises tomorrow!" She groaned at the thought of the gruelling routine awaiting her. At least today provided a short respite from Josh's continual demands.

"Too *fat!* You've hardly got an ounce of spare flesh as it is after all those workouts you've been doing. Anyway, it'll do you good to put some meat on your bones. We can't have you wasting away to a shadow!" Elizabeth scoffed good-naturedly while the others heartily agreed.

"More like a *mammoth* if I had to eat at *your* restaurant every night – look at all this food!" Lara chuckled in reply, enjoying the camaraderie after being away for so long. As much as she got on with her fellow inmates, there was nothing like family to make her heart glad. She turned to her daughter. "Better watch out, Munchkin, or you'll soon be putting on piles of weight from all those carbs you were worried about before coming home to stay!"

"Oh, *Muuum!*" Nikki rolled her eyes at the childhood name as a burst of laughter came from all sides of the table.

Before tucking into the generous spread, everyone joined hands as Charles prayed, "Father God, we thank you for your Son as we celebrate his birth, for all your bountiful blessings and the delicious variety of food spread before us. We give thanks even more so for Lara being able to join us today, and we ask for your continued help to build her strength so she can be up walking again very soon – *and* serenading us with that fabulous voice. It's a real treat having her safely back with us ... even if she *is* rather a handful at the moment!"

With furtive glances around the table, those listening on couldn't help breaking into amused smirks. Charles had been carrying Lara around the house ever since her arrival, so she definitely had turned into a handful for him at least.

"And bless the hands that prepared this meal" —Elizabeth and Nikki were suddenly on the receiving end of several affirming smiles and nods— "and we ask your blessing on this food and our time together."

For a fraction of a second Charles paused, and then he couldn't help himself. "Be with those we all love who can't be here today" —Suzie sent a quick look her sister's way and noticed Lara catch her breath and then swallow hard— "and continue to keep Nikki safe as she celebrates this special day and throughout the year to come – especially when she's using that swish new saddle on Jasper! And let them gain many years of pleasure – and safety – from it. Thank you for all your plentiful gifts. In the name of our Lord Jesus Christ, Amen."

Ignoring the pain in her heart, and as a way to keep everyone else from dwelling on that one line and focus on the other cheeky one instead, Lara playfully pitched her unopened bon-bon down the table. "What's this about me being a handful! How *rude!*"

With a loud guffaw, he ducked his head as the whole table resounded with relieved laughter. In the time-honoured tradition, she then broke out into a husky rendition of *Happy Birthday,* and the others soon joined in. Even though her voice was far below its usual clarity, the atmosphere around the table was just like old times. This was the seventeenth time the mother and daughter had shared Nikki's birthday with Adam's parents – the first when she was just five years old – and each one held significant memories for all of them.

Raising a champagne glass, Lara's natural beauty mingled with a hint of regret, although her eyes sparkled as she looked across at her daughter. "I can't believe my baby girl is now twenty-one years old. I'm just sorry I wasn't there to cater for all your friends last week, sweetheart. I hope you didn't mind. I wasn't too sure how I'd cope being around that amount of people just yet."

"Of course, I didn't. We all had a great time, but today is perfect. This is exactly what I wanted with all the family around, truly."

"Well you're the absolute joy of my life and the other beat of my heart – everything a mother could ever want in a daughter. I'm proud of the fun-loving, gorgeous little girl you were, *and* for the talented, caring and considerate person you've become. I wish you every happiness and continued success in all you do. To Nikki – my special blessing..."

Everyone around the table raised their glasses, toasting the young woman with three rousing cheers.

It certainly was a great day for celebration.

Chapter 43

The mouth-watering lunch was over, and everything cleared away. With a satisfied sigh, Lara confirmed it was the best meal she had eaten for a very long time. Charles carried her back to the recliner while Nikki took Jasper for a quick ride to break-in the new saddle. Jack followed his cousin and was happy watching from behind the fence-line as she and the trusty mount completed a complicated jump sequence. The young boy was looking forward to a much-anticipated ride once the spirited gelding had settled down.

Suzie and Ben offered to clean up while Elizabeth and Charles chatted with Lara in the living room. Soft strains of traditional Christmas Carols drifted from the in-wall speakers located throughout the house and made for a relaxing atmosphere.

When the sudden chime of the doorbell echoed through the living area, the husband and wife turned quizzically to each other.

"Were you expecting anyone?" Elizabeth asked as he got up to answer it.

"No, were you?"

"Not at all. I've no idea who it could be."

Hurrying out to the foyer as the two women continued chatting about the day, Charles' eyes lit up as soon as he pulled the door open.

"Merry Christmas, Dad!"

The older man's face broke into a huge welcoming smile. He knew this wasn't just fate ... more like divine intervention. "*Adam, my dear boy!* What a *wonderful* surprise! But what are you doing here? I thought you were in Sydney when we spoke on the phone this morning..."

The newcomer's smile matched his father's. "I was! I just flew in an hour ago. I hoped you might be up for a visit from a lonely old traveller."

"Of *course* we are ... oooh, I can't believe you're here! This is the best Christmas *ever!*"

Charles grabbed his son and pulled him close, slapping his back over and over again as Adam manipulated an armful of gifts to return the hug.

"It's great to see you. And this is just the welcome I needed! Christmas in Sydney isn't much fun without family, and I hated the thought of you and mum being on your own today, so I jumped on a plane at the last minute."

"Come in, come in!" Charles' expression softened when he noticed the sudden shimmer filling his son's dark eyes.

Pulling him into another warm embrace, he couldn't miss Adam's deep sigh as he clung to him. It was obvious all those gruelling months spent searching for Lara were taking their toll and being with family was all he craved.

"Well actually, we're not on our own," Charles added when they broke free and he was able to look into his son's eyes again. "We've had some very special visitors drop by – I think you might remember them."

That beloved voice was instantly recognisable to the woman sitting just out of their line of sight. His mellow tone had always been at the forefront of her thoughts.

Lara's heart was racing at the thought of seeing him again ... until reality hit. Turning to Elizabeth in dread, her eyes filled with unshed tears. In desperation, she shook her head as a frown creased her brow and the word '*Nooo!*' fell silently though emphatically from her lips.

She looked around frantically, trying to work out how to get away before he could catch a glimpse of her. Then she remembered the wheelchair waiting on the terrace hidden from view, too far away to be of any use. The wretchedness of her situation threatened to overwhelm the panic-filled woman ... while her heart maintained that powerful drumbeat in her chest.

There was absolutely nothing Lara could do. Destiny had taken matters into its own hands, choosing to intervene while her injuries ensured she remained captive to its bidding.

Charles led the way into the living room. The looks he and Elizabeth exchanged were of joyful astonishment. There was a gleam of hope shining in their eyes evident for anyone to see, though Lara was too busy trying to cover her legs and hide any scars to notice the silent messages.

As soon as he came around the corner, Adam was completely oblivious to everything except the beautiful woman with chestnut hair seated directly in front of him. She was dressed in his favourite shade of blue and had the appearance of an angel in the soft afternoon light spilling through the window behind.

His mouth fell open as he came to an abrupt halt, almost dropping the armload of presents on the floor. Wordlessly and moving like a robot, he deposited them on the coffee table, while those piercing eyes Lara recognised so well held hers captive. When he eventually did manage to speak, his voice was breathless as though having just run up a very steep hill.

"*Lara!*"

All it took was hearing her name spill from his lips for all those old defences to come tumbling down. She had heard it uttered countless times every day of her life, though none of them had ever been coated with this amount of emotion ... or pain. To hear it slip through his lips again was enough to make it seem to breathe with new life.

Any thought of fleeing was gone the instant she looked into those never-forgotten eyes. She was powerless to stifle the cry rising out of her spirit. "Oh, Adam ... my love..."

The loud emotion-laden lament made him groan with longing. It was everything he had been yearning for during all of those long and lonely nights making up a lifetime of years. He crossed the room at a run and fell on his knees beside her. Cradling the face he adored with hands seeping with tenderness, every inch was covered in desperate kisses as two small tears rolled slowly down her cheeks.

And all the while his gaze held hers for what seemed like an eternity.

All of those months filled with pain and heartache melted away as she drowned in his captivating dark eyes – soul windows that once upon a time had given her spirit nourishment and strength. And today was no different. She fed from his intense stare ... and Adam did the same. Letting out another heartfelt groan, he clutched her against his chest as though terrified she might disappear again.

Neither of them noticed when Elizabeth and Charles slipped away to join the others in the kitchen. This was a private time of reunion and rebirth. It was important these first few moments were theirs alone to savour and cherish.

Every millisecond evolved into a new form of forever as the reunited lovers breathed each other in ... and once-empty arms now held close what had always seemed an unattainable dream. For the first time ever, they felt as free as eagles, soaring above an ocean of longing to ride the thermals of reunited souls.

When reality stole in bringing with it a fresh wave of hope, Adam touched her face with gentle fingertips, once again looking into those bluest of eyes. "I don't *believe* this ... my beautiful *darling Lara!* I had no *idea* you'd be here. Do you know how long I've been searching for you – wondering where you were? And no one seemed to know. It was as if you'd just dropped off the face of the earth. Oh, my sweet, sweet love, where have you been hiding?"

The moisture trickled from her eyes, making them sparkle like freshly cut diamonds. Lifting a gentle finger, he wiped every drop away, unaware his face was awash with its own steady stream now released at last from a dam held in check for so long. Her hands came up and deftly stroked his cheeks, not only gathering up those soulful droplets but also responding as a blind person – anxious to fasten onto everything familiar through each loving skin-stroke. He turned a little so his mouth touched the tips of her fingers with his lips, hungry to taste every part of this unexpected dream come true.

The large lump in Lara's throat restricted her raspy voice to rise above a whisper as she felt and watched his tender ministrations. "I'm *sooo* sorry, Teddy ... I had to go away ... I couldn't help it ... just don't ask me why, *please*." Every phrase dripped with pathos and remorse.

"But didn't you get my note? I left it with a bunch of roses against your door months ago. I have *so* much to tell you." Grasping her hand, the desperation in his eyes broke her heart.

There was no place to hide from the amount of hurt she was about to inflict by revealing she knew about his marriage breakup, as well as break the news regarding her subsequent and deliberate disappearance. Swallowing hard, all she could manage was a slow and contrite nod through a barrage of regret that went so deep it caused the words to stick in the back of her throat.

And she was right ... the agony in his eyes was even more intense as the telling gesture registered in his still befuddled brain. Watching his reaction, she felt as though a knife had pierced her heart ... and his.

Lara's hand fell limply into her lap when he dropped it like a hot iron. Slumping back on his haunches, Adam's tone was incredulous. "You *knew?*"

With a loud cry, she clung to the front of his shirt, trying to pull him close again. "Oh, my darling, please don't look at me like that. I can't bear to see all the suffering I've caused you. Adam, you *have* to believe me ... I wanted so much to be with you, but there was nothing I could do."

"But *why*, Lara? What could *possibly* have kept you away once you learned about Trina and I splitting up? I don't understand..." His chin dropped onto his chest and a loud groan rose in his throat. "I thought you must've stopped loving me..."

Now it was her turn to cradle his face with soothing hands. Pressing her lips against his forehead, she whispered an earnest, *"Oooh, Teddy..."*

Her heart was breaking, but she had no idea how to put it together again.

Once again, those haunted dark eyes sought out hers. *"But why?* What other reason could there be for you to hide from me like that? Even Mum and Dad didn't know where you were."

She had to close her eyes from the force of this last heartbreaking statement. A small sob bubbled up from her throat. How could she have incriminated his parents in her ruse? It was inevitable he would eventually find out the truth.

Feverishly, she stroked along two deep ridges of frown lines where they crossed his brow, trying to erase them with her fingertips. "Oh my darling, I'm *sooo* so sorry." She swallowed hard. He could almost taste the potency of her anguish as even more cutting words trudged from her soul. "They did know ... but believe me, it wasn't their fault. They begged to be able to tell you ... over and over again ... but I said no ... to be honest, I *forced* them not to say anything.

You mustn't blame them for my pigheadedness."

Everything was becoming far too confusing for him to comprehend. Wrenching her hands away, he needed an unhindered view of her face. "But why would you *do* that? And I can't believe they agreed to go along with something so cruel knowing how much I love you. It doesn't make any sense."

He scanned her face, determined to get to the bottom of why she was being so secretive. All Lara could do was look him in the eyes with an expression filled with deep regret.

He shook his head when she didn't answer. "I just don't understand ... they *knew* how frantically I was searching for you!"

"I can't give you an answer, Teddy. Just believe me when I say the reason would've hurt you too much, and I couldn't bear to cause you any more pain after everything else. You've been through enough already." Her hands once again sought out his face to offer a degree of comfort.

Anxious to hear the truth, though deeply afraid whatever she was hiding would break his heart, he grabbed hold of her arms. Using more force than intended, he squeezed them hard as his face pressed close to hers. "Is there someone *else?* Have you *married* again? Is that what's going on? *Tell* me, Lara, *pleeeaaase.*" He grasped her left hand only to see it was bare.

Leaning in with a heartfelt groan, she caressed his lips with hers, willing him to believe her as she vowed, "No, my love, I could *never* marry anyone else."

Adam let out a loud cry and pulled her into his arms again, claiming her mouth so forcefully their teeth collided. The desperation behind his relief was obvious, even though he was still left fumbling in the dark. With eyes closed, he breathed in each breath as it slipped through her parted lips, as though his soul was trying to draw in her spirit to force the truth out. No matter what her reasoning, he was determined never to let her go again.

Displaying a fervour long still remembered, she clung on and returned his kisses with the same degree of passion. He recognised her whimpers from all the other times they had been together like this – lost in their own private universe. The impact of hearing them again spurred him on even further to find out exactly what was going on. No one kissed with this much abandon without being deeply in love. So what was she hiding?

Overwhelmed by the long-lost craving revitalising every pore in their battle-weary bodies, Adam had to pull away. He was afraid of losing control. Even so, his hands still grasped Lara's tightly as he stared her down, willing her to tell him what was going on.

But still she kept silent.

Frustrated, he shook his head. "That's *it!* I'm getting to the bottom of all this and if *you* won't tell me then maybe Mum and Dad *will*. But *you're* coming with me – *no arguments!*" He scrambled to his feet and tugged at her hands.

"*I can't...*" Two simple words cried with such utter despair it made him stop in his tracks.

Instantly, a look of bewilderment overshadowed all of that former frustration. "*Why* can't you? Baby, what's going on? *Tell me!*"

Snatching her hands away, she thrust them over her face, neither willing nor able to look at him now the time had come to finally reveal the truth.

From out of the corner of his eye, Adam spied Suzie coming in from the terrace. She was pushing an empty wheelchair in front of her. Their anguished exchanges had carried out to the kitchen. Wanting to save her sister from the agony of further inquisition, she had decided to take matters into her own hands.

He caught sight of the grief in her eyes and turned back, pulling Lara's hands away as a look of hopelessness made his skin turn pale.

"Whose wheelchair is that?" Suddenly everything fell into place and his mouth fell open. "*Dear God, Lara ... what happened?* You *have* to tell me!"

Tear-soaked eyes searched his and her croaky voice once again came out as a whisper. "It's mine, Teddy." Hearing his sudden gasp, she had to swallow hard to summon up the courage to go on. "The day after André's first concert I was involved in a car accident." She could feel his pain as it poured from his eyes, but she couldn't stop. The words needed to be said once and for all, even though she could hardly speak because of the battle going on with her emotions after witnessing firsthand his shock and disbelief. "The car I was driving went over the side of the mountain while I was on my way to visit Claud—"

A powerful moan emanated from the pit of his stomach as he sunk to his haunches beside her. "*Noooo....*"

"It's okay. Please don't cry, my darling." Gentle thumbs brushed his tears away.

"But what happened to *you?* Your voice sounds so different ... and why a wheelchair?" Finding it all too hard to comprehend, he pulled away and looked her up and down. A thick film of tears blinded him from noticing her scars.

"They needed to operate on my throat and it damaged my vocal cords ... that's why I sound so different."

His gaze moved to her neck as a shaky thumb reached out to touch the small section of puckered flesh hiding behind an expensive sapphire and diamond necklace. He was too upset to register she was still wearing it.

"It's okay. Don't be afraid to touch ... the scar doesn't hurt anymore."

And then it dawned on him. She hadn't moved her legs the whole time they had been speaking. His searching gaze travelled down to where her toes were peeking out from below the long dress and then back to her face.

She nodded slowly. "Yes, sweetheart, my legs are partially paralysed. The doctors aren't sure if I'll ever be able to walk properly again. I can manage a few steps, but only by clinging to the exercise bars. It's been a slow process, and there's always the chance I may never fully recover."

A sob tore from his throat. "*Oh, my darling*, why didn't you *tell* me? I would've come to you. I can't believe you've had to face all this on your *own*."

Lara paused, trying hard to swallow another lump as she peered at him through blurred eyes. Her heart felt like a lead weight after witnessing the amount of pain he was in and knowing she was the cause of it. He'd already been through enough.

"I haven't been on my own, Teddy. I've had Mum and Dad as well as Nikki and Suzie with me ... and Luce." She dropped her eyes at the look of anguish on his face when he realised his best friend's wife was in on the secret too. Swallowing hard, she slowly raised them again. "They've all been there for me throughout this whole ordeal."

"And *Jeff* too, I suppose – that *mongrel!* What about *me! I* could've helped, too." In a matter of seconds, his tone went from anger to frustration and finally to despair. "Or don't I matter enough anymore?"

Knowing how heartbroken he would be was the precise reason she had kept silent. He had seen enough heartache in his life already without adding another whole layer that may go on forever.

"Of *course* you do, sweetheart, and that's exactly why I didn't say anything – I couldn't bear having you see me like this. I *know* how much you love me ... that's why I knew it would hurt you too much."

He got up off his haunches and knelt in front of her again, moving even closer to search her face. "It's *because* I love you that I want to share everything – the good *and* the bad. Please don't shut me out. You need *me, too*."

Somehow, she had to convince him. "I can't, sweetheart. Me being like this will only hold you back, and I don't want to hamper your career." She gestured to her crooked legs, imploring him to understand. "You have a whole future ahead of you, both here and overseas ... I'd just be a burden and a hindrance."

His hands grasped hers with frustration. "No, you won't. You're more important than *anything* else. Besides, I can always design houses or office blocks while you get better. I've already started building a home for us overlooking the Glasshouse Mountains. Didn't you read that in my note?"

She nodded sadly. "Yes, I did ... and I adore that you want to do all that for us, especially up there where it's so peaceful, but you need someone who can travel from place to place supporting you the way you deserve. I don't want to have to wait at home for months on end constantly wondering how you are and wishing I could be standing by your side."

He stroked her hair, pleading with his eyes. "You won't have to. I'll ask the producers to find someone else for the shows I'm already contracted for, at least until we can get you back on your feet. I'm sure they'll understand when they hear why. You said you've already taken a few steps. If we work hard together, I know we can do it. *Please,* darling, let me help. You're my *life!* You always *have* been ... from the very first instant you burst through that old theatre door. And we've wasted too much time already, *please* don't make us wait any longer."

Lara glanced across to the doorway and four sets of eyes sent their own poignant plea. They knew everything he said was right. Finally, she came to the same realisation.

Reaching out to touch the beloved silver patch at the front of his hairline, now less discernible amidst the salt and pepper, she drew him closer and murmured against his lips, "I'm *sooo* sorry, my darling. I didn't mean to be so cruel. I truly thought this was the best thing for both of us. Can you ever forgive me?"

With a loud sigh, he replied, "Only if you promise never to do anything like that again ... *ever!* It's been *agony* wondering where you were all these months."

Tender smiles replaced the former anguish and despair, while joined mouths brought a much-needed form of healing. This time their lips were gentle and loving rather than desperate and hungry, on a new journey to rediscover the familiar. Their eyes remained open, searching one another's soul in that old familiar way, fearful of closing them in case reality once again became a longed-for dream.

Exchanging delighted smiles, the others tiptoed into the room. When the reunited lovers spotted them out of the corner of their eyes, they separated – although not too far. Just far enough to welcome the family into a tight circle.

"Well, it's about *time!*" Elizabeth remarked with a loving smile, coming over to put her arms around both at the same time. She kissed their foreheads with a motherly smooch. "I was ready to give up on ever seeing this day arrive. But it couldn't have happened on a more perfect occasion!"

Before anyone could respond, a loud voice caused the whole family to turn towards the doorway.

"Oh, yeah, *that'd* be right! Stealing the limelight on *my* special day!"

Fresh from riding Jasper, Nikki was both astounded and delighted to see her mother and Adam together. With a squeal of joy, she hurried over to take Elizabeth's place, grabbing the beaming couple with both arms and squeezing them tight. At long last, this was the family she had always longed for.

Adam swept her up in a bearhug, holding her close and breathing in that unique fragrance that took him back to when she was a little girl. Apart from their brief conversation a year earlier – the one following Lara and Mark Sinclair's performances in *A Little Night Music* – many years had passed since they had last spent any real time together.

Back then, he had been lost in a world of longing – too distraught to take in what was going on. Seeing her now, he was bowled over by this mature and confident young woman instead of that shy schoolgirl gracing a college stage on the receiving end of all those well-deserved accolades and awards.

Nikki clung to his neck and wouldn't let go, reminding him of other welcoming hugs all those years ago. The loving gesture made him realise just how much of her life he had missed.

When they eventually came up for air, he stood back and held her at arm's length, taking in all the changes with an admiring grin. "Who's this stunner I hardly recognise and what happened to that cute little Munchkin I used to know?"

She gave a happy chortle followed by a dismissive wave. "Oh, she's long gone – and from the look of all this, it seems you'll soon be putting up with a hormonal daughter instead of that little kid who drove you crazy warbling *My Favourite Things* all the time!"

The room filled with laughter as his hands went up in the air in mock horror. "*Oh, no* ... anything bar that! Two gorgeous women in my life and both liable to burst into tears at the drop of a hat! Heaven help me!"

From the chair beside them, a playful backhand landed on his arm, while another well-aimed shot from this long-lost daughter made contact with the other one. Both women laughed as they exchanged identical thumbs-up at their perfect timing.

"Watch it, Mister," Lara responded, "or we'll *both* gang up on you. Then you'll end up rueing the day we ever came back into your life!"

"*Never!* That, my darling, would be *impossible!* Anyway, back to you, young lady" —he raised his eyebrows and sent a cheeky smirk Nikki's way— "If I remember correctly, it was more like 'My *Faborite* Things'!"

Blushing profusely, she jabbed at his arm. "Shoosh! Don't remind me!"

The others let out a chorus of loud chuckles and nodded, recalling more of her cute expressions as Adam broke into a mischievous grin. "Mmm, let's see if I can remember some more ... uuummm..."

She screwed up her nose and poked out her tongue. "Don't you dare!"

Bending down, he landed an affectionate peck on that cute upturned nose. The faint touch of his whiskers made it tickle, which in turn made her giggle, and she swatted him away with another well-aimed blow.

Lara's heart melted as she watched all their tomfoolery, delighted to have so many wonderful reminders from days of old. Noticing her expression, the love in Adam's eyes was plain to see when he bent down and nibbled lovingly on her bottom lip.

Nikki's irreverent sneer at this blatant display of canoodling soon had him make a beeline for her cheek, depositing a loud smooch that everyone could hear.

The whole room resounded with laughter, especially when Ben called out, "You tell 'im, Niks! Who does he think he is waltzing in here and taking advantage of your mother like that!"

The banter between them all was just like old times when fun and laughter had been the main ingredients for any family get-togethers.

Seeing the playful exchanges being tossed to and fro between the man she adored and her precious offspring made Lara realise just how foolish she had been to keep them apart for so long, although the heartbreaking decision had been her only choice at the time.

Adam was suddenly reminded of his and Nikki's last encounter. "Hey, Munchkin, I'm really sorry for being so vague following your mum's performance last year. That was awfully rude of me, especially not even recognising you to begin with."

"It's okay, I understood. You looked so sad it was easy to tell you were only thinking about one person that night." The trio exchanged pensive looks. "I'm just glad to see you're finally together after all this time."

"Me, too," he responded with a heartfelt nod.

"I've longed for this day for so long. Mum's needed you so much, despite making out she could do it all by herself ... as usual! I wanted to contact you, but she wouldn't let me."

Once again he glanced between them, reaching out to take their hands, and his gentle smile melted everyone's hearts. "Well, thank heavens the Man Above intervened or I probably would never have found her. But I'm sorry I wasn't there for you too, Nikki ... this must've been a terrible ordeal for you. I'm afraid your mother is one stubborn lady when she makes up her mind. I learned that a long time ago..."

The look he and Lara exchanged eluded to the countless years wasted and she mouthed the words, "I'm sorry," as her eyes held his captive. A gentle kiss pressed against her cheek was positive assurance all had been forgiven.

Before the mood could change to one of regret, Suzie declared, "Okay, now it's my turn." She made a beeline towards Adam with her arms spread wide. "It's so good to see you again, my old friend. This has to be the best Christmas ever!" Pulling him close, she met her sister's gaze over his shoulder and sent her a loving wink. "I'm thrilled to bits for all of us."

He held on tight as a ripple of belonging raced through his veins. "It's so good to see you too, Suze. Gosh, I've missed you ... it's been *way* too long."

"Sure has. We've been waiting ages for this day to happen, but it's worth it to see the three of you finally together again. I've missed you too, but not half as much as my stubborn sister and her precious girl."

She ruffled Nikki's fringe similar to the early days when her niece was just a little tot.

Elizabeth bustled around pouring long glasses of punch, ecstatic to have what she had always considered her extended family finally under one roof.

Charles was so overcome by emotion, he couldn't speak through the lump in his throat. All he could do was place a strong supportive arm around his son's shoulders and blink away the tears. For sixteen sad long years, he had waited for this moment. Adam could sense what his father was going through and hugged him close.

When they eventually drew apart, Lara took Charles' hand in hers, squeezing it tightly as an offering of thanks for all his years of patience, love and support. The soft-hearted man bent down to kiss the top of her head and she caught the watery glimmer in his eyes. His chin quivered as he tried to hold himself together and it was easy to see he was too choked up to say anything. As far as the proud patriarch was concerned, today's surprise was the best gift of all.

For over an hour, the room echoed with laughter and excited chatter as catch-up stories were shared and old memories reminisced over.

Along with his look of wonder to finally have his soul mate back again, whenever Adam's gaze fell on the chairbound woman happily joining in the conversations around them, there was also a deep shadow of sadness for the ongoing effects of her injuries. Noticing how often Lara had to use her hands to manoeuvre her legs to change position was enough to break his heart all over again. His only consolation was the fact that he could now ease her burden by giving of both his time and ongoing support – no matter how long it took.

Whenever their eyes met, the love flowing between them was like a drawbridge spanning a yawning chasm ... constantly drawing them back home.

§

Adam couldn't wait any longer and went outside to grab the wheelchair. Lara watched as he came towards her and quickly tried to mask a sudden rush of sadness as he tried to negotiate the unfamiliar contraption around the furniture.

Please Lord, let there be a time when I can walk by his side again.

Gentle fingers brushed against her hair as he bent down and whispered, "I'm going to steal you away for a little while. It's way too long since we had some quality time together – just the two of us. Do you mind?"

Lara's smile was all the confirmation he needed as she raised her arms. With a loving wink, he couldn't resist and stole a quick token from the mouth he had been hungering for as he lifted her into the chair on wheels. She was lighter than he remembered and it was easy to tell her legs had lost a lot of their muscle tone.

Once again, he groaned inwardly. *Oh Baby, if we'd been together, you never would've gone over that mountainside. I'm the one who should've been behind the wheel to ensure you were safe. How many more obstacles will we have to face 'til we reach the other side of our Everest?*

Lara's arms wrapped themselves around his neck for the few seconds it took for the transfer. Just like him, she was quick to take advantage of their closeness, except it was his earlobe receiving her love offering instead.

Instant shivers ran up and down his spine. It was the only catalyst he needed to send any thoughts of gloom far away. "Mmm, I've missed that feeling ... just wait 'til I get you alone!"

The muffled groan from the back of her throat let him know she was experiencing the same yearning as she whispered, "I can't wait..."

He wheeled her out to the terrace, and their immediate perception was of a bright new world – no longer seeing it through eyes clouded with emptiness and longing. An exciting new future stretched ahead of them, albeit one bound to hold both frustration and disappointment while they laboured to bring her legs back to full strength. But in spite of Lara's condition, their love was as strong as ever, providing more than enough incentive to bring a smile, along with some much-needed hope, back into their spirits.

Adam even managed an over-the-top quickstep as he pushed her across the grassy strip leading to the gazebo. Lara looked back at him with an enchanted grin, still having trouble believing everything that had happened. To see him so carefree, despite the initial shock when he learned the truth, did her heart good. Because he was a novice at manoeuvring the ungainly device, trying to negotiate a small tiled lip along the edge by pulling her backwards caused the chair to tip to the side, and almost sent her tumbling onto the ground. The pair burst into loud giggles as he tried to right it again.

"Whoa! Sorry, Baby ... I think I might need a driver's licence to steer this old thing!"

"At least it'll give me more incentive to get *out* of it with you at the wheel!"

"Oh, is that right! Obviously, you haven't changed much, you cheeky little humbug!"

Another burst of laughter split the night as he pushed her towards the bench seat. With some more careful moves, he managed to position the chair close to his legs and sat down, ensuring they were facing each other.

"There, that's better. Now I can look at you properly without having to share you with everyone else ... at least for a little while."

When Lara grimaced and tried to pull a patch of hair over the scar on her forehead, he bent close and touched the spot with a loving finger. "Don't ... you're just as beautiful as you always were ... *and* just as desirable."

Breathing a heartrending smile of relief, she reached out and softly caressed his cheek.

It was the perfect response to push any further fears away. Two sets of eyes and hands became mesmerised with a delicious sense of wonder to find themselves in such close proximity with no constraints.

"I still can't believe you're here, my sweetness," Adam breathed as he softly stroked her hair, while the adoration in their eyes fed two hungry souls.

This new form of endearment brought a delighted smile to her face. "I can't either. I feel like I need to pinch myself just to make sure I'm not dreaming." Her fingertips were as soft as the tip of a feather when she stroked along his strong jaw-line. "And I like being your sweetness. You've never called me that before."

Adam took her hand and pressed it hard against his cheek, as though only by physical touch could he truly believe she was actually there. "Down through the years, most times it was only the sweetness of your memory that kept me going, so that's how I've come to think of you."

"Oh darling, that's so beautiful – I love it! But I'm so sorry for keeping you at a distance while all of this has been going on."

"It's been hell wondering where you were. I've been searching *everywhere* – ringing everyone I could think of, desperate to find out where you could be. It was as though you'd become an elusive butterfly, always just out of reach."

Lara's eyes immediately went to her wrist, to the delicate gold and opal butterfly bracelet – the one she always wore on special occasions – and his gaze followed hers. It wasn't hard to recognise the gift purchased from a merchant on Florence's Ponte Vecchio now resting where it belonged. Since their reunion, Adam had been so captivated by her face he hadn't even noticed it until now. Unable to resist, one of his fingers began to outline the fragile shape, while his gaze moved to her hand where a recognisable ring still circled her finger.

Instinctively, his thumb moved down to stroke the glittering sapphire, placed there with a heartfelt vow so many years ago. All the while, dark eyes feverishly searched her blue ones. Lara knew exactly what he was thinking – their spirits still responding as one.

When she gave a tiny nod, Adam removed the magnificent ring from where he had placed it on that far-away day in a suburban coffee shop. This was the first time it had been off her finger since then. Noticing the stark white circle left behind – a sliver of flesh the sun hadn't kissed in all that time – he realised she had kept the promise made all those years earlier.

He pressed his lips against the pale imprint, almost as a tribute to her faithfulness, before they shared a touching smile. Then with her left hand in his, he slipped the band onto the finger it was always meant for. And in a similar gesture made so long ago, those same lips now caressed the shiny blue stone, only this time because it had found its true home at last.

"Lara Jennings, will you please give me the honour of becoming my wife as soon as possible? We've always belonged together and had to wait far too long already. I don't want to spend any more time apart than necessary."

His divorce would still take several months to come through, and from the looks of things, Lara's stint in rehab would take up most of that time anyway.

She touched his mouth with hers – gently gnawing on those lips she had been deprived of for what seemed like an eternity. "Yes, my love, with all my heart, yes ... just as soon as we can ... well, as soon as I can get out of this old thing and walk down the aisle to you!"

The joyous relief contained in Adam's cry of victory brought a similar response from his soulmate. Instinctively, she bit down on her bottom lip as the emotion of the moment bubbled up in her spirit. From out of the recesses of his heart, Adam recognised the token gesture – one that had only been a mirage for so many years.

"Have you any idea how much I've loved you all this time?" he whispered into her mouth, breathing in the essence of this much-loved kindred spirit – his other half.

"Not as much as I've loved you," Lara teased, savouring the familiar taste of him.

"Don't you believe it," he chuckled, determined to outdo her.

With a sudden lunge, she claimed his mouth in a deep kiss. It was so passionate, any further attempts to try to outdo one another were soon forgotten.

For countless minutes, small whimpers and soft groans were their only accompaniment, until the strains of *Silent Night* floated through the windows of the mansion and down across the lawn like a gentle serenade.

A poignant memory invaded the intimate moment and he lifted his head to caress her lips with a loving forefinger. "One Christmas Eve, after drifting off to sleep, the echo of that same carol wafted from the television in my hotel room. For a moment there, I thought you'd come back to me..."

She brushed her cheek against his open palm, as though embossing his unique texture onto her skin. "Oh sweetheart, I remember that night. I even sent up a prayer for you to be watching ... it was meant especially for you."

"I thought so." For the slightest of moments, his voice wavered. Holding back a sob, he pulled her head onto his shoulder, as if by having her close he could erase all the sad memories from that night. "When I woke up and saw you on the television, I realised it had only been a dream. That was the first time I fully understood why I always longed for sleep. It was the only place we could still be together."

When he looked into her eyes again, Lara could see all the pain of missing her etched in their depths.

With a strangled cry, she cradled his hand in hers. Even though it was impossible to dance in the normal way, a ballet begun a lifetime ago – one that had been patiently waiting in the wings for too many years – now returned to centre stage, both on their flesh and in their hearts. At last, they were free to unlock the intricate harmonies bottled away for so long.

As the afternoon sun filtered through a cluster of tall gums lining the riverbank, a duo of hands danced unrestrained to this newly-restored symphony of love ... while adoring eyes held each other captive.

§

It was nearly an hour later when Nikki came looking for them. She couldn't help smiling at the faint murmurings of tender endearments and soft laughter wafting through the trees.

It's about time you two realised you were always meant to be together.

She hated intruding, however, Elizabeth had sent her to round them up.

Rather than embarrass the reunited lovers by her unexpected appearance, she called out from a few metres away, "Hey, you two lovebirds, there's a huge spread on offer up at the house – it's time you came back to join the real world!"

When she came around the corner, Adam dragged her onto his knee so they were all huddled together in a close-knit circle. "This *is* the real world, young miss ... here with my two favourite girls. What more could a man want!"

It was the perfect way to end this private time of reconnection, though they lingered for a few minutes more to revel in being a family again. Lara proudly boasted about how well Nikki and Jasper were doing on the competition circuit, before raving about the variety of theatre roles their daughter was being offered.

While he listened and responded, Adam couldn't believe how the day had turned out. *What if I hadn't followed my instincts to fly home this morning...*

He didn't dare contemplate the answer.

A sudden call disturbed their musings. "Hey, you three out there, have you gotten lost or something? Hurry up, dinner's getting cold!"

"Come on, we'd better go. That's Mum, and she's sure to send out the dog squad if we don't go back and sample whatever's on offer."

Lara caught the slight note of regret in his tone and figured it was because another goodbye was looming – even though it was a much shorter one. She pressed in to touch his lips with hers one more time, and their eyes met in gratitude for all they had just shared.

Clasping hands, the mother and daughter smiled at each other as Adam wheeled his beloved soulmate back to the house. For someone who had lost so much throughout his lifetime, at last he had everything he would ever need.

§

Suzie was first to notice the new home for Lara's sapphire ring.

"Oh *wow*, you've already *asked* her! That's fabulous – another wedding in the family. This is the *perfect* Christmas!" Those sparkling cornflower blue eyes – just a shade lighter than her sister's – flashed between the two of them as she gushed out a flurry of well wishes.

The others quickly gathered around, and Elizabeth bustled in from the kitchen, exclaiming in delight as her eyes filled with tears.

"This is the best news *ever* – we're going to have a proper daughter-in-law *and* a grandchild! *Oh, thank you, Lord!*" Her hands flew together with a loud clap as her gaze rose to the heavens before coming to rest once again on the newly engaged couple.

Charles quickly draped a caring arm around his wife's shoulders, and she deposited a robust kiss on his cheek. "Isn't it wonderful news, Grandpa!"

"It sure is, Grandma!" he reiterated, pulling Nikki into their cuddle to convey his joy.

"And this is the best birthday present I could ever ask for – my family finally complete and I have my own set of *grandparents* – thanks heaps, you two!"

A delighted smile was sent her mother and soon-to-be father's way. It wasn't long before they were all exchanging boisterous kisses accompanied by tight hugs of congratulations. It was no surprise to see the family's responses, though the reunited lovers were still overwhelmed at the way the day had turned out.

The rest of the afternoon flew by with all of them eager to catch up on everyone's news. So much had happened over the years, including Suzie and Ben's marriage, and Adam was quick to offer his own enthusiastic best wishes. Though both men had only known each other for a brief period when Ben and Suzie first started dating, they remembered their first meeting during another special Christmas and quickly fell into that same easy camaraderie.

Jack was watching from the fringes, so his father called him over for an introduction to this new uncle. It wasn't long before all three of them had their heads together, comparing models of cars and then game consoles – a PlayStation 2 or the Xbox. Lara settled in her chair nearby with Suzie and Nikki on either side, listening in on this friendly debate and exchanging huge grins.

Charles and Elizabeth snuggled up next to each other on the couch, revelling in seeing how their family had grown in just a few sweet hours. Every now and then, he leaned in to give her a loving peck on the cheek. Today was so different from anything they could have envisioned before a grieving teenage boy had come into their lives.

Lara and Adam were never really apart, as though an invisible cord bound them together. The happy pair were constantly reaching out to touch one another's hands or faces, while fervent eyes continually sought out their mate.

As dusk began to descend, Lara heard the crunch of a heavy vehicle's tyres coming down the driveway, and her heart sank. It was time to burst the bubble – at least for today – and she hated leaving the family behind. Despite being physically exhausted from all the excitement, especially as this was her first outing in several months, she didn't care. All she could think about was the loneliness contained in the rehab centre's four walls. The last thing she wanted was to leave her family, especially now that Adam had come back into her life. Unfortunately, she couldn't keep the driver and other patients waiting ... and thankfully tomorrow now held the promise of her soulmate always being part of her life.

Adam hadn't heard the mini-bus arrive. He was too caught up in the thrill of being with Lara and Nikki again. It was only when a shadow crossed her face that he realised something was wrong.

"What's the matter, Baby? Are you in pain? Here let me help." He grabbed a cushion to place behind her back, worried that sitting upright for so long was causing her discomfort.

"No, sweetheart, I wish it was only that. Sadly, it's time for this fairy-tale to come to an end, at least for today."

The doorbell suddenly let out its loud chime, and he understood what she meant when Charles went to answer it.

"Do you really have to go just yet? How about I drop you off later tonight."

"Oh Teddy, I'd love to stay, but it's time for my meds. Besides, I was only allowed out if I promised to be back before seven-thirty. I'm so sorry ... there's really nothing else I can do."

"Well, in that case, I'll be over to see you first thing in the morning – promise!"

"You'd *better!*" she grinned, wrapping her arms tightly around his neck and planting a firm kiss on his lips. "I hope you realise I'll never be able to sleep now."

Through several deep kisses to make up for lost time, he murmured into her open mouth, "I won't either, and for once I don't care! I've spent so many sleepless nights missing you, at least this time there'll be a smile on my face imagining what I'll be doing to you in a few short hours…"

She gave an embarrassed giggle as he went on. "*And* we're going to get you up and walking in no time at all. But you'd better be prepared to find me a hard taskmaster 'cause I'll make sure there's no slacking off from those all-important exercises. I want to see you walking down the aisle to me as soon as possible!"

Lara knew his threats were only words with no substance. He was the gentlest man she had ever known. More than likely, she would be the one pushing herself to get those stubborn legs moving, while Adam would be insisting she take it easy. After even these few short hours, she knew without a doubt his love would never change, no matter what the outcome.

Happy in the knowledge this was something they could tackle together, she taunted, "You're on! I love you, my darling, and I can't wait 'til tomorrow!"

Following another lingering kiss, Adam seized another chance to hold her in his arms. Quickly scooping her up, he carried her outside while Charles followed along behind with the wheelchair. The older man was unable to disguise a grin as Lara took advantage of the situation by nibbling on his son's ear and neck. Adam squirmed to get away and tried to stifle several groans from the delicious sensations she was causing as he climbed on board. The other patients witnessed everything, and their rousing applause, along with a few catcalls, filled the confined space, much to Lara's embarrassment and Adam's delight.

He couldn't help laughing while the chair was locked into its allotted space and then snuck a loud kiss as he lowered her into it, which sent them all off again. Playfully, she punched his arm and whispered, "Stop encouraging them!"

His face was beaming as he bent down to kiss the tip of her nose. "Oh, but it's *so* much fun! See you tomorrow bright and early, beautiful lady, and thank you for giving me the best Christmas *ever* ... *and* it's only the first of many! I'm sorry I didn't have a present for you, but I'll be sure to bring one tomorrow."

A caring finger reached up to caress his cheek. "You've *already* given me the best gift ever. Merry Christmas, my Teddy!" Her nose crinkled in the old familiar way and his answering wink brought them full circle ... to the place where both of them knew they were safe at last.

Nikki was standing beside the window, a happy onlooker to all their exchanges. Her heart leapt to see her mother so happy after all the recent traumas and that stupid stubbornness to keep Adam in the dark.

Out of the corner of her eye, Lara caught the mischievous smirk. With her eyebrow raised and the glimmer of a grin, she called out, "Happy birthday, my precious girl ... and don't *you* dare give us any cheek after this lot! I've waited a long time for this night!"

"What? *Me!*" came the innocent reply as she tried to stifle a chortle.

"Yes *you*, young lady," Adam said with a mock scowl, joining in the fun.

"See, he remembers what you're like, even after all these years! Just remember I love you despite all that exasperating cheekiness you come up with at times!"

"I love you too, Mum – heaps and heaps. Bet you have sweet dreams tonight!" Her teasing chuckle made everyone laugh.

Adam bent down and placed one last kiss on those already thoroughly devoured lips, to the accompaniment of a few wolf whistles, another round of applause and some envious giggles thrown in from the other patients.

"Okay, you two lovebirds, let's get this show on the road," came from the driver.

With one final flourish, Adam sent all of them an over-the-top bow before scurrying outside for a last word of farewell to his newfound love through the window. And similar to all those other times in the past, their hands stayed linked until distance pulled them apart.

Lara's face shone as she leaned out to wave goodbye to her entire family. This was the first time they had all been together for over fifteen years – since that fateful morning when Trina begged her to let Adam go. Today was completely different and the culmination of all that had come before. There were no more dark clouds on the horizon – even the aftermath of the accident was nothing compared to having her beloved back where he belonged.

§

Later that night, the lovers made good on their word. Neither of them could sleep ... but they didn't care. After several hours of resistance, Adam gave into temptation and dialled the number of the rehab centre. At first, the night nurse hesitated in putting his call through until she noticed the light under Lara's door and decided to make an exception. After all, it was Christmas and the spirit of goodwill still prevailed.

Lara answered before the second ring had even completed its cycle and there was a catch in her voice. "Adam…"

"I just wanted to send sweet dreams to my best girl. I figured you were probably still awake."

"I am ... I can't sleep. Every time I close my eyes I see your gorgeous smile. Then my heart starts racing and I'm wide awake again!" He could hear the excitement in her voice, and his grin grew wider. "I can't believe you've come back into my life to stay!" Just as suddenly, her tone turned serious. "But do you really want to stay, Teddy? I truly understand if you decide it's all too hard now that you know what's happened..."

As much as she couldn't bear the thought of them being apart again, the last thing she wanted was his pity or a sense of obligation forcing him to stay.

His gentle chuckle was enough reassurance. "As if you could *ever* get rid of me now! I'm here to stay ... forever ... or at least until you kick me out when I drive you crazy wanting to make love every night. After all, we have a lot of lost time to make up!"

"Cheeky boy! I seem to remember I was quite partial to making love with you, so I can't really see me kicking you out for a very long time," she responded as her happy giggle travelled down the line.

"Just as well! Anyway, my darling, I'd better say goodnight or the nurse won't let me in tomorrow. She gave strict instructions we could only talk for a few minutes, so I'll see you first thing in the morning."

"Okay, sweetheart, and thanks for ringing. This has been the perfect ending to a fantastic day! I wonder if I'll still dream about you now that I have the real thing back in my life again."

A loud growl came down the line. "You'd better not be dreaming about anybody *else,* or I'll be straight up there to remind you who loves you most!"

"Well, if that's the case, I'll start dreaming about Mark Sinclair or Anthony Warlow! That way I'll get to see you even sooner!"

"*Wash your mouth out, young lady!* Have you any idea just how jealous I was the night I saw Mark walking the red carpet with you on his arm? And don't get me started on what it was like seeing both of you on a stage together – that was pure agony."

"Oh darling, the whole time I was up there, all I could think about was you – I'm afraid you've spoilt me for anyone else. Sometimes I wonder whether I love you *too* much."

"Never too much ... but I'm glad. That's the way it's supposed to be and you'd better not forget it! I love you too, and with every part of me. 'Night, sweetness."

"Night, my love."

They hung up with huge smiles keeping any feelings of lonesomeness at bay. The call was just like all those others so many long years ago – late night whispers of love to help two lonely souls sleep through the night.

Adam sat in a quiet corner of his terrace for most of the night, in silent contemplation as he watched the shimmer of a brilliant full moon seemingly dance across the surface of the creek running through the property before it spilled into the lake. His soul seemed to sigh with contentment knowing it was also smiling down on the woman he adored. For a few evenings every month for so many years, the glowing disk had been his only real link to her – now there was no more wondering where she might be.

His gaze took in the full spectrum of the heavens with all of its beauty, and instinctively his spirit cried out.

You've brought Lara and me through the darkest of times, Father God. Even when I let both you and Trina down by being unfaithful, you never gave up on bringing about a way for us to eventually be together. I know it's asking a lot, but there's one more favour I need to ask. Please grant my beautiful fiancée the strength to walk and to use her magnificent voice to bless others again. She's never lost faith in you, but could really do with a miracle about now. I'm sorry I seemed to lose my way over these last few months, but I know you were always with me. Thanks for bringing back the only gift I've ever wanted.

As though compelled to enforce his plea with a vow to Lara herself, he whispered into the darkness, hoping that somehow she would sense his spirit reaching out to her. "I promise never to give you any reason to leave me again, Baby. I know exactly where my priorities lie now, and I'm going to make sure our new home is set up perfectly once you're ready to leave that place. I promise with all of my heart and every part of our future to do everything within my power to make you happy. Sweet dreams and may God bless you every single day you draw breath."

Several kilometres away in a small hospital room, the woman his pledge was meant for glanced out through the window and down onto a picturesque lake in the nearby park. Reflected in its waters was the silvery orb of a tranquil moon. Lara knew without a doubt this was a gift from her Creator – Heaven's way of joining two spirits across the miles – as she imagined the face of her beloved gazing up at that same body of light and thinking of her.

Thank you for never giving up on us, Father. We didn't deserve your forgiveness for the times we did the wrong thing by Trina, but I'm so grateful you've given us another chance. I pray you'll keep her safe in this new life she's making – I really am sorry for hurting her, even though she was never the wife Adam deserved. Please help her to find true happiness just as we have today.

And please help Adam as he comes to terms with these stupid injuries. Give him the strength to deal with seeing me crippled and scarred – I couldn't bear to see his pity once he realises the full extent of the accident. And please help me to do everything possible to get better so I can run into his arms again one day. I'm sorry I didn't trust either him or you to know what was best for me over the last few months. I really don't know how to thank you enough for bringing that darling man back into my life, but I'm so grateful and vow to love him with all my heart as well as honouring you for the rest of my life.

As her focus settled on the reality around her, she noticed a pewter sculpture with its enduring message standing on the windowsill. The sight of it brought a poignant smile and she searched through the bedside drawer, seeking out a notebook and pen. Her fingers began to dance across the paper as her heart filled with hope in a way it hadn't done for many months. It took several minutes to articulate everything in a way that spoke exactly from her heart. Eventually, she finished and folded the heartfelt message over with a satisfied smile ... while absentmindedly brushing a tiny liquid droplet from her chin.

One final thought came to her before she sank into a satisfied slumber...

You've lived in my heart since I was a lonely young mum – now we get to spend the rest of our lives together. God bless you, my darling, forever and ever.

§

The following morning just before breakfast, there was a loud rap on Lara's door. Before she could answer, a much-loved voice called out, "Hey, my sweetness, are you decent? Can I come in?"

Grabbing a nearby blanket and tossing it over her legs, Lara laughed, "I don't know about being decent, but of course you can. Hurry up and get in here!"

A welcoming chuckle joined hers as Adam crossed the room and swept her into his arms. "Just how indecent do you want to be? I've waited a long time for you, woman o' mine."

As much as she longed to make love with him again, Lara wanted to wait until she was able to come to him as the lover he remembered ... not partially paralysed, unable to move in time to his rhythm. Even more so, a part of her also wanted their true reunion to occur once they had made those sacred vows of marriage. She knew God had brought them together again and this seemed the most honourable way to thank him for all he had brought them through to bring them to this place.

The bluest of eyes searched his, begging forgiveness for what she was about to ask. "Would you mind terribly if we waited, Teddy? I know it's already been what feels like an eternity, but would a few more months be asking too much?"

It was easy for him to understand the path her thoughts had taken. Rather than having her feel uncomfortable or embarrassed, he was more than willing to submit to her request.

"Of course not, Baby. You're definitely worth waiting for, no matter how long it takes. Besides, I'd much rather do things the right way this time instead of carrying around those awful feelings of guilt like before."

Caressing his cheeks with the gentlest of hands, her eyes shone with gratitude as she claimed his mouth in a long, drawn-out kiss. When they eventually came up for air, he had to let out a very deep breath as a way to control the ribbon of desire racing through his veins.

Lara's keen ears recognised his reaction and she couldn't resist sending him a cheeky smile. "Just think of it this way ... it'll teach you self-control and give me heaps more incentive to get these old pins moving again!"

"You'd better believe it! I plan on coming out here every day to crack the whip. That way you'll be sure to exercise twelve hours a day!"

His grin was all the incentive she needed to keep the teasing going.

"Oh, is that right? Alright, well how about you take me down to the gym straight away 'cause I can't wait to show you just how much I've missed you! And after my edict last night about walking down the aisle, the sooner we get started, the better!" She dragged on his shirt collar, pulling him close again to hold his gaze as her lips brushed against his.

His eyes pleaded as he whispered, "Alright, but not quite yet. I just want a few more minutes here without having to share you with anyone else."

Despite the self-imposed restriction, this early morning tryst was everything they had imaged through the long hours of the night ... filled with laughter and wonder, passionate kisses – and the constant dilemma of trying to keep their desire under control.

At one stage, Adam had to come up for air with a deep groan, while the twinkle in his eyes and a huge grin gave away just how much he was enjoying himself. "Keep nibbling along my neck like that and I won't be able to keep our promise. You know what your lips do to me!"

"Oh alright, spoilsport ... and just when I was starting to enjoy myself!"

"We'll take this up where we left off *after* you've done your exercises," Adam promised through a loud guffaw, and with one quick swoop, he deposited her in the wheelchair sitting beneath the window.

From out of the corner of his eye, he caught sight of the pewter statue positioned on the sill catching the morning sunlight and stopped dead in his tracks.

"*Oh ... my ... goodness,* that's perfect! Where did you get it?"

She reached out and took his hand, the love in her eyes plain to see. "I found it many years ago in a little French boutique in The Valley. It *is* perfect and I couldn't resist. Now it goes everywhere I do – even to Italy! Often seeing it looking back at me was the only thing that kept me going. I've never forgotten what you said on the night we ran into each other in the backstage corridor following your performance in *The Sound of Music*."

His look was intense. "And I meant every single word. I've never given up hope either. You always were the light guiding me home."

§

And out in that eternal dimension unseen by human eyes, two delicate threads – one of amaranthine purple and the other burnished gold – wove around and through each other as though dancing to an imaginary orchestra. These two fine trails of silk spun from the centremost core of two human spirits, formed the word both had engraved on their hearts – the same one replicated on a lone leaf that still clung to the steadfast tree right at the centre of this unique work of art.

The *H* had been fashioned in old English script and the three letters following completed the cry that for so long had cradled their souls in its meaning.

Now that hope was born anew and the threads fashioning their story remained entwined around one another 'til the end of time.

EPILOGUE

7 July 2011 – Six-and-a-Half Years Later

Opening Night of Doctor Zhivago – A New Musical

The Lyric Theatre, QPAC, Brisbane

Lara was having trouble fastening the back of her gown. Just when she thought it was secure, the pesky silver clasp came undone again.

"Oh, I don't have time for this," she muttered to herself, trying once again to get the little blighter to do as it was bid.

"Here, let me help you with that," the deep masculine voice that still sent delicious shivers up and down her spine whispered into her ear. Powerless to resist, gentle lips took advantage of the moment to linger on that tempting lobe.

Shaking her head in feigned annoyance, she raised her eyebrows and peered through the mirror, sending an impish grin her husband's way.

Adam ran his hands across her bare shoulders. His lips slowly followed that same path, sending even more quivers through his wife's curvaceous body. All the while, those dark eyes held hers in the glass reflection.

This time she responded with a sensuous moan. "Stop it, sweetheart. If you keep that up, we'll never make it to the restaurant, and I promised Nikki we'd get there early enough to avoid rushing through dinner."

With one final caress and another gossamer touch of his mouth to her exposed ear, he answered, "Oh, alright! It's just as well I love you both. If it wasn't the show's gala opening, I'd be suggesting we go tomorrow night instead. You're almost impossible to resist, you know."

Laughing at yet another one of her husband's attempts to race her off her feet, Lara turned around and wrapped both arms around his neck. "I'll be all yours when we get home, I promise."

He caught her gaze and recognised the glimmer of need in her eyes. "I'll hold you to that!" he vowed and his sultry look displayed similar cravings.

With a sweep of his hand, he waltzed her around the room to the imaginary strains of their favourite piece of music. A sheath of burgundy silk floated around her ankles, while the Swarovski crystal-laden bodice captured the light and caused a scurry of pinprick reflections to dance across the walls. The cheery cottage bedroom suddenly took on the elegance of a Viennese ballroom as they swayed and dipped to the music swirling in their heads.

Lara was light on her feet, making their steps match perfectly. Only those privy to their story would ever guess only a few years earlier a wheelchair had been her main mode of transport. The long months of hard work had eventually paid off. Now they were able to travel the globe together whenever one or the other was gracing one of the world's famous stages.

Time had been kind to both of them. Their bodies were still firmly toned to take on the strenuous roles that regularly came their way, and those same striking good looks still brought admiring glances wherever they went. Only occasionally did their eyes betray a glimpse of the pain that had once almost consumed them ... thankfully, this only occurred when a sudden memory or piece of memorabilia flashed by, bringing with it reminders of what it was like having to live without their soulmate.

Tonight's outing was a very special occasion and the reason they were staying in the cute little cottage in Paddington instead of the sprawling home Adam had built for them overlooking the spectacular Glasshouse Mountains. The much-loved stars, along with their beloved daughter and son-in-law, had personal invitations to attend Brisbane's opening night of *Doctor Zhivago – A New Musical*. All four were looking forward to witnessing one of Lara's favourite, albeit bittersweet, novels come to life in this new and exciting way, even though the movie had been banned from her house for the emotional wreck it made of her heart.

It was a much-envied behind-the-scenes fact that Lucy Simon, the musical's gifted composer, had written the entire score with Anthony Warlow's exceptional voice in mind for the lead. She first had the idea when he was appearing in *The Secret Garden* at the very same venue. Following many years of hard work, her vision had now become a reality and this was the sole reason

Australia had been chosen for its first official season. The show had already opened to rave reviews in both Sydney and Melbourne. This time it was Brisbane's turn to be mesmerised by the tragic storyline brought to life by a brilliant cast and with the well-respected leading man in the title role.

§

"Mum, you look amazing! Whoa – what a knock-out! If I didn't know better, I'd say *you're* the star tonight. Where'd you get that incredible gown? Milan, I suppose ... on your last trip to Italy."

Lara blushed at the compliment. Only two years away from turning fifty, she still found it hard to receive any form of praise, so the admiration in her daughter's eyes caused the usual wave of self-consciousness to make itself known. And the same thing occurred when it came to her career. No matter how much time passed or how renowned she had become in theatre circles, a part of her was still surprised at all the attention sent her way purely for doing what she loved.

"Oh, stop it! Anyway, what about you! That dress suits you perfectly and I love your hair. Having it swept to the side like that is very Rita Hayworthish ... you look gorgeous!"

Where's my little girl gone – the one who loved making sandcastles and singing about her 'faborite' things? And who's this stunning young woman now taking her place ... and with a loving husband by her side?

"Doesn't she look beautiful?" Adam concurred, his eyes softening as he glanced between two of the three key women in his life. "Your mother's sure to be the belle of the ball tonight – I can't wait to show her off! And you're not looking too bad yourself, Munchkin – it's easy to tell you're mum and daughter."

As he draped a soft shawl-like jacket around his wife's shoulders to keep out the winter chill, his gentle hands caressed its fine texture. It was the garment he had purchased in Bolzano many years ago, still looking as good as new because of the quality of workmanship and fabric.

A dark, handsome man draped his arm around Nikki's shoulders, kissing her upturned cheek while sending her an affectionate grin. "I agree. They both look smashing and aren't we the lucky ones!"

Nikki smiled up at her adoring husband. "Only because you have to say that, my love!" The young couple were as much in love now as on the night they first met – the beginning of a whirlwind romance that had all of their friends turn green with jealousy.

"No, I don't – it's true. You captured my heart the moment I set eyes on you in that first leading role ... and nothing's changed. Well, apart from the addition of a cute little fellow waiting for us at home ... I think he's more than enough evidence to prove how much I care."

Adam's ears pricked up. "And how is my best little mate? We haven't seen him for nearly two weeks. That grandson of ours is growing so fast he's probably a foot taller already." The besotted grandfather's eyes lit up as he pictured Charlie tottering towards him on his chubby little legs.

They would be celebrating the little boy's first birthday the following week, with his very proud namesake and devoted wife making up the numbers. Charles and Elizabeth were now in their early seventies and both continued to live full and happy lives with no signs of slowing down. The combined families still caught up regularly whenever their busy work schedules permitted.

"Oh Dad, he's just as cute as ever and has me in fits of laughter, especially now that he's growing into a little person," Nikki replied, using the name she had adopted since their double wedding five-and-a-half years earlier. "His personality's so much like yours; it's no wonder we all love him to bits! You and Mum should drop by for lunch tomorrow before heading back to the mountains – then you can see for yourself. Charlie'd be over the moon, and we'd love to have you stay for a while."

§

The day had been glorious. The sun was shining brightly as the two brides dressed in equally stunning though totally unique gowns slowly made their way down the garden path. With Lara's arm safely tucked inside her daughter's to help keep her steady, their eyes remained firmly fixed on the two good-looking men dressed in morning suits of different shades of grey waiting for them under the gazebo on the river's edge bordering Charles and Elizabeth's garden.

When Nikki had first suggested combining the two ceremonies, Lara was adamant. "No sweetheart, this is yours and Daniel's special day. Adam and I don't mind waiting a little bit longer before we tie the knot. I want to be getting around without these stupid crutches when I finally walk down the aisle to him."

"But Mum, if we do it together, I can help you so that you won't need crutches – at least not for that part of the ceremony. Besides, you'll be walking me down the aisle anyway so let me do it for you at the same time! Come on; it'll make it extra special if we get married on the same day – a new beginning to all our lives. Uncle Adam, you tell her. She *always* listens to you."

"Well, I can try!" he laughed. "After all, it only took me a mere sixteen-and-a-half years to convince her we belonged together ... still, I'm prepared to take a chance just for you. Personally, I think it's a great idea!" He turned a set of pleading eyes to his fiancée.

Leaning close, Lara ran her lips softly along his cheek as though seeking forgiveness for the long wait, while an adoring smile brought with it a small amount of hope.

After much coaxing, eventually he managed to convince her and the day had

602

been perfect, just as Nikki predicted. There wasn't a cloud in the sky and hardly a dry eye anywhere when a galaxy of guests witnessed their union – especially his parents as they watched their foster son and the woman he'd loved with all his heart for nearly two decades become one. It had taken many months of hard work as well as loads of tears to bring them to this place, but slowly Lara and Adam had seen the fruits of their labour. Eventually, she was able to stand on her own two feet without the aid of parallel bars or a walking frame, and the occasion was one neither of them would ever forget.

It was towards the end of June 2005, the afternoon of Adam's forty-fifth birthday, when she first walked towards him with only a pair of crutches for support. His tears had flowed freely when she painstakingly took those first faltering steps before coming to a halt in front of him. Lara had been practising in secret for the past few weeks as his surprise birthday present. That same night Nikki was starring in her first professional leading role and Lara's milestone was the best good luck charm she could ever have wished for.

Little did anyone realise, the brand-new star would also meet the man of her dreams that very same evening, providing even more reason for them to share wedding days. The four major events would always remain entwined in their history, and after everything Lara and Adam had been through, she felt they had already waited far too long to delay getting married any longer. The ceremonies were planned for Christmas Day – the first anniversary of their reunion.

Once the eager young bride and groom had exchanged their vows, they willingly took backstage to witness her parents do the same. Afterwards, the whole garden echoed with loud cheers and hearty applause as the proud new husband took his adorning wife in his arms for the long-awaited and heart-stopping kiss. A rush of tears flowed freely down Nikki's cheeks and Daniel gently brushed them away with a loving smile. Adam and Lara's marriage had been years in coming, and yet it couldn't have been a more perfect time ... celebrating it together made it even more memorable.

To their delight, Jeff and Lucy had been asked to be the sole attendants for both couples. Suzie was too heavily pregnant with a surprise and much-awaited new addition to the family to be part of the line-up.

Jack was mortified when he was asked to carry the rings, declaring in an indignant voice, "I'm ten, Aunty Lara, only little kids in tuxedos do that!"

After being put in her place, the soon-to-be bride set aside her wishes and asked him to hand out the Orders of Service instead.

During the ceremony, Jack and his mother and father stood proudly beside Adam's parents at the front of the crowd, smiling broadly through a shimmering blur of tears. Lying in a pram beside them was a precious baby just seven months old, gurgling and cooing loudly after keeping those nearby thoroughly entertained while waiting for the bridal party to enter.

Charlotte had come into the world with all the gusto of her musical parents when her loud cry resounded around the delivery room. An exhausted Lucy and a much-relieved Jeff had looked down at the squirming bundle, astonished though absolutely delighted to find themselves parents at last.

Similar to his baby daughter, just before the service commenced, Jeff had inadvertently put on a one-man show by keeping the guests amused when it suddenly dawned on him all four wedding rings were stashed away in the same vest pocket. The look on his face was priceless as he spent the next few minutes trying to work out which set belonged to which couple. Eventually, both were safely tucked into opposite pockets to waylay any mix-ups at two crucial moments. An outbreak of chuckles could be heard rippling across the lawn and over the river from several of those watching on.

Adam had organised two specific treats for their honeymoon.

The newlyweds jetted off to Rome a few days later, fulfilling a vow made several years earlier. This trip gave them the freedom and time to explore the Eternal City's fascinating historical streets in depth rather than the short stopover of their last visit. Naturally, a visit to a favourite villa in Tuscany became part of the itinerary. Adam was eager to catch up with his old friends, Antonio and Claudia, to thank them and show how much he appreciated their love and care bestowed on Lara while she had been lying so desperately ill in a hospital bed.

The reunion had been a highly emotional time for everyone. Claudia and Lara had always presumed they would never see each other again after uttering those final goodbyes in the hospital grounds fourteen months earlier. Watching the women's teary greeting on their arrival, both men in typical displays of masculinity surreptitiously turned their backs to wipe away their own tears before anyone noticed.

For five days, the Tuscan villa became their new home. The honeymooners were offered the same suite where they had experienced the joy and wonder of discovering each other fully for the first time. As before, Claudia and Antonio did everything in their power to make the room perfect ... and with the same intimate hours of pleasure resulting from all their meticulous efforts. When it came time for Lara and Adam to leave again, the farewells were just as poignant as the last time. And as before, treasured memories of Antonio's cheeky ways, along with Claudia's culinary delights and kind heart, filled the scrapbooks of their minds to take home.

Before setting off on the overseas portion of the honeymoon, Adam had arranged one other just as significant location as the ideal way to commemorate their new lives together. The night of their wedding, along with two more, had been spent in another place close to both their hearts – the same secluded B&B

he had chosen following their arrival home from that first Italian holiday.

Dusk was just settling over Wategos Beach as he stood on the balcony of their suite on the edge of the coastal town of Byron Bay. Lara came over to stand beside him and gently pressed a small scroll made from the finest parchment into her new husband's hand. A gold satin ribbon held everything in place, and it was easy to see how much care she had put into the unexpected gift.

"This is for you, my darling. I wrote it exactly one year ago today ... following our late-night phone call on Christmas Day after we found each other again. The words came to me when I was looking at the moon's reflection on the lake just outside my window at the Rehab Centre. I've been waiting for the perfect time to give it to you – somehow I think today fits the bill."

His eyes misted over as he placed a gentle kiss on her forehead, remembering every iota of emotion resulting from that unexpected encounter. She snuggled into his shoulder as he unrolled the delicate paper. Even the simple salutation headlining the poem was enough to make him catch his breath. Wrapping a strong arm around his wife's shoulders, he pulled her close and let every word issuing from her heart flow into his spirit. The sound of waves lapping along the shore was the perfect accompaniment to this touching moment in time.

My True North

You were standing there before me; the years just flew away,
We were back when we were younger like it was only yesterday.
Yes, we have grown older; the passing time has left its mark,
Yet our beauty is still deep within – a candle lighting up the dark.

You spoke my name; you looked at me; those eyes I knew so well
Searched deep within my spirit, still capturing me in their spell...
Impelling me to trust in you, and stay with you a while
You opened up your heart to me; your words caused me to smile.

But also with those words of yours, a silent tear was shed
For all the lost and lonely years ... I miss you in my bed.
And not just unspent passion, or yearning for your touch...
Because you were my soulmate, I loved you, oh, so much.

I'm sorry for the hurt I caused, the pain that you endured
I never meant to break your heart ... of that be rest assured.
I only wanted the best for you; not to see you tossed to-and-fro
It broke my heart to say goodbye ... and have to turn and go.

My love has stood the test of time; it's been battered – beaten blue
When another man tried to take from me what always belonged to you.
I've missed you, my love, my soul has grieved on many a lonesome night
But today, seeing you, my heart grew wings for its eternal flight.

No wonder we feel the way we do when we speak of the things long past
They're deep inside the both of us and those memories will always last.
Yet 'we're' not gone the way we thought; that 'us' remains the same
We gave our hearts for always then, and that's how they will remain.

No matter where the time has gone, from now until henceforth
My love will always burn for you ... my Adam ... my True North.

With my love always ... Your Lara - 25 December 2004

While Adam was reading the touching lines, his heart ached at the poignancy behind her words. This was the Lara he had fallen in love with on that long-ago night while standing in the shadows of a suburban street near an old theatre house. The passing of time hadn't changed her – it had simply made her even more desirable.

With a deep sigh and eyes glistening, Adam pulled his wife even closer and the beat of their hearts kept perfect time. She couldn't resist and lovingly kissed the mouth that had so often been a part of her dreams ... while two rivulets of grateful tears mingled at the realisation tonight they had finally come home.

Home was wherever they were together ... and would be for the rest of their lives.

§

More than five years had passed since that memorable honeymoon night. With recent shared memories binding them even closer, the happy foursome sat around the restaurant table anticipating the upcoming show.

Nikki had been in awe of Anthony Warlow from the very first time she had seen him play the lead in *Phantom of the Opera* – a surprise fourteenth birthday present from her mother. These days, as a fully-fledged actress herself, her admiration went even deeper. She couldn't wait to see him in the demanding role of *Dr Yurii Zhivago*, and it was obvious to everyone how excited she was.

"The reviews from Sydney and Melbourne have all been glowing," Lara enthused as those sparkling blue eyes encompassed her family. "John Frost has done a brilliant job bringing it to Australia before Broadway beckons."

Though not game enough to admit it, deep down she felt a smidgen of apprehension at the thought of sitting through the heart-wrenching love story all over again, especially with it being put to music. An emotional score could always set her off, and Lara dreaded coming away a blubbering mess like the first and only time she had witnessed Boris Pasternak's novel come to life. Suddenly a vivid flashback came back of the night Lucy had tried to cajole her into watching the movie and her just as adamant refusal to revisit all of that gut-wrenching emotion. Thankfully, tonight Adam was by her side instead of just being a faraway dream.

"I've heard Lucy Maunder, the young actress playing the role of *Lara*—" Nikki's mouth suddenly fell open and she grabbed her mother's hand. "Oh *Mum*, I'm sorry. I'd forgotten the main character's name. How could I have missed the parallels between the two of you? Are you going to be okay?"

Lara squeezed her back and gave a reassuring smile. "Of course, Munchkin, I'll be fine ... but thanks for caring."

"Course I care – I've only got one mum!"

"And I've only got one precious daughter ... now, what was that you were about to tell us about Lucy?"

"Oh, just that the other day I was reading about her online and several reviews were absolutely raving. Most were about how she's doing a fabulous job portraying *Lara's* feistiness as well as her vulnerability, while a heap mention her incredible vocal range. I can't wait to see her tonight. Hey, hang on, didn't you see her mum perform while you were doing that benefit in Sydney?"

Lara had to think for a minute and then her eyes lit up. "Oh yes, of course – Anne-Maree McDonald! *Now* I know where I've heard Lucy's name before. I'd forgotten they're mother and daughter! And you're right. I flew down to perform at a fundraiser for the AIDS Trust – back when you were in Italy for the school exchange program, I think. If I remember correctly, I decided to stay on for a few days after receiving an invitation to hear her sing.

"That's right, and I can still remember your phone call to me afterwards singing her praises!"

"Gosh, you've got a good memory! Yes, she has a marvellous voice, and is obviously much-loved by her many fans from the reams of praise I heard in the foyer afterwards. Apparently, while she was still quite young, Anne-Maree was a principal soprano with The Australian Opera, which only goes to prove her calibre. I'm pretty sure the programme's bio said she also appeared in the television series *Prisoner* at one stage, so not only can she sing like a lark ... she can also act – and obviously very well."

"Oh wow, one of the girls I shared a room with in Sydney was obsessed with that show. When she came for a visit a couple of years back, I remember watching a few reruns on YouTube. It was a popular series from what she said."

"It sure was and received excellent ratings, too. But it must be over ten years since I last saw Anne-Maree. She was an absolute stunner back then, although I'd be surprised if she's changed much – such a classical beauty ... reminded me of a young Elizabeth Taylor. From everything I've read, she's now a well-respected musical director and conductor who still likes to raise her voice for a favourite song if the opportunity arises! Oh and she also tutors at NIDA as well. Such a busy woman..."

"Really? Rats! Wish she'd been there when I was. But didn't you say you'd actually met her that night?"

"Mmm, you're right, I did! In fact, I met *all* of them – both Anne-Maree and Stuart Maunder – Lucy's dad – as well as Lucy herself. Strange how it didn't register when I was going over the cast list for tonight's show, although I was concentrating more on the fact that Anthony has top billing!"

She sent her husband a cheeky wink and wasn't at all surprised to hear a loud groan come from his side of the table.

"Oh, no, don't tell me you *still* have eyes for him!"

"Don't worry; you'll *always* be my main man, Teddy."

"Just as well!" he growled and sent an over-the-top glower her way.

Lara's hand came out and flicked his arm. "Oh, stop it!"

Both Nikki and Daniel laughed at this unexpected round of entertainment as Lara offered up a few more titbits from those days.

"Now I remember. When I met them, Anne-Maree was appearing at a gala event at the Opera House. I believe Stuart was Executive Producer for Opera Australia around that time."

Nikki was fascinated and leaned in closer to encourage her mother. "Well, talent obviously runs in their genes. But Lucy must've only been young then because one article stated she's only in her mid-twenties now."

"She was – I'd guess about fifteen or so at the time, and I'll never forget what a special rapport they all shared. I'm not at all surprised to hear she's been getting great reviews – they're a very talented family. Stuart was once the Staff Director of The Royal Opera at Covent Garden and performed in several renowned Gilbert and Sullivan productions himself. I know Anne-Maree's appeared at some of the more famous music halls in London, as well as others around the world. She even sang at Dame Joan Sutherland's seventieth birthday celebration! It's easy to see why theatre and performing are in Lucy's blood."

"Goodness, you sure are a fan, my darling," Adam piped in again.

"Absolutely! I bet I'm one of her *all*-time fans – albeit from a distance. I've followed her career for ages, even if only through reviews and word around the traps. Sadly, I haven't had the chance to see her in anything else since then."

Nikki came in again. "Well, with a pedigree like that, I'm not surprised Lucy sings like an angel! But as a singer and actor herself, it can't have been easy growing up in her mother's shadow." She turned to Lara with her eyebrows raised playfully and gave a friendly smirk.

"Oh really ... has it been that bad?" Lara wasn't exactly sure how light-hearted this last comment was meant and grimaced at her only offspring. "I'm sorry, Munchkin."

"It's okay, Mum. It just comes with the territory, so I've gotten used to it – besides, it just makes you work harder, which means it's a good thing in lots of ways. I'm sure it's been the same for her from everything I've been reading. I stumbled across an interesting article with the headline *Golden Girl: Lucy Maunder* when I was checking out the reviews. It sounds like she's totally down-to-earth, and her parents are really supportive according to the interview – so we're sort of in the same boat, although I doubt I'll ever be in her class."

Nikki was bubbling over with enthusiasm. As much as she would have given anything for the coveted role herself, the young actress always had a good word to say about her peers, and she was genuinely pleased for Lucy.

"Hey, don't put yourself down, young lady – you have a fabulous voice!" came a stern reproach from her mother's side of the table. "Anyway, I'm not surprised they're a close-knit family. They certainly came across that way when I met them all those years ago. Now I come to think of it; I remember seeing a few flyers around advertising a couple of shows they put on as a family. Sounds like something I'd enjoy. Maybe Dad and I will catch one if ever it coincides with breaks between our projects."

"Do you remember what they're about?"

Lara's hand flashed in a dismissive wave as she sent her daughter a cheeky grin. "Oh, nothing you'd be interested in! One showcases nostalgic tunes from days gone by, and the other's just a tribute to Richard Rodgers of the famous *Rodgers and Hammerstein* pairing.

At the mention of her favourite musical's duo of songwriters, Nikki's eyes twinkled. "Oh, *Muuummm*, stop teasing! And don't you *dare* leave me out if *that* one ever comes to town. They'd have to have *some* of the numbers from *The Sound of Music*, surely!"

Lara well remembered the fascination a little girl once had with the popular movie – and still had, if the truth be known. "For sure; and it's a date!"

"Great! Then maybe Lucy and I can swap stories afterwards about what it's like to have famous parents!" Her gaze flitted between both Lara and Adam as she sent them broad smiles. It wasn't hard to recognise the pride in her eyes.

Adam smiled and reached over to squeeze her hand. "Who both have talented daughters..."

"Thanks, Dad."

"If you're lucky, maybe you'll get to meet her tonight after the show," her mother replied.

"Mmm, that'd be excellent and maybe a few others from the cast. Anton Berezin's appearing in one of the supporting roles. He's an incredible actor – I've wanted to work alongside him since he was in *Cabaret*. He's Anthony's understudy for *Yurii's* character in this one and doing a brilliant job from everything I've been reading, especially after poor Anthony tore a calf muscle during the last rehearsal before its Sydney preview. Imagine the odds of something like that happening only a few hours before the first show!"

"It beggars belief. Such a shame – poor guy," Adam chimed in. "The whole industry was buzzing with the news."

Nikki shivered as she imagined the scenario. "It all happened so fast, and Anton had to fill in with hardly any preparation. It must've been so daunting for him."

Lara nodded gravely. "And from everything I've heard, he did a marvellous job, especially when you think of all the pressure he would've been under. With Anthony being one of the industry's biggest drawcards, it must've been quite intimidating for Anton having to face that first audience when they were expecting to see Anthony walk out on stage."

"I reckon – it's no wonder I admire him so much," Nikki answered.

"And thank goodness his injury was healed within a few days or else it would've been so disappointing for both Anthony and Lucy Simon, especially when she composed the score purely with him in mind," Lara continued. "I was listening to an interview with her on the internet only the other day where she declared, 'This is my *Yurii Zhivago!*' when he visited her home in New York City a couple of years ago. I also remember chatting to Susan Schulman when she directed *The Secret Garden* here in Australia back in the 90s sometime and she told me much the same thing. I managed to get along to see that one too, and he was fabulous. No wonder Ms Simon wanted him for this one."

"Well I can't wait to see it tonight – the whole show is bound to be amazing," Nikki responded, looking at her watch anxiously.

After listening to all the chatter about an industry in which he was only a bystander, Daniel butted in. "Well, I'm looking forward to seeing it too, if only our dessert would hurry up – that mud cake sounded delicious!"

"You'd better wolf it down quickly then, honey. I don't want to miss one second, and they won't let us in if we're late!"

"Don't worry, we've got oodles of time still," Lara assured them both with a kind smile. "Let Daniel enjoy his dessert, especially after he's had to listen to all of us prattle on for so long."

"Sorry, darling. Typical actress – words are my life and I forget to shut up a lot of the time," the young woman answered, realising she had monopolised the conversation for most of the meal. Reaching under the table, she squeezed her husband's hand.

He sent her a loving wink, along with a smile of reassurance, and pressed his lips against her cheek.

Hurrying along the riverfront leading to the theatre a short time later, the excited foursome passed a quaint little Nepalese Pagoda set on the edge of a lush rainforest. Lara and Adam exchanged loving looks when they remembered a special visit to Expo '88 and standing in each other's arms on that exact spot.

So much had happened over the years and yet the pagoda still looked much the same, despite having been ravaged by a series of severe torrential storms followed by a sea of devastating floods hitting the river city only a few months earlier. Thinking about the tragic story they were about to go and see, the stalwart structure was a timely reminder of how their love had been buffeted and battered, but still managed to remain steadfast.

§

The family found themselves seated in the centre of the fifth front row when the house lights dimmed. A heavy black curtain hung before them, embellished with the silhouette of a line of cut-out chairs. They were fashioned as a single panel running down the centre from top to bottom and offered a subtle hint of what was to come. Soft light filtered through each one, illuminating an elegant chessboard-patterned floor on the stage behind. The anticipation was so intense you could almost hear a pin drop as they waited in the stillness.

From out of all this silence, two sustained strains of a single chord rose from the orchestra pit. These were followed by a haunting few bars floating from the deep throats of a duo of cellos. Goosebumps ran across Lara's skin as the stirring music swirled around them. Unable to control an excited shiver, she tucked her hand into Adam's arm just as the curtain went up and a chorus of voices joined in.

On the black and white patterned stage, a young boy stood before an open grave. A group of people dressed in black paid homage around the yawning chasm, sombre as the Russian winter in which the scene was set.

The opening number was like a piece of intricate embroidery sewn together with lyrics instead of thread to define the contrasting class system in pre-communist Russia. Clever stanzas wove together *Yurii* and *Lara*'s tragic tale over an unfolding expanse of time. From both ends of the stage, these two young teens, living vastly different lives, drew the audience into their worlds.

His depicted a young boy growing up to become both a caring doctor and sensitive poet in a splendid home filled with love, pride and privilege through the kindness of his adoptive parents. Lara's existence as a poor young dressmaker from a single parent family portrayed a young girl trying to make a

611

living in a back-alley hovel while being continually abused by her mother's rich, arrogant lover. Holding her in his spell, this dastardly suitor manages to entice Lara into doing his bidding, no matter how desperately she tries to break free.

As the passing of time takes these two young strangers into adulthood and *Yurii* comes to terms with the opportunities lying before him through the generosity of his patrons, suddenly Anthony's powerful voice filled the auditorium with the question, *"What will my future be?"* The talented performer moved from the wings to centre stage, holding the audience mesmerised – similar to Lara's experience while watching him perform in *Les Miserablés,* back when she and Adam had sat side by side in a darkened theatre for the very first time on the eve of rehearsals for *My Fair Lady* in Sydney.

She gave an expectant shiver and squeezed her husband's arm as the two main characters moved from one heart-wrenching scene to the next, their stories continually interweaving around and through those tumultuous times in early-twentieth-century Russia. The lyrics captured every nuance of emotion and it was easy to understand why *Yurii* found himself drawn over and over again to the irresistibly beautiful young woman whenever their paths crossed.

The first glimpse they have of each other is in the most unlikely of places...

Fed up with the abuse meted out by her formidable lover, the teenage *Lara* embarks on a sinister plan – with a loaded gun in the ballroom of *Yurii's* family home. Much to the fiery young dressmaker's dismay, her aim is off, and another lies wounded instead. The concerned newly trained doctor witnesses everything and questions what would cause someone of her tender age to risk not only her reputation but also her life once the authorities find out. As she runs off into the night, his eyes follow her with another question, *"Who is she?"*

A few years later the young couple accidentally meet up again on a Moscow street. Even though both have since married, they sense an immediate and inexplicable bond, though the looming war and their individual situations ensure nothing can come of it.

In the middle of Act I, the dramatic storyline reveals their enduring agony while fighting to control the strong feelings of love now threatening to consume them. This is their own personal conflict set amidst the battlefields of World War I, far away in the frozen wastelands of this vast country. It is here they meet up again while tending to the wounded in a frontier hospital.

Despite *Yurii's* marriage to *Tonia*, his childhood companion still residing in Moscow hundreds of miles away, and *Lara's* to *Pasha*, an impassioned revolutionist with no time for gentleness or trivialities and now seemingly missing on the frontline, they can no longer pretend indifference. A dead soldier's love letter to his sweetheart is the catalyst to bring out the depth of feeling both of these lonely souls have been hiding for so long. For a few short weeks, they experience what it means to be loved for themselves without anything from their past defining them.

As the war draws to a close, once again their worlds are torn apart ... both sent back to pick up the pieces of their old lives with no way of knowing whether they will ever see each other again.

Yurii trudges home to a city now lying in ruins and a wife, who despite caring deeply for him in her own way, will never understand what drives the passion pulsating inside her husband's heart. He is consumed with a fervour of patriotism for a beloved country now thrust into the grip of atrocious conflicts ... and memories of a vulnerable though tempestuous young woman whose soulful eyes will forever haunt his dreams.

Lara returns to her small hometown in the Ural Mountains not knowing whether her missing husband is alive or dead. And still, deep inside her soul, a hidden passion endlessly simmers – for a caring and sensitive doctor who writes stirring poems that tug at her heartstrings and looks at her with eyes filled with compassion. For the first time in her young life, she understands what it means to be treated with tenderness and respect.

The unfolding tale depicts a country neither of them recognises any more. Separated by hundreds of miles and using any means possible to stay alive in the bleakness of a homeland soon to be thrust into the throes of revolution, the pair try futilely to subdue memories from a period of time that will always live on in a secret place in their hearts.

When *Yurii* realises the necessity to flee with his family from Moscow and the cruel regime now ruling there, the only safe place available also presents him with an unexpected opportunity to see *Lara* again. Loyalty to his family name and honour for his reputation are in sharp contrast to the burning need to be with the enchanting nurse who continues to capture his thoughts. Wherever he goes, this internal battle threatens to tear him apart.

§

When the curtain came down on the first act, Adam looked across and found his wife battling to control her emotions over a tale so similar to their own – a moving love story repeatedly thwarted by the direst of circumstances.

"Oh sweetness, are you okay?" A look of concern accompanied his whisper as a caring hand reached out to caress her knee through the silken fabric.

She could only nod until the lump in her throat subsided and then the words faltered when she finally managed to murmur, "Their story ... it's so like ours. I know we've seen it before on the small screen, but to have it play out live in front of us – and especially with such stirring music – brings back all of those long, lonely years wondering where you were and whether you were happy."

"Oh Baby, I know what you mean. I was feeling the same, and not knowing how you were was the hardest part of all."

"And those heart-wrenching lyrics – *I breathe you in, I feel you on my skin ... you melt away the cold and pain and fear* – I know exactly what that feels like. So many times I'd try to imagine your lips on mine ... longing to feel your breath filling my mouth again ... bringing me back to life. Sometimes the only thing keeping me going was remembering what it felt like having you beside me – I'd lie awake for hours imagining your skin against mine and your eyes looking just as they are now." She looked up at him as he brushed a tear from her cheek. "I didn't think it would affect me this much after so long."

He lifted her hand and moved his mouth along the tips of her fingers. "I'm not surprised at all. I can still recall how much that movie affected you. You were heartbroken for days, remember?"

Lara nodded, trying hard to hold back the tears. "Mmm, I was a mess." She ran those same fingers along his cheek and held his gaze. "But it was only because I didn't want to contemplate having to go through what they did, especially that tragic ending."

He leaned into her palm and his voice trembled. "Thank goodness an inner voice told me to book a flight that Christmas Day. I can't imagine going through life without you now. Our fate could've been much the same as theirs if I hadn't listened..."

"I know – and I've thanked God over and over for listening to your parents and our daughter's prayers instead of mine."

All Adam could do was nod as his lips touched the tip of her nose – closing his eyes while trying to push away that other dreaded outcome.

Her breath warmed his chin. "I don't know about you, but having their tale of heartbreak set to such a magnificent score underpinned with those poignant lyrics adds an even deeper dimension. And don't Anthony and Lucy's voices blend beautifully..."

"I know what you mean and they sure do ... the perfect pairing if you ask me. Whoever cast her knew exactly what they were doing. She's the perfect symmetry for his tone and skill."

"Absolutely and I can't believe the timing. What are the odds of the two of us being in Brisbane tonight rather than at least one of us off working somewhere else? All I can say is, thank God! I'd hate to have missed out on seeing this in our hometown."

"I agree – I'm so glad we were free, even though it looks as though the musical will have just as profound an effect on you as the movie once did. Please don't go all maudlin on me again."

She sent him a grimace through the makings of a smile. "I'll try not to..."

Nikki was just as moved by the epic tale. When the family made their way to the bar for an interval drink, she linked arms with her mother.

"If that's how it was between you and Dad, I think I'm beginning to understand what it must've been like being apart for all those years. My heart breaks though, knowing you had to go through everything by yourself. Why didn't you ever tell me how hard things really were?"

Lara stroked her hand. "Thanks, Munchkin, but you couldn't have done anything. It was just the way things turned out and I had to get on with life – but I always thanked God you were there to fill my days." Swept back in time, her expression turned wistful. "It's hard remembering back to the agony of all those years. I missed your dad so much – so badly that all I did was ache for him. Having been in love yourself, maybe you can understand what I mean."

"Mmm, I think I do, although we haven't had any obstacles like those you faced, thank heavens. I guess that's why you never wanted to watch the movie."

Nodding sadly, Lara remembered the wretchedness of those days. "I didn't want to have to deal with seeing all of their heartache again; not when mine was so raw. Your father and I had already watched it in Sydney when we were down there for *My Fair Lady,* so I knew how it ended. The plot was too painful, and I didn't want to have to face the fact that our story might have a similar ending."

Adam caught the last part of their conversation when he joined them toting a tray of drinks. His expression was sombre as he handed Lara a glass of Moscato. "It nearly did, my darling ... by a truck on a steep hillside in Tuscany."

An image of her misshapen legs filled Lara's mind for an instant, but soon the life returned to her eyes as she answered with a smile, "But *now* look what we have! A wonderful life together, a beautiful daughter who's followed us onto the stage, a son-in-law who's fitted into our family right from the start and an adorable little grandson who lights up our lives in the best way possible. What more could we ask for?"

Her gaze flitted from one to the other and Daniel sent her a sincere smile. He knew most of the details of his parents-in-law's story and admired their stance in trying to do the right thing by Adam's first wife. After the warm welcome he had received into the family, the young man was very happy they had found each other again.

Nikki leaned across and dropped a loving kiss on her mother's cheek. "I love you, Mum ... and don't ever forget how much."

"I know you do, sweetie, and I love you too ... big as the sky." Both mum and daughter exchanged tender smiles to hear the old expression from Nikki's childhood. "Now stop all this sad talk, or you'll have me blubbering like an idiot again!" Lara foraged around in her clutch purse for a tissue to blot beneath her lashes so the thick coats of mascara didn't run any further.

Out of the corner of her eye, Nikki spied an old school friend she hadn't seen since their teens. Grabbing Daniel by the hand, she sent a hurried excuse to her parents before rushing over to say hello.

One of Lara's comments brought back a long-forgotten memory for Adam. This was his first real opportunity to share something which had been locked away in his heart for many years.

Brushing a stray wisp of hair from her cheek, he whispered close to her ear, "In answer to your earlier question ... there's one more thing I wish we could've asked for – our own child ... a little person created by both of us."

She looked into his eyes with an expression of deep longing visible behind those dark, wet lashes. "I would've given anything to have carried your baby in my body. I often used to dream about what it would've been like ... but we both know it was impossible."

His gaze was unflinching. "Once upon a time I was thinking about having my vasectomy reversed ... then something happened, so there was no point anymore."

Lara gasped as a rush of unshed tears filled her eyes again. Just as quickly, she tried to blink them away, searching through the sadness to find an answer to what he was saying. "When? Tell me, Teddy, please?"

She felt his loving caress against the back of her hand. "Just after we'd been to the Blue Mountains for the day. Nikki was in the bathtub when I came in to find the two of you splashing water at each other ... you were having so much fun, and it made the perfect family picture. I remember thinking what it would've been like if that was you with our child. Nikki would've loved a baby brother or sister and the thought of seeing you pregnant with ours was all I could think about until..." He swallowed hard. "Trina came to Sydney a few weeks later, and suddenly all of those dreams were snatched away."

His words pierced her heart. If only she hadn't listened to the other woman's pleas. Lara had only been twenty-seven when they parted ... young enough to have carried several of their babies.

"Why didn't you tell me? I never would've said goodbye if I'd known ... I knew how much you longed for a child of your own. I remember the day Nikki started school and how heartbroken I was wishing I'd been able to have your child ... if we couldn't be together at least then I'd always have a part of you with me. Oh, darling, I've squandered so much of our lives. I'm so sorry."

Adam wrapped her in his arms and pressed his lips against her forehead. "I never had the chance. Anyway, I'm the one who's sorry. I vowed never to tell you. But hearing your comment just now and watching that tragic story come to life confirms how foolish we've been to waste so many years."

"Do you know what? As much as it hurts, I'm really glad you told me – just the fact you were willing to go through all that means everything. I love you with every part of me, Teddy, and we would've made beautiful babies if only we'd had the chance. But in my heart, Nikki's as much your daughter as she is mine. I've always thought of you as her father – the only one she ever knew – and she loves you almost as much as I do."

"How come you always know the right thing to say ... that's exactly how I feel about her," he whispered against the fragile skin of her eyelids.

Before she could respond, the sound of a bell heralding the second act soon had them scurrying back to their seats. They didn't want to miss one second of the moving tale.

It wasn't long before the swelling strains of the orchestra indicated the curtain was about to rise again. Lara took Adam's hand in the darkness rather than just holding onto his arm like earlier. It was almost as though she needed the comfort of his touch to convince herself the narrative playing out on stage would never impact their lives again.

§

The opening scene drew them in straight away and she sat mesmerised, especially when a distraught peasant woman lamented to another how a band of Red Soldiers had stolen her man away.

On stage, the fictional *Lara* tried to reassure her broken-hearted friend through the words of a song – metaphors that were clearly very dear to her own heart. Each line spoke of finding traces of the man she loves in the subliminal everyday things around her. The lyrics were poignant with imagery depicting a deep-seated yearning for a lost soulmate.

The talented young actress playing the challenging role was able to characterise *Yurii's* beloved muse with absolute conviction. So much so, the level of emotion she displayed meant several audible sniffles could be heard wafting around the darkened theatre.

In the fifth row, Lara grasped her husband's hand. He could tell she was recalling the many instances seemingly innocent little things from their months together had brought back memories during all of those long years of separation. Catching just a glimpse of the tall towers on Mt Coot-tha was one, although there had been countless others.

Gentle fingers caressed her palm, willing her to come back to him instead of getting lost in the sadness. Through the intensity of his wife's grip, he could sense how deeply the lyrics were affecting her, especially having them surrounded by such a rousing score.

Following more plot twists illustrating the lead characters having to endure the monotony of routine while hankering for their soulmate, the storyline moved to the separated lovers meeting many months later in the library of *Lara's* hometown. It was a touching scene expressing all of the heartbreak that came with seeing each other again after so long. Adam looked across and noticed two tears trickle down Lara's face as she recollected similar encounters in their own lives. And just like her, his heart ached at the memory of a stolen kiss in a quiet back corridor after her long-awaited comeback to the stage.

Cleverly, the lyricists were able to interweave not only *Yurii* and *Lara's* heartfelt reunion into touching stanzas, but also the anguish of their spouses – *Tonia* and *Pasha* – along with that of *Komarovsky, Lara's* despised abuser from when she was a teenager. Positioned in different areas of the stage, these five figures – three men caught in the spell of one woman and two women deeply in love with one man – lament about the different methods they each use to cope while yearning for a beloved soulmate.

Underpinning all five tales lay an undisputed truth: no matter how hard someone may search for love; in the end, it is love that finds them ... along with the torrent of emotions that keeps them company all the days of their life.

Both Lara and Adam could empathise with the emotive sentiment. Without meaning to, they had experienced an instant attraction from that very first meeting, and the pull on their hearts had been too strong to resist – love had found them even when they weren't looking for it. Likewise, even though they had been forced apart on two separate occasions – and once for endless years – the depth of their love had never waned. Instead, it had constantly drawn them back to their other half.

Lara had to keep swallowing a huge lump as her eyes followed the central players. She felt as though her heart was breaking for them.

One of the most moving scenes was when *Yurii* went missing in the bleak, harsh wastelands of central Russia. Neither his lover nor his wife has any idea *Lara's* missing husband – now the leader of the Red Army – is the instigator of a plot to take the doctor captive. *Pasha* knows this is his only way of ensuring his rival is barred from being with the woman they both desire.

When *Tonia* hears of her husband's disappearance and then learns of his affair with a young woman in the nearby town, she plucks up the courage to confront *Lara,* wondering if she has any idea where he might be. From either end of the stage, both of them break into a haunting duet outlining the ordeal facing each one – two women in love with the same man with no clue as to what has happened to him. They also share a mutual wariness as to how much either one should reveal about the extent of their heartache. By the final stanza, the two women reach an understanding of *Yurii's* need to have each of them in his life. And much to their surprise, these unlikely allies realise they can actually feel him closer when the other one is near.

As the touching interaction between these two rivals unfolded in front of her, Lara sat rigid in her chair, hardly daring to breathe. She was remembering another confrontation in a Sydney hotel foyer when Trina had pleaded her case ... that defining moment when everything had changed. A split second in history when Lara realised for the very first time the other woman's need, along with an understanding of the strength of Adam's commitment to a vow made many years earlier – even though it was far removed from what he truly wanted. Lara well knew the anguish that came from loving a man who belonged to another, and her heart ached for her namesake now singing on that lonely stage.

The man sitting beside her shifted uncomfortably in his seat. Adam hadn't been present when this same scenario had occurred between the two women in his life. He felt overcome with shame at the thought of having placed them in such an awkward position because of his cowardly indecision. The parallels were suddenly too close to home when he remembered his terrible anguish following Lara's decision to let him go. Both hands clenched as he tried to swallow.

Within seconds, the scene changed again, and the horrors of war riddle the faces of a huddle of seasoned soldiers. Trapped in the frozen wasteland, they try everything in their power to stay alive. *Liberius*, a zealous partisan, is prepared to use any means to dull the reality around him, even stealing morphine from some of *Yurii's* dying patients. His callous attitude brings a wave of utter despair from the sensitive doctor.

A clever character actor who appeared to be in his late-twenties portrayed the Red Army soldier, and his powerful voice carried across the audience. Nikki had already met Luke Joslin a few years earlier when they were both involved in a production put on at the Riverside Theatre in the western suburbs of Sydney. She had been thrilled to read he was involved in this production, especially after seeing him in another popular show the year before. Back then his role had been of a comedic nature, now it was exciting to see him take on the persona of such a heartless character.

As the plot moved to when *Yurii* returns to the village of Yuriyatin after escaping from the clutches of the Red Army, Lara's heart was in her mouth, remembering this was one of the most heartrending scenes in the movie.

Bedraggled, half-frozen and close to death after trudging hundreds of miles in the dead of winter, the starving doctor finally reaches the safety of his lover's porch, only to collapse in a heap at her door. For many years, he had suffered from a bad heart, which made the terrible journey even more arduous. Overjoyed to have him home again, though distraught to find her beloved in such a shocking condition, Lara drags him back from the threshold of death through her gentle ministrations and loving care.

When *Yurii* learns his wife and only child have fled the country with no means of finding out where they are, he is shattered. As much as he loves *Lara,* his concern and affection for both *Tonia* and *Sasha* have never dimmed, and he could never wish any harm on his childhood sweetheart. Even so, along with the sadness comes the realisation he and *Lara* are free at last to share the life they have always dreamed of.

With aching tenderness, Anthony and Lucy raised their voices for the stirring number *On the Edge of Time*. Every line dripped with the raw emotion of reuniting with a kindred spirit. Those in the theatre sat spellbound as the pair held each other while crooning sentiments outlining those early fateful encounters ... when two young people experienced love and forgiveness in all of its fullness for the very first time.

The passion-filled lyrics continued with even more earnest assurances – expounding on the bond uniting them and confirming it had always been there spurring them on throughout all the countless years of separation ... and constantly with the hope of one day finding their true soulmate again. The musical bridge offered a sad insight into the long years of separation until, eventually, the number closed with the very reason they had survived – to love one another freely and faithfully, even beyond the realms of time.

Every line touched Adam and Lara's hearts as if the entire creative team had been a witness to the story forming their lives. Those final few strokes from the lyricists' pens perfectly captured the culmination of this new life they now shared. Once again, the tears trickled down Lara's cheeks as she sat enthralled by the degree of poignancy both actors brought to their roles. She gave no thought to wiping them away. Instead, each drop fell unnoticed on her breast while her gaze remained fixed on the reconciled couple.

Then much to the audience's dismay, the unfolding love story suddenly fractured and split. The reunited lovers' renewed feelings and shared life only continue for another few weeks until the direst of circumstances forces *Yurii* to send *Lara* out of Russia under the protection of their old nemesis, *Komarovsky*. This cunning villain who had taken *Lara* against her will over and over again as a teenager, the same man who had instigated *Yurii's* own father's death, comes offering a failsafe means to keep them safe. The heartbroken doctor acknowledges if she remains with him in Yuriyatin, the authorities will most likely arrest them both and send them off to labour camps. Though it breaks his heart, such a threat is enough to convince *Yurii* this is the only way for *Lara* to have any chance for survival.

The scene was a heart-wrenching display of despair and sacrifice. Tragically, the young lovers separate with no forewarning this is the last time they will ever see each other.

Adam could feel the emotion building in his wife and gently squeezed her hand as his only means of comfort in the crowded auditorium. She clung on, glancing into his eyes while her own were awash with tears ... until once again the onstage drama commanded their attention.

When the narrative moved forward to show the passage of time, in a sad twist of fate the final scene mirrored the opening – mourners standing around an open grave on a cold winter's day. Only this time it is *Yurii's* final resting place. Along with a presiding official, two other dark silhouettes stand vigil beside this open fissure in the ground – *Lara* and their teenage offspring now left to grieve. The mother and daughter stare down at his unadorned coffin resting deep in the frozen earth.

She had been pregnant with *Katarina* when *Yurii* sent her away with *Komarovsky*. Their departure meant the father and daughter never had the chance to meet, though *Lara* had always kept his memory alive so *Katarina* could come to know him through the emotive poetry born from his gentle spirit.

Now this same woman – the one who had always loved him despite being separated for countless years – speaks into the yawning abyss as she introduces *Yurii* to their daughter.

From her seat near the centre front, Lara's heart ached as she recalled the futility of years Adam and Nikki had spent apart because of her fateful decision. All she could offer was a silent prayer of thanks that life had turned out so differently for them. Even more distressing was watching the other *Lara* fall to her knees, crying out in brokenness for the love she still felt and the pain that comes from living without her other half.

As a final tribute to his life and work, the grieving mother and daughter, there to honour the man lying in that stark, lonely grave, raise their voices to croon lines from one of *Yurii's* much-loved poems. Light snowflakes begin to fall when a group of mourners representing those touched by his work down through the years also join in. Poignant verses fall from their lips – ones *Yurii* himself had written in those lonely final years – each one adding to the exquisite stanzas he and *Lara* had already crooned to one another on his return from the war.

In these dying moments, Lara watched spellbound as the other *Lara* moved to the front of the stage as though singing to his spirit – the only means she has left to communicate with the man whose love has always been her lifeblood.

With hearts aching, those in the audience suddenly found their eyes drawn to the figure of a man emerging from the shadows just left of stage. It didn't take long to recognise this was *Yurii* returning to his beloved in spirit form. Those on stage fell silent – including *Lara* – as his voice rings out while he moves across to stand beside the still irresistibly beautiful woman who has held his heart captive all of his adult life. His eyes never leave her, and for a miniscule moment it appears she is aware of his presence when the glimmer of a smile touches her lips, as though recognising her soulmate's familiar tone.

For the first time in almost a score of years, the reunited twosome stand side by side, looking out to the horizon across the divide to the only future left to them. And while holding every onlooker's heart captive, *Lara's* voice once again blends with his, soaring above the sadness for the touching concluding line of the haunting duet...

"I know when life is through, my love will live ... in a ray of light ... in a distant chime... on the edge of time with you."

To the mellow strains of one final sustained note, the stage lights dimmed. All that remained was the figure of a man ... this caring poet and devoted doctor bathed in a single ray of light, while a distant chime tolls out its sad song – the perfect accompaniment to those heart-wrenching closing lines.

A hushed stillness fell across the audience as the last note faded away – except for a few muffled sniffles as several patrons discreetly dabbed at moist noses with already damp tissues. Then as one, the audience erupted into deafening applause – in gratitude for a stirring score surrounding a tragic tale delivered with all the passion and soulfulness required of a dedicated cast.

Lara clapped along loudly with a steady stream of tears pouring down her face, memories of those long-wasted years once again uppermost in her mind as her heart broke for the separated lovers. As crazy as it seemed, she wanted to turn the clock back fifteen minutes and actually become part of the storyline by rushing up on stage and begging *Yurii* not to let *Lara* leave without him. In her mind and heart, any threatening danger from the authorities was nothing compared to the tragedy of never seeing each other again. She well knew the desolation that came from years spent apart with no hope of reclaiming any of that precious lost time.

This musical had touched her heart like no other ... whether simply as an audience member or actually performing in one herself. Deep down, she sensed the tragic love story was far more than a fictional tale. Then from some place locked away in her high school memories, she recalled reading the author of the novel had based it around a woman he had once loved while married to another.

No wonder you were able to reach inside and touch my soul.

Her gaze never faltered as the cast took their bows. When the ensemble and supporting actors came forward to receive their share of well-deserved praise, Lara was one of the first on her feet, applauding loudly and calling out *"Bravo!"* or *"Brava!"* to each one.

When it was Lucy and Anthony's turn to come to the front of the stage, Adam was already standing alongside his wife, enthusiastically acknowledging the superb character portrayals by two exceptional stars. The waves of applause grew even stronger as the audience continued to revere the talented troupe, along with the accomplished orchestra led by the skilful baton of musical director, Kellie Dickerson. Both Adam and Lara had worked with her themselves, so they were familiar with the exceptional magic flowing from her spirit through that slender piece of wood.

But sadly, every curtain call eventually has to come to an end and the magic put away for another day. It was time to put this one to bed for the night, though both Adam and Lara were certain the lasting effects from such a moving experience would remain with them for the rest of their lives.

As they made their way out of the theatre, Lara had difficulty speaking due to a deep sense of connection to the tragedy she had just witnessed. She was overwhelmed with feelings of gratitude at the thought of how truly blessed she was to have her husband by her side when their story could so easily have ended with her sitting in a wheelchair, alone and still pining for the love of her life.

Recognising so much of herself in the principal female character, Lara had been unable to take her eyes away whenever Lucy was on stage. Her delivery and diction had been faultless, while the clarity and emotion she brought to each number was a credit to her ability – almost as though the character had taken up residence in her heart.

Being well acquainted with the feelings that came from playing such a deeply moving role, it wasn't surprising Lara felt an instant rapport between herself and the talented young actress. The blending of Lucy and Anthony's voices had been exquisite and was the perfect icing on the cake to outstanding performances.

Following an emotional few hours, she went off to the ladies' room as soon as they left the main auditorium to repair her make-up. Re-joining her husband a few minutes later, all trace of those earlier tears was gone, and he sent a caring smile her way.

"Are you okay, sweetness?"

"Yes, I'm fine now, don't worry. *Grrr,* I should've known I'd be like this after watching that movie!"

"Which is exactly why I love you as much as I do. You wear your heart on your sleeve, my darling, so I never have to doubt how much you care."

She squeezed his hand and sent him an adoring grin as they followed Nikki and Daniel downstairs.

Due to their connections, the family had received invitations to the after-party, so they hurried out to an area set aside for the cast and VIP guests to mingle. Scores of purple and red lights turned the whole space into a regal-looking square, clearly in an attempt to usher in a taste of Imperial Russia to the sub-tropical city. They were in time to see the cast walk the red carpet and Nikki managed to send a quick wave to Luke Joslin, the young actor who had taken on the role of the sinister *Liberius*, as he filed past. He recognised her immediately and responded with a big grin and wave of his own.

Flashbulbs burst from all corners of the walkway and made for a kaleidoscope of colour. QPAC's entire forecourt looked like a Winter Wonderland with magnificent ice-sculptures illuminated by a rich purple hue positioned in several prominent places. Even the title of the musical blazed in gold lettering across an overhead rooftop made of huge purple shade sails. Wherever they looked everything oozed with the elegance of olden-day Russia.

After listening to several speeches and rewarding everyone involved with a rousing round of applause, the family made their way to *Lara's Bar*, a venue catering exclusively to the cast, crew and special guests following the premiere event.

Nikki leaned in close and whispered in her mother's ear as she pointed to the bar's name, "Looks like they knew you were coming tonight, Mum!"

Adam answered before his wife could think of a response. "Yep, they know a good thing when they're onto it, just like me!" He sent her one of those tender winks she knew so well and a familiar wrinkle of her nose was offered in reply.

Luke, Nikki's former co-star, wasn't hard to miss, towering over a handful of cohorts surrounding him. A thick shock of dark hair made him easily recognisable, along with his cheerful ever-ready grin.

Catching sight of Nikki, he beckoned the family over to where some from the cast were mingling in a quieter section away from the noisy dance floor. As they drew closer, Lara noticed he was standing beside a stunning young woman with dark curly hair caught up loosely on the back of her head.

It wasn't hard to recognise her as the delightful young teenager she had met in Sydney years earlier, now all grown up to become the talented actress who had just portrayed the fictional *Lara* with such finesse. She was chatting happily with several of her peers as a ready smile lit up her dazzling eyes. Long, dangling earrings framed her face, enhancing features that gave the appearance of being flawless. A delicate lace and chiffon gown in champagne pink perfectly emphasised her shapely silhouette and drew several admiring glances.

As soon as they were close enough, Luke pulled Nikki into a warm hug.

"Gidday, old friend!" she laughed, hugging him back. "Gosh, it's good to see you."

"Hey, Niks, it's great to see you too!"

"Wow, tonight was amazing! I felt so proud watching you up there."

Those twinkling dark eyes looked her up and down as he raised his eyebrows. "Thanks, kiddo! And don't you look gorgeous! I'm glad you could make it, but how come you're here? I thought you had a new gig coming up in Sydney…"

"Oh, yeah, but that's in a couple of weeks. I wouldn't have missed tonight for anything. And congratulations on landing such a dynamic role – it's sure different to anything I've seen you in before. You did a brilliant job. Bravo!"

Having witnessed him taking home a prestigious Helpmann Award as well as receiving a coveted Green Room gong for another show the year before, she wasn't at all surprised to see him carry this one off with so much panache.

His face beamed to hear her enthusiasm. "Thanks, lovely! I'm glad you enjoyed it. Being offered a place with this cast is a dream come true, and you're right ... it is different to anything I've done before. We're all having a fabulous time and it's incredible to be involved in such an epic show."

"I'm sure it is! Oh, and I caught your weekly blogs on the official website, as well as all those excellent backstage interviews you did with the cast. It was a bit of a buzz to see your cheeky smile again – still a mischief-maker from the looks of it!"

He laughed and punched her arm playfully. "Says you, who was the instigator of so much mischief when we worked together in Parramatta! I'm glad you caught them, though. It's been a hoot!"

"I bet it has. The minute they announced it was going to be playing the east coast, I started following everything you put up."

"Oh, that's great. It's been fun making them, and a real thrill to be part of this talented bunch."

"And all those interviews are now showing on YouTube too! You'll soon be famous around the world!"

"Yeah, sure! It'd be nice though. One of my mates mentioned they were out there." He gave her another hug. "Gee, it's good to see you again! You look terrific, and I hear you've been getting plenty of work." With a warm grin, he nodded his head to include the others standing just behind her.

"Yeah, it keeps coming so I can't complain! Now I suppose I should introduce you to my family or else I'll be in *big* trouble. Luke, this is my husband, Daniel ... actually, didn't you two meet once before."

The two men shook hands firmly. "Yeah, that's right – at the Helpmanns, I think. Hi, Daniel, it's good to see you again. Thanks for bringing your good woman along tonight, mate."

The other man laughed. "Are you kidding – I couldn't keep her away! And it's good to see you again too, Luke. Congratulations on a great show."

"Thanks. I'm glad you enjoyed it."

They exchanged a nod and another smile as Nikki extended her hand to include her parents. "Luke, this is my mum and stepdad – you've probably heard of them around the traps ... Lara and Adam Peters." She sent him a conspiratorial wink, remembering how many times she had boasted about them over a late-night supper following one of their shows.

Once again, Luke extended his hand. "Of course, who hasn't in this business! It's an honour to meet you both."

Adam took the younger man's hand and his grip was firm. Lara's warm smile confirmed she was happy to get to know him better after hearing a few amusing stories from when he and Nikki worked together. She moved a little closer to touch his arm in greeting and sent a friendly nod his way.

Adam was first to reply. "It's an honour to meet you too, Luke, and what a brilliant job you did up there!"

"Oh, thanks very much, Mr Peters. It's good you could make it tonight, although I must say it's a bit strange to think you were in the audience. I'm usually the one watching you on a stage! I'm in awe of your work and have followed your career since before I graduated."

"Oh, my, thank you. But please drop the formalities ... just call me Adam. It was a real treat being able to sit back and take everything in rather than only seeing titbits from the wings between scenes. And you're not doing too badly yourself with those two well-deserved awards last year – congratulations! I was able to catch one of your performances when you were in Sydney."

"Wow, thanks. I'm glad you managed to get along to see it, but how did you find the time when you're always so busy yourself?"

"When I saw your name in the line-up, I remembered you'd worked with Nikki, so I stayed on an extra night once *Carousel* was done. She was telling me you've taken on a bit of directing work around the traps, too."

Luke looked surprised at Adam's pronouncement, and his unassuming grin encompassed both the father and daughter. "Mmm, I have. There've been a few now and hopefully more will come my way when *Zhivago* finishes its run. It's a challenge being on the other side of the curtain or camera, but I'm loving the experience."

"Oh, that's right. Nikki mentioned you directed a few for *Giggle and Hoot* on the ABC as well – our little Charlie loves that show, so I've probably seen your work without realising. Good on you and all the best with everything. I hope many more opportunities come your way."

The two men shook hands again. "Thanks, Adam; I appreciate your encouragement. It's been good to finally meet you after this one kept singing your praises when we were working together."

Both men laughed when Luke gave Nikki's arm a friendly nudge.

"Sorry," the older one responded with a wry grin, "she can be a bit of a broken record once she gets started."

"Oh, Dad, I'm not that bad!" Nudging both of them with her elbows, she turned from Adam to her former colleague. "And watch it, you! Stop telling tales!"

"Well, it's true!" Luke grinned at her father and sent him a surreptitious wink. "None of us could ever shut her up – all she ever did was rave about how proud she was of both you and her mum. I remember when you were playing *Javert* in

Les Mis at the Opera House ... she kept nagging all of us to get along to see her 'amazing dad'."

"And you did and everyone thought he was wonderful – see ... I was right!"

Adam quickly dismissed his stepdaughter's boasting by rolling his eyes and flicking his wrist. "Oh, don't listen to her – she's just a little bit biased! Now, I'd better shut up so my better half can offer you her well wishes, too." He leaned in close and whispered, "But whatever you do, don't call her 'Mrs Peters' – she thinks it makes her sound old and decrepit!"

Lara caught the cheeky remark and landed a friendly punch on her husband's arm. "*Adam, stop it!* Don't listen to him, Luke. I *adore* being called Mrs Peters! After all, it took long enough to happen!"

Luke tried hard to stifle a snigger as he turned to Lara. "Well, it's a real pleasure to meet you at last, *Mrs Peters*." He emphasised the last two words with a telling smirk and it was obvious he was partial to a bit of fun.

She laughed. "Oh, get out of here – it's Lara to you. And I'm so glad to finally meet you after this one's rave reviews about your work." Her gaze brushed over Nikki before turning to him again. "But it's a wonder I'm not grey and wrinkled from putting up with all of my husband's carry-on these last few years – as you can see, he's a bit of a tease, but I do love him to bits!" This time Adam was on the receiving end of a cheeky smirk.

The culprit made a play of wiping his brow in an exaggerated motion. "Phew, just as well! What do you reckon, Luke? Managed to grab me a good one here, hey!"

It was obvious the husband and wife were still very much in love when their hands met and held on tightly through a flurry of chuckles emanating from the others.

Happy to join in, the younger man's gaze swept her up and down with a mischievous glint. "You sure did ... and from what I can tell, Lara, you'll never have to worry about looking decrepit ... *nor* about growing old!"

Placing her hand on his arm, she gave it a playful squeeze. "Thanks, Luke – that's very kind of you. It's nice to hear *you've* obviously been brought up with manners!" A teasing scowl was aimed in Adam's direction before she turned once again to the other man. "Please take no notice of my husband – it's plain to see he's not to be trusted!" After exchanging more laughter, she leaned in close again and brushed her mouth against Luke's cheek in a proper greeting. "It's a real pleasure to meet you. Nikki was quite vocal when you were walking the red carpet, raving on and on about how clever you are."

"Now you're making *me* embarrassed! Anyway, you've certainly raised a talented daughter – clearly, she takes after her mother!" Another mischievous grin was sent Adam's way before he addressed Lara again. "I've been to several of your shows over the years – I had to just to shut her up! You should've heard her raving on and on about your work on *The King and I* a few years ago. She's one very proud daughter, *and* with good reason." The smile he offered carried a hint of concern, and she could sense he knew a little of her story. It wasn't surprising when they were all in the business, and most especially when the accident occurred less than a week after that particular production closed.

Her response was warm as she squeezed his arm again, recognising his caring spirit.

"Thanks and I can assure you we feel the same about her. And from all her accolades, you're someone we definitely should be keeping our eyes on. It sounds like you've been a busy young man and I wish you every success in the future!"

His expression turned sober when he responded with a heartfelt, "Thank you, that means a lot."

Lara's gaze then turned to encompass others from the cast grouped around them. "And what a triumph tonight! You all put on a brilliant show – thanks for giving us a fabulous night of entertainment. Oh and, Luke, I meant to add, I really enjoyed the amount of passion and menace you put into playing *Liberius*. Congratulations!"

"Thank you. It's an honour to receive any form of praise, and even more so from someone with your experience," the young man responded, echoing the thoughts of several others on the receiving end of her heady acclaim.

Their euphoria was already sky high after the success of the evening. To receive such high commendation from a performer with one of the biggest reputations in the industry only added to the excitement.

"Well, it's true. I've been an emotional wreck all evening. Such a heart-wrenching storyline put to a stirring score ... and the script and those lyrics perfectly conveyed the emotion of the novel. I was in tears several times, although I feel sorry for those close by who had to listen to my blubbering through a lot of the scenes!"

Luke's expression highlighted his empathy. "Don't worry; apparently it happens quite regularly from what we've all heard! I know I feel pretty special to be involved, and we've received fabulous responses from southern audiences."

Others from the cast nodded and murmured enthusiastically.

"Well, you're sure to receive the same in Brizzie after tonight's marvellous performance," Lara responded, once again including them all with a grateful look and warm smile.

"We sure hope so!" he said, exchanging excited grins with the young woman standing closest to him. "Anyway, I'd better introduce you to a good friend of mine – the talented young lady who portrayed the most tragic character of all.

Oh, and as you may have noticed, she's a bit of an enchantress on stage, especially during the wedding night scene! Lucy Maunder ... Lara and Adam Peters."

Both Adam and Lara chuckled when the actress landed a jocular punch on his arm for offering such a 'glowing' introduction. They vividly recalled the alluring image of a semi-naked figure rippling across a black backdrop during that one particular scene.

"That wasn't *me* ... it was just a likeness on a screen, you rat! And if you remember correctly, it just happens to be one of the most emotional numbers in the entire show!"

Lucy joined in the spontaneous laughter rising from her playful reaction. Her captivating hazel eyes turned to meet Lara's blue ones as she held out a welcoming hand and addressed both the husband and wife together.

"Please excuse my *friend* ... he's incorrigible! But like him, it's such a pleasure to meet you both. I'm sure neither one of you has any idea how much I admire your work."

Her manner was enthusiastic, and yet Lara could detect the faintest touch of endearing shyness in Lucy's greeting.

Smiling kindly, she took the young woman's hand in hers. "It's a pleasure to meet you too, Lucy, and thanks for those kind words. You probably don't remember, but we actually met several years ago – you were only a teenager at the time." Lara gently squeezed her hand, remembering a pretty, young girl and the delightful rapport she shared with her parents.

Lucy's eyes widened as a quizzical smile crossed her face. "Did we? I'm sorry, but I don't remember – I was probably too young to realise who you were back then."

"Oh, don't worry. Your mum was the star that night; I wouldn't expect you to remember me."

"Well, it's a thrill to meet you properly after seeing so many great reviews about your work."

"Thanks, Lucy, but don't believe everything you read!"

"Oh, I know what you mean ... some journalists will write *anything* for a headline!"

Both women shared commiserating smiles and a couple of knowing nods.

"But I've been to several of your shows, and each one was amazing," Lucy continued. "I absolutely adored your portrayal of *Anna* a few years ago. I missed the tour Luke mentioned, but was glad the powers that be reprised the show again for a longer run. Travelling to all the capital cities was the best way to prove to critics you were back and as strong as ever. I was in the audience when they brought it to Sydney. It was so exciting to see you gracing our stages again!"

Naturally, Lucy had heard about the accident and followed the headlines when Lara made her big comeback.

"Yes, it was the perfect way to get back into the industry. I was blessed to be given the opportunity when no one really knew whether I had the stamina for it – especially those sweeping dance numbers!"

"And you did a splendid job! I'm so glad audiences around the country had a chance to see you in that role again. I grew up watching all the old musicals, and *The King and I* has always been one of my favourites."

"Oh, mine too and thank you. I'm so happy you enjoyed it! It's an excellent role to play ... but I must commend you on doing a superb job out there tonight. *Lara's* such a gripping character and your voice is just exquisite. To be able to see your interpretation of my favourite character from one of my all-time favourite novels captured my heart – I was completely enthralled. Every single audience member was privileged to see you bring her to life so beautifully – I'll never forget how much your performance touched my heart."

"Oh, Lara, thank you. What a lovely thing to say. To know you've moved someone that deeply is every performer's dream ... but I don't have to tell you that!"

Lara sent her an affirming nod and a generous smile. "Well, it's true, and you deserve all the applause."

"Goodness, I'm flattered, thank you again. It certainly is a dream role. In fact, out of all the characters I've played, she has to be my favourite."

"I'm not surprised. She's always been a favourite of mine, too."

"Really?"

"True! I've loved that book since I was a teenager. Then the movie came out and she captured my heart all over again. But tonight was extra special."

"Oh, I felt the same as soon as I read the script and it made me even more determined to land the role. Even though *Lara* appears to have such a strong personality, there's also a fragility that touched my heart – but then I love how she's also so spirited and full of life ... and the way she adores *Yurii* adds the perfect amount of intrigue and romance." Lucy's mouth suddenly fell open, and her eyes twinkled as she realised the coincidence. "Oooh my goodness, no wonder you feel such an affinity with her! I love the name Lara, and if you're anything like her, I'm sure that hubby of yours is a very lucky man!"

The young actress glanced at Adam with a grin. He laughed and nodded enthusiastically, and his playful wink soon had her breaking into a giggle.

Lara caught her husband's response and nudged his arm with a well-placed elbow. "Hey you, don't go giving away our secrets!"

The trio exchanged amused chuckles, despite Lara's face turning a delicate shade of pink.

When Lucy found the courage to look Lara's way again, there was a heartfelt look of regret in her eyes. "I'm so sorry; I didn't mean to embarrass you!"

Lara's smile was sincere as she reached out and patted her hand. "Don't worry; it's fine ... I'm well used to my hubby's teasing ways! But in all seriousness, I doubt anyone else will ever be able to portray Pasternak's mysterious heroine the way you did tonight. You've certainly made *Lara* your own, and I'll never forget one moment of seeing you bring her to life with so much credibility. My heart kept breaking over and over – brava!"

Now it was Lucy's turn to blush, and her captivating eyes sparkled like before. "I think a powerful score and a virtual truckload of stirring lyrics had a lot to do with it! Amy Powers and Michael Korie have written the most beautiful lyrics to capture the essence of his story."

"I couldn't agree more. They're some of the best I've ever heard – a breathtaking interpretation of the novel, with excellent meter and rhyme. To having them underpinned by that sweeping music turned it into a pure feast for the senses. But don't sell yourself short, young lady. It takes real talent to convey the level of emotion you showed tonight."

Again, the young performer's attractive face portrayed a bashful grimace – this time to be on the receiving end of such high commendations from someone she admired so much. "Thanks, Lara, it's a relief to be able to do her justice. I only wish I could remember meeting you before – I feel awful."

"Please don't – it was a long time ago, so I wouldn't expect you to remember. But after seeing your mother perform, and knowing of your father's many achievements, I'm not at all surprised to find you have such a wonderful gift yourself. And from what I've just witnessed, we'll be reading about your exploits on stage for many, many years to come."

"Thank you! What a lovely thing to say. Mum and Dad are my role models, so I've been very fortunate." From the expression on her face, it was easy to see how much she admired them.

Another charming smile touched Lara's lips as she reached over to squeeze the young woman's arm. "Well it's true, and you certainly deserve it. Nikki was telling me earlier how you won a *Bound for Broadway* scholarship. It must've been exciting to have the opportunity to train under some of Broadway's finest ... and in New York no less. What a fantastic achievement! No wonder you were successful auditioning for this one."

Lucy's response was even more confirmation as to why she had so many devoted fans – and why a new one had just been added to the mix. There was just the slightest hint of humility overlaid with an appealing show of graciousness as she thanked Lara once again.

Adam leaned in and added, "And I agree completely with my wife. You were phenomenal out there and gave us all a wonderful night of entertainment!"

Just as she was about to answer, others from the cast sidled over and started jostling Lucy's arm.

Laughing at their not-so-subtle hints, it was obvious they weren't going to let up until she complied. "Okay, okay, wait your turn, you lot! Lara, Adam, I think I need to introduce you to some of my roguish cohorts, or I'll never live it down!"

"Hi everyone," Lara grinned as she greeted the newcomers collectively, while Adam responded with an inclusive nod as his eyes travelled from one to another. His broad smile was a good indication of how amenable he was to meeting them.

"Okay, well here goes." Lucy took a deep breath and extended her hand to the first in the line-up. "Lara, this fine fellow is Jamie Way. He played that indomitable comrade who knows how to entertain an audience with a lively jig. And I'm sure you noticed how easily he adapts to other characters, including a flag-waving Red!"

Lara took the young man's hand and leaned towards him with a welcoming smile. "Oh yes, I remember both characters well. Well done, Jamie! I must say you captured the arrogance of that overbearing fellow down to a tee ... and I enjoyed his unique little dance. It managed to bring a light touch to a depressing situation."

He returned her greeting with a broad smile of his own, looking dapper in a black outfit that matched the colour of his hair. "Thanks, Lara. It's pretty incredible being involved in this production and I'm so pleased you enjoyed it."

"I most certainly did, and I must congratulate you on that splendid voice. Fans are bound to be lining up to see you perform in the years to come."

"Wow, thank you ... I can only hope! Just being here is a dream come true. The whole experience has been incredible, and I have to keep pinching myself!"

"Hey, don't underestimate your ability. You deserve this time in the spotlight."

"Gee, thanks heaps. It's sure been a blast and to be honest, I'm not sure I want it to end."

His enthusiasm was contagious and those standing close by murmured in agreement as Lucy continued with the introductions.

"And, Lara, this young lady happens to be Caitlin Berry, who played my mother when I was a teenager right at the beginning."

"Hi Caitlin, it's lovely to meet you. Thank you for entertaining us so well."

"Hello, Lara, it's an honour to meet you. I'm so glad you enjoyed yourself. We're having a fabulous time with all of our changing roles."

"Yes, you do seem to have a few from what I could tell – as do most of you!" Lara added, looking around at the others.

Several offered affirming nods as Lucy gestured towards an attractive young blonde woman standing next to the dark-haired Caitlin. "That's right, and would you believe this gorgeous creature, also known as Stephanie Silcock when she's out of costume, gets to play my character as a teenager. You may have noticed she also morphs into *Yurii* and *Lara's* daughter right at the end."

"Oh yes, of course. I didn't recognise you with all that gorgeous golden hair, Stephanie – so different to the dark-haired beauty of the show. You did an excellent job and managed to move me to tears at the end with that moving tribute beside *Yurii's* grave. Well done!"

The pretty actress, looking resplendent in a full-length carmine-red gown, was ecstatic to receive such high praise. "Gosh, thanks very much, Lara. That's exactly the response we were all hoping for. It's super exciting to be involved in the show."

Stephanie looked across to Lucy who had also shared the scene, and the pair exchanged generous smiles.

"Well, you did a splendid job – both of you – so inspiring," Lara replied. "Thank you for a truly memorable experience – one I'll never forget."

The two young women nodded in appreciation and Stephanie mouthed a grateful, "Thank you," as Lucy went on. "And as you well know, Lara, with the poetic licence of musical theatre and the wonders of wigs and makeup, Caitlin might've been cast as my mother, but as you can see, she's actually a bit younger than me!"

"Oh yes, I noticed! I've been there myself a few times – and sometimes the other way around. I don't know about you, but it helps to keep me grounded!"

Knowing nods and another flurry of laughter came from everyone as Lucy added, "Oh, yes, definitely! And both Stephanie and Caitlin also played eye-catching nurses, as well as Moscovites looking for a new home."

"And they also take on a few other minor characters where good-lookers are needed!" Luke joined in with an amorous grin, pretending to ogle his attractive cohorts.

"Typical of you, Luke! You're such a flirt!" Stephanie added with a roll of her eyes and an infectious giggle. "But you should see the costumes flying backstage between scenes, Lara. It's a madhouse ... and so much fun!"

Her vivid description had everyone chuckling and nodding in agreement as images of those few moments between scene changes synonymous with backstage life filled their minds. Anyone in theatre knew full well ensemble players often had several roles to fill – and often back-to-back – to keep costs within budget.

"Well, it's certainly been lovely to meet you both," Lara added with a dazzling smile. "And you're right, Stephanie, it *is* so much fun! Don't you just love this life and the incredible range of characters we get to play?"

"It's fabulous!" she answered, and her eyes glowed. "I wouldn't change my life for anything. It's all I've ever dreamed of – well, this and partnering a young Rudolph Nureyev in Swan Lake!"

A few of her colleagues nodded, and one called out, "And you should see Steph dance. Her suppleness is amazing; we're all sooo envious!"

"Well, in that case, I'll be sure to come along when they cast you in a dancing role," Lara responded with an encouraging squeeze of the keen dancer's arm. "It sounds like you have quite a fan club!"

"Oh, thanks, Lara! It would be an honour to dance in front of you, and I'll be sure to get tickets to your next show."

"Thank you, that would be lovely. And make sure you drop by to say hello afterwards."

Stephanie could only grin and nod, feeling a little tongue-tied to be singled out like this. Lara dipped her head in acknowledgement with a caring smile before turning to Caitlin again. "And what about you – I bet you love this life! You certainly looked like you were enjoying yourself out there tonight."

"Absolutely ... treading the boards is a real buzz! Sometimes I have to pinch myself to believe I'm really here – I just love this life!"

"I can tell – that dazzling smile lighting up your eyes is a dead giveaway – and from what I saw up there, you're doing a terrific job!"

The brunette tried unsuccessfully to hide her delight to be on the receiving end of such acclaim from someone with Lara's reputation. "Thank you, but I can't imagine doing anything else."

"Neither can I, Caitlin," Adam joined in. "I wouldn't have met this gorgeous lady if it wasn't for a little old theatre just across the river." He placed a loving arm around his wife and gave her waist an affectionate squeeze.

Lara looked up at him with a loving smile and landed an affectionate peck on his cheek. "Mmm, that *was* a memorable day."

The others exchanged happy smirks as he turned once again to Caitlin. She was wearing an eye-catching hot pink gown that drew several admiring looks from others in the crowd mingling around the exclusive bar area. "You did very well tonight, young lady – firstly as the mother of a teenager and then with all those other roles. Good on you!"

The young woman's cheeks matched her gown to be on the receiving end of his praise as well as Lara's. "Thanks, Adam. I'm glad you enjoyed it. It's an absolute thrill to be involved in such an iconic show."

Lara joined in with an enthusiastic grin. "I'll bet! And nothing comes close to the adrenaline rush when another curtain rises ... nor the mad scramble backstage. I wish both of you every success in the future."

Both Stephanie and Caitlin send her a grateful smile before Lara turned to a few others still waiting patiently to meet them. When a good-looking man with a distinctive bald head and thick moustache elbowed Lucy in the ribs, she responded in kind and with the same amount of gusto.

"Alright, alright, I won't forget about you, Toddy!" she quipped. "Adam, Lara, this talented fellow is my old mate, Toddy Keys, who I accidentally shoot during the ball if you remember! Sorry, Toddy, nothing personal!" she added with an impish giggle.

Rolling his eyes, the newcomer pretended to scowl. "Don't worry, Luce, I'll forgive you – this time ... oh and the next, and the next *and* the next!" he added, remembering there were still many more shows to go.

"Gee, thanks, you're all heart!"

Their playful attempts to lighten what had been a sombre incident was typical of the camaraderie found amongst those involved in this line of work.

Turning to Lara, he was quick to add, "It's an honour to have you come along to see us, and even better to have the chance to finally meet you. From what I just heard, it sounds like you enjoyed the show."

"I did – very much – and it's nice to meet you too, Toddy. Thank you for a thoroughly convincing performance. I'm glad to see you're okay after this one's bad aim!" Lara said with a chuckle, tilting her head in Lucy's direction.

There was a twinkle in his eye as he sent a scowl his co-star's way. "And the sad thing is that she's never learnt how to aim the blasted thing for the whole run, so I keep getting shot over and over! Thankfully, they aren't real bulle—"

Lucy's elbow dug him in the ribs again with a well-aimed jab. "Well, it's no wonder I keep targeting you when you treat me like this! And if you're not careful, next time I'll take you into the forest instead of that grand old ballroom and do a proper job!" She turned to the husband and wife team and shook her head in fun. "See what I have to put up with ... he's a real shocker!"

Everyone burst into peals of laughter, while Toddy placed a contrite arm around her shoulders. "Sorry, Luce, I'll be nice in future, promise!"

"You'd better 'cause I've usually only ever got good things to say about you!" she retorted with another cheeky smirk. Her eyes rolled in mock disdain as she once again addressed Adam and Lara. "Despite his terrible character flaws, as you would've noticed, our multi-talented Toddy turns into a passionate soldier before morphing into a communist authoritarian later in the show – he's a real Jack-of-all-Trades and very versatile ... and has a glorious voice for such a brazen man! Sometimes he *actually* sends shivers down my spine..."

"Ah, now that *is* better!" the jovial actor laughed, turning to Lara and Adam with a twinkle in his eyes. "Don't worry about us; we're always taking the Mickey out of each other! Anyway, it's an absolute thrill to meet you. I've followed both of your careers over the years."

The two men shook hands warmly as Adam responded, "Thanks, Toddy. It's very nice to meet you, too. You did a brilliant job tonight, well done ... and Lucy's spot on, you most certainly do have a glorious voice! Definitely gave me shivers and producers are bound to come knocking after hearing you in this."

"Thanks, Adam, it's a real privilege to receive such high praise from someone with your standing in the business. I only hope you're right!"

"I'm sure I am, in fact, you've done very well already from an article I caught about your work in *The Pirates of Penzance*. The reviews were most impressive, so I'll keep an eye out for your next venture," Adam responded as they shook hands again.

Toddy sent him a surprised look before adding gratefully, "Gosh, thanks again, and I look forward to seeing you further down the track then."

They sent each other a nod of mutual respect as Lucy turned to the attractive young woman waiting next in line.

"Now, Lara and Adam, I'd like you to meet Elise McCann, one of our swings who fills in for most of us – and usually several times throughout a season."

Lara smiled as she took her hand. "Hello, Elise, it's nice to meet you. I recognise you from *Mamma Mia*. You did a great job, and I'm happy to see you're part of this production too. Any show would be lost without their swings!"

"It's good to meet you too, and thanks, Lara. I'm glad you were free to come along tonight. And *Mumma Mia* was a real hoot. We had heaps of fun working on it. Not quite the sombreness of this one! I've always been an admirer of your work and attended several of your shows. Your voice is wonderful."

"Oh, what a lovely thing to say, thank you. I've certainly been blessed to find my niche." She turned again to include the others. "As have all of you."

A chorus of grateful acknowledgements flowed from their ranks as Lara's gaze fell on the woman standing beside Elise. She had dazzling eyes and dark hair caught up in a loose knot at the top of her head. Her gown was a glittering cocktail number that fell to her knees.

"Hello, I remember your delightful smile from that lively wedding celebration. And looking at those eye-catching pins, I think I recall them from earlier tonight – on stage, maybe!"

The attractive brunette grinned and executed a half pirouette that offered another glimpse. One of her lines had been about the new Russian regime ushering in a time when women could wear the pants in the family. The scene then called for the actress to lift her skirt and display a pair of frilly pantaloons below.

"See, I knew I recognised them!" Lara declared with an admiring nod and warm smile. She quickly extended her hand. "Hello, I'm Lara. It's lovely to meet you, Johanna."

The young woman's captivating brown eyes lit up with surprise when she realised the popular star knew her by name. "Hello, Lara, it's an absolute pleasure to meet you, but now you have me intrigued. I'm sure we haven't met before."

"No, we haven't, though I've been to a couple of shows starring 'the delectable Johanna Allen' – as a tabloid I read recently declared – and I must say I was suitably impressed. You have an amazing voice and obviously a great reputation from the calibre of work coming your way."

"Goodness, thank you. I'm flattered! It's because of you and a few other big names that I decided the theatre was definitely my cup of tea. I went to see *My Fair Lady* as a teenager and have never forgotten the impact your voice and acting skills had on me."

"Heavens, that was a long time ago – now you're giving away my age!" Lara offered with a friendly laugh. "Although I feel honoured to have made such an impression – how about we be each other's groupies then!"

"Oh, okay, you're on!" the younger one responded with a grin.

"Great, I look forward to it!"

It was obvious they had found a kindred spirit, and both women exchanged heartfelt smiles as Lucy turned to the final person waiting in the line-up.

She introduced him with a flourish of her hands. "And finally, Lara, I'd like you to meet Ben van Tienen, who not only plays the piano like Beethoven, he's also our highly gifted assistant musical director. We couldn't do anything without these guys backing us up in the pit – as you well know."

"Oh, I sure do. They're the backbone of us all. Beautiful work, Ben – a masterpiece delivered exceptionally well by a talented group of musos. Please give our best wishes to Kellie, too. She's one of my favourite conductors."

"I certainly will, Lara – and mine too! Thanks for being so generous. It's a magnificent score, and we're privileged to be able to share it with others. The degree of depth and mix of light and shadow make every bar a pure pleasure to play."

"And I second everything my wife just said," Adam joined in with an adamant nod. "Tonight's performance was a stirring interpretation of a superb score coming from one of the best in the business. You can all be proud of fuelling the raw emotion displayed by the audience. I caught several whispers saying how moving the production is, as well as many lamenting the fact that no cast recording was ever made."

"Yes, we were all disappointed a CD didn't eventuate ... although, most of us are still hoping – fingers crossed! Anyway, I'm glad you made it and maybe I'll get to play for one of your shows one day – both of you!" His friendly grin included the two stars.

"We look forward to it!" the husband and wife chorused.

Both men shook hands before Lara gave the young musician a grateful hug. "All the best, Ben, and I meant what I said. We really couldn't do what we do without you guys hiding down there in the dark doing what you do best!"

He nodded his head in thanks, and they spent the next several minutes chatting with the cast as a whole, discussing various other projects some already had in the pipeline once *Zhivago* finished its run.

Off to one side stood a long line-up of fans waiting to congratulate the cast. With a farewell wave, the majority of the excited bunch went off to sign programmes and receive some more well-deserved acclaim. The hour was late, and it was time to let their hair down and party after putting so much effort into such a brilliant opening night. Nikki and Daniel were near the bar mingling with a few other cast members she knew from past productions.

When Adam looked at Lara and inclined his head towards the entrance, she nodded and they both turned to Lucy and Luke once again – this time to offer their goodbyes.

"Well, it's certainly been a treat being able to congratulate the two of you on an outstanding opening," Lara said with a warm smile. "Thanks for a marvellous night of entertainment and for introducing us to all your talented mates. I think it's about time we gave you young folk a chance to kick up your heels rather than standing around with a couple of old fogies. Off you go and enjoy yourselves."

She offered Luke another warm kiss on his cheek, and he returned her gesture, along with an affectionate hug.

"It was great to finally meet you too, Lara. Thanks again for coming tonight. Hopefully, we'll run into each other again not too far down the track."

"I'd like that, and I'm sure we'll be seeing your face in many more great musicals, along with your name displayed in a heap of directing credits, too," she added with an adamant nod before her gaze fell on Lucy again.

The two women embraced warmly. "And I know I'll be seeing you grace our stages for a very long time to come!" Lara continued, reaching out to stroke the ebony-haired young beauty's cheek. "You're a delightful young woman, Lucy, and hugely talented. It's been a real pleasure catching up with you again. Please give my best wishes to your parents."

Lucy's enchanting hazel eyes sparkled when she reached out to squeeze Lara's hand. It was a strange feeling to see the admiration in the older one's eyes directed her way when Lara had been Lucy's role model at various times while tackling a role the more experienced actress had already mastered. "Of course I will, and I'm sure they'd send theirs back to you. Mum really wanted to be here tonight, but unfortunately she had a gig herself down in Melbourne, while Dad's in Sydney directing an opera – the joys of being part of a theatrical family!"

"Yes, that's what we're finding too – Adam or Nikki are invariably involved in something else when I'm opening a show, although sometimes we get lucky!"

"Oh, of course, and I'm not surprised! And thanks for being so generous with your encouragement and support, Lara – you've been most kind and thoughtful. I'm so pleased you were able to share in tonight's celebrations – I love the electricity of opening night – and thrilled you stopped by for a chat."

"It was my pleasure, and I meant every word. You have a very exciting future ahead of you, young lady!"

Lucy responded with a radiant grin. "Thanks again! I just adore this industry, and I'm over the moon our glorious musical was able to affect you so deeply."

"Best musical *ever* – without a doubt. You're a true star – I mean that. Australians are very blessed to have you lighting up our stages – not just in this one, but in many more to come, I'm sure."

"Now I'm really blushing!" The two women shared affectionate smiles as Lucy's face turned a deep shade of pink. She quickly covered the evidence with her hands as her eyes sparkled. "Now look what you've done!"

"Don't worry, we can just pretend it's a healthy glow, then no one will know the difference!"

Lucy laughed. "Thanks, I can only hope! But I'll be sure to catch your next show if I'm in town. That way I can come backstage to offer my congratulations ... and maybe leave you with a healthy glow!" The pair laughed and squeezed hands as Lucy went on. "It was a thrill to meet you again – even though I can't remember the first time, sorry."

"Don't worry ... it was a long time ago, but I could never forget those stunning eyes of yours, nor that beautiful smile! Take care, and I look forward to catching up again – hopefully, sometime soon."

Luke shook Adam's hand and his smile was huge. "I'm so glad you dropped by to say hello. It's been tremendous to finally catch up after hearing so much about you from Nikki – and all of it glowing, I might add!"

Adam's eyes shone with fatherly pride. "I think she's a little bit biased somehow! But I wouldn't have missed tonight – you portrayed *Liberius* with so much spirit." He turned to include Lucy in his response. "And to add to my wife's sentiment, I'm sure you both are going to have long and successful careers. All the very best for the rest of the season. We'll be sure to come back before the final curtain call." Lara hooked her arm through her husband's and nodded eagerly, while he just smiled down at her and patted her hand. "I doubt I'll be able to keep this one away. You've definitely touched her heart in a way I haven't seen before."

"He's not wrong – wild horses couldn't keep me away!"

"Then I'll look forward to seeing you again," Lucy responded with a happy chuckle.

Exchanging tight hugs, Lara added one last heartfelt sentiment. "Chookas, Lucy, and please take care ... the music world needs your exquisite giftings for many years to come."

"Thanks, Lara, what a generous thing to say. I wish you and Adam every happiness and a great big chookas in all you do, too."

As the husband and wife waved farewell to the two young stars, they were already looking forward to seeing them on stage again in the coming weeks. Being between projects, they had nothing else demanding their time for the next couple of months.

Exchanging heartfelt smiles at how well the night had turned out, they wandered over to say goodbye to their daughter and son-in-law, who were chatting happily to more of her peers on the other side of the cordoned-off area.

Much to Nikki and Daniel's surprise and delight, Luke had extended an invitation for them to stay on for the after-party. The family of four exchanged warm hugs, along with promises from Lara and Adam to pop in for lunch the following day. It would be a lovely way to spend some quality time with their adorable little grandson before heading back to the country estate.

With a sense of sadness at having to leave behind such a memorable night, Lara and Adam made their way through the other guests to exit via the riverside entrance.

It felt as though their own story had been leading them to this very moment in time. Strolling along the riverbank and gazing across the dark expanse of water to the lights of the city, his hand softly stroked hers ... continuing the ballet begun so long ago.

Crossing the Kurilpa Bridge with its colourful array of changing hues lighting up the night sky, they paused for a moment to gaze across to four tall towers standing on a distant hillside. The flickering red lights had always been a drawcard for their eyes. Lara instinctively bit her bottom lip when Adam folded her in his arms. This insignificant little gesture was the ever-present symbol lying at the very core of their love story. Unable to resist, he bent down and pressed his lips against the ones he had always hungered for since their first meeting.

"See that hill over there, my darling. It will always be our special place, just as you will always be the love of my life," he murmured, savouring her breath when it mingled with his.

"Mmm ... and just like you'll always be my other half, Teddy. I feel complete whenever we're together *and* thoroughly loved. You've always been my other heartbeat."

For what seemed like an eternity, he gazed into the sapphire blue eyes of this fascinating woman who had changed every portion of his life and still made his heart race – the same one whose spirit had kept him a willing prisoner for more than twenty years. A wave of emotion welled up inside and left him speechless, and he had to blink away a sudden rush of tears.

But there was no need for words. Lara saw everything he wanted to say in those familiar dark eyes – the ones that had visited her dreams and been her closest companions through all the lost and lonely years. Since one never-forgotten meeting on another stage, it felt as if every part of her drowned in their depths with every glance ... and deep in her spirit was the certainty she would always be safe there – until it was their turn for that final chime to ring out. And even then, she knew with a certainty he would live inside her spirit forever.

Throughout almost a lifetime of separation, they had never given up hope. Now a gentle voice once offering comfort in the midst of all those hard times whispered another assurance deep into their souls...

"I made you kindred spirits – now trust in my faithfulness to take care of you ... until the end of time."

§

And in that forever dimension only seen by the angels, a swathe of rich silken threads used to form an intricate tapestry never faulted while fashioning another unique image in this exquisite lifetime masterpiece. To the strains of a renewed symphony, a pair of entwined spirits danced around every memory and keepsake already making up this beautiful canvas.

It had been a long and painstaking work. The Master Craftsman smiled with satisfaction as he formed one last delicate stitch to complete the shape of a treble clef ... similar to the one hanging around the woman's neck.

And alongside the familiar symbol, this same Artisan fashioned a phrase inside a stave of parallel lines...

You were always there ... beyond the dark ... lighting my existence...

Every lost moment had been worth the pain for the life they now shared. And the words of an exquisite song, telling the story of two lives that in so many ways mirrored their own, accompanied the rhythm of their footsteps as Lara and Adam slowly made their way home to the little cottage on the hill.

ON THE EDGE OF TIME

Lyrics by Amy Powers & Michael Korie – Score by Lucy Simon

When you spoke, you broke me open, set my mind and body soaring.
Every word I still remember, every whisper carries through.
In your eyes, I saw the starlight, like a beacon, never dimming.
In your arms, I was forgiven, lifted higher, born anew.

You were always there, beyond the dark, lighting my existence.
You, my answered prayer, my midnight sun glowing in the distance.
Daring me to dream, blazing from afar...
One star to guide me through, 'til I was here... on the edge of time with you.

You showed me a place where hope was real, not a mere illusion.
One unguarded space my heart could heal from its mad confusion.
Sheltered from the storm, in your warm embrace...
A grace I never knew, I know at last ... on the edge of time with you.

All the pain ... all the years of silent despair
All at once disappear ... like mist in the air, like mist in the air.

Let me share unhurried days – what days are left – in your love's protection.
Hold you in my arms, so I can feel God in his perfection.
This is why I lived – this I know is real –
To feel the way I do, forever free, forever true... on the edge of time with you.

Now, as shadows fall, you are the night ... softly you surround me.
Stars become your eyes, the wind your voice whispering around me...
Rising in the glow of the candle's gleam...
One dream forever new, my life is here ... on the edge of time with you.

Pure as summer rain, the autumn sun dancing on the river...
Frost upon the plain, the seeds of spring waking with a shiver.
Groves of silver birch, ageless and serene,
Grow green beneath the blue, as seasons pass ... on the edge of time with you.

(a)

You, the sea ... I, the shore ... eternal we blend...
Moving on evermore ... a line without end, a line without end...

I ascend beyond the pale, above the storm, breathing in your spirit.
Though my heart is frail, and death will come, I no longer fear it.
Nations rise and fall ... tyrants come and go...
I know when life is through, my love will live...
In a ray of light ... in a distant chime ... on the edge of time with you.

For those readers who would like to experience Anthony Warlow and Lucy Maunder performing the first four stanzas and bridge of this wonderful piece, I encourage you to visit the following website:

https://www.youtube.com/watch?v=RTYBbFMGS5k&NR=1

If you would like to hear the final five verses, make sure you get along to a performance of this fabulous show, which opened on Broadway on April 21, 2015. For lovers of fine music, I promise you won't regret it! And if you missed it the first time, another production is bound to be coming to a theatre near you in the not too distant future. At least I hope so, for your sake.

In the meantime, a Broadway version is available on the following website, where you can listen to all the songs from this glorious production over and over:

http://www.broadwayrecords.com/cds/doctorzhivago

ONE FINAL TRIBUTE

During the many months it took to write this series, another haunting tale kept me company every day.

Fearing the details would fade from my memory, one day I sat down at my computer and the following stanzas were birthed in my soul, hopefully as a way to capture the perspectives of both the cast and audience during the final Australian performance after having the privilege of witnessing that very poignant finale from the front row of QPAC's Lyric Theatre.

THE GOOD DOCTOR'S FINAL CURTAIN CALL

To honour a beloved tale from the pen of Boris Pasternak, the creative team of

Doctor Zhivago – A New Musical

gave his novel a brand-new interpretation through the exquisite form of music. To honour those who brought it to life on a stage, I offer my sincere & heartfelt thanks always for the final performance of this haunting production held at The Lyric Theatre, QPAC, Brisbane on 14 August 2011.

Part 1

A single black curtain hangs fully suspended –

Dark drapery embellished with a fine silhouette ... one single panel of chairs

Veiled shadowy forms wait in readiness in pin-drop silence...

Blackness all-encompassing, where spreads a chequered floor...

As elegant columns frame its form.

Two sustained notes emerging now –

Long-held tension spills over as actors' eyes flit one to another ... this is it

It's time – there is no going back now ... one last breath before...

That velvet cloth rises – to reveal a kneeling youth before an open grave...

In a winter snowstorm.

Haunting bars drawn from a cello's throat –

Dance from the fingers of an invisible musician huddled in a recess below

Above, citizens of Moscow strut that stage ... two sets of contrasting lives...

There in a beloved land ... soon to be hurled into turmoil and pain...

And still, the boy keeps his vigil.

An epic storyline ... passionate, poignant –

Tales of this youth now grown older – a brand new doctor oozing grandeur, privilege

While far across this city, an exquisite beauty ... young girl having to wrestle the advances...

Of an arrogant older man ... who should have known better...

His constant lust overshadowing all else.

Two contrasting lives – like those earlier lyrics –

Depicting a duality of different worlds – never ever intended to cross the other's path

As the grandiose dreams of this medicine man ... underpinned with strong aspirations...

Of wholeness granted to needy ones ... and a penned passion for his country...

Forever burns within his soul.

Meanwhile, this young, tender beauty fights each long day –

Seeking new life – desired not only for beauty's sake; also her true worth – that intended purpose

'Til, a zealous revolutionary emerges ... grasping her heart's flickering flame...

Offering days, nights born of intrigue, passion ... underpinned with promises...

Of a desperate and savage war.

Part II

Perfect night for a much longed-for announcement –
Yurii's kind patrons' elegant ballroom – now host to a daughter many lovingly admire
Dance Mazurka with her, beloved doctor ... dip and sway Moscow's society cream...
Until, a shot rings out – smoke wafting from an ugly gun ... now dangling...
From that other beauty's hand.

This woman ... this vision now captured –
Within his heart of hearts – a kindred spirit's image nestled in a new home ... a medico's memory
Her sad countenance forever haunts wanderings, in and through endless alone years...
To wasteland battlefields in the bleakness of frozen Mother Russia...
That other love of his heart.

A poignant unrequited love letter –
Breaks open barriers on a simmering passion ... now at last able unfettered to soar
Words lovingly wrenched out of like-souls, their true heartfelt emotion...
Baring pure similar hearts with daring – aching, reaching out ... touching another...
Its twin – its other half.

'Til snatched away once more by war-winds –
More endless years spent apart ... battles raging around evermore-entwined hearts
Seeking, searching how to dwell without another – that forever-kindred spirit...
To forever wage own costly private wars – across bloodstained fields ...
Of lost, empty – and lonely souls.

This healer, loath to risk fine reputation –
Last morsel of his in a city once and always loved ... now lying desperate, desolate
Still, those mesmerising eyes haunt him daily – despite a feverish struggle to push away ... forget...
Until, unable – she's part of him – his other half ... ever silently seeking out...
Reaching for her comfort ... that warm shelter.

Part III

Yuriyatin – small town so far away –
Refuge for a family torn apart – seeking shelter, comfort ... peace from an upside-down society
But, wait ... out of mistiness of time, a memory – *Lara's* life is there ... he *must* not go...
That other world ever waiting ... slumbering – to sweep away all that is familiar...
But he must, he has to.

"Must stay away from that village" –
His strength ensures hurt for no one ... stay busy idle hands and mind ... remain occupied
"You *must* write, husband mine. Go – do research ... bring books back," his wife's plea...
Discerning not she was sending this kind doctor, never fully hers – back to another...
His one true love.

"Lara!" – It is he, beloved ... longed-for voice –
Dragged unbidden from a treasure-house ... kept locked away in a lonely desolate heart
Set free only when dreams flood her bed ... while yearning his form instead...
Now he's there – bone of her bone ... flesh of her flesh – other half of her whole...
Her one true love.

Meagre weeks to be their lot this time –
Guilt ... pure ravaging hunger for a woman he should never have – not his, another's ... now gone.
"Come back, my almost-husband" – Lara's cries in vain ... he lurches away...
Then, straightway taken captive by one once close to her heart – now leader of...
A rebellious army dealing in treasonous ways.

Cold, hungry ... fervently tending sick, wounded –
Out in more frozen wasteland ... far from all he's held dear – at the whim of a mad man
Memories ... clear bright eyes haunt long days, wrestling a torment of life spent alone...
Worse than those gaping wounds Yurii tends ... is the yawning chasm in a heart...
Where she still dwells.

Part IV

Long years pass ... wasted years ... alone –

Far from that kindred woman – Yurii's life's blood – joy of his mind, heart ... true soulmate

Stumbling now ... countless never-ending footfalls tread snow-laden paths...

"Is that her porch – that haven of heaven – or are my eyes playing tricks on me...

Like my heart?"

"Yurii!" – It is she, beloved ... longed-for voice –

Dragged from a threshold of death, cradled once more – safe, warm ... a refuge embrace

Love-comfort, healing – all things beloved to bring back wholeness ... peace...

Those arms forever hungered for ... her lips, sweet as nectar...

Bringing nourishment to his very core.

Two separate souls ... now entwined together –

Unending – one begins as the other finishes ... one long cord of love ever unbroken

Sharing, caring ... happiness at last – first portion for two barren lifetimes...

Until ... voice dredged from ages past – old nemesis – thief of childhood-innocence...

And taker of Yurii's beloved papa.

Out of darkness, this enemy emerges once more –

"I *won't* go – *please* don't make me," a heart's cry to her beloved ... now falling on deaf ears

"You *must*, my dearest darling – safety's choice first for you *and* our child"...

"*Promise* on our love you *will* come to us, husband of my heart...

Papa of our precious offspring."

Heart stalwart ... cold killing lies ... desperate promises –

Each necessary to save her life ... and his ... and that gift lying silent in her womb

"*Go, Lara,* I *beg* of you, leave *quickly.*" ... "*No,* Yurii, *never* can I leave you"...

His final stance ... adored beauty thrust from safety's arms...

Only shelter for his weakened heart.

Part V

Broken now ... poetry reams his only companions –

Tales of love for his country ... and a woman haunting constant yearning dreams

His sleep, not her only dwelling place ... wind-whispers too carry Lara's voice...

Bearing a lost soul home to that daily refuge – her heart ... where no other can touch...

Just him alone.

More lost years – lonely ... so cold –

Where now warm loving arms giving comfort and shelter? Gone now, forevermore...

Misty shadows of his imaginings – "Lara-love, ever softly you surround me"...

Myriad poems capture her beauty, where once eyes gazed in love...

Finding wholeness each new day.

'Til, another open grave ... a forever home –

Residence of a doctor, poet ... lover – unknown beloved papa of a replica daughter

Lara's gentle whispers to this half-empty abyss – destined to nestle his cold, lonely coffin...

Her sad voice touched with haunting poetry – Yurii's penned stanzas of ... a beloved country...

Dear child lost ... and a cherished soulmate.

"Goodbye, my love, my only love, beat of my heart" –

This beautiful woman – now older, tho' still irresistibly beautiful as that first long-ago glimpse

Calling to her other half – uttering poignant words fashioned for a mirrored soul...

Forever their 'now' – floating on a chime ... in a ray of light ... on the edge of time...

One again.

Part VI

For the final time that sombre drape falls silent to the floor –

Putting end to this tale ... as last onlookers are struck silent, willing more from the lips of these...

Consummate professionals donned in garb of yesteryear ... standing silent, sad...

Over, done ... finished ... no more will they together grace a darkened stage...

Mesmerising us.

Tears unchecked create flowing rivulets –

A journey over now – complete ... poignant, passionate ... friendships enduring forever

Both on stage and off ... while a haunting score and stirring lyrics accompany...

So many yet unspoken words, similar to his, chase an awaiting destiny ... witness bearer no more

To this tragic saga.

Go gently into your eternity, beloved soulmates...

...with sincere and heartfelt thanks... Jennifer Larmar – 29 June 2012 ©

ACKNOWLEDGEMENTS

This edition is the author's new Aussie version and the culmination of a two-volume series entitled *'Til The End Of Time,* which began with *Silken Images.* It has certainly been a labour of love and without the support of many people, the series would never have come to fruition. I've tried to remember each one here. For any I may have overlooked, please accept my humblest apologies. All errors in any form are mine alone.

To *Lucy Simon,* composer, and *Amy Powers,* co-lyricist – two of the major creators of *Doctor Zhivago - A New Musical* – whose enthusiasm from the moment I began this journey has been both overwhelming and incredibly encouraging. Thank you for being my motivation to take this plunge into a new career and for those delightful gifts from your personal treasure-troves of creativity. They certainly have given me the incentive to keep going! I wish you every success as your exquisite production now travels from stage to stage around the world, showcasing your brilliance.

To *Jamie Way,* one of the cast members of *Doctor Zhivago - A New Musical,* who has the most generous heart and was always willing to answer my many questions about this fabulous show. Jamie, your readiness to help whenever you were able – and in whatever way you could – has been a wonderful addition to my memories of that glorious production and brought a huge smile to my face. Thanks heaps, Mr JWay!

To *Hannah Brown Gordon,* New York Literary Agent, for expert critiquing of my work and style. It was an honour to be included as one of only a handful of upcoming authors to be granted a one-on-one session with you at the Brisbane Writers' Festival in 2013. Thank you for providing excellent ideas to enhance the storyline and for offering so much incentive with your kind and encouraging words to *"...get it into readers' hands as it's something lovers of romance will want to read."* I can only hope I did your advice justice.

To *Chrisstie Matthews,* Publishing Manager and Lead Designer at InHouse Publishing, Brisbane for her painstaking work to design the eye-catching covers for the Aussie paperback editions of both this volume and its sequel *Silken Images.* And to *Caroline Mackay,* Editor and Client Manager, for organising my first Aussie paperbabies ready for printing. Thank you for putting up with a pedantic author and listening to all my ideas with a smile and being willing to take them onboard.

To *Kerrie Smith*, who blessed me more than words can ever say when you wanted to go to Italy to look after Lara – and take Adam with you. This just shows your gentle heart and is one of the reasons I love you dearly. Thank you for your support in so many ways. You made the journey that much sweeter.

To *Jessica O'Connor*, a true fan of musical theatre and a delightful friend. Thank you sincerely for that surprise dedication of my favourite song, *On The Edge Of Time,* when it was played over the airways of Northern England on the BBC's *Songs From the Shows*. I was overwhelmed by your thoughtfulness and it's a memory I will treasure forever.

To *Gena and Steve Cavini,* delightful friends and welcoming hosts who provided the photo for the front cover of this new edition. The image is of the picturesque alfresco area at the back of their Yackandandah B&B. It reminded me of sitting in a courtyard in Tuscany back in 2009 and is the perfect depiction of both of those breathtaking parts of the world.

To *Candice Fung*, a talented young artist who knew of my admiration for Lucy Maunder as well as my love for this special musical and offered to recreate my favourite scene. That drawing now graces the back cover of this novel, while another she created of Lucy alone hangs in my study spurring me on to write.

To *Helen McConnell*, award-winning photographer and former colleague who kindly offered her services to take the portrait photograph on the back cover. Just wish I looked that good all the time!

To *Kaye Cooper*, editor extraordinaire and special friend, for your willingness to go over my work with a fine-toothed comb, offering suggestions and picking up all those silly little mistakes, along with a few much larger ones, made after spending many long hours in front of a computer where all the words had run into each other! You've been patient, kind, encouraging and most of all a true friend. For all those things – and so much more – I'm truly grateful.

To *Liz Sykes,* a special lady who offered to undertake the arduous task of reading through the first edition of this very large tome one last time, seeking out typos and punctuation errors when I'm sure you had far better things to do with your time. I sincerely appreciate your willingness to delve through my latest offering with new sets of eyes for this final edition. And *Liz*, please thank your lovely hubby for his marvellous critique. It came at a time when I was starting to wonder whether I should be doing this at all. He's a man I admire greatly, both for his integrity and wisdom. Not surprisingly, I was quite overwhelmed ... and felt extremely honoured.

To *Karen Jones*, an avid book worm, fellow book reviewer and good friend who willingly agreed to run her keen eyes over this final Aussie version. Thanks heaps, for your good heart and some much-needed encouragement.

To *Lea Ford,* my cousin and friend who has been so supportive and suggested I use my former moniker as a nom de plume. Following some trepidation after being subjected to all sorts of teasing as a child with the various pronunciations of an unusual surname, it's a joy to honour my father by carrying his name forward … at least on a book cover. Thanks heaps, Lea. And just so readers are aware, it was always meant to be pronounced La'mar, not like the animal, nor a Tibetan guru as some throughout my younger years were prone to think!

Always to my loving parents, *Les and Lily Larmar*, who taught us kids the value of doing the best we could in everything we put our hands to, along with living to help others. Sadly, I fall short too many times. Thankfully, the foundation of your training and teachings have always stayed with me. Though you're no longer here with us, I will always love you both and give thanks for all your love, prayers and support over the years.

To my much-loved daughter and delightful grandson, *Sascha* and *Darien,* who have brought more joy into my life than either of you will ever know. My heart sings whenever I think of you or see your smiles. My greatest prayer is that you will be wise, be kind and remember how much you are loved by both your loving Heavenly Father and a mother who was given the best gift of all when He entrusted you to her care for what now seems such a short space of time.

And to my husband, *Steve*. Thank you for your patience when I got lost with these characters night after night rather than in your company, and for dragging me away from the computer to go on relaxing Saturday drives in the country or to a beach to explore even more of this beautiful world we live in. I can only reiterate from last time, thank you for your patience and for giving me the freedom to write without making me feel guilty – and for your willingness to pick up this very long tome and go through each line one last time, seeking out any elusive typos or blunders that a 'worded-out' writer so easily misses.

To the talented *Willie Nelson* for his poignant rendition of the beautiful song *Always on My Mind* – lyrics that always touch my heart ... and sometimes bring a tear.

To the classical brilliance of *André Rieu,* who has the ability to mesmerise audiences wherever he goes and take them into a world of elegance and grandeur for an unforgettable few hours to the strains of some of the best composers the world has ever seen. The concert described on these pages are simply a figment of my imagination, however that picturesque little Italian town did have the honour of hosting three shows in a similar vein in September 2003 only a year earlier. So, using the freedom of a writer's imagination, I decided to take him back there again so Lara could join his talented group of performers for another magical night under the stars.

To the brilliant Ludwig Van Beethoven and his haunting *Moonlight Sonata* – a piece which has stirred my soul from that very first taste as a small child when my father would sit in our high-ceilinged living room, while each note floated around every crevice and corner of our beautiful old Queenslander-style home.

To so many wonderful musical productions which have travelled the world over and given captive audiences lyrics and scores which have stirred our hearts over and over again – especially the brilliant *Phantom of the Opera;* a few lines of which can be found on these pages. Also, the inspiring *Les Misérables* for a storyline and musical numbers that never fail to bring me to tears. These were my two favourite musicals of all time – until another came along and just pipped them at the post!

And again, to the magnificent countries of *Italy* and *Austria* whose people and places had me mesmerised from the moment I stepped foot on your ancient soil. Whenever I think of those magical days, I'm transported back to picturesque towns whose streets ooze with history and enchantment. One, in particular, is Cortona, perched high on a hilltop in Tuscany where, on a glorious autumn day in one of your beautiful piazzas and on the steps of a stately church and town hall, I was fascinated by the comings and goings of your delightful townsfolk. One day I hope to go back so I can write about you all over again.

The highest honour for any writer is to know their characters have touched another's heart. I sincerely hope those on these pages have touched yours in some way and made you smile – and maybe even shed a tear.

With heartfelt thanks ... Jennifer Larmar

ABOUT THE AUTHOR

Jennifer Larmar, her nom de plume, was born in Brisbane, Australia. Only weeks after turning seventeen, she moved to Wellington, NZ for a working holiday. When her father died eighteen months later, she returned to Australia and then moved to Canberra for six years where her daughter was born, before settling back into her home state of Queensland for many years – from the contrasting landscapes of the Sunshine Coast to an apartment in the Brisbane CBD. She now lives with her husband in the serenity found in the foothills of the Victorian High Country.

For many years, Jennifer and her favourite little girl lived beside one of the beautiful beaches edging the Sunshine Coast. Now Sascha and the author's only grandchild live in Melbourne and she visits them as often as possible. 'Rhino' is the delight of her life and some of her best days are those spent with him and his mother. As she says, God created books and little people to make growing older a joy!

Raised in a musical family, she studied piano and was involved in school and church choirs. As a child, Jennifer enjoyed putting pen to paper in prose or poetry form, often for family and friends for special occasions. Over the years, she has written the lyrics to several pieces, including the anthem for Wellers Hill State School – a state government primary school located in Brisbane – which the students still sing every Friday during assembly. In the 80s, she was part of a musical duo, penning lyrics with a folk/gospel singer/guitarist/composer and performing in coffee shops together on weekends. This love of music saw her treading the boards in several amateur musical theatre productions on the east coast of her beautiful homeland.

Following a multifaceted career path, writing has become her passion. Apart from spending time with her 'other heartbeats' in Melbourne, sitting in a darkened theatre, being involved in music of some form, or travelling across this vast and intriguing planet discovering new and exciting places – and drooling over horses (!) – there is nothing she enjoys more than sitting in her study bringing beloved characters to life while taking them on journeys around the world. As Jennifer says, *"To me, writing is like going on holidays every day without the expense. I can take my characters anywhere, to do anything ... and all from the comfort of my study..."*

The two-part series *'Til The End Of Time* is her first foray turning a love of writing into a career. *Silken Images*, Vol 1 and *Fractured Symphony*, Vol 2 are available from InHouseBookstore.com.au, the main headline post of her Facebook page https://www.facebook.com/JenniferLarmar/, all Amazon's online stores, her webpage http://sbandta.wixsite.com/jenniferlarmar, and selected bookstores – or if you contact the author personally via her Facebook page or the official website, she offers them at a discount rate plus postage – and with a tasty little treat included!